A Draft of R...

Had I been asleep or unconscious? Had I woken? I had the sense that I might have been absent for a second or a year: that, finally, the question of time lapsed was impossible to ask or sensibly answer. No sooner had my sense of my own presence resumed than I wobbled and fell, finding myself on an unadorned stone path through grey-green grass which led to the portico of some great house. The stone of the house's exterior was as grey as the grass, as grey as the sky; the windows looking down on me reflected white like the eyes sometimes seen in the blind. I knew when I looked up I would see no sun, not even a bright spot where I might imagine it lurked behind the clouds; but I craned my neck and scanned the sky anyway. When I returned my gaze to the grey, featureless plain on which I stood, I saw someone looking at me from the doorway: so I walked the little distance to the portico and climbed the steps.

The man in the doorway was Tanaan. His black eyes repeated the void into which I might or might not have recently fallen; no, they were the green-grey of the Ruillin in winter. Usually I could guess whether a Tan's age should be estimated in decades or centuries: with this man, neither was the right unit to use. But the only lines on his face had been created by laughter, and nearly all of those few were around his eyes. His clothing was rich, but it followed no fashion I had ever seen or read of, and every pattern and weave showed grey upon grey upon grey. His bottomless eyes appraised me; he made not even a pretense of a smile.

"What are you doing here?" he said. "You're early; she's not here."

"What?" I said, reflexively, glancing past his shoulder to the interior of the house. The one room I could see was empty even of furniture; the place sounded vacant and smelled of dust.

"You're too early," he repeated, as if I should have some idea what he was talking about.

I shook my head, opening my mouth to protest.

"Look you, don't think I'm unaware of the havoc you intend. I'm telling you: this is not the time."

That was a code, or shorthand: it should have meant something to me. The Tan held my gaze as if waiting for its intended meaning to sink in, watching me with the patience of someone to whom time is of no relevance.

Except, of course, that this was not the time.

"Ah," he said finally. "I see. Never mind, then; time for you to go back. Here—" He produced from some inner pocket of his fancifully-cut coat a flask of cut crystal and unstoppered it. Whatever lay within gleamed greener than emeralds, fractured into a hundred different tones of green behind the facets of the glass. He offered it to me.

"What is this?" I said.

"Good for what ails you," the Tan answered. "Time to go back."

"Is this—" I couldn't think of the phrase in the Tanaan language; I gave up and reached for the arcane term. ". . . a deoch diarmaid?"

Something that might have become a smile flitted about his mouth and then changed its mind. "A draft of forgetfulness?" He shrugged. "More like a draft of remembrance."

And how could drinking send me back to where I had started, if I correctly understood the rules of such encounters? Wouldn't it, rather, bind me here?

The Tan sighed again. "No. I am not the fool here. Drink."

I did. Some liquor lighter than brandy, richer than wine, carrying the scents and flavors of a dozen separate flowers, flowed through my mouth and down my throat. Suddenly the eyes that met mine were as green as the liquor I had drunk. I blinked—and realized the grey grasses surrounding the house were a garden, my would-be host's clothes were so many colors at once that they should have offended my eyes, and a party that paled any debacle I had yet been involved in was going on in the house behind him. I caught the barest hint of clear blue skies as I collapsed.

the Shadow
of the Sun

Barbara Friend Ish

Copyright © 2010 by Barbara Friend Ish
Interior maps by Ari Warner Copyright © 2010
Sigil Copyright © 2010 by Rachael Murasaki Ish
Cover design Copyright © 2010 by Wynette A. Hoffman

First Trade Edition – published 2011
Printed in the United States and the United Kingdom

ISBN 978-1-936427-01-7

MERCURY RETROGRADE PRESS
6025 Sandy Springs Circle
Suite 320
Atlanta, Georgia 30328

www.MercuryRetrogradePress.com

Library of Congress Cataloging-in-Publication Data

Ish, Barbara Friend, 1963-
The shadow of the sun / Barbara Friend Ish.
p. cm. -- (The way of the gods ; v. 1)
Summary: "First of an epic fantasy series that explores the nature of deity and man's relationship to beings known as gods"--Provided by publisher.
ISBN 978-1-936427-01-7 (alk. paper)
1. Magic--Fiction. I. Title.
PS3609.S48S53 2011
813'.6--dc22
2010052946

Dedication

For Mark, fellow dreamer and love of my life, partner in all things. Your belief and support buttress my feet on the ground and lift my wings on the air.

An céad míle buíochas
A hundred thousand thanks

I am grateful each day for the people who let me share my dreams with them: who make writing and publishing and becoming fully human possible. First credit must go to my husband Mark: *nasclethéan*, patient first reader, and insightful critiquer, who gives me the space in which to dream and a reason to return to consensual reality; who adopts my dreams as his own and helps me bring them to fruition; who welcomes me into his dreams as well. He makes the journey a joy. So too I treasure the support of my children, Daniel and Rachael, who have become in adulthood two of the friends I am most proud to have. Thank you for having the grace to see my utter geekishness as cool and for your patience with the exigencies of living with an artist for a mother.

Thanks also are due the family of my birth: my parents, Patric and Thresa Friend, who named me for a paradox and then had to live with the consequences; my siblings Jen, Chris, Sean, and Mike, who welcome me into the wondrous mayhem of their lives. My mother introduced me to some of the SFF authors who shaped the writer I have become; my father taught me to love language, and showed me where my brain was and how to engage it despite the consequences. To them are due a certain amount of the credit for my good points and none of the blame for my many failings.

Another thousand thanks are due my dear friend Sonja Benjamin, healer of bodies and souls, sister in the dreaming hut. Without her, none of the things I do would be possible, and her friendship enriches my life.

No book goes to press without a robust support team; this one has had an embarrassment of riches in that regard. First thanks and last go to my friend, dream editor, and personal armsmaster Brett Shanley, who sees all the way to the center of the earth and who gave me the tools I needed to crack open the parts of this tale I hadn't yet brought to fruition. Thank you for your unending patience, your insight, and your willingness to talk endlessly about punctuation—and most of all for helping me dream my dream.

I am grateful beyond measure to Wynette Hoffman, not only for her magnificent work on the cover but for all the years of friendship and companionship in the wild places of publishing; a steadfast writing partner, she showed me the possibility of living the dream and offered me tough love when I needed it.

So too I am thankful for the contributions of Ari Warner, whose maps bring this story to life—and look beautiful doing it—and of Rachael Murasaki Ish, who developed the sigil that graces the cover and the scene-breaks of the Trade edition.

My early readers, including Wayne Fishell, Thresa Friend, Wynette Hoffman, Edward Morris, Leona Wisoker, and of course Mark and Rachael Ish, made this book a better tale than it would have been. I am grateful for their insights and patience with my process.

I am indebted to James Kempf and Anthony Thomas of Cliché Studios for the creative genius and many pleasant hours that went into the development of games and other expansive ideas for my world. Thank you for much fun and learning, and for helping me stretch my ideas in directions that would never have occurred to me otherwise.

Thanks also are due all the Mercury Retrograde authors and staff who work and play and dream with me: Zachary Steele, Edward Morris, Danielle Parker, Larissa Niec, and Leona Wisoker, who reminded me to drink my own Kool-Aid and was patient with me while I did it; in this regard Mark and Rachael Ish and Brett Shanley must be mentioned again, as must James Kempf. Mercury Retrograde would be nothing without them.

Contents

Hakaid the Shadow of the Sun

And open the Abyss

Let the heir of Tilimya
Woo the Virgin Star

Join the Sun and the Moon in Darkness

Thus results the Union of Silver and Gold

Blend the Essences in the Vessel of life
The Elixir etythe
Earth, Fire, Water and Air to command or release at will
In the Crucible where pain is ecstasy and Death is Life
Hidden is plain

The reach of the Shadow of the Sun is infinite

Aballo Grimoires Collection no. 1012: Aechering, Grimoire no. 22

The Shadow Working

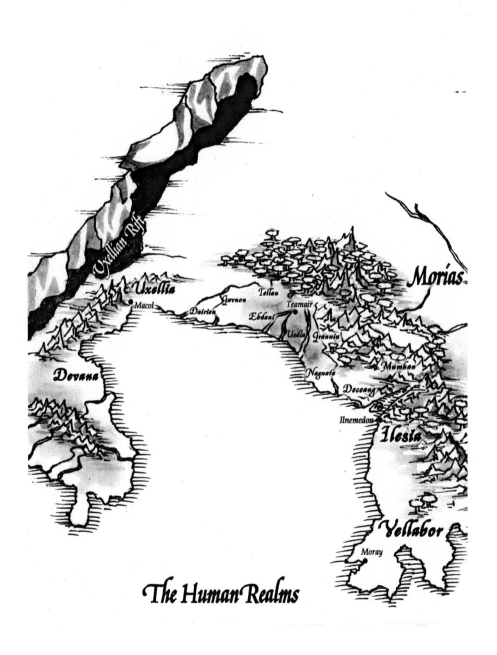

The Human Realms

Ilnemedon: Harpist Gorsedd Map Collection no. 135

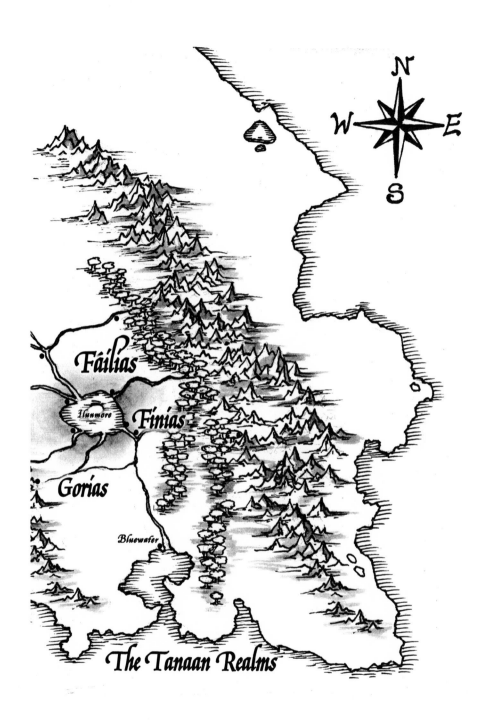

Fáílías

Ilunmore   Fínías

Gorías

Bluewater

The Tanaan Realms

The Human and Tanaan Realms

Chapter 1
Long Live the Righ

The smell of magic woke me. Immediately my heart was hammering, my throat tight; the terrible delight of raw arcane power washed over me like frankincense on mountain air. Scents and colors I hadn't tasted in a decade teased open parts of me long held closed, telling me things mundane senses never could. Death rode on tones of crystal from secret velvet darkness between the stars, wrapped in the purple-gold caress of spidersilk and aromas of peach and shocking blue. The magic hadn't originated with the ard-righ's wizard Athramail, whose signatures and workings regularly peppered the air of Ilnemedon; it wasn't the doing of any of the small-time charms dealers who haunt the back rooms of Ilnemedon's taverns and the ships that ride the winds up and down the Ruillin. This was a power blacker than any of those men could imagine and a thousand times more seductive; I struggled to wrench my awareness closed, to wrap a thick blanket around my senses, above all not to let my mind stray to the place where that intoxicating song originated. Just before I retreated into my mental cocoon, I felt the arcane circuit complete and felt the ard-righ die.

Intoxication fled; revulsion and guilt raced through me in its wake. My own harsh breathing echoed against the dark ceiling and unlit walls. The memory of a sunlit glade threatened to breach the surface of my mind; my palms itched. The place in which I'd slept for the past five years shrank into a prison cell. I threw myself out of bed and dressed, then sat before the dying fire and waited for the cannonade that would mark the ard-righ's death

Poor Athramail. Not even the Prince of the Aballo Order of wizards could have warded off that attack. But that wouldn't stop the old man from flaying himself half to death with guilt, nor would it necessarily spare his life.

And poor Coran: for the next three minutes, or maybe five, a son—and then, forever, an orphan and righ. It is the gravest of cruelties that for a man to ascend the throne, his father must die.

Frigid wind beat against my back as I rode up the mountain to Mourne Palace: making outrageous lies of the Ardan-eve garlands that lay trampled all over the road, sending the tail of my hair forward to flutter like crows' wings in my peripheral vision. Spring never comes kindly to Ilnemedon; the cold wet wind off the Ruillin persists well into summer, seemingly until the moment when the city turns into a sauna. In ten years I'd grown accustomed to this, but this afternoon the lowering clouds and biting air felt like a portent.

Who would choose this holiday for an arcane assault? The first light of spring is a time that favors growth and the seeding of great beginnings, a time so steeped in women's energy that only emergent need would persuade most wizards to draw power. The death of the ard-righ and the chaos that would ensue couldn't serve the beginning of anything. Even did one of the other righthe delude himself that he could win the ard-righ's throne, no Aballo wizard would wield that black power.

Even if they would, none of them could master it.

A flock of ragged crows haunted the palace as I rode up the final, steep ascent to the gate: perching on the lichen-spotted bastions, wheeling between the parapets and the steel-grey sky. Men on the bastions threw stones at the crows, trying to drive off the ill omen. It was too late for that, of course; and the crows were far from the only thing out of sorts here this afternoon. I didn't recognize either of the men standing guard at the gate—which I should have expected, as palace security is the responsibility of the tanist, and yesterday's tanist had become today's righ. But this afternoon the usual swordsmen at the gate were augmented by flashmen on the wall.

Strange days indeed when a royal will stoop to using flash-weapons, even if it's not his own hand wielding them. Worry for Athramail raced through me again; but a second look at the wall showed me the emerald sparkle of Athramail's power between the stones, occluded by shadow and invisible to the uninitiated eye. Usually I did my best to ignore the wards, but this afternoon they were a minor comfort: Athramail yet lived, yet held the post of House Healer to Ilesia, despite his failure last night.

The new guards challenged me, skittish as a pair of two-year-old racers on their first track.

"Good afternoon," I said, showing them two empty hands but not dismounting. I refused to acknowledge the flashmen on the wall. "I'm Ellion

Tellan."

The guards at the gate exchanged nervous glances. Ilnemedon is not a city in which it is wise to offend a stranger, particularly not an armed stranger who is a head taller and several handsbreadths broader in the shoulder than most men of the warrior class. But today, their first day on duty outside an unfamiliar gate, the guards were more afraid of letting the wrong man pass.

I could guess at the tallies being conducted behind those nervous eyes: a warrior knows another at a glance, and in this case the problem was complicated by sufficient evidence of wealth that there might be unpleasant consequences for them if they refused me entry in error. The one on the right had the look of a horse about to spook: I kept my hands still, my eyes steady, my attention on the men at the gate rather than the ones on the wall. If one of these two startled, it might well be the flash discharge that reached me first, and in this wind the telltale smell of ozone might not hit me before the bolt did. And I didn't want to find out whether I'd violate my vow and draw the power necessary to raise an arcane shield, not with the memory of the working that had killed the ard-righ so damnably fresh.

"Er—your name's not on the list…" ventured the guard on the left.

"Truly?" I retorted. "A *list*? Where is this thing? The names of all the people who come and go from this place every day would make too long a list for anyone but a bard or a harpist to memorize. So it must be in your pocket. Look again."

Spooked Horse twitched in a way that bespoke a hand about to reach for a sword; reflex sent mine to my own hilt. Immediately Spooked Horse's partner, a redhead whose nose had suffered more than one encounter with someone's fist or the pommel of a sword, rushed forward to grasp my horse's headstall. The beast reared, nervous as usual. Ire flared in me; a senseless hope that one of the flashmen above us *would* fire came on its heels.

"Back away!" I snapped. "I am Ellion Tellan. I am on my way to visit the righ. If you can't remember your list, go get someone who can."

"What is your business in Ilnemedon?" Spooked Horse rejoined.

"My *business*?"

"Tellan's clear on the other side o' the world."

I cast him a withering glance. "*I* live *here*. For five years now. Unless I miss my guess, *you've* been standing on a wall in Carrickfergus until quite recently. At this rate you'll be on your way back by nightfall. Open the fouzhir gate!"

Spooked Horse half-drew his sword, striding towards me; the redhead reached for my horse's headstall again. I smelled ozone. Terrible anticipation crackled through me.

"Fools!"

I glanced towards the voice, through the bars of the gate. Den Donard, who had gone to bed last night as leader of a royal son's personal contingent and been awakened as First Armsmaster to Ilesia, stood there now, scowling at the guards. I knew I should be relieved, but need tingled in waves across my skin. I willed myself to a semblance of calm.

"Damn your empty heads!" Den snapped. "I don't know how you did things out at Carrickfergus, but if you're to stand guard duty in Ilnemedon you've got to learn to recognize people! That's the ard-harpist!"

The redhead blanched, withdrawing his hand; Spooked Horse flushed and unlocked the gate.

"Your pardon, Lord Ellion," Den said. "The—the righ will be pleased to see you."

I nodded and rode through. "Even Lugh Lámfhada had difficulties getting inside the gate on at least one occasion. But those men are a waste of perfectly good arms."

Den shot them another dark look.

"Congratulations, by the way," I said.

Den grinned. "Thanks."

"This doesn't mean I've seen the last of you on the sparring grounds, does it?"

"Tell me when you'll be there, and I'll strap on my ugliest armor, just for you."

The seneschal showed me to a sitting room in the royal residence, a space as grey and black as the city outside. No lamps were lit, despite the gloom. Coran Mourne, new righ of Ilesia, ard-righ-apparent, stalked along the curve of the room's outer wall, crushing a visible path in the intricately woven rug and chewing on a thumbnail. He was already dressed in white, his usually luxurious fall of blond hair cut short in mourning and the righ's torc with its gleaming eagle-head finials looking uncomfortably tight around his bull neck. He glanced up as I ducked into the doorway, fixing me with eyes that spoke of strategic wheels turning behind them and a need for blood. After a second the tension and grief in his broad face eased.

"Ellion!" Coran said, crossing the room to embrace me. "Great Lord Ilesan—" He touched his fingertips rapidly to his lips and heart: an atypical prayerful gesture. "It was good of you to come!"

"I'm so sorry," I said. I clasped Coran tightly. A man's transition from tanist to righ seems to be even more confusing for the people around him, as if that could be possible. Everyone else would be tentative and withdrawn with Coran for the better part of a twelvenight; I would not be a part of that sudden emptiness. "What happened?"

"Cuill—wine. The ard-harpist and I will have wine," Coran said to the seneschal. The man bowed and withdrew.

Coran stepped away and resumed his course around the edge of the room, periodically glancing through the slits at the crows wheeling outside.

"The kharr," he growled. "Naturally, the fouzhir kharr. Athramail thinks it was the Bard's Wizard who opened the breach."

I nodded. The man called the Bard of Arcadia, the leader of the rebel kharr, had recruited a renegade wizard to his cause. No one knew who the renegade was: the appellation *Bard's Wizard* had been inevitable.

"It wasn't—The breach wasn't in the outer wall," Coran said, still pacing.

"Where, then?"

"Here. The residence."

"Fouzh," I said. The arcane part of the job had been very subtle, unless the Bard's Wizard were here himself. To work inside another man's arcane defenses without disrupting them is next to impossible.

"Was he captured?"

"The assassin? The *spy?*" Coran shook his head. "The gods granted me no such pleasure. For all I know, the man still walks within these walls."

Coran turned and retraced his steps to the far end of the chamber, his face a map of the methods he would have used to extract every possible scrap of information from his father's murderer. Suddenly he stopped, looking at me.

"Damn it all, where is my head? Ellion, will you sit?"

"It's not necessary—"

"Yes." Coran stared as if his enemy's name might be written on my forehead. Some decision manifested in his eyes. "I have need of you today, my friend. Let's sit."

Coran's footman brought wine: a Vellabori red, unwatered as the new righ preferred it. Its familiar woodsmoke-and-cherries aroma wafted past me as he poured. Coran settled, with exquisite gentleness born of countless broken articles of furniture, into a chair that would have swallowed most men whole; his immense muscular frame made the chair look in perfect proportion to the room. I took up the seat opposite. One of the pleasures of our friendship was time spent in the company of a man with whom it was easy to feel the world was too small, rather than my own size that was amiss: a small moment of rightness in a day that seemed in danger of spinning out of control. I offered the righ a little salute with the glass.

"Abu al-righ," I said, *Hail forever*.

Pain twisted Coran's face. He drained his glass quickly and refilled it.

"I'm sorry," Coran said, voice gravelly. "The day came far too fast. Let's not—How about a game of chess?"

"Chess?" I echoed. I was tempted to break my long-standing moratorium against looking into other people's minds. I knew Coran as well as any man; what horrors could I possibly find in there that would outweigh what I carried inside myself? But I'd learned the hard way that knowing too much about what goes on inside other men's heads makes it difficult to like them. And Coran was the only real friend I'd had in ten years.

"If you like," I said finally.

We set up the board in silence. Once we began to play, Coran stopped glancing outside at the crows, and the conversation turned to calmer topics: the arrivals of Coran's tiarna and other vassals for tonight's pyre; the expected improvement in the weather in time for the ceremony; the feast being prepared for afterward. Coran was an excellent chess player, but I had seen all his strategies before, and the one he was developing could only be characterized as *tired*. In five moves, he would land his king's admiral to the queen's side, and that would be the beginning of my checkmate.

"Of all enemies, a bard," Coran said. "How does a man defeat a bard? He shouldn't be able to do what he's doing at all."

I made a sympathetic noise and moved my king's knight into position.

"Who musters for him?" Coran continued. "Who commands the companies in the field?" He sighed. "Of course it's not like that." Out came his queen's wizard, right on schedule.

"No, it isn't." The kharr didn't have a proper army: just spies, and pirates, and farmers and tradesmen who suddenly took up makeshift arms. I saw no honor in any of it, just madness in the name of a false god. I sidestepped the trap awaiting my queen three moves hence and moved a pawn instead.

Coran sat back in his chair, surveying the board with a look of disgust, then turned that same look on me. "You already know. Damn you."

He sighed and looked down at the board again, plotting a new strategy.

"I shall be grateful to have your sharp eye beside mine, when the time comes to order the strategy at Teamair," Coran said without looking up.

I flinched. Coran was right to be thinking beyond the election of the next ard-righ to the battles the ard-righ must lead, and to expect that he would be the one the righthe chose. But the high throne of the ard-righ of all the nations should have been mine, and it would bypass me through no one's fault but my own.

Finally, realization hit me, with all the force of a charging destrier. I knew what would happen this spring: a Grand Moot. I had known since the ard-righ died. But now I really grasped what a Moot would mean. It would take place on Bealtan Day; my old teacher Amien would summon all the righthe, and probably a number of tiarna, to the Moot grounds outside Teamair. They would all be there, every man I had spent the last ten years avoiding: Amien and Uncle Pariccan; Sanglin and Dandem and every other wizard I knew. I would be summoned, too; and to refuse the summons of the Prince of the Aballo Order means absolute exile.

Every man of Tellan would know all the details of my disgrace, and everyone else would soon hear the tale: the untimely death of my parents, the way Uncle Pariccan raised the Tellan tiarna against me and wrested the righ's torc from my neck. As long as Pariccan failed to produce a male heir, I was, arguably, once again next in line for the Tellan throne; but that would never happen. Tellan memory is longer than that. It would be as if ten years of self-imposed exile had never been.

I slumped back and leaned my head against the top of the chair, staring at the shadows on the arched ceiling.

"I need you beside me now, Ellion," Coran said. "You're the only man in Ilnemedon who can keep me honest."

I laughed. It sounded empty in my own ears. I felt Coran's gaze on me again: I sat up and met the righ's eyes.

"Listen, I know—Look, there's no point in discussing ancient history," Coran continued. "But you and I both know you're absolutely wasted as a harpist."

"Ah, Coran," I began, pushing the chair back from the table.

"No, really. Listen. You are one of the great military minds of our time. You should be ordering the field, not singing about it afterward."

There was no arguing with this truth. I could have ordered both the military and the arcane aspects of the war creeping eastward across the human lands, from the ard-righ's throne. It was what I had been born to do.

"I have decided to grant you the Tiarnate of Louth and the title of Ard-Tiarn," Coran said, grey hawk-eyes steady on mine. "And I'd like you to stay on here in Ilnemedon as War-Lord."

Not merely tiarn, but ard-tiarn: *Lord Most High*. My hand itched for my sword and someone to turn it on; but of course I had surrendered my blade at the palace door. Coran's affection for me had always been unqualified; he was the one man to whom my undefined status didn't seem to matter. But the new righ was a proud man. If I didn't accept the title, the insult might be more than our friendship could bear. And there was no way I could accept.

"Hell, you could marry that woman none of us ever meet—What's her name?"

"Laverna," I said, before I could control the impulse. Shock flashed in Coran's face: Laverna is a goddess of the old religion, the patroness of whores.

I shook my head, rising. "There's no woman, Coran. It's kind of you to offer, but you of all men should understand I can't—"

"Can't *what?*" Coran's fair face flushed. "It's not as if I'm asking you to lay aside a title! That ship has long since sailed!"

With a gale-force wind in the tail. But to accept Coran's offer would remove me irrevocably from the rank of royalty, however dark and ill-explored a corner of that rank I might now occupy.

I bowed, throat tight. "I thank you, my lord. Your offer is beyond generous. But what I need you cannot give me, and my presence among your peerage would be nothing but a source of strife."

Coran's grip on the glass tightened visibly. I wondered remotely whether it would snap. "Hardly more than your presence among my vassals' wives!"

I bowed again. "My military mind remains ever at your disposal—"

"If you truly think a deposed righ of an upstart backwater commands more honor than the ard-tiarn of Ilesia, you're a greater fool than anyone imagined!"

An upstart backwater. Only the righ of Ilesia could hold such a view of Tellan, the nation chartered by the goddess Tella Herself. But Coran was angry, and with good reason: I inclined my head.

"I'm sorry. I will miss your father—but I have absolute faith in you. I'll see you this evening."

"Get the hell out."

The interior of my apartment in the Harpist Gorsedd Hall had grown impossibly dark and confining. I could barely breathe for the staleness of the air. How was it possible I had thought this place comfortable? I stalked through the outer rooms, fighting down the temptation to sweep the stacks of memoranda and correspondence and the half-completed score from my desks, smudged the heel of my hand through the note one of the lords of the gorsedd had scrawled on the slate beside the door, and strode into the private chambers.

What insanity had I been pursuing for the past ten years? Where had I gotten the idea that the Harpist Gorsedd was in any way relevant? *You should be ordering the field, not singing about it afterward.* Even that was only a half-measure of approach to the truth. But all the bridges between me and the things that mattered had long since collapsed in fire, and I'd been the one applying the torch. All that was left to me now was to play the role I'd spent these wasted years building.

Tradition rather than fashion dictated what I put on for the ceremony: formal mourning white, an uncomfortable color relieved only by the double-handbreadth of gold that is my right by virtue of royal birth. When I was fully dressed, my hair brushed into a proper fall, I went and stood in front of the wardrobe to stare at the speckle-feathered cloak, the ard-harpist's mark of office, and work my mind around accepting the inevitable.

There was no question that I must wear the cloak tonight: it was a necessary part of the protocol for representing the Harpist Gorsedd at a state funeral of its host nation. I had spent years earning the right to wear it, and every other man in the gorsedd would mortgage his firstborn for the privilege. But tonight the speckle-feathered cloak felt like a mummer's costume, not something befitting royalty. How could it embarrass me to wear something other men sacrificed their personal and social lives trying to win? The gods seemed more perverse than usual.

At sunset I joined the procession up the mountain, the feathered cloak heavier on my shoulders than a full harness of armor, to witness the dead righ's cremation and pay my respects to the living one. Coran barely glanced at me: a behavior that, on such a day, wouldn't have merited a moment's thought if I hadn't just turned down the most generous gift a righ could offer a foreign-born man. My heart felt as if it had been replaced by an anvil.

The dead righ already lay atop the pyre, surrounded by knights from his personal contingent, when the procession arrived. Airships bobbed in the skies around the summit, the silks of their canopies rippling with the colors of houses whose ranks were insufficient to merit places at the pyre and the fires in their braziers winking against the darkening sky. The competing breezes raised by their windcallers pushed the air of the summit into strange swirls that whispered seduction against the back of my neck.

Coran stepped into his proper place at his father's feet, pale face reflecting exhaustion; his brother Niall, now also his tanist, stood at his right hand, facing south. The tanist's torc, which until yesterday had graced Coran's neck, hung loosely about Niall's slender sinewy throat. I stood well back among the tiarna and other dignitaries of Ilesia, allowing them precedence at the pyre. I could see over the tops of most of their heads, anyway. Athramail stepped into the customary spot for a wizard, facing east, and began calling the fires to the pyre's compass points.

"All glory to Lord Ilesan, by Whose Will the Waters of Chaos quickened into Life," Athramail sang, wind rippling in his ceremonial robe. He cast fire from his knob-knuckled hand to the wood piled near the ard-righ's head, igniting the pyre. My palms and fingers tingled. But I must not open myself to power, not ever.

"All glory to Lady Tella, by Whose Will the Air of Thought condensed into Form," Athramail sang. Fire sprang up in the wood at the ard-righ's feet. Had the goddess been watching me, that last time? Shame erupted inside me. Before my parents' deaths, before my entire life collapsed, She'd always been watching over me. There was no reason to believe She hadn't seen everything. She'd certainly had no use for me since.

"All glory to Par, Lord of Warriors, Whose glory Conary Mourne served and Whose favor will yet set Conary among the heroes at the Feast Hereafter," Athramail intoned. Fire sparked at Athramail's gesture, and for half a second I found myself in Tellan again, standing at the foot of my father's pyre wishing I were the one who had died. I wrenched myself back into the present.

"All glory to Lady Ara, Whose bounty nourishes all Her children." The pyre blazed yellow and orange, billowing white smoke towards the darkening sky. A short distance away, as deeply buried in the crowd as I, pale-haired round-hipped Findabhair, wife of an important Ilesian tiarn, caught my eye with a significant look. Fatigue washed over me; I closed my eyes. Historically speaking, this wouldn't have been the most indecorous moment at which I slipped out of a gathering with a wife not my own; but tonight, it just seemed too banal.

"A warrior comes to the Great Feast, bedecked with the badges of his battles," Athramail intoned.

I chanted the expected response with the rest of the crowd: "Lords and Ladies, welcome him!"

"A lover returns to the One he has missed, bringing stories and songs of glory!"

"Lords and Ladies, welcome him!"

"May he sit at the Great Feast, ride with the Great Hunt, enjoy the accolades of a true warrior. And may he greet us when we arrive at the Gate!"

"Lords and Ladies, welcome him!"

Athramail stilled. A silence broken only by the crackling of the fire settled over the crowd. The fire climbed steadily across the well-seasoned wood and engulfed the bier. Within a minute, the ard-righ's body was no longer visible, and only the fire remained, brilliant yellows and oranges sliding through deep reds and elusive hints of cobalt and green, blazing against indigo sky. Arcane consciousness wrapped stealthy tendrils around my mind, and for a moment I relaxed into it. Then I realized what I was doing and wrenched myself into the ordinary moment, clenching my teeth around profanity. Coran glanced at me, meeting my eyes across the tops of a hundred heads, then returned his attention to the pyre.

During the procession back down the mountain, men were already talking about the war in the west and the upcoming Moot. They traded all the same stories my own sources had brought me a twelvenight or more ago as if they were fresh. My mind slipped forward to the Moot again.

It was too easy to imagine what it would be to ride into Teamair for the festival as ard-righ-apparent, to perform the triple sacrifice on Bealtan Eve, to step up to the high throne in the Star Chamber, to order the battle strategies. I would have been the first ard-righ who the wizards of the Aballo Order couldn't lead by the nose; I would have deployed my resources to consolidate my power, rather than yielding it all up to the Order as ard-righthe always do.

But that long-expected future wasn't coming. Instead, I would be present in the Star Chamber as ard-harpist on Bealtan Day, swearing fealty to Amien with the rest of them, enduring all the cheek-cuts and left-handed comments of wizard and righ alike.

How proud my father had been, showing me around Teamair during the Moot at which Conary was elected ard-righ! The stars in my birth chart were clear, and my father had reveled in what they portended, even though the man knew he would already be dead when the day of my election came.

How crushed he would have been by the current circumstances, if he were alive.

There wasn't even any comfort in the fact that death had spared my father the humiliation. His death was my fault, too. I couldn't face the Moot, or the summons that was coming. I couldn't look any of those people in the face again.

There was no possibility of defying the Aballo Prince's summons—and only one alternative. When Amien's herald arrived in Ilnemedon after the feast of Estra, the man would find me gone.

Chapter 2

Stranger in a Strange Land

Wake up.

I opened my eyes, elation sweeping through me: the goddess's voice in my mind was a miracle. But a blade arced down through the darkness towards my throat.

I grabbed the assassin's wrist and twisted, deflecting the knife, grappling for a second hold and trying to kick him away. He hung on stubbornly; we tumbled over the side of the bed to the floor. I cracked my shoulder on an unfamiliar bedside table and scratch-landed on a wool rug, fists still full of assassin.

Where was I? The assassin rolled on top of me, twisting his wrist in my grasp; I pushed and rolled us over again. Fear forced my mind into a sort of spurious wakefulness, but everything still felt unreal. I leaned on the man's throat, grappling for the knife, while the man yanked on my hair and rolled on top again. My spine scraped across a painful transition between the rug and a hard plank floor. I struggled to wrap my fingers around the hilt, wrenched the knife free, and stabbed the assassin in the chest.

Blood splashed sticky and warm over my skin. I pulled the knife free, releasing a torrent that showered me again. Gods, I was a fool! I shoved the assassin's inert body away, throat clenching and heart pounding; I scrambled to my knees for a look around the room.

Once I'd wiped my eyes clear, I saw: the assassin and I were alone. Everything looked unfamiliar; I felt as if I might be enmeshed in one of those dreams of waking from a dream. But then my brain shook off sleep like a dog emerging from a river, and I remembered.

I wasn't in Ilnemedon; this was why everything looked strange. I knelt in a guest chamber at Tyra, the summer home of the legendary Tanaan Lady Carina of Finias, heroine of a ballad and a war four centuries past. And, at least when I retired this evening, no one here had seemed interested in killing me. A shudder tripped up my spine.

Lady Tella had spoken to me. After ten years of silence, after the wreck I'd made of everything, She finally had words for me again. She'd intervened to keep me alive, when She could simply have allowed my life to end on a fool's errand in an alien land. Had She decided to grant me a second chance? Hope flickered in my chest, but for the moment that was just a distraction. I yanked the tight-fitting hood from the assassin's head.

The man was human, and still alive. His breath came in shallow gasps. He sported well-made clothing, expensive boots, and a top-quality knife. The weapon was well balanced, either new or well cared for: much like the knife I always tucked into the concealed sheath in my right boot. Hatred overtook me: I'd left the human realms almost a twelvenight ago; the bastard must have been tracking me for at least that long. But my father's security master had spent years drilling this lesson into me: the time for emotion would come later. First I must understand.

"Who?" I said.

Predictably, the assassin said nothing. I grimaced and laid the blood-streaked knife on the polished planks of the floor, well out of the assassin's reach, then pushed back his sleeves, exposing his wrists and forearms to the moonlight. A gorsedd harpist in Regia, who had kept me well supplied with unusual tidbits of intelligence until that city fell to the kharr, mentioned seeing a peculiar tattoo on men he knew for kharr insiders: a redsnake coiled around the wrist. But the assassin's wrists were unmarked. Did this mean he wasn't kharr, or merely that he hadn't earned the tattoo?

I wrenched the assassin's head to one side, pulling aside the blond tail of battle-bound hair and looking for another sort of tattoo at the base of the scalp: a stylized sun rendered in black, the mark of the Order of the Hidden Sun. Devotees of the god Par, members of the Order of the Hidden Sun hold beliefs so blasphemous they would all have been exiled long ago, if they weren't the best spies and assassins in the world. The man's neck was unmarked: whoever wanted me dead was neither tiarn nor royal. And that eliminated every readily-imagined enemy and agenda.

I sighed and looked into the assassin's glazing eyes. The man was going to die, but it would take a while. I knew what I had to do.

Feelings didn't matter here. I needed to discover who had purchased my death, and that easily outweighed the things I might endure when I touched the assassin's mind. None of what I must do was a violation of my vow to give up magic: telepathic work is not an arcane operation, no matter what the uninitiated may think. A born telepath is little more than a man blessed with hearing among a society of the deaf. Nevertheless a knot of cold formed in my middle. To encompass the mind of a dying man is dangerous at best, and far too often fodder for weeks of screaming nightmares.

No time to waste: I braced myself against the pain and dying-disorientation that would spill into me at the contact and brushed the man's consciousness with my mind. But where I should have found a man's mind, I encountered a wall.

I sat back on my heels. Who was this man? Men who study the writings of the wizard Ransmith know how to shield against a telepath; I had seen those shields before. The wall around the assassin's mind was unlike any of those: a prickly fog that resonated in my teeth, rather than the impermeable fortress a wizard trained in Ransmith's methods would use. I sensed none of the tell-tales of Talent that allow members of the initiate to recognize one another: the assassin was neither wizard nor druid nor windcaller. And yet his mind was shielded. I searched the man's drawn face: his expression betrayed nothing. His eyes wavered between my face and things only the dying can see.

I drew a deep breath and touched the shield again. It wouldn't be possible to force and shatter; but if I could stand the resonance, I might slip through.

Hello? I sent.

The man didn't seem to hear: he wasn't a telepath, then. Nor did he seem to notice when I gritted my teeth and dove through the disquieting electric fog, trying to ignore the lightning that shot up my spine and gathered in the back of my brain.

Pain and breathlessness welled up to swallow me; the room swirled and sparkled towards deeper darkness. A miasma of guilt and grief invaded my consciousness, lodging painfully in my chest and throat. *Fireproof bastard*, the assassin thought. *Why wouldn't you die?*

I foundered for a second, nearly losing track of the contact. *Fireproof?* What the hell did that mean? With an effort I hung onto the link, pushing further inside.

The assassin's mind came into focus, and a face condensed out of the misty shimmer surrounding me: the same visage that stared at me from every mirror I'd ever encountered. Through the assassin's eyes my face was unfamiliar, almost inhuman: intense and forbidding, its high planes and deep blue eyes awash in moonlight and stark shadow, its jaw as uncompromising as a knife at the ribs.

Who? I thought. My hard-edged face melted into a memory of a half-famil-iar knife in my hand and a faintly-moonlit room condensing around me, a pair of startling blue eyes snapping open just a second too soon—

—gut-wrenching slide out of normality into nowhere, darkness falling away beneath me until even the sensation of air rushing past is gone, lights spinning and flashing in unnamed hues at the edges of vision—

—a golden-hued city basking in sunlight and summer warmth, air hum-ming with unrecognizable languages and immense gleaming buildings scraping a lavender-and-indigo sky—

—a beautiful, improbably-dressed Tana with eyes the color of emeralds, black hair swirling around her as she spins to face me—

—a cramped ill-lit corridor suffused with acrid odors; a prickle of sudden defenselessness across my back; ageless golden eyes fixing on me in white-hot menace as the weapon in my hand explodes—

—smoke in my eyes and blood in my mouth; the flaming remains of an earth-and-timber roof sailing down to pin me to a smoldering floor—

I couldn't breathe. Was that blood in my lungs? Would they find the time to torture me before I drowned? I very nearly hoped they would.

Suddenly I found myself again. The sensation of finding my own mind from *outside* nearly splintered me. I clung to the tenuous connection, released the assassin's mind and pulled back, the fog of the assassin's failing awareness and the cloud-occluded stars of the man's thoughts swirling backwards around me as I mindsailed away. I was getting rusty; I had nearly drowned in that death; and who would have come in after me? Sweet Lady Tella, when had I become such a fool?

Finally the assassin's pain-wracked face and battle-bound blond hair came into focus again; cold shivered through me as the lightning in my spine and hindbrain fizzled out. The assassin was too far gone to yield up anything coherent: there was no reason to prolong his suffering. I took a second to be sure my voice would sound steady before speaking.

"Shall we end this?" I said.

Something happened to his mouth, something that might have become a smile but then edged towards despair. He gave a barely perceptible nod.

I nodded in return. I picked up the knife again, drew it across his jugular and through his trachea. I sat back on the ruined rug as the life flowed out of the man, trying to sort through the meager senseless clues I'd acquired; but I couldn't get my attention off the assassin.

This was far from the first death I had witnessed, far from the first man I had killed. Nevertheless there were words that should have been said, and I could have said them. The assassin could have used the assistance of someone who had walked the other side, and I knew the way. But those duties were the prerogatives of a place I had left behind. Now I could only offer dispatch, warrior to warrior; to do more would have been a lie.

My Talent was becoming a rusty knife, grown both less effective and more apt to accidentally harm. I still smelled power everywhere; it had grown only more intoxicating in ten years of my refusing to yield to its call. But the skills that allow wizards to wield power safely were stiff with disuse.

And yet Lady Tella had spoken to me, for the first time in ten years. She hadn't forgotten me. She still had use for me. She might even have decided to forgive me. I had to find some way to become worthy of this second chance. I must understand what She required.

But first I must figure out who had initiated this attack. Who hated me this much, and why?

The halls of Tyra House stretched endlessly in the dark. My improvised blanket kilt dragged me slower still. My chest and arms still bore smears of blood; the stuff was begininning to dry in my hair, pasting it to my head and face. Now that the emergency was over, my mind spun over the attack and its context, seeking purchase. I wasn't likely to discover who had set an assassin on my trail until I returned to the human lands, but I reeled at the irony: only after I spent a twelvenight alone on the road had the man finally pulled off an attack—while I was a guest of the royal Tanaan House of Finias.

What had the assassin been doing since I left Ilnemedon, on all the days and nights when I presented a far easier target? Where were the Tanaan protocols and readiness for household attacks? How could a noble house this ill-prepared survive? In a human nobleman's house, in a situation like this—no. In a human house, there would *be* no situation like this. The responsibility of protecting a guest is understood to be a geas overriding every other, and no danger would be allowed within a bowshot of a guest's room at night.

Unless, of course, the host had decided to murder the guest himself. That would be the gravest of all possible violations under human law; but who knew how the game was played out here, among people whose ancestors had been gods? Every story and song about the Tanaan is clear: there is no predicting, let alone really understanding, what Tanaan might decide to do. Gods know my experience with the one Tan I ever thought I knew had borne that out.

Surprising how being in the Tanaan realms brought all those memories out of the dungeon where they belonged. I shoved them aside for the hundredth time this twelvenight and turned my mind to the problem I might yet solve.

If no human can understand their moral codes, even Tanaan politics must be driven by power and necessity. I was a perfect stranger here; no one in Finias had any reason to kill me. The fact that I didn't matter in Tanaan politics, whatever they might be, should have protected me. There should at least be a night watch or household security master I might call upon, someone to whom I could report the royal House of Finias's complete failure to uphold its guest-responsibilities.

I trailed cold fingers across the cabinets and presses spaced at intervals along the walls, trying to maintain my orientation between the areas of scant moonlight. I peered down darkened corridors, beginning to wonder whether anyone else remained alive.

A half-familiar knife in my hand; startling blue eyes snapping open just a second too soon: the memory leapt out of my head to flash against the darkness. It had come from the assassin's mind, and my own had called it up in a senseless attempt to focus on something: I recognized the eyes, just as I'd recognized my own face through the assassin's vision. This was the assassin's last coherent memory, the beginning of the man's attempt to take my life. Why was the knife only half-familiar?

I couldn't find anybody; the entire wing in which I'd slept lay in darkness. Why were the guest rooms in the most insecure spot in the house? They should have been on an upper floor. I walked across the cold smooth marble of Tyra House's grand reception space, then entered the opposite wing. The dining room and sitting rooms stood on this side, I remembered. In some of the oldest human houses, servants' quarters are tucked away beyond the public areas. Maybe I would find someone of sufficient authority to handle my problem back there.

Another assassin-image surfaced behind my light-deprived eyes: a gut-wrenching slide into nowhere, lights flashing at the edges of vision. I staggered, catching myself against a heavily-carved linen press. My bloodstained blanket began to un-kilt; I stopped to resettle it. I didn't know what to do with this incomprehensible image. I'd never seen anything like it. Most likely it was just a dying-hallucination.

A golden-hued city basking in sunlight and summer warmth, air humming with unrecognizable languages and immense gleaming buildings scraping a lavender-and-indigo sky. A faery realm? The elusive paradise of Hy-Breasaíl? A dream? I didn't know. I shook my head, trying to regain focus on the here-and-now.

The only areas beyond the public ones were the kitchen and the laundry, both of which were dark except for banked fires on the hearths. I was the only two-legged creature in either place.

More ghost images: *a beautiful young Tana with eyes the color of emeralds, black hair swirling around her as she spun to face me; ageless golden eyes pinning me as the weapon in my hand exploded.* I'd never seen a Tana before this journey; even after a twelvenight in the Tanaan realms, they still seemed like myths come to life. None of the Tanaan I'd met here in Finias matched the intense warrior beauty who flashed in the assassin's mind and was gone. But the golden eyes: those seemed familiar. I had the sense that I ought to remember who those eyes belonged to.

Eventually I found myself in the marble-floored reception space again. I walked out to the center and looked up. Deep galleries on the second and third floors receded into cavernous darkness; the ceiling, which I remembered as delicately frescoed and perhaps four stories high, lay completely hidden in shadow. Evidently the Tanaan felt no more need for night-lighting in their houses than they did for security for their guests.

Enough was enough. Proper projection could have filled the space with my voice, almost effortlessly; instead I channeled mounting frustration into a shout.

"HELLO?" My voice reverberated from the ceiling and the galleries, bouncing like a rock skipping around the interior of a well. In very little time the galleries filled with people, who I sensed as disturbances of the air and deepenings of the shadows rather than really being able to see or even hear them.

Someone lit a lamp: a Tan of typically elongated build and inestimable age whose dressing gown seemed not to have been buttoned properly. Nevertheless he carried a strange, otherworldly grace.

Light struck me heavily in my dark-strained eyes. It splashed a small puddle of illumination across the southeast corner of the second-floor gallery, exposing a lissome blonde Tana with a couple small wide-eyed children clinging to her shift—and caught sparks of magic in three dozen pairs of Tanaan eyes arrayed around the shadowed balconies.

Ripples of dismay ran through the galleries, and murmurs of *blood* and *Beallan*: the Tanaan word for *human*. Most of the eyes drew back; but a few leaned closer, as if for a better look at some exotic animal in a cage. I stood at the bottom of an observatory well, scions of the gods looking down on me; but this time I stared up at people rather than stars. For a moment awareness of mystery encompassed me. Then I remembered.

"Hello?" said a Tan I couldn't see.

"Hello," I answered, pitching my voice to the far side of the third-floor gallery for lack of a discernible target and hanging on to my civility. "Good evening."

Or was it morning? I set the problem aside.

"There is a dead would-be—" I realized I didn't know the Tanaan word for *assassin*. "—murderer in my room…"

If minds had gears as some composers are fond of fancying, mine would have been grinding on Tanaan declensions. "And I'd appreciate it if someone could get the body out of there…"

The sharp edges of Tanaan diphthongs felt like burrs rolling around in my mouth. "And I'm going to need a bath."

Silence stretched in the ill-lit hall. I couldn't even hear any of them breathing.

"…Anybody?" I said finally, putting real effort into sounding reasonable.

"Ah, yes," said a Tan I couldn't see, after another pause. The Tyra seneschal? It seemed I should recognize the voice. "If you would be pleased to return to your room, Lord, I'll join you there in a moment."

Someone should have brought me a towel. Instead I stood across the chamber from the assassin's corpse, rivulets of dried blood on my chest and arms, while attenuated Tanaan servants flitted in and then scattered like rushes before a wind. The flush of combat ebbed from me; fatigue took its place. How long had I slept? Two hours? Three?

I looked around the room. The fireplace at the center of the exterior wall stood clean and empty; the drafty flue was probably too narrow to admit a man. I hadn't touched either of the windows this evening, all too aware of the security hazard they represented. The glass still appeared untouched. I needed to go outside and see if the man had come in that way—and then shut the window behind him? Why?

Eventually a herald in the unmistakable white-and-gold of the Aballo Order glided into the room. I startled. Sweet Lady Tella, had Amien sent a herald all the way out here to find me? How had he known where to look?

"Tiarn Ellion," the herald said.

Another start of surprise jolted me: the herald was no Ilesian bard or failed Aballo initiate, but a Tan. He must be a member of Lady Carina Finias's staff. His dramatic facial bone structure verged on unpleasant angularity, as those of Tanaan often do. His high prominent cheekbones, delicate jaw, and large wide-set eyes might have been beautiful—again I thought of Deaclan—had he weighed ten pounds more. He had the stretched, wispy look all Tanaan seem to share—and no excuse for passing himself off as a herald that I could discern. A herald should know better than to call me *Tiarn*.

The herald's unnerving grey eyes took in my bloodstained body and improvised blanket kilt. His gaze slipped away, to the corpse and the blood soaking into the patterns of the rug. The Tan's translucent skin faded past the color of snowflowers and kept going.

I glanced again at the door behind the Tan. It was undamaged; it had still been locked when I opened it after the assassin died. Had the assassin managed to pick the lock without damaging it, then locked the door behind him when he entered the room? No professional would go to so much trouble to cut off his own escape.

Focus, I reminded myself. *Contain, then investigate.*

"Where is your security master?" I said.

The herald winced. "Tiarn, Mor Rishan is aware that Beallan customs are different from ours…"

Rishan Murias here? With his Lady en route to their home. How were they going to celebrate Bealtan, two hundred miles apart?

"But among the People it is taboo for—for a person under a death vendetta to accept hospitality from—"

"What?" I snapped. "What about his responsibility as host to ensure a guest's safety?"

The herald made a gesture a human would intend as half placation, half supplication. I supposed it meant the same thing here. Probably.

"Tiarn, Mor Rishan regrets this—incident, as I'm sure you do. He would like nothing better than to… resolve things simply and quietly."

I sighed. "Yes. That is exactly what I'd like."

The herald bowed. "Thank you, Tiarn. Mor Rishan will see you after you bathe."

I waited out in the house's front yard, away from the sights and smells of dead assassin, while servants heated enough water for me to bathe. Mountain air lay cold across my bare skin. I watched Telliyn climb towards her zenith and paint the disorganized garden in pale light, turning Lady Tella's intervention for me over and over in my mind.

Wake up. What did that mean? A simple enough instruction on the surface, it had been sufficient to save my life; but nothing She said had only one layer of meaning. Was this a call to return to Her service, to rededicate myself to the vows I'd taken at Aballo so long ago?

That was wishful thinking. I could return neither to Aballo nor to Tellan. Nevertheless the memory of the night She called me to Her service washed over me, and the mountain chill of Tyra became the fierce caress of the wind off Lady's Lake on the Tellan family estates; the lush terraced gardens spread out below me, awash in moonlight and sparkling with the dancing jewels of countless fireflies. A cloud descended from the mountain on the opposite shore to kiss the surface of the water, and awe shivered through me.

Moments like this were why the Tellan family lands are sacred ground. That land and those lakes belong to Lady Tella; the Tellan clan are Her elect. Lady Tella and Ilesan, the Lord of Gods, created the universe out of chaos, with the tumultuous embrace of Air on Water. Air belongs to Ilesan; Water is Tella's. Rivers, lakes, and seas are Hers. Places in which Air touches Water are sacred; this low cloud touching Tella's high mountain lake was an echo of the moment of Creation.

Rather than pulling on my jacket against the unexpectedly fierce cold, I let the wind blast into me, feeling it as the power of the Moment. Lady Tella, always a benevolent presence at Sliavtel, gathered around me so closely that my mind exploded with rapture. Joy tingled in every portion of my being.

Ellion. This was my Lady's voice in my mind. I'd heard it in dreams for longer than I could recall; this was the first time She'd spoken to me while I was awake. The brandy glass slid from my hand. If it landed on the stone of the terrace, it made no noise I could hear. *I require you.*

"I am ever Yours, Lady," I said, as remotely and perfectly conscious as if this, too, were a dream.

Not fully. Not yet. Come to Me.

There was no need to ask where She wanted me to go; the mystery of the wizards' retreat had occupied my dreams for months. How long had I been waiting for this Call without realizing it? How long would it take to reach Aballo?

But just as quickly as it came over me, the moment collapsed, and I stood covered in blood and an improvised blanket kilt, outside a house of no security and little more welcome, aching for Her hand to settle on me again.

Wake up. If it wasn't a summons, what did it mean?

By the time the servants had heated enough water for me to bathe, dawn cast pale shimmering light on the windows. Evidently they were cold-hardened by the long mountain winter: it never occurred to any of them to light the brazier in the bathing room until I finally asked someone to do it. I remembered a time when I was less affected by cold than anyone I knew; now I saw how soft I had become in Ilnemedon's southern air.

Finally things in the bathing room were as settled as they were going to get: I dismissed the servants, unwrapped the blood-soaked blanket, and slipped gratefully into the water. I had to wash my hair several times before it finally felt clean.

When I returned to my room, the assassin's corpse was gone. So was the bloodstained rug. Morning had brought color back to the room, but it had little power against the pervasive mountain chill: the white silk of fresh bedding glowed like new snow among dark hardwood furniture and drapes of deep red and green, but the floor under my bare feet felt as cold as summer frost. The floor had been mopped, but several servants were still trying to restore order to the room.

I evicted them and began to dress; in short order the need to look for clues from the attack overwhelmed my need for warmth. I walked around the room buttoning my shirt, examining everything.

The windows seemed untouched, the harp case and bags I'd carried from Ilnemedon undisturbed. The glass sported streaks left by a cleaning cloth, but also a certain amount of dust. The flue of the fireplace was definitely too narrow to admit the assassin's muscular shoulders. My sword and knife remained in the wardrobe where I'd left them, along with my newly-acquired assassin's blade.

There was no way the assassin could have entered the room while I slept: door locked, windows untouched, flue inaccessible. I'd exercised the simple precaution of checking every possible hiding place in the room before lying down. If I hadn't awakened to his knife in my face, I wouldn't have believed he'd been here at all.

Shortly Rishan Murias arrived. He didn't look four hundred years old. I don't know what I expected of one of the heroes of the great war against the renegade wizard Nechton, but he was both less commanding and less exotic than my imagination had built him up to be.

Nevertheless, if his hair was snow-white, his face remained as firm as a fifty-year-old man's. He had a rider's legs, and the straightness of his spine brought his fine-boned head up to the level of my eyes. But in typical Tanaan fashion, Rishan lacked ruggedness. He seemed as if a warrior who met him on the sparring ground might accidentally break him.

Rishan opened his mouth and then closed it again. His command of Ilesian was adequate, but he obviously couldn't figure out how to address me. Neither could human nobility, so I probably shouldn't hold that against him. Still it pricked me.

"Lord Rishan," I said.

The Tan turned his head; diffuse light touched the depths of his black eyes. Legend holds that Tanaan eyes gleam like cats', but that isn't the truth. The minute filaments that make each human iris unique lie deeply hidden in Tanaan eyes, giving them an abyssal aura. Moments when light illumines those depths feels like suddenly seeing all the way to the bottom of a glacier lake.

"I must apologize for the damage to your house," I continued. "If I'd been awake…"

Rishan waved dismissively: the rug was ruined, but other than this I'd wrecked nothing. Again I waited while the Tan considered his next statement.

"Ellion," he said finally.

I bristled. I didn't expect any title from Rishan: *sian* or even the Tanaan *ouirr* would have been enough. But tonight I was not even to be acknowledged as a man of honor, an equal.

"It is I who must apologize. It has been centuries since this sort of thing happened among Dana's People…" Rishan trailed off.

What had happened to Rishan Murias and Carina Finias, the Tanaan who played such critical parts in the wizard Nechton's defeat? Were those songs every bit the fabrications I knew the romantic ballad about Carina to be? Should I doubt the other historical eipiciúil of that period, too? I should have known better than to hold out hope that something, finally, would live up to the songs. *Sweet Lady Tella, I was a fool to expect—*

I stopped the thought. I was mind-shielded, a simple precaution when dealing with a known telepath; but a consciously-framed thought can still be accidentally broadcast, despite the cleverest shield. And Rishan's Talent was a strong one. Anyone who had studied the history of Nechton's War knew this. I must remember even my thoughts weren't secure here.

Contain, then investigate. It is every security master's axiom. At least I was the only living human at Tyra tonight: were I careful, news of the price on my neck might not spread. It was reasonable to hope that, with the assassin dead, I would remain relatively safe until I turned up alive in the human realms.

"Was there any sort of perimeter on the house this evening?" I asked.

"Any… no. I assure you, we will spare no effort to discover who this man was."

I managed a humorless laugh. Rishan clearly had no idea how to conduct such an investigation, still less how to do it without attracting attention. The less involved Rishan was, the safer I would be. I pushed a curl of wet hair out of my face.

"No point in that," I said. "This was a professional. Any identity he might have had is long gone."

Rishan nodded, angular face still. An uncomfortable silence descended.

"I understand you'll be leaving us this morning," he said finally.

"Heading downriver again," I said, relaxing a bit at the more neutral topic. "I hope to catch up to Lady Carina before she reaches Finias and—"

"Who told you Mora Carina was en route to Fíana?" Rishan's alien stare searched me like a stiletto.

"Your pardon, sian? When I arrived yesterday evening, everyone agreed that the mora was on her way to…?" I frowned, some disconnected memory hovering just out of reach. The one map I'd found that covered the eastern areas of the Tanaan lands had borne no label near the summer capital but *Finias*, the nation's name. I'd concluded the city and the nation were eponymous. Was *Finias* the nation, *Fíana* the summer capital? "…Fíana? To make preparations for Bealtan."

Rishan shook his head, pain in the angles of his brows and narrow mouth. "The city? You mean Irisa."

Now I remembered: I'd heard, long ago, that the Tanaan call their lands and Great Houses by different names than humans do—though I could no longer recall who told the tale or exactly what they'd said. *Fíana* must be their word for *Finias*.

"And the mora on the river is the *young* mora, my daughter," Rishan continued.

Was this Tanaan coyness or another language problem? "Then where might I find the mora Carina?"

Rishan looked away, shrugging one shoulder: a Tanaan gesture that can mean anything from *Leave this topic alone* to *Your guess is as good as mine*.

"Then the young mora…" I said.

Rishan glanced at me, then returned his gaze to something behind my left ear. "Will be invested at Bealtan. Seven years have passed; Letitia attains maturity this spring. All the clan leaders agree it's time."

"I regret that I was unable to attend the mora's pyre," I said.

"I had heard you were an intelligent man," Rishan grated, glaring at me. "There *was* no pyre." He turned and swept out of the room, dressing gown billowing behind him.

In the kitchen, I coaxed a cup of unidentifiable tea and a sort of breakfast roll from a pretty Tana who might be twenty or two hundred, wishing I could come back later and enlist her help with unraveling the tall tales one hears about Tanaan women. But the single most important skill a harpist can cultivate is knowing when he is out of a tiarn's good graces and it is time to move on. It was definitely time.

Discreet inquiries confirmed the best theory I'd been able to spin: Lady Carina Finias—Fíana?—rode out of her stable yard one hot spring day seven years ago, and no one had heard from her since. No one knew where she had gone or why. Alive or dead, interested in her people or not, she was about to be succeeded by her daughter. It seemed a sorry end for the heroine of *The Ballad of Carina*.

But it wouldn't scotch the wheels of my plan. I'd spent the better part of a month traveling, and the death or disappearance of the potential gorsedd client I'd come to meet wouldn't send me back to the Harpist Gorsedd Hall. Not when I knew what would be waiting for me there: Amien's herald, and a summons to the Bealtan Moot. I couldn't refuse the summons. The best I could do was be halfway to Hy-Breasaíl when it arrived—and stay away too long for it to matter. This year, I would spend Bealtan among the Tanaan.

Chapter 3
Journey of a Thousand Miles

After two days of following the river back towards the city, I finally spotted the young mora's barge. Two barges, in fact: in the typical fashion of royals everywhere, the lady clearly found it necessary to bring every comfort, member of personal staff, and hanger-on wherever she went. A group on the first barge sang the sort of neverending travel song that makes harpists want to take their own lives rather than endure the repetition for another mile; the second barge was quieter and seemed to be carrying more gear than people.

I cued my horse for greater speed; he leapt forward, seemingly relieved at the change in pace. Within moments I had closed the gap between myself and the barges almost enough to make shouting upwind worthwhile. Someone on the first barge rose, looking back at me: a Tana with gleaming blonde hair whose face was obscured by the angle of the early evening sun. Within seconds half the people on the barge had turned to stare, so I waved. A number of them waved back; the barges pulled in to shore, and I stopped and dismounted to wait for the passengers to disembark.

Once the gangway was in place, the Tana who had first spotted me walked across—carrying a book. This must be Letitia, the young mora: she appraised me frankly, brilliant green eyes clear and steady on my own for long enough that most men would have looked away. I didn't want to, though I was pleased to move on to other aspects of her person when a tall young Tan stepped across the planks behind her, the sound of his boots on the wood snaring her attention. They were like a matched pair of two-year-old racers: blond and arrestingly beautiful, almost eerie in their similarity, their typically elongated Tanaan physiques and their evident youth giving them a coltish air. She was the leader of this team: he paused at her elbow, a book of his own tucked against his lean frame and his body angling towards her even while his abyssal blue eyes examined me with an analytical, protective air.

"Hello," she said evenly in the Tanaan language. Her voice had a pleasant, unaffected musicality, as those of most Tanaan do.

"Mora Letitia?" I said. She nodded; I bowed, and she nodded again, in the manner of a royal recognizing a person of lower rank. She had no way of knowing, of course; I would grant her the error for free.

"I am Ellion Tellan, the ard-harpist." I paused, gauging whether she'd understood. How much could a Tanaan, even a Tanaan royal, be expected to know of human gorsedd and craft organizations? "The leader of our gorsedd," I elaborated, using the Ilesian word.

She nodded. "Isn't Tellan a country?"

Had she deduced so quickly who I was, or was the query born of absolute naïvete? I couldn't tell.

"Yes," I said, disciplining myself to meet her gaze. "But the Harpist Gorsedd is based in Ilnemedon, in Ilesia."

Her exotic face turned analytical. "So your name is Tellan, but you live in Ilesia."

"Yes."

"Ah." She glanced around, so I did, too. People crossed from both barges, unloading gear and personal possessions and establishing a camp with an efficiency that suggested long routine. Men set up tents and cook-fires; a gaggle of young, pretty Tana giggled and whispered and threw me a series of curious, speculative glances while spreading a cloth and some pillows beneath the branches of a birch; a group of lithe blond archers of both sexes arranged targets for practice. All told, the archers and the rest of the young mora's contingent numbered only one more than a bare dozen. The utter unconcern with security I'd seen at Tyra seemed a sudden bastion of safety. How did these people survive?

"This is my…" The young mora and her male mirror-image shared a quizzical glance; he raised his eyebrows. "Consort, Iminor a Dianann."

We bowed properly to one another. Why did he look embarrassed? Or was I misreading a Tanaan expression that meant something else altogether?

"Sian," I said, and silence settled among us again. Apparently it would be my task to drive the conversation: I grasped at the surest topic among those few who regularly read.

"What are you reading?" I said to the mora.

Surprise blossomed in her face. "You rode here from Ilesia to find out what I'm reading?"

I laughed. "No. You stepped off a barge carrying a book. Most people wouldn't take a book onto a boat. What if it fell in? How would you ever replace it? But you didn't seem at all worried, so I wondered what you were reading."

Finally she smiled, shaking her head. She turned the book in her hands, gaze on the old leather of the obviously well-loved, expertly-tooled cover.

"Philosophy, in the Ilesian language," she said. "I'm told it was my mother's favorite."

And there it was, just that quickly: the opening I sought. "I was saddened to hear of her loss," I said, which—against all reason—was true. "She was… a great lady."

Suddenly the young mora's eyes were on mine, surprise and something that might be hope written in her expression. "You knew her?"

A man could lose himself in the depths of that gaze. For a brief flicker of time I felt as if I had slipped into an old fireside tale.

"By reputation only," I said. "I had looked forward to meeting the heroine of the song."

"The *song?*" she echoed, so incredulous that I wondered whether I'd used the wrong word; she exchanged another look with her young consort.

"Don't tell me you have never heard it," I said.

She shook her head. "I've never heard any of your music. I can't believe— why would Bealla have a song about—"

Abruptly she was staring at me again. There are stories that claim the gaze of a Tana can render a man incapable of falsehood, or irrevocably capture his heart, or both. I knew better than to believe old tales, of course. But my throat tightened anyway.

"You are the leader of your harpist organization," she said finally. "Does this mean you can play?"

I fought down an incredulous laugh. "Yes. Would you like to hear the song?"

"Yes."

I nodded. "One moment. Excuse me, please."

I swept a courtly bow and walked back to the place where my horse waited, seemingly content for once. I unlashed my harp case from the saddle, slung the speckled-hide strap over my shoulder, and returned to the spot in which the young mora and her consort stood, surrounded now by the gaggle of Tana I'd seen preparing a picnic-nest under the tree. They tried unsuccessfully to look as if they weren't watching me approach, giggling and whispering to Letitia. Was it possible Tanaan were as curious about humans as we are about them? Once I'd had the thought, I realized how obvious the answer was. Finally the mora laughed and shooed them off.

"Mora," I said, and bowed again.

She smiled. "Would you come and sit with me? My companions of the chamber have prepared a spot for us, and it can't be possible to play that thing standing up…"

I smiled in return. "Thank you," I said, and followed her and her consort to sit on the blanket beneath the tree. The young Tan wrestled a bit with his scabbard as he settled, as if it were an unaccustomed encumbrance; I restrained a puzzled frown.

It is Tanaan custom for the women to rule; I understood this, strange as it was. The Tana arranging her skirts about her and tucking a pillow beneath her elbow *just so* would soon be the nearest thing the Tanaan nation of Finias—or

Fíana—would have to a righ. This would make her consort the next thing to a riga: royal. I couldn't fathom how a royal could avoid becoming a warrior, even did he also find time for scholarly or artistic pursuits, as this Tan evidently did.

The questions I wanted to ask were rude: I stored the information as a piece of the puzzle that didn't match any I had discovered so far and opened my harp case.

"With your indulgence, Mora," I said, glancing at her. If she was embarrassed by her consort's discomfort with his scabbard, she hid it well. I pulled the harp free and set the case aside. "It hasn't been tuned in days…"

She nodded, unsurprised; I pulled the harp key from my pocket. A Tana brought and served wine for the three of us. I settled the harp against knee and clavicle and began tuning while the serving-girl lingered, staring a bit. Finally the mora shooed her off again.

The familiar routine of tuning took the edge off all the strangeness around me; for half a second I wished I were back in the solitude of my studio in the Harpist Gorsedd Hall. But Ilnemedon was the last place I should be right now, and I was in the midst of an experience few humans are lucky enough to have. I made a deliberate effort to appreciate where I was, tuning with half my mind while I took in the scene with the other.

A collection of pretty, brightly-colored tents had sprung up across the meadow in which I sat; twoscore blond, exotic people in elegant silks moved among them. The sun's last ruddy rays glanced from the strikingly-enamelled helms and breastplates of swordsmen as they bouted. Somewhere meat roasted over a campfire. Dragonflies performed an iridescent aerial dance above the river, which flowed almost soundlessly into sunset-tinged mist; to my left, beyond the meadow, trees laced golden with evening climbed northward out of sight. Shadows stretched away from me, deepening. There must certainly be songs no one had ever written in all this.

"I came to Fíana," I said to the mora, "to speak with your mother about taking on a new gorsedd harpist. Our records show that she retained one, a very long time ago."

"Really?" Again she was incredulous.

I nodded. "At first I thought her taste for our music might be unique among your people. But now that I see your interest in things Ilesian—" I nodded towards the book beside her, then glanced at her consort's book and recognized the title with a small shock.

"And yours as well, sian," I said to him. "Beannchar on siegecraft, isn't it?" And why would a noncombatant read Beannchar? "An excellent volume; so much of it still holds true…"

He nodded slowly, analysis in his depthless blue eyes. Had he but grey eyes and black hair, he would have been Deaclan's double; they had the same lean, muscular physique, the same high, graceful cheekbones and narrow jaw. Even the analytical look was familiar to me, though in Deaclan's eyes it had shared the stage with the unmistakable light of magic. The realization made something strange and uncomfortable happen inside my chest; I pushed the thought aside.

"Well," I said to the mora, keeping my sudden agitation out of my voice. "A harpist of the gorsedd would be a rich resource for you, and a nice change of pace from your own bardic works. Do you retain a bard?"

"I—No. My father does…"

"But you will be invested at Bealtan, I understand."

She nodded; I reached for the grace stroke. "So this would be a good time to begin expanding your own staff."

Her curious expression collapsed into a frown.

"I—I suppose it is," she said, as if I were the first to suggest that her staff should meet her needs.

Clearly it would take until Bealtan at the very least to develop any sort of understanding of the Tanaan realms.

"So," I said. "This is *The Ballad of Carina.*"

I raised the harp to my shoulder again, began a musical walk down a lane so familiar and well-worn I could have played through the whole thing while asleep. But this evening, sitting in a meadow with a Tana who probably hadn't reached her third decade, the tired standard roared suddenly to life. This was Carina's daughter, the living incarnation of all the outrageously worshipful imagery in the song; Carina herself couldn't have been much older than Letitia was now when the events of the song took place.

Who had she been, that Carina? Usually when I played this song I thought about my old teacher Amien, who centuries later still seemed to carry an inextinguishable torch for the Tana. Surely there had been more to her than Tanaan beauty; the Prince of the Aballo Order has ample opportunity with women of great beauty in royal courts across the human realms. Carina was a Talent, the stories say. Was that why Amien lost himself in her?

I sang my way down the path the verses traced: Carina on a sojourn at the royal Tanaan court of Murias, completing the nuptial negotiations that would eventually make Rishan Murias her consort; word of the menace posed by the renegade wizard Nechton reaching all the way to that remote land; Carina traveling through lands rocked by war between Nechton's forces and forces loyal to the true gods, finally reaching Nechton's stronghold at Macol; Nechton's defeat at the hands of her incomprehensible magic and the subsequent rout of his armies in the field; Carina's return to the mystery of the Tanaan lands and the human realms left to remember and rebuild.

The more I learned of the history of that period, the more Carina had come to seem the next thing to a goddess to me. It was very strange to look at her daughter, who so matched the physical descriptions in the song, and consider the possibility that Carina might have been this young and delicate and yet somehow managed to defeat the greatest arcane talent ever to cross the threshold at Aballo. For the thousandth time I wondered how she had accomplished it. What power or technique she had mastered that Nechton was unable to counter. How many other secrets of Tanaan magic lay hidden on this side of the world.

How many of them Letitia knew.

Letitia stared at me in intense silence after I finished, wearing a look that suggested the entire eipiciúil might be an elaborate joke and the punchline had been lost in translation.

"Did you write that?" she asked finally.

I smiled. "It predates me by several hundred years."

"But it's *true?*"

Surprise overtook me before I could control my expression. Most historical ballads are composed of layers of fancy and winners' self-justification, only leavened by a few nuggets of inescapable truth. I had already spent more years picking them apart than I'd spent on any other area of study, and this one fared better than most: there were no untruths I was aware of in its verses, only areas of history that are beyond the purview of historical balladeers.

Everyone agreed Nechton's power had so far outstripped that of any member of the Aballo Order that no living wizard could have hoped to defeat him: even in the private chambers of Aballo, this fact was beyond debate. Arcane scholars—not least Amien himself, who had apparently spent considerable time with Carina—were still at a loss to explain her power and how she had defeated the renegade. And of course there was no accounting for the motivations of the Tanaan, who could easily have stayed on their side of the mountains and waited out the crisis. They have the lifespans for it, after all. But none of the ballad had proven untrue thus far: merely unexplained.

"As far as anyone knows," I said. "With eipiciúilae this old, it's hard to find anyone still living who remembers the events."

Among humans, that would have played as a humorous understatement; Letitia just gazed at me. And finally it occurred to me that Amien must know *exactly* what had happened; if I had correctly read between the lines of his stories, he and Carina had been together for much of the war. I wished I could learn what he knew about the backstory.

But not so passionately that I would talk to him, of course.

"Do you know of a reason why I should suspect it?" I asked Letitia.

She sat back with an exasperated sigh. "No. I just—Endeáril! Why was I never *told* any of this?"

Why, indeed. Human men drive their sons—and anyone else unable to escape—to distraction with the boredom of endless war stories. Shouldn't Tanaan warriors do the same?

Unless the arcane battle had left Carina scarred in ways that only other members of the initiate might understand. Unless the duel had shown her things about herself that no man should have to carry inside him, things about which she was too ashamed to ever share the burden. Unless she had broken vows, destroyed her connection to her gods, caused the deaths of people she loved.

I shook off the bleak imaginings. That was my story, not hers. There must be a much simpler explanation.

"Mora," I said quietly, "I couldn't begin to guess. But sometimes... Sometimes it's impossible to talk about engagements like that... afterward."

Once again her gaze locked on me, and I was sinking into the emerald sea of her eyes. Some quality about her gaze felt like innocence; was this the transcendent, ageless wisdom of the Tanaan one hears so much about? And what was the source of the grief in her depths?

Was this a mysterious, ageless creature out of a legend, or a woman barely out of girlhood missing her mama? Both possible truths wavered in my head; I couldn't decide.

"When did it happen?" Letitia asked. "This war?"

"A little less than four hundred years ago."

"So she was young."

"Very young. Possibly no older than you are now."

The mora bristled. "Why, how many winters have *you?*"

Suddenly I felt as if I had sailed into a mined harbor. How was I supposed to know where the mines lay?

"Twenty-eight," I said mildly, presenting her with a calm, even gaze. The belligerence in her eyes softened; I should have smiled, but magic walked red and black up my spine, sparkling in dark seductive hues around the edges of mundane vision, and my head was shifting to accommodate it.

It was an unimaginable stroke of good luck: I'd stumbled into an arcane engagement between two of the legendary Tanaan mages. The fact that I was likely to be caught in the crossfire troubled me far less than it should. I was about to see something no human had witnessed in centuries.

But no: there was no answering flare of power anywhere in the meadow, no court wizard on Letitia's little staff. What was going on here?

It was an error in judgment, one I'd probably regret within minutes, but I cast a tendril of awareness towards the arcane onslaught approaching the meadow's northern border. I encountered no answering mental presence here, either: the black energy racing towards me stemmed from a remote working. Its vehicles included a group of dead souls tethered to undead bodies.

Cold horror gripped me, and I discovered myself on my feet, fingers curled around the hilt of my sword. Such workings are violations of the code every Aballo wizard vows to uphold; but apparently the Tanaan weren't bound by any sort of moral convention. And no one in this meadow seemed to have even a glimmer of what was bearing down on them.

"Get to the barges," I said to the mora, hardly aware of the words leaving my mouth. Iminor stood beside me, seemingly following my gaze. But I couldn't focus on him: a contingent of horsemen rode out of the trees, and though dead they were unmistakably human.

This wasn't Tanaan magic at all. Whoever had set an assassin on my trail had decided to escalate beyond all the bounds of warfare, arcane or otherwise, and I had just put dozens of innocent people in mortal danger. The best I could do now was draw the attack away.

"Mora, *now!*" I barked, all pretense of courtly manners lost, and sprinted to my horse. He stared wild-eyed, ears pinned: predictably miles ahead of his dim human rider at recognizing battlefield magic. I vaulted into the saddle and spurred him towards the onslaught; he snorted and dug in, muscles rippling as if he might turn and bolt in the opposite direction instead. I swore and slapped his hip with the flat of my sword, and he leapt forward, racing diagonally across the meadow. Iminor and Letitia shouted words the wind swept away before I could hear them; people ran in a dozen different directions; the riders thundered straight across the meadow as if unaware my faster mount would have me in the woods before they reached the place where our paths intersected.

I stole little glances at the riders as I raced away: pale and still-faced, they were resplendent in scarlet coats and meticulously-articulated spidersilk mail. Their huge black destriers, full of mane and fetlock, rumbled across the meadow like an approaching storm. I could feel myself beginning to stare even while I urged my horse faster: eyes snared by the grace and precise co-ordination of the contingent, the aura of power shimmering around them, the seductive hint of almost-visible tethers to a crystalline will trailing in their wake: the elusive connections tantamount to an invitation, for a wizard with the fortitude to look into the truth of the black power that fueled them. Surely learning the source of that energy was not a violation of my vow, merely a necessary gathering of intelligence about an unknown enemy. Surely no one in this meadow would be surprised when the riders took to the air like the Wild Hunt of Hy-Breasaíl, and no one would blame me when I followed.

They bore directly southward across the meadow. They weren't going to intercept me; they weren't even going to try. I wasn't their target.

I sucked in a lungful of suddenly-cloying air and wheeled my horse towards the campsite. The undead horsemen rode without slowing through a hailstorm of Tanaan arrows, undeterred and unbloodied by the hits they took. They reached the fringes of the camp before I did, swords busy among the Tanaan. Power flashed against my skin like sparks from a campfire; the Tanaan were dying instantly, on contact: not of their wounds, but of the sudden draw of their life energies into their attackers. Whoever had crafted those dire ghouls was using a depletion spell to power them: it was simultaneously terri-ble and elegant, and the accidental splashes of energy arcing against me made my throat knot with horror even while the pleasure of the power sprinkled itself up the length of my spine. The riders had slowed, but they weren't stop-ping; and the part of my mind that had trained to manage battlefield deploy-ments drew all their separate trajectories into a single pattern and saw their target: Letitia.

Moments like this were why I always found myself choosing overbred Dáirine lighthorses: the horse followed my cues as if he'd been waiting a twel-venight for them. He cut and wove through the chaos to the place in which Le-titia raced among the tents, shouting and harrying her panicked staff towards the barges. I leaned down and plucked her from the ground as we galloped past, swinging her up and around behind me. She grabbed two fistfuls of my jacket and jammed a shoulder into my spine.

"No!" she shouted. "What are you doing?"

And I'd thought her push against the ground as I lifted her had been a help-ful, intelligent choice, possibly the result of extraction drills. Well, we'd argue later; I just wheeled us back towards the woods and spurred the horse faster.

"Those are *my people* dying back there!" Letitia shouted in my ear.

Or we could argue now. "*You* are the target of the attack!"

We jumped and cleared a little stream trailing across the meadow. Letitia gasped and bounced against me, then clutched more tightly at my jacket. I glanced back: most of the warriors of her contingent still stood, but they were not organized. Her attackers would take them apart that way, and a lighthorse carrying two can't outrun a destrier for long. We would have to make a stand; I needed reinforcements and a spot in which to deploy them.

"Fíana!" I shouted, which served to catch the attention of most of the war-riors. "Fíana! To me!"

We raced to the treeline, and I glanced back, satisfied that the warriors finally understood where their lady was and were following me, then scanned our surroundings for a spot I could use. There was nothing: just darkening meadow and shadowed trees and a horse who was tiring under the extra weight. At the edge of the woods, I reined. There was no better choice than the trees.

"Well, then, that's it!" I said. One should address noncombatants as gently as possible during combat, but it was perfectly obvious that not only the remains of Letitia's contingent but all her attackers were following me, and the attackers would reach me first. My voice was not as gentle as it should have been. "Please tell me you know how to climb a tree!"

"What?" Letitia shrilled.

"Fouzh!" I said. We were well and truly buggered, then. Maybe I should try to dodge among the trees a while, counting on my greater maneuverability to peel off a few of them and perhaps buy her contingent some time. My horse's sides were heaving.

"*Of course* I know how to climb a tree!" Letitia snapped. Her voice sounded strong, but her otherworldly eyes were edged with tears. "But this hardly—"

"Up you go, then," I said, schooling my voice to a semblance of calm, and maneuvered the horse so we stood beside a hefty oak. "Don't come down until I say!"

She didn't move. The riders were closing in, and some treacherous voice in the back of my head suggested that it would be far more expedient to manage this situation magically; that it might be the only way anyone survived to embellish the tale. It would be all too easy to allow the shift in consciousness that was trying to overtake me. My throat clenched with the need.

"Mora, *move!*" I barked instead, tossing a glare over my shoulder at her.

"All *right!*" she retorted, wrenched the voluminous folds of her dress aside, and scrambled up on the horse's back. She pulled herself up to the lowest branch with surprising nimbleness for a woman wearing half a wagonload of silk; I edged the horse away. I was nearly out of time: I drew my sword.

"Go as high as you can!" I called; and then the first ghoul was on me, blade crashing against mine as we closed. A composer who intended to entertain would have called my opponent *it*; the possibility of a human man enchanted beyond death cuts too close to the bone to go down easily with beer. But this had been a human man: a trained warrior, quite possibly a nobleman; even in death his muscles knew combat, right down to the sinew. His dead gaze made my throat tighten even as I parried, and his emotionless face, green-cast and purple-lipped as it was, angled to take in every motion rather than spending all attention on my sword. My riposte was an action of will, not the automatic motion it should have been; again and again I found the dark power that hung on him dragging my mind towards arcane awareness, while my opponent rushed in to claim the moment's advantage.

I knew arcane history well enough to recognize that the only sensible target on this opponent was the head: it must be severed completely from the neck to break the spell. And I couldn't allow even so much contact as my knuckles grazing the artistically-worked guard of his sword, or I'd find myself infected with a deadly depletion spell. But awareness of the spell nearly snared me;

his blade screeched down my own, and suddenly we were far too close. The magic driving him sparked against my skin. I shook it off, hauled my traitorous mind closed, and turned my attention to the fight.

By the time I dispatched him and discovered that even decapitation will not make an undead man bleed, three more arrived to take his place. I maneuvered hastily against the trunk of the tree Letitia had climbed and dove into the all-but-hopeless task of fending off a growing body of attackers without any substantial shift in stance. When a shout rose nearby and a second sword rang against an opponent's blade, there wasn't time for more than a glance between me and my new ally—but I nearly lost the rhythm of my engagement in surprise. Of all the Tanaan warriors in that meadow, the first to arrive had been Letitia's consort. This was no noncombatant, after all.

"Ouirr harpist!" he shouted, blade sliding against his opponent's as he fought for control. "Don't let them touch you!"

I nodded, parrying rapidly to the left and fending off an attack from the right with a sidelong swipe. The sword jarred in my hand. "Go for the heads!"

Five more Tanaan swordsmen arrived. The odds were growing less dire. But I was astonished again: two of the warriors were Tana, and they were competent. Another Tan raced in, planted his feet, and attacked a ghoul's sword arm.

"The *heads!*" I barked again, and severed another. Still no blood. It should have been a relief, but its absence unsettled me.

One of the Tana shrieked a battle cry that sounded strangely like "Bastard!" and, despite the fact that she was as horseless as the rest of the Tanaan, nearly severed a ghoul's head. It dangled, bloodless and evidently still aware, against the ghoul's chest; the dead man swung again, narrowly missing her.

"Lord of Light!" the Tan who had just arrived croaked, and finished the job. Another down; a dozen or so to go.

"There's one in the tree!" Letitia yelped from someplace in the branches above us. I swore and glanced around for an opening in the swarm of horsemen around me; on the other side of the massive trunk, an unarmed Tan swung a fallen branch at the ghoul dangling from a bough: once, twice, and on the third blow the dead man fell. One of the Tana was on him by the time he hit the ground, taking his head with a single stroke. My distraction left me so vulnerable I had to duck beneath two simultaneous attacks, then swing my blade above my head so I could remove my face from my horse's neck without touching steel.

Little by little we whittled away at them. Our opponents were as varied as any group of living men might be, though they all shared the same greenish pallor, purple lips, and dead eyes. There was a weird synchronization to their rhythms, as if they all moved to the beat of the same mad inaudible drummer—and an oddly high proportion were black-haired. Either they shared some form of communication I didn't recognize or the wizard behind this assault was monitoring them directly: when, at length, we eliminated their numerical advantage, they simultaneously disengaged and withdrew, riding away across the now-dark meadow and leaving their fallen comrades behind. One of the Tanaan warriors ran a short distance after them and then stopped.

Suddenly everything was quiet. Telliyn's waning crescent failed to penetrate the shadows of the trees beneath which we stood. The fewer attempts people made to pick their ways among the fallen ghouls and their quite possibly active spells without adequate light, the better.

"Hold a moment," I said, glancing around the group of warriors to gather their attention. Then to the Tan who stood in the meadow, I said, "Get us some torches, please?"

One of the Tana detached herself from the edge of the group and ran towards the river with him. Their blond hair streamed behind them, pale in the fading light, as they ran. I glanced up into the tree, but I couldn't see Letitia.

"Mora, please stay put until we can get you down safely," I called, then looked around at the warriors again. "Anybody hurt?"

"I can climb down a tree!" Letitia snapped. Even knowing where to look, I still couldn't see her. She must have climbed a good way up.

"Minor wound on my forearm," one Tan said calmly, studying his wrist in the scant light.

And yet he lived. Was the depletion spell only active when the ghouls were—I repressed a shudder—*feeding*, then?

"Without touching any of these ghouls?" I said to the spot in which I thought Letitia's voice had originated, trying to sound composed. "Have patience, please."

I must make a point of watching the young warrior and try to find an opportunity to examine his wrist. I glanced at him again, trying not to seem obvious, but he just shook his hand the way a harpist who has played too long might shake the fatigue from his muscles and shoved his fingers into his sword belt with a gesture that suggested long habit. We all stood there in uneasy stillness, waiting for the torches to return.

After a few minutes the warriors I had dispatched returned with torches, moving more slowly than they had on the way out. Torchlight restored detail to their faces: the Tan's lean visage was grim, the Tana's angular cheeks wet with tears.

"Tru, are you hurt?" the Tan who seemed to be the leader of the contingent said.

"No." Her voice was thick, but her terse answer invited no discussion.

We picked our ways out of the battleground by torchlight, stepping carefully to avoid the fallen bodies of the attackers. It might have been the site of any skirmish, except that there was no blood. Once all the Tanaan were clear of danger, I led my skittish horse out, then walked back in to collect Letitia. I heard her moving around up there; I thought I heard silk rip. Then, abruptly, she dropped to the ground, defiance in her lovely face.

She wavered, flailing to catch her balance; without thinking I grasped her arm. For half a second she relaxed into the contact—then turned a wrathful look on me.

"Thank you," she said, the civility of her tone belied by the razors of her gaze.

I nodded, recognizing the fear that lay beneath her anger. Of course a ruler must not show his subjects vulnerability, particularly not when things are at their most dire. She was far from the first ruler to choose this solution to the problem, but still I wondered at such behavior in a Tanaan. I realized I had expected grace, even here; and though I recognized my own foolishness I had to fight down disappointment. Had I not just rescued her? Had I not—had we all not—acquitted ourselves well? But there was no point in starting a discussion that would be nothing more or less than an argument.

"Mora, would you follow me?" I said instead.

Her jaw clenched visibly; she nodded. I began retracing the path I'd used to get my horse to safety. Letitia stepped towards the more direct route—then wavered again, obviously on the verge of unconsciousness. Suddenly I realized she'd become entangled in the magic surrounding us, even though she'd touched nothing. Perhaps Carina's Talent ran true.

The morae of Fíana do not faint, she thought. The clarity of the broadcast surprised me all over again: this possible Talent was a telepath. She seemed unaware of having broadcast the thought.

"Mora—" I grasped her arm. She shuddered, clutching at me with her free hand: gaze suddenly, desperately vulnerable.

She straightened, but her gaze was still absolutely open on mine, and something inside me was melting.

"I'm *all right*," she said, in a tone that conveyed quite the opposite. "What in the Sweet Lord's name…?"

I sighed. "Some very black, very deep magic. Magic is in the blood of the morae of Fíana, I understand; it's little wonder you feel it so. But you *will* be all right. It can't touch you if you don't touch it."

She nodded, let me take her hand, and finally followed the path I chose into the clear. The warriors who had stood with me gathered in a loose knot, watching the mora approach. Another shudder wracked her, but then she lifted her chin and crossed the grass toward them as gracefully as if traversing some grand reception hall. Finally she stopped and glanced at me again.

"Right, so—" Her voice was strangled and abruptly gone. She delicately cleared her throat. "Tiarn Ellion Tellan—"

Oh, sweet Lady Tella. "I am not tiarn," I said quietly.

A frown flickered across her face; she smoothed it away and nodded. "These are Nuad a Dianann, Fíana's armsmaster—" This was the Tan I'd identified as the leader of her contingent: a grey-eyed Tan whose professional demeanor never cracked, even in the midst of losing warriors under his command, but whose alien gaze suggested contained torment. We exchanged grave nods.

"Mattiaci a Be Chuille," the firebrand who had tried to pursue mounted ghouls on foot, "Vandabala a Nemain," who had apparently survived a brush with an enchanted sword, "Eber a Fea, and Cantrusteihiae a Argoen, who everyone calls Tru, mem—"

Letitia's voice faltered again. "Members of my personal guard."

I gave and received nods there as well.

"Cainte a Fea, my chef, and Mabon a Bóind, ship's mate; and of course Iminor a Dianann, who you've already met."

Nods all around. Finally we were done.

"Thank you all," Letitia continued. "All of you are the reason I am alive. Should—should I expect to find more of our companions still living?"

"A few, on one of the barges," Tru said quietly.

Letitia nodded. "We'll go to them first. Then we'll attend—" She stopped, swallowing. "To our dead."

If there were only a few Tanaan left here and a few on the river, the number of pyres she must be contemplating would leave her exposed for a very long time.

"Mora, the sooner you are behind Irisa's city walls the better," I said.

Letitia glanced at Nuad, who nodded rueful agreement.

"Well, we can't very well leave our people here!"

She was right, of course; but her protection outweighed the need. Surely a group of people who weren't the targets of horrifying arcane vendettas could be sent back to handle the issue, once she was safe.

But I was a stranger here, and Letitia had evidently not been trained to handle personal attacks gracefully. Doubtless my opinions on funerary choices would be unwelcome. I pursed my lips, waiting for a better opening.

"In Hy-Breasaíl..." Eber said slowly. His face, like the rest of his muscular body, was unusually stocky for a Tanaan, more like a human's conformation; and at the moment his features were screwed up in concentration. "Morae had their pyres on boats..."

"The second barge?" the tillerman said. "But—"

He sighed, resigned. Every face I saw reflected understanding: sacrifice a barge, and they would save hours or days of tree-felling and pyre-building. They might even save their mora's life.

Letitia sighed, too. "You're right, it's fitting. Nuad... Who can I spare for that task?"

Nuad looked around, shaking his head slowly. "I will stay with you, and I'm certain Lord Iminor will too?"

The young Tan nodded.

"Sian," I said to the armsmaster. "If you can use an extra pair of hands, it would be my honor to serve your dead."

Surprise registered on Nuad's face; he offered me a hands-clasped bow of the sort that Tanaan protocols reserve for royalty. "Ouirr, the honor is ours."

The barge was loaded with bloody Tanaan corpses laid shoulder to shoulder, from end to end. The deck sagged towards the water. There was no wizard to call the fires, which struck me doubly strange in the wake of the attack we'd just endured: Letitia lit the barge with a torch, and several Tans poled it away from the bank. We all stood for an uncomfortably long time watching it burn, while my back crawled with anticipation of another attack, and I wondered why a mora on the verge of her investiture would travel with a chef and a military guard but no arcane support. It didn't seem the time to ask the question, but it burned on my lips.

Eventually everyone climbed aboard the other barge. I led my horse across the gangway without waiting for invitation or permission and settled him at the rear, near the tillerman's nest. Even after we'd pulled away from the bank and into the center of the night-dark waterway, I found myself scanning the woods on the northern bank, as if the—*surviving? Remaining*, I decided. As if the remaining ghouls might be expected to regroup and storm across the water.

The undead cannot cross water. As long as we remained on the barge, the surviving members of Letitia's entourage should be safe.

Assuming we didn't crash in the night and lose the second barge.

At first the people around me circulated among their companions, consoling one another and grieving their dead, while the remains of Letitia's military guard manned the poles and attempted to steer the barge through mountain snowmelt and the inevitable thickets of detritus it brought in. Eventually the noncombatants settled into restless, exhausted sleep, and the silence was broken only by the sounds of Tanaan guardsmen poling away debris. I scanned the northern bank as it slipped past, then turned and surveyed the southern bank for good measure. All was quiet. Letitia had settled on a pile of sandbags, shredded skirt spread around her, and assumed a posture for all the world like that of a druid in meditation.

I felt my gaze lingering in a way that any observer would certainly judge improper. But I couldn't overcome the fascination. Torchlight cast her long, sleek hair in a dozen hues of white and gold, and with eyes closed, her face was as remote and mysterious as any goddess carved on a temple wall. Her delicate frame was as long and lean as a teenage boy's, but there was an inexplicable femininity to it, and the conformation of her breasts within that wrecked dress made me itch to peel it away and see what wonders lay beneath, even while some nameless thing inside me ached to wrap awareness around the exotic energies her meditation had raised.

She shifted; she sighed without opening her eyes. I glanced away hastily lest she catch me staring, then experienced a pang at missing contact with her meditation-altered gaze. There would have been a melding between us, one unlike anything I had ever experienced. Probably unlike anything any human man had known. I steeled myself against the need and fixed my eyes on the northern shore again.

Papa?

I startled at the broadcast. It was Letitia. Immediately, involuntarily, I was staring again.

Papa?

Letitia? The sleepy mental voice was unfamiliar, but it must be Rishan's. Why were they broadcasting rather than engaging in direct telepathic contact?

Papa, I—we've been attacked, Letitia broadcast.

What? Rishan's broadcast sounded horrified. And he didn't even know what had happened yet. *Just wait, old man,* I wanted to say; I was on the verge of broadcasting myself.

This must simply be their way. It was infectious; and I remembered the stories of the late-night telepathic contacts Rishan had established with the legendary Armoan Lanas during Nechton's War, contacts that eventually led to the hero bringing the Essuvians into the fight.

In camp this evening, Letitia broadcast. *A—a group of... Oh, Sweet Lord, I don't even know what to call it.*

What? Rishan broadcast again, sounding yet more agitated. Was this what Rishan's contacts with Armoan had been: so much mental shouting across the world? Had they imagined they were the only telepaths in existence?

Across the barge, Letitia gave voice to a small, strangled noise. *Papa, it was sorcery.*

Holy Mora, Rishan moaned. *What happened? Is everyone all right?*

No, Letitia broadcast. The pain in the thought tore at my throat. *We lost— Oh, Sweet Lord Endeáril, we lost Sirona and Caicer and—* A cloud of grief erupted in the aether, half-choking me. *Only twelve of my people are left.*

Ah, no. Rishan's grief hung about me now, too. I felt as if I were eavesdropping: it discomfited me. *C'choiri, what happened?*

Letitia transmitted the equivalent of a shrug. *They rode in. I don't—I don't know how to—They didn't even seem like real people.*

What?

I don't know. It was as if the Wild Hunt had put on matching outfits and come into daylight.

I had to fight down a laugh.

They started off Beallan—beautiful in a terrible scary way, totally silent... but when someone killed them, they didn't seem to die... unless—ah, unless someone chopped off their heads.

Sweet Mora. Rishan sounded shaken. *Whose were they?*

Letitia broadcast the mental equivalent of a head-shake. *I don't know. Red and black uniforms?*

Red and black? Rishan broadcast. *That doesn't sound like Banbagor... Who else could—No.*

What? Letitia broadcast.

No Fíana clan would stage an attack on you—certainly not so close to the investiture. Not even Be Chuille would use sorcery. Surely there would have been a chal-lenge...

We lost people from every clan, Letitia broadcast. *Who would sacrifice their own—*

Rishan broadcast a word I didn't understand, but which I suspected was a Tanaan profanity. I hoped I would remember it later.

Where are you now? he broadcast.

On the barge again, headed downriver. Mabon says we should reach Irisa morning after tomorrow night.

Rishan nodded, somewhere in his house at Tyra. *How many of your guard remain?*

Four, not including Iminor or the harpist.

Irrational resentment flared in me. Yes, I'd introduced myself as ard-harpist, but then I'd saved her life. And yet she reduced me to the inconsequential thing.

The harpist? This time Rishan's broadcast crackled with distaste, which I knew was meant for me. *The zhamin with the—*

Zhamin is a Tanaan word for which I'd never heard adequate translation, though I knew it meant human—and not in a complimentary sense. But Rishan's venomous broadcast shifted abruptly into an image of a golden-feathered eagle clutching a redsnake in its talons. A moment of arcane consciousness raced through me.

Rishan was a seer, the stories said. Had I just become entangled in a vision?

51

Damn it, I'm sorry, Rishan broadcast. *I had hoped you might avoid him.*

Papa, he saved my life. For the first few minutes he was the only one who understood what was going on.

Another eagle-image blasted through my mind: this one was as black as moon-dark. Rishan swore again.

I'm dressing, he broadcast. *We ride within the hour. I will be in Irisa within fourteen hours of you, Daughter. Secure the gates the minute you ride through, stay on the barge until you get there, secure Ériu House as well. And by all the goddess—by Endeáril's name DON'T assume you know what that harpist intends. I swear demons follow him.*

I sighed. No man was ever enhanced by eavesdropping.

I promise, Papa, Letitia broadcast. *Be careful. I'll see you in two days.*

Be safe.

Letitia opened her eyes. I was snared in her gaze before I could look away, still too strange with that little hit of arcane consciousness to guard against the wonder of her eyes. A door inside me that had long stood closed creaked open, just a bit.

"Mora," I heard myself say. "You weren't sleeping." I should have given it a question-inflection, but the opportunity was past by the time I realized my mistake.

"Talking to Papa," she replied. "To Mor Rishan."

"You're a telepath," I said, with grand mastery of the obvious.

She nodded solemnly. "It didn't seem to be of any practical use, before tonight." She looked around the barge, at the guards patiently plying their poles. "A lot of things didn't."

I tried and failed to imagine a world in which guards didn't seem as necessary as water to a royal. I wondered where the wizard who should have been watching over her was tonight. But a royal house's security arrangements are its own business, not topics of polite conversation with outsiders. My curiosity didn't matter. Instead I reached for the thing that would keep her talking, driven by a wish for a connection I didn't understand.

"Sometimes it's impossible to recognize what's real."

"Until afterward," she agreed.

I nodded.

She curled up in the middle of a pool of torchlit silk, wrapping her arms around her knees. "Mindtalk works better at home—when we're together."

"Really?" I said. "Why?"

"Why shouldn't it? We're farther apart."

"Yes, but it's not as if you're using your ears," I pointed out. "Maybe it's only harder because you *expect* it to be."

Aether knows no distance, after all. But she frowned at me, as if I had overstepped my bounds again. Finally she looked away, and I sighed. The legends do not paint the Tanaan as quite so touchy.

But the flickering torchlight fell softly on her, making her hair glow and her dress gleam, and I remembered that she had been in mortal danger and seen dozens of her people, doubtless many of them friends, die tonight. And those are not things to which women are accustomed.

What was needed here was a new topic: something neutral.

"You began telling me, earlier, about the book you were reading," I said. "It belonged to the mora Carina?"

She looked at me again, and in her alien eyes I saw regret. "Let me see—here."

She reached for the book, opened it to a page someplace in the middle. "'Each moment holds the opportunity to step back onto the path of the gods, to choose the gifts with which the gods created us,'" she read. "'Redemption may lie in great acts, but the possibility of harmony with the gods is inherent in each breath.'"

Wonder shivered through me; my throat closed up. It had been so long since I'd felt the Hand of the goddess on me—but this passage, from Letitia's lips, felt like an invitation to return to Her. Holy Lady, was it possible I had actually stumbled onto my proper path—here, in the wilds of Fíana?

"You've read it?" Letitia said.

I was half enmeshed in arcane consciousness already; as far as I could tell, she and I were the only people still on the barge, and the river we traversed might or might not occupy the mundane world.

I shook my head, altogether snared in her gaze. "Beautiful ideas. Who wrote it?"

"A man named Cullinn."

Disappointment crashed down on me: I knew that name. The Cullinns ruled Ilesia before the arrival of the true gods—before Ilesia was called Ilesia. Little has been heard of them since. The conclusion was unavoidable: this work predated the true religion; this call was not for me. A chilly night on an unfamiliar river resumed existence around us.

And yet I couldn't shake a sense that my path lay here, with Letitia. Why?

"You know his work, then," Letitia said, as if I'd guessed a surprise she'd planned, disappointingly ahead of schedule.

"I... No. I've heard the name. But his philosophy—" Abruptly I bumped up against the edges of my Tanaan vocabulary and had to search. "Is... earlier than the arrival of our gods."

Letitia frowned pensively. "So Bealla don't read his work anymore?"

I offered her a regretful smile. "Modern sages teach that who a man is... is in the hands of the gods. His stars ordain his fate."

Her pensive frown shifted to an expression of annoyance. "So everything we're ever going to do—is already known? That can't be!"

"Of course it can. Why do you think seers dream true?"

"Why do you bother to get out of bed in the morning?" Letitia retorted.

"What?" I blurted.

"If you can predict what is going to happen to you, for the rest of your life, why bother going through the motions? If I had known how this trip was going to turn out, sure as the Lord breathes I would have stayed home!"

And there it was. Why was this harder to face than a contingent of undead warriors on battle-trained destriers? Abruptly I was like the canopy of an airship when the fuel runs out; I found it necessary to sit down on the deck.

Why bother going through the motions? If my stars, which seemingly marked me for ard-righ but had instead concealed a lifetime of infamy and shame, were correctly understood from the outset, would everyone around me have built me up so high, then turned away when the inevitable fall came? Why didn't knowing I was shot through with evil, somehow cursed by too-portentous stars, make it easier to bear? Would I have done anything of importance differently, if I'd understood—or was I doomed to carry out this string of damnable, ignominious failures, no matter what the contents of my mind?

"Why do you bother, if that is what you believe?" Letitia said, softly this time.

My throat clenched. I manufactured a laugh.

"Damned if I know," I said in Ilesian, and stared out at the north shore again.

"Letitia?" Iminor said from the front of the barge. He laid down his pole and threaded his way to the rear, fathomless eyes flicking from her to me and back. "Is everything all right?"

Letitia nodded. "We were just... discussing philosophy."

Iminor nodded solemnly, but his face darkened into distrust. And suddenly it was just like so many conversations in so many ballrooms in Ilnemedon, only without the pleasure of having the woman. I rose, brushing dust from my hands.

"Sian, if I may, I'd be pleased to take a turn with the pole," I said.

The Tan bowed, but his suspicious eyes didn't change. "Indeed, ouirr, I thank you."

Chapter 4
Who Treads Here

No mortal eye has seen them, but the poet's soul, it knows:
Fáilias and Murias, Finias and Gorias
Earth's treasure, Sea's delight, City of Wind and Soul of Fire
Who treads here will return transformed
Or mad, or not at all.

'T*he* song had been in my head all day. As the barge approached the city of Irisa, I discovered I was humming. I'd been through here on my way out to Tyra; and of all people, I should know better than to believe old songs. There was no reason for this place to cast some sort of glamour over me, as if I were a farmer on his first trip to Ilnemedon.

But if a twelvenight of traveling up and then back down the river had lent Fíana a certain familiarity, something about the city and its environs ensnared me in untoward wonder: some aura, perhaps, of centuries upon centuries of people descended from gods; people whose names graced songs that I had studied and performed. Maybe it was nothing more than the soft magic of watching the sun rise over these storied lands. Whatever the reason, today my whole being echoed with the wonder of the place in which I traveled. I peered around each bend of the river as we approached Irisa, naïvely open to all of it, even while some cynical portion of my mind strove to hold itself apart.

Every so often for the past hour, the barge had floated past derelict towns and unused harbors. Canted stone turrets and crumbling houses peered from gorse riotous with yellow blossoms; decaying piers shrugged into still waters amid fleets of cranes. I seemed to be the only one surprised by the decay.

Broad smudges of smoke on the western horizon captured everyone's attention, however. I would have thought the smoke portended nothing more serious than early-season brush fires, a regular phenomenon on the plains of the human lands; but the taut faces on the barge suggested nothing normally burned here. If the song had a basis in reality, then, it must be Gorias, not Finias, that the composer styled "Soul of Fire". For a pleasant change, the descriptives in the descending half of the verse were correctly paired with their referents. It almost compensated for the fact that at least one of the names was wrong.

More and more of the land we passed had the appearance of cultivated fields. Once-elegant houses crumbled amidst expanses of rice and pastures occupied by the storied red cattle of Finias: creatures of no evident magic, roan-coated rather than sporting the scarlet pelt of some dandy human nobleman's dyed-coat mount. I should have seen the cattle as further evidence that the place I traveled was a mundane land populated by people with no concept of security or evidence of commerce. Instead I found myself thinking about the songs of the great *Siege of the Brown Bull*, that song-cycle so old no human scholar can accurately fix its age, and wondering whether any of the cattle I saw descended from that illustrious bull's line.

Up ahead, in the center of the water, a river light stood: a white marble confection nearly as tall as the immense light towers that guard Ilesia at Donruil. I'd seen this on my previous visit, too: but from the shore, not from the water at its very foot. From this angle it seemed the work of a god, too airy and fragile to sustain its own weight without divine aid. I craned my neck for a better look as the barge passed by—and then the river opened into Irisa's broad harbor, an expanse of mirror-calm water scattered with islands. To the north, ancient town-houses delicate as seafoam stretched away beyond sight, interspersed with windmills so tall and attenuated they could only have been conceived by Tanaan minds. Rather than sails the windmills had long, slender blades, which gleamed silver as they spun slowly through late-afternoon light. Their smooth tapered columns pointed like long white fingers towards the sky.

Out in the harbor itself, westering sunlight dazzled on quiet waters. In the distance a businesslike fortress perched on an island that was little more than a huge rock. Other islands rode lower, invisible except as smudges atop the water.

"Welcome to the City of the Winds, sian," Letitia said.

My head snapped around of its own accord. The Tana stood within arm's reach, her mass of gold-silk hair radiant in the waterglow. She smiled and met my gaze, the mystery of her bottomless emerald eyes magnified by Fíana's sunlight-saturated atmosphere; but tension around her high brows and in the tendons of her slender neck belied the ease of the greeting. If her gaze never wavered towards the smoke in the west, her deliberate inattention to the problem made me want to steal a glance in its direction. Nevertheless this oddly quiet place was her home, and she had made the effort to welcome me as her guest: the first such reception I'd received in Fíana. Honor demanded that I play my part; and something more complex than desire drove me to give that performance all the charm I could muster.

I bowed. "I can't tell you how many songs tried to capture this. It's easy to see why they failed."

Letitia waved dismissively, but this time her smile was genuine. "Ouirr, it's only the harbor. Save your superlatives for my home."

"Are those windmills?" I asked. "I've never seen their like."

Letitia nodded. "They were built by the first mora of Fíana. They still supply all the water for the eleven islands and half the coastal towns."

"Amazing," I said. "How do they work?"

Letitia's smile faded. "I'm not sure. No one is. Iminor's been working with a group that's studying them, trying to learn enough to go beyond maintenance."

"Any luck?"

Letitia smiled ruefully. "Here and there. Iminor could give you a more complete answer. The part I understand is that we've got to regain not only building techniques but forging knowledge as well."

"Lost knowledge is a painful thing."

"You have no idea."

"You might be surprised."

Letitia shot me a penetrating look. Had I crossed another unmarked Tanaan boundary? If I couldn't keep my foot out of my mouth, I might find myself evicted from the Tanaan lands long before Bealtan.

The barge approached the fortress. Neighboring islands climbed out of the water, the depths between them spanned by bridges that looked too insubstantial to sustain a man's weight—much less the horse-drawn wagons their width suggested. Clearly this place should be viewed from the water, not from horseback at the harbor's edge. Finally I could see that the windmills I'd thought situated on the harbor's southern bank actually stood on the islands, among more of the delicately-wrought town-houses. Some of these exhibited the subtle decay of buildings long vacant.

"Kykia, here on your left," Letitia said quietly.

"What's here?"

"Merchants' homes, mostly. At one time other royal clans maintained feasting halls there…" Letitia shrugged. Questions piled up in my throat, but this time I sensed the unmarked boundary: I kept my mouth shut.

We passed through a narrow channel between the island and the fortress. Across the water, a tall island crowned with larger buildings climbed skyward on the right, while two more river lights jutted out of the water on the left.

"Now we're in the central harbor," Letitia said.

"Lovely," I said, mostly because it seemed expected. The place was beautiful, but it was uncomfortably quiet. I wondered what it had been like before decay set in—and why the place had faltered at all. This was definitely in the class of questions that would get me hastened towards the door.

"Euros on the left—originally the domain of traders who dealt in silk, spices, cedar, and precious metals from the Beallan lands. Irisa was the termination point for seafaring ships; from here goods went upriver to the Devadore, whence they traveled to Fáill, Muir, and Banbagor."

A better harpist would have memorized all those names and facts; I just let most of it wash past me, looking around. Nevertheless the words *Fáill, Muir, and Banbagor* snared my meager attention: these must be the Tanaan names for the nations of Fáilias, Murias, and Gorias, just as Finias had turned out to be Fíana. The song—and all the maps I'd seen—were wrong four times over.

"And now?" I asked. This couldn't be a rude question: she'd opened the discussion. But the tension around Letitia's mouth deepened.

"Now the growers on Apilio meet the demands of Fíana's silk trade. And it's been centuries since anybody built a ship big enough to take to the sea, so the need for cedar just isn't there. Skira on the right, with Ériu just visible behind it."

I squinted more closely at the right-hand island. Now I could see that what I had taken for one island was actually two, and the height I'd spied was part of the farther isle. What must it be to rule a place whose greatest days lie in the past? A human righ is charged with leaving his nation better than he inherited it; from what would the ruler of a place so obviously diminished take her pride? When she dreamed of restoring her nation to its legendary glory, what form did those dreams take? I gazed around at the stillness of the once-bustling harbor, trying to imagine where I would begin; a surprising surge of melancholy washed through me. I realized I'd stopped listening to Letitia's narrative.

"You can't see it from here," she was saying. "And behind Ériu are Zephyr, Boria… and Apilio."

Praise Tella, a name I recognized from earlier: I scrambled to make a contribution to the discussion. "Where they grow silk."

"Exactly."

"Which they trade with whom?"

This earned me another penetrating look. "The other clans."

"*Clans?*" Was there no longer any trade with the other Tanaan nations?

"Banbagor has not been in the habit of international trade since the beginning of my mother's reign," Letitia said, as if this explained everything. This unmarked boundary felt like a precipice. Tanaan should be accompanied by signalmen who can warn unsuspecting humans away from dangerous areas of conversation, the way harbormasters employ lighted buoys to keep ships out of the shallows.

I bowed again. "I thank you for the tour, Mora. Your harbor is the fairest I've ever seen, made only lovelier by your radiant presence."

She smiled; I was headed back into safer waters. "I look forward to welcoming you to my home."

The barge docked in front of an octagonal tower of white marble decorated with reliefs that I guessed were wind gods. The three gods visible from the pier were busily summoning storms, dumping rain, and propelling a ship with breath from ballooning cheeks. The sundials mounted below them read slightly later than five hours past the zenith: twelfth hour, they would have called it in Ilnemedon. I couldn't remember how they expressed time here.

A pair of wispy blond Tans met the barge, long lines of horses in tow: far too many mounts for the small, exhausted party that disembarked. The stable-boys' high-planed faces shifted through puzzlement to horror as Nuad quietly explained that most of the horses must be led home riderless. Letitia closed her eyes for a moment, visibly struggling for control, then led the rest of the people off the barge. I waited until everyone but the tillerman gained the shore before coaxing my own horse down the swaying ramp. By the time I stepped onto the pier, the rest of the party had already mounted.

"Sweet Lady," Iminor said to Letitia, reaching across the space between their horses to gently grasp her hand. "Nuad and I will see to the security of the isle."

Letitia nodded, still downcast. "I'll see you for dinner, then."

"If not sooner," Iminor said.

"The clan leaders—"

"I haven't forgotten. Remember Grandma is madding this month."

Letitia sighed. "Hurry back." She watched Iminor and Nuad ride for a few seconds, then looked around at the remains of her escort. Her gaze settled on me. "Ouirr Ellion, would you ride with me?"

"I would be honored," I replied.

Ériu House stood on the height I had seen from the harbor, surrounded by orchards and gardens as disorganized as Rishan's environs at Tyra. Aromas of lilacs and apple blossoms filled the air. The slow ride up the height seemed to soothe Letitia; within a quarter hour she returned to hostess mode. As we crested the path to the orchards that surrounded the island's summit, the house came briefly into view. As grandly scaled as any human royal residence, Ériu House was built of exquisitely-worked marble so pale it glows in the sunlight, even more delicately wrought than the structures in the city below. Cupolas and cornices, roofs and towers: all are carved of the same radiant stone, surrounded by a garden that was preparing to announce Bealtan with a riot of blooms. But the crest of the path leveled and passed into the orchard, and the house was hidden again.

"I see now that you were right, Mora," I said. "I should have saved my praise."

Letitia laughed. "The credit is due the mora Ernmas, Fíana's third mora. I don't know how many battles can be laid at the front steps of that house."

I gave her a quizzical look.

"Ah, a tale that never crossed the mountains? That's odd: supposedly one of the players did."

I found myself smiling. I'd used that sort of tale-tease more times than I could count. "Mora, if land-rule ever becomes tiresome for you, you should consider becoming a bard."

She granted me a flourishing horseback bow. "Mora Ernmas Ériu, the third mora of Fíana, wanted to build the finest house in the world. But the greatest architects and stonemasons lived in Fáill, so that was where she had to travel. Fáill was proud of its ascendancy, and the mora of Fáill was quite content that her house outshone Fíana's; the architects and stonemasons held their secrets as closely as ever, and no amount of gold would buy Mora Ernmas anything more substantial than a meal.

"But while she was in Fáill, Ogma a Eithne, the greatest of Fáill's architects, fell in love with Mora Ernmas. He followed her back to Fíana in secret and offered to build her this house. She paid him more than anyone had ever paid for a house, though he swore he didn't care about the gold at all. The story goes that they made love in each and every room, in each staircase and alcove, before the house was complete."

Human folklore is full of men who succumb to the spell of Tana. They invariably destroy their lives to win these elusive creatures, and then one wrong word or unfortunate astronomical conjunction takes even that away. The Tana disappear; the men succumb to ruin. Why should the Tanaan tales be different?

"Of course," Letitia said, "there was war. As soon as the mora of Fáill discovered Ogma had gone to Fíana, she began a campaign to win him back. When Mora Ernmas announced her undying commitment to Ogma, the mora of Fáill sent no gift but war-chariots."

"So who won?" I asked.

Letitia smiled. "Well, neither of them, really. In the midst of the confusion, Ogma slipped downriver to Bluewater and took ship to the Beallan lands."

For a moment, the surprise actually took my breath away. Stomach-aching laughter followed on its heels, beyond any hope of control. I clung to my horse, knowing I looked the fool; most of the Tanaan stared at me, amused but nonplussed. Didn't they see the hilarity?

"Ah, dear gods!" I gasped when I could speak. "Leaving both of them looking like fools! That's the best twist in the tail I've heard in months! Rest assured the story will cross the mountains now."

The path climbed again; we entered the gardens surrounding the house itself. Somewhere beyond sight, a spring or fountain murmured. Lilac petals littered the path; blossoms on the verge of opening nodded on the breeze. The curves and cutwork on the house's exterior gleamed in the sunlight, glowed in the shadows: as serene and sensual as an ancient river goddess bringing forth blessings in a headwater grove.

"How tranquil this place is," I said. "You'd hardly realize you were in a city."

Letitia nodded. "I've never been sure why they bothered building Tyra. There's nothing here anyone would need to retreat from—well, except the clan—" She hesitated, mouth twisting: as if catching herself in an indiscretion.

"A problem all royals share," I said.

This time her smile was one of gratitude. "Of course. How do Beallan royals handle the problem?"

I smiled. "Build summer houses, mostly. The tanist of Ilesia—excuse me, the righ now—favors sailing expeditions."

"Where does he go?"

"He won't say!"

We both laughed. The sharing felt more satisfying than it should have.

Letitia reined in front of the house; the party stopped and dismounted. Tanaan servants streamed from the the front door, enveloping the shrunken group. Suddenly, for no reason I could discern, I remembered the horde of Tanaan servants who descended on me and the dead assassin in the guest room at Tyra. *Among the People it is taboo for a person under a death vendetta to accept hospitality*, Rishan's herald had said.

"Mora Letitia! Look at you!" a tall, redheaded Tana exclaimed.

"Hello, Etan," Letitia said.

"Oh, can't you just smell the estrus coming!" Etan cooed.

"Etan," Letitia said, warning.

"Sweet Lord, yes!" another Tana said. "How she glows! Look at the whites of her eyes — almost the same shade as her teeth—"

"*Flidais!*" Letitia said.

The group surged up the stairs; I stepped back, letting them pass.

"Bet she's been all over Lord Iminor!" Flidais said to Etan, nudging the redhead conspiratorially. "Oh, Sweet Lord, remember—"

"*Enough!*" Letitia snapped, stopping. "Could we focus on what matters here, *please*? I almost got killed! My friends are dead!"

"What?" Etan asked. Flidais clutched Letitia's arm, staring.

"Orna?" Flidais asked. Letitia shook her head.

"Grian, and Aibell—"

"And Sirona, and Caicer, and—" Letitia's voice broke. "And the list goes on and on. And everyone who made it home needs to rest—Etan, please have the assistant chef prepare dinner tonight. Cainte is exhausted."

"Mora, no," the chef said. "I wouldn't dream of it. Not with the clan heads—"

"Haven't you trained her, then, Cainte?"

"Why do you shame me, Mora? Let me cook."

Letitia sighed. "At least get her a bath, Etan. Ouirr Ellion—" She paused, looking around, finally spotting me. "What are you doing down there?"

"Mora, I—" What did one say in this situation? *I'm afraid I can't come in because of this price I hadn't realized was on my neck*? That just sounded stupid.

"When I was at Tyra," I began, "Mor Rishan made it clear—"

"Oh, *fie!*" Letitia said, descending the stairs again.

"Well, his herald said—"

"Ouirr Ellion!" Letitia stopped less than a pace away from me and tilted her head back to meet my eyes. She laid a delicate hand on my arm; the rest of the world disappeared.

"You must understand," she said softly, "a woman's first Bealtan is a rocky time for her father. He cannot be held accountable for what he says for at least a month beforehand."

Several seemingly-unconnected facts coalesced in my head. Tana don't function the way human women do; they come into sexual maturity almost a decade later, into estrus only once a year. Of course that time must be Bealtan! And all Tanaan still celebrate the old Bealtan rite, which the human religion reserves for the wizards and the righthe. A memory tried to breach the surface of my mind; I fought it back down.

"The fact that my Bealtan is also my investiture—" Letitia glanced away, shaking her head. It was too easy to imagine how she would look in the glow of a Bealtan fire. No wonder Rishan was on edge.

"Papa is impossible right now, ouirr Ellion," Letitia said. "It is not his fault."

Were this true, and none of what Rishan had asserted at Tyra valid, his herald would be far from the first retainer required to spout nonsense by a nobleman's temporary insanity.

"He is concerned for your safety, I'm sure," I said.

"If anyone is improving my safety, it's you. Please—" She took my arm in a gesture both courtly and disconcertingly sensual. "Come inside."

I should refuse, but I really didn't want to. "Lady, it is impossible to tell you *no*."

"Just as it should be," she said, throwing me one more intimate glance. She escorted me up the stairs, past the staring knot of servants and retainers, and into the house's reception hall. The walls in here were the same as the house's exterior: so pale that sunlight seemed to glow right through. An immense chandelier of transparent glass hung above us, singing softly in the breeze.

"Ah," I said. The chandelier chimed in response to my voice. "I feel as if I've seen this place before."

"Then it's tied to your destiny." Letitia smiled as if she were reciting an amusing superstition, but I found myself staring at her, the cold hand of some unknown god on the back of my neck.

She shrugged. "That's what the wisewomen say."

I nodded. The people on the stairs followed us inside, finally, and the chandelier chimed again.

"Ouirr Ellion Tellan, these are Etan and Flidais a Ériu. Etan is Ériu House's seneschal, and I commend you into her best care. Etan, please ensure that the ard-harpist's every comfort is attended."

"With pleasure, Mora."

"Welcome to my home, ouirr Ellion," Letitia said, ensnaring me with her emerald gaze again. "Be at rest here. I look forward to seeing you at dinner."

I bowed. "Your hospitality is legend."

Chapter 5
Into the Mystery

Ériu House seemed a world away from Tyra. A pretty, pale-haired Tana brought a tray of fruit and cheese and a decanter of wine to my room before I had so much as settled in there; Etan, the ageless blue-eyed seneschal, offered me a bath and a guide should I wish to explore the city. I gratefully accepted the bath, but not the guide. It would feel good to spend a few hours in one place.

After a bath I wandered the elegant corridors awhile, then walked out to the broad portico overlooking the gardens. Evening cast rich golden light over the riotous flower beds and seemingly-random paths; the breeze set flowers dancing and lifted my unbound hair from my shoulders. I breathed in lilac and narcissus, mind turning once again to the assassin at Tyra and Lady Tella's intervention to spare my life—and the attack against Letitia. Tempting as it was to see a connection between Letitia's enemy and mine, I knew better than to imagine they might be the same person. Even extrapolating from the formerly-human ghouls sent against her to the conclusion that her enemy hailed from my side of the mountains would be a logical error. It was much more likely that some other Tanaan royal's mage had chosen to reanimate human rather than Tanaan warriors as a matter of simple political expediency—or that some Tanaan royal or tiarn had hired a renegade human wizard.

Naturally the idea of a renegade wizard put me in mind of the Bard's Wizard, the man who had assassinated the ard-righ on Ardan Eve—and the up-coming Moot. Agitation swept over me; I strode down from the portico and out to the disorganized gardens.

All the royals in the human world must be preparing to leave for Teamair, along with every trader, mummer, and pickpocket—and every patronless harpist, druid, or champion—who could possibly make the trip. Coran would sail out of Ilnemedon within days. Deneth Cooley of Ebdani, who was work-ing day and night to look unaware of his planned nomination to the throne of the ard-righ; Ilesia's sworn enemy Conwy of Deceang, who would stand for the post as well; even damnable Uncle Pariccan: they would arrive in plenty of time for the festival. I should have been there, too: not as I was now, deposed and disgraced. I should have been there as ard-righ-apparent. This should have been the greatest month, the greatest Bealtan of my life. I seethed as I hadn't in a twelvenight, scattering the artfully-arranged gravel paths as I paced.

It was far too easy to imagine the scene developing at Teamair even now. The next month would be an endless series of dinners, tournaments, parties, and other ostensibly social gatherings at which deals were brokered, would-be retainers sought patronage, and tiarn and righ angled for the best alliances they could make. The ard-harpist ought to be there, even if the man from Tel-lan couldn't. Would the rest of the lords of the gorsedd send someone in my stead? I had forgotten how not to care.

Gradually my anger cooled towards something heavier but no less painful: just as always. I began to see the garden again, to absorb the artful chaos of it, to hear the birdsong and feel the soft harbor air. Undisciplined tree cover encroached much closer than the distance of a bowshot on the house, compro-mising household security and infusing the garden with a warm spice aroma. The pale peppery fragrance of early spring flowers blended with the forest aroma, a herald of oncoming bacchanalia. By Bealtan this garden would be a botanical orgy. Within the twelvenight Letitia's staff would string holiday gar-lands: a ritual that would be repeated in every hamlet, city, and capital across the world. How would they decorate Teamair this year, with no ard-righ to have final say over the theme?

What would it be to celebrate Bealtan at Teamair and Uisneach as ard-righ-apparent? The weight in my chest increased; imagining splashed across my consciousness before I could forestall it. The grand parties hosted by all the serious candidates for the post of ard-righ would be the least of it: everything of importance would take place away from the crowd. The Triple Sacrifice: by tradition the ard-righ must perform the ceremony on Bealtan Eve. A holdover from the old religion, it would be blasphemy on any other night, even though the men who perform it no longer invoke those old Names: facing down the stallion singlehanded, dedicating one's killing strokes to the gods; waiting while druids remove the hide of the sacrifice and a wizard dreams prophecy within.

On an election year, each of the serious candidates for the ard-righ's throne finds some quiet place in which to perform the ceremony on Bealtan Eve. For the ard-righ-apparent, the presiding wizard would be Amien himself. Had that sacrifice been mine to perform, there would have been a depth and richness of shared experience between me and Amien: one such as there hadn't been since the night of my initiation into the Order.

That had been a Bealtan Eve, too. I had been the last to know what Amien planned. I'd been expecting a Bealtan Eve observance of the sort men outside the initiate are supposed to perform: dedications to Lady Tella; stories and songs of the Lady's Champion, the hero Cúchulainn. Not until later did I understand the nature of the true Bealtan Eve observances and how closely the illicit ones attempt to imitate them.

Memory infiltrated me, surrounding me with the stone-walled arcane workshop in which I'd studied at Aballo. The place bore Amien's unmistakable stamp; his energies lingered on the leather bindings of books and the very stones of the hearth. But the signatures of all the previous Princes of the Aballo Order resonated in this place, too.

Aballo had been empty all day. Most novitiates and initiates spend Bealtan at home; most of the wizards in residence leave the isle to fulfill holiday duties in places without permanent druidic appointments. The halls echoed with quiet. I couldn't figure out why Amien had kept me and the senior members of his workshop at Aballo; I couldn't understand why Amien delayed lighting the Bealtan fires, summoning everyone to the workshop at sundown instead.

Candlelight cast the place in magic. The heady scent of amnivaren in the censer mingled with the dark complexity of the powerful-smelling brew Amien had made, stretching my awareness wide. I tingled with a need I couldn't name. When Telliyn climbed over Aballo's walls, her light entered through the window to pool in the center of the floor: casting the rest of Amien's workshop in even greater mystery. Red-headed Sanglin, Amien's right hand, herded me into that crystalline space at the center of the room, handed me a cup of Amien's brew, and drank with me. The brew made my head even more uncertain than amnivaren; something in me trembled on the verge of letting go, and I wasn't sure what would happen if it did.

Sanglin held out his hand for my empty cup; I fell into the magic in his brown eyes, and without warning I found his mind tangled with mine. This happened occasionally, accidentally; typically I controlled it, pulled myself back into myself. Tonight I couldn't remember how.

Sanglin's affection suffused me. I didn't question when the man pulled off my clothes and Oregen wrapped the ceremonial robe around me; I didn't question when I realized Amien and dark-haired Dandem had taken up compass-point positions opposite Sanglin and Oregen. I turned to Amien; the familiar arcane signatures that always hung about him had become the crackle-and-hum of an imminent storm, and the controlled wildness of magic overlaid the fondness in his coal-black gaze.

Amien smiled. "Cast the circle, Ellion."

Now, finally, I understood. This was to be my formal initiation into the Order. It was months ahead of schedule: Ildan, the fall equinox, was the expected time. For the moment the date seemed wholly irrelevant.

I knew what had to be done; I'd seen the process hundreds of times. I must invoke the gods and goddesses at the four compass quarters; I must visualize Them with such conviction those visualizations manifested. I must channel and direct the energy that would form the protective circle for tonight's working, drawing it in brilliant arcs from point to compass point. Now, finally, the delicious energy that always flowed in a circle would run through me. The need coursing through me redoubled; this time I could put a name to it. It was magic I craved.

I raised my arms and invoked Ilesan, Lord of Gods; my visualization of Ilesan sprang into being behind Amien. The god's long dark hair, piercing black eyes and chiseled ageless face looked exactly the same as when anyone cast a circle; something in my middle took flight. Par was as ready to my mind: browner skin than any human, curly black hair and wild golden eyes, the sinewy arms and shoulders of an archer.

When the circle began in the quadrant between Them, the energy rippled through my body like a lover's touch. Laughter welled in my throat. The circle manifested exactly as I visualized: gold rather than the typical Aballo green. Sanglin stirred, but no one said anything; nobody ever used gold, but anything other than black or red would have been acceptable. Gold felt right in a way I couldn't have explained.

When I invoked Tella, the goddess Who manifested looked real enough to touch, more present than either Ilesan or Par. Tonight She was even more beautiful than any visualization I had ever seen: Her white skin purer than the light of Her moon, Her long hair blacker than the spaces between the stars. The pleasure of channeled energy intensified again, blending with the first surprising tingle of readiness. I forgot to banish it. Ara's cascading golden hair, exotic amber skin and voluptuous curves were pale in contrast to Tella's beauty and wondrous presence; but She was there, and the circle closed just as it should.

I grinned, which was not exactly proper. Magic flowed intoxicating as wine throughout my being. I had felt the ability within me all along, but a wizard in his novitiate is never called upon to work magic. Until tonight, it had all been study. Now I felt ready to do anything; but I wasn't sure what *anything* might be.

Amien met my eyes again, face just as pleased as my own must be. The wizard closed the distance between us, reached up and laid his hands on my head.

The second phase began: I hadn't expected this, either. Under Amien's coaching and commanding touch, for the first time I channeled Ilesan's Element of Air, blown abruptly into awareness too wide to control. For a moment I couldn't see; I lost track of my body, too far gone with the ecstasy coursing through me to locate the mundane world. When I found myself again, Oregen stood in front of me; together we drew down the power of Fire. It lit me like a chandelier; again I reeled with the wild delight of it. But this time I managed to control the madness. This time I knew who I was, when Sanglin took Oregen's place.

Sanglin met my eyes, smiling. Rapport suffused me. Sanglin was the only member of Amien's workshop with whom arguments never turned bitter; the only one able to look past the shock of the questions I asked, who didn't seem to care that I was royal. Together we invoked Water: Lady Tella's bailiwick. Without speaking, the goddess Who stood silent behind Sanglin stepped out of Her position at West, walking through the sudden silence to stand within arm's reach.

Without thinking I dropped to my knees, hearing Amien and the others fall to the floor around us. Tella's gaze fixed on me, Her beautiful moon-white face full of pleasure and pride. She seemed lit from within; taller than I'd expected. I marveled at the delicacy of the bones of Her face, at Her small perfect mouth. Her long black hair hung like a curtain around my face as She leaned towards me, too perfect to touch. She didn't speak aloud, but reached out to touch my cheek, delicate hand warm against my skin and heady scent enveloping me. Rapture blasted through me, erasing everything but my Lady and the sparkling pleasure of magic.

What a gem you are, Ellion Tellan. How fitting that you have come this night to stand before Me.

I reeled: this was Bealtan Eve. Lady Tella was comparing me to Cúchulainn: the one who took his initiation on Bealtan Eve at the hands of his own goddess, the one who spent all his mortal days as Her favorite. As a member of the Tellan royal family, I had felt my dedication to Her inevitable; but if I'd all but taken Her favor for granted, never had I imagined myself as Cúchulainn.

Truly I am pleased, She continued, amber eyes inescapable.

"Lady—" I said. But I had no idea what else to say. I stared up at Her, an almost painful joy washing over me.

She smiled again. *Be true in your practice, Dear One. Doubt not that we will meet again.*

She straightened up, turned and vanished into an incandescence that dazzled my eyes; I wavered reeling on my knees, the world spinning beneath me as the heady smoke of amnivaren crowded around. I was still in Amien's workshop, and Sanglin was staring at me.

I couldn't think of anything to say. Silence encompassed the room, but the rest of them were climbing to their feet. It wasn't done, the ceremony they had brought me here to complete. There was no need to discuss whether or not it was appropriate to finish. Dandem stepped into the center of the circle before me; but his brown eyes were haunted, and he stood just slightly to the right of the place in which Lady Tella had. When he touched me, the trembling of his cold hands raised gooseflesh on my skin.

Amien called the Bealtan fires afterwards; the rest of us passed through the flames in the ritual of purification. But tonight it felt less like purification than completion. The flames were a caress so distracting that I forgot myself until Sanglin yanked me and my smoldering hair out of the fire.

"Would it kill you to do things the normal way *once*?" Sanglin barked.

I laughed, but no one else did. Amien offered me a bittersweet smile that did little to conceal the worry in his gaze.

Had he somehow known, even then, how I would wreck things? My insides clenched at the thought—but the conclusion didn't fit the facts. He would never have kept me on at Aballo if he did. I pushed aside the dark imaginings crowding around my edges, seeking awareness of the here-and-now and finding myself in the midst of a half-wild garden painted gold and burgundy by the setting sun. A Tana I hadn't yet met walked the path towards me: gait schooled to the sort of casualness that never quite conceals the plan behind a seemingly-chance meeting, pale green eyes meeting mine with a smile. Sunset cast her red hair in a dozen shades of fire.

"Ouirr," she said, closing the distance between us and extending a hand in the manner of a woman who expects a kiss on the wrist. I took it, obliging the unspoken request, and discovered well-developed calluses on her fingertips.

"Lady," I said, meeting her gaze with a questioning look.

She grinned. "Good eve, ouirr. I am Macha Ciena a Nemain, Ériu House's bard."

I surprised myself with my lack of surprise at meeting a female bard. After Letitia's female herald and female seneschal, a female bard seemed almost commonplace.

The mundane world wrapped comforting arms around me; I grinned without planning it. "You and I have much to discuss."

"Indeed we do, ouirr. May I show you my studio?"

"Only if you show me via a route that leads past my room. I would never live down the shame if I left Fíana without playing with you!"

She gave me a smile and took my arm. The smolder in her glance would have meant she intended to do far more than play with me, if she were human. For all the tales of wanton insatiable Tana one hears in the human lands, however, I was still trying to sort out which were deliberate signals and what was allure as impersonal as the enticement of flowers to a bee.

Inside the house, lamplight cast the chambers and courtyards of Ériu House in a completely different kind of glamour than had greeted me this afternoon: high ceilings receded into purple shadows; strange flameless lamps spilled golden pools of light over pale marble and richly woven rugs. My room was dark, but my harp lay exactly where I'd left it: I scooped up the case by the strap and strode back into the lamplight. Macha cast a speculative glance over my harp case and took my arm again.

"Dear gods, what a relief it is to finally find a colleague here!" I said as we walked across a courtyard. "I needed background on your politics a twelve-night ago!"

Macha laughed. "Wheels within wheels, it is. Choose a place to start."

"Thank you. The mora will be invested at Bealtan."

"Yes."

"Then who's in charge now?"

Macha grinned. "A perspicacious question, and one for which there's no easy answer. This situation has not occurred within anyone's memory or knowledge; everyone is making up the song as they play. The lady passed the age of responsibility several years ago; she's been leader of Clan Ériu since."

"But not mora," I said.

"How could she be mora before estrus?" Macha said, as if it were perfectly obvious.

"So the moraship is heritable by the Ériu clan?"

"Theoretically no, practically yes. In theory any clan leader could assemble a coalition and take it herself. In practice, since warfare ended…"

For half a second I lost focus on what she was saying. Since warfare *ended*? How was such a thing possible? Even could a ruler get everyone else to stand down, how would the ban be enforced without arms?

"…it's become impossible for anyone else to take the Gáe Assail."

"The what?"

"The Great Spear of Fíana?"

I'd thought that weapon a myth. The Great Spear had originally belonged to Lugh Lámfhada Himself. It had been the most feared of all Tanaan weapons, too powerful to be managed by any but its owner.

"It exists, then," I said, unable to keep the astonishment from my voice. The Tanaan did not practice war, but they were in possession of the greatest weapon ever forged.

"Of course!" Macha released my arm and swept through an open door. The last shreds of daylight and the sound of her heels on marble hinted at her motion across a darkened room. She paused, turned up an oil lamp, and gestured me inside.

"Glass of wine?" she said as I entered. Her hand was already on the decanter.

"Thank you." I set my harp case on a table and looked around. The room was of a size that would have indicated a well-favored royal appointment in the human lands, rich but not ostentatious with rugs on the floor and hangings on the walls. A door on the right-hand wall led to an inner chamber: a bedroom, I guessed.

"How does a mora choose a consort?" I asked, crossing the room to take the glass Macha offered. She gave me a little salute with her glass and another promissory smile; I returned both.

"There aren't set rules," Macha said, leading me to a settee. She sat down beside me. "Historically, most choices have been about cementing alliances between royal houses; that's how Mora Carina came to choose Mor Rishan."

Macha smiled. "Actually, *she* didn't choose him. Her mother, Mora Berecyntia, did. Mora Carina actually had her eye on a bard..."

I laughed. "But Mora Berecyntia had access to the usual methods of forcing royal children into the appropriate marriages."

"Just so." Macha laughed too.

"So was Lord Iminor... Mora Letitia's choice?"

Macha shrugged. "They've grown up with the expectation. Royal blood is scarce these days. She's clearly not *in love* with him, though she does love him."

"And he's totally devoted to her."

"Totally. In this day, it's enough."

"It's about as good as it gets for royals, in any day," I observed. "Were they married when she reached the age of majority?"

"Lord of Light, no! Ouirr, among Dana's People, no one marries before estrus. And morae rarely take consorts before their investitures."

"Keeping the lines of inheritance clean."

"Just so."

"Then their marriage is scheduled for this summer?"

Macha nodded. "Bealtan Day."

"It's going to be a busy Bealtan."

Macha's sidelong glance, delivered with all the sensual languor of decades of practice, promised hours of Bealtan busyness. "Very, very busy."

"I can't wait," I said. For a moment we were both silent, just slightly too far apart for a kiss.

"So," Macha said, a new huskiness in her voice. "If you had to choose one song to cross the mountains this month, which would it be?"

There was no need to consider the issue. "*Fare and Fir.*"

"It's yours?" The perfume in her hair enveloped me, permeating my brain. I shook my head. "It's older than our written records."

Macha laughed. The motion of her breasts very nearly made me lose track of the topic.

"So much for your one chance at immortality."

I shrugged. "I am ard-harpist first, a composer second."

"You shame me." A wicked grin spread across Macha's face. "Now I've no choice but to play you *Carin and Allanin* rather than one of my own compositions."

"*Carin and Allanin?*"

Macha rose and crossed the room to retrieve her harp. "Written by Allanin, the bard I mentioned earlier. It's not a bardic work per se: there's no lyric or recitative. But it's arguably the ultimate achievement of our harp tradition."

She sat beside me again and began checking the tuning of her harp. It was reasonably close to the true: she must have tuned it earlier in the day.

"Allanin a Fea was the first person then-Lady Carina brought onto her staff," Macha said, adjusting a string. "She was several years past the age of responsibility, but Mora Berecyntia was little more than three hundred years old: Carina had no expectation of ascending to the clan leadership, much less the moraship, for at least a century. She had a house built on Kykia and took up residence there. Allanin had a magnificent studio—it would make you drool, ouirr—but apparently he gave no sign of actually sleeping in that bed. Rumors floated through reception rooms and feasting halls: Carina would marry her bard. He was not merely of the Fea clan, but a son of the House of Fea itself, and it hadn't been so very many centuries since the leader of Clan Fea was a mora… You get the idea."

I smiled. "Some things never change, on either side of the mountains."

"Mora Berecyntia had other ideas, of course. There were still a lot of raw feelings after the war with Fáill the century before, so she wanted to strengthen ties with Muir. And the mora of Muir had a son who was reasonably close to Carina in age…"

"Rishan."

Macha nodded. "Oh, there was drama and slamming of doors. Carina swore she would marry her bard; Mama threatened exile. Evidently she did cut off Carina's allowance…"

I laughed.

"And Carina rode to Muir to begin the nuptial negotiations, but not before she'd sworn her undying love for Allanin. He wrote this song for her, as a sort of send-off I guess—or perhaps he wrote it later. We're not completely sure. At any rate, the story that goes with this song is that their devotion to one another was unwavering, their passion—" Macha met my eyes, a mischievous one-sided smile on her lips.

"Unequaled before or since. The bit about the passion may be true, but as for the devotion… The truth on that front seems to be that she was completely besotted with him until she fell for a Beallan wizard during your war against the renegade sorcerer."

Amien: I knew it immediately. The old man had been obsessed with Carina and her mysterious power. He wouldn't admit it, but there was no question they had been lovers.

"The Prince of the Aballo Order," I said.

"Is that who he was?" Macha said. "He very nearly wrecked Fíana's succession."

She set the harp key aside and adjusted the harp against her shoulder, raised her hands to the strings, and met my eyes. The invitation in her gaze was unmistakable. I gave her a smile that promised all she could handle and more.

Carin and Allanin was pure seduction. If I hadn't been curious about the mystery of Tana, if she hadn't already made it perfectly obvious her allure was personal and meant for me, the song would still have made plans for unlacing her dress begin arranging themselves in my mind. It became nearly impossible to focus on committing the song to memory. She glanced at the strings occasionally, when large-scale jumps in the melody made navigation necessary, but mostly she played to me. The pale green depths of her eyes and the soft shadows on her long neck drew me inevitably closer, until the only gentlemanly thing to do was to nuzzle against her hair as she played. She leaned into the contact; I pushed her hair aside so I could explore the back of her neck with my lips.

"We can exchange songs later," she said, and laid the harp on a chair.

The love of a Tana didn't measure up to the rumors. It was pleasant enough, as loving with any experienced and willing partner is; but the mystery the stories suggest simply wasn't there. Even her body held few surprises for a man who had spent enough time studying those attenuated forms to develop a sense of how they must look beneath their clothes. Had I truly come out here hoping the enchantment in the songs was real? Of all men, I should have known.

Chapter 6
This Sort of Thing Never Happens at Home

As I approached the reception room in which Letitia's dinner guests were to gather, I heard the sounds of a harp. Good: there would be at least one familiar face present. I found a pleasant smile with hardly any effort and stepped into the doorway, discovering the room already full of elegantly-dressed Tana: Macha of course, occupied with playing some song I must find time to learn; but no one else I recognized. All the Tana looked up as I stepped into the doorway; every conversation in the room expired simultaneously, and I found myself confronted by a dozen pair of otherworldly Tanaan eyes.

I'd seen this sort of speculation on entering ballrooms and reception halls across Ilnemedon: I knew what it meant. I'd bedded one of their own, and the tale had spread in the faster-than-time-itself way of particularly juicy gossip. Now everyone present was trying to figure out whether I was worth the effort, whether Macha had satisfied, and a minor host of other questions I was too ignorant of their politics to work out. I filled the sudden stillness with the most elegant bow I could muster and said, "Good evening."

A chorus of *Good Evening* and speculative glances echoed back, so I stepped into the room. Someone else crossed the threshold on my heels; I turned to see Letitia. She was once again dressed in a gown befitting a mora in her home court: ornately-woven silk in a palette of blues that made the emeralds of her eyes sparkle like stars on a moonless night. But even those eyes couldn't keep mine from the distraction of the necklace she now wore beneath her torc: a finely faceted teardrop diamond, roughly the size of my thumbnail at the base, which was certainly enchanted, sparkling with energies of unfamiliar and fascinating flavor. She met my eyes; her tense distraction dissolved into a regard that made the tales of Tana one hears in the human lands flit across my mind. She'd heard the gossip, too: this was evident in the odd mix of speculation and disappointment in her eyes.

"Ouirr Ellion!" she said, sealing the spell of her otherworldly gaze with a smile, and took my arm. "Have you met everyone?"

"Not yet," I said, smiling down at her, and let her introduce me all around.

Tonight she seemed to have worked out appropriate labels: I was introduced as ard-harpist, which position she explained well enough that I didn't feel more than a moment's impulse to correct her. Most of the Tana around her turned out to be Fiana's clan leaders, who seemed to occupy a position somewhat greater than a human tiarn: evidently these women were the leaders of what they call great-clans, each of whose septs seem to be as numerous and diverse as the clans of any human nation. Letitia introduced all the clan leaders by name, but they fluttered around like so many birds; I found it difficult to sort out which was which. I just smiled and bowed to each of them, content to remain no more than a matter of base gossip in this company. One price on my neck was enough.

Letitia had just introduced Tiaran, the leader of Clan Dianann, when Rishan stepped into the doorway. Instantly his animosity prickled like the charge of lightning across my skin; I lost track of the old clan leader's too-penetrating silver eyes, meeting his venomous gaze. I nodded politely, but he spoke telepathically to Letitia, eyes on me the while.

Daughter!￼ he broadcast, the thought carrying a wealth of horror and disappointment. *What is that zhamin doing here?*

A frown flickered across Letitia's face; she smoothed it away. I tried to pretend I hadn't heard the transmission and turned my attention politely on Tiaran, who appraised me thoughtfully. Her eyes made me feel the need for a mind-shield, but a mind-shield can deaden the awareness to more than consciously-expressed thoughts; and clearly I'd missed some subtext during my last encounter with Rishan, which was the last time I'd used one.

"You've had a long journey, young ouirr," Tiaran said.

I felt my eyes seize on the place in which a new tooth was growing in her mouth: a pale sliver protruded from the spot in which an incisor was missing, looking for all the world like that of a child in the throes of cutting permanent teeth.

*That **gentleman** saved my life,*￼ Letitia broadcast, in tones of long-suffering patience. *He is my guest.*

I wrenched my attention away from Tiaran's tooth and tried to fix it on her face without giving in to the entrancement her eyes invited, barely hanging on to the conversation I was supposed to be holding.

"Yes," I said. "Almost a month now. I rode through the old Essuvian rangelands and Banbagor; someone here told me I might find the mora at Tyra, so I rode out there."

Rishan broadcast the equivalent of a violent head-shake. *Listen! You don't understand what you're dealing with!*

"And find her you did," Tiaran said. A certain abstraction in her gaze made me suspect she was as able to hear and distracted by the silent argument being broadcast around us as I.

Rishan was still ranting. *He should not be in your presence! Particularly not under these circumstances.*

I nodded. "Though not until I was on my way back here. We met on the river, as she sailed home."

Oh, sweet Lord Endeáril, Letitia thought: clearly not an intentional broadcast, merely a thought fueled by frustration. *Please get me through to Bealtan.*

A Tan was expected to be insane on the eve of his daughter's first Bealtan, I remembered. I felt an unexpected pang of sympathy for Letitia.

"Odd that you missed one another on your way out," Tiaran observed.

Papa, Letitia broadcast, obviously marshaling her patience. *You've got this all wrong. He is not—*

I nodded. "I can only guess they sailed straight past me while I crossed one of those places where the trail leaves the bank."

Zhamin are animals, each and every one. They do not respect our ways.

Was it true what his herald had said at Tyra: that among the Tanaan, a man with a price on his neck was not supposed to accept hospitality? Letitia had made it all seem of no consequence this afternoon. Or had I been merely hearing what I wished? Maybe I should have stayed outside, found some other place to lodge in the city, made my way upriver to see the other Tanaan nations.

Letitia cast a dark glance across the room at Macha, who was suddenly very busy playing. She didn't understand what Rishan meant; she thought his only agenda was her continued virginity. I felt a blush begin to creep up from my neck.

"What made you decide to travel so far from your home?" Tiaran asked.

Already he— Rishan broadcast.

Papa, enough! Letitia snapped. *I've heard all about it already. He saved my life. You owe him thanks. Stop being rude!*

I couldn't speak truthfully about anything tonight. "Some centuries ago, the mora Carina was a client of the Harpist Gorsedd," I said, willing myself to meet her eldritch eyes.

The old Tana smiled knowingly. "That's only an errand. I asked you why."

"Just needed a change, I suppose."

Tiaran cast me a dubious glance. "Whatever you run from only winds up following you." She glanced past me, at Rishan; Letitia followed the old Tana's gaze and flushed. "But you knew that already, didn't you?"

Daughter—

Stop embarrassing me in front of Lady Tiaran.

"Letitia," Rishan said, somehow managing to infuse the name with both cold and an odd deference. "A moment, please?"

Letitia's mouth twisted. "After dinner, Papa. Our guests have waited long enough."

Suddenly Macha stopped playing, as if she'd absorbed some cue that eluded me; Letitia drew herself up with all the grace of a riga and walked from the room, staring pointedly at Rishan until she passed through the doorway. I stepped aside, allowing the clan leaders precedence, but Tiaran claimed my arm and pulled me into the midst of the progressing Tana, a cat's smile playing about her lips. Rishan followed us into the corridor.

"I owe you thanks," Rishan said. His manner would have been considered faultless in the high court of the ard-righ at Teamair, but the tension around his otherworldly eyes suggested the words passed his lips with all the pleasure of a kidney stone. "I understand you were the one who recognized the sorcery during the attack on Mora Letitia, two nights hence."

I bowed, but the shocked exclamations and rustling of silk among the gaggle of Tana entering the dining room robbed the gesture of impact. By the time I had straightened up, only Letitia's eyes remained on me.

"It is my pleasure to serve the mora," I said, meeting her enchanting gaze. The slow smile on her lips would have ignited an entire cord of wood.

"*Sorcery?*" shrilled one of the Tana, a creature even more angular and elongated than the rest.

"Now you understand why I have been so distraught, Scene," Letitia said.

"Sweet Lord, yes!" Scene said, twisting a handkerchief in her long fragile hands. "I would have been absolutely devastated to think that one of our Fíana sisters would do such a thing!"

"Though it's hardly more comforting to think of Banbagor engaged in the practice," said Tiaran.

The Tana around her nodded fierce agreement, but once again I was confused. All the songs and histories—the Breasaílian histories in particular—portray the Tanaan as great mages. When the Tanaan took Hy-Breasaíl from the demons who held it before them, it was their magic that carried the day. The humans who took Hy-Breasaíl from *them* were only able to defeat the Tanaan mages because of Talents who took their secrets to their pyres. And yet this was far from the first indication I'd had that the Tanaan were steadfastly averse to magic. Were the songs I had learned yet more lies? Or had something on this side of the mountains changed?

Inside the dining room, Letitia settled in her place at the head of the table. Rishan took up the opposite seat. The Fíana clan leaders, Rishan's herald, and a group of Tana who apparently constituted Rishan's and Letitia's shared staff sat down around them. I, who had for some reason been blessed by the gods, was seated in the Tanaan place of honor for a guest, at Letitia's left hand: sufficiently far from Rishan that the ill-will in the old Tan's stare didn't do more than redden the tips of my ears. Iminor and his distrustful blue gaze, seated directly across from me, seemed almost benevolent in contrast.

"How did you recognize the sorcery for what it was, at distance?" Rishan asked as the servants began pouring wine. "Is that sort of thing common among—" His gaze flicked briefly from me to Letitia; the word *zhamin* hovered in the air of the room, but something in Letitia's answering stare seemed to rob the old Tan's intent of its charge.

"Bealla?" he finished.

Letitia sighed.

"Well," I said, toying with the stem of my glass. "I wouldn't say *common*— and what does generally occur bears... little resemblance... to what we saw."

Half a twelvenight among the Tanaan was improving my ease with the language, but when conversations progressed beyond pleasantries, I still found myself racking my brain for words.

"Arcane attacks against Beallan great houses are fairly rare," I continued. "There are—strict codes governing how magic can be used in warfare; wizards are enjoined from making direct attacks on... magical noncombatants."

I frowned. "Though recently, of course, the Bard's Wizard has broken all those codes..."

I glanced around the room: all the Tanaan regarded me expectantly. All those weird eyes staring at me ignited a little spark inside me, as if I had been magically transported to the famed battlefields of Maige Tuireadh.

"Ah, I see I've been remiss," I said. "Has news of the war not crossed the mountains?"

"No," Letitia said, as if grateful for the distraction. "What of this war?"

"A rebellion," I said. "Led by a... an insurgent called the Bard of Arcadia."

Letitia was suddenly intent.

"Arcadia?" Iminor echoed, puzzled.

I shook my head. "A mythical place. There are those who say it's real, those who maintain it's a—" I concluded I just didn't know the word I needed and threw in the Ilesian word, hoping my audience would follow. "Cipher for Hy-Breasaíl—well, for what Hy-Breasaíl should have been, in their estimation..."

"A *cipher*?" Iminor repeated, forming the Ilesian word carefully and looking even more perplexed.

Damn. I shrugged. "You're not expected to believe the man is really from a place called Arcadia, nor necessarily that he's a bard at all. Certainly he's not a gorsedd harpist... It's—a code, a kharr code."

Iminor nodded, still puzzled. Letitia was profoundly thoughtful.

"At any rate... Five years ago the kharr—the rebels—overthrew the capital of Uxellia. Since then the rebels have taken the entire nation of Uxellia, as well as cities in Dáirine and Gavnon—and the Liis region. This winter they—" I *still* didn't know the Tanaan word for *assassin*; who would have thought I'd need it? "Murdered the ard-righ. Intelligence suggests Dáirine and several cities in the central region may be about to fall. The Prince of the Aballo Order has called a Grand Moot for Bealtan, at which the College of Righthe will elect a new ard-righ—and define their... strategy to eliminate the kharr. It's not my war, not by any stretch of the truth—"

I spread a regretful smile around the room. "And—I apologize—not exactly dinner-table entertainment. Clearly the City of the Winds is the place to celebrate Bealtan this year." I offered Letitia a little salute with my glass, feeling Rishan's glare.

"We don't share your taboos about serious conversation over dinner," Letitia said, shooting Rishan a warning glance. "Please continue, if you would. Your rebels are breaking the rules of war?"

I nodded. "Their leader—this so-called Bard of Arcadia—has recruited a renegade wizard to his cause. No one seems to know who he is, but evidently he's a man of considerable power and little regard for humanity. The things he does are—totally unacceptable. Wizards are required to take an oath at initiation..." I shook my head. "I couldn't give an accurate count of noncombatants—noble, common, and bondsmen alike—he has killed."

"The rebels have a grievance?" Rishan asked. His tone was oddly mild.

"No," I said, then hesitated. Once again I wished for a signalman to show me a path through Tanaan waters that wouldn't exhaust my welcome.

"Gentles," I said slowly. "I respect the fact that the Danaan have their own gods…"

"Goddesses, mostly," Letitia said quietly.

I met her eyes. "Just so. But the kharr have a false god. They bring his image into town on a cart. What begins as a traveling… unsanctioned—devotional… becomes a—" Once again I had completely exhausted my meager command of the Tanaan language. Was the word I needed shared between our tongues, as so many of the words having to do with religion are?

"Saturnalia of the worst sort." This time, it seemed, I'd gotten away with it: everyone appeared to understand. "All dedicated to this—god. At some point in the revel, there's a sort of… tidal shift in the city. The fortunate loyalists are the ones who get out."

"Beallan history has been a long series of religious wars," Rishan said. The condescending curl of his lip made me want to rearrange his expression by force. "The Ilesians, for example."

"Ah, yes," I said, with a smile I didn't feel. Only Rishan would reduce the arrival of the true gods to an internecine squabble. "And Nechton."

Rishan glowered.

"So you've seen this sort of thing before," Letitia said, laying a hand on my arm. Her eyes held absolute fascination; a thrill swept through me. She would make a particularly satisfying conquest, if Rishan knew what was going on. Just one more reason, as if I'd needed another.

"Arcane warfare?" I said, deliberately turning my full attention on her. "There are countless tales, at least half of them… unsubstantiated. The Aballo code prevents the wizards involved in an arcane battle from talking about it to anyone outside the initiate. When it's done properly, only the wizards involved in the battle are certain it's taking place at all. At this moment I can't recall any truly blatant arcane battle more recent than Nechton's War, and most of the really noteworthy displays seem to have been much earlier."

It was a pity, really. The spectacular arcane battles described in the older histories never lose their power to thrill.

"For example: the storm that foiled the Cullinn righ's final attack on Tellnemed during the Ilesian War—an arcane storm. It rained rain, but also slugs and firespiders and mud. That was less… subtle than what you'll usually see today, but quite effective. Even today, though, wizards use weather to—influence—the outcomes of battles on the field."

Finally I realized there was no hope of expressing myself precisely in this language. I could only use the words I knew to their best advantage. I relaxed, relieved of my usual harpist's compulsion to find just the right word, and allowed myself to simply tell the tale; I paused for a sip of wine.

"Today it's a much less dramatic business—though the argument can be made that subtlety requires more skill. Contemporary arcane warfare includes tampering with an enemy's chariots, ships, fortresses, weapons—while enhancing the patron's… in certain cases, destroying the enemy's fortifications altogether—though, as usual, magical noncombatants can't be harmed… gathering intelligence about enemy movements and positions and more—clandestine—things… Protecting one's patron psychically, with ward-spells… warding a place so it becomes completely impenetrable, both physically and, we hope, magically."

If I hadn't vowed to give up the practice altogether, would I have chafed against the restrictions placed on modern wizards? No doubt I would have. I had never overcome my hunger for the thrill; in the end it was the thing that undid me. Today the thought of even the watered-down arcane warfare my contemporaries practiced raised an ache of unfulfilled need in me.

All the songs I'd learned that touched on arcane battles; all the grimoires and histories between whose lines I'd read, teasing out the details of the magical engagements: they roared to life in my head, as they had so many times before. I was still talking, but hardly aware of what I was saying: magical imagining had commandeered my brain.

"But that's only the opening phase of a really expert battle. Among wizards with a real—flair for this sort of thing, the game shifts into a canter with protecting the patron against other wizards' workings and intelligence-gathering efforts, and countering the spells that have already been laid. Some of the best workings involve undermining the other wizard's work in ways that are not immediately apparent, so all looks secure and people depend on it.

"This is where the real artistry begins. Seeking out the structure of the spell, learning its heart, changing it—without leaving your name on what you've done, if you're very good. The other man thinks his illusion holds, but all that remains is the sort of spurious visual effect that those on the inside expect to see. Or the network of a righ's personal wards may appear to be intact, but now there are places that can be penetrated, and the assassin who knows where and how to strike the righ will find the job a simple one. Counter-spells and counter-counter-workings, so subtle and complex that even wizards who aren't party to the conflict can't follow their internal mazes…"

I returned to myself, unsure what magical zone I'd occupied, and discovered I was smiling, my eyes fixed on nothing. I had the uneasy sense that I had forgotten the language issue altogether, and had slipped into Ilesian—or even, gods forbid, the Tellan language. I manufactured a little self-deprecating laugh, shaking my head, and glanced around the table. Most of the faces reflected various flavors of puzzlement—except Rishan's, which was a mask of barely-contained horror.

"Have I seen that sort of thing before?" I said finally. "No. I didn't realize the—" I nearly said *Tanaan*, but caught my lapse into Ilesian just in time. "Danaan had a similar system."

"We don't," Rishan said.

"Oh?" said Tiaran, her moon-pale gaze as challenging as any man's. "Then what are they doing, out in Banbagor?"

Sweet Endeáril, how did those two wind up on the same end of the table?

I startled. At the other end of the table, both Rishan and Tiaran turned swift astonished glances on the young mora. The old Tana barked an apparently genuine laugh.

"Your pardon, young ouirr," she said to me. "Typically we are a better behaved people."

"You mean, typically we aspire to be," Letitia said, casting a withering glance at Tiaran.

Tiaran grinned, showcasing the place in which a new tooth was growing. My uncertainty about the right course of action evaporated: I might be violating Rishan's taboos, but Letitia cared not at all. And there were puzzles to solve.

Old women grew new teeth here. Magic had gone the way of the old gods, but my hostess wore an enchanted gem. Competent warriors were unaccustomed to wearing swords. It was going to take far, far longer than Bealtan to make any sort of sense out of all this, and were I serious about pursuing Letitia, I might need the time anyway. Watching Rishan seethe while I did it would only add spice to the chase.

Was there really any reason to hurry back to Ilnemedon? I would only find myself dealing with assassins and uncomfortable political situations, and regretting opportunities ignored.

I grinned at Tiaran. "No blood lost."

Give them time, someone else thought. Rishan scowled again, but Letitia's mouth twisted with suppressed laughter. She moved abruptly, as if kicking someone under the table. That someone could only be Iminor: I looked across the table with renewed interest. How many telepaths were in this room? Now I suspected it was as common among the Tanaan as the tales suggest.

"I've been thinking," Letitia said, with the deliberate casualness of someone steering a discussion back into safer waters. "About the work they're doing with the city windmills. Iminor, you said before we left that Budd thought the problem lay in smithcraft?"

Iminor nodded. "There's knowledge they've lost, as usual. There are days when I wonder why the ancients didn't just *write things down*..."

"In the early days after the Transition—and in Hy-Breasaíl as well... the great smiths were also great mages," Rishan said thoughtfully. "Budd's problem may have less to do with smithcraft than magecraft."

Iminor grimaced. "In which case the knowledge is lost for good. That would certainly explain why they just can't seem to get the forge temperatures right."

"I wonder if they still have the craft in Banbagor," Letitia said, too casual.

Banbagor? Why all the sudden talk of Banbagor around this table? Was it possible they had intelligence that suggested Letitia's mysterious enemy lurked across their southern border? I tried and failed to remember which Tanaan nation Deaclan had called home, and wondered whether the one Tanaan ever to take training at Aballo had returned to this side of the mountains after everything fell apart. He had been as unafraid of the dark corners of magic as I had, back then. What if he had continued his explorations rather than withdrawing in horror of what we'd done?

The room felt suddenly cold. But the Tanaan still seemed to be talking about windmills. Iminor raised a pale eyebrow at Letitia, meeting her eyes.

"Indeed," he said. "I wonder."

Among human nobility, a dinner to which guests are invited is considered incomplete until the men have retired to a sitting room for brandy. But Tanaan dining requires far less ceremony. After the last course had been completed and everyone sat toying with wine glasses or bits of dessert, Letitia stood and stepped away from the table. The rest of them rose as if they had been waiting for the signal.

Little knots of conversation gathered; Tiaran was busily organizing some clan-leaders-only gathering that must take place without delay. Macha met my glance for an instant, and then her eyes slipped away, and she remembered some errand that propelled her from the room. I sighed: I'd been on both sides of that transaction in the past, but I'd hoped only for an opportunity to learn another song or two. Now I didn't know how I'd fill the time before sleep. I joined the trickling exodus from the chamber and wandered through the elegant corridors until I found my room.

Someone had lit a lamp and turned down the bed. A book lay on the table beside the lamp: I crossed the room to pick it up.

As soon as it was in my hands, I knew: this was the book that had belonged to Carina, the Cullinn volume of philosophy Letitia read to me on the barge. *Each moment holds the opportunity to step back onto the path of the gods, to choose the gifts with which the gods created us. Redemption may lie in great acts, but the possibility of harmony with the gods is inherent in each breath.* The words had been echoing in my head for two nights. My need to discover the next point of Cullinn's argument was a hunger in my chest.

I laid the book down. The last taboo volume I'd read was Aechering's grimoire. Hadn't that gotten me exactly where I was tonight? The room felt suddenly stuffy, my throat tight; but I was on the first floor again. There was no way I could open a window. I would go for a walk instead.

Lamps like pale bubbles illuminated the paths of Eriu House's garden. Once out of reach of the lamplight spilling from the house's windows, the etheral globes were the only source of light: Telliyn had already passed her third quarter and wouldn't rise until later, while Arliyn was too early in her cycle to appear in the evening. I walked with my feet on a softly-lit path and my head in darkness, the Cullinn quote rolling around in my brain. *Each moment holds the opportunity to step back onto the path of the gods.* That moment on the barge returned to me: Cullinn's words raising a feeling almost like the Touch of the goddess in me; my sudden sense of having stumbled into destiny. It was tempting to conclude that Letitia was sufficiently important to Lady Tella that I should take whatever action was necessary to discover Her Will. That I should read that contraband book and seek understanding.

But that was just wishful thinking: a wish for Lady Tella's attention, and a wish to read yet another blasphemous text. I was only seeking an excuse to do what I knew I should not.

I followed the twisting paths around the house and down the hill behind it, a restless itch beneath my skin driving me farther and farther from the summit. At the bottom of the hill, a gate stood open: so much for Rishan's admonitions regarding Letitia's security. Beyond the gate, a bridge stretched across the water and out of reach of the lamps. The span looked no more substantial than the ones I'd seen from the barge this afternoon. I stepped through the open gate and onto the bridge, trailing my hand along the cold smooth marble of the rail. Water burbled and murmured beneath me; wind blew my hair back from my face.

Beyond the reach of lamplight, stars sprang to life across the reaches of the sky. With Telliyn still below the horizon, even the faintest of the stars were easy to see, and the thick-clustered stars of the Way of the Gods stretched like a moonlit highway across the vault. I paused in the middle of the span, looking up. The constellations here occupied nearly the same positions as in Tellan, but my mind leapt to the hill outside the observatory at Aballo, to the night Deaclan and I spent sharing a skin of wine, staring up at the stars, swapping night-sky stories from our homelands. There had been so few moments of peace between us; but that night, I could imagine us partnered as nasclethéana. He had never failed to challenge my ideas, never deferred to what everyone imagined the stars said about me. That night it felt like the possibility of true honesty.

To the north, Cúchulainn did battle with the Dragon. On the other side of the bridge, the Descending Goddess spread her arms high above the horizon, while the Hound ran away to the west. The Eagle hid behind the trees on the opposite shore. What stories would Deaclan have told about those constellations? I couldn't remember anymore. What pattern would he have seen in the strange parallel occurrence of renegade wizards on both sides of the mountains? What if one of those renegades were Deaclan himself?

At least he would still be practicing. An untoward spark of jealousy ignited in my depths. That was the wrong response: I should be horrified by the idea of someone with whom I had shared workshop experiences, someone I knew, being capable of what I'd seen in that meadow. But all I could feel was anger at the idea of him still practicing after all these years, while I had laid it aside: of course he was capable of it. I was, too. I followed the bridge across.

Was this island Apilio, where they grew silk to trade with other Fíana clans? Or Zephyr, where conversations I'd overheard suggested cattle were pastured? It was hard to see evidence of either occupation: the trees blocked what little light the stars provided, and I could barely discern the path, let alone the breed of the trees around me. How do mulberry trees smell?

I was about to turn back rather than lose myself in the darkness when I spotted light through the trees. Torchlight, almost certainly. Unfamiliar energies teased at my edges. In the human lands, I would have filed the seductive energetic aroma as magic; but the Tanaan no longer practiced sorcery. So what did I smell? I walked closer until light and shadow resolved into a clearing illuminated by seeming moonlight, in which a group of Tana were... dancing? I wasn't sure; I stepped closer again. Tendrils of pale green and lavender wrapped themselves around me; aromas of strawberries and rain-soaked air filled my lungs. Power sparkled up my arms and across my scalp, unlike anything I'd ever tasted: subtle rather than strong, a charge that might linger on the skin. Pure delight shivered through me, overlaying the fascination of the scene.

The Tana in the clearing were dancing, moving in a circle like a group of wizards at a working: hands joined, hair unbound, and absolutely naked, bathed in a light reminiscent of the glamour Tanaan cast in old songs. Their chant sounded like something I ought to remember; if the words weren't clear, the purpose was: protection. Whether one called it *prayer* or *a working*, the intent was the same.

I recognized several of the Tana from dinner: was this Tiaran's urgent meeting? In the center, obscured from the shoulders down by forest growth and moving Tana, stood Letitia: at once tantalizing and shockingly vulnerable. She needed protection, but prayer to some Tanaan god or goddess who might or might not exist wasn't the answer: she needed a wizard of her own to stand against the renegade.

Each moment holds the opportunity to step back onto the path of the gods, to choose the gifts with which the gods created us. Why shouldn't that wizard be me?

My imagination leapt ahead of my judgment: I could visualize a counter-working that would turn the renegade's undead warriors against him, redirect his every intention in ways impossible to recognize until too late. All I would need to begin to learn and grasp those energies I'd sensed in the meadow, to prepare to directly engage my enemy, was a second attack on Letitia. Anticipation raced through me: the reasons for the conflict between Letitia and her unseen enemy didn't matter; neither did the inevitable casualties. It would all come down to the final engagement with the renegade, to the test of my power against his. If that wizard really were Deaclan, it would be no more than the resumption of a duel that had been suspended rather than decisively won.

Finally, late as usual, the horror of what I was contemplating caught up with my conscious mind. My breath lost its way in my chest. Letitia needed arcane protection, but that wasn't what she would get from me. I needed to get the hell out of Fíana. Right now.

Letitia had been in the bath: this must be the reason Etan made me wait to see her. Her hair trailed dark gold down her back, red-touched by firelight, dampening the silk of her dressing gown until the line of her back was visible through it.

"Good evening, ouirr." Letitia smiled, gesturing for me to sit.

The stories of men driven mad by the love of Tana: finally, I glimpsed the slim ray of truth that myths always harbor. It would be easy for a man to make himself crazy around these women. Half a dozen times since we met, I would have sworn I could have made an advance and been well received—but Letitia was Tanaan, and committed, and I was too old for romantic fantasy. It would be easy for a man possessed of less reason to trip and fall.

"I know you've a great deal on your plate," I said, ignoring the chair she offered. "But I haven't forgotten the business for which I came, and I hope you won't either. I'll be leaving in the morning, with thanks for your gracious hospitality. But I'll be back next spring, and we will try this conversation again."

"Really?" Letitia said. I wasn't sure whether I saw disappointment in her face. "I'll be leaving in the morning, too: for Banbagor."

"What?" I blurted. "You should be under guard in this house with the walls buttoned up, not riding across the countryside!"

I'd forgotten courtly manners again, damn it. It would be a relief to rediscover equilibrium, someplace beyond Fíana's borders. I cleared my throat.

"Mora," I finished lamely.

Letitia smiled away the lapse. "It turns out—My new herald explained this to me, once we were back in the city… Evidently there is a very old tradition of settling grievances among royal houses, by provocation to war before a mora's investiture."

I sat down. "Settling a grievance."

"Evidently Banbagor was the source of the attack two nights ago."

"But I thought the Danaan had no means for such an attack."

Letitia shrugged. "So had I, but things are strange out in Banbagor. The tradition is clear: I must go to them to settle the dispute."

"That's insanity! Ride out and offer yourself to your enemy?"

"No, the rules for this transaction are dressed with steel. I should be absolutely safe en route—though we're likely to be monitored. I assume you're on your way to Banbagor anyway; I'd be pleased if you'd travel with me." She met my eyes.

Was she creating an opening for me, then? Or was I over-interpreting? Damn it, why had I bedded Macha? I'd been through this before: bedding a member of household staff makes it impossible to pursue the Lady without things getting ugly. Now my only hope lay in obviating the gossip by confessing my crime—and praying the Tanaan's famously lax expectations regarding sexual fidelity weren't just another myth.

Looking embarrassed was easier than I'd expected. The hesitation with which the confession must be delivered came just as readily.

"Mora, I would relish the opportunity to travel with you again. But I— Mora, before you make that invitation, you should know… This evening, I had—an encounter with… a member of your staff."

I pursed my lips and turned my face to the fire, to give her time to arrange hers in the appropriate expression. Through my lashes, I saw disappointment: she hadn't been sure of the rumor, after all. Then she smiled, every inch the mora.

"How sweet you are, sian," she said. I looked at her again, accepting her generosity with a small smile. "Whatever pleasure a member of my staff may have had of you is a blessing, not a crime to be confessed. It changes nothing."

Now, inexplicably, I was embarrassed. And at least some of the rumors were true. The song wormed its way through my brain again:

Earth's treasure, Sea's delight,
City of Wind and Soul of Fire
Who treads here will return transformed
Or mad, or not at all.

How could I walk away from this? Wasn't I smart enough to handle it? Gods only knew whether a human would ever receive such an invitation again. What the hell.

My room didn't look any different than it had twenty minutes ago; but while I was out, Fíana's numinous quality had begun to reassert itself. The decanter of wine on the desk beside the door gleamed; the facets of the glasses beside the decanter sparkled. The fireplace offered a warm welcome, already stocked with firewood and flanked by tools that were as pristine as if they had never been used. The hangings on the walls, the wardrobe across from the windows, even the washstand in the corner: all were worked with artistry and unabashed grace, fitting for the residence of a legend. Even the transparent blue haze at the edges of my vision seemed to belong in this magical realm into which I'd stumbled. I pulled off my jacket and began unbuttoning my shirt.

A garotte flashed past my nose on its way down from the top of my head. Without thinking I tucked my chin into my chest and threw myself backwards. The assassin and I fell, the garotte finally loosening from my neck as I tumbled sideways and cracked my head against the the footboard of the bed.

I rolled into a crouch. "What the fouzh is this?" I barked.

The assassin advanced again. I tried to grab his head, but he blocked my left arm and and gripped my right, throwing me across the room. I landed in an upside-down heap against the door, remotely aware of my own stupidity, righted myself as quickly as possible and scrambled to my feet. Before I found my footing, the assassin was on me again, all shadowy clothing and standard black hood; we crashed backwards across the narrow desk.

My head slammed against the carved marble of the wall; my scalp scraped on the rough textures. The desk shuddered; the decanter and glasses on its surface chattered. I grabbed the decanter by the neck and slammed it against the back of the assassin's head, showering us both in wine and shattered glass. I thrust the assassin away and pushed myself to my feet as the man tumbled to the floor. Wine ran into my eyes.

The assassin swept my feet from beneath me; the desk rocked as I bounced to the floor. The jagged neck of the decanter rolled from my fingers. I scrambled backwards and grabbed it, leapt to my feet, and launched myself at the retreating assassin. The man seized a poker from the rack beside the fireplace and spun towards me, swinging the implement backhanded like a farmer wielding a broadsword. I ducked under the stroke and drove the broken neck of the decanter into the man's neck. The assassin staggered backwards, then swung the poker sidelong and connected with my skull; pain exploded through my head. The man dropped to his knees, the poker falling from his hand; my own vision was wavering, but I reached down and jammed the neck of the decanter in more deeply, twisting. I shoved the man away as my legs crumpled beneath me.

At first my only awareness was of pain in my skull. Gradually I remembered the pain was an indication of a problem I hadn't yet solved: I opened my eyes. This was even worse; there was something in them that stung. Half-blind, I stumbled to my feet and crossed the room to the washstand; splashed water on my eyes, picked up the towel and wiped my eyes until they were clear. The towel was bloody now: no surprise there.

I put a hand to my head, experimentally. There was a tender area roughly the size of my fist, which was puffy, and a sticky gouge more than half the length of my thumb. At least it was all scalp: there would be no need to explain it to anyone, once I'd gotten cleaned up. Gods knew Rishan and his staff weren't going to be interested in discussing this breach of security with anyone, either. My hand came away covered in blood and shards of glass. The towel smelled of wine.

I looked towards the spot in which I'd fallen. The rack of fireplace tools lay toppled on the hearth; the poker had landed a short distance away. Blood pooled on the hearth and soaked into the rug. But the assassin was not in evidence.

I reviewed the situation again. The towel in my hand was covered in blood; my shirt was stained with wine. The rug was even bloodier than the towel. My head was tender to the touch. Everything added up: the fight I remembered was real. But the man who had bled to death on this rug was gone.

I shook my head. It hurt. This conversation with Rishan was going to be even less pleasant than the last one.

"Well," Rishan said. "Here we are again. What have you done with tonight's body?"

"I rather thought you had it," I said.

Chapter 7
Goodbye, Hello

I took my time in the all-but-empty dining room, savoring the only hot breakfast I was likely to get in half a twelvenight or more. Morning sunlight cast bright slabs across the dining table and sparkled in the glass beside my plate. The pounding in my head had receded to a dull ache, and a day of fresh air would rid me of the rest. It would be a relief to finally put permanent distance between Rishan and myself.

A footfall sounded in the doorway; the muscles between my shoulder blades tensed in anticipation of another uncomfortable conversation. But the Tan in the doorway was Iminor, whose clothes already exhibited the tattle-tales of time spent on horseback. Relief made effortless the smile courtesy demanded.

"Good morning, sian," I said.

"Good morning," Iminor replied, with a typically reserved answering smile. "I thought I'd be breakfasting alone, I'm so late."

"But you've been busy," I said. "I have no such excuse."

Iminor shrugged and settled into a chair. "There's always more to do at home than on the road. By tomorrow I'll be as much at ease as you."

"I had no idea a royal consort would work so hard."

Iminor shrugged again. "I'm not royal. I'm sure there's nothing I can tell you about this situation, ouirr; it means I've got to work twice as hard."

"Indeed," I said, nonplussed, and sipped tea.

"Well, it comes with the territory, doesn't it?" Iminor said earnestly, meeting my eyes with the first frank gaze he'd volunteered. "Were it not for the Deluge, Letitia's consort would have been a royal from Fáill or Muir or Banbagor. That's my great good luck, but I'll spend each of my days earning it."

This was not the first time the Deluge, whatever it was, had been mentioned in passing; but the name matched nothing in the scant Tanaan history I knew. Now I wished I'd thought to ask Macha about this topic rather than the matter of the Tanaan succession: she was the only Tanaan I knew who didn't grow prickly for incomprehensible reasons, and there was no way I could jeopardize this morning's fragile, unlooked-for rapport. Maybe if I kept him talking he'd drop clues I could use.

"Earning it?" I echoed.

"Why do the goddesses elevate any of us to such positions? Nobody knows."

This wasn't true: I knew a man was born royal if a god or a goddess looked favorably on him, if his fate furthered Their designs. And he retained that status only as long as he continued to do so. But it would accomplish nothing to point this out. I toyed absently with a breakfast roll, appetite waning.

"Being royal or semi-royal or royal by marriage means we have an obligation to serve our people," Iminor continued. He had never looked me in the eye for so long. Rishan must be keeping quiet about last night's assassin. "It's the one true justification for having been set apart."

"Yes," I said.

"And not having been born to this position, I've got to work twice as hard simply not to be judged insufficient."

"Landing in a place to which you weren't born is a profoundly uncomfortable thing." A truth on either side of the mountains, apparently.

"And yet I'd do twice as much, were my lady or the Holy Mora to require it. The gift I've been given—" He meant Letitia: I understood. "Is worth ten times what I could ever give in return."

I smiled ruefully. "It's a wise man who appreciates what he's got without having to lose it, sian. I wish I'd been half as enlightened as you when I was your age."

The stablemaster and his crew swarmed around the yard in front of Ériu House, preparing the mounts and gear for Letitia's retinue. My own horse wasn't in evidence yet, though I spotted my harp case and pack amid the caravan-load of gear waiting in the portico. Rather than standing and staring at the Tans as they worked, I wandered down the garden path again, too restless to go back inside.

Countless songs and apocryphal stories swirled around in my head: human wizards drafted into wars between Tanaan courts; human women kidnapped, sometimes willingly, by Tanaan righthe as concubines or brood mares to supplement the shaky Tanaan reproductive ability; human champions seduced by Tanaan morae to further their ambitions. How many of those stories began with something as simple as an invitation to ride to the neighboring court? Was I going to spend Bealtan celebrating the old rite among the legendary Tana—or risking my neck in support of agendas I wouldn't understand until too late, if at all?

I probably ought to be worried.

"Ouirr, good morning," Letitia said.

My head followed the sound of her voice, of its own accord. The Tana stood at a branching of the path, on the fork I would not have taken on my own: mysterious emerald eyes illuminated by filtered sunlight, river of golden hair braided into a thick plait—and, by all the gods, wearing pants. It was an eminently sensible wardrobe choice for travel; I had seen Letitia's guardswoman Tru similarly attired. But on Letitia, pants left me no recourse but to stare.

"Now, that just isn't fair," I said. "How do you expect the Banbagor spies to concentrate on their work?"

Letitia laughed and took my arm; a thrill rippled through me.

"Ouirr, even on this side of the mountains, we know enough to mistrust the honey-tongued harpist," she said, guiding me down the path on which she stood. "Come with me; I was just about to visit the Mora's Spring."

The path opened into a small grove of apple trees. Bees buzzed among the blossoms. At the center of the clearing stood a small outcrop of pale pink granite, which water or tools had carved into a series of descending pools. A spring issued from a cleft in the rock, spilling down through the small pools to fill a larger basin below. Narcissus bloomed around the perimeter of the basin, their perfume so heady my brain whirled. An odd seductive power pulsed here, in much the same way as at any human sacred site; but it felt different from any such place I had ever visited.

"Come," Letitia said again, releasing my arm. She bent to grasp and dip a small metal cup into the water. "The Holy Mora welcomes all travelers."

She offered me the cup; once again I could see the alien priestess who stood naked in the midst of a secret grove. I took the cup reverently, in both hands, sipped and handed it back. The water was as cold as mountains in winter, fresh and flavorful as only spring water can be. Her fingers brushed mine; her gaze captured me, making it impossible to look away. She drank, too, eyes still on mine.

"Your wonders never cease," I said. "The power of this place is so different from our sites."

"Yes?"

"Oh, yes," I said. "The energy here is all about… the opening of ways. Inviting things into themselves, creating space in which things can become. It's almost the opposite of the power sites Beallan wizards use. That magic is about bending reality to one's will. Creation or destruction by force. This feels… upside-down." I smiled; she returned the smile, but now I wasn't sure my words had made sense to her. Maybe it was just that these weren't mysteries she was allowed to discuss. "In a rather wonderful way."

"Mora."

I looked towards the entrance to the grove. Etan was there, still-faced as any human righ's courtier. Abruptly I was aware of how close together Letitia and I stood; but to back away now would be an admission of things I didn't want to confess.

"I am sorry to interrupt," Etan said. "Your caravan is ready. Shall I assemble your retinue?"

"Thank you," Letitia said, smiling as confidently as if she stood within a hand's breadth of men not her consort every day. Etan curtsied and withdrew.

"Right, so," Letitia said. Her mouth twisted into half a smile; she reached up and touched my forehead. "The Holy Mora's blessings on you, traveler. May you find the path easy beneath your feet."

I stepped back and bowed. "Thank you."

Letitia smiled and took my arm again and led me back out of the garden. The house yard was even more crowded than a few minutes ago. Not only horses and stable hands but most of Letitia's retinue stood in the yard, restless; suddenly the unease I should have been feeling all morning crashed down on me. The horses in the front half of the train seemed agitated, as if there might be a snake nearby; the stable hand holding mine looked on the verge of losing control to the stallion's vibrating nerves. Iminor's and Nuad's were faring better under their riders' experienced handling; Letitia's was fretful but well-controlled. I added the stable hand who drew my horse to the list of people who would be relieved by my departure.

"Zhev," Letitia whispered, hesitating. She was abruptly pale.

"What is it?" I asked.

"Stupidity," she said, barely more audible. She closed her eyes for a moment, shaking her head. "Do you know, for a moment I actually expected my companions to be here."

Her companions of the chamber: I had almost forgotten about those deaths. All the Tana waiting to travel with Letitia must seem pale substitutes for the young, vibrant ladies with whom I'd seen her giggling on the evening we met. I laid a hand on her arm, wishing the rules of propriety would permit me to offer better comfort.

"This grievance had better be big," she said. She lifted her chin and straightened her spine.

"Good morning," she said, pitching her voice to encompass the yard. Everyone responded in kind. She released my arm and walked up the length of the nervous incipient train, introducing or re-introducing me to everyone: Cainte the chef, who sported a sword on which she rested a hand, meeting Letitia's gaze with a challenging look and daring Letitia to object; the new herald Boanna, who wore pants and a long-tailed coat in the typical style of heralds on the road—but whose personality was lost to me in the intellectual dissonance of a Tanaan herald wearing what the back of my head knew to be the Aballo colors, despite the fact that they were clearly Fíana's colors as well; Etan's assistant Flidais, the new guardian of Letitia's chamber, who accepted the reintroduction in a gentle way that made it clear she didn't expect to replace Letitia's recently-deceased favorite; and three fresh-faced daughters of the Ériu clan, who were aquiver with their opportunity to serve the mora as maidens of the chamber. Except for Flidais and the new maidens of the chamber, Letitia was the only one among the party who wore neither blade nor mail: her vulnerability made the skin on the back of my neck crawl, even though I understood this was a part of the bizarre protocol we must follow.

"And of course you remember Nuad, Fíana's armsmaster," Letitia said. Nuad and I exchanged bows again. "Nuad, are you ready?"

The armsmaster nodded and laid a soothing hand on his nervous horse's neck, battle-bound blond hair bobbing against his white-and-gold enameled armor. "Your guard will meet us at harborside."

"Carina?" someone behind me said. The consonants were properly formed, not elided as Tanaan usually render them. "Lady?"

I turned towards the voice. The front door of the house swung open, and Rishan and Etan stepped out to the portico. But it was impossible to focus on them: the person standing behind Letitia, hand tentatively outstretched, was Amien.

"*Amien?*" I blurted.

The wizard wasn't looking at me: rather at Letitia's back. His head snapped around in my direction, and our eyes met. Power rattled up my spine; buried memories of magic dashed themselves against the inside of my skull. Amien seemed not to have aged in ten years: his unruly lead-grey hair and age-lined face were the same as ever. But his typically regal bearing was blunted, as if he were unsure of his reception, and his black eyes were full of pain.

"What the hell?" Amien said.

I shook my head, swallowing a torrent of words. Halfway to Hy-Breasaíl wasn't far enough by half.

"Ouirr?" Letitia said, turning to me. As her face came into view, the wizard's equine visage shifted into crushing disappointment.

I cleared my throat. "Mora Letitia Ériu a Fíana, allow me to present Amien Cughlin, Prince of the Aballo Order."

More arcane energies knocked against my awareness: black and red crowded around the edges of my vision, coalescing into a fog that even mundane eyes might see. Letitia granted Amien a deep nod; the wizard stared at her for a moment before executing a courtly bow. The new herald yawned audibly; Nuad blinked and shook his head as if to clear it.

"You are—Carina's daughter?" the wizard said, voice even more gravelly than usual.

The power at my periphery wasn't Amien's: his signatures were all in greens, and he avoided anything that hinted at darkness as if it might kill him. So why did I feel I knew this energy swirling through the Ériu House yard?

Letitia nodded; Amien glanced away, swallowed, and returned his gaze to her face.

"Then I believe the news I carry is for you."

All three of Letitia's new maidens of the chamber tumbled gracelessly to the ground; the herald staggered, reached out to support herself against her horse's flank, and collapsed. A cocktail of lavender and valerian washed over me, and a circuit completed itself in my brain. Somewhere far away, a wizard whose name I didn't know had launched a briocht of irresistible sleep, channeling it through something I could almost sense nearby. There were no undead Wild Hunt here today, but the mechanism and the author of this working were the same. The wonder was not why I recognized the signatures, but why it had taken me so long to place them.

"The fog," Nuad gasped.

"Hold your breath," Rishan mumbled from the portico.

"It's not that kind of fog!" Amien snapped, and rattled off a counter-spell. The air cleared; reflexively I shook my head. But by the time I'd drawn another breath the fog was back, falling like a thick cloak over the entire yard.

"Fouzh!" Amien drew himself into the crane position: left boot balanced against right knee, left hand tucked into the back of his belt and left eye closed; all power trained up from the earth through his right eye and hand.

Here it was: the attack I'd wished for only last night. Drawing those energies into myself and dismantling the spell from the inside would be easier than drawing my sword; arcane awareness settled over me, and for half a second Letitia and Amien, the fog, and the horses and stableboys who occupied the end of the train were all I could see. Merely breathe that power into me, and I could begin to engage Letitia's enemy. The madness of magic would make everything permissible. Only later would I awaken to what I'd done.

Amien shouted out a second briocht; I shook off arcane awareness and reached for my sword as the fog wavered and then resolved into something both thicker and brighter. Several Tana cried out in panicked voices, no longer visible among the haze; I heard people begin running, towards what I couldn't tell. But it didn't matter; within seconds I heard them hit the dirt, doubtless asleep. My head whirled with the onset of a valerian slumber.

I groaned: there was no sane choice here. Stave off arcane awareness and succumb to the spell; or allow the shift in consciousness to overtake me and try to control the madness it would cause. At least I might be marginally effective while awake.

Amien shouted again: the incantation that would raise protective wards around the yard. As if that would help, when the conduit Letitia's enemy was using must be right here with us. My head whirled faster; I breathed in the fog, feeling it dissolve in light against the back of my throat, and as my head shifted into magic it suddenly became possible to see through the all-encompassing sparkle around me. Once again Amien and Letitia, a couple of stable hands, and the last seven horses in the train sprang to vibrant life in my vision, while everything else faded to grey mundanity. I tingled with the need to grasp and rechannel the energy, to seek out arcane awareness of my enemy; instead I drew my sword, raced across the yard, and beheaded the closest stable hand. Why hadn't I noticed his pallor and blue-purple lips the moment I entered this space? Letitia shrieked; but no blood followed my sword.

"What the hell?" Amien shouted.

"Básghilae!" I shouted back. "The last seven in the train!"

"So you kill a stable hand?"

I swept my blade through the throat of the second stable hand who smelled of enchantment, finally unsurprised at the lack of blood. This time Flidais, whose supposed horse he'd been holding, shrieked in chorus with Letitia, put out a hand to steady herself against the being she thought was a horse, and collapsed.

"Fouzh!" I barked. "You've got a better idea?"

Iminor and Nuad staggered towards me, swords bared; Amien cast a bright green flare of arcane power at the horse in front of me, and it went down. The bolt passed within inches of me; my throat burned with need. I could take both Tans, even without the spell that had stripped them of all but the last shreds of consciousness; it would be ten times more satisfying to end the encounter magically. But Nuad just grabbed Letitia's arm and stumble-pushed her towards the house, and Iminor planted himself beside me, leaning against my off side without seeming aware. The horse began climbing to its feet, wisps of smoke curling from its hide.

"The heads," Iminor said with remote sagacity, just as the remaining horses broke ranks. Amien cast at each of them in turn, and they all went down: coats black and smoking, the muscle beneath their hides partially exposed. But most of them began climbing to their feet again. Nuad and Cainte stumbled in to strike at the two closest to the house; Iminor chopped at the neck of the first Amien had struck. Amien swore and rushed in with sword raised while I raced to waylay one that attempted to slip around the outside.

How does one fight a horse? If a man is unhorsed in battle he can easily find himself on the ground trying to defend against a mounted enemy; a battle-trained destrier will kick and bite a man on foot as readily as he will another horse, and the most effective defense is a sword to the horse's neck. I buried my blade in the correct spot for such a slaughter; but of course the blood that should have sprayed across my body didn't come. The animal turned a gaze of detached recognition on me—but beneath that detachment, I thought I saw both intelligence and despair.

I scrambled backwards and chopped at the beast's neck; the animal turned to advance on me again. I wished for a poleax. My blow jarred against vertebrae, knocking the horse over but not severing the head. The light blades the Tanaan carried must be even less effective.

More bolts of power sang across the yard; Amien swore and swung his sword again. Smoke rose from several of the horses, but two were already regaining their feet. Across the yard, Letitia slipped down the steps of the portico and scurried to the back of the disintegrating train.

"Mora!" Nuad shouted, voice raw with frustration and fatigue. A horse reared and kicked out at Cainte, clipping her in the chin and caving in her chest; she fell, sword clattering across the yard, succumbing to the death spell before her body hit the ground. I chopped at my horse's neck as if it were a tree, finally severing it, then turned and bolted towards the one that had killed Cainte. But before I could reach it, Letitia was there, swinging a small cauldron by the handle and connecting with the horse's skull. A hollow gong rang through the yard; the horse collapsed.

"Fouzh!" I heard myself shout. "Letitia!"

"Mora, *inside!*" Nuad barked; Letitia dropped the cauldron.

I reached the downed horse and removed its head with a series of grisly chops, finally severing the head just as the beast began trying to regain its feet. When I looked up Nuad was wielding the discarded cauldron—and Letitia had picked up another. It bounced ringing from the head of a horse, which wobbled to its knees but began to right itself. Amien cast at the creature, the bolt flying within inches of Letitia's face; Letitia leapt backwards with a little shriek as it fell.

"Letitia, GO!" I shouted, running towards the horse she'd stunned. She shot me a look of frustration and ran towards the portico, tossing the cauldron to the ground. An immense black stallion raced past me and Iminor; nothing stood between the horse and the Tana. I shouted and threw my sword as if it were a spear and this insanity my pre-coronation horse sacrifice; I ran after it. The horse from which I had turned lunged to its feet.

"Amien!" I shouted. The wizard cast at the horse charging in my wake. The bolt passed so close behind me that I could feel the energy against my back. My sword penetrated the neck of the stallion chasing Letitia, knocking the beast to its knees. Halfway between the horse and the house, Letitia tangled in a downed horse's lead and fell.

Things shifted into unnatural clarity, as they so often do on the field. Letitia disentangled her feet from the lead; I leapt onto the horse's back—booted feet only; direct contact meant death—and yanked my sword free. The horse scrambled upright, catapulting me skyward. I was vaguely aware of Rishan's slitted eyes on me, where he lay paralyzed by the briocht. I sailed through the air and tumbled into the horse's path, crashed bruisingly to the ground and rolled to my feet, fighting for air and clutching the sword, as Letitia ran towards the door. My head began throbbing again. The horse closed in behind me: too close for either me or Letitia to outrun. There was no choice but to stand and face it. I spun towards the animal; Nuad shouted an oath.

This was how it felt for a righ to stand against the stallion, to know that the balance between order and chaos rested on this one divinatory sacrifice; that failure would mean far more than the loss of one's own life. Six hundred years ago, a man standing in this place on the night before his coronation would have dedicated his next stroke to the god Esus, just as the spear-thrust would have been performed in the name of Turenn Thunderer. Today it was all for Letitia.

After an interminable half-second, the moment of inevitability came: the stallion was committed to this path, too massive to change trajectories. And I was too great a fool to run. Its gaze locked onto my own, the rage of the goaded stallion tempered into something colder but no less singular. I raised my sword, and the horse charged into it, knocking us both to the ground. I rolled away, just in time to avoid contact, reaching for the knife in my boot. What I was going to do with it I had no idea.

Amien's blade sliced down through the horse's neck, severing the spine. Iminor completed the job with a swift final stroke. Abruptly the yard was quiet; the fog sparkled into nonexistence.

"Sláinte," I muttered, rising. Amien stared at me for a moment, then laughed: a harsh, humorless sound.

"There's a hide in which you couldn't pay me to dream," the wizard said, in the ironic tone he used after something went terribly wrong in the workshop.

"What?" Letitia shrilled.

"The hide of the sacrifice," Amien said, surveying the yard. "They use them for divinatory—Hello, what the hell?"

The wizard strode past Letitia to the place in which the train had fractured into chaos. I swore and followed: I saw it now, too. The decapitated horses were no longer horses, properly speaking. Hides were disappearing; hooves had become hands and feet. A similar change was taking place where I had first engaged a horse: the headless animal had already taken on a distinctly human shape.

"Oh, what hell is this?" Letitia moaned.

"Everybody, don't touch anything," Amien said. "Let's go slowly and get things sorted out."

Chapter 8
News from Elsewhere

Amien worked arcane wards around the house. They shimmered in every shade of green: an impenetrable circle of sliding hue that stretched upward from the ground, towards the sky and out of sight. I didn't realize how deeply I'd been dreading the appearance of an assassin or some arcane onslaught until the wards closed and the tension in my back relaxed.

There was no peace in the sitting room to which Etan conducted me and Amien and bade us wait for Letitia, however. Amien and I stood staring at one another from opposite sides of the room, while I cast about uselessly for some neutral topic of discussion that might drown out all the things I couldn't allow myself to say. When Rishan entered the room a moment later, relief washed over me: Amien could take up a conversation with him, and I could fade into the hangings. But within seconds it was clear they had nothing civil to say to one another, either. I drew in breath to sigh, then had to release it slowly so it wouldn't be audible. Silence hung in the room.

Finally Letitia arrived: fresh-cream skin muddied by the green light pouring through the windows, emerald eyes glittering with pain. Her fingers twined around Iminor's with visible intensity; she released him reluctantly and cast a tormented glance around the room.

"Gentlemen, be at ease," she said absently. I restrained a humorless laugh, watching as she crossed the room to sink into a chair.

There was nothing for it, now: I followed the rest of them into the sitting area. Rishan and Amien beat me to the remaining chairs; I settled at the undesirable end of the settee, allowing Iminor the closer seat. Silence descended again.

"Ouirr," Letitia said finally to Amien. "Forgive me. In all the—" Her voice disappeared; she swallowed and went on. "I'm afraid I've lost track of your name."

Amien looked astonished. "Amien Cughlin, La—Mora. Prince—"

Sudden recollection flashed in Letitia's face. "Of the Aballo Order of wizards," she finished. "I'm sorry, I'm very—My head's not working very well right now."

Amien nodded.

"You came to bring me news."

Amien nodded again, preparing to speak.

"And got far more than you bartered for," Letitia continued, and astonished me with a frank glance. There she was again, suddenly: the alien priestess who required my defense. And this time the appreciation in her gaze was unmistakable. I offered her half a smile.

"That seems to be happening a lot lately," she said at length, gaze still on mine.

"Yes?" the wizard said.

"They tell me it's Banbagor," Letitia said, glancing at him again.

Amien frowned.

"The Mora of Banbagor," Letitia continued. "A grievance? My heralds keep dying, but evidently an attack on the mora-in-waiting right before investiture..." She frowned. "But I was on my way to make formal answer. They're not supposed to attack again if I do."

"Mora, this attack didn't come from Banbagor," Amien said.

"What?" Letitia turned a look of incredulous bewilderment on him.

"This is what I came to—This is why I'm here," Amien said, his gruff voice turning to gravel again. "Truthfully I expected..."

"You expected Carina," Rishan snarled.

Amien glanced away. "Yes. But I—I see now that I... misinterpreted."

It was far more satisfying than it had any right to be to see Amien so discomfited. He looked at Letitia again, frowning. The room grew uncomfortably still.

"No," he said finally. "The intelligence we've received remains what it is. And it has certainly been borne out this morning."

"What are you talking about?" I said before I thought better of it.

The wizard met my eyes: grief, fear, and anger warring behind his practiced reserve. "About a month ago, a kharr spy was captured at Carricolig—the seat of the Ebdani righ," he elaborated for Letitia, then glanced at me again. "Under torture he yielded intelligence of a plot... against the Lady of Finias."

My head snapped around for a look at Letitia before I could control it. The events of the past three days reshuffled themselves in my head, all of them showing Letitia to be even more defenseless than I'd imagined.

"Against who?" Letitia said to Amien.

"The Mora of Fíana," I said gently. "Our names for your lands are different…"

She stared at me. Her lids fluttered. *The morae of Fíana do not faint*, she thought.

"Are you telling me…?" she said in a thready voice. "The kharr. These are your rebels? You spoke about them at dinner last night?" It seemed a very long time ago.

"Yes," I said.

"Why would your kharr want to kill me?" she asked: not wailing or whining, but simply, absolutely bewildered. My throat ached at her defenselessness; and I realized that was precisely the question.

I shook my head and turned to Amien. "Sometimes torturers find things that don't exist," I reminded him.

"At first I thought so, too," the wizard said gravely. "But a few nights later, a herald in the service of a minor Ebdani tiarn was found murdered on the road to Tonagal. His pouch was damaged, but one of the remaining missives contained instructions for a tiarn in Ilesia… to do everything in his power to ensure that Ilesia offered Finias—Fíana—no succor… And promised rich rewards after Ilnemedon fell."

Anger sparked inside me. "The Bard of Arcadia. They're threatening Ilnemedon, now, too?"

"Where's my herald, by the way?" Amien said, touching off an entirely new flavor of irritation in me.

"Your what?" I said, with a passable attempt at innocence.

"The one I sent to the Harpist Gorsedd Hall?"

So he had known where to look. How much did he know about my last ten years? My irritation flared into anger.

"How long ago was that?" I said, maintaining an innocent expression but surprisingly defenseless against the ire creeping into my voice. "I've been away from the city for a couple of twelvenights…"

Amien's mouth twisted. "No doubt they've been enjoying the peace."

I manufactured a laugh.

"*Why do they want to kill me?*" Letitia shrilled. I turned back to face her, abashed.

"I don't know yet," Amien said gently. "I'd like to keep you safe until we figure it out."

"How do you propose to do that?" Letitia said. "The green wall's pretty, but—"

"It's temporary," Amien said. "This place is indefensible—"

"We've got extensive history to the contrary!" Rishan snapped.

"The power sources here are *all wrong!*" Amien retorted, frustration and something that might be fear boiling up in his tone. The Tanaan stared as if he had declared the moons built of glass, but I found myself nodding: it explained much about the encounter out in the house yard. Attempting to bank any serious working against the upside-down power in this place would be useless.

"I can't work with what you've got out here!" Amien continued. "Great— Dear gods, these energies are unusable! Didn't you see, out there in the yard? None of those horses should have gotten up again, Básghilae or no!"

"What?" Letitia said.

"There is a *reason* I've held my position for four hundred years, and it isn't because I can't take some no-name druid from gods-only-know-where who can cobble together dead bodies and depletion spells! But what you can channel here just spreads out into… nothing!" He looked to me as if for confirmation; all I could do was nod. Letitia still looked completely bewildered.

"Mora, we were talking about this, this morning…" I reminded her.

"We were?"

What had she thought we were talking about? "The energies in your sacred sites?"

"Oh! Yes." She met my gaze again, and abruptly the smolder that hung about her when we were alone was back. My mind skipped from that tantalizing moment at the sacred spring to the alien priestess who stood naked in a sacred grove—to Bealtan. Did Tanaan custom restrict a Tana to a single performance of the Bealtan rite—or was it reasonable to hope I might steal some of that magic for myself?

How was it possible I was even thinking about this now?

"The energies are a problem?" Letitia said faintly.

"The energies are *impossible*," Amien said. "We've got to get you to Aballo."

Excitement and dread collided in my chest.

"What?" Letitia said.

"Let's just rein that one in *right now*," Rishan said, low-voiced. His pale, green-shadowed face was abruptly flushed. "The last time you promised to escort a member of this family—"

Suddenly Amien was on his feet, chair sliding away behind him. He grasped his sword; his chest heaved. He and Rishan stared as if trying to bore holes through one another's skulls.

"No man, not even one of the lords of the order, may ignore the summons of the Aballo Prince," Amien rasped. "Nevertheless I begin and end each day with the wish that I had forfeited my life and done just that."

"So do I," Rishan rejoined in a profoundly unsympathetic tone.

Amien spun away and strode to the window. The sounds of everyone breathing seemed unnaturally loud.

"We should be able to reach Aballo in nineteen or twenty days," Amien said to the window. "I have sent word to the High Chief of the Essuvians, requesting that she meet us with reinforcements at Banbagor, but—"

"What about the wildfires?" Letitia interrupted. "Wait—*twenty days*? I can't be gone that long! My investiture is in twenty-four!"

Amien laughed humorlessly. "This war has been going on for five years, now. I can't guarantee that we'll have it mopped up on time for your investiture!"

A strange desperation manifested in Letitia's face. "Maybe it'll just have to wait."

"Letitia! " I blurted. Sweet Lady Tella, when had my mouth developed a will of its own? All I did out here was speak out of turn.

"Mora," I said, in a more appropriate tone. "Do you understand what is happening here? The Bard's Wizard is targeting you. Every resource the kharr can spare will be applied to your death. If Amien can't find the power to keep you safe out here... You must agree to go to a place we can defend."

And had I really just volunteered to spend the next month working with Amien? I'd gone mad and hadn't noticed.

"But Aballo?" Letitia said reasonably. "Does it have to be there?"

Gods, no. Anyplace would be better, with the possible exception of the kharr's captured capital of Macol. But Amien shook his head, whether at Letitia or me I wasn't sure.

"Aballo commands the most reliable power sources in the world," he said, sounding reasonable again. "The tides alone make the island difficult to approach, and the harbor's completely inaccessible unless you know the release spells. And we have *walls*," he said to Rishan. "Yes, Mora, it must be Aballo. I cannot guarantee your safety otherwise."

"There are wildfires between here and Banbagor," Letitia said. That must be the source of the smoke I'd seen from the barge yesterday.

"Yes, arcane fire," Amien said. "It pursued me as I rode; it's no coincidence, I assure you."

"And a plague of locusts between here and the sea," Letitia said, as if she thought she'd won an argument.

But Amien just nodded, unsurprised. "That's what I felt. Well then, Mora, we should probably discuss traveling via the Muir Pass. I may be able to contact my second from Ilunmore and—"

I lost focus on the argument. Traveling via the Muir Pass would take us through the center of Tanaan society and culture, through cities about which I'd spent countless hours reading and more hours dreaming. I'd taken the shorter route to Fíana: beyond Ilesia's eastern borders and north, across the highlands and through Banbagor. To tread the celebrated shores of the Devadore, to visit the College of Bards at Arian and learn from their loremasters, even to see the wonders of the sacred isle of Ilunmore—these things would be more than sufficient compensation for a month in Amien's company.

"Muir?" Letitia's voice escalated into shrillness again, snapping me back into the moment. "How long is *that* going to take?"

Amien shrugged. "Longer. Twenty-two, twenty-three days? If we can charter a ship at Goibniu, we can shave off a few days... But this close to the Moot, we can't plan on that."

Letitia buried her head in her hands. "How do I know these two attacks came from the same place? What if the first time it really was the mora of Banbagor, and I go through Muir to Aballo rather than making answer to Banbagor—and Banbagor goes right on attacking Fíana? How could I call myself Mora then?"

"Mora, there's no way it wasn't the same wizard both times," I said.

"Can you prove it?" she retorted.

Not without discussing any number of topics I'd give much to avoid. I grimaced. "No."

"If Banbagor wanted to settle a grievance with you, they wouldn't make it impossible for you to get to them," Amien pointed out.

"Unless they just wanted to make it look like I refused."

"To what end?" I snapped. Letitia rewarded me with a look that suggested I had stepped out of line again—as if I were some inconsequential tiarn. My frustration flared higher; I mustered my patience.

"Letitia, what would the mora of Banbagor accomplish by removing you as mora of Fíana?" I said, with far less irritation than I felt. "It's not as if she could become mora of Fíana as well, is it?"

She turned a wrathful glare on me, meeting my stare with mouth set in a way that made it very clear I was treading the edge of my welcome. I held her gaze, too frustrated to care. Amien had found me, anyway.

After a moment she sagged, then gathered her dignity and rose. "I need to meditate," she said, and left the room.

More than an hour had passed. Rishan and Amien had gone directly from the sitting room to a private chamber nearby; I couldn't imagine them drinking brandy together after the baleful stares they'd exchanged, but I didn't hear shouting or furniture breaking, either. I wandered aimlessly among Ériu House's elegant corridors and courtyards, waiting for an opportunity to make a graceful exit.

Why had I thought I wanted to spend a month or more in Amien's company? With him here, Letitia had all the arcane defense anyone might require, and it was clearly a matter of very little time before one of us lost patience with another and said something everyone involved would regret. Maybe I'd come back next spring; maybe I'd take a wrong turn on the way back to Ilnemedon and miss the Moot after all. Maybe I'd sign on as a Nagnatan mercenary and get it over with: it was strangely difficult to imagine going back to Ilnemedon at all, whether as ard-harpist or simply as some man the ard-righ used to know. I wondered where a man could get a skin of brandy in this city.

"Ouirr Ellion," Etan said quietly.

I looked up: the Tana stood in the doorway to the courtyard I wandered, green-lit and downcast. I met her gaze evenly, sharing her grief and my rising despair.

"If you would return to the sitting room, the mora will join you in a moment."

I nodded and followed her inside. As I approached the sitting room, I saw Rishan walk in. Amien hurried towards me from the opposite direction and planted himself in my path.

"You didn't tell them who you are?" he said, black eyes incredulous. "Great Lord Ilesan, Rishan thought you were a harpist!"

I manufactured a laugh. "My lord, I *am* a harpist. A good one, as it happens."

"Pheh," Amien said, spun on his heel, and stalked inside.

Letitia was already there, in the same chair as before, golden hair and fresh-cream skin muddied by green shadows and sudden age in her eyes. She had the air of someone who had been sitting alone for quite some time.

I bowed and entered the room. "Mora."

"My lord."

She gestured for me to sit; I took advantage of the opportunity the moment afforded to adjust to my sudden change in stature—or tried to. Something very strange was going on in my chest. I glanced at her again as I settled, and found her gaze still on me. Iminor entered the room and settled beside me again.

"I appreciate your grace in giving me time to collect my thoughts," she said finally, sounding so much older than a Tana on the verge of her first Bealtan that I ached to wrap my awareness around her, to seek out the cause or cure. I held myself closed.

"I will surprise none of you," she continued. "My investiture must wait. I cannot become mora under these circumstances; there will be no safety for anyone here until this situation has been resolved. My lord Amien, I would be grateful to accept your offer of sanctuary at Aballo."

It was done, then. Amien nodded gravely, face still.

"My lord Ellion," she said, turning her depthless eyes on me. "I will not ask you to ride with me on this journey. The war against the rebels is not your war: you have made this plain." Her eyes were as intent on mine as if we were the only people in the room. Objections tangled on one another in my throat.

"But, my lord, if you volunteered—I would not turn you away."

I could feel Amien staring at me. Rishan rose abruptly, chair sliding away behind him, and strode to the window. I rose, feeling the inevitability of it, and presented myself on one knee. I met Letitia's eyes and offered her my sword.

But there was no way I could make the crossing to Aballo.

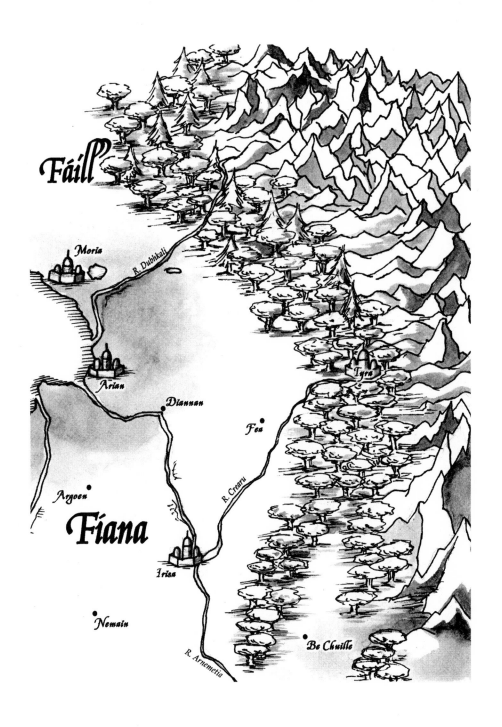

Northern Fíana and the Devadore

Chapter 9
Leading the Blind

Cainte the chef, Etan's assistant Flidais, and Letitia's herald Boanna were already arrayed on funerary biers in a hall that was probably a ballroom on happier days. I discovered I wanted to pay respect to Cainte, even though we had barely known one another: the Tana had the soul of a warrior, whatever her profession, and she had died in Letitia's defense. I stood beside her body, looking at her fine-boned face: does every Tana become a goddess in the stillnesses of meditation and death? I tried to apply myself to the question, hoping it would distract me from the energies Amien was raising in the opposite wing. But the battle for calm was a hopeless one.

Amien had insisted on working personal wards for Letitia before we set out: a sensible last line of defense for the Bard of Arcadia's latest incomprehensible objective. But the wizard was clearly having as much difficulty with the working as he'd had with the Básghilae out in the house yard: again and again power surged at the edges of my awareness, only to fade like the smoke from a cheap candle. He must be half-insane with frustration; the surge-and-fail of power was making me itch for violence. Finally I admitted I wasn't giving the dead their due, murmured an apology, and strode out to the house yard.

The house was surrounded by wards, of course: I'd forgotten. They hung like drapes of green magma suspended from some unimaginable height, blockading everything beyond the edge of the portico. I could have opened a portal and slipped through, but the thought of entangling myself in Amien's working was even less appealing than the still air; I just stood there, hand on the pommel of my sword, waiting: for what, I did not know.

A moment later Amien strode out to the portico, fuming.

"Ah," I said without thinking. "Got it?"

"Fouzhir torc," he muttered.

"What?" I said blankly.

He gave vent to an explosive sigh. "Her torc! The Mora's Torc of Fíana! I couldn't get the wards past the damned thing; she finally had to take it off. Great Lord Ilesan, get me the hell out of here!"

I nodded.

"She looks exactly like her mother," the wizard said, staring at the wards around the house.

I nodded again. "I had wondered."

Amien nodded, too, as if the fact were yet another irritation. "*Exactly*."

For a moment we were both silent. Finally he sighed.

"Well, I'd better take these things down," he said. "We leave in half an hour."

"Well, then," I said. "I'll see you in a bit." I turned and strode back inside, in search of some way to while away half an hour that didn't involve Amien.

When I returned, the yard was busy again, with a more compact train that carefully skirted the places in which someone had heaped wood and kindling on top of Básghilae corpses and set them alight. I hoped for the sake of everyone who must remain here that the upside-down pyres worked—and wondered where they would hold the proper pyres for Letitia's dead retainers tonight.

Amien already stood beside his horse, impatience written in his every motion; Iminor shot me a look of pure venom as I stepped down from the portico. We hadn't even held a conversation since this morning's battle; how had I managed to offend him? I gave him a nod, because a civil response to anger tends to end such matters quickly, one way or another, and applied myself to checking my horse's tack and ensuring that my gear was properly lashed. By the time I finished, Nuad, Letitia, and Rishan had arrived. Rishan glared at me, too, then turned a look composed of equal parts injury and frustration on Letitia. She just sighed and climbed into the saddle, the spidersilk of her artistically-crafted mailshirt rustling; so I followed suit, surveying the train. For the moment we were a party of five with a single pack horse: a much more sensible proportion for travel than this morning's mummers' parade.

"Don't bollocks this one up," Rishan said to Amien.

The wizard's mouth twisted. "Kiss my ass, old man. Your words will inspire me all the way to Aballo."

"See that they do."

"Is there anybody who still likes you?" Amien retorted. "Nuad, let's go."

Nuad glanced at Amien, Rishan, and Letitia in turn; Letitia gave him a nod, and he cued his horse.

"Be safe," Rishan said to Letitia, sudden vulnerability in his face. A little noise escaped her; she reached out and brushed his outstretched fingers as she passed.

Rishan turned his depthless black eyes on me as I fell in behind her and Iminor; suddenly his voice was in my head.

Surprise me. Do the right thing.

Long habit sent sarcasm racing to my lips; but suddenly I felt the import of this thing into which I'd stumbled. I met his gaze and nodded instead.

A double contingent of guards waited for us at the base of the slope, as Nuad had promised: ludicrous and resplendent in the same white-and-gold enameled armor I'd seen on Letitia's previous contingent, the Fíana standard fluttering prettily in the light onshore wind. They came to order as we rode down to meet them; Nuad dismounted and presented each guard to Letitia in what was clearly a ceremony of high tradition. Among them were Mattiaci, Vandabala, Eber and Tru, the surviving members of Letitia's last contingent—and three Tana besides Tru.

All the Tana except Tru hailed from junior septs of the Fíana clans, I noticed: what truth might I glean from that? It seemed reasonable to assume that a position on the Mora's Guard was an honorable one; the preponderance of Tans who hailed from primary clan houses seemed to bear that theory out. So if rank helped secure a position in this organization, what did it mean that the males tended to be of higher rank than the females? I had insufficient information, as usual.

There were two members of Clan Ériu among the group: Ogma, who hailed from a junior sept, and Neide, who was of the clan house itself. Letitia stiffened visibly when Neide was presented; he winked at her, with head tilted a bit so most of those present couldn't see. But she made no objection to her kinsman's inclusion in the party.

Finally the presentation was complete: all twenty-four of them stood in a long line before Letitia, battle-bound hair stirring in the wind and well-worked armor gleaming. She glanced at Nuad, then looked out at them again.

"Thank you, Nuad, these guards will do admirably," she said, in what was clearly the expected conclusion to the ceremony. I wondered whether I imagined relief in the line of Nuad's shoulders.

"Mora," Amien said, an undercurrent of frustration in his tone.

Letitia stiffened again, then turned a warning gaze on the wizard.

"Lord Amien," she responded in a tone that left no doubt which of them was in charge of this expedition. Astonishment raced through me: no human righ would have the effrontery to put the Prince of the Aballo Order in his place, certainly not in front of observers. A human would have known better than to think he would be the last one standing. What freedom must it be for a Tanaan mora to answer to none but her gods.

But Amien looked frustrated, not surprised; and I remembered his first appointment had been to the staff of Mora Bebhionn of Muir, Rishan's mother. I was torn between satisfaction at his discomfiture and an uneasy sense that Letitia's condescension towards the Prince of the Order translated into disrespect for the true gods.

"Mora," Amien said again, gaze locked on hers. "I do not dispute Ouirr Nuad's selection of your guards, but the manner of their outfit is wholly unacceptable!"

Letitia bristled; the wizard shook his head and pressed on.

"Our objective is to get you to Aballo *safely*—to attract as little attention to you as possible. This contingent is quite obviously in the service of a tiarn at the very least, most likely a royal!"

"Would you prefer they looked like a band of highwaymen?" Letitia snapped.

"Yes!" Amien retorted. "A Tana traveling under such guard, with the Bard of Arcadia's bounty on your neck most assuredly a public thing by now—"

"Fíana's honor—"

"Will not keep you alive!" Amien's voice escalated perilously close to a shout. He stopped, surprise in his equine face. Letitia's translucent skin was abruptly several shades paler. A horse stomped nervously; everything else was silent, except the Fíana standard dancing in the wind.

Nuad cleared his throat; Letitia looked at him, and he bowed.

"Mora, I regret—but I believe Lord Amien is right. May we have leave to re-outfit before your departure?"

Letitia stared at or through him for several seconds before replying.

"Of course," she said finally. "How long will you need?"

Nuad produced a look of profound regret. "Half an hour, Mora."

Letitia just nodded, but Amien sighed.

"Be quick," Letitia said. "We will wait here."

The sun was edging towards noon when we finally crossed the harbor and began following the river north. The Tanaan didn't ride in proper ranks: rather in a disorganized, shifting series of clusters that seemed, if not relaxed, more comfortable than the situation warranted. Mattiaci and Vandabala teased one another for looking tired; I looked at the younger Tan with renewed concern, remembering the brush he'd had with an enchanted sword, but it soon seemed clear both Tans had spent last night carousing. Letitia moved among the clusters of guards, speaking with each member of the party as they rode, Iminor doggedly in her wake. I recognized what she was doing, and the impulse was a sound one: warriors need to feel a sense of connection to the person they are assigned to protect. But if we were attacked in this disorganized state, with no one quite certain where the mora was or what their immediate responsibilities might be, the outcome could only be disaster.

I glanced at Nuad, who consistently occupied the rear of the shifting mass. He seemed alert, even anxious, apparently monitoring the entire party and the terrain around us; after a few moments more I realized everyone in the group was similarly aware of our surroundings, even while they chatted with the mora or their fellows. There was no carelessness among them. The reality was much worse.

I rode forward and fell in beside Amien, who had assumed a position at the front of the pack. "My lord."

The wizard shot me an inquiring glance.

"I need to rearrange your planned schedule," I said.

Amien grimaced. "Why should you be any different?"

I manufactured a laugh. "I'd like to stop about an hour before sunset, leave us some time to drill with the contingent. Battlefield tactics—they have none." If someone had told me a year ago that speaking the Ilesian language would ever feel like a return home, I would have laughed.

Amien gazed at me for a moment, as if to assess whether I might be joking. Finally he shook his head with a humorless laugh.

"Would you like to make the announcement?" he said, with the air of a righ inviting a visiting tiarn to begin the evening's dance.

I shook my head. "I'm going to deal with Nuad."

Amien raised his eyebrows and shrugged; I dropped back to ride beside Nuad.

"Ouirr," I said, "how many of this contingent are experienced fighters?"

Nuad glanced at me, then forward at Letitia. I followed his gaze, then had to push aside the distraction. All the qualities that make spidersilk mail the choice of everyone who can afford it served only to heighten her allure. I must be sure to avoid riding behind her.

"Oh, they're all tournament champions," Nuad said. "It's a requirement for admission to the Mora's Guard. The Arian woman in particular will polish your..." He cracked a reluctant grin.

Oh, sweet Lady Tella. "Yes, but how many of them have experienced *combat*?"

Suddenly all of Nuad's attention was on me.

"Oh," he said gravely. "Well, Matti, Vanda, Eber, Tru, and me. And Lord Iminor, of course."

As I'd suspected: only the people who had stood with me in the meadow, on the night I first joined them. These were people who spoke about the end of warfare as an established fact, after all.

I nodded. "Ouirr Nuad, with respect—there are significant differences between battle and a tourney."

Nuad nodded emphatic agreement. "Oh, Lord of Light, didn't we see that!" he groaned. "Eight champions lost in five minutes!" The sudden grief in his face tore at my throat; then, just as abruptly, his professional demeanor returned.

"If you would," I said carefully, in tones pitched for his ears alone. "There are things I could show you..."

Nuad glanced at Letitia again, then turned a look of intense gratitude on me. He nodded. "Teach us."

We stopped on a bluff overlooking the river, a place that seemed to serve both as a campground for travelers and a shrine to the Tanaan goddess Lys. Lys is one of three primary goddesses, I learned: a sort of junior dignitary to their great goddess Dana, a huntress and seer and—if the statue in the place was a proper likeness—so severe and angular that her virgin status might or might not be voluntary.

News of the contingent's changed mission and the training I planned had spread among the group during the afternoon: the mood was serious as the contingent set up camp, and more than one of them cast surreptitious, anxious glances at me. The clusters I'd observed on the road this afternoon persisted in the disposition of the camp; finally I realized I was seeing factions. The remaining members of Letitia's previous contingent claimed the space nearest the nest that Iminor built for Letitia; the others spread out in threes and fours. My first priority must be to accustom them to working as a unit—but I was distracted from planning tonight's lesson when I realized Vandabala was unwell, after all. He looked greyer than he had at noon, and his companions— including the Tana, Tru—left him to rest while they divided the tasks of setting up their campsite among themselves.

I looked around, trying to locate Amien so we could discuss the situation— and spotted Letitia standing at the edge of the bluff, leaning across her horse's withers and staring at the westering sun. I couldn't see her face, but even from this angle it was clear she had taken on a subtle glow. I stared, momentarily unable to summon the will to look away. Echoes of her unearthly illumination wafted on the air of the campsite; without thinking I breathed them in, tasting a warmth like roses in summer against the back of my throat.

A different power surged at the edges of the clearing. The next breath I drew tasted of death. I glanced around: as many as half the trees at the southern perimeter were shifting into human shape, drawing weapons from the deadfall at their feet; more slipped in from the east. Again Letitia's enemy had augmented his forces: this time they had nearly double our numbers.

"Fíana!" I shouted and drew my sword.

"To arms!" Nuad called and flung himself into the saddle. Most of the Tanaan followed suit and launched themselves towards the Básghilae—who had arrayed themselves with a row of pikes in front, swordsmen behind, and no apparent concern for the fact that their shapeshifting had left them nude. Amien raced in from the far end of the camp, casting at them as he ran. The first bolt caromed crazily and struck the statue of Lys in the face, severing her nose. I ran past him to engage the Básghilae, several members of Letitia's first contingent in my wake.

Amien shot me a glare. "I could use some *help* here!" he barked.

"I'm giving you all I can!" I moved to close with the Básghilae. But before I got there, several mounted guardsmen galloped past, as if they actually thought they could slip between the pikes to engage the ghouls.

"No!" I shouted. "Fools! Stop!"

"HALT!" Nuad roared behind me; but momentum or bravado carried the knights forward. Horses slammed into the pikes and screamed; Tans were thrown spurs-over-helmet to land helpless among the swordsmen at the rear, who dispatched them within seconds. Amien cast another bolt of power across the campground; this one swerved towards me, and I had to duck to avoid it.

"Fouzh!" I snapped, glaring at the wizard. "If you don't want me here—"

"Shut up!" he roared. "Help me or shut—" Again he let fly; this one finally hit home, and one of the pikemen went down. Another group of Tanaan horsemen poured towards the breach. Nuad was among them. So, unaccountably, was Letitia.

"Letitia!" I shouted.

Horror broke across Nuad's face; he wheeled his mount to intercept Letitia, blocking her progress. All at once the Tanaan were in disarray and Básghilae were racing towards her.

"Riders!" I shouted. "Guard the mora! Iminor, Mattiaci, Eber, Tru—with me! On foot!" I slipped into the opening between the pikemen; the place dissolved into chaos. Tanaan horsemen encircled Letitia, fighting Básghilae; other Tanaan warriors engaged undead swordsmen on foot. Letitia's handsome kinsman Neide fell back before a particularly vicious attack, lost his footing and toppled backwards off the bluff.

"*Neide!*" Letitia howled and slipped between her defenders, sword raised. Básghilae across the campsite turned towards her; Nuad roared frustration, hauled her summarily from the saddle, and spurred his horse into the center of the group defending her.

There was nothing for it but to dig in and whittle away at the Básghilae. Little by little, as darkness gathered at the bases of the trees and stretched across the campsite, we reduced their number—until finally, just as on that first night in the meadow, we overcame their numerical advantage and they withdrew. This time I found myself staring after them, trying to guess at the Bard of Arcadia's plan. To send Básghilae so far from his base of operations, wherever it might lie, was a huge expenditure of magical resources; presumably the Bard needed his wizard for other operations as well. Why spend so much on an objective that made so little sense?

I looked around the campsite again and discovered Amien staring at me, bewilderment and frustration in his face. I met his gaze; he shook his head and turned away.

Far too much time passed before Letitia finally agreed to halt the search for her kinsman's body; not until it was too dark for even Tanaan eyes to discern much, and Iminor quietly pointed out that she was endangering the living with her hunt for the dead, did she allow herself to be persuaded to move out.

We walked this time, horses in tow, following the dusty road along the river by torchlight. Finally we reached a place Nuad declared possible to defend: a little crannog so long abandoned that the edges of the artificial island were beginning to fray. We crossed a narrow, crumbling causeway and found ourselves in the midst of a bracken-infested, deserted homestead. Once again the Tanaan set about building a campsite, this time by torchlight; Amien stood in the center of the little yard and cast wards around the island, calling the true gods to each quarter in turn. The incantation echoed inescapably in my head and tried to force itself past my lips; I held myself closed, but power teased at my edges.

When it was done, I realized I had forgotten about tending to my horse; the brush felt like something alien in my hand, and Amien had caught me staring.

"Ellion, a moment?" he said gravely. I nodded and followed him away from the campsite, across the tiny would-be island, to stand among the bracken at the base of the ward-wall.

For a moment we stared at one another in silence. It felt different than it had this morning; now the words bubbling up in my throat held no rancor. But they were just as impossible to speak. He seemed shorter than he had during my days as his student; there seemed to be more white in his hair now. Maybe it was just that I wasn't used to seeing the top of his head.

"What's this business with the sword?" he said finally. "This contingent is full of swordsmen; I need *help*."

Dread caught at my chest. "I'm giving you all I can. I can't—"

"You of all people should understand what we're up against!"

It felt like an accusation of a hundred crimes, all of which I had committed. I forced myself to meet his black eyes, seeing myself reflected in a dozen hues of green: a sad shade of the man whose deep connection with the goddess had rendered unnecessary the ethical caution practiced by the wizards around him. Or who had thought it did.

"You've got my blade," I rasped. It was yet another flavor of humiliation that the ard-harpist could allow his voice to sound like that. "Don't ask me to work magic."

"Letitia?" Iminor's voice echoed across the crannog.

"Mora?" That was Nuad. Immediately Amien and I glanced around and then back at one another, anger forestalled.

"What the hell?" I muttered, striding back towards the campsite.

"Great Lord Ilesan, how can a Tana get herself lost on a warded crannog?" Amien groaned behind me. He stopped, and I paused to look back at him, realizing what he was doing: seeking Letitia through his connection to the arcane wards he'd worked for her this morning. His gaze was immediately abstracted; then just as suddenly he nodded and strode past me, preceding me into the campsite.

"She's here," he said to the frantic Tanaan. "She's on the crannog, and she's safe."

"Good, but where is she?" Iminor said.

Amien looked thoughtful. "I'm... not sure," he said after a moment, gaze focused on senses arcane. "I'm not—" Suddenly he was speaking Ilesian again. "—a clairvoyant; all I get from this is impressions. Bracken? She's sitting in bracken?"

That didn't narrow it down, not here.

"And she's—" He frowned. "In... amhain—no, machnamh—in trance? Meditating?" He returned to the present moment, glancing around at the group. "She's meditating," he said, nodding.

"Oh Sweet Lord," said Iminor, evidently the only Tanaan present who understood Ilesian, and strode out of the campsite. At a word from Nuad most of the guardsmen spread out as well; Amien watched them go, guilt in his face. I was just turning back to my neglected horse when the wizard gasped; my head whipped around of its own accord.

"What?" I said.

"Ah, damn... They scared her," the wizard said, voice rough. "Fouzh but I hate it when they cry."

I nodded.

A moment later Letitia stalked out from behind the crumbling homestead, most of her escort in tow.

"Lord of Light, can't a woman *meditate* in peace?" she snapped, no trace of tears in her face or voice.

Amien bowed. "I will try not to let that happen again."

With so many new guards eager to distinguish themselves in the mora's service, there was no need for me to take a watch. Nevertheless, sleep was all but impossible. Amien spent the night struggling to keep his wards active, trying one power source after another; again and again the surge-and-fail of power sent me bolting from sleep. Finally, an hour or so before dawn—or so I guessed, in the absence of stars by which I might check my internal clock—I gave up trying to sleep and lay in my bedroll watching the wizard, who alternated between staring at the fire and pacing the camp's perimeter. Finally he stopped, glaring at me.

"Well?" he snapped. "What have you to say?"

I sat up and met his eyes. "Nothing, obviously."

"Damn right, nothing!" the wizard retorted. "He has a right to criticize who has a heart to help!"

The wards guttered and collapsed; without warning the entire flow of energy mapped itself across my consciousness: the power center Amien had tapped; the energy of the wards smearing across the aether like smoke-rings in a sudden wind—and the cold, crystalline consciousness at the opposite end of the flow: the wizard who had torn the working from beneath Amien like so much tissue; a black awareness that felt like someone I ought to know, someone I might turn out to be. For half a second it was as if our eyes met, across some indeterminate distance; I found myself standing in the midst of my rumpled bedroll, sword in hand and all the hair on the back of my neck saluting. Across the narrow channel, barely visible in the first glimmers of daylight, mounted Básghilae waited.

"Fouzh," Amien said tiredly.

Chapter 10
Tuned to a Dark Mood

Dianann House is a much more modest structure than Ériu House: if the latter is a riga, the former is a noblewoman who welcomes widowhood as an opportunity to concentrate on scholarly pursuits. Nevertheless it has tall, solid walls; and after three days of fighting and two anxious half-warded campsites, I had never seen anything look lovelier.

For the past three days, it had seemed the Bard's Wizard anticipated our every decision. It wouldn't be so hard to explain his predicting we'd make for Dianann: there are only so many possible destinations for a party following a river, and Dianann House stands right on the water's edge. But as we traveled that long river road, Nuad—who, like Iminor, hailed from Dianann—let me teach him quietly about the use of terrain in staging an ambush. Twice he anticipated places we should be wary of and led us onto lesser trails—where we found ourselves under attack anyway. Finally, on the third day, we remained on the river road, riding into the place sensible tactics said we should avoid and counting on our opponent to again anticipate the detour—and endured yet another ambush: not in the expected spot on the river road, but rather a short distance afterward, at the precise moment when we stood down. It was as if the Bard's Wizard, whoever he was, could somehow see what we were doing. But Aballo has not trained a wizard capable of physical magic who was also a clairvoyant since the great Tol, and the one farsensing orb created since

Hy-Breasaíl was destroyed at the end of Nechton's War.

It made no sense. It made the skin on the back of my neck crawl. I counted a party of almost-untried warriors lucky to have conducted Letitia this far, even at the cost we had endured: half our number, by the time we rode through the gate.

Standing in the yard when we arrived was Tiaran, the ancient Tana with eldritch eyes and knee-length silver braid I remembered from dinner at Ériu House: pleased relief breaking across her face and heartfelt grin revealing her half-grown new incisor, as if she'd been waiting there for a while. I startled, astonished, but Letitia just cast an exhausted, unsurprised glance in my direction.

"The Dianann is a wisewoman, ouirr," she said quietly. "Iminor and I were betrothed because of a vision she had; I cannot recall her ever being surprised by anything."

"What was the vision?" I asked. But the seer in question was crossing the yard towards us, and the stable hands were beginning to crowd around; Letitia shrugged, reined and dismounted, so I followed suit. Tiaran embraced Letitia without preamble, leaving the younger Tana struggling against sudden tears.

"Come inside, child," Tiaran said quietly. "The bath water is hot."

A little noise escaped Letitia. "Your hospitality is legend," she said, the courtly words hanging on the edge of a sob.

Tiaran kissed Letitia on the forehead, released her, and turned to Iminor and Nuad, who she grabbed in a fervent double hug, kissing each of their brows.

"Well done," she said, emotion creeping into her voice. "Very well done indeed; who needs a bath?"

"Lord of Light, Amma," Iminor croaked. "The longest bath ever!"

"*Pra-nu*," Nuad said.

I controlled the startle with an effort, then had to fight down the impulse to laugh at my own foolishness: few humans outside the initiate use that phrase, which invokes the attention of the gods to a prayer or act of magic. For people descended from gods, it seems, it is nothing more than an expression of fervent agreement.

Tiaran released both Tans, smiled at me, and offered a courteous nod. "It's good to see you here, young ouirr. I had looked forward to your visit."

Again I fought down a laugh. I hadn't known this place existed, much less planned to come here, and she'd been waiting for my arrival. But her attention was already on Amien, who she greeted with a deep, nimble curtsy.

"And Himself!" she said. "Truly you honor my house; never before has one of the Lords of the Order graced us with a visit."

Amien bowed, smiling for the first time since I'd seen him in Fíana. "Your hospitality is legend. My lady, with your indulgence, I'll need to ward the house."

"Ah," Tiaran said, as if he had just handed her the missing piece of a puzzle. She nodded gravely. "I'm sorry—I should have realized... I'll need a few minutes to prepare."

"Of course," Amien said, equally grave.

"May I make you comfortable in the meantime?" she said, taking his arm and turning towards the house.

"I'm sorry, I dare not," Amien replied. "Ours is… a formidable opponent." He glanced at me; my throat tightened.

Tiaran frowned thoughtfully. "I see no attacks on this house this night," she said slowly. "But if your goddess tells you otherwise…"

Amien bowed. "It is not my god that speaks, but simple caution."

Tiaran nodded. "That, too, has merit. I will have my men inside the wall in a few minutes. Be at ease, my lord. Will the rest of you come in?"

I looked at Amien, trying with minute gestures of eyebrows and eyes to remind him that the answer had better be *yes*: to refuse to stand down when her men held the walls would be a terrible insult. He seemed to understand, though I could see the surrender pained him.

"Thank you, Lady. We are honored to accept your welcome and protection," he said with creditable smoothness. "I will remain out here, and offer your men what support I may, until you are ready for warding."

Tiaran smiled and looked around at the group. "Be welcome in," she said, took Letitia's arm in her own, and led the group across the yard.

For half a second I wavered on the edge of decision: it felt profoundly wrong to leave Amien to handle arcane defense alone, exhausted as he was. But it wasn't as if I could actually draw power, so what would be the point? My throat tightened again; I turned and followed the group towards the house.

"Ellion," Amien said behind me.

I stopped and turned towards him, giving him an inquiring look; he cast a glance around the yard, which was rapidly emptying, and up at the walls. The men on the walls were spaced for the watch, not defense; there was no one within range of a normal speaking voice.

"It's been… a long time," the wizard said slowly, black eyes intent. "Much has changed—but much remains the same. You were… the most promising Talent I ever taught. And I need your—"

I shook my head vigorously. I couldn't draw enough breath.

Suddenly the accusation was back in his tone. "What happened to the man for whom limits didn't matter, who turned Tellan upside-down to answer the goddess's Call?"

"He displeased Her," I grated.

Shock flitted across Amien's face; but he didn't hesitate. "A youthful mistake. Surely—"

"If you believe *that*—"

"So *this* is Her Will? You waste your Talent, you jeopardize lives with your inaction, you—"

"I have no idea what Her Will is anymore!" I blurted—then wished more fervently for death than I had in a long time.

Amien stared at me; half a second later he remembered to close his mouth. Wind whined through the gate as someone pulled it shut.

Silence stretched between us; Amien's face was grave and still, but his eyes were full of alarm. Just like the day he arrived in Tellan, after everything fell apart.

I managed a stiff nod, spun on my heel, and crossed the yard with what little dignity I could muster. I could still feel him staring after I pulled the door shut.

When Vandabala failed to arrive for dinner, I finally remembered: he'd been ill since we set out from Irisa, and he'd had a brush with an enchanted sword. I should have been on top of the issue much earlier; and if my suspicions were correct, he needed Amien, not some garden-variety healer.

But Amien needed rest and food, even more than the rest of us; the green walls of the wards hung solid tonight, but his face had developed a hollow look. I waited throughout dinner, where he sat at Tiaran's left hand and seemingly developed an instantaneous friendship with the seer, trying without much success to carry my share of the dinner conversation.

No one present seemed in significantly better spirits than I: which was to be expected, I supposed, as the tableful of warriors with whom I sat had been raised with the expectation that war was a game confined to the tourney field, not an endeavor at which competent fighters might die. During a lull in the conversation, Letitia looked across the table at me, a question struggling towards birth on her lips.

"Lord Ellion," she said finally. "Would you educate me on the topic of the Bard of Arcadia?"

I felt myself stiffen, then remembered: the Tanaan have no taboos regarding serious topics at table. The conversation could hardly do more damage to the mood in the room. I pursed my lips, but controlled the impulse to look into my plate rather than meet her bewitching gaze. For a moment I stared at the enchanted diamond that dangled beneath her torc, trying to figure out where to begin.

"Our knowledge of him is limited, I'm sorry to say," I said finally. "At first he seemed little more than a curiosity: a small-time bard in Macol playing in taverns that catered to tradesmen. Even then, from what I've been able to glean, no one outside his immediate circle knew his true name: he was simply *the Bard of Arcadia*, even though no one could have said where Arcadia might be or how he had become its bard. It's hard to say exactly where his influence spread when; by the time I became aware of him, the main thrust of his mission seemed to be... evangelism for the god Esus, one of the gods that were worshipped by—" I nearly said *humans*. "—Bealla before the arrival of the true gods six hundred years ago."

"So this bard worships a god no one else believes in anymore?" Letitia said, puzzled. "How does that...? Who would...? Is that the basis of the war?"

I offered her a rueful smile. "No. Half the boat captains on the Ruillin still worship the old goddess Laverna, and no one cares except their wives."

Amien shot me a look; I raised my eyebrows, daring him to dispute the point, and he turned back to his conversation with Tiaran.

"So the Bard of Arcadia has... unusual religious beliefs, but that's not what's at stake," Letitia prompted.

"It isn't," I agreed. "The issue is that he—and the kharr who follow him—

are working to overthrow every ruler everywhere."

Letitia frowned. "And replace them with what?"

I shrugged. "The god Esus, perhaps?" The humor eluded her, and every Tanaan around the table, though in the corner of my eye I saw Amien quirk a wry grin. I shook my head. "It's anarchy he's advocating, Mora. With himself at the head of the mob."

Silence settled over the table. Some taboos should not be violated.

"He hasn't managed to overthrow all the rulers on the other side of the mountains yet, correct?" Letitia said finally.

"Correct."

Letitia nodded. "Well, my lord Ellion, I am no scholar of warfare, but it seems strange that he would—" Her calm tone disintegrated. "Put so much effort into killing *me*."

"Letitia," I began.

"Really, if whatever this Bard's agenda is—doesn't it seem much more likely to have something to do with, say, the mora Carina? As I understand it, she is known on your side of the mountains."

Now Tiaran was looking at Letitia as if she'd said something insightful.

"Didn't—Lord Amien, am I mistaken or were you, too, expecting to meet the mora Carina on your arrival at Irisa?"

The wizard nodded. "Yes, that's true; and it brings me to a question I've wanted to ask." He swallowed, the exhaustion in his face overlaid by grief. "What happened to the mora Carina?" His voice had gone to gravel again.

"I—don't know, Lord Amien," Letitia said.

For a man trained in truth-sense, the difference between the truth and a lie is as easy to hear as a harp string that has gone off its proper pitch. Even through the pain in Letitia's voice, it was plain: her answer, while factual, was far from true. I controlled the impulse to slip into her mind and try to ferret out the things she had chosen not to say, but found myself staring at her anyway. In my peripheral vision I saw Amien doing the same.

Letitia looked into her plate, toying with her food, then spread her gaze between Amien and me. "Truly there has been no word of her in the Beallan realms?"

And that question was an attempt at misdirection: she didn't know the answer, but at this moment she was more interested in getting our focus off herself.

"Letitia," I said, patience thinning. "Would we both have come out here looking for her, if there had?"

The Tanaan left the dining room in the same unceremonious style I had observed at Ériu House. I spoke Amien's name as he escorted Tiaran from the room. He met my gaze without speaking, something I couldn't quantify in his eyes, and nodded. I remained behind as Iminor took up his habitual spot at Letitia's elbow and the shrunken contingent followed them from the chamber.

Within a minute Amien was back, staring at me from the doorway.

I nodded. "Vandabala. Do you know which one he is? He's one of Letitia's original—one of the group that is always in closest proximity to her."

"Are we talking about the one who's ill?"

I nodded again. "On the night of our first engagement against the Bard's Wizard—let's see, that's three—plus another—six nights ago in total… Vandabala took a minor hit from a Básghilae weapon."

Amien flashed me a look both accusatory and alarmed.

"He seemed fine at the time," I temporized. "The Básghilae weren't actively feeding at the time, just trying to get to Letitia—and it wasn't until we were on the road these last three days that he began to show ill effects…"

Amien shook his head. "So have you investigated?"

Guilt flared inside me. "No."

"And now you want me to do that, too."

I couldn't help it: I glanced away. Nevertheless his glare set my face burning. "My lord, I—"

"Being uncertain of the will of the gods is the human condition, Ellion," Amien snapped. "Welcome to the realm of mortals." He turned and strode away.

I slunk out of the dining room, climbed the stairs to the room I'd been allocated for the night, and picked up my harp: I just wanted to hide and play through the pain. But a harpist who is a guest and does not share his music with the household violates a geas older than human memory: were I to play tonight, it must be in the house's great room, where everyone had gathered. I sighed, slung the strap over my shoulder, and went back downstairs. At least playing would give me an excuse to avoid conversation.

Everyone looked up as I stepped into the room, faces displaying varying mixes of surprise, anticipation, and pleasure.

Tiaran smiled. "My lord, you honor us."

Against all reason, I felt a flush rising on my cheeks. I bowed. "It is only my pleasure I share with you this evening," I said: the expected reply.

"Allow us to make you comfortable," Tiaran replied. Iminor rose from his seat beside Letitia and adjacent the fire, ceding the desirable seat in accordance with the same protocol that requires a harpist to share his art.

I held up both hands in the required refusal. "My lord," I said, shaking my head.

Iminor had been well schooled, or else the protocols were the same on this side of the mountains: he bowed and stepped away to stand behind Letitia's chair. I bowed again and accepted the seat; servants brought a new chair for Iminor and installed it on Letitia's other side, then set a goblet of heroic proportions on a low table before me. I found myself smiling, surprised: I couldn't think of a human tiarn whose household would be this well-prepared. Usually a harpist only receives this sort of honor in a royal house.

I unpacked my harp, pulled the key from my pocket, and began tuning as the servants poured wine for everyone present.

"What would you hear this evening, Lady?" I said to Tiaran.

Even here she did not falter. "Whatever pleases you, my lord."

I accepted her gracious answer with a nod and a small smile, then applied myself to tuning the harp as conversations resumed around me. Tiaran sat speaking with Nuad; several of the knights played a card game I didn't recognize, with a deck that bore an eerie resemblance to the ones I'd seen fortune-tellers use; Letitia held a book but seemed to be staring through the narrow window on the opposite wall, at the green curtain of the wards. The mood in the room still verged on despair: a wise harpist would play something to lift a warrior's spirits, probably a lay of the great warrior Cúchulainn. But I didn't want to hear about him tonight. I tuned the harp to my dark mood, then finally realized what key I had chosen. The harp was ready to play *Fergus in Exile*. So was I.

I struck the opening chord; they all looked at me. Even Letitia laid the book across her lap. Firelight caught in Tanaan eyes, and I remembered: most of my audience didn't understand Ilesian. I must tell them the tale in the Tanaan language if they were to have any appreciation for it.

I let my hands wander over the strings, teasing out bits of the chord progressions in the song, dallying with snatches of the melody, and looked around at my audience again: of the twenty-four who had stood at harborside three days ago, twelve remained—thirteen, if one counted Vandabala, who lay in a bed upstairs. Some of the eleven fallen had been lost to superior fighters, but more to inexperience with real warfare; I still hadn't trained them, and what little I could do before we set out in the morning was unlikely to spare any life but Letitia's. They were dying in a war that had nothing to do with them: as if they were the pawns of some restless god in an ancient tale.

Renewed dread bit at my throat. The song in my hands was appropriate for them, too: far too appropriate. A wiser harpist would stop and re-tune, play something else—but suddenly I saw that the key and the melody fit their mood as well as mine. Wherever I finally ended up, this was where we must begin. I paused, sipped lean but subtle red wine from the herculean goblet, and began again.

"This song comes from a very large song-cycle about the War of the Brown Bull," I began, introducing a snatch of the Brown Bull's primary theme with my left hand and returning to toying with the current melody. Sparks of recognition lit in eyes all around the room, which shouldn't have surprised me: no one is certain how old that cycle is. If the Tanaan turned out to know the work, if against all odds I returned as ard-harpist to Ilnemedon, I must bring the fact back with me, just in case it was the missing piece to some historian's puzzle.

"This is the story of Fergus, who was born to be righ but tricked into giving up the throne to his nephew Conor," I continued. "He was a man of honor, and he served the righ his nephew faithfully, never giving sign that he was anything but content to be a mere lord and the greatest warrior in the realm. Where Conor needed him, he went, whether to fight or to make peace—and so it was natural that Conor should call on Fergus to restore the peace between him and his nephew Naisi.

"The trouble between Conor and Naisi arose because of Dierdre, the most beautiful woman ever to walk the meadows of Hy-Breasaíl."

The Tanaan were nodding.

"Ah, you know the story of Dierdre?" I said, smiling, and let her theme ripple briefly across the strings.

"When she was born, a seer prophesied that she would be the most beautiful woman in the world—and that she would marry a mor," Tiaran said grave-ly. "And she would be the cause of war and the ruin of the country."

I nodded. "And so Conor decreed that he would marry her himself, think-ing he would avert the doom and possess this great beauty—but the gods laughed at him, as They so often do, and rather than marrying him she eloped with his nephew, Fergus's beloved friend Naisi.

"Conor remembered the prophecy, at least for a while—and he didn't fight Naisi for her, and let them run. And when he saw they would not return no matter how they were pursued, he sent Fergus to offer peace. In peace Fergus and his sons brought them back to court, Deidre and Naisi and Naisi's broth-ers—but again the gods toyed with Fergus, and he was forced by a geas to temporarily separate from the party on the evening of their arrival. Naisi and his brothers were betrayed; Fergus's sons fell defending them, and all were lost; and Conor captured Dierdre after all. But she would not have him, and when the opportunity arose she killed herself—and when Fergus returned and saw how Conor had betrayed his trust and killed his sons and his beloved friend, he swore vengeance."

"And he took his warriors and left Ulaid to take service with the great Mora Maev," one of the Tana said softly.

I looked across the room, hands pausing over the strings: it was spare, sin-ewy Easca who had spoken, a flavor of intensity I didn't understand in her am-ber eyes. She'd been quiet since our first night out of Irisa: only Letitia seemed to mourn the loss of her kinsman Neide and our failure to give him a pyre more deeply. I wondered for the thousandth time at the way the right song will open lips that not even strong drink can move.

"Yes," I said to Easca. "And together they plotted the war and the ruin of Ulaid that was prophesied at Dierdre's birth."

I shifted from toying with the chords to playing the progression as written, and brought in the melody with my right hand. The low, dark notes hummed through the harp's sound chest, resonating against my clavicle; even the open-ing verses whispered the betrayal of men and the cruelty of gods. I barely remembered I had an audience this evening, half-losing myself in the song. It unwound itself under my hands, carrying me along. When it was over I lifted my hands from the strings and finally took in my audience again, awash in the familiar feeling that the harp had transported me elsewhere for a time. The Tanaan looked as worn by the musical journey as I felt—and Amien stood in the doorway, expression haunted.

"My lord," Tiaran said softly.

I met her shining gaze.

"Thank you," she breathed.

"It is only my pleasure," I murmured; she shook her head.

"Thank you," she repeated.

I offered her a grave nod. Amien cleared his throat, and a knot formed un-der my breastbone. The look on his face was clear: I'd been right about Vanda-bala, and the Tan's situation was as dire as I'd feared. Amien stared at Letitia as if trying to figure out how to frame the news he must deliver—and sudden recognition flashed in his face.

"Mora!" he said, something that might be amusement running beneath his tone. "I am a fool!"

She frowned, puzzled. "I doubt that very much, my lord."

Amien shook his head. "The gem you wear."

Letitia touched the diamond that dangled beneath her torc. "It belonged to the mora Carina."

Amien nodded. "Iliria."

"What?"

"Its name is Iliria. I... made it for her." Abruptly his gaze was on something in the far corner of the room. "To use... in the war against Nechton. I didn't realize—"

Absolute consternation manifested in Letitia's face; her narrow fingers closed around the gem as if she might pull the chain from her neck without bothering to unclasp it. "My lord Amien, is this—? The necklace is ensorceled?"

The wizard shrugged. "It's not a weapon, but rather... a tool. I'm sorry, this was not the time—there are other things... We should speak of this later, Mora."

Letitia nodded.

"What I came to tell you—" Amien cleared his throat. "Mora, Vandabala—"

She shook her head, pressing the fist that grasped the necklace to her mouth.

"I understand he—took a minor hit with an enchanted blade? At your first encounter with the Bard's Wizard?"

Letitia swallowed, looked at the rug, nodded. In my peripheral vision I saw Mattiaci reach out and grasp Tru's hand.

"Mora, I'm sorry to say that—even though it seems the ghouls were not—feeding?—at the time... the blade itself carried a spell that is slower to work but no less deadly."

"But can't you—?" A note of protest crept into her voice. "My lord Amien, if the Prince of the Order cannot rid a man of sorcery, then one must wonder—"

Amien shook his head. "I'm sorry, Mora. Any explanation I could give gets very technical, very fast. The spell is a contact-spell—anyone who touched the weapon from either end would succumb to it. And it's tied to a power source so dark I can't even see what it is."

"But you must be able to do something!"

Again Amien shook his head. "The spell's got a nasty hook. It's worked so any wizard who attempts to heal the victim—will become ensnared by the spell himself. I couldn't heal Vandabala; I'm sorry. All I could do is go with him."

Letitia wrapped her arms around herself; the book in her lap slid down the silk of her skirts to the floor, and a map slipped out from among the pages. Iminor leaned down to reach for it, but she dropped suddenly to the floor and retrieved book and map before he could lay hands on them. She closed the book carefully and laid it with equally deliberate care across her knees, there on the floor, and looked up at Amien again. Her face was composed, but her eyes shone with unshed tears.

"How—long?" she said finally.

Amien sighed. "A few hours, probably."

Letitia nodded. For a moment the room was silent. Amien moved as if he would withdraw.

"Lord Amien," she said suddenly.

"Yes?"

"Should I assume… that all our opponents' weapons are so ensorceled?"

Amien sighed again. "Probably."

Chapter 11
Beyond Death

1 knew I was dreaming, because we were back in the little grove, Letitia and I, on the island that lies in the shadow of Ériu: Zephyr, perhaps, or Apilio. Tonight no circle of Tanaan clan leaders surrounded her, and tonight she wore the ceremonial mask of the Bealtan priestess: not a full-face mask, but the sort of domino that reveals the lower half of the face, adorned with feathers and jewels and the iridescent skin of something I would have guessed to be a dragon if such beings existed outside Hy-Breasaílian tales: all shifting in color and form in the way things will when a wizard steps out of ordinary reality into the places where the magic happens. I wasn't wearing a mask: no priest this Bealtan I, just a man who would steal a bit of Bealtan love. Nevertheless I remembered the ceremony, because no man who performs that sacred marriage ever forgets it, and I knew the proper order of things here. I was not at all certain I would follow it. This was only a dream, after all.

There are times when it is incumbent on a wizard to let the dream show him its own face, even though he knows he dreams: when it is a message from the gods, or a dream-sending from a brother wizard. But this was just a wish-dream about something that was never going to happen; Letitia would be at Aballo by Bealtan, and I would be far from there. So I stretched out a hand to trace the silken curve of her jaw, to follow the delicate line of her neck, to explore the exquisite structure of her clavicles and the little hollows beneath them that led inevitably to the wonder of her breasts.

All at once the mystery of it caught up with me, and a tremor skipped up my spine; the warm scent of roses in summer washed over me, and sparkling delight wrapped itself around and raised rills of rapture all over my arms and back. My breath caught in my throat; her emerald gaze, somehow intensified by the otherworldly mask, transfixed me; and without waiting for the little movement of the head a woman makes when she is inviting a kiss I rushed in to claim it, and her wondrous flavors and textures exploded across my awareness. I should do this with style—such a wonder as the seeming myth of a virgin Tana demands no less—but between one breath and the next I was lost to reason, and the only thoughts I could form concerned touching her in ways that would make her tremble even harder than I. Gently I enfolded her, all the skin of my body singing to me the delight of hers, and drew her to the ground, knelt beneath her and drew her across my lap: in this, at least, I would practice the ritual properly, ceding her the control while I warred pleasurably to escalate the pitch. Even a man who may no longer be a priest should be allowed to worship. But suddenly Amien was there, in full ceremonial regalia as if he were on his way to call the Bealtan fires, and with one glance informed me that I was once again bollocksing things up. And just that quickly I felt myself begin to shrivel.

Any man with a modicum of Talent and training should be able to direct the flow of a dream. It should have been effortless, aware of my dreaming state as I was.

"Get out of here, old man," I said, and willed him away. But he just frowned and shook his head.

"You're going to have to do better than that," he growled. "What makes you think you've earned the right?"

Letitia glanced from Amien to me, as if seeing me for the first time; astonishment manifested in her face. And then, without preamble, she was gone, leaving me kneeling naked and suddenly cold in the midst of the grass.

I startled, suddenly awake in the pre-dawn light, profanity dying into a whisper on my lips. My heart pounded in my ears. After a few seconds I realized it *was* pre-dawn light I saw, and not the green of Amien's wards: I threw myself out of bed, flung on my clothes and grabbed my sword, and raced downstairs before I'd fully buttoned my shirt. I pelted into the house's narrow portico, just in time to see Tiaran cross the yard to the place where Amien stood at the center and take his arm.

"And now to bed, my friend," she said with firm gentleness. "My men have the watch."

He smiled down at her, a tenderness I had never seen in him playing about his lips. "Witch. I am undone."

She chuckled. "You stand with your back to mine. And take a nap for a few hours. Come." She drew him across the yard while he cast a final glance around the wall. Men stood atop it, silhouetted against the dawn-streaked sky; early morning light traced the curves of bows and the pommels of swords. It looked so ordinary that the reality of it hit me like an unexpected charge: those were Tanaan men up on that wall, I was on the wrong side of the mountains, and none of those men was likely to have any real idea what to do if something more dire than a boar approached this place. Warfare had ended here—at least until the Bard of Arcadia turned his eye on a Tana who could do him no conceivable harm.

Amien let Tiaran draw him up the steps into the portico—and finally caught sight of me, where I stood paralyzed just outside the door.

"Gods grant you strength," he said: the traditional blessing a wizard gives to a colleague who steps up to share the burden of warding a place for safety. But his tone made it an accusation, and his black eyes might have melted steel. I stepped back without thinking, glancing involuntarily at the floor. Tiaran's gaze swept from him to me, the light of analysis in her silver eyes.

Rest well, my lord, I should have said: it is the traditional response. But my throat was full of guilt, and I could only stand mute while he stepped inside.

When their footsteps receded behind me, I sighed, buckled the sword belt around me, and finished buttoning my shirt. I should bind my hair back into a tail, but I'd left the thong inside and had no desire to risk encountering Amien again: I crossed the yard, found a place in which someone had stood a ladder against the wall, and climbed up to walk the perimeter.

Dianann looked peaceful from here: dawn stretched peach and pale green across the river, less than a quarter mile to my right; mist rose from its rippling surface. Rice fields spread out from the base of the wall to the terraced slopes half a mile or so to the west. At the top of that ridge a lone cowherd was already driving three dozen head—bizarre that after so much time I still tallied cattle automatically—up to the day's pasture. Squint, and I might imagine myself in some remote corner of Tellan. I shook off the dread that thought engendered and began pacing the top of the wall.

There were no dust clouds in the distance, no telltale sunlight on metal: none of the indications that a force is moving in the vicinity. The Tans on the wall gave me wary looks and wider berths than necessary on the narrow walkway as I passed, while I took in the appalling nature of the weapons they carried: the bows were functional, sufficient for hunting, but every edged weapon I saw looked as if it had been pulled from some trunk not opened in centuries and returned to service with only the barest of preparation.

Lady, have mercy on them, I thought. *Let us be gone from here when the Bard's Wizard finds us next.*

I followed the curve of the wall northward, scanning the northern and eastern horizons. Across the river, homesteads dotted the areas beyond the rice fields, surrounded by pasture lands, well-maintained groves of oak, and fields of something I couldn't identify at this distance. To the north similar farmland followed the curves of the river, until the elevation on the eastern side of the river dropped away to a valley still cloaked in early-morning mist. Beyond that valley, I knew, lay the great city of Arian, tonight's destination. Anticipation mounted in me again: today, finally, we would enter the central territory of the Tanaan nations: the great inland sea of the Devadore and the summer capitals of the Four Realms. I'd spent years reading about those places, about the magnificent cities on the Devadore and the sacred isle at its center. These were the great centers of Tanaan learning and culture, and I had many questions that could be answered nowhere else. I peered at the northern horizon, hoping to catch some glimpse of the fabled orichalus roof of the Fíana winter palace: legend holds the gleam is visible as far away as the isle of Ilunmore on a clear day. But the weather to the north was too cloudy, or perhaps the elevation here was insufficient: I saw nothing but grey skies fading into grey morning mist.

Reluctantly I tore my attention from the places I hoped to see tonight: the collegial centers of the Tanaan brehon and bards that are mentioned in the histories; the elegant architecture and tree-lined boulevards of the courtly district. The Tanaan sentries on Dianann House's northern wall were as wary and ill-prepared as their counterparts on the other side of the house; below, inside the wall, the kitchen gardens and stables were quiet.

Arian would be quiet tonight, perhaps all but empty for the season. I knew I shouldn't expect too much, knew I would be better served to plan the training I would finally do for Letitia's contingent this morning than to cast my mind forward and form expectations that would leave me disappointed in all the little ways Irisa had. But when had a human harpist ever visited Arian and heard the Tanaan bards in their own enclave? How far into the reaches beyond the human knowledge of history did their eipiciúilae and learning go? Did their bards know the true history of Hy-Breasaíl, and how would that history compare with the few garbled scraps we humans have? How was it possible I could afford to stay there only one night?

If I survived the trip to Aballo, I would have to make a point of returning to Arian. Perhaps in the fall.

If I were to survive this trip, I'd better put some thought into training the remains of Letitia's contingent. Properly-trained knights would have spent months drilling on unit tactics; human knights who aspired to commands of their own would have been educated in at least the core philosophies of battlefield theory and served as junior officers in campaigns run by their elders, their betters, or both. All I could do this morning was distill the corpus of knowledge Letitia's knights should have, down to the core that might allow me to keep her alive all the way to Aballo. I needed to preserve their lives as long as possible, of course—if for no reason other than the fact that she really couldn't afford to be more thinly covered than she already was. But there was no question which life must be preserved at any cost. The question, as usual, was *why*.

I walked the wall; my mind ran over all the same strategic terrain it always did. Finally I decided, for at least the fifth time, to focus our scant training time on unit tactics: teaching them to form proper ranks and useful defensive formations, focusing their minds on the unit rather than their continued fascination with distinguishing themselves and building their own reputations. As if any of them was likely to survive long enough for their reputations to matter.

My throat knotted; the faces of the surviving Tana in the contingent flashed in my mind. Broad-faced, steadfast Tru; sinewy, brooding Easca; quiet Bruane with her red-gold hair and brows that resembled the wings of some exotic bird: how was it possible that I could allow them to continue on a mission few male warriors could be expected to weather, when I knew their lesser strength was likely to be the first thing overmastered in any encounter? How could I ask as much of them as I did of the Tans? And how would Letitia survive if I tried to spare them?

It was a problem I couldn't solve. The only sane thing to do was to set it aside. Every commander knows that some of his men will die. I couldn't spare any of them and hope to protect the rest. But there was still a knot under my breastbone as I climbed down the ladder at the northern edge of the gate, crossed the stream that slipped across the kitchen gardens and through the portcullis before spilling into the river a dozen feet outside the wall, and made my way to the stable.

Quiet hung in here, broken only by the sounds of horses in stalls; sunshine filtered through unglazed, open-shuttered windows to cast beams of light through the dusty air. The stablemaster and his hands must be up on the wall carrying obsolete weapons and watching for things they would have no clue how to address: it would be unreasonable for me to demand that one of them come down and tack out my horse for me. I plucked a winter apple from a bin beside the door and strode down the dimly-lit passage, peering into the stalls.

Finally I spotted my horse: he seemed pleased to see me, after his fashion, and eagerly accepted the apple I offered. Today he seemed not particularly put out by taking the bit: progress.

"Well, then, old man," I said to him, hefting the saddle into place. "Ready to show those other fellows the ropes?"

He snorted; I shrugged. It was a ridiculous question: this horse had been bred for racing, not battle. When I bought him this winter, there had seemed no reason to choose a practical beast over one that was a pleasure to ride. I could only see my own folly in hindsight, as usual.

I patted his shoulder and bent to fasten the girths. The ground shifted beneath my feet; blue haze gathered at the edges of my vision. I staggered away from the horse, straightening up; the beast whinnied alarm; a sudden rush of air at my back announced the attacker behind me. I shifted to grab the assailant and threw him over my shoulder; he collided with the horse, who squealed, reared, and bounced the man back into my face.

We tumbled to the hard dirt floor in a breathless heap; I had barely enough time to form a quick impression of yet another assassin's hood before the man squirmed to right himself and instinct sent my hands scrambling for his throat. My fingers found no purchase on the slick fabric of the hood; he came at me again, knife gleaming in the muted light; we grappled and rolled amid the straw while the horse continued to whinny, buck and carry on above us. On my back again, I nearly got my fingers around the hilt; at the last second the assassin shifted his grip and drove the tip into my palm. Instinct took over again: the only thing more useless than a harpist with a severed tendon in the hand is a warrior who can't grip his weapon. The assassin drew back just enough for a killing blow to the heart—and the horse's hoof connected with the back of his head. His eyes rolled back; I grabbed the knife and drove it between his ribs. I was a fool; I was lucky; I rolled the assassin off my body and scrambled to my feet, cast the knife into the dirt at the other end of the stall, grabbed the reins and showered the horse with soothing touches and reassuring lies until he finally subsided into quivering, as far away from the assassin as possible.

Finally I turned back to the man, closed the distance between us and yanked the hood from his head. He bore an intriguing superficial resemblance to the assassin at Tyra; but that blond battle-bound hair and warrior's build could have belonged to half the men in the Order of the Hidden Sun. Or whatever organization or noble house had managed to spawn this insanity.

But the resemblance wasn't superficial. Once I walked around to stand in front of the assassin, it was easy to see: the man looked exactly the same as the assassin at Tyra. It was the same man.

It couldn't be, and yet here he was: the same face, the same scar on his right cheekbone, the same half-conscious grey eyes. Twins are nearly always exposed at birth, but a few survive: it was possible this man was a twin. But both twins wouldn't develop a scar when one was injured. And no human, living or dead, could survive a pyre like the one whose smoke sailed up from Tyra almost a twelvenight ago.

"Who the fouzh are you?" I blurted. Of course the assassin said nothing. I wasn't sure I would have believed any answer he'd give, anyway—and then I realized I shouldn't have expected any answer at all. The undead do not speak. They are incapable. Revulsion swept over me: I'd been dancing with a corpse.

But inevitably my mind seized on the puzzle he presented. The Básghilae we'd been fighting since that night on the Crearu: they were exactly what I would have expected, had I ever taken the time to consider how such a working would turn out. In fact I had taken them to be the best possible outcome: though obviously dead, they exhibited no signs of decay. But if that were the best possible outcome for reanimated dead, then what the hell was *this*? This man was warm; he bled; his muscles felt strong. Deep effort or sudden pain could surprise a grunt from him. It would never have occurred to me that he might be dead, until I realized he couldn't be alive.

I stared down at the assassin, watching blood flow and eyes glaze, and tried to catch my breath. What about the damage I inflicted at Tyra? I slit this man's throat; I watched this man die. Surely the undead cannot die again—and if, against all logic, they do, then wouldn't it slow them down? How would they heal? And how could it have happened this quickly?

Someone not among the initiate might have said simply, *magic*, and left it at that—but of course I knew better. Magic has consistency and logic, even if that logic is not of the everyday sort. One must work with physical reality, unless one is dealing with exclusively spiritual matters. And here was physical reality, staring me in the face and breaking every rule I knew. Finally I had to know: I pulled back the assassin's collar, trying to see what had been done to him.

The assassin's neck was clean. As if the broad slit I opened across his throat had never been. Again horror gripped me. I straightened up and walked away.

If the Bard's Wizard were the author of the Básghilae we'd been fighting for the past seven days—and that was the only reasonable conclusion—then who was doing this? Whoever had crafted this working was operating at a level beyond even the wildest hopes of the Order. He needed no infectious death-spell to accomplish his aim: this was a precision strike. And it was directed at me. Suddenly I was freezing, despite the warm air around me.

But just the same, the wizard in me had to know more. I walked back to the dying—dead?—man and opened his blood-soaked shirt. His body looked like any professional warrior's except for the wound in the chest. The chest wound didn't look as if it would heal on its own: it pumped furiously, bubbling blood down the man's side like a scarlet spring.

Fully functioning undead. How was this even possible?

The assassin's body was also decked with old battle scars. Some were fresher than others; a few were more recent than a month, including an impressive one across the assassin's midsection that looked as if it should have killed him. And there were bruises on the man's body, no more than a twelvenight old.

How could he have bruises from a few days ago and no signs of the mortal injury I'd inflicted—not to mention the pyre? My head shifted; a ripple of unreality echoed through me into the hard dirt floor. This must be how Cúchulainn felt, when he accepted the green god's challenge and sliced off the god's head—and the god got up and put it right back on.

I realized I was pacing towards the door of the stall again, before I knew where I was going; within three steps I knew what I must do. I'd thought this man defeated at Tyra. But seeing him die hadn't been surety enough. Clearly even immolation on a pyre wouldn't do more than slow him down. The one thing I could think to do now was to follow the prescribed course of action for defeating the undead: decapitation.

It would be a gory job, but I was already covered in blood. A single swift stroke with the sword would do it. Then my biggest problem would be the body. A wizard with this level of ability bent on my elimination was a clear signal that my blood-price was astronomical—and someone was prepared to pay. Public knowledge of it would guarantee my death. I had to dispose of both the body and the head.

How? The river seemed the likeliest option, if I could manage it. Once the body was in the river, the current would carry it in the opposite direction from the route I would take. A sudden, ludicrous image of the assassin's body floating all the way downriver to Irisa, Rishan spotting it and recognizing my handiwork, flashed across my mind; I surprised myself with a short bark of laughter. But first I had to get it to the river: across the kitchen gardens undetected, up the ladder carrying both a body and a head—and either hope I could fling both far enough to reach the river or come up with some explanation that would get me back inside the gate after I climbed down. Assuming none of the Tans on the wall saw what I was about.

First things first: the decapitation. I turned back towards the assassin, reaching for my sword and swallowing my distaste—and then realized he was gone.

Gone. Again. How? I looked across the stall: the hilt of the assassin's knife still protruded from the dirt. My clothes were still covered in blood; the cut on my palm still oozed. It was just the same as that night at Ériu House, except this time I'd been conscious the entire while.

A shaky sigh escaped me. The assassin wasn't going into the river: I was. There was no choice but to wash off all this blood, to try to act as if nothing unusual had happened this morning. And I had damned well better figure out who was capable of this and why they would bother. But I had no idea where to begin.

I was still thoroughly, embarrassingly soaked when Letitia's contingent assembled in the yard at the front of the house, with nothing to do for it but fall back on a decade's experience of practicing bravado in untenable situations. Gathered on the steps of the portico, Letitia's knights greeted me with a variety of expressions ranging from nonplussed to fascinated; Tiaran, who, for reasons I couldn't fathom, had decided to observe our training exercise, addressed me with a thoughtful gaze and a reluctant quirk to her lips. Letitia met my gaze in a smoldering regard that brought this morning's Bealtan dream roaring to life in my head. For a moment I forgot how I'd intended to begin, even forgot the way the silk of my shirt stuck to me. With an effort I dragged my mind back to the lesson.

"We don't have time," I began, looking around at them, "for you to learn what you should. This morning you will learn what you must. All the knights here this morning are competent warriors; the fact that you're standing here proves that. This morning you must learn to fight as a unit. As of now, there is no such thing as individual glory—not even individual glory in death. The only glory will come when the mora arrives at Aballo alive. Distinguish yourself before then, and most likely you're compromising the mora's safety and that of your fellows."

There was restless, disgruntled shifting among the contingent. Iminor shot a few targeted, quelling glances; Letitia wisely kept her attention on me, as if the lesson were the only thing worthy of notice.

"This morning, we'll be learning and practicing the things experienced companies do to protect one another and execute their strategic objectives," I continued. "We'll be learning to form and move in close, serried ranks—so close that a glove tossed into the air in the midst of an engagement couldn't find its way to the ground. We'll learn to use the crown formation and to make the terrain work for us in an engagement. We will work together. Effectively. At every moment, we will remember the only thing that matters is the safety of the unit and the mora.

"Meanwhile—" I looked at Letitia again; immediately my concentration began to waver. *Focus.* "The mora will be learning her role—which involves not trying to behave as if she is a member of this contingent, and allowing her knights to do their work."

Now Letitia looked outraged; Tiaran was frankly amused.

"This is no tourney-game, and the sword in her hand is a contingency plan only." Her eyes met mine unwaveringly, but now her smolder was of a completely different sort. "When she disrupts the operation of the contingent in a battle, she only endangers her knights. It is her job to stay behind the lines, or at the center of the formation, and let them do their jobs."

Letitia opened her mouth as if to protest. I just raised an eyebrow; Iminor shot her a look even more forbidding than the ones he'd turned on Semeon and Ogma a moment ago. Renewed pique flashed in her green eyes, but she nodded.

"Well, then," I said, looking around at all of them again. "If everyone is ready, let's mount up. We'll start with the serried line."

I climbed into the saddle; the contingent stepped down to the dirt and crossed the yard towards their horses. At the far end of the compound, someone pulled the gate wide, and a horseman rode through. I recognized the face of Letitia's kinsman Neide immediately; this time, finally, I wasn't fooled. Behind me, Iminor said, "No", very quietly; Tiaran's hand snaked out with astonishing speed to grasp Letitia's wrist. I spurred my horse into an immediate canter, racing towards the horseman: drawing my sword and removing the Básghil's head as Letitia's cry of joy gave way to a bone-freezing scream. This time the lack of blood made my stomach turn.

I reined and leapt from the saddle just in time to see the horseman topple to the dirt and the riderless horse wheel and bolt back out the gate. By the time I had formed the thought of shouting for the Tans at the gate to close it, the horse was out and Easca was on me, sword bared and bloody vengeance in her shrieks.

"Easca—" I began, but she was beyond hearing. I parried her first two strokes, reached out with my sword and caught her hilt with the tip of my blade, flipping it from her grasp. I grabbed her, hugging her against me; she thrashed in my grip.

"I'm sorry," I said. "Easca. Look. Listen. No."

She stilled for a moment, then started again. I grasped her more tightly and glanced over her head, across the yard. Letitia stared at me, betrayal in her emerald eyes, and extracted her wrist from Tiaran's bony fist. Tiaran sank to the ground.

"I'm sorry," I said to Letitia. "I know—" I swallowed against another wave of nausea. "I know how it looked. But that was not your kinsman."

Letitia sat down abruptly, there in the center of the yard. A shudder wracked Easca, and finally she stilled; she pulled out of my grasp without speaking, wiping tears from her face, and crossed the yard to retrieve her sword. I walked past the knot of horrified Tanaan gathered around the decapitated Básghil corpse, towards Letitia.

"Sweet Lord of Light," Iminor croaked suddenly. "Everybody *back up!*"

The knot loosened; I glanced back at them, already knowing what I would see: the headless body that had seemed to be Letitia's kinsman wavered, shifting into the form of a dead human. Suddenly Letitia was on hands and knees, crawling towards a bed of lady's fingers at the portico's edge. *The morae of Fíana do not vomit in public,* she thought, and contradicted it.

I dropped to my knees beside her; she sat back on her heels, wiping her mouth with the back of her hand. Without thinking I reached out to embrace her, to do and say whatever I must to erase the betrayal in her gaze—and then remembered: I was soaking wet; more than two dozen pairs of eyes were on us; and I wasn't sure where the line of propriety fell on this side of the mountains. I let my arms drop again; further disappointment registered in her gaze, and she looked away.

Amien bolted from the house to the portico, clothing rumpled and the tail of his hair askew. "What the hell is going on?"

I sighed. "We were just having a graphic lesson in what it means to be Básghilae."

Amien grimaced, nodding. "My lady?" he said to Tiaran.

"What it means to be—? *What?*" Letitia shrilled.

Tiaran shrugged, still on the ground. "You would think that, after all this

137

time, it wouldn't knock me from my feet to see a vision come into daylight."

Letitia craned her long neck to stare up at the wizard. "Lord Amien, I keep hearing this word, but I get no explanation!"

I turned to look at her, surprised: the Tanaan had understood readily enough the concept of a renegade wizard attacking with undead warriors; but none of them seemed to want more than the bare facts. Magic might be part of their history, but now it was sufficiently taboo that they grew visibly uneasy each time the topic was raised. Even Letitia had seemed content to know no more than tactically necessary. Until this morning.

"Mora," Amien began in a distracted tone, crossing the yard towards Tiaran. "You need to—"

Letitia's hand sliced through the air. "I need to *understand*!"

Amien stopped. For several seconds they stared at one another. No one moved.

"My lord," I said. "I believe the mora is right. She does need to understand. Her knights do, too."

Amien looked from me to Letitia, pursed his lips, and nodded. Now, finally, the gaze Letitia turned on me was warm.

"You may recall," Amien said to the group gathered around the table in Tiaran's dining hall, "the story of the Breasaílian god Dian Cecht and His well of rebirth."

"Yes," Letitia said, sounding oddly relieved. "An ancestor of mine, in fact."

My head snapped around for a look at her before I could control it.

"Truly?" I said. I had known the Tanaan were the descendants of gods, of course; but the idea of Letitia being able to trace her line to one in specific made my head swim. Suddenly the idea of a nation merely chartered by a goddess seemed small.

"Oh, yes," Letitia said, actually smiling now. The warriors around us settled more deeply into their chairs, tension lifting from their faces. "Dian Cecht was the father of Ernmas, who became the mother of the goddesses Ériu, Banba, and Fodla. It is from Ériu that Clan Ériu takes its name."

I found myself smiling as well. "And—"

"*If* I may continue," Amien snapped.

I inclined my head; but I knew I was still smiling, amazed. "Your pardon, my lord. Every so often I am reminded that I am a harpist."

Amien's mouth twisted. "I was raised with the expectation of inheriting vining estates, and you see how that has turned out for me."

"Please continue," Letitia sighed.

With one final squint at me, Amien turned back to her. "Well, then. Dian Cecht and His well of rebirth. At the second battle of Maige Tuireadh, when the Danaan were doing battle against the Fomor, Dian Cecht laid spells on the well of Slane—and after each night of the battle, the Danaan brought their dead to the well, and Dian Cecht restored them to life. Wizards have been trying to recreate that working for centuries—mostly with very little success. No one has ever succeeded in truly restoring the dead to life."

Except whoever was trying to earn my blood-price, apparently. Where had he learned to do what even the Bard's Wizard couldn't?

"All mortals can do, it seems, is create undead," Amien said.

All the Tanaan nodded, waiting.

"The Básghilae we've been fighting," Amien continued. Some troubling thought crossed his face; he interrupted himself: "The name originates with the most successful worker of undead, the renegade Nechton, who was the first to develop undead that were in any way sustainable."

Affront mounted in me; I'd seen this sort of misdirection before, indeed been coached in it, like every student at Aballo: *Don't allow yourself to be forced into giving your patron too much information. Those outside the initiate are better off without knowledge that might be used unwisely. When cornered, obfuscate.* I suppose many wizards believe the philosophy, but it is clearly just one of a hundred methods of keeping power in the hands of the Order: I'd seen that even before I left. And it wasn't even relevant here: either Amien was operating from sheer force of habit or it was his intent to teach the Tanaan that trying to get information he wasn't prepared to volunteer would only end in headaches.

"Before him," Amien continued, "all anybody could manage were ghouls that—well, they didn't last very long, and parts tended to fall off, and—"

"Lord Amien," Letitia said firmly, "I find the history of these things interesting but perhaps not to the *point.*" I wanted to cheer.

Amien sighed. "Always the same story. No ruler ever has time for the answers to his—her—own questions. Mora, give me five minutes, and I promise the understanding you crave."

Letitia sighed and gestured for him to continue.

"Our knowledge of his methodology is limited," Amien said. "He had originally gone to Macol to take an appointment as House Healer to Uxellia, but—"

"*House Healer?*" Letitia echoed, in the way a person will when a memory has been incompletely brought to mind.

"The title given to a sorcerer in the employ of a Beallan royal house," Iminor said. "Theoretically the sorcerer's fealty is due the royal house, but in reality they all still look to Aballo."

Amien turned a look of frank astonishment on the young Tan. After a moment his mouth quirked into a reluctant grin. "I would be pleased if you would make a point of not expressing that opinion to any royals we happen to meet between here and Aballo. I really don't need the headache."

Iminor just gave him a modest half-smile.

Amien cleared his throat. "By the time the renegade began his work in this area, he had cut off all contact with the Order. So what we know about his operation is sparse. We do know that he used a well, in much the same way Dian Cecht did—and that he used slain warriors, for the most part. Now I suspect the Bard's Wizard has somehow managed to lay hands on copies of his grimoires—"

"His what?" Iminor said.

"Grimoires. His...notes and records, recipes and methodologies. His books of spells. Every wizard keeps his own."

I couldn't decide whether to hope Amien was right: Nechton's grimoires were assumed destroyed, along with the farsensing orb he'd created and the rest of his workshop, around the time of his defeat. During my wilder days I'd thought the loss of those things a terrible blow to arcane history; today the idea of someone actually practicing from those works, whether copies or the original volumes, made cold gather inside me.

"So what we're seeing is the same as what..." Iminor trailed off.

"Nechton," Letitia said quietly. "Like in—the mora Carina's song."

The Tan shot her a surprised glance, then continued, "It's the same as what Nechton did?"

Amien shook his head grimly. "It's better. The Bard's Wizard has used those methods as a jumping-off point. I'm not certain what power source Nechton used to sustain his Básghilae, but these use a contact-depletion spell."

The Tanaan all wore expressions that suggested they had grasped at understanding, and it had slipped between their hands. *When cornered, obfuscate.* All at once I'd had enough.

"They draw the life energies from whoever they can touch," I said quietly. "From whoever comes in contact with either the Básghilae themselves or with their weapons. It's why we lost so many on that first night."

Letitia's translucent skin turned paler still; she nodded.

"Among other things, it means that there may be no definite—span of usefulness for these Básghilae," I said. "We can't just wait them out."

"Also, it seems clear that this wizard has incorporated contact-shapeshifting into this working," Amien interposed, and drew breath as if to continue muddying the water.

I interrupted him again. "Which means these Básghilae can assume the shape of anything they touch."

"Lord... *Endeáril*," Iminor said, voice raw. "So when we saw Neide this morning, that..."

"That wasn't the person you knew," I said.

"It was just a—sort of effigy," Iminor said.

"Neide was not there," I temporized. "But the person you saw afterward..."

Renewed horror flared in Iminor's blue eyes; he glanced from me to Amien. "The *person*?"

"Where did you think they were coming from?" I said. "These aren't clay figures come to life in a fireside tale; these were real human men, all of them! They are just as much the victims of this renegade as Neide and Vandabala! Maybe more so."

"Ellion," Amien said.

"No," I said firmly. "They need to understand. Being ignorant of the truth does not protect people from it. It only hampers their ability to judge what they see. It only robs them of the vocabulary they need to deal—"

"So you would have me teach from Aechering in workshop?"

I felt myself flinching physically, stung. The presence of grimoires like Aechering's and Ransmith's in the library at Aballo, full of arcane techniques and areas of philosophy that are too dark for Aballo's tastes, had been a point of contention before I arrived there and doubtless continued as such after I left. I had made no attempt to conceal reading those works, but I hadn't shouted out my insights on those grimoires at dinner, either. It is a sort of unspoken codicil to the Aballo code: those few of us who read the darker works do not speak about them, and those who judge us for it pretend not to see. Of course Amien must blame all my failings on my taste in reading material.

"Knowledge never harmed anyone," I grated.

"No, men do that," Amien snapped.

"A man not educated in the use of the sword will pick up a cudgel, if the time has come for killing."

"Gentlemen," Letitia said.

"Then by all means, let us stop checking weapons at the palace door!" Amien said.

"Give me the choice between that and a situation in which no living wizard has any idea how to address our collective enemy, and I'll take my chances at dinner!" I said.

"No—living...?" Letitia said faintly.

"If both my dining partner and I are educated in the use of the sword, I guarantee there will be courtesy throughout the meal!" I pursued.

"I would be more inclined to accept that if good men hadn't already died at the table!" Amien retorted.

Too late I understood what he'd meant. While I'd been arguing about giving the Tanaan the knowledge they needed rather than restricting them to what little Amien wanted them to know, he'd been talking about me. I should have known he would lay my father's death at my feet, should only have been surprised it took him so long to come around to it. For half a second my father's face was all I could see: the belated, horrified comprehension in his gaze the last time his eyes met mine. I was on my feet, and I didn't remember rising. Instinct had sent my hand to the hilt of my sword, and the irony of wanting to draw on Amien in a dining room was so thick I could barely breathe. I spun away from the table and left the room.

I walked, fast and purposeless, until I found myself in Dianann House's entry hall, then yanked open the door and strode out to the portico. Once again I was trapped by the green wall of Amien's damned wards. I needed to run; I needed to fight someone; my hand was on my sword again, but there was no one out here on whom it would be right to turn it. I just stood there, staring across the yard at the wards while my mind spun with heinous black impulses, until Iminor stepped out the door to stand nearby.

"Lord Ellion," he said slowly.

I turned to look at him, startled: it was the first time he had addressed me so.

"At this moment, the mora is in a private chamber with Lord Amien..." His otherworldly blue gaze shifted. *We're talking now,* he broadcast.

Let me know. That was Letitia's voice. A deep pang of need for the closeness of mind-to-mind contact washed through me; unexpected jealousy flared in its wake. The last telepath I had known was Deaclan. Even the months when we hated one another were charged with an intimacy I hadn't known since.

Iminor focused on me again. "...asking him not to force her to choose which of you will accompany her on this journey, because she needs you both. It is my task to make the same request of you."

Sudden heaviness weighed on me, as if I were wearing a full harness of mail. I sighed and glanced away, casting about for something besides the damned wards on which to focus.

"I regret," I said. "Naturally I will apologize to the mora."

"That's not necessary, ouirr," Iminor said quietly. "She just needs—we all need—you and Lord Amien to resolve whatever—" Suddenly he stopped, turning a look of profound concentration on me.

"When Lord Amien arrived at Ériu House," he said. "That was not the first time you two had met."

I sighed again. "But it was the first time we'd spoken in about ten years."

Iminor drew in a hissing breath. "Not a happy reunion."

"No," I said, staring at nothing again: no longer hoping the conversation would end of its own accord, but not willing to hurry it along, either.

"What matter lies between you?"

His name is Deaclan, I thought. Always paired off against me in Amien's workshop, always driven into tighter and tighter competition, as if it would prove something when one of us finally gave into the frustration. As if Amien had a right to act surprised. As if any act of redemption would ever be enough to balance what I'd done. I glanced at Iminor, framing a suitably acid reply, and once again all I could see was the similarity between him and Deaclan. Suddenly Iminor's eerie beauty made me angrier still. I wrapped my right hand around the rail of the portico steps to keep it from grasping the sword.

"I am a disappointment to him," I said in Ilesian. "In fact it is probably no exaggeration to say I am the bitterest disappointment of his very long life."

"Ouirr, I don't—did I understand you?"

"To promise resolution would be a lie," I said to the rail. "I can only promise that I will do everything in my power to ensure things remain civil, and apologize for my lack of composure this morning."

"We are all under a good deal of strain," Iminor said.

"It will get worse before it gets better," I replied, and walked the steps down from the portico.

"Ouirr," Iminor said. I stopped but didn't turn back.

"What it means to be Básghilae," he said. "This morning you told Amien we were... seeing what it means to be Básghilae. I don't remember all your words, but that phrase—I'm sure of that phrase."

My throat clenched. I forced myself to face him.

"The matter from which Básghilae are made," I said, voice inexcusably thick. "Is dead warriors. Mostly men who died in battle against the Bard of Arcadia and his allies. Essuvians, most of them; I can't help but wonder whether—had Amien's plans to rendezvous with High Chief Rohini of the Essuvians and her men come to fruition—whether any of those men might have recognized some of the Básghilae we are fighting, from when they were alive."

Iminor leaned against a pillar, face absolutely white.

"The problem—the real problem with being Básghil..." I found it necessary to clear my throat. "Is that Básghilae are not just puppets. The spell binds the dead man's soul to his reanimated body. The soul is what makes the function."

"Lord of Light," Iminor croaked.

"Those dead men—are still in there, somewhere. They're aware; they just have no will, no choice. Sweet Lady Tella, if there's a worse fate, I don't know what it is—to be used for evil, to know you're doing evil, to not even be able to choose the release of dying, to see..." My throat dried up. For a moment we were both silent.

"It is a mercy, then," Iminor said at last, very quietly.

I looked at him.

"Killing them. Ending it. It's a mercy..."

"To the enchanted man," I said, nodding. "Yes, it is."

Chapter 12
The Deluge

Once again we were late in setting out. As we traveled the river road north from Dianann, I quizzed Letitia's knights periodically about the terrain we traversed, making them apply their lessons from our training session. At first they debated tactical issues as solemnly as a group of high-ranking brehon adjudicating a royal divorce, the events of the morning fresh in their minds; but as the road unrolled behind us, and the sun came out to cast everything in the fresh light of spring, they began to relax their white-knuckled grips on the reins and actually showed signs of enjoying the exercise. Eventually Bruane, she of the red-gold hair and bird-wing brows, looked around at the group, mischief in her face, and said, "And how would you handle an ambush here?" in what was evidently a hilarious rendering of my accent, inserting broad trills where the *R*s should be and completely eliminating the impossible-to-pronounce *cthlwhch* diphthong from the question.

Suddenly all the knights were laughing. Even Iminor, who had worn a haunted expression since this morning's meeting, smiled.

"Oh, come now!" I laughed. "Let me hear even one of you speak Ilesian! Letitia and Iminor, you don't get to play."

"Uh… *fouzh*," said stocky Eber, grinning.

"Cread… hon?" offered Greine, looking for all the world like an apprentice who has found the keys to his master's liquor cabinet.

"Oh, your mothers would be so ashamed," I said, shaking my head in mock dismay.

We rode on, as the road twisted away from the river over rising terrain, and soon the gathering forest gave us opportunities to discuss attacks from cover. Gradually the road narrowed and began to look as if few people traveled this route; eventually it became a track just broad enough for a single horseman, and the group quieted and arranged themselves in a narrow file. Then, abruptly, we crested a steep incline—and the forest and the track stopped. Before us, the ground fell sharply away, treacherous slopes of crumbling grey shale spilling down to a deep bowl that stretched, barren, away beyond sight. Everyone stopped, spreading out along the edge of the ridge and looking down.

Sulfurous vapors wafted up on a cold, wet wind; clouds hung over an area at the base of the ridge that I would have called a lake—except that no body of water I had ever seen was yellow. Stunted bracken and scrub grass clung to the rocks here and there, but nothing taller grew within sight. The very earth breathed of tragedy and the aftermath of rage; it gathered in my throat, even more searing than the sulfurous fog.

"What the hell is this?" Amien croaked. For a moment everyone was silent.

"The Deluge," Easca said at last. "Lords, I know the way."

"Get up here, then," Nuad said sharply.

"The *what?*" Amien said.

Again silence fell over the group. A quick look around the contingent revealed most of them staring at the devastation with the sort of fascination with which one addresses a truly horrific wound: horror, I noted, but no surprise. As if such a scene were no more than should be expected. Letitia's horror was overlaid with guilt, Nuad's with the sort of dismay a commander wears when he's overlooked some detail that will cost lives.

"What happened?" I pursued.

They all glanced at me. Only Easca seemed willing to meet my gaze. Letitia's guilt gave way to humiliation.

"Nuad, how long to Arian?" she said.

"Easca?" Nuad said.

"*Mora?*" I said.

Easca shrugged, the long tail of her golden hair drifting on a wind that now carried both sulfur and the tang of iron. "Call it six hours, ra?" She glanced at Letitia. "Six to eight."

Letitia turned her face in my direction, but her eyes were on something above me and to my left. She shrugged one shoulder. "Ouirr, that is a discussion... better left for—the other side."

I hung onto my patience with an effort. "Mora, this wind tastes of the aftermath of magic."

Letitia flushed and looked away.

"If there is—"

"It is the Will of the goddess you taste, ouirr," she said, voice strangled. "And long past. Indulge me: it is a tale for later."

Iminor shot me a warning glance; I gestured frustrated acquiescence and turned to Nuad.

"Easca, take the lead," Nuad said. "And set a reasonable pace."

She nodded, slid from the saddle, and led her horse past Letitia to a thin hint of a descending path. Even that label over-glorified it: nothing distinguished the route Easca chose but a slightly higher proportion of parched dirt showing among the shale. She slip-stepped carefully, shale falling away beneath her feet and skipping towards the base of the rise, trailing dust that rose in grey-white puffs on the dank air. Her roan gelding picked its way gingerly in her wake. After a few moments of watching, the rest of us dismounted; Nuad followed Easca, Letitia slip-sliding precariously on his horse's heels. Iminor followed her, and Amien; I hung back and let the rest of them proceed before me: peering ahead and trying to get some sense of the desolated zone through which Easca planned to lead us, catching my lower lip in my teeth as shale spilled away and horses and knights scrambled to retain their footing. The devastation stretched, jagged grey and swathed in shifting plumes of smoke or fog, north and east beyond sight. Finally the last of Letitia's knights descended, and I followed him down into the shale and dust.

Skirting the poison-yellow lake, we picked our ways across uneven, rock-strewn ground to a cluster of huge weathered buttes. Beyond them, the plain opened into seemingly endless distance. After a few moments of scrambling across the treacherous, broken flats, Easca led us to a surface I would have guessed a dry streambed—though what would flow through here I wasn't sure. We mounted and began to ride again.

Mist gathered around, stinging against the eyes and throat, then blew away; the path rose and then dipped into a deeper hollow, where the ground lay caked in red-orange mud and grey ash surrounded a steaming pond of vibrant aqua hue. Another rise and we were crossing an elevation punctuated by steaming sulfurous vents around which the rocks were crusted with crystals in a mosaic of brilliant hues. No birds flew overhead; there was no sign of game large or small. I tried to imagine how the places through which I rode could be the Will of a goddess, no matter how stern.

Many of the cataclysms of history can be traced to the workings of the gods, of course: there are very old stories of the gods of Breasaíl leveling the strongholds of Their enemies, and some songs suggest the isle of Hy-Breasaíl itself may have perished in a war among Them. Even Lady Tella destroyed the once-great city of Esunertos; but that was because Esunertos was the seat and final bastion of Her enemies, the worshipers of the old god Esus, and Esus's followers would not accept the true religion. I had traveled the road that skirts the site of Lady Tella's final battle with the Esusdians; that destruction could not compare to what I saw around me. The idea of a goddess visiting this on Her Own people sent cold into my core.

We traversed the fractured, poisoned plain for hours. Here and there we passed outcrops and buttes of strangely melted aspect; sprinkled at irregular intervals were bodies of water, but all of them venomous: green with floating patches of sulfur-yellow; the rust-red of a peat bog, surrounded by bituminous black ooze; waters chalky white and steaming amid brick-red mud-flats; ponds that might have seemed safe except that the water boiled. One spring exhibited the brilliant teal that men who sail deep into the southern ocean speak of; but the black rime covering the rocks at its perimeter was a clear warning. The knights passed the canteens back and forth until they were all empty; when the sun was high we halted on a rise tall enough to let us stand, temporarily, above the low-hanging bands of noxious fog. But there was no water for the horses, and the feed we carried was too dry to go down easily without it.

Even here, the party spoke little. Several of them paced around the top of the rise, but they seemed to have stopped trying to absorb their surroundings. Letitia stood a little apart from the group, hugging her own arms and staring morosely northward; Iminor's head was tilted back, his eyes on the sky. I examined the wasteland in which we stood in all directions, as much as was possible through the fog and smoke, trying to discern whether the Bard's Wizard might be preparing another attack. I saw no signs of mounted parties besides our own—but visibility was too poor to be certain.

From this vantage point, it seemed as if the earth itself had ignited, like a pan left too long on a fire; as if some lingering coals might lurk in the crevices, trailing smoke and waiting for their next opportunity to light up the sky. As if whatever happened here had almost, but not quite, run out of fuel rather than been brought to a definite end. I wondered whether I imagined the hatred I felt still lurking here, the smoldering embers of something that surpassed any rage that ever fueled the cruel, angry things I'd done. And were I not imagining it, whether that made me less terrible and dangerous a person than I thought.

Probably not.

As I made my slow circuit of the top of the rise, I came upon Amien staring west: face drawn with dismay, eyes fixed on the far distance.

"What the hell is all this?" I said to him, sotto voce.

He startled, glanced at me and shook his head. *"The will of the goddess,"* he muttered. "I don't know. I can only assume it happened after my last visit here. You have any sense of it?"

I shrugged. I didn't want to talk about the things I'd felt. He would understand far too much, as always. "Anger. You?"

Amien nodded, eyes still on the horizon. "Something that would reach all the way from the Abyss to kill us, if it could."

For a moment I felt as if that something stared at me across the realms: as if its animosity were personal and meant for me. The hair on the back of my neck rose.

"Lords," Nuad said, snapping me back to the present moment. "The mora is ready to ride."

I glanced around; Iminor held Letitia's stirrup for her, and she swung tiredly into the saddle. I stored the information: the days were so long as to defy belief, this far north; but the party's range must be measured by the extent of Letitia's stamina rather than hours of daylight. I nodded and returned to my own horse.

We rode down into the acrid vapors and resumed threading our way past this thing the Tanaan called the Deluge: this event that, I now saw, was also a place. Our shadows turned to stretch and lengthen behind us; I began to feel as if we had become the victims of some cruel joke, and we would ride northward until we all expired of thirst, surrounded by undrinkable waters. Clouds gathered, somewhere above the noxious fogs; the world plunged into grey shadows, and visibility shrank further. Eventually the terrain began to rise again, steadily gaining in elevation. Clusters of melted-looking buttes gathered to the left and right. Letitia began to sag in the saddle. Dirt gave way to grey ash and pockmarked basalt, garish ponds to pools of bitumen; we crested a steep rise, and the river came suddenly into view below us.

I was not the only one who exclaimed with relief. The party hurried down to the water and dismounted; knights bent to the water beside their horses. I scooped out a handful: it had a metallic tang, but it was swift-moving, and I judged that Easca at least would have known whether it was to be avoided this far north. After a deeper drink I refilled my canteen, then rose and looked around.

Bare, scarred basalt stretched away in all directions, relieved only by occasional areas of broken ground in which moss and low grasses clung to life. Even the river supported only narrow fringes of bracken and a few stunted, gnarled trees. Across the river, similarly barren land rolled away beyond sight. I turned, scanning northward—and spotted a glint of wan sunlight on metal at the top of a hill. Worry seized at me; Letitia was far from the only person too tired to face another attack. But immediately I realized what I saw: one of the immense sculptures that grace the Twin Hills of Arian. The serene, beautiful city I had read about lay in ruins around it.

"Sweet Lady Tella," I said without thinking. Tanaan heads up and down the line snapped around in my direction; in my peripheral vision I saw them follow my gaze, then heard their collective gasp.

"Mora," I said. "*That* is Arian?"

Letitia flushed; after a moment she gave a reluctant nod.

"What *happened*?"

"I—" She swallowed, then visibly gathered herself. "Ouirr, let us speak as we ride."

After days of informality, yet another outbreak of courtly language from her lips: I felt myself stiffen, forced myself to nod as if the change in tone were of no consequence. Nuad called the party to order; Iminor helped Letitia into the saddle again; we followed Easca across the windswept barren, towards a broken wall I guessed had once enclosed the great city of Arian. I nudged my horse into position beside Letitia and Iminor; she looked at me, then glanced away.

"Mora?" I said quietly. "This is the Deluge. This was Arian. Now…?"

Letitia sighed.

"After the Transition, Dana's People came to the Four Realms and settled around the Devadore," she said to her horse's ears. The bardic recitation was easy to hear in her voice: someone, probably Macha, had drilled her on this passage until she could recite it letter-perfect.

"On the shores of the Devadore they built their capitals: Moria in Fáill, Senia in Muir, Uriah in Banbagor, and Arian in Fíana. In the summers the morae tended to their lands; the morae Ériu made their summer capital at Irisa, and while the summer ships sailed they remained in residence there. When the seasons turned, the morae of the Four Realms returned to their capitals, gathering around the warm, life-giving waters of the Devadore as if around the Lady's Hearth, and the graceful city of Arian outshone them all. People came from all over the Four Realms to take the waters and the healing air; the brehon and the bards held their conclaves at Arian, and the city rang sweet with the learned discourse of the brehon and the songs and tales of the People's great bards."

Letitia fell silent. No one spoke; for a time only the sounds of horses and the occasional pop and hiss of a steam vent competed with the moans of the dank wind.

"But then?" I prompted.

Letitia seemed to sink further into the saddle. Again her gaze fell on something in the vicinity of her horse's ears.

"The Holy Mora lost patience with Her people, with their prideful sorcery and petty wars," she continued, so quietly I had to strain to catch the words. "And so She sent the Deluge, as discipline and warning, that Her People must mend their ways, cease their grasping at powers not intended for mortals, stop their fruitless battling. Fire rained from the sky; the summer capitals fell and the Devadore died."

The wind moaned, grasped the tail of my hair and tugged it sideways. Letitia must have been the despair of her tutors.

"*And?*" I said.

"Enough!" Iminor barked. "Lord Ellion, I don't know how it is in the Beallan lands, but among the People it is considered rude to humiliate one's host!"

I couldn't help it: I stared at him, stunned. The Tanaan thought this obscene waste was somehow their fault? Why couldn't they see that the blame lay with a goddess Who was anything but benevolent? Finally I shook my head.

"Your pardon, Mora," I said quietly, acutely aware of Iminor's cold stare. "Clearly your people are much holier than mine. If our gods rained fire as punishment for warfare and magic, the Beallan realms would be a slag-heap on which the flames never died." I reined and let the escort pull ahead of me, and took up a position at the rear.

The opening in the ruined wall through which Easca led us had probably not been one of Arian's main gates: it was situated on a northwest bearing, flanked by two simple pillar-stones. Or it had been: the one on the right had fallen and lay blackened as if by lightning, encrusted in lichens of pale grey-green. Nevertheless the road had once been broad and solid even at this minor gate, and it still showed a clear path up the hill.

We followed the broken paving-stone through a landscape of tumbledown buildings that even now showed ripples and sprinklings of quartz and other luminous minerals. Gnarled trees sprang up every so often, in many cases from the rubble of the buildings themselves; like everything else here, they bore streaks and swaths of lichens in hues I had never imagined possible. Here and there a building or an enclave still stood; but all were vacant and blasted.

As the road twisted this way and that, the immense sculptures on the two neighboring hills slipped in and out of view behind buildings and trees: the scales that marked the place that had been the central enclave of the Tanaan brehon, and the harp that stood where the College of Bards had made its home. The sight of that harp increased the heaviness of the grief in my chest every time I saw it. So much music and knowledge lost. Would humans ever find the truth that stretches beyond our oldest histories, find some way to separate the facts of Hy-Breasaíl from the fictions and maybe even discover where the isle lies? The College of Bards in Arian had been the last remaining place I could think to inquire.

No one spoke; the sounds of our horses' hooves echoed mournfully against the ruined stone. At the top of the hill, the avenue we had traveled opened into an immense square. Here, oddly, many of the buildings still stood; but the western side of the square lay covered in an immense heap of multicolored rubble that could only have been Fíana's summer palace. Tragedy gathered in my throat again; I reined without really thinking about it, slid from the saddle, stood staring across the square. The sounds of the party continued across the square, presumably down the hill; but I stood as improbably fixed as a tree whose roots had tangled in a building.

After a moment Easca stood beside me, looking out across the tumble of stone.

"That was Atzila, the summer palace," she said quietly. "It was built of seven colors of stone: white and green marble, goldstone, bluestone from Fáill, pink, red and grey granites—and red-streak basalt from Muir. They say the gleam of the orichalus roof could be seen from Ilunmore."

I nodded.

"At the center of this square arose the Ithaldach spring, famous for the rainbows of the fountains built here and the healing properties of the water. It's probably still there, under the rubble; but no one can find it now. No one knows where the water has gone."

I nodded again; for a moment we stood silently looking across the terrible waste. From this point the lonely harp sculpture was easy to see.

"On that hill there," I said, "where the harp stands. That was the College of Bards."

Easca looked at me, surprise in her face. Wind blew a strand of red-blonde hair across her face, but her gaze never left mine.

"Yes, Lord," she said. "The sculpture was wrought of findargat—gods-metal. It's indestructible. Even the argentel crystal that makes the strings gleam like that is still in place." She sighed. "It's the only thing that still stands, over there. The College of Brehon is a little better, but not much."

I glanced around the square again, taking in the rest of the buildings. The one nearest me stood, and it looked reasonably sound; I stepped closer, to the steps leading down from the square to the shadowed entry. I peered through the gaping doorway, but it was dark inside. Stepping down to the entryway, I laid a hand on the smoothly-worked doorpost—and magic tumbled through me: the subtle power of the music in a bard's hands. But this wasn't one bard: hundreds, maybe thousands had passed through here, each carrying musical energies that raced up my arm and sprinkled themselves across the small quiet spaces of my mind. Almost without conscious decision I stepped inside; and even after all this time and all the malevolent intent outside, the energies of this place welcomed me in: I stood in a tavern, and countless seasons of stories and songs, the magical strains I knew and others I had hoped to learn flowed through and around me: beauty and the sort of hunger that can only be expressed in music, far more than one bard's best work. But after that brief swell, the energies of the place went quiet, and the tragedy of its emptiness caught up with me again.

Easca stepped inside, her amber eyes intent on mine. For a moment we stared at one another in silence.

"I've spent a lot of time walking these ruins, Lord," she said finally. "Trying to understand. Trying to see how a reasonably-good people could so anger a good goddess that She would do such a thing to Her Own people."

Pain gathered in my throat.

"And you know what, Lord? I don't understand. If there's evil in this place, I can't find it."

"I know," I said softly.

"Is it—?" She hesitated, glancing away. The blonde tail of her hair gleamed in the subdued light.

"I am of the clan house," she said finally. "I won't be a member of the Mora's Guard forever. Eventually I will be the leader of Clan Arian, this clan no one else likes to admit still exists—as if pretending Clan Arian is just a sept of Clan Dianann can erase all this." Her gesture encompassed the tragedy around us.

"In thirty years, or fifty maybe, I will come home," Easca continued. "To lead my people, to stand with them in defense against whatever comes across these wastes. That's my responsibility, to stand for my people. And so I wonder—"

She stopped again, swallowing. I waited, watching her. She'd already said more than she had since Irisa.

"If a goddess does evil," she said finally, voice hardly more than a whisper. Her eyes were still on something behind me. "If a goddess does evil—is it still incumbent on Her people to worship Her?"

Her unvoiced thought hung on the air, as easy to hear as if she had said it aloud: *Or should they stand against Her?* Finally she glanced at me again, watching me while somehow managing to avoid meeting my eyes.

Cold gathered inside me; for a moment I couldn't find my voice. Easca waited as if I were some high-ranking brehon and my judgment might settle the matter.

"Well," I said. "In *The Siege of the Brown Bull*, when Conor betrayed Fergus, it was meet for Fergus to take his men and leave Ulaid, to stand against the righ who had betrayed him so."

Outside, the wind keened.

"But you could argue," I said, "that the vows of service the men of Ulaid gave the mora Maev, which ultimately required them to fight against their own countrymen, were the source of much of the evil that arose in that war."

I sought her gaze; now, finally, her eyes met mine. Had their goddess's wrath fallen differently, might Easca have been mora of Fíana, while Irisa lay in ruins?

"I don't know," I said quietly. "There are questions for which none of the songs or sages has an answer, on either side of the mountains."

Easca nodded, silent, and followed me as I stepped back into the bitter air.

Chapter 13

Crossing Over

Easca and I caught up to the rest of the party at the river-crossing to the village they now called Arian. Heads turned as we rode up; every face I saw wore the certainty that Easca and I had been dallying, and reactions to that imagined fact ranged from amused speculation to outrage. Letitia wasn't looking at us: rather across the river. But the glance Iminor turned on me was toxic.

So be it. It was nothing I hadn't seen before, of course; people leapt to conclusions about what I'd been doing to whom several times a twelvenight. In Ilnemedon it was tiresome; here, unexpectedly, it stung. But I refused to acknowledge any of it. Instead I looked past the group to the river we must cross.

The river ran even swifter here than where we first came out of the sunken waste, tumbling and frothing over the remains of a structure that must once have been a bridge of astonishing form. The span had been built in sections, punctuated by tall bastions and massive, improbable ropes of still-gleaming steel. Where the first section should have stood, only metal ropes trailed and twisted into the water. Farther out, one of the slender bastions had broken like a felled tree, carrying another section of the span with it. Other sections lurked, barely visible, a few feet below the tumbling water. The setting sun made the submerged sections wink in and out of visibility and cast long shad-

153

ows from the bastions and the bluffs on the opposite shore: rendering the demands of the span's center and the conditions at the other end impossible to estimate. What I did know was the crossing would require us to navigate slick, steep banks, swim the horses to the edge of the remaining span, and then alternately ride, ford across submerged sections, and swim again across the missing areas: a treacherous operation even under reliable light. Meanwhile, even if most of the women in the party still sat strong in the saddle, I didn't need to ask whether any of them was tired; and Letitia's form had grown distinctly soggy.

"Well, then," I said to no one in particular, "clearly the sensible thing to do is camp on this side, and make the crossing in the morning."

Even more heads whipped around in my direction.

"What?" Amien snapped. "We need to get across the river! Everyone needs shelter, and rest; in the village we'll be able to find an inn—"

"Really?" I said to Easca; she grimaced and shook her head.

Amien's mouth twisted. "And over on *that* side of the river I'll have at least a chance of building decent wards! That place—" Amien gestured at the city behind us. "Is evil."

"No," I said. "There's no evil there, just sadness. We should be able to find a building that's safe enough to camp in; if the Bard's Wizard attacks again, we won't be endangering noncombatants—"

"If he attacks again, I want to be standing on magically-usable ground!"

"The party is tired!" I retorted. "This would be a treacherous crossing for *fresh*—"

"I know you don't *care* how difficult the arcane work is—"

He stopped suddenly, staring at me; I stared back. This time, I knew, everyone in the party was certain that the person who should be eliminated was me. Oddly, I couldn't even care about that, only about the anger—and fear—in Amien's gaze.

Fear of what? Of me? Of all the things I couldn't allow myself to do—or all the things I *might*?

I glanced away.

"You're right," I said finally to the air behind his right shoulder. "I am more concerned with the safety of the party, and of the noncombatants in that village, than I am with arcane convenience. But the decision is the mora's."

I glanced at her: now, finally, she met my gaze, something in her eyes that would have destroyed entire cities if it only had the power.

"We go forward," she said, low-voiced.

I inclined my head, throat clenching.

"Easca," Nuad said peremptorily.

Without a word she rode past me, threaded her way through the party without responding to the cold stare Letitia turned on her, and cued her horse down the steep bank. The gelding plunged into the water, which broke over the saddle bow and beat the creature disconcertingly sideways—and then the horse surged forward through the water, and my impulse to charge in after Easca subsided. A moment later the horse scrambled onto a submerged section of the span. Nuad followed Easca into the water; Letitia glanced at Iminor, but he just stared at her, frost in his blue gaze. She shrugged and cued her

154

horse forward.

Her delicate white mare had not been conceived for such a challenge: I drew in an involuntary, hissing breath as it slipped down the steep banks and plunged into the water. For a moment it seemed Letitia would be swept away by the current. Iminor cued his horse as if by reflex, then sensibly reined and gave Letitia room to maneuver in the narrow crossing. Finally the mare found some purchase or reserve of strength and began to beat her way across the water to the bridge. By the time her rear hooves were scrambling for a foothold Iminor was already in the river.

The rest of us followed them across, one by one. I unlashed my harp from the saddle and slung it across the center of my back, hoping it might remain dry. It was a strange, balance-wrecking encumbrance; I wondered how harpists who can't afford to maintain horses are able to tolerate the annoyance day after day. All at once I realized I was tired, too: far more worn than a day's ride warranted.

Finally there were only two of us left on the near bank. Manannan, the old man of the contingent—which meant he might have seen anywhere from fifty to two hundred years in the mora's service—gestured courteously for me to precede him. When I wasn't riding at the back of the contingent, he always seemed to be: clearly he was accustomed to that place of responsibility and took pride in upholding it. Nevertheless I was about to decline when Letitia and a horse screamed in unison.

I looked out to the center of the river: Letitia had missed the connection at the far end of a broken span and clung to the back of her desperately-swimming mare as the horse was swept helplessly downstream. On the span behind her, Iminor wrenched his horse's head sideways and charged directly into the water. Farther ahead, redheaded Rathacht had been dragged into some underwater hazard in another missing section. For one horrifying moment horse and rider hung, obviously impaled on whatever had snared them; then the water wrested them free. Without further thought I cued my horse into the torrent, as if I could catch up to them and do something of use from here.

I gained the first section of the bridge; across the river I saw Iminor submerge briefly as his horse neared Letitia—and then his head reappeared beside her just as her horse foundered. He hauled her from the saddle into the water; I hurried my horse across the span to the next place we must swim, hardly aware of the water in my boots and the cold of the wet silk plastered across my middle. By the time I had reached the next span, Iminor had Letitia clinging to his saddle as they swam towards the far bank, but her bedraggled mare was nowhere to be seen. I passed through one of the little bastions, hurrying my horse towards a spot from which I could see what was happening—and the beast stumbled as we came out the other end, dropping suddenly onto another section that lay a few feet below the surface. Fierce, chaotic currents dragged us sideways; once again cold water swirled into my boots. This was the spot where Rathacht had been swept off the span, I realized. I glanced into the darkening water at my left hand, spotting a wicked-looking tangle of stone and metal.

"Courage, old man," I murmured to the horse, and did what I could to throw my weight against the force of the current. After a few moments of struggle the horse scrambled onto a section of the bridge whose surface lay above the water, and I glanced at the far bank. Just a little farther now. Most of the party had already gathered at the far end of the span; Letitia and Iminor were scrambling up the bank less than half a mile away, and Nuad led a group towards them at a gallop. By the time I reached the far bank, Letitia and Iminor lay amid the bracken at the verge, a cluster of knights dismounted around them.

I reined, dismounted, and patted my horse's neck. "Good work, boyo," I murmured to him, glancing around.

The village huddled much closer to the banks of the river than I had realized. The houses, small weathered-looking dwellings, all stood on squat platforms of cobbled stone; there seemed no distinction between the village and the rice fields around it. Some houses were entirely surrounded by plots of rice and could only be reached by narrow, raised earthen walkways. Other homes occupied ground high enough to support small vegetable gardens. Sunset light shimmered on the water in the rice fields, made silhouettes of the women stealing a few last minutes in vegetable plots and the children playing on the walkways. From the southwest corner of the little village, men drove skinny cattle in from some range I was certain even they didn't refer to as pasture.

A group of riders swept in from the northern edge, hooves thundering against basalt and splashing through rice paddies—and as the Básghilae took their first victims, my head shifted into magic, whirling into ur-reality too fast for me to stop. Through the village they came, slowing as they took the lives of noncombatants but never really stopping. Once again the energy of the Tanaan on whom they fed tingled against my skin, kindled the invisible series of lights that traces a wizard's spine, knotted my throat with warring pleasure and horror—and then, suddenly, the leader of the Básghilae contingent was close enough for me to see his dispassionate green-cast face, his hollow despairing eyes—and unexpected comprehension of the working required to create his kind blasted me open, beyond human reason. Half a second's echo of the power their maker channeled shot through me; my apprehension of the cataclysmic fusing of their souls to life energies not their own sparked meteors in my mind. Fierce need raced through me; my throat grew so tight I could barely breathe, and the sounds of my own harsh breath rasped in my ears.

Down the riverbank, Letitia gave an inarticulate cry of despair; Nuad called the knights around him to arms. Revulsion swept through me; my sword was in my hand before I realized I was reaching for it, and I discovered myself in the saddle. I spurred the horse out to meet the onslaught.

I knew better than to bring emotions to battle; I knew all the ways fury, fear, and despair reduce the effectiveness of a leader. But anger and the need to destroy blazed through me too powerfully to shunt aside: I heard myself roar, waded into the first engagement with a crashing impact of sword on sword that resonated in all my bones and knocked the Básghil from his stirrups. I leapt to the ground after him and separated head from body with a stroke that was satisfying for half a second. I wanted desperately to hack the corpse beyond recognition. But behind me I heard Letitia's knights racing up the narrow swath between the bluff and the river, and I forced myself to set that satisfaction aside. Instead I scrambled back into the saddle and spurred the horse into the path of the next rider.

He was still fresh, almost sparkling, with the lives he had just absorbed. I wondered whether I could pull those energies into myself: whether I would survive the contact with his undead flesh. Some saner part of my mind recognized the madness of the impulse, recognized the energies that drew me had cost any number of innocent lives; and suddenly I had to swallow against nausea. Again horror and revulsion drove my sword, made it almost impossible to resist the impulse to follow the defeated ghoul to the ground and hack the corpse to unbloody pieces.

A different magic flared nearby, its flavor too bland for me to do more than recognize its presence. A bolt of green flew in my peripheral vision: Amien. I should have been surprised when it swerved away from its target at the last second, but I was already occupied with destroying the next Básghil. The wrongness of his existence drove my sword: the blade hummed satisfyingly through the air, bit rewardingly into flesh. When this one fell, I found breathing a little easier. I looked up, heart still pounding—and realized I had lost all awareness of the field.

Oh, dear gods. If I couldn't order the battles for the Tanaan, then what was I doing here? Hastily I swept a glance around: Nuad stood with six of the knights—all three women among them—in a tight, mounted half-crown pinning Iminor and Letitia against the riverbank while Básghilae swarmed all around, trying to create an opening. As I looked, Easca knocked a ghoul from the saddle—and Iminor slipped around the back of the formation, sword bared, running to take the Básghil on foot. I shouted, but it didn't make sense even to me; nevertheless Iminor cast me a guilty glance as his first stroke hit home. Closer to the bridge, Amien engaged in an all-out melee with another group of Básghilae, aided by Manannan, Fiacha, and Greine. They were heavily outnumbered, and had allowed themselves to become trapped in a depression that was probably a streambed during the rainy season. Luachran, stocky Eber, and young Semeon, who had been Cainte the chef's grand-nephew, lay dead nearby.

There was no question where I was most needed: I spurred the horse towards Amien's melee, taking the first Básghil from the higher ground at the rear. It wasn't much of a rear-guard action, but it was enough to shift the balance of the engagement. The knights in the hollow attacked with renewed vigor; the Básghilae shifted focus to accommodate the new front. I still wanted to follow every Básghil I defeated to the ground.

Eventually, we eliminated their numerical superiority, and they disengaged and withdrew. But there was no satisfaction in it: I knew the deaths of three knights were my fault; and I couldn't stop remembering the unearthly, horrifying delight of the energies the attackers had released, feared to identify the character of the tremors that raced up my spine. As darkness closed in we gathered our dead, and the two groups converged in the zone between our engagements. It felt as if we should have embraced, should have congratulated one another on surviving; instead we all stood still for a moment, staring dumbly at one another. Letitia glanced at me, abject shame in her face, and looked away; my own humiliation made nausea gather in my throat again.

"It should be easier," Iminor croaked finally. "Knowing that you're doing them a favor. Knowing that it's not their fault. It should be easier to feel mercy."

"But I still just hate them," Mattiaci agreed, eyes on something at the far end of the village.

Everyone fell silent.

"We should get inside, Lords," Easca said after a moment. "Arian is not a place to be outdoors at night."

"Lead on, then," Nuad said tiredly, and swung into the saddle without giving the order.

The group mounted, Letitia on the black gelding that had been Luachran's, and followed Easca northward on the riverbank. I hung back, taking up the rear again, mind full of things against which people should bar the night door.

The village of Arian had more dead to mourn tonight than we. And of course their shock was far greater. For us, now, the only shocks of Básghilae attacks came from inside our own hearts and minds.

The villagers had already scooped up their dead and scurried inside; only the horse-trampled fields and gardens showed that something had passed through. But as we followed Easca down the narrow, winding path through the village, I heard wailing from more than one house—and felt eyes on us behind the shutters of several others.

The house to which Easca led us was her own: the home of the clan leader, Alba Arian. It was too small to accommodate even a dozen guests; and we weren't many more than that now. Though it stood on a large enough patch of dry land to support what appeared in the fading light to be a vegetable garden, it could only be reached via an earthen walkway; and even Easca wasn't certain how to accommodate so many horses or where we might build pyres in this waterlogged place. If Letitia had hoped for some sort of ceremonial welcome on her first visit here, she must surely be disappointed.

Easca reined in front of the house, hesitated, then said quietly, "Lords, let me fetch the Arian. She'll know what to do," and slipped from the saddle. She raced across the narrow walkway and banged a fist against the door. Within seconds it opened, revealing a grief-stricken Tana whose age might be measured in decades or centuries, who wrapped Easca in an immediate embrace and began weeping in earnest.

"Mama," Easca said quietly, a note of protest in her voice. "We've the mora outside, with a—oh, Lord of Light, with a Beallan sorcerer and a group of—"

"The mora?" the older Tana echoed. "Of what?"

Easca gave voice to a humorless laugh. "Of Fíana, Mama."

Easca's mama looked up, scanning the group without releasing her daughter; then abruptly she straightened.

"Right, so," she said, smoothing hair back from her face. "Let's go."

Mother and daughter crossed the little walkway towards us, the elder sweeping the group with a gaze that missed little and romanticized less. We all slid from the saddles as if this were some sort of inspection drill; finally the clan leader stopped and, evidently unable to deduce which of the Tana the mora might be, dropped a swift, general-purpose curtsy to the group.

"Welcome," she said.

"Mora Letitia Ériu a Fíana," Easca said, manner flawless but a neutrality in her voice that suggested politics passing human understanding. "Allow me to present the Arian, my mother Alba Arian."

Letitia attempted a soggy curtsy; exhaustion and waterlogged spidersilk nearly pulled her to the ground. Just in time Iminor grasped her arm.

"Lady, your hospitality is legend," Letitia said.

The Arian swallowed what I suspected was a laugh. "I'm sorry, we favor safety over protocol here these days. Please come in."

"Lady," Iminor said smoothly.

"The mora's consort, Iminor a Dianann," Easca murmured.

The young Tan bowed, as perfectly courtly as if his clothes weren't still dripping; the clan leader curtsied to him, but her growing impatience was evident.

"Lady, with great respect—we've sixteen horses and three dead of our own. I assume you'd prefer we didn't bring them all...?"

"Lord of Light," the clan leader said. "Ouirr, you're right. Easca—we should be able to make room for the horses in the barn. I'll send Erc to run for Badra..." She paused, the strain of solving problems beyond her own village's tragedy plain in her face. "I know you'll want to prepare your dead. We can build cairns in the morning—" She frowned, as if she'd just apprehended another problem. "—but I don't know—"

Simultaneously the group gave a collective gasp of horrified understanding.

"*Cairns?*" Letitia said. "Lady, we need to build pyres!"

The clan leader nodded ruefully. "Lady, how many trees have you seen out here? Since the Deluge we have had to... find other ways."

"But we're not storing vegetables!" Letitia protested.

The clan leader sighed. "Lady, our wisewomen carry an unbroken tradition from Banba, who was priestess on Ilunmore. They all agree that the cairn stands in for the Great Barrow on Ilunmore and the Lady's Underground Ways."

"Lady," Easca said quietly to her mother. "You're debating outdoors."

The clan leader glanced at Easca and sighed. "You're right, Daughter. Lady, we can talk more about this inside; let's get you in for the night. I'm afraid I don't know where we can properly honor your dead tonight; you'll be stepping on one another in here as it is."

"Maybe upstairs?" Easca said quietly.

The clan leader grimaced. "There'll be little dignity in that trip."

Easca nodded ruefully.

"Well, bring them in; we'll sort it all inside," the clan leader said.

"I— Thank you, Lady," Letitia said, plainly unhappy.

The clan leader nodded. "We'll settle your dead, and I'll send my son to fetch Arian's—herdsman, and then you can settle your horses. It's a bad night all around, but we'll sort it."

"Thank you, Lady," Letitia said again.

Manannan, Greine, and Fiacha followed Letitia and the clan leader inside, carrying the bodies of the fallen knights. Seconds later a young Tan bolted out the door and down the walkway, stopped just long enough for a swift embrace with Easca, and raced out into the village: Alba's son Erc, I guessed. The rest of us stood silent in the gathering dark, waiting for the knights to return. A zephyr skittered down the street, carrying wild, unfamiliar energies that raised gooseflesh on my exposed skin. My heart ramped up its pace again; renewed desire for things I knew better than to touch swept through me, and I bit down hard on my lower lip.

Finally they came back down the walkway; we mounted and followed Easca through the village to a wattle-and-daub barn. The doors were already flung wide, and lamps burned within; we dismounted, led the horses inside, and did what we could for them in the small space not occupied by cows. My own horse rolled his eyes at the close quarters and constant jostling; but at least by now he was acquainted with his fellows, and they could share warmth as their coats dried. I hoped he would find some peace tonight, once all the people cleared out.

The clan leader's house proved just as cramped as I had surmised: surely the smallest, meanest dwelling in which a noblewoman of royal ancestry had ever resided. The first floor was all one room, lit by rush lamps and a pungent dung fire. The three fallen knights had been carefully laid out in the center. The second floor lacked stairs: only a stout ladder led through an opening in the first floor ceiling.

We stacked our soggy packs in the corner near the door, piled damp mail and weapons in the farthest reaches of the room. There was no remedy for our sodden clothes but to stand near the smoky little fire; I chose the clammy embrace of wet silk over smelling like a dung fire for gods-only-knew-how-long, and took up a spot against the opposite wall instead. Alba's daughter Ailbhe brought bowls of water subtly scented with heather, so the Tanaan might prepare the dead according to their custom; Tru, Bruane, Easca and even Alba and Ailbhe fell to the task immediately. Amien walked quiet circles around them: banishing the dark energies wafting towards the corners of the room, murmuring prayers for safe crossing to the heroes' reward. None of it seemed to have much effect on the depletion spell; I could barely see the knights' bodies through the traces of magic that hung on them: a shimmer of shadow in colors that mundane eyes never see. But if Amien saw it, he said nothing.

"Lady," Letitia said. Now that she'd removed her armor, I saw: she no longer wore the enchanted diamond. The well-worked Mora's Torc looked oddly plain without it. I wished I had finagled some opportunity to examine it more closely before she realized what it was; I wondered whether it had been lost with her horse.

Alba looked up, chagrined. "Your pardon! I have taken your—"

Letitia shook her head, face set in a way that made it perfectly clear she considered the task outside the mora's purview, and shifted the book she'd been carrying since Irisa from hand to hand.

"I need to meditate. We'll be sailing to Ilunmore tomorrow. Where—"

"Ilunmore?" Alba echoed. "How?" She cast a glance around the group.

"I... have an idea, Lady," Easca said quietly, not looking up.

"Really," Alba said, but Easca just kept bathing Luachran's wounds. The clean scent of the heathered water permeated my head, warring strangely with the shimmer of the depletion spell.

"Is there someplace I can have quiet?" Letitia pursued.

"I—" The clan leader shrugged. "Upstairs." She cast a glance towards the ladder.

Letitia followed her gaze, then nodded stiffly to the clan leader and stepped towards the ladder. "Nuad," she said peremptorily, and climbed through the opening in the ceiling.

Nuad's face didn't change, but the set of his shoulders spoke of resignation. He followed Letitia up to the second floor.

"Ilunmore?" Alba said to Easca. The idea flitted through my head that there was significance to the juxtaposition of heather, which is sacred to Lady Tella, with the residue of the depletion spell. But there wasn't time for me to examine the thought before it faded into the smoke from the pungent fire.

Easca's shoulders sagged, too; she didn't look up from her work. "Mama, we're escorting the mora to the Beallan lands; she also plans to make the pilgrimage at Ilunmore along the way—" Something in the clan leader's face or posture made her stop.

"The pilgrimage," Alba said, no gentleness in her tone. "Has she been invested, or not?"

Easca sagged further.

"And yet she's mora."

"Mama, do you want to talk Irisa politics tonight? We're leaving in the morning."

Mother and daughter exchanged stares. Several of the Tanaan sitting around the little table and leaning against the walls shifted uncomfortably.

"How do you plan to get to Ilunmore?" Alba said.

Easca sighed, sat back on her heels, and wrung out the cloth she was using. "I'm going to talk to Indech," she said, and rose.

Nuad climbed down the ladder. "Easca, you're first watch."

"*Ra?*" Easca said, incredulous. Her fair face flushed. "With respect, Ra, I've only one night—"

Nuad's hand sliced through the air. "The mora asked for you specifically."

Alba frowned. An anger that suggested far more history than this one injustice gathered in Easca's face.

"Who better than the one who knows the territory, she said."

"Ra, you know—"

"Easca, get on it."

She cast Nuad another aggrieved, incredulous look; crossed the room to gather her mailshirt and weapon; spun on her heel; and stalked outside. The door closed behind her with sufficient impact to shake the frame.

"Nuad," Iminor said quietly, and went to stand among the armor in the farthest corner of the room. Mattiaci and Tuiri moved closer to the fire, expressions bland. A strange little ripple of upside-down power, reminiscent of the energy I'd tasted at the spring in Letitia's garden at Irisa, washed past me; a tremor skipped up my back. I had to find something else on which to focus.

"She needs you to stand up to her when she's wrong." Of all things, why Iminor's barely-more-than-whispered words were what came through to me at that moment was beyond my capacity to understand. "She gets emotional;

she needs you to—"

Upside-down power rippled up from the floor, swirled around me like a whirlpool, pulled my consciousness towards places I couldn't allow it to go. Heather and some exotic aroma I couldn't identify infiltrated me. This time I realized what had snared me: the energy of Letitia's meditation. Was it so much stronger than it had been on previous nights?

Arcane consciousness sank velvet talons into my brain. In another thirty seconds I would no longer have a choice. I pushed away from the wall and strode to the door.

"Lord?" Bruane said, looking up from the floor with concern in her gaze. Her red-gold hair reminded me of someone, of some argument I'd left unfinished.

"Ellion," Amien said, in a tone that would have irresistibly fixed my attention, were I still a member of his workshop. But the mayhem gathering in my brain made it impossible to focus on him.

"Excuse me," I said, opened the door, and stepped outside.

Will-o-the-wisps hung over the rice fields, for all the world like stars fallen to earth and so numerous that the entire village had taken on a faint blue-green glow. The air sparkled and danced against my skin, whispering of energies that awaited the grasp of someone who knew what to do with them. Out in the narrow excuse for a road, Easca spun towards me, unearthly light casting her in strange glamour and tracing the fine edge of her swiftly-drawn sword.

"Lord!" she breathed.

I nodded and strode down the walkway. "I'm just going to get some air." Maybe things would be less eldritch beyond the rice fields.

Easca shook her head. "Lord, this is no place for an evening stroll."

A hollow laugh escaped me. "Nevertheless, I'll be back," I said, and walked down the road to the river.

Telliyn waxed towards her first quarter, nearly at her zenith. Her light bathed the swift current and barren shore in a pale glow, made the bracken clinging to the banks into the feathers of some underworld bird. Across the river, the lonely sculptures on the Twin Hills of Arian gleamed. I turned north, away from the places where Básghilae corpses lay, following the river until the rice fields and will-o-the-wisps faded into darkness behind me.

Moonlit basalt stretched away from the river into limitless distance, meeting the pinpricked darkness that arched above. Telliyn stood on the near side of the bright smear of the Way of the Gods, Arliyn across that divide. The sky was starkly cloudless tonight; stars twinkled in myriad subtle hues. The wind still carried hints of sulfur and iron—and energies whose names I didn't know but longed to learn, harbingers of powers far stronger than the things Aballo wizards are trained to tap. Those energies infiltrated me, creeping through chinks in the wall I tried to throw around myself, raising illicit thrills up the length of my spine. It reminded me of something, this sensation of standing on the verge of knowledge that could blow Aballo's understanding of magic wide open. No more than two heartbeats passed before I realized what it reminded me of, and the memory swept over me before I could forestall it.

In my mind I was in Tellan again, astride a new and glorious stallion I hadn't yet named, halting him almost mid-stride in a little, fir-infused glade on the southern edge of the Tellan family lands. Everything felt renewed this month, delighting my senses and my spirit; even this place through which I'd ridden a hundred times held an eldritch glamour I'd never noticed before. There was something here, a sense of presence like and yet unlike the closeness of the goddess I so often felt in a ceremonial circle: something half-familiar I sensed but couldn't see; and I sent every sense, arcane and mundane, questing after knowledge of it. I gathered the reins in my left hand, turning the horse all the way around, peering into shadows. Something shimmered in my peripheral vision, but when I turned my head towards it I couldn't see anything there.

There are times when a wizard knows better than to trust his eyes. On a whim, I shut mine.

There was definitely something here. It had been waiting for me, as patient as if time had ceased to exist.

Hello? I thought, not projecting it. I heard no answer, unless the near-laughter of wind in the treetops was a reply.

Earlier this twelvenight, on my return from Aballo, I had made the sacred marriage on Tellan's own soil; my bond with the goddess, like my bond with this nation I would one day inherit, felt utterly complete. But surely other gods had walked these lands before the arrival of the true ones; how surprising would it be for older forces to call my notice now? At Aballo, more timid voices would have been calling for me to draw back, to be wary of straying from the path, as usual; I missed them not at all.

A rider approached from the south: I opened my eyes and turned the horse again, until the the shimmering enigma hovered behind my shoulder and the place in which the path left the glade lay straight ahead. And on that path, entering the clearing, Deaclan: had he ridden all the way from Aballo seeking me? Half a twelvenight's journey through lands I knew he had never seen. For a second I was almost happy; until this moment I hadn't realized that, against all reason, I missed the constant tug of awareness of his awareness. But his luminous eyes, silver in a circle, were storm-dark today; his sensuous mouth twisted into something that wasn't a smile. Now I understood what had brought him here: two years of competition and his escalating hatred; the itch for a dance that our superiors at Aballo would have stopped before it really began. The welcome I had almost offered twisted inside me; anger and multilayered arcane lust rose up in its wake. I drew the defensive habit of irony around me and smiled.

"Ah, but you've missed the party," I drawled.

Deaclan gave an elaborate shrug. "You were the only one there who didn't know it was dull."

I made some tart retort, but neither of us was listening; the ground on which my new horse stood erupted in flames. The young stallion reared, panicked; I vaulted backwards, rolling into the landing and casting at the Tan as his shield shimmered to red-purple life. I drew the golden sparkle of a shield around me and scrambled to my feet. How many months had I been waiting for this moment? We should have done this long ago.

Look at this. It wasn't a telepathic sending, and it wasn't my thought, but it was inside my head anyway; and suddenly I was aware of the energy in the clouds scudding down from the north. This evening, those clouds would be a storm on the palace compound. Right now, that power was a tingle of delight along my spine.

I grasped the power and turned it on Deaclan. It crashed against his shield. For a moment I was alight with energy broader than anything I'd ever found in myself, stronger than any sacred source. The flash faded, leaving afterimages in my eyes and a broad ring of scorched and smoking earth around the Tan. He met my eyes as the echoes rolled through the forest around us, gaze full of unspeakable words that made my throat knot up.

The flash came again; this time I wasn't the one who had channeled it. It crashed against my shield, making my ears ring and my head momentarily uncertain. But when I reached inside for energy to cast at Deaclan, I found something just as delicious and wild as the lightning I'd channeled a moment before, and the part of me that wasn't always human made me forget about everything else.

Look at this. It was not my thought, again. This time I couldn't have cared less whose it was.

Show me, I thought. And whoever/whatever it was, it did. I stretched; the ground and trees and mountains and clouds receded below me, and the world curved away from my eyes. Everything was dark, except for the world far below and the brilliant glow of the sun hanging in the distance behind my left shoulder. A half-visible river of cold dark fire streamed above me, sparkling close enough to touch.

I grasped it. I found myself again, reached back to the place where I stood inside a wisp of golden energy; and I let the cold darkness blast through me. Deaclan's shield flashed and vanished; his gaze was a reflection of the terrible beauty in which I'd tangled, of all the joyous anger and awful lust we'd been taught never to satisfy. My own ungovernable laughter echoed in my ears. More riders approached: two horses moving at a brisk easy gait, following the trail I'd ridden only moments ago. I should stop. What Deaclan and I were doing was inadmissible.

But I didn't care if we were discovered; I didn't care who saw. Deaclan had brought this battle into *my* preserve; I would owe no apology. And I burned with the need to find out what would happen: not just this dance, but the things that would come next. I cast even wilder power at Deaclan; without warning my shield boiled away; I deflected the force Deaclan flung at me, brain ringing with the impact. Wood snapped with a lightning crack as a tree broader than my outstretched arms toppled across the space at my left hand.

Take a look at this. Incomprehensible brilliance flooded my mind; power blasted into me, too fierce to contain. I laughed again, full to bursting with raw anger and delight. The Tan I might or might not reduce to ashes began to shimmer, his motions oddly slow as he cast again. There wasn't time to work another shield; I would deflect the charge, sacrificing another tree or two and then turning the brilliance boiling in my brain into the final onslaught of the engagement.

The casting came at me; simultaneously I realized who was riding into the glade. My parents, attired for riding and relaxed for the first time since the days of feasting and preparations for my sister's wedding began, had stolen a little time for themselves. They weren't ready to understand what was happening here; they still radiated unease when someone mentioned my time at Aballo. This was more than they could bear to know. Deaclan's casting hit me; my awareness of them tangled up with the way I deflected his power.

It was wrong. I knew it even before the motion was complete. I tried to pull it back, to absorb into myself the destruction I'd shunted aside. I didn't know how I'd survive it, but I knew my chances were better than theirs. Brilliance flared again, the flash outside me and the mayhem within echoing so I lost track of where each began. For a fraction of a second my father met my eyes. I dimly sensed more hoofbeats approaching: at a canter this time. Then half the clearing exploded.

The shock of the explosion washed through the glade, blowing dirt into my eyes and mouth. A bit of burning lace flashed past me and was gone. A howl ripped up from my core, igniting my throat; Deaclan stared at me, his white-hot anger melting into fear. Fintan's horse clattered to a stop between us.

I had never bothered to work it out: how many years before Deaclan and I began our initiates at Aballo had Fintan completed his. He'd been House Healer to Tellan since I could remember. Usually he seemed impossibly narrow-minded, ineffectual; today he leapt into action. He worked a binding that separated Deaclan from the rest of the glade and immediately turned a forbidding stare on me. I barely saw any of it; all I could focus on was the blasted place in which two horses and two riders had disappeared. A horse's severed head dangled in the branches of a tree. A woman's riding boot—I knew whose it was, but couldn't allow myself to form the thought—balanced precariously upside-down, as if its owner had decided to dive into the earth. Nausea vied with the intolerable pain in my chest. There was nothing to do but stand and stare.

I stared, mind full of whirling black emptiness and tears streaming until I forgot about trying to focus my eyes. I startled when a hand closed around my arm. I blinked; gradually the world swam back into focus.

The sun had dipped down below the hostile ground; clear daylight had faded into the long orange glow of sunset and the charcoal shadows of trees. I'd been standing there staring at nothing for hours. Deaclan and Fintan were gone. None of this mattered. Dica, my father's seneschal—oh, gods, my seneschal now—stood in front of me, wiry hand grasping my arm and shadow-smudged eyes searching my face.

"Lord?"

I startled. The voice wasn't Dica's. The hand on my arm belonged to Easca, and her moonlit face was full of concern.

"Lord, do you know where you are?"

For the space of a breath I thought I was in Tellan. But I stood in the midst of barren basalt: stars stretching above me, wild energies caressing my skin and teasing the edges of my mind. Now the hunger they roused in me just made me ache.

"Hell," I said, offering Easca a wry smile.

Her answering smile held no more humor. "That place is sometimes mistaken for this one," she allowed.

I tried and failed to formulate a witty reply.

Easca nodded as if I'd said something insightful. "Lord, will you walk in with me?"

"By all means," I said, and fell in beside her. "This is no place for an evening stroll."

Her mouth quirked. We lapsed into silence, keeping company with our private thoughts. Finally it occurred to me that I had once again managed to compromise both her honor and her safety with one thoughtless act.

"I thought you had the watch?" I said, as if it might shift my attention from today's lengthening list of failures.

Easca shrugged. "Lord Iminor came and claimed it. But you didn't hear it from me."

"I will add it to the list of things I failed to observe today," I said, eyes on the barren horizon.

"Tomorrow will be a better day," Easca said after another long silence. "I spoke to Indech a little while ago. He knows where the old yachts were dry-docked. And he says if we can get one into the water, he's sure he can sail us there."

I nodded, digesting this. "People here think he's mad, am I right?"

Easca's head whipped around for a look at me, astonishment written in her face.

I shrugged. "People always think men who dare difficult things are mad."

Easca nodded silently.

"Women, too," she said after a moment.

Chapter 14
A Draft of Remembrance

Easca's kinsman Indech had redder hair than I had seen since Sanglin, who had been Amien's right hand while I was at Aballo. And still was, I surmised, though I didn't open that basket of snakes with the wizard. Indech wasn't as young as his obviously radical ideas had made me expect; but as is the way with Tanaan, I couldn't form any useful estimate of his actual age. He led us past the place where the river Arnemetia veers to the northeast; we trotted up a narrowing channel, towards an immense wall of rock. Too vast an edifice to call a bluff, it rose to an improbable height, stretching east and west beyond visibility: as if the land on which we rode had dropped suddenly away, or the area we approached had risen like a loaf left too long. It seemed the stream we followed would come to an abrupt end at the wall; but as we approached, I saw: the stream issued from a cleft at the wall's base. Indech paused long enough to kindle a torch and led us inside. More than one of the Tanaan cast anxious glances backward as we rode in.

Before long, the ceiling of the passage dropped, and we had to dismount and lead the horses through the water. I began to despair of my boots ever drying out. But the stream grew shallower and narrower as we walked, eventually veering into some side corridor. We continued northward, through a tunnel of damp basalt. Rivulets streamed down the walls; odd colonies of fungus caught the light of Indech's torch and glowed, in colors rarely seen outside wizards' dreams. Eventually daylight showed ahead, and we walked out to the shore of the Devadore.

The water stretched away to the horizon, shockingly bright blue-green and stippled at the shore with white-foam waves, beneath a sky that had gone steel-grey with a ragged tissue of clouds. Mist rose from the water's surface in wisps of rainbow hue. Several of us walked to the shore.

"Don't drink," Indech said behind us. "Better to stay out altogether."

The dry dock lay a mile or two to the east, apparently; we mounted and Indech led us up the black-pebble beach—not to a warehouse, but to an immense cave on the shore. We walked in: it was too vast for Indech's torch to give any sense of what might lie within. Amien called an arcane light and tossed it into the dead air, where it rose for an improbably long time, glowing as it grew, revealing a space easily the size of Mourne Palace in Ilnemedon. An astonishing array of ships stood tethered to the walls or anchored farther out, white-frilled water lapping at their hulls. Someone gave a low whistle.

"Mabon would give his right—" Mattiaci stopped. "Pardon, Mora."

Letitia waved dismissively.

"Who do all of these belong to?" she said.

Indech shrugged. "No one living, Mora."

"Which one should we use?" she asked after a moment.

"That depends," Indech answered. "Do any of you know how to sail?"

The knights looked at one another. Indech grunted.

"Once we're out on the water," Amien said slowly, "I can call you a wind. I'm not a trained windcaller; I won't know without you telling me just what wind direction or speed you need... "

Indech gave the wizard a slow, thoughtful smile. "That's all right, Lord, I wouldn't know how to order one in a way that would make sense to a sorcerer. But we'll sort it."

"Indeed." Amien smiled. We all looked out at the ships again.

"Which could we get the horses on?" I asked. "Can we use this first one, here?" It stood only a few feet away from the narrow ridge on which we had gathered, which seemed to suggest easy access; but I had little knowledge of ships. Beyond the fact that it had two masts, and the deck stood higher above the water than a man on horseback could reach, I could have given little useful description. It looked well-made enough.

"It would be the easiest to maneuver out," Indech said thoughtfully, but his eyes were on another ship, which stood anchored a little distance out in the water. I didn't know what made that ship more attractive. He shrugged, wistful.

"How will we get it out, once we're aboard?" Letitia asked.

"There's a sluice-gate at the entrance," Indech said. "Once we open it, the water will rise enough for the ship to move freely. I think the ancients must have towed them in and out..."

"If they were using windcallers, they might have moved the ships with their minds," Amien observed.

Everyone looked at the wizard again. He smiled, just a little.

"Yes, I expect I can," he said. "With Indech's help."

And so it went. Indech climbed a crumbling rope ladder up the side of the ship, and after a few moments let down a gangway across which we could lead the horses. My horse balked at the way it swayed underfoot and had to be persuaded to each step. Tru, crossing behind me, clucked in sympathy—for the horse, I suspected.

"Nobody's happy, sweet boy," she crooned to him. "Everything is stranger than the last. You'll be all right."

I looked at her, and at all the other troubled Tanaan faces. Most of them had been getting farther from home each day, I realized, and now they were about to sail away from their native country: assuredly for the first time in their lives. Only Indech looked happy at the prospect.

"Courage," I said to Tru, but pitched my voice so the rest of them would hear it. "Remember the undead cannot cross water. We can be sure of almost two days of peace once we're under way."

A number of faces brightened at that thought. The tension around Tru's blue eyes relaxed, and she crooned reassuringly to my horse as I coaxed him to take another step, and another.

"What's his name?" she said.

"What?" I said, reflexively, barely looking up.

"His name?" she repeated.

"Oh!" Another step. Soon we would gain the deck. He'd been calm enough on Letitia's barge on the Crearu. "I haven't named him yet. Well—that is to say—he's got a name, a show name, but those show names aren't real names."

"A show name? Like for the races?" Tru said.

I nodded. "I always like to wait and see what name would fit a horse before I give him a private name."

"So he's new," Tru said. "Good boy!" she added, evidently for the horse's benefit, as he set a tentative first foot on the deck.

"I've only had him a couple months."

"Any names so far?" Tru asked.

"I've decided against Nervous Wreck," I said, smiling. "I don't think it would be good for him to hear that all the time."

"That sounds like a racer name, anyway," Tru said with an answering smile.

Eventually we all gained the deck, and Indech slipped into the water and swam to the sluice-gate. After some struggling, he opened it. The entering wave raised every ship by several feet and swept Indech straight past the one we had chosen. He was still coughing and sputtering when he climbed onto the deck again.

Once everything was settled, he freed the ship from its tethers, then went to stand beside Amien at the prow. Energy prickled across my scalp as Amien enveloped the ship with his will and moved it slowly away from the wall, adjusting under Indech's coaching, and nudged it through the little channel into the Devadore.

The mist I had seen from the shore enveloped us; the sun was a pale, flat disk peering through tattered ribbons of clouds. The knights and I divided ourselves into two crews and did our best to follow Indech's instructions for raising and manning the sails. When the first tentative breaths of Amien's wind filled the sail I was manning, pleased wonder shivered through my middle, surprising me: it had been a very long time since I had any sense of the ferries on the Ruillin as anything but routine, and even my first time aboard a boat manned by professionals had not given me this sense of the everyday magic involved in a ship's flight across water. Indech grinned like a madman; even Amien looked happy.

Once we had the ship on the correct course, there was little for the rest of us to do but gaze at the scenery. Out on the open water, the mist dissipated. The sky held onto its tattered clouds and steel-grey hue, but now I could see all the way to the horizon. The ship danced and skittered across the waves; several of the knights grew notably green around the edges. Tru, Mattiaci, and Manannan leaned against the rail at the back of the boat and watched Fíana recede behind us until there was nothing but water in every direction. Most everyone else clustered in the ship's prow, looking forward as if they might glimpse Ilunmore before it climbed over the horizon. Though I knew better, I found myself doing the same.

What would we find at Ilunmore? As recently as yesterday I had looked forward to this part of the journey, even more than I had anticipated visiting Arian. I had spent more hours than I could count, at Aballo and afterward, collecting everything written or sung about Ilunmore that is available to humans. Even now, I could call to mind the maps of the island on which I had spent so many dreamy moments, could see the vision of their great goddess that the Tanaan had projected on their sacred isle: the mountain at the island's northern shore they call the Great Barrow, which corresponds to their Lady's Head; the Temple Mount at the Lady's Heart; the mysterious lake-within-a-lake they call the Lady's Womb. For days I had looked forward to finding some high point from which I might see that vision for myself, might contemplate the other as-above-so-below mystery that is projected on the isle: the five concentric circles into which the ancient Tanaan divided the isle by taming the rivers, and the echo of the heavens those rivers created. I knew Aballo had been modeled on the structures at Ilunmore's great temple, from the fourteen gates, thirteen galleries, and twelve-times-twelve stelae to the layout of the enclave entire; the idea of walking the paths of the original raised a strange longing in me: as if seeing those places might bring me back, after so much time, to stand face to face with the goddess.

The precision of the celestial alignments at Ilunmore was said to exceed even those at Aballo. But I had found no record of any human actually setting foot on the Tanaan sacred isle. I had looked forward to finally pacing out the galleries and confirming the symmetries of which I'd read, and perhaps even talking with one of the Tanaan astrologers. Now, of course, I wondered how much of their ceremonial center still stood. And I suspected there would be no one to talk with who wasn't on this boat.

Listening to the Tanaan converse as we sailed across the Devadore, I realized everyone had his or her own agendas for the visit, and I had somehow failed to notice the most important of all. There had been nothing of it in the histories I'd read. While any Tanaan might make a religious pilgrimage to Ilunmore, it seemed no mora could be invested without making that journey. There were sites she must visit, ceremonies she must perform—and the whole royal progress culminated in a visit to the summit of the Temple Mount, where stood the Tuaoh Stone: the great god-stone that once marked the center of

Hy-Breasaíl.

"The *Tuaoh Stone*?" I blurted. The stone was another of the treasures of Hy-Breasaíl that no one, at least no human, knew how to find: just like the Great Spear of Lugh Lámfhada, which Macha had so casually mentioned the Fíana morae holding at Irisa. Some of the histories mention the presence of the Lia of Fáilias, the Fáillian righ-stone, at Ilunmore; but the Lia Fáill is only one of several stones that people claim to be the lost Tuaoh. I'd always thought the tales of the Lia Fáill as the true Tuaoh a conceit of human harpists, not something to be considered seriously.

All the Tanaan gathered in the prow looked at me, nonplussed.

"Yes, the Tuaoh Stone," Iminor said finally. "Before the Deluge a mora couldn't be invested without a visit. It was where the goddess would designate Her favorites."

I laughed, surprised. "Which of you is carrying the Great Sword Fragarach, then?"

Letitia gave me a puzzled little smile. "That is the treasure of Banbagor."

I swallowed a second laugh. "Of course." *Next you will tell me they are making soup in the Great Cauldron at Muir*, I thought, but didn't give it voice. Once I was sure my voice would sound composed, I added, "You plan to visit the Tuaoh today, then?"

Letitia nodded. "This evening. First we visit the Lady's Womb, and bathe in the waters."

A sudden image of all of us bathing together skipped across my mind. The idea of not only Letitia but also Easca, Tru and Bruane in the nude competed with that of Iminor and Amien in similar condition. I wasn't sure what showed in my face, but the wizard chuckled.

"By *we* she means the Tana," he said. "By tradition only the outer circle is open to men."

"Oh," I said, unable to restrain my disappointment: I would miss the wonders of Ilunmore's sacred geography, after all.

"We will suspend that, today," Iminor said smoothly. "It was traditional for a mora-in-waiting's approach to the Tuaoh Stone to be witnessed by the priestesses at the temple. Today the mora will make do with us."

I glanced at Letitia, waiting for her polite protest of the phrase *make do*. But she was abstracted, her gaze on the far horizon and a tension that looked less like anticipation than apprehension on her lovely face.

"Lord Amien, I understand you need visit the Tuaoh Stone as well?" Iminor continued as if there had been no lapse.

The wizard nodded. "I may be able to contact my second from there. We may be able to arrange reinforcements as early as Goibniu."

He was right: whether or not the Lia Fáill was actually the Tuaoh, it was a power stone, and the Temple Mount must be a potent power-site. It should make a useful location for a dream-sending.

Iminor nodded, too. "No doubt the Holy Mora will lend you Her aid."

I wondered how anyone who had ridden through Arian yesterday, who sailed on a centuries-old relic of a ship across a sea rendered toxic by that goddess's Own Hand, could maintain such misplaced faith. But I didn't give it voice, and I refrained from looking at Easca. I no longer doubted their goddess truly existed, but I knew the best we could hope for was to escape Her notice.

No sooner had I birthed the thought than it began to worry at me like an underfed dog with a bone. Amien planned to step into their holiest of holies and tap one of their greatest power objects. How could She fail to notice? What if the Tanaan were right and the Deluge had been Her declaration of a ban on magic in Her lands? Might a human be granted an exception, or would he be singled out for yet greater wrath? I spent most of the remaining voyage trying to imagine how we might protect Amien without abandoning the idea of contacting Sanglin, but the only idea I came up with that might actually work was attempting the operation myself: no better than Amien taking the risk in some ways, far more dangerous in others. I stared out at the water and chewed my lip. The hours dragged.

Eventually Ilunmore climbed over the horizon: first the peak of the Temple Mount, then shortly afterward the Great Barrow. Gradually the shore came into view. The mountains surprised me: I had always imagined the sort of great, rugged peaks that define the landscape of Tellan. These were smaller, more weathered: like the prominences that line the Ruillin.

Even before we gained the shore, I saw: Ilunmore was as ruined as Arian. The gardens of which I had read were gone, and only bare black basalt and the occasional stubborn stunted tree had taken their place. The cove into which we sailed had once boasted a graceful marina; now it was all Indech could do to find a place where we could tie off and disembark.

On shore, everyone stood for several moments, looking around. The edge of the wrecked marina abutted a wide path of white quartz, speckled with egg-shaped stones of pockmarked black, that stretched north and south beyond sight. This must be the Way of Endeáril, the devotional path of the outer circle. The motif of the inverse night sky is sacred in any context, from the white-and-black granite of the ceremonial center at Aballo to the speckled-hide harp case that only one of the Lords of the Harpist Gorsedd may carry. The Way gleamed, stark and strange, amid the island's black basalt: like an echo of the Way of the Gods that divides the night sky.

Leading east, towards the Temple Mount, the remains of a broad processional road stumbled across the broken surface of the island; the low, relief-carved walls that had once enclosed it were little more than trails of rubble on either side. In the distance I saw a bridge rise up from that road: the span across the outermost of the river-rings, I guessed. That must be the path an arriving mora would follow.

"Well, then," I said finally. "Do we take separate ways?"

For a moment no one spoke. Iminor and Letitia exchanged a glance; she nodded.

"Tru, Bruane, and Easca will accompany me to the Lady's Womb, and then to the Temple Mount," Letitia said quietly. "I'll make the devotions at the sacred spring below the temple. If we can find the Inner Ways, that's how we'll come up to the Tuaoh Stone."

Iminor nodded, too. "The rest of us will take the Way of Endeáril to the Great Barrow. After, we'll come up the Outer Path to the temple summit."

"We'll meet you there at sunset, then," Letitia said, trepidation in her face. "Give me my pack?"

Iminor reached for her hand with a reassuring smile. "Already behind your saddle, milady."

Letitia glanced back at her horse, surprised, then produced a smile. "Thank you."

Iminor smiled again. Letitia climbed into the saddle, so the rest of us did, too. For a few moments we sat and watched the women ride away. I knew each of the men around me felt the unease of leaving the mora with so few blades, and each must be working his mind around the strange fact of temporary safety in his own way. Then we turned our horses north and followed the Way of Endeáril along the barren basalt shore.

Every so often, we passed elaborately-carved stelae, which stood beside the Way on the seaward side. A number of them had fallen or broken, and few of them looked stable; most bore splotches and streaks of lichens in a variety of unnatural hues. The stelae made a complete circuit of the island, hugging the Way of Endeáril, I learned; and each told the story of some episode in the lives of the Lady's Consort Endeáril or the hero Cúchulainn.

No matter that Cúchulainn was mortal, and human; the Tanaan had claimed him for their own and installed him with their god on Ilunmore itself. Reeling at the utter strangeness of it, I could barely absorb the story the first standing stone told. Our lore teaches that the god Lugh fathered Cúchulainn on a mortal woman; the Tanaan, I learned, believe that Cúchulainn became the god Lugh: after his encounter with the Green God that is described in the classic *Fare and Fir*. I didn't ask if they knew the song; the Tanaan with whom I rode were far too busy relating the portions of Cúchulainn's life covered by the stelae we passed for my benefit, tripping over one another in their eagerness to tell the tales. When some detail finally made me realize that the Tanaan consider Cúchulainn an avatar of their great god Endeáril, the whole thing snapped into place for me: Tanaan warriors, almost to a man, adopt Endeáril as their particular deity for private devotions; Cúchulainn, the greatest of mortal warriors, folds quite neatly into the story of Endeáril—especially into their version of the episode of the goddess's kidnap into the underworld and subsequent rescue, which was the topic of this series of stones.

As with many of our oldest histories, we share the essentials of that tale with the Tanaan. In human lore it is the young goddess Ara Who is kidnapped by the Lord of the Underworld. Among the Tanaan, their great goddess Dana is tricked by Donn, their god of the dead, into killing Her Consort Endeáril, and further deceived into swallowing the Acorn of His Soul; and finally, defenseless in Her grief, kidnapped into Donn's domain: all because Donn has tried and failed to fairly win Her Hand. There was no bardic recitation in the version the Tanaan knights told me as we rode, but they loved the tale as well as any warrior loves a lay of Cúchulainn.

And a tale of Cúchulainn it turned out to be: in their version, with the goddess kidnapped to the underworld, and Her Consort no more than a spark of life in Her belly, it falls to Her champion Cúchulainn to effect a rescue. Mortal though he may be, Cúchulainn crosses the barrier between life and death and lays siege to Donn's great House; even here, Cúchulainn's reputation has preceded him. And rather than risk the destruction He fears Cúchulainn might wreak, Donn releases the goddess back into the world of the living, and She gives birth to the god en route.

A worthy interpretation, I judged, but in the end it worked out muddy. I tried and failed to make what I had heard resolve into a sensible whole. In Tanaan lore, Cúchulainn became Lugh after his encounter with the Green God; yet Cúchulainn was trapped in the underworld after the goddess's rescue, being mortal and unable to return once he had made the crossing. So was the god Lugh in the underworld?

The Tanaan temporized. They exchanged puzzled looks. *No*, they said; *well, maybe, during winter-dark.* And then, finally, *Lord, don't you know you can't expect these things to line up like pickets in a fence?*

Well, yes, of course I did. But I never remembered until I hit that unresolvable knot. The Tanaan seemed relieved when the entrance to the Great Barrow drew into view and I gave up the futile effort.

The Great Barrow on Ilunmore, I knew, held the skulls, the ashes, and in some cases the long-bones of the morae of the Tanaan nations. The entrance to the barrow-cavern stands only feet from the shore, facing southeast: too close to the true for an alignment with midwinter sunrise. I wondered whether it might be situated to catch the first light on the Day of the Dead. Whatever the case, the exterior walls at the entrance are painstakingly inlaid with brilliant argentel, clear crystals nearly as hard as diamonds which the Tanaan hold in even greater esteem: making the black basalt twinkle like a moonless night. Inside we would find more argentel: inlays of spirals in endless profusion that stretched farther into the mountain than even midsummer sunlight can reach.

But all these things of which I had read and heard paled beside the thing no human source could have told me: the Great Barrow is not merely the burial chamber of the Tanaan's great leaders. They maintain it is literally the path to the underworld, the doorway through which the ancient Tanaan emerged from the Lady's Underground Ways during the time both our races call the Transition, the period of retreat from Hy-Breasaíl.

I stopped in the entranceway, stunned: staring at Tuiri, who had carried most of this afternoon's tale-telling and who tossed this shattering fact over his shoulder as if it were just one more feat of Cúchulainn. For a moment I suspected I was having a problem with the Tanaan language. Maybe I had caught a whiff of mine-gas.

"Do I understand you?" I managed finally. "A man can walk down that tunnel and find himself in…?"

"In the House of Donn?" Tuiri said. He shrugged. "That's how my Amma tells it, Lord. I don't know anyone who's tried it."

"No indeed," I breathed. Truth be told, I was far less compelled by the idea of visiting the Tanaan underworld than finding a route to Hy-Breasaíl. But even were such a thing possible, there wouldn't be time this afternoon. No, this was another thing I must put off for some quieter period.

Nevertheless, I trailed after the Tanaan into the Barrow. Most of them had followed Indech and his torch beyond sight; I walked a little distance inside: watching slivers of sunlight spark in the argentel spirals in the walls, finding myself infected with their awe at this sacred pilgrimage site. As poorly used as the island outside was, all the inlay work here seemed to be intact. A stray sparkle above me caught my eye; I looked up and realized that the spiral inlays stretched right up the walls and across the curve of the ceiling: some larger, some smaller, some spinning left and some spinning right. Some joined at the tails to make three-petaled or nine-petaled whirligigs. All the spiraling sparkles made my head threaten to spin into magic; by the time I regained my sense of the here-and-now I stood alone.

Echoes of men's whispering skittered into the chamber from one of the corridors that stretched back into the cavern. What were they finding back there? I walked carefully into the deepening dark, to the corridor entrance. I spied the faint glow of Indech's torch a little distance within, and followed it down the passage for much longer than the teasing light from the entrance had suggested, fingers trailing against the densely-carved wall in an effort to keep my bearings. I walked as quickly as I could, trying to catch up, but the light ahead dimmed and receded altogether, and finally I was left in utter darkness. Of course they were faster; they had a torch.

Still I pressed on, increasingly curious, keeping my hand on the wall. The wall fell away from my hand: the path had branched again, and I stood in darkness too dense to discern anything but the sounds of my own breath. If I couldn't locate them now, there would be no sensible choice but to turn back. I stretched out my arm and found the wall again, and took two steps down the right-hand corridor, trying to catch some glimpse of the light—and something shifted. Without thinking I opened up arcane senses, trying to understand what I had stepped into; some power I couldn't identify surged around me, and suddenly I felt nothing beneath my feet. Air rushed into my face. Lights flashed at the edges of vision; for half a second everything flared into a black-speckled white inverse of night. Then even the darkness was gone.

Had I been asleep or unconscious? Had I woken? I had the sense that I might have been absent for a second or a year: that, finally, the question of time lapsed was impossible to ask or sensibly answer. No sooner had my sense of my own presence resumed than I wobbled and fell, finding myself on an unadorned stone path through grey-green grass which led to the portico of some great house. The stone of the house's exterior was as grey as the grass, as grey as the sky; the windows looking down on me reflected white like the eyes sometimes seen in the blind. I knew when I looked up I would see no sun, not even a bright spot where I might imagine it lurked behind the clouds; but I craned my neck and scanned the sky anyway. When I returned my gaze to the grey, featureless plain on which I stood, I saw someone looking at me from the doorway: so I walked the little distance to the portico and climbed the steps.

The man in the doorway was Tanaan. His black eyes repeated the void into which I might or might not have recently fallen; no, they were the green-grey of the Ruillin in winter. Usually I could guess whether a Tan's age should be estimated in decades or centuries: with this man, neither was the right unit to use. But the only lines on his face had been created by laughter, and nearly all of those few were around his eyes. His clothing was rich, but it followed no fashion I had ever seen or read of, and every pattern and weave showed grey upon grey upon grey. His bottomless eyes appraised me; he made not even a pretense of a smile.

"What are you doing here?" he said. "You're early; she's not here."

"What?" I said, reflexively, glancing past his shoulder to the interior of the house. The one room I could see was empty even of furniture; the place sounded vacant and smelled of dust.

"You're too early," he repeated, as if I should have some idea what he was talking about.

I shook my head, opening my mouth to protest.

"Look you, don't think I'm unaware of the havoc you intend. I'm telling you: this is not the time."

That was a code, or shorthand: it should have meant something to me. The Tan held my gaze as if waiting for its intended meaning to sink in, watching me with the patience of someone to whom time is of no relevance.

Except, of course, that this was not the time.

"Ah," he said finally. "I see. Never mind, then; time for you to go back. Here—" He produced from some inner pocket of his fancifully-cut coat a flask of cut crystal and unstoppered it. Whatever lay within gleamed greener than emeralds, fractured into a hundred different tones of green behind the facets of the glass. He offered it to me.

"What is this?" I said.

"Good for what ails you," the Tan answered. "Time to go back."

"Is this—" I couldn't think of the phrase in the Tanaan language; I gave up and reached for the arcane term. "...a deoch diarmaid?"

Something that might have become a smile flitted about his mouth and then changed its mind. "A draft of forgetfulness?" He shrugged. "More like a draft of remembrance."

And how could drinking send me back to where I had started, if I correctly understood the rules of such encounters? Wouldn't it, rather, bind me here?

The Tan sighed again. "No. I am not the fool here. Drink."

I did. Some liquor lighter than brandy, richer than wine, carrying the scents and flavors of a dozen separate flowers, flowed through my mouth and down my throat. Suddenly the eyes that met mine were as green as the liquor I had drunk. I blinked—and realized the grey grasses surrounding the house were a garden, my would-be host's clothes were so many colors at once that they should have offended my eyes, and a party that paled any debacle I had yet been involved in was going on in the house behind him. I caught the barest hint of clear blue skies as I collapsed.

I had a much-too-immediate view of rough-hewn basalt. The edges pressed uncomfortably into my face. Now, finally, there was torchlight.

"—on? Ellion! What the hell!" That was Amien. He skidded to a stop beside me, dropped to his knees to peer into my befogged eyes.

I pushed myself onto my side and began formulating a strategy for climbing to my feet. My mouth still tasted of flowers; the heady vapors of the liquor still warmed my throat. Now I could see I lay in the Barrow's entry chamber, not the corridor in which I'd lost my way.

"Where were you? What the hell was that power surge?"

I stared blearily into the wizard's face. I wanted to tell him everything: he was the only person I knew who was likely to understand. I'd almost forgotten the thrill of walking realms beyond the mundane; I couldn't get the statement *You're early; she's not here* out of my head. It rang of purpose, of some truly important mission awaiting me. And gods, I wanted something I did to finally matter, wanted to stop being the one who wrecked things at the critical moment. But I'd seen that look on Amien before: back at Aballo, right around the time the goddess started making public Her interest in me. This time I knew better than to discuss extra-mundane encounters and their meanings.

"What?" I said. "Right here."

Amien shook his head.

"I think I caught a whiff of mine gas," I extemporized. "Maybe you did, too?"

Amien shook his head. "There was definitely something... Something—arcane."

"Hunh," I said, and pushed myself to my feet. Reality performed a little spiral dance; I ground my tongue between my teeth to make it stop. "Isn't it time we—"

"Fouzh," Amien whispered. Even in the torchlight I could see he'd gone pale, and his eyes were on something no one else could see.

"What?" I said softly.

"Letitia," he breathed. "I've lost her. The wards—"

Evidently I was not the only one unable to continue listening. The entire party rushed out of the cavern, scrambled into the saddles. Nuad, Iminor and Tuiri conferred briefly about the most efficient route to the Temple Mount, and then we were galloping southwest down a road as wrecked as the one Letitia had taken. After a moment I realized what we'd forgotten to try.

"Iminor!" I called over the noise of pounding hooves. "Have you tried—" Damn it, what was the Tanaan word for a telepathic sending? "Mindtouch?"

Iminor reined, throwing the party into confusion. Several knights overshot him before bringing their horses to heel. The Tan stared at me.

"How...?"

I was even less interested in discussing this matter than what had happened inside the Barrow. No good would come of them realizing I heard their broadcasts.

I shrugged. "I'm not a fool." That was a lie, of course. "Have you tried?"

Iminor shook his head; his gaze turned on something inside his own head, or something too far away for eyes to see.

Ti? the Tan broadcast. *Letitia? Are you all—*

Im! Letitia's thought was as subtle and unmistakable as the scent of roses on the air. Relief flooded through me; the tension in Iminor's shoulders dissolved. *Where are you?*

On our way to the Outer Path. You?

Just coming out of the sacred spring below the temple. It's all so... I don't know.

Iminor nodded, there in the saddle. *Ti, Amien lost track of you a little while ago. Is everything all right?*

All right as it can be. I'll see you at the— Even through a broadcast not aimed at me, I heard the depth of dread that made it difficult for her to form the thought. *...summit?*

See you there, Iminor broadcast. He turned his eerie blue eyes on me for a long, weighty second, during which I did my utmost to look as tensely curious as the rest of them; finally he looked at the wizard.

"She's all right," he said.

"What happened?" Amien asked.

Iminor shrugged. "Nothing out of the ordinary, as far as I can tell. She'd just bathed in the sacred spring at the temple. Everything—" Amien smacked his own forehead; puzzlement manifested in Iminor's face. "Seemed... fine?"

Amien shook his head. "The spring. The power of the spring must have knocked out her wards. I'll have to rebuild them tonight..." He sighed. "Assuming that's possible here at all."

We started down the road again, more slowly this time. We crossed a broad bridge flanked by low, relief-carved walls, of which entire panels had fallen away. I looked down, but what the space suggested had once been a river of respectable breadth and depth was now a sad furrow of black basalt carrying only a trickle at the very bottom. On the far side stood a once-grand, circular building of pale-pink granite. Carvings of snakes wound up the blasted pillars; the roof had been wrought in the shape of an immense rose, but half of it seemed to have melted away. As one, we reined and stopped, gazing at it. Any temptation to walk inside was quelled by a huge gap running straight from the center of the portico to the gaping door.

"The Precinct of Tiana," Iminor murmured. "I wonder if Her moon-temple stands."

We wouldn't find out today, I knew: that temple is the centerpiece of the island's southern quadrant. Or had been, perhaps. Subdued, the party continued on the southwest road, crossing another barren river-ring to the Precinct of Lys. It hadn't fared any better than its sister. All the structures here were of bluestone where the Precinct of Tiana was pink granite, and all the motifs I saw in Lys's territory spoke of the archer, the owl, and the hunt; but their great goddess had been just as unkind here. Grottoes lay smashed; elaborately-carved stelae canted at insane angles, partially submerged in the basalt. I thought again about what Amien planned to do this evening, and cold gathered inside me.

In the Precinct of the Sun we turned south, onto a road that followed the curve of the all-but-empty river channel. Here, everything was worked of red stone: marble this time. In the Tanaan system, the Sun belongs to the great goddess Dana, but that hadn't spared this precinct Her wrath. In the sun-circle that stands at the entrance to the Temple Mount's Outer Way, five of the fourteen standing stones leaned against one another like men stumbling home from a tavern, three lay smashed across the broad ceremonial road, and two were missing altogether. Most of the capstones lay in surprised tumbles at the circle's edge. We stopped again, and this time Amien slid from the saddle. I sighed and followed suit, and we stood as near the center as fallen stelae would allow, looking around. Westering sunlight sliced between two of the canted stones, casting the wizard's steel-grey hair in gold.

"Great Lord Ilesan," Amien said, in a tone that made it into a prayer for understanding.

I shook my head. "Wrong Person to ask."

"Ah, dear gods, these alignments..." Amien shook his head. "I had hoped—" He waved unsaid words into nonexistence and returned to his horse. I looked past the remains of the ring, to the mountain on which the temple stood, wondering.

I knew what it is to be so angry that rage drives everything, of course. But I also knew that, even when rage pushed my conscious mind to a perch from which it did little more than observe the madness, I never lost the ability to choose my actions. I might do any number of unacceptable things in the name of anger; but even for this mortal, there was no such thing as true loss of control.

Who would do such a thing to Her Own sacred site?

I would get no more answers than Amien, of course. Finally I climbed back into the saddle, and we rode on.

The Outer Way to the temple spirals up the mountain like the inlays in the Barrow. We alternately walked and rode, giving the horses what rest we could; but the long northern day was drawing to a close, and we must reach the summit before it did.

It is one thing to read about a temple being carved straight into the heart of a mountain; another thing entirely to see it, to ride the broad spiral up its exterior that is the least of its wonders. Even in ruins, it robbed me of breath at every turning of the path. I wished I might have another day to walk its corridors, to see the places where the sun can be sighted at known times from any given point within, even in the deepest depths; to watch the constellations climb into the windows created for them and mark the passing hours by their dance. As the northern and eastern sides of the mountain sank into twilight, I spied the lights within the mountain, recognizing the same unreal flameless glow cast by the lamps at Ériu House. Now, finally, I understood what I saw: yet another of the ancient Tanaan's forgotten magics, which still went about its business without any help or attention from those who no longer remembered how it works.

Finally the Outer Way crested the summit. We stopped and dismounted, looking across the shallow platform that capped the mountain. An immense sun-circle of bronze-flecked goldstone had once stood around the now-bare ceremonial ground; the remaining stelae and capstones gleamed against a sky streaked with every possible color of gold, orange, and red. The only thing standing within the wrecked circle was a pale blue-grey stone. I wondered whether it really was the Tuaoh.

If so, it was shorter than I had expected, no taller than me. Veins of brilliant colorless crystal spiraled up its length, catching all the hues of the sunset.

"We'll stay here, outside the circle," Iminor said. He spoke quietly, but somehow his voice carried. Finally I realized how strangely still the air was for a mountaintop. Was this, too, some trick of ancient engineering? "The mora-in-waiting must be the only person to step into the circle until the goddess has had Her say."

"Her say?" Amien said.

"The mora-in-waiting comes up through the Inner Ways and crosses the circle to the Tuaoh Stone," Iminor said. "The stone creates a connection between the mora and the goddess. If the goddess approves the choice, She gives a sign."

"Such as?" I found myself speaking just as softly as they.

Iminor shrugged. "The Stone has been known to hum. Sometimes it's just that everyone on the summit feels Her Presence and approval. For one mora—Boanna of Fáill, it might have been—the Tuaoh's veins began to glow."

There seemed to be a great deal of room for interpretation, especially if the sun hit the stone just right. Iminor nodded as if he'd heard the thought.

"This is the same type of stone the central shaft of the Gáe Assail is wrought of," he said. "There are stories of the core glowing through the cutwork on the housing, when the Spear was well-wielded by a mora in battle…" He cast a questioning glance at the wizard, who nodded thoughtfully, eyes on the putative Tuaoh Stone.

Was the stone magically responsive, then, like the crystals that are the hearts of flash-weapons? Might it, too, store and then release energies on command? In a certain respect, the stones at any sacred site can be thought of in that way; but now I began to suspect this was a more powerful or at least a more responsive stone than flash-crystal. Were the effects in the Tanaan histories the results of true interventions by their goddess, or just tricks of magically-knowledgeable women? If there were some trick to it, how could a Tana born long after a prohibition on magic be expected to have the knack?

On the other hand, if their goddess were not actually involved, whatever its innate power, the stone should be safe for Amien to use to launch a dream-sending to Sanglin.

I couldn't decide whether to hope for the Presence of their goddess to bless Letitia's candidacy, or not.

Suddenly Letitia was there, stepping out of some alcove to our left, walking slowly up the steps to the platform. She was dressed like a mora again, in a simple but elegant gown of white silk. Sunset light illuminated her unbound, golden hair, tangled in the torc at her throat. Easca, Tru, and Bruane clustered in the doorway behind her. Everything was quiet as she crossed the platform and stopped in front of the stone. Finally, after an interminable second, she stretched out a hand to touch it.

Nothing happened.

My heart ached for her: I couldn't have named a greater pain than rejection by one's goddess, unless it was suffering that rejection in public. I must find some quiet moment to tell her my theory about the operation of the stone: that this might not be about her malevolent goddess at all.

After a moment that stretched until I could barely control the impulse to intervene, she withdrew her hand, tilted her head back to look at the sky. I stole a glance around the summit, seeing puzzled analysis in Amien, heart-wrenching pain in Iminor, quiet horror in most of the knights—and a strange stillness in Easca. Unexpectedly Easca caught my gaze; she flushed and looked away.

"Right, so," Letitia said finally in a thready voice, spun on her heel, and walked back across the platform towards the door to the Inner Way.

"By your leave, Mora…?" Amien said quietly.

Her head whipped around in his direction, astonishment displayed in her face.

"I should try to get a message to my second," he finished.

She nodded curtly and stepped down to the narrow margin around the sun-circle; Amien drew a deep breath and walked to the stone.

I had never attempted a dream-sending from anyplace but Aballo, and then only as a training exercise; nevertheless I knew the drill. Amien proceeded exactly as I had been taught, settling himself in a meditative posture with his head and back against the stone and his eyes on the setting sun, removing his mind from ordinary consciousness and entering the trance-state of aisling, which is the most effective for sending a dream. I couldn't have guessed at the dream-sending's precise content: nasclethéana tend to develop shorthands that serve them from the ceremonial circle to the dreams they send one another when apart. But I knew the intended message: *Relay to Brinner, House Healer to High Chief Rohini of the Essuvians: Amien asks the High Chief to meet him and the Lady of Finias at Goibniu, eight nights hence.*

When he stretched out his awareness to encompass the stone, I felt it, a tingle against the edges of my awareness and a flavor of lightning on the air. I'd been wrong: if there were a trick to using the stone, this operation should have set it glowing or humming. I felt Amien's mind wrap around the stone, felt the way he called its power into himself so he could bounce it back out to the aether as a sending strong enough to reach a wizard at the other end of the world. Suddenly a pulsing, blue-lightning flavor blanketed the mountaintop, and Amien was slumping to the ground.

I had never heard of an earth-power nexus too strong for a fully-trained wizard, but it seemed clear: he was overwhelmed by this one. This wasn't that gentle upside-down power I kept tasting in the Tanaan lands, but something huge and raw. I shouted, but Amien didn't hear me; without further thought I bolted up the steps and across the ceremonial platform, throwing my consciousness between Amien and the stone, making myself into a wedge that might wrench them apart.

Something started to hum.

I reached the stone; I leaned down, scooped up the wizard, turned back the way I had come. He was lighter, wirier than I expected; the hum seemed to be coming up through the soles of my boots. It filled my ears, escalating to a roar like a cannon; all the hair on my arms and the back of my neck stood at attention. It was exactly like the split-second between tapping into a stormcloud and bringing the lightning to ground.

I swore and ran, racing off the platform and ducking Amien behind one of the remaining stelae. As suddenly as it had started, the roaring stopped; the lightning gathering on the mountaintop dissipated. I brought the wizard to the ground as quickly and gently as possible, knelt beside him, laid an ear against his chest. His heart beat wildly, echoing in my throat. His skin was far too pale.

"My lord?" I said. "Amien!"

He didn't seem to hear; I sent a thin thread of consciousness into his. His mind still echoed with the preternatural roar.

When it came to telepathy, Amien was deaf as a twenty-year-old dog. There was probably no point in trying to send him composed thoughts. But some part of his rattled mind was aware of my presence; he stirred, there on the ground. I smoothed a hand against his hair.

"There, now," I said softly, mind still half in his. "All is well. Breathe, and come back."

His eyelids fluttered; he startled into consciousness, nearly launching himself to his feet. I laid a hand on his shoulder, holding him fast.

"A moment, my lord," I said. "Do you know where you are?"

He shook his head slowly, there on the ground. "I dreamed—" He drew in a surprised breath. "Fouzh. I'm here. That was… I'm not sure the message got through."

"Perhaps we'll try again at the Nemetona on the Black," I said gently.

He nodded. The color was returning to his face.

"It *is* the Tuaoh," he said. "On Hy-Breasaíl, it used to roar. You've read Pirtanien?"

Oh, damn, I had. Before they moved the stone during the Fall of Hy-Breasaíl, before it took on the name *Lia of Fáilias* and evidently lost its voice, the god-stone's recognition of the righ had been marked by a sound described as a dragon's roar. Finally I realized the Tanaan weren't so much watching Amien as staring at me.

Dear gods, would this day never end? How many ways would the hideous gods of this place find to torment me? It was nothing but a tease, to dangle righship in front of me in the Tanaan lands.

Still, that sad part of me who would perform any feat necessary to return to the place that should have been mine: he was ready to leap at the chance, ready to imagine a scenario in which the first righ of the Tanaan in millennia might be elected ard-righ at Teamair. I wanted to knock my head against the stone beside me. Gods, I was a fool!

I shook my head: it started out directed at Amien, but after the first shake I was shaking my skull at the whole ridiculous situation.

"There were several different stones that were claimed to be the Tuaoh after the Fall," I reminded him. "The Lia of Fáilias was only the best known."

He just gave me a quizzical look.

"My lord, I'd like nothing better than to get you off this summit," I said, changing the subject. "Can you walk with me to the Inner Way?"

The wizard smiled. I'd seen that look before, too. I still wanted to knock my head against a stone.

Chapter 15
In the Abode of Immortals

The interior of the temple yet retained the exquisite design and delicate carving I'd read about—where it wasn't crumbling into heaps of debris. We camped for the night in the topmost chamber, surrounded by an arcade of windows situated to frame the zodiacal constellations as they performed their nightly dance. An open, circular hearth at the center of the round would have provided warmth, had there been wood available. The group clustered around it anyway, faces illumined by the ancient arcane lamps, gnawing on jerky and hardtack and swapping stories about what they'd seen on their sacred isle. Amien allowed himself to be persuaded that rebuilding Letitia's wards might wait until he'd slept, and curled into his bedroll in a shadowed corner. Letitia picked up her pack, announced her intention to meditate, and walked down the stairs leading to the next level. Every time I looked up from the horse-tack I was feigning to clean, I heard some conversation abruptly cease, found some Tanaan knight pretending he or she hadn't been staring at me.

"Well, then," I said when frustration began making my hand itch for my sword. "I spent years reading about the structures of this temple. I'm going to go see how much of what I read was true." I climbed to my feet, nodded to the group, and walked down the staircase opposite the one Letitia had used.

At first I just paced, trying to outrun the anger. Gradually the bubbling ire quieted, and it became possible to pretend I was in this place alone. I began to truly see the galleries I traversed. Tales I wavered on the verge of identifying marched, danced, flew, and battled their ways along the inner walls, facing down the arcades that opened on the stars. Ancient arcane lights concealed behind columns and places less obvious bathed the crumbling frescoes on the ceilings with crisp, unforgiving illumination. The galleries sloped almost imperceptibly downward; gracefully curving staircases eased more abrupt transitions. Every so often, an arcade opened into an alcove, creating a space like a balcony that might have been intended for meditation or simple, pleasant stargazing. In one such alcove I discovered Letitia.

"Sweet Lady Tella!" I blurted, unaccountably startled.

Her head jerked upward; for several seconds she stared up at me from her seat on the floor. As the pounding of my heart slowed, I took in what I should have seen immediately: she had changed back into her travel clothes and re-plaited her hair. The enchanted gem that had once belonged to Carina dangled between her hands, catching and fracturing the white-golden light of the lamps. Gradually it dawned on me that I must be the last person she wanted to see this evening.

"Your pardon, Mora," I said quietly, offered her a brief bow, and turned to retreat. I would find my own alcove in which to hide. If only someone had thought to pack a skin or three of brandy.

"What happened in the Barrow this afternoon?" she said, forestalling me.

Oh, damn. "What?"

She cast me a glance that left no doubt she saw through the pretense of confusion. "I've been hearing some interesting tales. You found the Lady's Underground Ways? Or was it the House of Donn?"

"Dear gods," I sighed. "I caught a whiff of mine-gas. I suspect Amien did, too. Maybe some of the knights, as well, if you're hearing stories like that."

She stared at me for an uncomfortably long time. I returned the gaze without knowing why.

"Who are you, Ellion Tellan?" she said.

I had sung this moment in a dozen songs. Bizarre to be standing in the middle of it. I knew my lines; I was to confess the truth of everything: the way the goddess Called me from Tellan to Aballo, the hundred ways She publicly marked me for Her own, the twelvenights Amien spent trying to persuade me to stay on after my initiate, his obsession with my succeeding him to the Prince's throne despite the fact that the stars marked me for ard-righ. Letitia's lines were equally inevitable; but the redemption they offered would be nothing but lies.

I manufactured a laugh. "There's a question for the sages."

She stared at me.

Finally I shrugged, spreading my hands. "I am what you see. A man with a penchant for wrecking things who managed to get thrown out of his own country. A professional liar, as all harpists are. Someone who would be more than he is."

She looked abruptly down, at the dangling diamond. "Wouldn't we all."

I took a step towards her. I knew it was a mistake, but my feet seemed to have an agenda of their own. "You are the mora of Fíana."

Her head snapped up again; she fixed me with the gaze of a wounded she-wolf. "Really? On whose authority? You, who the Stone acknowledges? Who the goddess—" Her voice vanished; she glanced away, towards the stars.

I stepped across the gallery, leaned against the relief on the inner wall. The visage of some immortal or avatar I didn't recognize crumbled at the contact; I straightened hastily.

"The goddess has no great love for me," I said evenly.

Letitia gave voice to a humorless laugh, face still turned towards the night. *She will take my blood and leave my bones for the crows,* she thought; my throat closed. I fought down the impulse to contradict her. It took me longer than it should have to come up with a different approach.

"I don't put too much stock in what happened up there," I said finally. "Amien didn't realize... Letitia, there are half a dozen different stones that are claimed to be the Tuaoh. Amien didn't know what he was tapping."

Letitia glanced at me again. "Are you asking me to believe the goddess doesn't speak through the Stone?"

This was dangerous territory: I shook my head quickly. "I'm suggesting that some things the Tuaoh... does on its own, maybe. That arcane manipulation might yield unexpected results."

"So the Stone recognizes you, but you think the goddess doesn't?"

This way lay madness. "I'm suggesting the Stone's behavior may have less to do with my presence or anyone else's than with what Amien was doing." I wished my heart believed it; I hoped she did. "And that you are the mora of Fíana, but—well, maybe there are things you need to do before your investiture."

A split-second's image burst forth from her mind and washed past me: the interior of a trunk, a jumble of metal buried beneath jewel-encrusted robes.

"Yes," Letitia breathed, relaxing suddenly against the wall. "There are things I need to do." Just as abruptly her spine tensed again, and a frown creased her face. She looked at the necklace for a long moment; the pendant swung, winking in the arcane light. I wondered about the intent of the spell or spells Amien had wrought on it, about its intended use. *It isn't a weapon,* he'd said at Dianann. *But rather... a tool.*

"I need to become the mora Fíana requires," Letitia said to the stone.

Sudden, unexpected pride for her shot through me.

"I have been a child," she continued, eyes still on the diamond. "I had thought simply being, and the little services I perform for the Holy Mora... that they were enough. That it was reasonable to rely on others to protect me, to attend to all the things beyond those little responsibilities in my behalf." She looked up at me again. "I need to become the mora my mother was, and her mother."

I fought off the smile warring for control of my mouth. "I would say you've gone a very long way down that path already."

Letitia blew out a little, dismissive breath, almost smiling. She folded the necklace into one fist and fixed me with an analytical stare. Her eyes caught the arcane light, rippling with a glow of gold; something nameless skipped up my spine, and for the first time in days I saw the alien priestess in her, the avatar of some goddess far more benevolent than the One she served. This was a mora anyone would follow, a being whose gaze could illuminate the innermost reaches of a man. The habitual shields I held around myself dissolved.

"Tell me true, Ellion Tellan," she said; and though the Tanaan do not practice sorcery anymore, I felt the words as a binding on me. "Would you be mor?"

My breath knotted in my throat, blocking the lie I should have told. I was powerless against the need to look away.

"Yes," I said softly to the stars beyond the alcove. "But not of Fíana."

"Ahhh," Letitia breathed.

I swallowed. My throat was still impassably tight.

"In that case, there is something I would ask of you," she continued after a moment.

Again I faltered, and hated myself for the weakness. Finally I summoned the will to meet her eyes.

"Teach me what a mora should know of warfare," she said. "I must learn to contribute to my own defense; I must be able to make decisions and to see when my advisors are wrong. I'm not so foolish—" Her voice caught. "As to imagine that I can persuade you to serve me always. Though I know I would already be dead ten times over, were you not here."

"You want to learn strategy?" I said.

"And I must be competent with the sword," she answered.

That was a lost cause. I knew without crossing my blade with hers that she would never be able to defeat a competent warrior. I should restrict what I attempted with her to defensive tactics.

But that, of course, was a prior admission of defeat. No tactic, however clever and safe, can serve a warrior past the point of exhaustion. The only true defense is winning.

I inclined my head. "Mora Letitia Ériu a Fíana, I will teach you all I can in the time we have together. Strategy you will have ample opportunity to learn along the way, and it will be my pleasure to instruct you. Weapons training will be for evenings, or other times of safety and rest. But—"

"Ellion—"

"But," I said again. "You will agree to remain behind the lines or within the formation during engagements, and let your knights do their work."

She sagged like an airship with the fire extinguished. "While they continue to bear all the risk."

"To do otherwise puts them at greater risk," I rejoined.

"And when I am competent?" she said.

If, I thought. *A very great If.* "When you are competent, then we will decide together how to deploy your resources. Mora Letitia Ériu a Fíana, I offer you my service under these terms."

She gazed at me in silence for a moment. Still I saw the priestess in her, and tried again to steel myself against the impulse to surrender.

"Lord Ellion Tellan, holder of secrets, speaker of none, I accept your offer. You will have my devotion to your tutelage, my trust, my gratitude, and any other boon you would name." She glanced away. "But one."

"That boon I would never ask," I said softly. "I know too well what it would cost."

"That I believe, my lord," she said, just as softly.

This time, finally, I had the presence of mind to protect the reputation of the Tana with whom I'd found myself alone. I sent Letitia back to the temple's topmost chamber ahead of me, reasoning she was the one whose protracted absence would raise concerns. By the time I returned to the chamber, most of the knights were asleep, and Letitia already lay curled in her bedroll. She met my eyes as I walked in, calmer than I could recall ever seeing her, then collapsed almost instantly into sleep. I unpacked my bedroll and settled in an empty patch near the door.

From this angle, the Tuaoh was a massive, grey-on-grey silhouette against the stars. The stones of the sun-circle around it glistened in the moonlight, their golden hue faded almost white by the moons. The impulse arose in me, fey and nearly irresistible, to walk out into that space again, to see what would happen. It took me a very long time to fall asleep.

Chapter 16
Living with the Loss

Amien had been right: inside the temple at Ilunmore, he couldn't raise power that made any sense to him. He couldn't rebuild Letitia's wards. I surprised myself with a desperate itch to try; I wanted to see if I could hold my mind in a way that could accommodate the energies in this space. I had the sense that, if I surrendered to what they were rather than trying to force them to be what any Aballo wizard would expect, I might be able to work with them.

Amien might well be, too. But the man who told the Prince of the Order how to conduct a working could hope for no better outcome than a challenge to try it himself. I kept my mouth and my mind firmly closed.

In the Precinct of the Consort, Amien tried again. He and Letitia withdrew to a sheltered spot while I tried to ignore the reason why. The privacy was at least as much for her as for him: the crafting of personal wards is a working that must be performed with the subject nude. I tried to study one of the ever-present stelae, tried to absorb the tale of Endeáril's wooing of the goddess Dana. I couldn't help thinking about what it would be to let my hands hover within a hair's breadth of her skin, to trace all the curves and angles of her form starting from her bare feet to the crown of her unbound hair, to feel the energies unwind themselves against my fingers and palms and direct them into a net of safety around her. After the third time I lost track of the thread of the tale of Endeáril and the goddess, I gave up and walked to the shore, and watched the white foam race into oblivion against the rocks. I felt each attempt Amien made, felt the repeated blooms of upside-down power I just knew a wizard could work with if he would accept the way they must be romanced rather than forced; in short order the ideas of seducing arcane energies and Letitia unclothed got irretrievably tangled in my head, and I couldn't so much as look at her when Amien finally gave up and they returned.

"We'll try again at Uriah," he growled by way of greeting. I nodded, and we returned to the ship.

Back on board, we headed south, manning the sails under Indech's direction as Amien provided the wind. For a couple hours, the isle of Ilunmore slid past to our west; the stelae tracing the Way of Endeáril kept pace with our flight, barely visible across the water. Then, abruptly, we passed beyond the southern edge of the isle, and we were on open water again.

I felt no anticipation for reaching the shore today; landing would mean our respite from Básghilae attacks was over, and we must endure seven days before we might hope to meet reinforcements. The faces of the Tanaan displayed unease at least as great as my own; only Indech smiled.

He planned to ride back to Arian, I learned: the ship was not one a man might sail alone. But now that he had proven it possible, he expected to recruit other sailing men of Arian, planned to begin learning the ways of the old ships and exploring the shores of the Devadore to see if any of the western Tanaan survived. I wondered whether trade might once again become possible for the Tanaan, and smiled to think of Letitia's being the reign under which their faltering nation blossomed again. But I left Indech to hatch the plan for himself and turned to scan the horizon for the approach of land, dread turning in my chest.

Eventually, inevitably, we landed, at the edge of another demolished marina. The once-great city of Uriah, the former Banbagor winter capital, spread in wrecks and tumbles along the shore, mercilessly illumined by a perversely brilliant late-afternoon sun. The only thing standing within eyesight was a sun-circle just beyond the edge of the marina, which seemed improbably intact. Onshore wind sent the tail of my hair fluttering forward. Something inside me sank as the gangway dropped onto the broken stones of the dock.

"Zhev," Iminor muttered.

I turned to look; I hadn't realized he stood beside me at the rail. His mouth twisted in approximation of a grin; he manufactured a laugh.

"Sorry," he said quietly. "Just nerves. I was getting used to feeling safe."

I shrugged. "A common sentiment."

I looked at the sun-circle again, curious. The stones weren't as tall as the ones on Ilunmore: man-height, no taller. There were no capstones: this must be a very old circle. But the stones seemed precisely-shaped, at least from here. And they were dark-hued, which intrigued me. I collected my horse and coaxed him down the gangway, then left him to nibble at the green things peeking up through the broken ground of the shore. I wanted a closer look at the sun-circle. Iminor and a few of the knights followed me, discussing the strange color of the stones; abruptly Iminor gave voice to a hiss of distaste, murmured something about seeing Letitia settled and turned back towards his horse. After a moment the rest of them followed.

My curiosity was undiminished. Red-streak basalt is an unusual choice for a sun-circle, true; but now that I had seen one in basalt, I wondered why no one ever builds them so. It seemed to me the perfect medium. Bright daylight erased any separation between the stones and the long shadows they cast: one flowed seamlessly into the other. I had never seen a better statement of the essential union of light and dark, that truth so deep few even among wizards are prepared to entertain it. After a moment I realized the perfection with which this stone revealed that concept might well be the explanation.

The circle seemed to be situated for a western entrance: I walked around to the far side and stood for a long moment looking at the stones. The carvings were less weathered than I expected. I noticed Amien standing beside me.

"Strange what stands and what falls, isn't it?" he mused uneasily. I nodded and stepped into the circle, hearing him follow.

The air in here was different: my throat tightened at the wild, dark energies in this space. If danger had a smell, this was it: delights that mundane senses would never experience knocked at the edges of my awareness, begging for me to open up and let them in. Some small, sane sector of my mind observed a second, broader ring of sighting-stones spaced at intervals a short distance away and automatically began cataloging the dates they must mark. Meanwhile my boundaries were melting; I couldn't quite remember how to hold myself closed. I thought I saw one of the stones move, and turned.

Just in time to see it melt into human form.

"Fouzh!" I spat, hardly aware of speaking. I glanced around: Amien and I now stood surrounded by naked, armed Básghilae. Between the inner and outer circles, most of the Tanaan were already scrambling into their saddles; Letitia shouted at Indech, pulled him up behind her saddle as seconds stretched into improbable distance and the knights encircled her. I found myself drawing automatically back-to-back with Amien, discovered my hands occupied by my sword and knife, and wondered remotely at how easily I had shifted into the fighting habits of the Order. The circle of Básghilae closed around us; Nuad shouted for the knights to focus on Letitia rather than taking the bait Amien and I had become; arcane consciousness wrapped itself around me, unbidden. It was a thing I should not allow.

"Start with the Bow?" Amien said evenly.

Just the same the shift was necessary. Men everywhere believe the wizards of the Order hold fighting secrets they do not share; the truth is the esoteric disciplines feed the military ones, flowing one into the other like basalt stelae and the shadows they cast. In battle the Forms become fighting postures; expanded consciousness allows two men standing back to back to fight as one. Neither of us would survive this encounter if I didn't allow the shift.

And after all, how many times had I found my mind open to the arcane senses lately without doing any harm? I could do it one more time.

"Perfect," I said, much more calmly than I felt. I had settled into the position even before he suggested it. But I couldn't allow myself to wonder at that non-coincidence; the Básghilae were on us and training had taken over. My blades sang in my hands; Amien and I danced together, from the Bow to the Phoenix to the Crane and on into forms I hadn't executed in years. It should have frightened me how fast it all came back; it should have served as a warning, the onset of that glowing feeling of near-union with a partner in the Work; all I knew was the way we covered one another's blind spots, the way I parried, feinted, double-engaged for him and he for me was the closest a mortal can expect to come to the union all of us seek.

And I accepted it as one more inevitability when I looked across my blade to the Básghil I had engaged, and saw behind the ghoul's dead eyes his maker. Finally I saw how he watched me, whoever he was: how this whole thing had started with Letitia and expanded into something that would become about him and me. How little difference there was between us, in the final analysis—except, some hideous voice inside me suggested, for the fact that he had thrown off his chains.

I had only to choose, and I could be the same. Instead I took the Básghil's head. But when I engaged the next ghoul, the same awareness lay behind his eyes.

"Fine," I heard myself say. "Fouzhir fine." Amien's blade swept into the space between us, parrying the stroke he was right to fear I'd miss. I compensated for the opening he'd left on his off side with my sword, slowing the rushing blade just enough for his slashing counterattack. We shifted a step to the left, as one, turning on an unseen axis. The pleasure of it caught me again.

"Come get me, then," I said to the man behind the ghoul, and allowed near-union with Amien to encompass me once more. The dance took me; the Básghilae became one more fact, like terrain and the direction of the blazing sun, that influenced the steps and forms and strokes Amien and I chose, and I avoided their eyes. I was surprised and oddly disappointed when they disengaged and withdrew.

For a moment Amien and I just stood, back to back with our fists full of weapons, in the midst of a macabre circle of headless men; the remaining Básghilae rushed away to the southwest and all but disappeared behind dilapidated buildings and the blinding, nearly horizontal glare of the sun. Automatically I tallied the Tanaan: they were all in the saddles, still in a full crown formation with Letitia and Indech at the center, breathless and flushed; headless corpses littered the ground around them. The unreasonable, soaring joy of a battle well-fought swept over me. Amien and I glanced over our shoulders at one another, still moving simultaneously—and simultaneously laughed. That took me, too: we laughed loud and long, throwing our arms around one another with blades still in hand while the Tanaan stared at us from their saddles.

"Dear gods, it's been too long!" I said without thinking.

"Yes," Amien said, meeting my eyes. And in one of those moments in which shared arcane awareness is very nearly a substitute for telepathy, I saw all his anger and resentment melt away, saw him return to a place in which his student would become his successor and all his desires for the future would be answered by the fact of my presence. And for that moment, all I wanted was to give him everything for which we both yearned. But then I remembered, and wrenched myself into ordinary consciousness.

He understood, of course; we were too enmeshed for him to do otherwise. He turned away; we sheathed our weapons and picked our ways out of the circle of dead men. Longing for things I would never have wrapped heavy chains around my heart.

We made our goodbyes with Indech and rode south through the rubble-choked streets of Uriah, looking for a place in which we could camp securely for the night. Indech would be perfectly safe from Básghilae, of course: the danger followed us. In two days he would be home, beginning to pursue his dreams; we would be someplace in the wilds of Banbagor or Muir, trying to remain alive. But I knew better than to cast my mind too far forward in the midst of a siege: I turned my attention to the problem of shelter for the night.

I had already decided that a place which must be warded would not do: that we would take watches tonight, and Amien must be allowed to rest. But I had not yet discussed it with him, and he still wasn't looking at me. There were too many unsaid words between us for something so mundane to get through. I left him and Nuad at the front of the party as we rode out, and dropped back to the rear. To my surprise Letitia reined and fell in beside me.

"Well," she said without preamble. "What should I have learned?"

That no matter why I engage in arcane awareness, I will find some way to bollocks things up, I wanted to say.

"What did you observe?" I said instead.

"That was a trap," she said thoughtfully. "The Bard's Wizard had set things up long before we arrived."

"Yes," I said.

"He knew where we would land," she continued.

"That wasn't hard to predict. The only sensible destination from Ilunmore is the Muir Pass."

Letitia nodded, digesting this.

"But it was a very good trap," I said. "Worse than that, actually. It was diabolical."

She cast me an inquiring glance.

"He could easily predict where we'd land today," I elaborated. "And where we'll be going. Concealing the Básghilae so we would step away from the safe ground of the ship into a place in which they could overwhelm us was a good strategy, and though we've seen that before, we weren't exactly on guard for it, were we?"

She shook her head. "We should have been, though."

"How?" I said. "If we start suspecting that everything, everywhere, actually conceals Básghilae, we're just going to start spooking ourselves. We'll be doing his work for him. We need to be vigilant—which, if you'll notice, your knights were. We need to be ever ready, all the way to—" Unexpectedly my throat tightened. "Aballo. But you don't want to wear your knights out jumping at shadows. Nuad has them tuned to just the right level of awareness."

Letitia cast me a thoughtful look, then nodded.

"What was difficult about this ambush—give points to our enemy on this one—"

She turned a look of frank horror on me; I shrugged.

"Letitia, respecting your enemy is the first principle of warfare. I don't like his objective, and I find his methods horrifying, but beyond that I've got to respect his strategic ability. If I get emotional about it, I'm going to make mistakes born of emotion. Keeping emotion out of it can be hard on the battlefield, but there's no excuse for failing to do it when we're just talking about strategy."

Letitia gave me a long, troubled look. "I don't know if I can be that cold," she said finally.

Her words landed like an unexpected blow. It took everything I had to avoid showing how they rocked me. Me, cold? My greatest fault lay in how very many things could make me *feel*, in how often I failed to control my responses. I glanced around, assessing possible campsites and reassuring myself that the Básghilae were not staging a second ambush in these streets, to give myself time to sound calm.

"I'm not asking you to be cold," I said finally. "Just to remember that your enemy is a real, intelligent man—very intelligent—and that everything he does makes sense. And if you can engage the discipline necessary to study what he does and how, you can learn things about him that you can use to develop your own strategy. I can tell you he's doing that very thing with us."

She drew in a swift, dismayed breath.

"This is what I'm talking about," I elaborated. "Concealing the Básghilae under shapeshifting and illusions is a sensible, even predictable, tactic. What made his use of those techniques terrible, and excellent, is how well he tailored what he did to *us*."

Fear widened her eyes; I began to doubt the wisdom of speaking military truth with her. But I had given my word.

"Our enemy chose to conceal his forces in a way that was guaranteed to draw us closer," I said. "Any wizard—or scholar," I amended quickly, sudden panic rising at how close I had come to revealing myself, "could be counted on to find an intact sun circle in the Danaan lands… as irresistible as a salt lick in winter. Of course we would draw close."

Letitia nodded.

"What was diabolical about that trap was the circular arrangement, which was everything we thought we expected—and which very quickly had Amien and me pinned. He drew us all in, then separated the most experienced warriors from the rest of the party—and, what's worse, we became bait he then used to try to draw your knights away from protecting you."

Now she was growing pale.

"Nuad handled that beautifully," I said quickly. And fortunately it was true. But any temptation I felt to discuss the truly horrific level of intelligence our enemy had about us died. And the subtexts I'd read in the attack were beyond discussing—with anyone.

Because if the primary objective of that attack had been the expected one, our enemy now had a well-defined secondary objective: me. He had read me like a text in a library, and we still knew nothing about him. No one builds sun-circles of red-streak basalt; but I had found it irresistible. Any sane wizard would have taken one whiff of the energies in that space and backed away; instead I wanted more. If I had glimpsed him through the eyes of his Básghilae, today and during that engagement on the Arian shore, he'd been studying me for far longer; and he was undeceived by the lengths to which I went to conceal my Aballo past. I was the chink in Letitia's armor.

Protests flared inside me, as if there were someone present with whom I might argue. Letitia needed me: not only my blade but my expertise. They would never successfully order their battles without me.

But I looked ahead, down the line of warriors, and I knew that wasn't true: not anymore. Though unready to lead an army, Nuad had firm command of unit tactics now; and the Tanaan had become a unit. One in which, against all odds, women functioned as full members. Letitia's coverage was sparse; she still needed reinforcements. But whether I constituted an asset or a liability to this party was an open question, because our enemy had learned my greatest weaknesses; and he understood what drove me well enough to use my failings to draw me in. Because there was something inside me that was essentially the same as something inside him.

From now on, it must be counted on that he could trap me, and I would not even see where the blinds lay until I had stumbled into them. My only hope—Letitia's only hope—was for me to avoid arcane awareness, to stay away from anything that sparked arcane desires. Those were the things he knew he could use against me. I couldn't allow that to happen again.

"So what's the lesson?" Letitia asked.

I reeled with the impossibility of discussing it. Then I remembered: she was talking about the simpler problem.

"What do you think?" I said. For a while she was silent. The sounds of hooves on broken paving alternately echoed and muffled against buildings in various stages of collapse. Somewhere ahead in the line, another conversation too subdued for me to follow threaded between the hoof-falls. Ruddy sunlight cut nearly horizontal paths between the buildings, splitting the world into strips of brilliance and expanses of shadow.

"Learn as much as you can about your enemy, so you can tailor your attacks?" Letitia ventured finally.

I met her eyes and nodded.

Pride at having gotten it right sent a smile breaking across her lovely face; then, abruptly, the implications of the lesson crystallized visibly for her, and she stiffened.

"He's miles ahead of us," she said softly.

"Yes," I said. "What's worse, it really is true: there's no question he can see us during attacks, through the ghouls. He's learning more about us with every engagement."

"We need to learn more about him," Letitia murmured.

I nodded again. And then I realized the best way to do that was through arcane methods, and cold settled over me.

Several minutes passed in silence broken only by the sounds of horses' hooves and the wind moaning in shattered buildings. Then the road we traveled widened into a broad square. To one side, near a broad expanse of mixed rubble and eerily graceful architecture I suspected had been the Banbagor winter palace, stood a tower perhaps three or four stories in height. As a written language Danaan comes to me only with difficulty, but I astonished myself by instantly absorbing the sigils that marked the tower's exterior. Half a second later I realized that was exactly what I saw: sigils, glyphs of arcane language and intent. I reined, astonished, just in time to see Amien, at the front of the line, finally do more than glance at the tower and rein as well. The rest of the party straggled to a stop.

"Well, this looks likely," Nuad said cheerfully.

Ah, no. I knew what I saw: a sun-tower dedicated to gods that predate the Tanaan Transition, the original gods of Hy-Breasaíl. I wondered whether the Tanaan who lived here at the time of the Deluge had any recollection of the original dedication of this monument; and I itched to walk its every yard, to unravel the spells that had gone into its stunningly-crafted masonry. It was exactly the sort of thing I now knew I should avoid.

"Fouzhir hell," Amien said. He glanced at me and immediately away. I felt my face flush.

"What?" Letitia said to me, as if I had seen a revelation of the goddess in some household object.

"A sun-tower," I breathed.

"Yes?" she pursued.

I shook my head. I couldn't figure out where to start.

At the other end of the line, Amien shook his head, too. "No. We can't use this. No way will I be able to raise power here."

"My lord, there are plenty of us here for watches."

The words had come out of my mouth. I felt my lips and tongue move. But I had no recollection of deciding to speak. I should be arguing vigorously in favor of any other campsite, should spend the rest of the evening pretending I had never read those sigils.

"Absolutely," Nuad said brightly. Mixed dread and excitement leapt in me. "Lord Amien, you should rest tonight. We have no guarantee we'll find places we can protect with arms alone for the rest of the journey."

Damned if he hadn't absorbed every word I'd ever spoken in his presence. There was no arguing with his logic.

"But I also need to work personal wards—" Amien began, guilty relief spreading across his equine visage.

"Choose any other space," Nuad said. Pleased, half-surprised confidence rang in his voice. "We will hold it while you work. And then you will have a night of rest."

The Bard's Wizard wouldn't attack again tonight: the fact was too obvious to even mention. Tonight he marshalled his forces; he never risked an engagement with even odds. Where his next force enhancement would come from I couldn't guess; but I knew we would see no more of the Básghilae until those reinforcements arrived. Didn't that mean I could afford to enjoy the wholly unanticipated miracle of an intact Hy-Breasaílian sun tower?

"I will take the parapet," I said. And while I kept half an eye on the horizon, I would see the stars as the ancient Danaan had. I was not altogether certain I would seek relief at the second watch. Neither was I certain I should be allowed to remain with the party. But I ached to walk into that tower the way a life-long drunk wants another drink.

Amien looked at his horse's ears, a guilty smile stealing across his lips. "So be it. Mora, I saw a little walled garden perhaps a block ago..." He cast her an inquiring look; she glanced at me and nodded.

"Easca and Tru, with us," Nuad said crisply. "Lord Iminor, will you ride with us or help the others secure the tower?"

Iminor gave him a thoughtful look, then turned a speculative gaze on me. "I go with my lady," he said to Nuad.

The six of them turned their horses and rode back down the battered street. I dismounted, and the knights who had remained with me followed; we set about unburdening our horses and seeing to their care. As the sun sank towards the horizon, I walked the perimeter of the tower, telling myself it was my duty to ensure it was as safe as we all surmised. But the shadows of ancient spells in the spaces between the stones commandeered my attention, and the sigils of protection and dedication to gods Whose names I didn't recognize but Whose faces flitted across my mind robbed me of any hope of focus.

By the time I had completed the circuit around the tower, I had deduced the hours and heavenly objects the windows were intended to frame, but I had far too little sense of the lie of the spaces around the structure. I thought it stood sufficiently separate for the watches to spot any approach on foot, although I had the nagging sense that several of the windows would be vulnerable to bowshots from the ruined palace. But I couldn't give the problem the attention it deserved. I sent Ogma, the best archer, to make the same circuit and deliver his own assessment; his eyes sparked as if he'd been singled out for some privilege, but I knew the truth: the party needed someone whose mind was focused to do what I had failed. Nevertheless my heart beat faster yet as I climbed the cracked stairs to the narrow door and stepped inside.

Chill lay on the stones of the interior, but wondrous mosaics decorated the floor and adorned a ceiling that soared astonishingly high above. Tiny tiles of gleaming orichalus had once spanned the impossible height of the walls; even now enough of them remained for me to sense how the chamber must once have glowed. I stepped into the wide-open circle, feeling as if I floated between the images above and below rather than having any sense of connection with the earth. Something I couldn't identify drew me to walk the stair that spiraled dizzily up the interior of the wall and through the ceiling to the second floor.

The setting sun cast this space in a blaze of ruddy gold. Even after all this time, memories of centuries of arcane activity shimmered in the air. Something that was not a chill swept up my back; my throat tightened until I could scarcely breathe, and my feet carried me into the center of the space, the spot in which any wizard would perform the bulk of his work. The thrill of magics whose names I didn't know crowded around. Bindings and curses, weatherworkings and spells infinitely more subtle, the ecstatic presences of unknown gods: all these things wound around and through me, so potent that I remembered in all the sinews of my body what it was to draw power, so insistent that I found myself blasted wide. When I reached the center of the room, the rapture of a hundred thousand workings pounded through me, in waves and gusts and staccato bursts of insanity I couldn't remember how to stop. I heard myself cry out; I shuddered with helpless delight, suspended beyond time and reason by the pleasure of the energies that had channeled through this space. Century after century of Danaan mages raced through my awareness, their curious minds and fearless hearts braving anything in the names of knowledge and power, their souls unfettered by rules and strictures and fear of condemnation, their actions guided by their affections and personal codes of honor. The pouring energies subsided into a tingle of rapture that fluttered over my skin; my chest ached with the loss of everything they had been and known and passed from mind to mind. I staggered and nearly fell; my eyes dazzled with the afterimages of a dozen setting suns. Manannan stood at the top of the staircase, staring at me.

"Lord?" he said.

I shook my head, tried to fill my lungs. Rapture played unabated over my skin.

"Unbelievable," I croaked. "Fouzhir unbelievable. How do you live with this loss?"

Manannan gave me a puzzled frown. "It was… before my time, Lord. I don't think I have any real idea how things were before."

I should be accustomed to this by now: the things that moved me most would forever play as madness to practically everyone I met. Such madness is a luxury even royalty can afford only in small portions.

I nodded. "Neither do I. I'm going to secure the roof."

Up another flight of stairs and through a door that opened *up* like the hatch of a hold on a ship, I gained the parapet. The cone of the roof rose up beside me, blocking the eastern sky. For half a second I was disappointed by what seemed an unfortunate architectural decision; then I realized the shape of the roof, wrought in reactive schists like the rest of the building, was intended to function as a focus for long-distance workings. Immediately my mind multiplied the concept, and I saw the sun-towers the Breasaílians must have used stretching across all the lands the songs tell us they ruled: the almost effortless cohesion of their empire borne on aetheric currents among their myriad towers. What must it have been, to live in a time and place in which magic was as ready to hand as any mundane tool and as well understood? If only we had some idea of how to get back to such a paradise.

I walked the circle of the parapet, the sunset-limned sky unrolling itself around the tower as I moved. Once I was certain all was quiet, I began the circuit again: slowly this time. The wreck of Uriah spread out to the east and west, but the tower actually stood at the southern edge of the city. Had we ridden another minute or two, we would have encountered the remains of the wall. Had this place been the palace, then? Or the College of Mages? The histories are notably quiet on where that center lay.

I stood for a long time looking south, across the darkening lands beyond the ruined wall: trying to catch some glimpse of the retreating Básghilae, trying to estimate the road we would ride tomorrow. The river Latis unwound lazily across the blasted plain, shallow waters reflecting gold in the setting sun. The road to the Muir Pass followed that river, I knew, but it was hard to pick out in this light. I saw no signs of anyone living within the tower's horizons; it all looked disturbingly like the lands outside the fallen city at Arian.

Eventually I walked the rest of the circuit, turning south, east, and finally north as the clouds blazed peach and crimson and some half-familiar zephyr of delight teased my edges. I felt I should recognize it; I couldn't lay hands on it. But as I came around the curve of the parapet, the last sliver of the sun winked across the wall at me, casting Letitia in gold.

Another man might have thought it a trick of the light: she should be a silhouette against the glowing sky, not readily visible. But a breeze skittered past her, stirring her unbound hair and carrying the delicate, unmistakable arcane aroma I kept smelling on her, and I recognized the flavor haunting the part of my awareness that mundane senses confuse with the throat: she was enmeshed in the same subtle magic I'd glimpsed on our first night out of Irisa, somehow absorbing the light of the sun. The scent of roses tickled my brain, though my nose knew there were no flowers nearby; a warmth like the memory of brandy filled my throat, spreading into a shiver of desire that tripped down the length of my body. I stood as if enchanted, drinking her in, afraid to move and startle her into mundanity. Amien's wards hovered on the edge of visibility, a net of green that shimmered in the hues of the emeralds that come from Tellan's deepest mines. She turned and looked at me, and I realized those emeralds were the same color as her eyes.

On the other side of the mountains, in places where the sort of language that coaxes a woman into bed had long ago become a reflex, I would have made that observation aloud. Tonight such wooing felt false. I couldn't remember the last time I had played those games with a woman: even that night with Macha at Irisa had been her idea, not mine. I wondered whether I had lost the knack.

And then Letitia's eyes met mine, and I forgot about everything else. There was no room for wooing here, only worship. If there are prayers one is expected to offer the avatar of the goddess Dana, I had no idea what they might be. I just stared, heart pounding in my throat.

"The Danaan no longer practice sorcery?" I managed finally.

And just that quickly the spell was broken, and a Tana wrongly clad in spidersilk mail stood before me, glancing away in embarrassment.

"No sorcery," she said softly. "Just a gift of the Holy Mora. It is of no practical use."

"The Touch of the goddess is its own justification," I said, just as softly.

She cast me a swift look of astonishment; then one corner of her mouth quirked into a humorless half-smile. "If anyone would understand that, I suppose it would be you."

She was thinking about the Tuaoh Stone, I realized. I shrugged and glanced away. There was no balm here but truth; to apply it was a strategic error.

"That is a thing I learned long ago, on the other side of the mountains," I said, embarrassed by my own foolishness, and turned to look out across the ruins.

Half a second later Letitia leaned against the wall beside me, avoiding my gaze with a similar pretense of surveying the horizon. "And last night?"

I shook my head, still unable to look at her. "If your goddess turned Her gaze on that mountaintop yesterday, I had no sense of Her presence."

In my peripheral vision I saw Letitia nod and glance back at the swiftly-disappearing sun—and dared to hope the matter had finally been laid to rest.

"So this gift," I said after a moment. At the eastern end of the sky, stars shimmered into visibility, pale diamonds against a cloak of deepening blue.

Soon the Swan would be visible. "Is it a thing given to all the morae?"

Letitia sighed. "I don't know. There were so many things my mother never had the chance to teach me."

She paused, brooding. "I feel traditions dying around me every day, and I don't even know what they were. I've lost count of the skills I lack. I suspect I haven't the faintest idea of the things that occupied my mother's mind, or her mother's." She looked at me. "How do I find out about these things? Who can I ask these questions, now that my mother is gone? I found her journal recently, at Irisa—" She glanced away again, as if this fact were somehow damning. "And I've been reading, and trying to learn…" She shook her head.

"But what one writes in a journal is not what one would pass to a successor, given the time," I finished.

Letitia nodded.

"Have you spoken with your bards?" I said. "The preservation of such things is their greatest responsibility."

Letitia sighed again. "Macha makes me… dream of slitting my own throat."

I surprised myself by laughing. Letitia didn't step away, but she shifted, and it was a motion of withdrawal. I forced myself to quiet.

"I'm sorry," I said. "I have memories of my own tutors that are just as fond. But surely Macha is not the only living bard in Fíana?"

"I'm sure others will find me just as lacking," Letitia said glumly.

"No," I said. "They won't. They will know you first as the mora, and any lack they perceive in your education they will pin on Macha, not you." I stood still for a moment, watching night spread across the sky. "People who knew us as children always seem unable to forget the children we were. It is no coincidence that every righ, without fail, eventually releases every one of his father's retainers."

Letitia nodded thoughtfully. A question fluttered in her face, then died. Abruptly I realized how many questions she chose not to ask, how keenly she saw the gulf between the things I thought and felt and the things I could allow myself to speak. A hundred secrets piled up in my throat, tripping over one another in their rush to be the first out into the open. I swallowed them all down.

"Do you want another strategy lesson?" I said. "I'm afraid there's too little light for sword-work tonight."

"Yes," she said, and glanced up at the moons. Telliyn stood directly overhead, half her face showing. Arliyn trailed behind, already full. The next few nights would be increasingly bright: better for in-camp training, but also better for nighttime attacks. And once Telliyn reached her completion, her waning would mark the rush of days to Bealtan. Bealtan Eve was little more than a twelvenight away, I realized. Strange to think how far away it had seemed, even as recently as Irisa.

"Thirteen days to Aballo," Letitia murmured, evidently to herself.

And six days to Goibniu, where we might meet reinforcements. Where Amien might hire Letitia a ship, all but guaranteeing her safe arrival at Aballo and relieving me, if that was the phrase for it, of the obligation to continue with the party. Where I might find it necessary to part company with them anyway, if today's total lack of self-control in the presence of the arcane didn't cease.

Six days. An eternity of ambushes stood between us and the relative safety of Goibniu. And yet the time seemed suddenly too short.

Letitia shook her head, eyes still on the sky.

"What?" I said, reflexively.

She shook her head again, glancing away. "I can't remember how I imagined that I might still manage to be invested at Bealtan."

I sighed. "I think there is a part of the mind whose sole job it is to imagine ways that things might return to normal, after our lives are taken from us."

Letitia glanced at me and visibly decided against asking a question. But I knew what she wondered, and the impulse to give her things she would not ask for overwhelmed me.

"As far as I know, that part of the mind never stops, no matter how many times the rest of you calls it a fool."

She sighed. And though I knew, assuming any of us survived, where Letitia would spend Bealtan, I couldn't imagine where I would be. I could not go to Aballo, not and refrain from giving myself over to arcane impulses that would only end in destruction. Whatever I might desire and dream, Iminor would have no competition from me that night. Amien would want me to accompany him to the Bealtan Moot; my heart shrank in me at the idea. I had to tolerate Coran being elected to the throne that should have been mine, but I wasn't sure I could bear watching it happen. And yet there would be no getting around the fact that I had received Amien's summons. Perhaps I should be hoping for relief at Goibniu: at least parting company at Goibniu would give me a chance to lose myself before the Moot. But that idea held no pleasure, either.

Gods, I was a fool.

"So, a lesson?" I said finally.

"Please," Letitia said, eyes on the sky again. "You choose the topic. One way or another, our time together is short."

Chapter 17
Blood-Price

For five days we fought our way through northernmost Banbagor: following the remains of the river road through areas of devastation like those outside Arian until we reached the deserted fortress at Helike, then striking west-by-southwest across league upon league of rolling, nearly featureless plains in which life gradually resumed. Three times we spotted Tanaan settlements; each time, Letitia bade us pass them by. The geas of receiving travelers who need shelter is as strong as it ever was, on that side of the mountains; but so is the one that forbids a man—or woman—under a death-vendetta to accept another's hospitality. We could not ask anyone for shelter, Letitia decided. Not after what had happened at Arian.

But after Helike there was no other shelter to speak of, and on north Banbagor's rolling plains visibility is measured in miles. The Bard's Wizard switched tactics to accommodate the terrain, as any sensible commander would: with little hope of surprising us, he harried us. Time after time, Básghilae dashed in swift as a flock of vultures, only the sound of their hooves giving any sense that they were of this world. They galloped in from behind and overtook us; they appeared suddenly over the crest of a hillock to our left; in the evening, when the sun was low and blinding, they came at us out of the glare. Not once did they dig in for a complete engagement: the attacks were swift hit-and-run affairs that gave Letitia's knights no time to form up, Amien no time to attempt the working of wards, me no time to give in to the temptation to meet their eyes. Each successive engagement made me more grateful for Letitia's personal wards. And, oddly, each engagement became a new lesson for Letitia. I was surprised by how quickly she learned, by the constant leaps in the sophistication of the questions she asked.

Our tactics shifted, too. There no longer seemed any point in denying the Bard's Wizard knew where we were going and by what route, or that our attempts at evasion were merely wasted miles. We rode straight across the plain, only adjusting our course when sun- or star-sightings told us we had strayed from our bearing. After Letitia stunned both Amien and me by asking whether the Bard's Wizard might actually use the signatures of Amien's arcane workings to locate us, he stopped working wards around our campsites at night—and we stopped suffering attacks the moment the wards came down. I wondered privately how long it would be before our enemy chose to exploit that; but in the mean time, Amien was as well rested as any of us, and I began to believe he would make it to Aballo without burning himself from the inside out.

I talked myself dry as we rode those empty grasslands, teaching Letitia as much and as fast as she was able to absorb. Before long I realized Iminor was listening, too, and included him in the discussion now and then. In the evenings, under the waxing moons, I began developing blade skills with her—and quickly realized that my predecessor in her training, whoever he had been, had committed the same mental error that very nearly ensnared me. She had only ever been taught defensive tactics. I growled at the injustice; she stopped, blade resting lightly against mine, and said quietly, "I'm not sure you're blaming the right person. I had never seen the point of mastering the sword. After all, blade handling in a mora is really only for show."

I had not known her capable of irony: it is not a thing at which the Tanaan excel. The surprise of it made me laugh until half the knights were staring at us, and then I completely failed to recreate the humor for them. Afterward, however, I began teaching her the knack of making one's defense count for offense, of finding an opponent's weaknesses and tells and using them against him.

And at that, she was a surprisingly adept student: particularly when it came to personalities. As the grasslands gave way to varied terrain and the beginnings of forest, and the party grew accustomed to her preoccupation with learning strategy and tactics, their interest in our proceedings faded; and she began sharing a variety of surprising insights with me, during quiet moments on the road and in camp. Through her eyes I saw how Amien picked fights with me when he felt he was falling short of expectations; how harshly Iminor judged himself when he failed to outperform her knights; how Easca hung on my words but gave Letitia herself no more than her due—and I saw how troubled Letitia was by her sense that she had failed to earn the Arian woman's respect. Gradually I realized how clearly she saw all her knights, how she yearned to be worthy of their service. It made me feel naked before her, wondering what she saw in me but chose not to share.

One night as Letitia and I crossed blades in the evening's training, Básghilae invaded the camp on foot, fading soundlessly into the circle of firelight. I pinned Letitia between myself and the fire, praying that the ghouls would no more brave fire than water, and we fought them off again—but Manannan took a minor hit shielding her from my off side. And as the Básghilae withdrew in yet another silent rush, and Manannan stood staring at the little cut on his hand, Letitia gave voice to a tiny moan and staggered away from the makeshift hearth. When next I glanced at her the sword was still in her fist, but her stance was strange; and she had the look a man gets when he's deciding how best to end his life on his own blade.

I covered the distance between us in two huge strides, clamped my hand around the hilt and wrested it from her, hissing, "Don't you dare. His honor means more than that."

She recoiled as if doused with cold water, eyes glittering as she met my gaze. Then she nodded and sank to the ground.

What must it be to know you are dead, and yet walk? My imagination failed to wrap itself around the problem. Manannan stared at his hand, stared at the fire, walked out past the circle of firelight on some errand I couldn't imagine. Ogma, who despite or because of the fact that they occupied the two extremes of the age span of the contingent, had formed a strangely close bond with Manannan, followed him to the place where light faded into darkness and stopped. I couldn't decide whether Amien should work wards around the camp or we should spare his strength and just admit the horse had left the barn. I felt as if time had frozen and trapped me on the spot.

"He's not losing forces with these tactics," Amien observed. With difficulty I quelled the startle. "There's absolutely no reason they can't come back in an hour."

I met his eyes, sighed, and sent Ogma out to bring the Tan back to base.

"Three nights to Goibniu," Amien said abstractedly, in an evident attempt to cheer himself. But I remembered how he had looked after three nights of trying to ward campsites on the way to Dianann; and I wondered who I would be protecting if I refused to help this time.

Naturally the Básghilae were there waiting when Amien's binding came down in the morning. I was not the only one who waded into the engagement with renewed passion. This morning the Tanaan displayed a fierce synchronization that seemed like something out of a song, shouting at each ghoul that fell. Manannan tore into the Básghilae with fey abandon, oblivious to the damage their blades could still do him; but neither Nuad nor I called him to task. I found myself seeking the awareness behind the dead eyes of each ghoul I engaged, though what I would do once I found it remained a question not only open but unexamined—and then, in the third opponent I engaged, he was finally looking back at me, and I knew: I dispensed with style, left myself open for half a second, and swept off the ghoul's head.

But the itch of revenge not yet won remained someplace deep in my chest. When the Básghilae disengaged and rode off, it took everything I had to refrain from chasing them. The quickness of my breathing had less to do with

205

exertion than with the need to track the Bard's Wizard to his base, to seek out and destroy whatever well he was using to create these ghouls, to engage the man himself. Swords would be only the beginning; and for those moments during which the fight still surged in my veins, I burned to throw aside any concerns about the methods and energies I might call upon in besting him. How could there be harm in using even the blackest of resources against a man who worked this much evil this casually? But even as I formed the thoughts, I knew they were the doorway to evil as great as what I wanted to defeat. I spent the first couple miles after we set out grinding my teeth.

A short time later, we were back on the trail that had once been the Muir Pass Road. The terrain climbed steadily as we approached the mountains; the forest closed in around us, until the sky disappeared behind layer upon layer of evergreen boughs. It put me in mind of Tellan—and the duel. For the first time in days I remembered my suspicion that Letitia's enemy might be Deaclan. I knew better, now. I would have recognized his mind as he stared at me from behind Básghilae eyes.

The road passed out of the woods again. Across a small sunlit plain, the road carved a visible path up the flank of a mountain. Here the hard riding began, I knew; but once we gained the pass, everything would grow easier: the terrain, the weather, the defensible structures of civilization. Once we reached the shores of the Black, the very waters would act in our defense. It was too early to even think about relaxing, but the presence of the mountains made me feel we might win through, after all.

In the midst of the open space, beside the trail, stood a single standing stone: a boundary marker, I realized. As we rode closer, I saw the barely-visible remains of another road, which joined the Muir Pass Road a few feet after the stone. By common, wordless consent, we reined, looking at the stone and the place where the other road had led northwest across the clearing to the woods on the other side. Iminor drew closer to the stone without dismounting, riding off the road until he could touch the words carved on its surface.

"Banbagor," he read from the side nearest the road. He cued the horse again and rode around to the opposite side. "Muir."

This had been the end of their mutual boundary, back when such issues mattered. Here travelers from the human realms had decided which road to take. I wondered what errands might have prompted their trips, tried and failed to calculate how many leagues lay between this spot and the closest of the settlements we'd passed.

"Aballo," Amien said decisively, pointing towards the mountain. Iminor cued his horse back onto the road, and we set out again; horror and grief at the evil of their great goddess overtook me once more. Suddenly I was doubly glad to be leaving the Tanaan realms behind.

From that point we rode steadily upward. This felt like northern Tellan: like the final day of the road from Aballo to the place I had thought of simply as *home*; like the trails to the mountain valleys in which we had hunted. The party with which I rode might have been any hunting party or pleasure-riding expedition, had the mood been better and the pace less urgent. For the first time in years, the names and faces of the pack of young Tellan men who had always trailed in my wake manifested in my mind. Sons of tiarna and seach, all of them: no doubt their lives had continued precisely as planned. No doubt Tellan was exactly what it had always been.

I could only hope none of them would make the trip to Teamair for the Moot season. If everyone of consequence in the Beallan realms knew I had lost my throne rather than relinquishing it voluntarily, until this spring at least they had known no more: whatever the men of the Aballo Order thought of me, they had closed ranks on this topic as effectively as ever. None of them disclosed to anyone outside the Order that I had once counted myself among their number, nor the circumstances surrounding my father's death. I was Amien's great failure, the loose thread that might prompt men of consequence to ask questions the Order couldn't afford. The wizards' silence outside the Order would remain absolute.

But the tiarna of Tellan knew I had taken training at Aballo. Their fear of what I was and what I might do had made it easy for my uncle to raise them against me. I had little reason to hope my presence at Teamair would fail to rekindle the old stories in the mind of anyone who knew—nor to hope that they wouldn't spread the tales during the season, drippingly juicy gossip they were. It was too easy to imagine how the stories would run. And I would have no defense against the truth. When we reached a wide spot in the punishing trail, and Amien reined to look out across the broadening vista, I seized the distraction with both hands.

"Yes," Amien said in a satisfied tone as the rest of us gathered around him. "This is what I remembered. It's been such a long time I wasn't sure how well memory served."

"What is this?" Letitia asked, looking around.

"A rest-stop," Amien said. "The caravans would stop in these places at midday."

"*Caravans?*" Iminor blurted.

Amien nodded, smiling. "It was your people who established the route; the caravans were almost exclusively Danaan. I traveled this road a few times, when I was in the service of the mora of Muir. There's always a stopping-point at midday on this route—and it was a long stop, several hours, when the caravans traveled it, and anybody who didn't keep pace with them was just borrowing trouble. I wonder whether the cook-houses at the campsites still stand." He dismounted and gave the horse an affectionate pat. The beast began to cautiously sample the local flora; the rest of us followed the wizard to the ground.

"There should be water nearby, a spring or something," Amien said thoughtfully, looking around.

"This was a well-established route," I said, astonished. "I've never heard or read about it."

Amien shrugged. "It's been my experience that the things everyone knows about are the least likely to be covered in the histories. I suppose it all seems too obvious at the time."

I shook my head.

"But yes: it was a well-established route. Danaan caravans, mostly fine-goods trade between the ports on the Ruillin and the Four Realms north of the mountains, via their outpost at Nimah on Lethin Isle."

"Nimah?" Letitia said. She looked at Iminor, who shrugged.

"Lethin Isle," I said, yet more incredulous. I knew the place, though I'd never set foot there: Lethin Isle stands at the northern end of the Ruillin, a few miles south of Goibniu. "I thought that place was vacant."

Amien smiled ruefully, spreading his gaze among us. "It is now. Centuries ago, before—well, before the Deluge, I suppose, though of course none of us on the Beallan side knew about the Deluge..." He cleared his throat, gaze on something far away. He shook his head. "People wondered what had happened to Nimah, of course. But everyone was just... gone. If anyone went all the way across the mountains looking for answers, the rest of us never heard about it. I suppose everyone at Nimah went home, to Muir... or what was left of it." He fell silent again, and turned his head to gaze out across the land below us.

"Were there... other such outposts?" Letitia said after a moment.

Amien seemed to snap back into the present moment. "What? No, not to my knowledge. Most Danaan trade was by sea; these caravans served Muir more than anyone else."

"Fáill, perhaps," Iminor mused.

Amien nodded. "Perhaps. I never really paid attention. Hell, I never set foot on Lethin until after Nimah... until after the Deluge." Again his gaze ranged after something I couldn't see. He shook his head. "I was a fool."

A wry, reluctant smile creased his face, and he looked at Letitia. "Over and over again. Well, then. If I recall correctly, they would unburden the horses at the break."

I nodded. "That's how they do it in the mining caravans in Tellan."

The wizard glanced at me. "You've ridden those trails?"

I nodded again, swallowing against the tension in my throat. Tellan's emerald mines are her greatest riches, greater even than her cattle. Of course I had ridden with those caravans, walked those mines, learned those miners' ways. I didn't want to talk about any of it. But the wizard just nodded, satisfied.

"Good," he said. "I'm sure your memory is much fresher than mine."

For an ordinary caravan on a mountain trail, the greatest fear—aside from the hazards of the terrain—is bandits. We had the Básghilae to worry about, of course—but also time: the measure of the opportunities Letitia's enemy had to muster his reserves after we knocked down his forces; the waning of the days before the Bealtan Moot; most especially the limits of the stamina on which Amien drew to ward our campsites night after night. It required an act of discipline for me to remain at the rest-stop long enough for the horses and riders to grow fully rested; when Telliyn rose late in the afternoon, within two days of her fullness, I had to fight long and hard against the impulse to urge my horse faster. When we arrived in the evening's campsite, and I looked across that narrow lumpy space to the trail rising onward after it, I knew we were in trouble: if the mountains truly were a two-day crossing, tonight's camp would have been in the pass itself.

"Fouzh," Amien muttered, looking around the campsite as we rode in.

"This isn't a two-day trail," I said, forgetting to school my voice to calm. It wasn't surprising that he'd forgotten so small a detail over the centuries; but that hardly eased the blow.

"I fouzhir *see* that!" the wizard snapped. "You think *you're* not looking forward to the extra night!"

I couldn't help it: I looked at the reins, at my hands. Guilt welled inside me. I would need new gloves soon; I'd ridden more in the past two months than in the previous ten years. A better man would offer to take on the responsibility for tonight's wards himself. But were wards really necessary or even desirable? They would certainly make us easier to find. Were I to attack this place, how would I go about it?

"Assault from above," I said, mostly to myself.

"What?" Amien said.

I nodded. "Hold off on the wards, will you? Let me take Ogma and Manannan and see what's ahead on the trail."

Amien gave me a skeptical look. "I don't like those odds."

I surprised myself with a grin. "If things get dicey, we'll send Ogma back."

"What?" the young Tan blurted, but Manannan gave voice to a wry laugh.

"Back in an hour," I said. "Two at the outside."

"Ellion—"

I didn't wait for the argument, just cued my horse and led the two Tans up the mountain. The shadows were long, but generous amounts of light still bathed the trail. Some parts of the trail held nothing but bare rock; such areas would grow only more frequent tomorrow. But tonight enough solid earth and low mountain grasses occupied the path to reassure me that no one had recently passed this way. Were the Básghilae behind us on the trail, then? Or had they taken another route altogether, planning an ambush on the other side of the mountains? I certainly wouldn't attempt an attack from below on this trail, not unless I was out of other options.

When the sun disappeared behind the mountain, I turned us reluctantly back towards the campsite. We had seen no sign of other riders on the trail; but that wasn't proof of safety. I wondered what exactly I had been hoping to find, what I would have done if only three of us had stumbled on a full contingent of Básghilae. Manannan was dead already, of course; but how would I have protected Ogma? I felt as if there were a deep pool of bitumen inside my own mind, and the answers lay within. But I had led two men under my command out here with me; the only thing to do was set the question aside and get them back to base before some other form of idiocy manifested.

Finally we reached the campsite. All was quiet, but Amien looked worn; I would have given my realm, had I still possessed one, for a skin of brandy. Fortunately no one here was in possession of such a thing. Shortly after we arrived, Nuad, Mattiaci, and Tru rode up from the trail below the camp. Had this been Aballo, and not a mixed-race party in the mountains, I might have kissed the armsmaster.

"All clear below, Lord," he said to me as they entered the camp. "If they're following us, it's from some distance."

I nodded, smiling without planning it. "Let's post watches tonight, then."

I turned to Amien. "My lord, I think we're reasonably secure here. Let's save your strength, and minimize our enemy's access to what you're doing."

The next day was more of the same: punishing mountain trails, a break at midday that required all my discipline to respect, and a second climb in the afternoon. By the day's second leg, some of the hollows and crags we passed bore traces of last season's stubborn snow. And this time, finally, at the end of the day's trail, the pass hove into view.

It looked lovelier than it had any right to: a long, surprisingly broad sweep of a hollow swathed in unreasonably lush green grass. Without discussion everyone began riding faster, eager to cross the final, narrow ledge and scramble up the last steep bank to the promise of rest just above. Even Iminor stopped looking nervously down from the narrows.

"There's a lake up here, if memory serves," Amien announced to no one in particular. "Too cold for bathing, even in summer, but I think I just might stick my feet in…"

I chuckled. "Spoken like a true southerner. I'm sure it's lovely."

Ahead of me, Iminor reined suddenly. "Wait—"

Something prickled up my spine. I looked past Iminor, at the crest of the bank leading down from the pass; one of our enemy's ghouls met my gaze. Of course it would be here.

The ledge we rode, though comfortably wide enough for even a laden caravan horse, couldn't safely admit two; and the bank leading down from the pass was too steep to allow any kind of speed on the way down. But that didn't stop the Básghilae from catapulting across the bank at a breathtaking pace, didn't keep the first rider from slipping past Nuad and heading into the space beside Amien, towards Letitia. I shouted, but from the middle of the train a man can do little in such a situation. But even as Nuad engaged the second rider and Amien sent a casting of power on a miraculously true trajectory to eliminate the one behind Nuad's, the wizard managed to communicate some signal to his horse that sent its rump wide, sent the first Básghil's mount tumbling off the ledge and down the long, jagged slope below. Several of us shouted; Iminor said, "Ti—"—and, apparently understanding, she backed her horse along the wall at our left hand and let Iminor slip past her on the outside. My heart leapt into my throat at the maneuver; for Iminor and his evident fear of heights it was nothing short of the act of a god.

Between one breath and the next, I felt something shift: not the ground, but something else I couldn't lay hands on, something immediate and perilous. I had a momentary sense of time stopping and lurching forward again. Amien let fly with two more bolts of green; two more ghouls fell limply from saddles. Behind me, I heard a muffled explosion—and above, the unmistakable sound of the face of the mountain giving way.

"Rockslide!" I shouted, half-mad with the impossibility of doing anything, sandwiched in the midst of the train as I was. All the horses in the train jostled a step or two forward, as if they might outrun it. Either I had the same instinctive response or my horse followed his fellows' lead. But the way was blocked, of course.

"Fouzh!" Amien yelled, turned swiftly in the saddle, and using his sword the way some druids employ wands or staves, cast a quick binding over the spot in which the party clung to the trail, then turned back to the battle. The binding shimmered in a thousand hues of green, translucent; from within the boundary I saw rocks and dirt and trees pouring across its exterior and plummeting into the gorge below. A secondary tremor shivered up the mountain's face, and the ledge collapsed behind me.

My horse's rear hooves scrabbled for purchase; I threw myself against his neck, and with a great surge of the hindquarters he scrambled forward onto more secure ground. Simultaneously the avalanche shifted above us; rocks veered suddenly sideways across the binding, sweeping the attackers nearest the front from the ledge. Nuad and Amien drew back under the cover of the binding, crowding everyone further; behind me, a horrifying gap separated me from Mattiaci, Tru, and the back half of the party. Bruane and Greine were gone.

There was nothing to do but wait for the slide to end: I slipped from the saddle to stand between my horse and the face of the mountain. I glanced behind me, across the gap, seeing the Tanaan on the other side slip out of their saddles as well. And between me and Mattiaci on the wall, under the preternatural stillness of the binding, I finally spotted a series of regular holes: the sort of holes a drill makes. I understood immediately, and desire to leap into a chasm gripped me: those holes were the outer faces of the sort of bores that miners make, to bury explosives in a wall of rock they want to bring down.

They had blown just a fraction too far away to take me. Instead Bruane and Greine had lost their lives. I knocked the back of my head against the wall; pain exploded through my skull. I wanted more, but I forced myself to stop. The Tanaan taboo against a person under a death-vendetta accepting hospitality made sudden, blinding sense: this was not just my blood-price anymore. Whoever intended to bring me down was no longer concerned about collateral damage; once again, I was a danger to the rest of the party. To confess the truth was to light a beacon far more dangerous than the arcane signatures of one of Amien's workings. If we got Letitia to Goibniu alive, it must be the last time any of them saw me, and I could not even offer a true apology. My throat knotted in anticipation of the look of betrayal I would see in Letitia's eyes, the disappointment I would see in Amien. I knocked my head against the wall once more.

Finally the avalanche stopped. People started moving; I forced myself to rouse.

"Wait," I said. "Give it a few minutes. Sometimes these things just pause." Green flared in my peripheral vision; Amien gave voice to a noise of satisfaction.

"They're still *there*?" Letitia said.

"They seem to be leaving, now," Amien said, still sounding gratified. "Dear gods, what a relief to be back in places with power I can use!"

After some measureless time of quiet, we agreed it was probably safe to move. Amien sensibly left the binding in place as the party filed forward, past Básghilae corpses and across rockslide rubble that shifted in ways that made me catch my breath each time a rider moved. Once Letitia's horse had scrambled across the rockfall to the relative safety of the grass above, I said quietly, "My lord."

"What?" Amien said, turning to look at me. Delight at having regained access to power sources he understood fairly radiated from him.

"The ledge... collapsed between me and the back of the party," I said.

The wizard drew in a swift, dismayed breath, asking questions with his eyes.

I sighed. "We lost Bruane and Greine. The rest of them are all right, but there's a gap in the ledge..."

Amien nodded, walking back across the ledge towards me. For a moment we stared at the gap in silence. He didn't seem to notice the bore-holes; maybe he just didn't understand what he saw. He hailed from vining country, not mining country, after all.

"We've got enough rope that we might get the knights across," I said quietly. "But the horses..."

Amien nodded again. "Then let's do the whole thing magically."

The shift in the head that precedes magic was ready, beckoning. But for all the ways I'd endangered the party since leaving Irisa, I had still managed to avoid violating my vow not to draw power. My sharp, indrawn breath was as involuntary as it was evidently infuriating.

"*Fine!*" Amien snapped. "Fouzhir fine! It wasn't as if I asked you to—" He expelled a huge gust of air, then looked out across the rockslide below us. After a second he raised his chin, still not looking at me.

"If you could step off the ledge," he said icily, "I'm going to need room to work."

For half a second I actually thought he meant I should do it the short way. Belatedly I understood. I nodded wordlessly, collected my horse, and climbed onto the green grass of the pass.

Ilnemedon: Royal Map Collection no. 886 (detail): The Ruillin

Chapter 18
The Last Time

Two days later, we rode into Nemetona, on the northern shore of the Black. The place is named for the shrine to Lady Tella there, which Owain Mourne raised to mark his conquest of all the Ruillin basin in Her name. I had looked forward to this arrival, not only for the irrational sense of civilization providing some measure of safety, but also because I had the sense that human cities and villages would feel like a return home. I was surprised to discover how strange Nemetona looked, how small and mean; something in the back of my head knew even Ilnemedon would seem pale and uninspired after the wonders of the Four Realms, diminished though they might be.

The weather turned sultry as we rode down from the mountains: strange for so early in the year, this far north. The spidersilk mail that had seemed a useful layer against the cold only yesterday had become my own personal sauna. Under other circumstances I would have taken arrival in the Ruillin basin as a cue to pull off my mailshirt: the cities of the northern Ruillin in particular may be a bit rough-and-tumble, and it is an agreed-upon fact that any sin committed on a Ruillin ferry short of murder or theft is left on board after one returns to land; but while I wouldn't consider wandering the Ruillin unarmed, neither would I expect to draw either sword or knife. On the Ruillin, mail is the mark of someone who makes his living by the sword, and most men find it simpler to keep their wits about them than to live with others leaping to conclusions. Most men are not trying to keep a Tana under a death-vendetta alive, however. I would rather sweat and give extra attention to courtesies than hope I could pull the mail shirt back on in time to cope with an attack.

At the outskirts of the town, Amien reined and turned to face Letitia.

"Mora," he said gravely. "The time has come for you to take off the torc."

"What?" she said, hand moving to her throat.

The wizard sighed. "We are about to be among people again. And by now everyone on the Ruillin knows about the bounty on the neck of the Lady of Finias. Your neck can't afford a torc just now."

"Are you taking yours off?" she snapped.

He frowned. "There's no need."

She glanced around. Her gaze rested on Easca, then returned to Amien.

"Lord Amien," she said. "For more than a twelvenight I have done everything you asked, whether it was necessary or not. I have come halfway across the world at your insistence rather than defend my own home, at the cost of dozens of lives. I have required my knights to put aside the dignity and standard of equipage they have every right to expect. Now you ask me to dishonor my clan?"

"Mora—"

She shook her head vigorously, drawing herself up to her full height. "I would ask you where it stops, but clearly that question is mine to answer. Lord Amien, it stops here!"

He shook his head, too. "That torc—"

"—is the pride and dignity of the Ériu clan, and not mine—"

"—says only one thing in the Ruillin basin this month—"

"—not mine to shed because it's inconvenient!"

"—and that is *Here is your bounty!*" Amien finished.

They stared at one another for several long seconds while the rest of us shifted uncomfortably in the saddles. Something in me ached for this apparent blow to Letitia's honor, incomprehensible though it was; but I knew Amien was right. Wasn't it just a torc, after all?

Then I remembered how I had felt the day I laid mine aside; and perhaps I understood, a little.

"No," Letitia said finally, low-voiced.

Amien's reins crumpled in his fists. Still the staring continued.

"Well, then, Mora," he said, venom in his tone. "You'd better put that cloak back on. Because if anyone sees that thing on you, no amount of fast talking will change anything."

"Fine," she said icily, and reached back, into her saddlebag. After a moment of fishing around, she produced the cloak, raised her chin to fasten it about her throat, and picked up the reins again, staring at Amien the while. The mere sight of the thick wool cloak on top of her spidersilk mail made sweat prickle across the back of my neck. "Proceed."

"As things stand, we're going to need a cover story," Amien said. "There must be some reason why two—Bealla—have ridden out of the Tanaan lands, in the company of half a dozen Tanaan guarding a woman of their own race." He paused, anger dissolving towards thoughtfulness. "If she's under guard, she's of noble or at least wealthy family. So why is she here?"

"Marriage," I said.

The wizard looked at me, gaze as chilly as it had been since the pass. He nodded.

"Tied, as all such marriages are, to territory or trade," he said. "I am in the employ of an influential trading family of Nagnata—No."

"No," I said simultaneously. "They're noble, of the tiarna, and they don't want to be named."

"Right," Amien said. "They're paying me obscene money to travel to… Banbagor—Gorias…" Several of the Tanaan stirred; the wizard raised a hand. "Practically no one on this side of the mountains has the faintest notion of the geography of the Four Realms, and I don't want the name *Fíana* to be part of this tale."

Letitia nodded slowly.

"I traveled to Gorias, in the company of the unnamed tiarn's wastrel son—"

"Ah, that would be me," I said lightly.

"Indeed it would," Amien replied, but his tone didn't convey any humor. "To retrieve the bride and finalize the trade agreement between this noble family of Gorias and the tiarn in Nagnata." The wizard paused, looking around at the Tanaan. "Her *brother*—" Amien looked at Iminor. "And several Gorias free-lances have accompanied the lady, to ensure that the agreement is properly honored once she reaches her destination."

"And that she arrives safely," I interposed.

"Yes," Amien nodded. "Her brother is focused on her honor, the others more on safety."

"Milady, I look forward to our impending nuptials," I said lightly to Letitia, then astonished myself by experiencing a ridiculous, lightning flash of something I couldn't identify in my chest.

She flushed; Iminor scowled at me.

I tossed him a grin. "Perfect. Just keep that up."

"Where are the knights protecting *you*?" Iminor growled.

I manufactured a laugh. "Ah, not only am I a wastrel and a rake, I'm an infamous duelist. Unless the knights get involved, I'm not worried."

Iminor's mouth twisted. "You are a fool, then."

I offered him an ironic horseback bow. "Now you are getting it, ouirr."

"Let's go," Amien said tiredly, and cued his horse.

The shrine at Nemetona stands in a small grove of cedars, near the shore—or, more properly, near the high-tide line. I sensed it didn't see much traffic: the power-nexus on which it sits was perceptible but not compelling, and the stones themselves bore little evidence of the sorts of energies that lay on a place in which regular devotions take place. Nemetona might be named for the shrine to Lady Tella, but the farther north one travels on the Ruillin, the more the worship of the old goddess of the Ruillin persists; I suspected She was the one getting the attention at Nemetona, despite the shrine. Laverna, goddess of the river and patroness of whores, never goes hungry on the Ruillin: not in the towns, and not on the water itself. Standing in this little cedar grove, the surprising truth came to me: if the kharr won through to these places, they might find more sympathy here than we loyalists liked to believe.

Unremarkable though the shrine might be, the territory itself compelled not only attention but a certain amount of awe. Here was power, though not power of a sort wizards are trained to use. I had never been so far north in this part of the world; the ferocious tides and huge tidal spans of the Ruillin basin reach their peaks in the Black and the Grey, and I stood astonished at the shrine-site: staring across almost half a mile of wet mud-flats, past the high naked docks stretching out into thin air and the sad beached boats at their feet, to the low-tide line. Experience farther south on the Ruillin had taught me that the waters would rise to meet these docks, buoy these boats, lap at the base of the rise on which the shrine stood in a matter of hours; and it was far from the first time I'd seen a Ruillin port at low tide. But farther south, the tides rarely pull all the way back from the shore. In the five years I spent in Ballarona I never saw it happen, though in fairness I spent little time at the riverfront while I lived there.

But at Nemetona, apparently, it is all in a day's routine. Little wonder Laverna gets Her due here, while Lady Tella receives no more than lip service.

The Tanaan stood similarly entranced, absently grasping their horses' reins, while Amien set about contacting Sanglin. After some discussion, we'd decided not to ask for a message to be relayed to Rohini: if we managed to secure a ship for charter at Goibniu, the reinforcements we'd requested would no longer be necessary; but we'd miscalculated before the last message, and Rohini was probably waiting at Goibniu this very night—while we must wait for tide and daylight before we could travel there. If she continued to wait for us at Goibniu, however, we would reach her before the relayed message did.

So tonight's dream-sending was composed more of information for Sanglin than anything else: the presumably welcome news that we had managed to cross the mountains, though we were running late; and instructions to follow if we were delayed so long that Amien might miss the opening of the Bealtan Moot. Tonight the sending proceeded without mishap, but by the time Amien was done, my mind had shifted predictably from the wonders before me to the looming disaster at Teamair. I pushed aside the dismal imaginings, turned my mind to calculating the days between Letitia and safety. Sailing on a ship chartered at Goibniu, she could be at Aballo in six days—with practically no concerns for safety en route. Cautious optimism was probably in order. I felt less joy than I should.

We rode to Nemetona's lone inn. It turned out to have only two guest rooms, both of which were already let for the night. I was pleased to see freshly-drawn beer and hot food prepared in a kitchen for the first time since Dianann; but tonight our company in the inn's main room was comprised of frankly-staring locals well into their cups—and the crews and captains of a couple of small-boats the tide had deposited at this end of the Black for the night, whose manners were no better. The men staring at the Tana in our party didn't improve the taste of the food, which turned out to be stew no more inspired than the stuff we'd been cooking over campfires for the better part of a twelvenight. We made a hasty meal of it, Amien arranged passage on one of the boats heading south again in the morning, and we decamped to Nemetona's boathouse.

On the way, I tried to figure out whether I should explain the scene in that inn to the Tanaan: the ideas humans have about Tanaan in general and Tana in particular; the expectation human men have that Tana are wholly wanton and ripe for the picking. I finally decided to let the issue lie: the Tanaan would be shocked; humans everywhere would turn out looking like fools of the highest order; I would sound a paranoid idiot; most likely all of the above. Tru and Easca were more than capable of protecting themselves from drunks in taverns, I reasoned; and there were still more men than women in the party.

Nemetona's boathouse stood at the far end of the little marina, at the edge of the mud-flats: during high tide it must stand half-in, half-out of the water. A single door opened from the path that traced the shore, and on that side the building stood no taller than boathouses anywhere; but the entire waterward side stood open, and as it stretched towards the water the building expanded downward, twice as deep at the waterward edge as at the shore. Inside, a packed-earth floor afforded space for loading and unloading; a walkway wide enough for a single horse traced the interior of the western wall. The water within the boathouse stood empty, and still considerably lower than the loading spaces. I guessed the boats that regularly sheltered here must be at the other end of the Black tonight.

Amien didn't cast wards around the boathouse: they would be visible from half the village, would raise questions we wanted to avoid. Instead he worked a subtle binding over the door on the landward side, which would alert him even from sleep if someone tried to enter; and we divided the night into watches again. It was my turn for the first watch; I settled inside the boathouse with my back to the wall, my jacket once again a welcome ward against the chill. I situated myself so I could see the door but with my attention towards the water.

Everything outside the boathouse lay painted in pale colors by the light of two full moons. The roofs on the other side of Nemetona looked peaceful, almost pretty, across the water. Inside, the boathouse echoed with the pounding of surf as the tide raced towards its height; huge swells roared across the water and crashed against the boathouse walls. The sound was hypnotic: most of the party lay down in the dry area of the boathouse and seemed to fall instantly asleep. Soon only Letitia remained awake: swathed in her cloak at the limit of the boathouse's interior walkway, face towards the water.

The energies her meditation always raised were fainter here, zephyrs of pleasure against the edges of my awareness that I discovered I could enjoy without danger of being pulled into arcane consciousness. Moonlight made a faint halo of her golden hair. Time stretched into strange, limitless peace, and I found myself relaxing, as if this were the sort of pleasure-outing that can make a man contemplate leaving his daily life for the illusion of unending quiet. There could be far worse ways to spend a lifetime than sitting ward for Letitia and her companions.

Abruptly I realized, with true and painful awareness of its immediacy, that tomorrow we would reach Goibniu. And there we must part company. I could not keep my promise to return to Fíana next spring, unless I dealt successfully with the price on my neck.

Letitia stirred; she turned and looked at me, moonlight casting her face in a luminance that grabbed me by the throat.

"These waters are amazing," she said, barely audible above the noise of the surf.

I might have lost the knack of wooing in the past two months, but I could still apprehend an oblique invitation: I rose and walked down the length of the narrow walkway, settling behind her on the weathered planks. From here the door was less visible, but the view of the lake was commanding: I told myself it constituted a reasonable compromise. For several minutes we just sat, watching the water race up to consume the land.

"By this time tomorrow we'll reach Goibniu," I said, still looking at the water. In my peripheral vision I saw her nod. "If we're able to charter a ship, the next morning you'll be sailing to Aballo."

Her head snapped around; she stared at me again. This time I couldn't meet her eyes.

"*I'll* be sailing?"

I swallowed. "You... will have no need of me, once you have a ship of your own. The undead cannot cross water; with a windcaller you can be out to sea in three days, at Aballo just a few days later. And I—" My throat closed; I swallowed again. "I cannot go to Aballo."

"*What?* Why?"

Oh, sweet Lady Tella. I could beat any man I knew at chess, but I hadn't seen this question coming? If it had been necessary to introduce this topic, shouldn't I at least have had a deflection ready? I cast about uselessly for something that was both true and admissible.

"Ah... let us say it is another of the places where my welcome has worn out," I managed finally.

Now her look was analytical. "Having something to do with the reason why you're so angry with Amien."

"What?" I blurted. "Letitia, you've got it perfectly backwards. *He's* angry with *me.*"

She gazed at me in pensive silence. Something in the way she held her mouth said I had probably lied. I hadn't, about that; but I had, about so many other things, by omission and commission both. I looked away.

"As you say," she said at last, and looked out at the water again.

Something inside me sank. On our last night together, I would leave things like this? A cloud passed before Telliyn's face; will-o-the-wisps in the marshlands to the east and southwest leapt into pale green visibility. I longed to speak the truth, finally; but there was none I could tell about this issue without confessing everything.

Maybe it no longer mattered. After all, she would most likely be on a ship little more than a day from now. But the necessity of caution snuffed out the impulse for truth, as usual. I could do nothing but gaze at her moonlit profile, trying to come up with some way to redirect the conversation, to keep her engaged with me. As if it mattered. As if it would go anywhere, even could I sail all the way to Aballo.

"I wish—" Abruptly I realized truth was sneaking out of me anyway, and my voice faltered; she turned to look at me again. "I wish I could have known you under other circumstances. In peace."

She met my eyes in a gaze so frank and intimate my throat closed again. My heart thudded against my sternum.

"I wish I had known you much earlier," I said. Before her commitment to Iminor. Maybe tonight I would be doing more than staring at her, if I had.

Her mouth quirked. "When I was a child."

I found myself smiling, and wondering why it hurt. "Yes, then. And when you were an old woman."

Her smile crumpled; she glanced quickly away. Once again I couldn't figure out how to fix things.

"I'm sorry," I croaked.

She didn't look at me, but a hand stole out from beneath her cloak to grasp mine.

"I am, too," she said quietly. "I'd better go to sleep."

Just as quickly her hand withdrew, leaving a lingering, immediate sense of where it had been. She rose and walked back into the boathouse proper. I forced myself not to gaze after her, to stare instead across the water, as Telliyn re-emerged from behind the cloud and painted everything in pale glamour again.

When I woke in the morning, the lake appeared to have drained once more. But the captain had enjoined us to meet him on the dock at midmorning; so after a cold breakfast we packed up our gear, saddled the horses, and took the short ride to the dock.

Morning light shimmered in the mud flats, glittered on the water. The *Tansy*, the boat Amien had engaged, still rode below the dock, but someone had dragged a gangway from the dock to the deck. Amien paid the captain the fare, and we coaxed our horses down the swaying gangway while the crew stared: mostly at the Tana. Amien and I stared back at them, twice as intently, and most of them got the message.

Even as the party straggled across, the water rose a few inches. Within half an hour, the dock from which we had embarked lay lower than the boat on which we waited. An hour after that, the tide stilled briefly and then began running in the other direction; the crew raised the sail; and we were gliding south across the Black. Relief broke across Tanaan faces at the knowledge that we were, once again, temporarily safe from attacks. Faster and faster the tide ran, until the flow of the water outpaced the wind and the crew lowered the sail again.

And suddenly, as sometimes happens on the Ruillin, on a ship in the grip of the tide, everything was glorious. Brilliant sunshine revealed all the subtle hues of gold and white in Tanaan hair, glinted on the hilts of their weapons and the mail they wore; the wind of our passage brought color to their fair cheeks, sent their cloaks whipping and warrior tails streaming. Easca's head moved as if she might be scenting prey on the lake air, beautiful and deadly as a hawk's; Tru laughed, evidently for the pleasure of the flight across the water, and the music of it made the crew stop what they were doing and stare once more. This time I let it slide. The contingent might have stepped out of a song, and even Iminor, with his unsmiling face and eyes that saw far too much, fairly sparkled. I wondered when this exotic company had come to seem commonplace, and how much beauty I had failed to observe in my preoccupation with survival.

All of them paled beside Letitia, however. The red of her cloak sang against the profound emerald green of her eyes; her hair glowed in the water-light like spun gold. I kept catching myself trying to commit her profile to memory, trying to memorize the way her hair escaped its braid to tangle in the pin on her cloak. As if any effort would be necessary. As if it might be possible to forget.

Sometime after noon, we reached the south end of the lake. The crew anchored the boat a little distance from the dock; we resaddled the horses and waited with barely-contained impatience as the crew brought the gangway into place. From the dock we stepped out to a little fishing village whose name I didn't know, where all the houses stood on stilts and a narrow, weatherbeaten walkway served in place of a street.

I'd heard about this crossing between the lakes at the head of the Ruillin and the river proper: at low tide the flats stretch perhaps two miles between the Black and the Grey to the north and the river proper to the south; as the tide rises it sweeps straight across to spill into the lakes, eventually dashing itself against the Nemetona coast and whatever corresponding town lies at the head of the Grey. Evidently the transition between the river and the lakes is unnavigable at any time.

I tried and failed to imagine what it would be to have the land on which one lived invisible for most of the day. A man would have to love boats to tolerate it.

"Ya got mebbe five hours afore ya c'n get out and cross the flats to Goibniu," the captain said as we filed off. "Then mebbe two hours afore the water comes up too high again. Don't wait for the water to clear; ya'll never make it. Just get right out there soon's it's shallow enough."

Amien nodded. "Thank you." He glanced around at us. "Five hours."

Five hours with nothing to do but wait for the tide to go out. I would willingly have postponed Goibniu and the parting that must come there as long as anyone asked; but this just felt like the gods having a laugh at our expense.

"Let's see if they've got a tavern," I said. "And get some lunch."

The place had a tavern, but the owner clearly hadn't been expecting anyone this early in the day. We found him in a chair with his feet up, repairing a fishing net, as we arrived.

"Ho!" he said as we walked in, feet slamming to the floor. His gaze slipped past me and Amien to the Tanaan, and his eyes widened. "Damn," he said softly, then seemed to remember his manners.

"Welcome," he said, eyes still on the group behind me. "Where ya travelin' from? And what c'n I do for ya?" The inflection on this last question was nearly innocent, but only nearly so, and I felt myself bristling. Suddenly his eyes were on me again, and a little of the wind went out of his sails.

"We're on our way from Gorias," Amien said, as smoothly as if it were the truth. "Bound for Goibniu after the tide clears. We need—lunch? Maybe some news?"

"Gorias, eh?" The tavern-keep's gaze flicked back to the Tanaan again. "Ya'll be Tanaan, then? I never—"

"Yes," Letitia said calmly in Ilesian, ignoring all the ways she might have corrected him.

He gave vent to a long exhalation that spoke of wonder, longing, and a strange sort of relief.

"What is the name of this place?" she asked.

For half a second his mouth formed a perfect O. "Land's End, Lady."

In my peripheral vision I saw Letitia nod. "Yes. It does seem to be. What does one eat for lunch in Land's End, sian?"

"For you, Lady, anything ya want."

She smiled and pulled off her gloves; he looked as if he might faint. "Anything you have is fine."

The man stammered something about getting something for the lady, sketched a bow, and hurried into the recesses of the weathered building. I hoped he would remember to bring enough for the rest of us. We all pulled off our gloves, jackets, and cloaks—except Letitia, who pulled at the throat of her cloak a bit but didn't take it off—and settled on the benches of one of two long tables in the room. The place was dim after all the light out on the lake this morning, but through the tavern's open back door, the water to the south was easy to see. How would we know when the tide was receding? The Ruillin stretched away beyond sight; the only thing visible on the water was the faint protuberance of some tiny island a mile or so distant.

After a moment the tavern-keep returned with a pitcher in hand. A young woman I guessed to be his daughter followed him in with a tray full of earthenware cups, cast a glance among the Tanaan warriors gathered around the table, and turned as red as Letitia's cloak. She distributed cups around the table and retreated in a haze of confusion; the tavern-keep began pouring: not ale or beer as I'd expected, but wine. Evidently he had decided a Tanaan Lady rated nothing less.

Letitia smiled graciously at him, but I realized how precarious a path we meant to tread here on the Ruillin: no matter what we said, no matter what adornments Letitia wore or put aside, anyone who had heard the tale of the bounty on the neck of the Lady of Finias was likely to connect Letitia with what they had heard. How could people who couldn't differentiate Finias from Gorias, let alone know their true names, do otherwise? I should be grateful for the prospect of chartering a ship at Goibniu and extracting Letitia from this mess before too many people had a chance to see her.

"Ya'll be here for the moon rites, Lady?" he said shyly as he poured her wine.

"The moon rites?" she echoed.

To his credit, the tavern-keep flushed. "They say the Tanaan practice the old religion," he said softly, with a surreptitious glance at Amien. "Is't true?"

She cast a quizzical glance at him, head cocked. "I couldn't say, sian," she said courteously. "Which religion is the old one?"

"I believe," I said quietly, "he means the worship of the goddess." I couldn't work out whether I was being helpful; more than anything else, I was curious to see where this would lead. "The goddess of the Ruillin still has many followers here."

Letitia nodded. "Yes, sian, we honor the goddess."

A smile broke across the tavern-keep's pale face. "Ah, then ya'll've come just in time. This eve's the moon rites, down at the Lady's Well." He glanced along the table again at Amien, who was studiously engaged in missing the entire conversation, looking lost in thought and staring out the door. "The Bealtan moon comes full tonight."

"And her sister, as well," I observed, borrowing the phrasing I'd overheard in taverns and ferries and places less reputable, up and down the Ruillin: *the Lady moon, and her little sister*. In certain contexts those phrases are not only epithets for the moons but euphemisms for the tender bits of a woman.

The tavern-keep shot me a look of frank astonishment, as if I'd cracked some sort of hedge-row code; behind him, Amien caught my eye with a glance that said he knew I was toying with the man, and he couldn't decide how to feel about it. Still, I couldn't have said whether *toying* was the right word for it at all.

"Yah," the man said finally, nodding, and turned to Letitia again. "Ya'd be welcome at the Lady's Well this eve."

"Thank you, sian," she answered gravely. "But they tell us we must cross to Goibniu while the tide is low."

The tavern-keep nodded, smiling. "Sure. The Lady's Well is on the way, and the low tide is the only time ya can visit. Ya c'n see't from here," he said, pointing out the back door.

I followed his skinny arm, frowning. "All I see is a little island, sian."

"Yah! Those are the Pillars 'round the Well."

I nodded slowly. "So when would a man make the crossing, if he were going to visit the Lady's Well, and make it to Goibniu after that?"

The tavern-keep's mouth folded into a thoughtful moue. "Hour before sunset, give or take."

"And how long is the trip to Goibniu?" Iminor said.

The tavern-keep's head swiveled quickly for a look at the Tan. It took him a moment to formulate an answer.

"Mebbe two hours," he said finally.

"Putting us at Goibniu around nightfall."

The tavern-keep nodded gravely. "Not much time to spare when the tide's this late in the day. Ya don' wanna miss the gate."

"No doubt," I said. All the cities on the upper Ruillin lock their gates at night. Getting caught on the riverward side of the gate at the rising of the tide didn't bear contemplating.

"Then we must leave as soon as we can," Letitia said decisively. "I don't want to miss the chance to honor the goddess. Tonight is our night for observances as well. Can you tell us as soon as it's safe to start out?"

A look on his face that suggested far more than information would have been hers for the asking, the tavern-keep nodded. She smiled; he murmured something about checking to see if her lunch was ready and retreated.

Lunch consisted of fried fish and pan-bread. Two months ago in Ilnemedon, I would have been completely unimpressed; today it was delicious. The caution with which the Tanaan approached the food made me wonder how I had looked at their tables.

After lunch, the waiting began. Several of the knights walked out the door through which we had entered to explore the weathered-plank street, evidently exhausting the possibilities of that amusement in a short while. All of us walked out the back door, through which the main body of the Ruillin was visible, to meander around another, narrower plank walkway that extended only to the edges of the building and peer across the water for signs of the tide beginning to recede. From here the so-called pillars at Laverna's sacred site still looked like a little island. Back inside the tavern, Tuiri dug out a bag of dice, and several of the knights began a game on the table at which we hadn't eaten, as if a different table constituted a change of scene. I unpacked my harp and began tuning it, realizing only as the sound chest came to rest against my shoulder how much I had missed playing. Everyone looked at me expectantly; I shrugged.

"I'm really just plinking around," I said. At the other end of the room, the tavern-keep's pretense of ignoring our proceedings evaporated into a double-take; abruptly I realized I'd thrown the Ilesian phrase into Tanaan without even thinking about it, and the Tanaan had all understood.

"And I haven't tuned it in half a twelvenight. With your indulgence, Mora," I said to Letitia.

She smiled wistfully and said, "As it may amuse you, my lord." And I found myself smiling in return: remembering the time I had first played for her on the bank of the Crearu a hundred years ago; struck anew by the wonder of this company and how far we had all come. But up the heels of that awareness raced the fact that it was all ending. I turned my focus to the business of tuning, though I could have done the job with a fraction of my attention, waiting for the wave of things I couldn't allow myself to say to pass by.

But instead of passing, it intensified. I shifted from tuning to playing: an unscripted song whose ending I couldn't predict, which evolved from phrase to phrase under my hands. There were no words; there could never be any words. I was a fool. I tried to lose myself in playing, but the people around me kept drawing my attention: Mattiaci rising from the dice game to draw Tru into an open space and dance to this song whose rhythms shifted from one moment to the next; Manannan, whose eyes had grown full of *last times*, crossing the room to pull the tavern-keep's daughter from the inner doorway and wordlessly draw her into the dance as well; Amien, face etched with some grief I couldn't identify; Letitia, whose face and hands and fragile bravery prompted phrase after phrase from my strings. And abruptly, although the song wasn't over, I couldn't play it anymore, because something inside me was ready to burst. I lifted my hands from the strings; I set the harp aside and strode out to the narrow walkway at the back of the room, feeling them all stare after me. For some minutes I just gazed across the water, waiting for rational thought to return. When it finally did, I realized how perilously far inside my walls I had allowed all of them to come. I must repair my borders or find myself making emotional mistakes of every sort.

An hour before sunset, finally, we were ready to set out. Iminor paid the tavern-keep, in silver of Fíana I felt certain the man would never spend; Letitia thanked him warmly for his hospitality, and he flushed to the roots of his thinning hair.

"Will we see you at the Lady's Well?" she asked as she pulled on her gloves. Sudden shyness came over him; he smiled a little, glancing at his shoes.

"No, Lady," he said. "Only horses c'n cross from here during the spring tides. I woulda needed leave hours ago, and go 'round by way o' the Grey, to reach the Lady's Well in time."

Regret suffused Letitia's face. "And we delayed you! Sian, I am sorry."

This time he dared to meet her gaze. "I'm not, Lady. There'll be other Bealtan moons. Ya're here today."

Out on the flats, I understood the meanings of all the puzzling things we'd heard about the crossing. I made the whole party wait while I unlashed the harp case from my saddle and slung it across my back: the water still rose to my horse's withers. The powerful southward flow of the tide would have quickly overmastered a man. But the tide withdrew steadily, and by the time we approached the rocks we had seen from the tavern, the water was no higher than my horse's knees.

The so-called pillars at the Lady's Well looked for all the world like melting stelae in a sun-circle made of wax. They seemed not manmade but sculpted by the tide: a fitting tribute to a river goddess. And unlike the quiescent shrine to Lady Tella at Nemetona, the place pulsed with arcane energy so strong that I realized just in time how automatically I was opening myself to its flow. I managed to hold myself closed, but I still felt the seduction swirling around me, raising little rills of pleasure up my spine.

No. No. If opening myself to power would be a violation of my vow, how much greater an offense would the goddess find it if the thing that finally seduced me was a site dedicated to one of the old gods? I didn't want to imagine trying to explain myself to Her. I swallowed against the temptation, gathering the reins in my fists as if I might grasp my sad excuse for control.

The flats climbed slightly as we approached the site; atop the rise, the mud lay exposed in ripples that showed the action of the tide. More than three dozen people already stood around the pillar-stones. At the base of the rise we dismounted, I gratefully pulled the harp from my back again and lashed it to the saddle where it belonged, and we walked up to join the crowd. A number of people looked at us, but most of them returned their attention to the goings-on within the circle, where three plainly-dressed women stood at the edge of a pool in the center, making offerings and reciting a prayer that sounded as if I should recognize it. Power hummed in my brain until I felt I might split open.

The ceremony wasn't long; by the time Telliyn had risen at the eastern horizon, the whole thing was over, and people had begun lining up to bathe in the pool.

"Like a sacred spring," Letitia observed in an undertone to Iminor. I had a sudden flash of her as a priestess in this place, making offerings, bathing in the pool. Did they celebrate Bealtan itself here?

"You're not going in?" Iminor answered, a wary edge to his voice.

A vision of a wholly unorthodox Bealtan, with Laverna as the Bealtan goddess and a Tanaan priestess as Her avatar, began to unfold itself in my mind. Instead of trees, a pillar circle; instead of the soft grass of a sacred grove, the welcoming waters of a sacred pool.

Letitia shook her head, stepping through the circle of melted stones. "But I'm going to make an offering."

The Ruillin is unpredictable and frequently harsh, but Laverna had never brought an entire people to its knees. Surely She was more deserving of Letitia's devotion than their goddess Dana. With Letitia as Laverna's priestess, who could resist the urge to worship here?

"Ti—" Iminor said urgently, voice little more than a whisper.

She paused, looking back at him.

He shook his head, distress written in his face. "We should go. It's getting late; the tide will turn soon."

She shook her head.

"What if you fall in—?"

She cast him an impatient glance, already unfastening the pin from her cloak. "I'm not going to fall in."

Letitia crossed the little perimeter between the stones and the pool, stood at the pool's edge with the pin in her hands. It winked in the light of the setting sun as she held it, face alien and beautiful in the stillness of her devotions. Even the priestess administering the bathing of the worshipers seemed unable to look away from Letitia; but then someone in the crowd at the other side of the circle shrieked, and everyone looked west. Galloping across the flats, sending water splashing in every direction, came a contingent of Básghilae.

"Avengers!" somebody shouted; suddenly everyone seemed to be running in a different direction. The human stampede surged through the circle of stones. Letitia's voice rang briefly above the throng, and she fell into the pool with a resounding splash. Iminor shouted—at me, I felt certain—but all I caught was *undead* and *water*. I knew what he meant, though: *The undead cannot cross water? The hell they can't!* But then the Básghilae took their first victims, and the splashing of those energies against my skin made me lose track of everything else.

It was only a second, I knew; but in that second I was completely lost. Rapture blasted through me, holding me fast; for that instant the source of the delight was completely irrelevant. But I had been trained to work through whatever energies might flow from a working, and that training took over: immediately every arcane sense I possessed was open wide, and the stray life-energies of a dozen people flowed through me and away.

I hadn't drawn power. I hadn't. But the hunger roared in me now, and as I raced into the circle with the Tanaan, claiming a place at the pool's western edge and the forefront of the onslaught, I saw the full truth of each of the ghouls that came at us. The first man I faced had been Essuvian; he was a cocktail of despair, the life-energies of a woman of Goibniu, and a surprising shot of the power of the Well at my back—and beneath that, beneath everything, the presence that was becoming all too familiar, the man called the Bard's Wizard. I didn't draw on those energies, though it felt as if I had arrived at a banquet hungry and then refused to eat; but I saw, behind the dead man's eyes, the clear and fearless awareness that drove everything he did. It would have been easy to open a direct arcane connection with the wizard. Instead I applied myself to destroying his masterfully-created tool. That is warfare, in the end: the deliberate destruction of things that men of talent have crafted with all their skill. I wrecked that effort and turned my attention to the next.

At some point during my next engagement—another Essuvian, flavored more with impotent rage than despair, who tasted of the recent lives of both a woman and a man—I realized that the Tanaan who stood with me around the Well had been replaced by horses; I spared a glance to my right and discovered Iminor mounted beside me, blade sliding and sparking against a dead man's as he fought for control. And then, suddenly, as I wrecked another painstakingly-crafted Básghil, my horse appeared at my left hand; and Manannan was offering me the reins.

I met his gaze, seeing all the honor of a warrior who has dedicated his life to the defense of people who need him, the knowledge of his life trickling away hour by hour, his determination to use his remaining days to serve the same ideals he had pursued all along—and his horrifying gratitude that whatever happened in the next few days, he wasn't going to end up like those ghouls. Sudden, soul-deep self-loathing swept over me. These dire ghouls I secretly admired, these energies that lit up every power center I possessed: they were the profoundest wrongs anyone had ever seen, and I didn't know the difference between good and evil anymore. I wasn't sure I ever had.

But in a sudden, blinding flash, I saw it now: this man who just wanted to use his remaining hours defending the woman who needed him; the innocent woman who required all our defense; the warriors who had committed themselves to the task despite dangers beyond anything they had ever imagined; the simple people who just tried to live right lives every day, to honor the gods as they understood them—those were the things to which I should commit my heart and blade. These black energies and dire workings were not only threats to the people I had mistakenly allowed myself to love: they were things that must be eradicated from my self.

I scrambled into the saddle; by the time I looked back to meet Manannan's gaze again he was gone. And the next Básghil was on me. I saw him just as clearly now, but now it was all different: the horror and despair of the man's entrapment tore at my throat; the waste of the simple lives he'd been forced to take in order to continue his unending nightmare raised a twisting revulsion in my chest. The awareness behind his eyes was colder, crueler than I had imagined a man might be. Loathing and ire welled up in me, drove my blade, made me burn with the need to use arcane means against him as well. The ghoul was down; the man I wanted to destroy was once again out of reach; I glanced around to locate Letitia and my next opponent—and spotted a newly-exposed path across the rapidly emptying flats, which led in the direction of Goibniu. I wanted desperately to engage my enemy again, but finally I was able to recognize that my first priority must be Letitia. She was in the saddle, like the rest of them, soaked to the bone but sword at the ready; I shouted, and they broke from their engagements and followed me across the flats, Básghilae on their heels.

Gradually our lighter, faster horses pulled away from our pursuers. But before long we came upon a group of people fleeing along the same path. I knew what would happen if we overtook them and raced for safety: a moment later, the Básghilae would overtake them too, and they would fall victim to the enemy. There was no choice; a swift glance exchanged with Letitia settled the matter, and I reined. We formed up, right there on the flats, as Letitia shouted for the people behind us to run. The Básghilae crashed into us, and the engagement began again.

The power they carried blasted through me, setting me alight even while the eyes of the first opponent met mine and my gut twisted with the horror of what I saw. He was trapped by evil; it wasn't his fault; but the pity I reached for was subsumed by hatred, and I wanted nothing more than to hack him to bloodless bits. I destroyed him, and the one who followed, and if I did either of them any service it was only by accident. I knew what they were, knew the manner of their making and the atrocity of their existence, and I could not rest until even their memories had ceased to exist.

Yet their memories would linger, and their energies would haunt my dreams, and my opponent knew it too. I suspected I was already as doomed as Manannan.

Finally the people we protected had run beyond sight; we broke away and fled again. Over and again we fought that rear-guard action, while the walls of Goibniu and the long, steep ascent to its gate hove into view—and the tide began to flow in the wrong direction. The waters rose steadily around us; each time we had to delay a little longer as the fleeing people behind us fought the flow, as energies I knew were evil but couldn't help craving knocked against my awareness and sought out the chinks in my nonexistent armor. My head whirled with desire; my throat knotted with horror; I gave up trying to reconcile the two and let the imperatives of the engagement take me.

Automatically my mind tallied fallen ghouls and Amien's increasing arcane success against them, the rising of the waters and the growing proximity of defensible walls; a sector of my awareness observed and approved the consistency with which the Tanaan bested their opponents, the way they protected each other's flanks, the unity with which the contingent moved. Finally the noncombatants behind us were racing up the ascent to the gate—and straight into market-day traffic on its way back home. The Básghilae seemed to spot the tangle and the potential victims at the same moment we did; ghouls we had not yet engaged stopped swarming around the edges of the fray and broke towards the people on the Goibniu gate road.

And suddenly Manannan broke away as well, overtaking them all, racing up the steep road to the place where sodden people had run up against local farmers and their wares. Even as we hacked our ways out of the fray to join him, he cut through the people on the ascending road like a herdsman among cattle, driving them all gradually up the rise. We outpaced the ghouls we had been fighting, but the ones who had broken away before us reached the Goibniu gate road first, and all of us dragged increasingly tired mounts through rising water.

On the gate road, Manannan had somehow managed to single-handedly turn the tide of people, and they were scrambling towards the gate with the first wave of Básghilae in pursuit. Water surged steadily up the road, faster and faster as is the Ruillin's way. The low wall separating the steep lane from an abrupt drop into the water disappeared beneath the racing tide; there was nothing to do but guess where it had been and press on, attacking the Básghilae from below as Manannan tried hopelessly to fight them off from above. Behind him, people cut donkeys and cart-horses loose from their burdens and hurried them through the gate, leaving an obstacle course of half-laden wagons behind. Manannan planted himself between two wagons, blocking the Básghilae's path, blade humming among three opponents simultaneously and apparently oblivious to the wounds they inflicted. We had very nearly won through to the spot he occupied when one of the ghouls separated his head from his shoulders and his body toppled into the rising surf.

A roar tore from my throat; I turned fury and some flavor of loss for which *grief* was too small a word on the opponents that remained between us—but by the time we had defeated them, the rest of the Básghilae were attacking from below. Nuad and I shouted the same instructions simultaneously; the knights re-formed with Letitia at the rear, covering her retreat through the racing tide. By the time she was within reach of the gate I realized I couldn't see Manannan's body anywhere, and the water was less than a dozen feet below the entrance. It was too late; it had been too late four days ago; I shouted at the knights until they were all inside, and as I rode through behind them, somebody slammed down the portcullis so fast I felt the wind of its passing on my neck. Seconds later a wooden gate crashed closed as well.

Letitia's skin achieved a heretofore-undiscovered shade of white; her eyelids fluttered, and she fell unconscious across her horse's dripping neck. Her sword slipped from her fingers and clattered on the stone at her horse's feet. Easca looked intensely thoughtful for a moment, then burst into tears.

"Well done," I croaked, looking around at the party. "Dear gods, well done. I need far more than one drink."

"Pra-nu," Amien said.

Chapter 19
A Night for Strong Drink

I had never visited Goibniu before tonight: its reputation as a rough, unappealing mining town had dissuaded me from ever making the trip. The place lived up to the reports: the streets we traveled seemed populated exclusively by gambling and drinking establishments; street vendors hawking food with smells that elicited wildly conflicting messages from my stomach; smithies and a jeweler or two, with shops already shut tight for the evening; and, perennial as wildflowers on the Ruillin and as numerous, women of the profession that is politely called *night butterflies*. But nothing I'd heard had prepared me for the energies humming in the air of this place: Goibniu vibrated with the power of the old gods, infiltrating my tattered boundaries until I ached with need.

Goibniu looks to the old smith-god for Whom it is named, the god of the forge and the underground ways that yield secret treasures; I felt the power rumbling beneath the earth of this place, wafting up from the smithies, swirling in the smoke of the smelters. And from the east, proximate and in a surprisingly-easy peace with the palpable presence of the energies underfoot, the raw power of the river swirled around the edges of my mind. None of these energies should move a man devoted to the true gods, but I couldn't shut them from my awareness or stop the thrills they raised along my flesh. I strove to pin my mind to the present moment, to hear the speech of my companions and see the mundane faces of things the people around me saw. I was not entirely successful.

Letitia was still pale and shaken, though she sat erect in the saddle and spoke in carefully firm tones; but it was the things running beneath her surface, the soft sparkle of a power whose name I didn't know, that commanded my attention. She'd lost her personal wards again: doubtless they had been knocked out by the power of Laverna's Well. The glow about her was all her own. Amien glimmered against the mundane people and things around us: his energies were familiar, as deeply lodged in my subconscious as the scent of home. Iminor cast a shadow that was more complex than the simple absence of light, though its flavor didn't compel me. I kept fantasizing about wrapping my mouth around Letitia, and the reasons for that were not entirely sexual.

The city fathers of Goibniu had never bothered with street lighting; we charted a path by the lamps outside the taverns and gambling halls, the light spilling through doors that opened as men came and went, the last fading streaks of scarlet and orange above the mountains to the west, the brilliant glow of two full moons. At the edges of the pools of light, night butterflies gathered like moths, the vibrant colors of their hair sparking under the lamps and the huge dark pools of their eyes seeming to swallow the night. The men we passed on the street stared frankly at the Tana, and a few of the more inebriated assayed tired come-ons; but the Tans in the party couldn't help ogling the night butterflies.

"Endeáril, look at that one!" Fiacha said to Ogma, grey eyes sparkling.

"No, her!" Tuiri added.

"Sweet Lord, where do they get those hair colors?" Tru said.

"They're dyes," I said. "Like for clothing? But these are made for hair."

"Unbelievable," Tru said, as we passed a pair of provocatively-dressed women sporting hair in vibrant shades of scarlet and blue and the floating silk scarves that are the signature of the profession.

"Hello," Mattiaci said to them, masterfully demonstrating his entire Ilesian vocabulary. Tru walloped him on the back of the head, without real malice.

"I could make a fortune selling belladonna in this place," Amien groused.

I surprised myself by laughing; but Letitia roused herself to say, "Belladonna? Isn't that...?"

"A drug," I said. "Yes. It's good for fever, but it'll give a woman who isn't ill fever-dreams. And eyes that look like that."

"Her pupils are huge," Letitia said.

"They all are," Iminor added.

I nodded.

"And that's... beautiful?" Letitia said, puzzled.

I laughed again, but this time with embarrassment for my race. The Tanaan all watched me, waiting for an answer; suddenly I was glad we were speaking a language the people around us couldn't understand.

"The idea..." I began, then glanced at Amien. "You want to take this one?"

He laughed. "Not a chance. You walked into it."

I sighed. "The idea is that belladonna eyes... look like Danaan eyes."

Now the glances I received ranged from puzzlement to astonishment.

"I... wasn't going to bring this up, but you might as well know: Beallan men everywhere, of every station, have—certain ideas about Danaan women."

Letitia raised her eyebrows, waiting for me to continue.

I wasn't going to explain it all. I couldn't. How can a man be expected to tell people he respects that his kind objectifies their kind, sees them as objects of fantasy and possible sources of enchantment? It was simply not possible to explain that a human man who looks at a Tana sees, beyond the natural beauty of their race, a person whose mind is occupied with little but sex, who has either such great need or so little discernment that the meanest and ugliest among men is likely to find his wildest fantasies satisfied; that a Tana who meets a man otherwise immune to her charms (that mythical creature) is likely to enchant him so he succumbs to her desires. We breathe these ideas like air in the Beallan realms; they seem reasonable until one has met the purported wanton enchantresses in the flesh and realized that they are all as different as human women are. But it was too humiliating to admit, too difficult to explain—especially with Bealtan growing so near, and the light of the lamps around us making it so easy to imagine Letitia in the glow of a Bealtan fire. Her eyes would be as deep with night-vision, as full of the gleam of emeralds, as they were now. Her gentle intoxicating power would fill every corner of my being.

I tried to clear my throat, but it didn't help. I should come at the problem from a different angle.

"Beallan women... aspire to the beauty of Danaan women," I said. I relaxed a little: I could get through this version. "I suspect the Danaan do not realize how very beautiful a race they are. How could you, when you see that beauty all the time?"

Letitia cracked a reluctant smile. "It has been a while since we've seen the honey-tongued harpist."

I felt myself flush, suddenly grateful for the poor light. "Ah, sweet lady, I am trying to speak truth. Will you hear it?"

Her smile faded. "Your pardon, my lord. Go on."

I nodded, unable to resist the urge to glance away. "Because—Beallan men... so desire the beauty of Danaan women, the night butterflies try to look like them." There: the worst of it was over. "Or what they imagine they look like, since most Bealla never meet a Danaan. Mostly what they go by is the songs—"

"The songs?" Letitia said.

I offered her a rueful glance. "Which praise the wonder and depth of Danaan eyes, which are sure to enchant a man—" Mattiaci guffawed; Tru whacked him again.

"Among their many other beautiful attributes," I finished lamely.

"Sweet Lord," Iminor said. "Bealla are insane."

I nodded. "Indeed, ouirr, every one of us."

Everyone fell silent, surveying the night butterflies again. Amien spotted the inn he wanted and beckoned; we all followed.

"Oh, I wish Manannan could have seen this," Ogma said.

"Especially the part about the drug," Tuiri added. "He would have *laughed...*"

Most of the party went directly down the alley between buildings, to the stable behind the inn. I followed Amien inside. The place failed to impress, although I had stayed in worse inns: it was reasonably clean and well-lit, with stout, scarred plank floors and walls half-timbered. I'd seen that style of building before: the plaster concealed not stone but packed straw or rushes, whose coating of plaster served to keep vermin out but would do little to prevent the spread of a fire.

Like most inns on the Ruillin, this one was set up to accommodate four men to a room—though a single bed was laughingly assumed to be enough for them all, be they lovers or strangers. We were now only eleven, so Amien let three, and paid extra for locks for the doors, using the name Rinnal Ruthin.

"Ruthin?" the innkeeper said, looking puzzled. "Why do I—? Oh! Somebody left a message for you!" He rummaged around in the cubbies of his desk, finally coming up with a folded piece of paper with *Rinnal Ruthin* written on the outside.

Amien received the page and unfolded it—and laughed.

"What?" I said.

"Note from my friend," he said, and handed it to me.

Sry we missed you. Inn w sausage & blood-pudding 3 dys. R.

R must be Rohini, High Chief of the Essuvians. I wondered which inn she meant, and why *sausage and blood pudding*, obviously a code, was funny.

"She remembered," Amien said wonderingly, taking the note and stowing it in his pocket as we walked out to collect our horses. His smile made me suspect the rumors about the nature of his relationship with Rohini might be true, after all. He had always maintained they were friends, no more, though stories suggested they had traveled together under different circumstances before she stepped up to the Uxellian throne.

"It's one thing to remember which inn I'd choose, but the name..." He smiled again, shaking his head.

"What does she mean?"

"Ah! She'll meet us at Ballarona." Abruptly he sobered. "Assuming we can't find a ship, of course."

"Of course." My mind skipped forward of its own accord: tomorrow morning we would part company. And I would have to choose between lying to him and humiliating myself at Teamair.

The wizard cleared his throat, and I knew his mind had run in the same direction. "Ellion, I—"

We stepped through the door. Our horses stood waiting at the hitching post—and Fiacha was with them, smiling at me as if I were the still-green knight who needed reassurance after a difficult encounter and he the one who had more scars than his companion had years.

"Let's see what happens with the ship," I said.

Amien nodded, and we mounted and followed the alley to the stable, where we claimed the last three stalls. I began unburdening my horse and discovered, as shocking as if it belonged to another, my harp case still lashed to the saddle. Of course it was soaked. I groaned, leaning my forehead against the saddle while grief welled in my chest.

"What is it, Lord?" Fiacha said from the stall across the corridor.

"My harp," I said, trying to sound calm. "Gods, how *stupid*..."

A harp can be replaced, of course, even one as rare and expensive as an instrument crafted by the talented Bernatel. And there was a chance that, if I pulled out the gut strings, it would dry without warping. And yet I felt as though a friend had died, and I had no one to blame but myself. I gathered up my meager discipline, unburdened the horse and saw to his care, then dragged my sodden bags and harp up to the room I would share with Amien, Tuiri, and Fiacha tonight. Tuiri and Fiacha went straight down the hall to the bath, as delighted by the opportunity as boys on their way to a pond at the height of summer; Amien deposited his belongings in a corner and went back out to ask around for a ship for hire. I sat down and unpacked my harp.

The speckled-hide case was so thoroughly soaked I feared even it was ruined; the harp felt sickeningly damp under my hands. I sighed and began removing the smaller, gut strings. They would surely shrink as they dried, pulling the harp irrecoverably off the true. The longer, metal strings I left in place, in the forlorn hope that they might help the drying wood maintain its shape. I pulled a towel from the wash-stand, dried the instrument as well as I could, and stood the harp on top of it, at a distance from the fire that I hoped would provide therapeutic warmth without drying it too fast. By the time I had pulled the last, wet things from my saddlebags and found places to drape them overnight, Tuiri and Fiacha had returned, so I left the false bottoms of the bags in place. The money hidden there would suffer no ill effects from the damp, after all.

I stood surveying the array of things that had seemed important enough to pack, a hundred years ago when I left Ilnemedon. They looked like supplies for another man's trip. I couldn't imagine why I had bothered with half of them.

Among the things I had packed and then more or less forgotten about was a razor. I took it with me to the bath.

By the time I arrived, only Mattiaci and Ogma remained in the room, and they were nearly dressed. The floor was slick, the air heavy with steam. I found a tub that didn't seem to be coated with half the mud of the Ruillin, drew fresh water, and mixed in enough hot to make it steam. As I pulled off my clothes, Mattiaci and Ogma left; I slipped into the tub and let the silence settle around me.

I washed; there was much of which I needed to be clean, but little enough that soap and water might solve. All the day's failures came crashing in on me, and I was helpless against the recollection of the illicit energies I had tasted: the seduction of Laverna's Well on the flats, the terrible rapture of the lives sacrificed to feed the Básghilae, the cold, horrifying elegance of the Básghilae themselves and the wild mixtures of energies they carried after they fed. All of these raced through my memory, raising thrills and shame in equal measure. During those seconds when I managed to push the recollections aside, the omnipresent subterranean rumble of the power in this place and the deadly seduction of the river raced in to torque me further.

Horrifying as all those things were, their implications were worse: they were tools my enemy could use to get through me to Letitia, forces that could make me lose track of the men who were my responsibility. Had I maintained focus on the flats today, would Manannan have left himself so open to death?

I knew the answer. Yet after the first time it became evident he was setting and pursuing his own objectives, when he handed me my horse, I had been so consumed by the arcane aspects of the encounter that I completely failed to bring him to heel. Little wonder he had died on the gate road, out of reach of men who might guard his flanks. Little wonder I'd wrecked a harp, a Bernatel-made three-octave double whose like most harpists will never see.

I shaved, remotely surprised that I had passed the point at which the stuff I shaved might be justly called stubble. Eventually I looked and smelled clean on the outside, but inside I was unchanged. I slid down in the water until my knees poked out into cold air and my skull rested against the rim of the tub, weight in my chest.

The door opened; Amien walked in.

"Hello," he said.

"Hello," I answered. "Success?"

In my peripheral vision, I saw him shrug. "An airship. There isn't a water-ship for love or money anywhere in this town."

I nodded as well as I might with my head on the rim of the tub, still staring at the ceiling. It would be tomorrow, then. Letitia and her companions would be far safer without me. I couldn't feel good about it.

Amien stopped mixing water in a tub and fixed me with a black-eyed stare. "What?"

I groaned and slipped farther down in the tub. "I wrecked my harp. The damn thing was lashed to my saddle the whole time we were out there with the water coming up around us, and I *forgot*. Oh, gods, how stupid am I! How could I let that happen? You'd think I'd pay better attention!"

Amien knew as well as I, of course: a harp is a sacred instrument, the vehicle not only of pleasure and learning but of the magical strains handed down by the Hy-Breasaílian gods. The proper care of a harp is a geas upon every harpist. But he shook his head.

"Manannan was a champion, and he knew his time was up," the wizard said gently.

My head whipped around of its own accord, and I felt myself stare.

"He chose his exit, Ellion."

I couldn't think of anything to say. Instead I hauled myself up and out of the tub, water surging in my wake like the incoming tide, and I knew I was still staring. There was a terrible heaviness in my chest.

"What?" Amien said, apparently in answer to my astonishment. "You've had that same look every time we lost someone—since Arian. If I can't—" He shook his head again. "It's not your fault."

Oh, gods. A wall inside me was crumbling, as if those words had been the release spell for a binding. From behind that wall, a great weight of grief and guilt came spilling out. But even as the forgiveness I hadn't known I needed threatened to shake me apart, I knew I didn't deserve it, knew Amien would never have said those words if he understood. I could barely breathe. And suddenly I wanted to punch him. Instead I spun away and put my fist through the plaster.

I'd been wrong: it wasn't just straw behind that plaster, though I'd managed to leave a fist-sized hole. My hand began to bleed. I pulled on my pants, gathered up the rest of my clothes, and walked out.

At the base of the stairs to the inn's main room I encountered a night butter-fly, a comely if perfectly mundane young woman with bright purple hair and a filmy blue scarf, who greeted me with a knowing smile and a movement of the shoulder that made me aware of the conformation of her breasts.

"Hungry?" she said, in tones that made it clear she wasn't offering food, surveying me from toes to hair with a great show of eyelashes and a languor-ous smirk.

But rather than falling into the dance with her as I ordinarily would have, whether or not I was interested in a metaphoric meal, I found my mind stut-tering like a cart with a stick lodged in a wheel. I blinked.

"Thirsty," I managed finally and brushed past her with an attempt at a courteous nod, then strode into the main room.

Even this was exactly what I had heard: with the exception of the Tana with whom I traveled, the only women in the place worked here. All of our party but Amien were already present, gathered around two large tables someone had pushed end-to-end. I noted with relief that they had all had the good sense to leave their mail in the rooms, and all were dressed for an evening indoors—except Letitia, who wore her cloak again. The fire on the hearth and the heat of the stove in the kitchen made the room too warm for the heavy gar-ment; her fair cheeks were flushed nearly as red as the cloak. Though I didn't precisely understand her choice, I saw the sense of obligation that underlaid it. My respect for her honor grew again.

None of the Tanaan seemed aware of the way men stared from tables all over the room, which I counted a blessing. They looked up as I approached, smiles breaking across somber faces. But as I settled at the table, Letitia's gaze fixed on the hand I'd smashed in the bath, and horrified guilt flared in her eyes.

"Your hand!" she said. "You're injured! Oh, Holy—"

"No, it's all right," I interrupted. "I'm just a fool."

"It wasn't a—?"

"Hush," I said quickly, waving her to silence. "That's not a topic for open rooms."

Her gaze shifted into a mixture of guilt and hurt.

"I'm sorry," I said. "And no, I managed to do it myself."

She nodded, but her eyes were on something behind me now. And there wasn't time to address it, because a barmaid had arrived at our table and stood staring down at me. Her dark hair surprised me after all the flaxen or red-blonde hair on the Tanaan and the vibrant hues on the night butterflies.

"Good eve to ya, sian," she said, somehow embedding all the flirtation I should have expected of a barmaid in that simple greeting.

"Good eve," I answered. The polite smile I offered was in no way up to the standard of charm I had once carried without half a thought. I had lost the knack, and that wouldn't do.

"What c'n I get ya?"

That was an opening through which a man might drive a team of horses. I tried out a more charming smile. "Something of which there's enough to go around."

The fun had gone out of it. All I wanted was a drink.

"Spirits," I said, including the others at the table with my glance. "This is a night for strong drink."

"Pra-nu," Letitia said.

"Brandy?" I said to the barmaid. "Or water o' life, if you've got it?"

Her disappointment at my failure to flirt vanished into anticipation of a healthy pile of coin. "Uisge-Beal—that we've got."

The blasphemous name, *Water of Beal*, didn't even surprise me. Of course everything here would be named for old gods. And all the gods knew I was in no position to judge.

Nevertheless anticipation of the relief of a decent drunk made my smile real. "And some dinner?"

"Stew? Or meat pies."

I'd seen enough stew in the past twelvenight to last me a lifetime. "The pies."

The barmaid looked around at the rest of them, then back at me. Even Iminor and Letitia seemed to be waiting for my cue.

"Ah, pies for everyone," I said. "Plenty of 'em."

She grinned and fairly bounced across the room.

"Have you seen Amien?" Iminor asked.

I nodded. "He's in the bath. Probably done by now."

"Did he find a ship?" Iminor pursued.

All at once I realized I hadn't told any of them except Letitia. Even Amien thought I would be on that airship in the morning. My throat tightened.

"An airship," I said, using the Ilesian word. I couldn't help glancing at Letitia. Her eyes conveyed all that might be said in this company: she remembered what I'd said, and she was both disappointed and frightened at the idea of my leaving her. And somehow, maybe because it was an airship and not a watership, she held onto hope that I would change my plan.

"An—A ship of the air?" Iminor said in Tanaan. His voice was even, but trepidation lurked behind his eyes. He feared heights, but he'd seemed to get over it after the pass. Those complex shadows gathered around him again, despite the lamps in the room; I blinked them away and nodded.

"You're familiar with airships?" I said. All the Tanaan looked at Iminor, obviously waiting for an explanation they could wrap minds around; but he shook his head.

"They—*fly*?" Ogma said, incredulous.

I nodded. "Essentially an airship is a huge basket with a great silk canopy, into which a particular sort of brazier blows hot air. The hot air makes it float."

"Do you know how to—sail one?" Tuiri said.

I shook my head. "They have captains and windcallers, just like ships of the water. You hire the ship and the crew both. All you do is ride."

"But you've been in one?" Tuiri pursued.

I nodded: I had. It was more amusing than sailing on the river, but not nearly as good as wearing the shape of an eagle. Though that was a thing I didn't do anymore, either. It struck me that there were a great many things I no longer did, and the things I didn't do anymore were vastly more satisfying than most of the things I still engaged in. Fortunately the barmaid turned up with a trayful of cups and a bottle of spirits, in glass.

Glass. I almost laughed. She'd taken our measure and brought the most expensive thing they had.

"Yah?" she said, meeting my eyes. And suddenly I just didn't care.

"Yes," I answered, and she set a cup in front of me, pulled the stopper from the bottle, and poured.

I drank; the familiar fire of uisquebae raced through me, sparking a memory of life-energies not my own that crashed through my being—and pushing everything just a little farther away.

"Yes," I said again, and set down my cup. She poured once more; the sound warmed my heart. "I predict we will need another soon."

"There's more," she said, and began passing out cups.

Once all the cups were full, Letitia raised hers, looking up and down the table. We all joined her salute.

"Manannan a Boind," she said, voice and face carefully composed. "A champion. A man of honor."

She drank, so I did too. Her eyes widened, and she paused after a sip, gasping in surprise, but all the knights tossed theirs back and slammed their cups to the table. I smiled and slammed mine down too, so Iminor and finally Letitia followed.

"Sláinte," I said, and poured more for everyone I could reach. I was at the end of the table, so my reach didn't extend far; I slid the bottle to Nuad, who met my eyes with a fey smile and poured for everyone else. Because I'd employed similar tricks in my own behalf, I could see that Nuad poured Letitia only a half-measure without making the difference apparent; I shot him an approving glance, and he astonished me with a wink.

This time Iminor raised his cup, and we all followed—just as Amien arrived. The air around him rippled with arcane presence. His black eyes saw me, perhaps truly, certainly in a way no one else had in years. He surveyed the table, cast a long look over me, then nodded and took up the seat opposite mine. By the time he settled, the barmaid was there with another cup. Nuad slid the bottle back to me, and I poured for the wizard.

"Another one of these," I said to the barmaid. "And some pies—Meat pies?" I asked Amien. "Or stew."

"Pies," Amien said, nodding. We all picked up our cups again.

"Manannan a Boind," Iminor said. "More years as a champion, and a member of the Guard, than everyone else put together."

We drank; we slammed down our cups. People at other tables glanced at us.

"Sláinte," I said again, and began pouring the next round. Nuad picked up where I left off. The barmaid brought two trays of steaming meat-pies, which smelled delicious. Nuad raised his cup this time.

"Manannan a Boind," he said. A strange smile played over his lips, then crumpled. "My teacher. My friend."

Again we drank; again we slammed.

"Sláinte!" Ogma said at the same time I did; Letitia laughed, whether at Ogma or at something inside her own head I wasn't certain. The mundane world receded a good distance, though I could still feel the power of the old gods humming around the edges of my brain.

"Meat pies," Tuiri said, as if it were a revelation. We slid the trays up and down the length of the tables so everyone could reach. This proved more amusing than anyone had expected. The pie tasted as good as only uisquebae can make tavern food seem.

"We have an airship," Iminor said gravely to Amien.

"Yes," the wizard said. "In the morning."

"How big is this thing?"

"Big enough for twelve," Amien said in a satisfied tone.

"Twelve *people*?" Iminor asked with the same grave courtesy and achingly precise diction. "Or twelve horses and riders?"

"Um," Amien said. "Fouzh. Yes, I had meant to…" He shook his head; unexpectedly I spotted a solution to my problem.

"Ni hanasa," I said; a catch-phrase harpists and wizards, and all men of learning, share: *Not hard.* It is what one says when called upon to explain something terribly complex, and it must be delivered without irony. Why it sprang to my lips I couldn't have said; but it made a kind of sense to me tonight that it never had except when I had stood in Amien's workshop, mind wider than the room with the presence of magic.

"I am the mora's ground crew," I said, and though something in me hurt at what I knew I must say, I smiled. "I'll get the horses to stable until you need them back—after all, you won't need them at Aballo."

Amien frowned, nodding. All the Tanaan except Iminor looked as if I had delivered terrible news. Easca visibly swallowed a protest; I couldn't look at Letitia. Iminor was still too controlled to allow the satisfaction in his eyes to manifest in his face, but the habitual tension went out of his body. I made a point of not noticing.

"And I'll get word to… your friend at the inn," I said.

The wizard gave me a long, silent look, as if he saw through my pretense of a smile to the things I couldn't afford to say.

"And we will meet again at the Fair," he said finally, black gaze fixed on mine.

"Fouzh," I said without thinking.

"Ellion," Amien said, layers of meaning in that one word. I looked at the hand I'd smashed again; he reached out and poured more uisquebae into my cup. I picked it up and slammed it back; he poured more for both of us, and we drank again.

"Bastard," I said. "Don't you understand that's the last place—"

"Don't you understand I need you there?"

"Bollocks!" I snapped. "That's why you've got Sanglin!"

"Try thinking with the other head!" Amien spat.

"Gentlemen," Letitia said in Tanaan, which made me realize we'd wandered into Ilesian; then she spoiled the effect by seeming to forget what she had planned to say. I reached for another meat pie; Amien poured the last of the uisquebae into my cup, and the barmaid turned up with the next bottle and another tray of pies.

"Praise—gods be thanked," Amien said, and began pouring for everyone he could reach.

"But is the Eridanus the River Cainte?" one of the men at the table beside us said to the other. "Or did the author mean the Arnemetia, in Finias?"

Immediately my ears seized on their discussion: I'd heard a hundred variations on the debate, in taverns up and down the Ruillin. The men at that table were sailors, probably captains; they were engaged in the endless, seemingly hopeless, effort to reconstruct a sailing route to Hy-Breasaíl. Every profession has its variation of the impossible search for that lost paradise: the sailors' is the most direct, but in some ways the most esoteric, because they are among the few who actually try to base their forays on old texts and quantifiable facts. I would be lost if left in command of a ship, of course; but the maps and texts, mutually contradictory things they are, I knew intimately.

"Gullion suggests there may actually be two rivers Eridanus," the other man said.

The first man made a dismissive noise. "That only proves he couldn't read a chart!"

My mind lit with remembering the ancient maps, imagining the lands to which these men would sail if they only knew how. Tonight their goal looked like Ilunmore in my mind: but an Ilunmore untouched by the wrath of a goddess, one that hummed with powers like I kept feeling at Goibniu. After a moment I realized I still sat in an inn, but the power humming around me was real, and the uisquebae in my cup was warming under the grip of my hand. I returned my attention to my own table and made another attempt at drowning desires I couldn't seem to escape; Amien met my eyes.

"First time in Goibniu?" he said quietly.

"Fouzh, this place *hums*," I said, then realized I was treading the edge of the uisquebae-soaked zone in which a man's mouth develops a will of its own.

Something lit in Amien's eyes, and I knew he understood, as no one else here would.

"Have you considered the idea that the smith-god Goibniu might be an aspect of Par?" he said.

A short laugh escaped me: I'd heard that sort of sophistry before. The energies rumbling beneath the stones here had nothing whatsoever to do with Par or any other of the true gods.

"Whatever lets you sleep," I said.

His mouth twisted, and he turned away.

"Letitia, annu," he said to her; the term of affection told me he was nearly as drunk as I. "We still have one more task tonight, you and I—"

I knew what he meant: he needed to rebuild her personal wards again. If I were he, I'd be wondering what it meant that the power of a sacred pool dedicated to an old goddess could knock out wards drawn on the new.

Meanwhile the sailors at the next table were still going round over an entirely peripheral problem. "But if you match the Hy-Breasaíl amber trade with the frankincense route, then it's the Uxellian Penninsula—" said the one to my right.

"Isn't the route traders took irrelevant in the end?" I said to him.

Both sailors looked at me, astonished; Amien shot me a quelling look.

"Pirtanien records that the ships sailed from Hy-Breasaíl *into the setting sun* after the Fall," I continued, "and landed at the mouth of the Riga."

"Ellion," Amien said, warning. As if it might be possible for us to be inconspicuous here, as if we might somehow pass through this place without leaving a trail of tavern gossip behind us.

"Who's the fool now?" I retorted, shooting a glance at the Tanaan and meeting his eyes again. The way we spoke and dressed, even the fact that our shirts buttoned rather than laced, marked us out: as foreign, as wealthy, as loyalists, as most likely noble. And the Tanaan were beyond conspicuous. How could a conversation with sailors that would fade into everyone's blurred hangover recollections change anything? The things people would remember were enough to expose us ten times over.

"So aren't you looking for an oceanic route?" I said to the sailors. "Something to the east?"

"The sailing routes from Finias lie to the east," the first man said. "Which means the *Arnemetia*—"

"Oh, you're missing the point," I said. "The Tanaan realms aren't Hy-Breasaíl!"

Both men looked past me, at the table full of Tanaan I occupied. Amien shot me another look.

"Letitia," he said. "While I can still stand, if you please?"

And suddenly the working he meant to perform roared through me, breathtaking and inescapable. Kneeling at her feet as she stood there unclothed, shot through with her gentle power as I raised sparkling delicious power of my own: to enclose her lean feet and legs; to trace the spare curves of her hips and the moons both great and small; to stretch up her sinuous spine and court the wonders of her breasts, delicate clavicles, and long white neck; to enclose all of her, up to her crown, in energies that would lend me constant awareness of her. But that would be only the beginning, because there would be ample opportunity to caress her along the way; to feel the silk of her skin under my hands, to touch her in ways that would raise shivers and quickened breaths and sweet unplanned sounds; to embrace her, love her, blend her magic and mine into something never before seen.

She glanced at me as she rose, and all my desires suddenly condensed into a very physical ache. My head whirled with need; I was on the verge of saying something monumentally stupid. If I had any ethics whatsoever, I would walk out of here now and never come back. All their lives would be longer if I did.

I glanced at the staring sailors and shrugged.

"I'm going for a walk," I said, and climbed to my feet. As Letitia and Amien walked towards the stairs, I strode out of the main room and into the street. The moons cast pale illumination over half-lit buildings; ground-floor shops all stood dark, but lights played in the windows on the floors above. Fewer men crawled the streets now, but their drunken shouting more than made up the difference.

I walked. I knew what I sought, but not where to find it, and I strolled rather than striding: studying the businesses I passed, gazing at the moons and the stars spilling across the sky while the fiery fog of uisquebae rolled around my brain, gradually admitting to myself that I had been right to never come here, and I would have been righter still to avoid this place tonight.

Farther south on the Ruillin, the gambling halls come in two varieties: the ones in which the stakes are fantastically high and yet the games are no more than amusements—and the ones in which the risk of the thrill outweighs the thrill of the risk, where men will cheat and attack one another for it. Goibniu is full of the latter. The former is the best of all possible places to find the sort of woman I sought: one who does not change the natural color of her hair unless it is to hide a bit of grey, and whose scarves, should she wear such adornments, are all meticulously finished and black. No one calls those women night butterflies; most men are unaware they exist at all. But there were no gambling halls of the right sort in Goibniu, nor a good tea-house or even a solid, reputable brothel.

But eventually, at the edge of the circle of lamplight outside a gambling hall, I found a woman who would do: a slender creature with hair as scarlet as Letitia's cloak and a blue scarf patterned with green. Her perfume carried the scent of sweet musk-rose, and it raced straight through my nose to my brain.

"Well, now, that is mighty fine," she said, looking me up and down with belladonna eyes that were probably blue when the drug wore off.

"I was just thinking the same thing," I said, and stepped closer.

She gave a throaty laugh and linked her arm through mine in a practiced gesture that brushed my wrist against her breast, pulling me away from the lamplight.

"Your inn?" she said, looking up at me.

I shook my head.

"I know a place, but it'll cost…" She shot me a sidelong, estimating glance.

"That sounds fine."

Her place was around a corner, an inn of the sort at which rooms can be had for much less than a whole night. It was less clean than the inn I'd left behind. The fees, for the room and for her, were what I expected; her rules were the same as they always are, unless one pays much more. Not that I wanted to kiss her, anyway. I just needed to drive things I couldn't touch out of my head and fill the space with things I could.

"What's your name?" I said as we stepped into the room.

She cast me a coy glance. "You tell me."

Oh, never mind, I thought. I smiled and shook my head, put the money on the table, stretched out a hand and let her bright sparkling red hair rustle through my fingers. Something inside me relaxed; the power under my feet and the power out on the water rushed in, swirling through my consciousness.

A laugh escaped me. "I'll bet it's Laverna."

"How did you know?"

I smiled and unwound the scarf from her neck, realizing out of nowhere that a scarf was what Letitia needed to conceal her torc. I unlaced her dress, slipped my fingertips down her body—but the power I wanted humming beneath my fingertips wasn't there, and of course I couldn't allow myself to raise it. Out of the fog of uisquebae and swirling illicit powers arose the knowledge that I was wasting everyone's time and meager sanity. That sex was the least of what I hungered for, and none of my cravings would be satisfied here. That I was the greatest fool in all of Goibniu, for that matter in any of the Beallan realms, and the one woman I wanted I would never have. I sighed and stepped back, bent to pick up the scarf. The color would highlight the emerald of Letitia's eyes.

"Love?" said the woman who was, for the moment, named Laverna.

I shook my head. "I'm sorry, I don't—" I didn't even know how to express what I *didn't*.

"You've already paid, though," she said, an edge developing in her voice.

I nodded. "Give me the scarf and we'll call it even."

She gave me a look that clearly said I was both drunk and insane, and there was no disputing either point. But she could buy a dozen scarves with the money on that table. I nodded, smiling a little at my own idiocy, and walked out.

The lamp was still on in the room in which the Tana were lodged. The light shone around the edges of the flimsy door. I knocked; behind the door, Tru said, "Who is it?"

"Ellion," I said: not loud, but certainly audible nevertheless. What a laughable excuse for security. I could put my fist right through that, too.

But then the door opened, and Tru stood looking at me with Easca behind her; and though they weren't wearing swords, Tru's was naked in her hand, and Easca stood with her hand on the hilt protruding from a scabbard on the table. Warmth washed through me.

"Locks are redundant with you two around," I said, smiling.

"Come in," Letitia said. She sat curled on the inadequate bed, back propped against the wall. A uisquebae fog still lay on her, but she held the book she'd brought along: Carina's journal, I remembered. Sudden, blazing curiosity about the things the legendary heroine had troubled to record raced through me. But just as quickly it was pushed aside by awareness of the wards that now skated around Letitia's flesh. I saw them only as a green glow at the edges of my vision, but the merest shift in focus would show me the physical net of the working.

I didn't want to see. I didn't want to think about what Amien had done.

"How was your walk?" she said.

I grimaced. "I hope you get to see more of the Beallan realms than Goibniu. This place is dismal."

Pain manifested in Letitia's face. "Tru, Easca, could we have a few minutes?"

"I—" I began, stunned. It was true that Letitia need fear no attack with me in the room; but I feared for her reputation.

But Tru and Easca nodded with grave courtesy, as if a woman being alone with me were in no way untoward, and it came to me in a foggy flash: the rules among Tanaan are completely different. The women own the property; they rule the nation. Their lives do not depend upon the opinions of men. I no longer believed any of the things I had been taught about Tanaan society,

246

including the received wisdom that no expectations of sexual fidelity exist among them; but I remembered how inconsequential my bedding Macha at Irisa had seemed: everyone knew by the next morning, but no one seemed to much care. And at Arian, when everyone assumed Easca and I had spent our time alone in the ruins dallying, more people had been amused than upset by it, and no one seemed to think any less of Easca afterward. In fact I now suspected the conquest had been considered hers rather than mine. Finally I saw how little I understood their ways.

"How do you say *meat pies* in the Beallan language?" Tru asked.

I told her.

"And *tea*?" Easca inquired.

I answered that question, too.

They nodded, satisfied, and left, closing the flimsy door behind them.

"I—brought you something," I said lamely, crossed the room towards Letitia, and pulled the night butterfly's scarf from my pocket.

"Ellion!" she said, as if I had brought her emeralds.

I shrugged. "It should be more comfortable than the cloak. Of course you won't need it at Aballo, but even in an airship it will take a few days…" The pain in her eyes made my mouth run dry.

"This is it, then," she said.

"I've got to handle the horses, and get word—"

"No lies," she said. "Not now."

I looked away. "No. Yes. This is where we part. You no longer need—"

"The undead absolutely can cross water," she said flatly.

I swallowed. "Mora, I cannot—"

"But *why*?"

I opened my mouth to deliver some courtly version of *I really don't want to talk about it*, but the uiesquebae hijacked it.

"Me on Aballo would spell the breaking of every vow I haven't yet violated," I heard myself say.

"What?" she breathed.

I stared at her, losing myself for some unquantified span of time in the emerald depths of her eyes. I had to get out before my mouth fired off again.

"I am sorry. Truly, deeply sorry; I wish I were—" Words lodged in my throat. I swallowed. "You're safer—" Oh, sweet Lady Tella, I couldn't say *that*.

"It has been a privilege," I croaked, once again unable to look at her; I bowed and beat a hasty retreat.

Chapter 20
Ship of the Water, Ship of the Air

Morning dawned grey and cloudy, but the light stabbed me in the eyes. Everything I owned was still damp. I packed it all anyway, even coiling the now-brittle gut strings into a side pocket of the harp case for no reason I could identify.

In the inn's main room I forced myself to eat, though getting the first few bites down was as great a struggle as it always is after that much uisque-bae. The Tanaan, evidently observing the time-honored practice of not letting anything pass the lips until one can be certain it will remain there, stayed in the rooms; but after a few minutes Amien joined me at the table. We ate in a silence born of mutual understanding and aching skulls. My head cleared and my stomach settled, though neither as much as I would have wished; but at least I would be able to step into the street without moaning aloud. I wished I'd brought a hat with a good wide brim. Perhaps after the airship launched I would wander around Goibniu again until I found one.

I paused between bites of porridge, looking at the wizard—and suddenly realized where I had developed the practice of forcing myself to eat: Aballo. It is de rigueur in that setting, understood by all: despite the most heinous after-effects of whatever mind-opening brew may have been used to facilitate a working, it is necessary for a wizard to be able to function again as soon as the brew wears off. Something inside me felt heavy; I wondered how many of the things I took for granted had grown from seeds planted during my time there. How much of what I was would never change, despite my heartfelt efforts.

Amien met my gaze. "What?"

I shrugged. "We are who we are."

"As the gods made us," he said equably, and went back to his porridge.

Eventually the Tanaan came downstairs. Hung-over Tanaan look essentially like hung-over humans, though for reasons I couldn't have explained their hangovers are funnier. Letitia wore the scarf: I absorbed this in a single glance, and immediately discovered I was unable to look at her further.

The launch grounds for airships lay just south of Goibniu's wall, across the road from the river. The airship's canopy, which had been crafted in a palette of blues, lay partially inflated across the vacant field, already tethered to one of the largest baskets I had yet seen. The basket still stood sideways, exposing the light planking of its base. A little distance farther from the river, another crew spread out their canopy preparatory to inflation. We drew up at the edge of the field and stopped, watching: perhaps a dozen men busied themselves around the airship, evidently controlling the canopy and adjusting the ropes and netting as the thing began to take shape.

In the center of all the wandering ropes, between the basket and the canopy, a spare, dark-haired man stood alone, almost entirely still, watching the canopy unfold. His right hand moved slightly, then went still again, though the arm remained a little distance from his side. That would be the windcaller: the magic-worker who can resist making irrelevant gestures has yet to be trained. Another man walked out of the opening in the canopy, said something in passing to the windcaller, and crossed the field towards us. He was tall and as lean as airship crewmen always are, dressed in leather from broad-brimmed hat to boots; his smoky eyes took us all in without evident emotion, though they lingered over the Tana.

"Mornin'," he said. "Sian, I see you are thirteen, not twelve."

Amien shook his head. "Our friend—" He indicated me with a nod. "Will be taking our horses. Friends, this is Conaig Munh, the *Aveta*'s captain."

"Mornin'," he said again; we all responded in kind. "Gentles, we'll have the ship ready in a little while. If you could stack up your things over there, we'll load them for you."

Letitia frowned, obviously on the verge of objecting; he held up a hand.

"Milady, that's the way we've got to do it. We've got to distribute the weight. Once the canopy rights up, and your bags and our supplies are aboard, we'll invite you into the basket. You'll want to put on jackets or what have you; it gets cold up there, and we may not be able to get your bags and packs back out before we land.

"Your destination is Tonagal in Nagnata, if I remember?" he said to Amien.

Amien smiled ruefully. "Aballo, actually."

The captain just raised his eyebrows. I wondered how many of his charters lied about their destinations until the morning of launch. He glanced at the Tanaan again, and then his gaze came to rest on Amien.

"That place is magically protected, sian," he said. "No one can—"

"I know the release spells," Amien said evenly. "When the time is right, I'll handle them."

Again the captain granted the wizard a long, dispassionate look.

"If we make our previous night's stop at Tonagal, that puts us off the coast of Aballo at the end of a flying day. You can't get us through, we'll go down in the ocean. I'll let you try it, but it'll cost you two extra days, because I'm not risking this ship. We go in from Damona, in Ebdani."

"No," Amien said. "We can't spare the time. I've opened that binding a thousand times, and—"

An odd, appraising shift occurred in the captain's gaze, but he shook his head. "Take it or leave it. Two extra days. Ten extra gold, and another ten for the risk. I told you, I don't fly into places under siege, and I don't take charters that put my ship or crew at risk. You don't like it, you're welcome to hire a watership, but I guarantee you won't get an airship captain to lay that bet."

Frustration gathered in Amien's face. Across the field, the canopy surged suddenly upward, righting the basket. Men raced around the ship in a practiced dance, holding the ship by the ropes as it shimmied sideways. After a moment they brought it to rest again and tethered it to stakes in the ground. By the time I returned my attention to Amien's argument, the windcaller strode up to join what he doubtless thought was a calm last-minute conversation.

"We're good," he said to the captain. Then he caught sight of Amien, and goggled; he stared at me in silence for a moment as well.

"My lord!" he said to Amien, sweeping into a bow that called to mind an albatross in flight. Relief and sudden worry chased one another across Amien's face; I realized I should have expected this. Windcallers are specialized Talents, and their power generally doesn't approach that of a man qualified to train or work at Aballo; but they have the same awareness of the extramundane as any wizard—and evidently the same ability to smell Talent on another man. Amien's torc could mean only one thing in this context. The wizard waved him off.

"Not here, if you please," Amien said gruffly.

The windcaller straightened up, swallowing, and glanced from Amien to me and back. "Lords, I'm Echtag Gand, and I took training at Matach. It is my honor to—"

"We really need to be quiet about—" Amien said.

"Who *are* these people?" the captain said to the windcaller.

The windcaller glanced at the captain; his gaze ranged over the Tanaan. Understanding dawned in his eyes.

"Your pardon, Lo—gentles," he said to Amien and me. "We will get you safely through, I give you my word."

"This morning they say *Aballo*?" the captain pursued, eyes on the windcaller.

The windcaller nodded, face full of wonder. "I've never been there, have you?"

"No, you fool, no one has, because the place is *sealed*!"

But the windcaller just smiled. "They will get us through."

"And we need to go in from Tonagal," Amien said. "We're running out of time."

The captain shook his head, resigned, but a certain thoughtfulness had developed in his eyes. "Who are you?"

Finally Amien smiled. "I told you last night. My name is Rinnal Ruthin, and we're en route to Tonagal in Nagnata."

"Just so," the captain said slowly, looking at the Tanaan again. "And from there to Aballo, though no one other than the Tonagal station needs to know."

Amien nodded.

"You still owe my crew an extra ten for the risk."

"Done," Amien said.

"Well, then," the captain said to the group. "Stack up your gear; make your goodbyes; tonight you sleep in Nemetona, in Mumhan. Sian, we agreed to half this morning?"

"We did," Amien said. We all climbed out of the saddles; the Tanaan removed the saddlebags and other burdens from their horses. Iminor kept glancing across the field at the airship, his trepidation in stark contrast to the satisfaction of parting company with me that I had seen so clearly last night and today. They stacked their belongings near the airship; they helped me string their horses onto a pair of long lead-lines. The airship's crew stowed things a few at a time, until the mound of belongings they had left disappeared into unseen recesses of the basket.

"We're ready, gentles," the captain called. Iminor gave vent to a deep, nervous exhalation. Grief, guilt and anxiety surged inside me. How could I let them go on without me? Letitia needed every blade she could get, and three nights stood between her and the guarantee of safety. But how could I even contemplate going with them, when I knew my unconquerable flaws and illicit lusts, not to mention the price on my neck, put them at risk? And no righ of a human nation had a better personal guard: not anymore.

I embraced each of the knights in turn, and we wished one another good luck. Most of them looked as worried as I felt, and Easca clutched me tight and long. I kissed her temple, finally, and stepped back, watching her follow the others into the basket. Nuad embraced me, too, drawing back to look into my face.

"Thank you," he said. "I will never forget the things you taught me."

An unexpected smile commandeered my mouth. "Few could have done what you did with this crew. It has been my privilege."

"The privilege was mine," he said, smiling too, and climbed into the basket. I turned and looked into Iminor's face.

He gazed at me in silence; shared understanding passed between us. He didn't like me, didn't like the way I looked at Letitia—or, I realized in a flash of mind-wrecking insight, the way she looked at me. And I would have been compelled to torment him all the way from Irisa for his stiff uprightness and narrow judgment, had the situation been less dire. And yet.

"We did this thing together," he said as if he'd been thinking exactly the same things. "And I owe you a debt I can't ever repay. Don't imagine I'll forget."

I nodded. "Be safe, and live long."

His mouth quirked in a reluctant smile; he climbed aboard. Now only Amien and Letitia remained. I turned to the wizard, and he caught me in a wiry embrace.

"This has been—completely unexpected," he said without releasing me. "I'm glad you were with me."

Pain clamped my throat shut; I nodded voicelessly, and he stepped back, meeting my eyes in a frank gaze.

"See you at the Fair," he said.

And now I was trapped. It occurred to me that I had been trapped when he turned up at Irisa.

"See you," I said.

He climbed aboard; Letitia met my eyes as if trying to decide what to say. I pulled her to me, burying my face in her hair, feeling her tremble through the spidersilk mail. I breathed in her sweet exotic scent, willing myself to remember. After far too little time, she drew back, eyes shuttered.

"My lord," she said, a dozen flavors of disappointment in her voice. Something wrapped cold fingers around my heart and squeezed. "Thank you."

Take it back, I wanted to say. Instead I bowed and stepped back, and she turned away. Iminor extended a hand to her; she climbed into the basket. A leather-clad crewman drew the door shut, and the men on the ground cast the stay-ropes to men in the basket. And they were aloft.

The ship rose like a smoke-ring, sure and graceful: coasting slightly northeast on the wind of the incoming tide. I stood and watched, head craning back to track its flight, as it rose higher than the city wall, higher than the trees at the field's southern edge, up towards the places where the thermals run. The ground crew had already lost interest and moved around pulling up stakes and doing other things I couldn't pay attention to; I heard a horse whinny, restive. But I couldn't stop watching. I felt as if some critical part of me had been loaded into the basket.

And then, as if out of the blue cloudless sky, the awareness crashed down on me: I had made a terrible mistake. I could have traveled as far as Tonagal with them and still avoided crossing to Aballo; Letitia might have had one more blade, might still have had an experienced commander, for another three days.

On the heels of that horrifying insight came another: I had been deceiving not only the others but myself. It wasn't fear of whatever accident in which I might embroil Letitia that had left me standing on the ground this morning, but fear of how it would feel to know I had failed: fear of watching more knights die and knowing I should have shielded them, fear of the pain of knowing my failings had harmed her. I wasn't protecting her; I was protecting myself. And my failure to try to overcome the ways in which I erred, my failure to give Letitia everything I might: those were far worse than whatever error I might have made in the course of giving her my all. There was no excuse for simply failing to try.

Sudden, frigid wind surged in from the mountains behind the city, beating downward and east towards the river. Dust and chaff kicked up from the field, pelting my face until it stung. Above me, the airship wobbled, its upward flight halted; it dropped as if pushed from a table, only recovering a short distance above the city wall. I felt the surge of wind the windcaller pulled in from the river, in my hair and in senses arcane—and felt the arcane power in the answering blow that pushed the ship back towards the river. The power the windcaller fought was severalfold stronger; I knew, without having to consider the issue, who its author was. There was nothing I could do but watch as the ship fell helplessly back towards the shore.

Within seconds it was clear the ship was going into the water. A great bubble of shimmering green manifested around the basket and canopy: Amien's work, I knew. We might be back in the human realms, but the power here still ran in the wrong direction for a man attuned to the true gods; when Amien's familiar signatures joined the next surge of air the windcaller summoned, the Bard's Wizard overmastered it anyway. I raced back to my horse: when they went down in the river, they would need whatever help they could get. It took all my meager patience to grab the lead lines and pull the horses along behind us, to harry them into speed; but I would need them, too.

We raced into the road, followed the airship half a mile or so south, then scrambled down the ragged slope towards the shore; the green bubble around the airship skittered east above me, throwing a moving shadow across my path. As the horse skidded down the last, treacherous yards to the bank, ship and bubble crashed into the water. They plunged into the oncoming tide—I hadn't realized how deep the Ruillin was so close to the shore—then breached the surface and settled. The racing tide pulled them north, towards the busy Goibniu docks.

I cast my awareness against the bubble, knowing Amien would recognize me in the shock that rippled around his perimeter—for a fraction of a second it was as if our eyes met, and all his frustration and fear raced through me—and flung the lead-ropes into the same place I had just touched. Just as they reached the boundary, the arcane shield vanished; water crashed over the edge of the basket, and the canopy sagged into the tide, but Amien had caught the ropes. For a second he met my gaze across the water, something I couldn't identify in his face; then the ship's crew had the ropes in their hands.

"Go!" Amien shouted; I cued my horse and he scrambled up the slope; I wrestled the ends of the lead lines free of the places I'd stowed them, pulled and gave the command. After a moment the horses got the message, and backed up. It wasn't enough to tow the ship in, but the basket held steady as the crew wrestled the sodden canopy out of the clutches of the tide. And then the lines went slack again; the basket lifted out of the water, seemingly under its own power, passed dripping above me, and landed on the road above. When I finally returned my attention to the horses around me, I discovered the lead lines trailing into the water; I gathered them and coaxed the horses back up the steep bank.

Everyone had scrambled out of the basket by the time I arrived. Amien met my gaze and smiled, in that rueful way he'd always had after things went wrong in the workshop; I found myself smiling in return.

"Missed you," I said to him.

He cracked a reluctant grin. But then I saw Letitia watching me and scrambled from the saddle to stand before her.

"Mora," I said. "I'm a fool. Will you let a fool try again?"

My breath hung in my chest as I waited for her answer. How could I blame her if she turned me away? She gave me a long look; and of all the things I saw in her gaze, trust was not among them.

"Don't leave me again," she said.

The words fell on me as a geas, and I inclined my head. "I won't."

She nodded as if the matter were settled; Iminor glared at me. But I knew she'd be serving me a dozen flavors of humility over the next few days.

Nothing for it but to endure. I'd brought this on myself, all of it. Time to shoulder the yoke, to figure out what to do next. There was little to discuss in that regard.

"When Telliyn is full, the ferries run in the morning," I said. "We'll have to hurry to make the tide."

"The undead absolutely can cross water," she said, meeting my gaze.

"But nothing can get on a boat once it's left the dock, not on the Ruillin," I answered. "It's the fastest way south. At Ballarona we may yet find a watership."

Letitia nodded; she glanced at Amien. "Is there reason to assume the—" She glanced around at the airship crew, who had unloaded all the gear, right there in the road, and now seemed to be untethering the canopy from the basket—and evidently gave up any hope of stealth. "Any reason to assume the Bard's Wizard can't or won't do the same thing again?"

Arcane noncombatants must not be harmed. It is the first rule of arcane warfare. But we all knew better than to imagine that rule moved our enemy. The dozens of people who would occupy the ferry with us would not be protected by the Aballo code.

Amien raised his eyebrows. "More hope than a reason: what he did this morning was magically expensive; it takes a tremendous amount of energy to bring so much power to bear at distance. I'm not sure how he managed to do it at all. It's... reasonable to hope that he's spent his—" The wizard cleared his throat. "That he'll have to rest before he can do something like that again."

Letitia fixed him with a penetrating stare. "Have you discovered where he is, then?"

The wizard looked away. "No."

"And yet you're confident he's some distance away."

Humiliation crept into the wizard's black eyes. "Mora..." he began.

And suddenly I'd had enough. It was one thing for her to humiliate me; Amien had been utterly steadfast.

"Letitia, if you've got a better idea this morning, we are at your disposal!" I snapped. "Save your humiliation for the man who deserves it, and let's do what is *possible!*"

She turned and stared at me again. Her chin lifted in that particular way that meant she was about to dig in her heels. I returned the stare. After several interminable seconds, the hardness in her face crumpled into desperate vulnerability, and my fortifying anger gave way to guilt again. She cast a shame-faced glance at Amien and nodded.

I looked around at the knights: while I wasn't looking, they had removed all the horses from the leads and returned the gear to the horses. Even Letitia's and Amien's possessions were back where they belonged. They all stood beside the horses, watching us argue—and more than one of them looked as if our arguing was a source of relief. Amien paid the airship captain the rest of the fare he'd agreed to, in compensation for the damage to the ship; and we all mounted and hurried back into the city.

Water was already spilling across the dock as we rode down the ramp to the ferry; the crew waved us urgently across and cast off the gangway as soon as we gained the deck. Amien paid the fare while most of the crew stared at the Tanaan; I interrupted all the staring by asking where horses were to be lodged during the trip. I got an answer, but I was still irritatingly aware of the bold gazes from crew and passengers alike as we dismounted and led the horses to the makeshift corral at the rear of the ship.

Nevertheless a sort of calm settled over me as the crew cast off from the dock and raised the sail. If we weren't safe, we occupied a zone in which the threats could likely be managed. We had a few hours in which to rest, gather our wits, and formulate another new plan. The ship's windcaller summoned a southerly wind; I gathered up the knights, leaving Iminor and his venomous stare with Letitia, and took them on an impromptu tour: it seemed to me that this was an opportunity to experience some of the merits of the Ruillin, and they shouldn't miss it. Not while I was here.

None of us was in the right frame of mind to truly appreciate the atmosphere of a Ruillin ferry, but at least the Tanaan took in the sights: the charms dealers and fortune tellers who haunt the salons of the lower deck, the floating tavern room and ubiquitous ferryboat card games and ever-present night butterflies. They agreed without discussion that a drink was in order after the disastrous flight, so after a full circuit of the lower deck they trouped straight past the stairs to the tavern room again, towing me along. Mugs of thick ale restored the color to their faces; the tension in their bodies unwound, just a little.

Now they were all ready to eat, finally, and I was hungry again, so we bought skewers of roast pork, sacks of roasted early potatoes and little fried fish and carried them up to the interior portion of the main deck, where a troupe of mummers was performing. Today's feature was a satire, but it had been more than a month since I left Ilnemedon, and I felt myself missing the nuances of their performance. And of course the Tanaan didn't understand any of the lines. After we finished eating, we walked back out to the open, to lean against the rail and watch the worn-looking mountains crawl past.

The power of the river infiltrated me again, swirling inside my body and mind until I felt the southward pull of the tide in the bones at the base of my spine and the spiraling currents created by the boat's passage as a whirlpool in the back of my mind. Something inside me relaxed, and a roaring energy swept into me; I shook my awareness free, but I was still unsettlingly aware of the forces acting on the ship I rode, the thin, bright, self-conscious energy of the windcaller in the high chair on the sailing deck above and the huge, uncaring power of the river herself. I tried again to focus on the mundane, to fill my attention with my companions and the things they saw, heard, and felt.

I spotted the island that must be Lethin in the distance, and pointed. "That's Lethin Isle," I said, raising my voice over the wind and rushing water. "Where Nimah was. Remember?"

"The trading outpost, before the Deluge," Easca said. "Lord Amien rode with the caravans."

I nodded; we all looked across the water. I'd never ridden this ferry route before today; but had I done so, I would have been one of the hundreds of passengers who pass Lethin every month without giving it a second thought. From across the water it gave no sign of ever having been inhabited, let alone by Tanaan. In these difficult waters, there was little reason to imagine it would have been. But today I wondered what it would be like to live in reasonable proximity to Tanaan, and yet have the life I thought of as normal. What it would be for people up and down the Ruillin to have regular contact with these wondrous alien people and begin to learn their ways.

"Hel*lo*," someone said behind me. I turned: it wasn't Mattiaci showing off his Ilesian vocabulary, but one of the mummers we'd seen inside, a wiry, compact, dark-haired fellow in the costume and makeup that can be the Rogue or the Lord, depending on the demands of the tale at hand; and he wasn't talking to me. Leave it to a mummer to have the stones to take a run at an armed Tana.

I glanced around: Tru and Easca considered him with speculative glances; Tru decided to treat the mummer to a smile. He mimed a sudden blow to the heart, grinning.

"I'm sorry, they don't speak Ilesian," I said to the mummer.

He glanced at me. "I don't mind," he said, and returned his attention to Tru. As the rest of us stood watching, he bowed; mummers dressed as the Damsel, the Farmer, and the Druid capered across the deck and began playing a dance tune on reed pipes and a little drum, and the Rogue performed an extravagant gesture of invitation to dance. Tru laughed and put her hand into his, and he led her straight into it, right there on the deck. Easca began dancing with Tuiri; people on the deck gathered until the Tana and their partners danced in the midst of a circle, watching and clapping along with the drum. Mattiaci and Fiacha meandered across the deck and wordlessly invited a couple of night butterflies to join the dance.

After a few minutes, the whole thing broke up, in the typical easily-distracted way of the ferries; but the Rogue bowed again, in extravagant mummer style, tucked Tru's arm into his, and began to promenade her around the deck, pointing out the sights beyond the rail. I knew she didn't understand his narrative; it was easy to see she also didn't care. She was an adult, I decided, and armed: there was no need for me to get involved. I wandered off to take in the sights of the eastern bank, such as they are that far north; I glanced down the length of the deck and saw Letitia and Iminor doing the same. Even from here I could see he stood close enough to feel her breath, and he leaned against the rail in a pose that made it impossible to miss the sword at his hip. I felt certain even the mummers were steering clear of Letitia, and my presence there would be neither welcome nor required.

He was her consort. I was a foreign man who couldn't even be counted on to stay the course. I had no excuse to feel jealous. I looked out across the water.

After a moment, Amien stood beside me. "Matti and Fiacha think they've made new friends," he said. "Someone is going to have to explain to the Tanaan about the night butterflies."

"And by *someone*, you mean me."

The wizard shrugged. "You know, the Tanaan have no concept of whoring."

I found myself staring at him, stunned.

"It's true. They've got what they call priestesses of loving, who serve in the temple to the goddess Tiana—but that's a sacred function. Sex for money… Well… I'm not sure they'll understand at all."

I shook my head. "I'm not sure I'll ever understand them."

Amien nodded, looking across the water. "I don't. Not in four hundred years." He pursed his lips, thoughtful, then cast me a sidelong glance. "But there is no pursuit more fascinating than a thing you cannot understand."

"I'm certain moths hold very similar conversations," I said. "Right before they plunge into lamps."

Chapter 21
The Dance

Dromineer lies halfway between Goibniu and the city of Ballarona. Now that I had seen Goibniu, I understood: that truth is more than geographical. The city of Dromineer has the same rough-edged quality as Goibniu, but the ferries run both north and south from there; in contrast to Goibniu's make-money-and-get-out sensibility, Dromineer has the sense of a place that might be satisfactory to men who have never seen the south. There are more inns, better entertainment of every variety, more sophisticated craftwork and better access to the stuff of daily life; men will bring their families to live there. But the streets are still thick with night butterflies, and even the baker is armed.

If the place had changed in five years, I couldn't tell. But I could count the number of days I had spent in Dromineer on my fingers, and I had never spent more than a night or two there at a stretch. Why would I, when I'd had a home of sorts in Ballarona and the ferries run every day?

At the top of the ramp leading up from the ferry, Amien turned unhesitatingly to the right. I would have, too; I could guess where he was bound. I would have made the same choice: there is no place in Dromineer more comfortable for a loyalist. Except.

I urged my horse a little faster, moved forward to ride beside him.

"The Caithdell," I said.

He glanced at me and smiled. "Great minds."

I shook my head. "I played there a few times, years ago. I'm not sure whether the proprietor remembers me, but—"

"He remembers you, I'm sure," Amien said gruffly, and led us past the Caithdell towards the next block.

"Once we're settled at the inn, I'm going back out," he said. "I want to try to get a message to Brinner."

I raised my eyebrows.

"Rohini's House Healer," he elaborated, as if I might have forgotten. I nodded again.

"I want to make sure she knows I'm serious about the rendezvous, and I got her message," Amien continued. "And I'm writing a letter to Sanglin that Brinner can hand him at the Moot—just in case."

I met his gaze for a moment. I wanted to assure him it wouldn't be necessary. Instead I just nodded again.

Outside the Ship and Anchor, Amien reined and cast me a faintly amused glance. "Never played here, did you?"

I shook my head again.

"Good."

We settled our horses in the stable and trooped into the inn. Late-afternoon sunlight lay fractured by the myriad tiny panes of the windows, speckling the scarred plank floor. Dark, narrow panels of wood lined the walls of the main room, which stood immediately to the right of the entry we occupied—and in which the mummers from the ship were already setting up for their first show of the evening.

"Hai!" one of them chortled; the rest followed his gaze to our party. Within seconds they had gathered in the doorway and were attempting to communicate with the Tana without benefit of words. Tru and Easca met them halfway in that effort, to the evident consternation of Mattiaci and Nuad; even Letitia smiled at them.

Amien let three rooms again, then hung back as the Tanaan began climbing the stairs.

"Can you direct me to a shrine?" he said to the innkeeper.

The man looked thoughtful. "Well, there's a shrine to Goibniu down by—"

Amien shook his head, impatient. "A shrine of the *true* religion?"

The innkeeper raised his eyebrows. I got the astonishing sense that he considered Amien's attitude narrow-minded and a bit rude, but that he was prepared to grant a certain leeway to a guest.

"A shrine to Par, out by the north wall," he said. "Not much traffic there, though."

"No doubt," Amien gruffed and followed me upstairs.

In the room, Amien deposited his burdens in a corner and went straight back out; I forestalled Tuiri and Fiacha as they began following him downstairs and gathered all the Tanaan in our room. Letitia, Tru and Easca were the last ones in; Easca shut the door behind them, and they all stood there looking expectant.

I cleared my throat. "This'll just take a minute. I didn't realize—" I cleared my throat again. There was nothing for it but to get it over with, like a dart that must be pulled from the flesh.

"Well, then, here it is. You've all met the night butterflies." They all nodded. "Do you realize what business they're in?"

"*Business?*" Mattiaci said, and I wondered whether I'd used the wrong word.

"How they make their living? Earn their money?" I said.

"How?" Tuiri said.

Oh, dear gods. "They…" Sell their affections. Rent their bodies by the hour. Lie for a living.

That last was no different from my profession, of course. Just pull out the dart.

"They will bed whoever pays the fee," I managed.

There. It was out. But the Tanaan just looked thoughtful. After a moment understanding dawned on Letitia's face.

"Oh!" she said. "Like the priestesses of loving in the Temple of Tiana."

"Um," I said. "Not quite. These ladies are not priestesses. They're… professionals."

They all looked bewildered. I should try a different angle.

"Here's what you need to understand," I said. "On the Ruillin, anything can be had for a price. You can hire a man to protect you, without him being sworn to you or anyone: he will do it for the money. You can buy another man's death, if you really want, by hiring an assassin. Though that will tend to come back to haunt you. And if you want—" Damn. "Loving, and you want it without the courting, you can hire a night butterfly."

The Tanaan were still frowning, but now it was different. They understood what I had said, but only intellectually. Letitia put a hand to the scarf, intense analysis in her face; she turned a penetrating look on me. I felt myself flush.

"Bealla are insane," Iminor said finally.

I shrugged.

"Have you ever—?" Mattiaci began. Someone, probably Ogma, trod on his foot or put an elbow into his ribs, and he stopped speaking; my blush intensified. I couldn't look at any of the Tana.

"Listen, if it's all the same to you I'd rather not discuss my sex life," I said, with a pretense of a smile. "And I'm not here to regulate yours. I just thought you should understand."

They all stared at me a few seconds more; finally Letitia said, "Thank you, my lord," and they all filed out. Mattiaci hung back until most of them had left, looking as if he might try his question again. Ogma grabbed his elbow and pushed him through the door, then pulled it shut behind him. Finally I was alone.

I spent a few minutes unpacking all my damp things and checking on the progress of my harp. It didn't seem to be buckling, at least not yet, but it still felt clammy to the touch. I set it a little distance from the fireplace, wrestled with the tinderbox someone had thoughtfully left with the extra wood beside the narrow hearth, and nurtured the fire into something that might spread a helpful warmth around the room.

By the time I reached the main room, the mummers were already performing for the early-dinner crowd—the same routine I'd seen earlier—and the

Tanaan had managed to order themselves mugs of beer. The room was still far from full, typical for so early in the evening; but this crowd included a decent percentage of women. I crossed the room to the bar and acquired a mug of my own, then claimed a seat at the end of the table.

The deep racing power of the river, the subterranean stirring of the smith-god's energy, myriad other energies whose names I didn't know: I felt them gather around me again as I settled into stillness. Not much traffic down at the shrine to Par, the innkeeper had said: little wonder for a place in which the old gods run so fierce and strong, but strange in the abstract. From the parapets of Dromineer's wall, on a clear day, one can glimpse the high places of Tellnemed: the place in which Lady Tella raised a man with too little Talent to become a druid to the power who changed the course of human history. How could a man look upon that place, even from across the river, and not see Her magnificence? I didn't understand.

My mind wandered; thoughts of Amien's current errand rolled across my brain. Seven nights to Bealtan Eve; eight days to the Moot. Five days stood between the party and Aballo, unless we managed to charter a ship tomorrow—and even the back-up plan depended on being able to hire a ship at Priaochan. It would be a close thing for Amien to reach Teamair in time, and he might have to fly there under his own power to accomplish it.

Even had I wanted to attend, keeping my vow might very well mean missing the Moot, now. Everyone of consequence must already be there.

I wondered what Coran was doing tonight: what party or reception he had hosted or decided to attend; what I would have been doing this evening, had things gone as planned and everyone's understanding of my birth chart been true. What things would be if I had never left Tellan for Aballo. If I had never left Aballo for Tellan.

So many roads not taken. There was no stepping back onto any of them. The gap between destiny and its fulfillment had swallowed me.

"Hey."

I snapped back into reality with a start. The mummer who played the Hero, a lithe redhead, stood over me: mischief in his face. I gave him an inquiring look.

"Where's your Da?" he said. "We've got somethin' he should—"

"He's not—" I began, then sighed. The less information volunteered, the better. "Out to visit a shrine. Back by dinner."

The redhead grinned and nodded. "We'll catch 'im then. Don't spoil the surprise."

I shook my head; I didn't even want to imagine what they had planned. When mummers get that look, it never ends well.

A fresh mug of beer landed in front of me with a thud; I looked up at the mummer attired in motley and made up as the Fool, the left side of his face black and the other smeared in white. He settled across the table from me, meeting my eyes with a performer's smile and an appraising look.

"Thank you?" I said. Free beer is never free.

"My pleasure," the mummer answered, and extended a hand in the easy style of the Ruillin. "Loeg," he said by way of introduction.

Back at Nemetona, we'd agreed on a cover story but hadn't invented names to go with it. If I were here alone, I could pick one and remember it; but I knew I'd never get the word to everyone in time for the deception to go unrevealed. Mine isn't a common personal name, but I knew there must be other Ellions, somewhere in the human realms.

"Ellion," I said, and clasped his outstretched hand.

He grinned and reached for his beer again. "Tell me a story, and I'll tell you one of my own."

I smiled. "Does mine have to be true?"

Loeg laughed. "Caisin's got a harpist coming in an hour. He'll tell pretty stories. Let's tell true ones."

I nodded. I probably wouldn't know the man who sat on the platform across the room. There are many gorsedd harpists in the human realms, and I had fewer acquaintances among the rank-and-file than among the lords of the gorsedd. Dromineer is of little consequence to the gorsedd's Ilnemedon-based politics. And there are plenty of harpists working the Ruillin who are not associated with the gorsedd. I could only hope tonight's harpist, whoever he turned out to be, wouldn't recognize me, either.

"You first," I said.

Loeg nodded and fixed me with a quizzical look. One painted eyelid drooped a little, as if in concentration. "Here's a good one—fresh out of Goibniu on today's tide. Seems a group of Tanaan defended the Lady's Well outside Goibniu from an attack by the Avengers of Esus." He paused, watching me; I kept my face still.

"Avengers of Esus?" I said in the coolest voice I could muster.

"Sweet Lady o' the river, you *have* been in the Tanaan realms, haven't you? For a long time, I'd guess." He fixed me with another penetrating stare. "The Avengers…" He shook his head: suddenly, deadly serious. "Some things even we don't joke—" He shook his head again.

"Then from out of the depths of hell
The hero met the riders fell."

I felt myself stiffen, saw his eyes shift into something far too knowing for a mummer. I recognized the verse, of course: the appearance of the Básghilae in the ballad *Armoan*, the stirring history of the great Essuvian hero Armoan Lanas, Rohini's great-to-the-I-wasn't-certain grandfather, and the role he played in the defeat of the renegade Nechton. That song and the *Ballad of Carina* encapsulate most men's understanding of the history of Nechton's War. No song more clearly portrays the Básghilae.

"Ah," the mummer said, eyes still on mine. "Y'know—And I'm telling the tale, understand, not writing it—More than one person thought it interesting that the Avengers never felled anyone at Goibniu, not until a party o' Tanaan turned up in the company of a couple of Ilesians…"

The breath had stopped in my chest. I was thoroughly out of my depth: he definitely had access to pieces of the backstory I lacked. I could fill in some of it: the Bard's Wizard was using Básghilae for far more than his mission against Letitia. They were common knowledge now, and my all-but-tasteless joke at Dianann had been uncomfortably close to the mark: the crimes and conquests the Bard of Arcadia committed were done in the name of the old god Esus. And the Básghilae—the Avengers of Esus—were understood to carry out the agendas of the Bard of Arcadia: which meant most or all of their offensives were against loyalist targets.

Which, I now understood, Goibniu was not. I was developing doubts about Dromineer as well.

"Well, what reason would they have?" I hazarded.

Loeg nodded. "Just so." He had another mouthful of beer. "So what do you think?"

I shook my head. "I think I missed a lot while I was away."

"Maybe so," Loeg allowed, and then a look of the sort I'd expect from a mummer came over him: speculative, mischievous, ready for the sort of play that ends in metaphorical, rather than literal, blood.

"Though I wot you've seen some things few men ever do," he said, looking down the table we shared with the Tanaan. All the mummers had gathered around the Tana, who entertained their practiced overtures with more warmth than politeness required. Letitia was actually talking to them. The Tans, meanwhile, had all adopted eerily similar expressions of neutrality.

Another flash of insight descended on me: expectations of sexual fidelity might exist, but the rules of it still eluded me; and their codes of gracious conduct forbid Tans from the time-honored methods of pummeling one another for stepping over the invisible lines, in fact require them to behave as if whatever the Tana in question might choose to do is her business entirely.

"What sent you all the way out to the other side o' the mountains?" Loeg pursued.

"Well—" I raised my eyebrows. As with any lie, the trick to making a cover story work is not giving it all away at once. "I'd never been there."

Loeg chuckled. "Who has? Y'know, when Sainrith wondered why a man would travel all the way out there, that's exactly what I said: *You ever been there?* A man's gotta see something new now and then. And then, o' course, there are the Tana…"

He cast me a speculative look; I shrugged.

"But then I got to thinking: a young man like yourself, he wouldn't take the longest booty-trip ever in the company of an old man. So…?"

"This would be my story?" I said, feigning resignation.

Loeg nodded. "It would."

"Well," I said, then manufactured a look of insight. "You'll know how it is. Being a mummer? I know you fellows have no problems with the ladies."

Loeg laughed and glanced down the table; I smiled.

"Eventually," I said thoughtfully, "a man has seen all there is to see of human women. So I thought I'd find myself a Tana."

Loeg chuckled. "You seem to have more than one. That seems selfish."

I shook my head. "No, two of them are knights."

Loeg goggled, eyes suddenly, comically wide in his black-and-white face; I grinned.

"It's true. I'd put them up against any man."

"So the Tans are—" Loeg looked speculative. "Free-lancers, as well?"

"I knew you'd get it," I said, with a look of surprised approval. "Most of them. Her brother…"

"That's the blond?" Loeg said, with another glance down the table.

"They're *all* blond," I pointed out.

He waved dismissively. "The lady in question is the one with the scarf, and the one who's glued to her is her brother."

I shrugged.

"He doesn't much like you."

I shrugged again. "His problem. I'm a likable fellow."

Loeg gave me a long, thoughtful look. "So who is this lady who travels under guard, with a couple of Ilesians?"

"I'm not—" I swallowed the protest. A man of Nagnata who didn't want people to place him wouldn't claim that nation, not on purpose.

"She's of good family, from Gorias," I said.

"Mmm-hmmm," Loeg said. "And she agreed to marry you. Because you are…?"

I raised my eyebrows. "I have a certain amount of charm."

"And yet she's sitting all the way at that end of the table," the mummer observed.

"I got here late. All the good seats were taken."

Loeg nodded. "That's a pretty tale," he said, with an inflection that all but called me a liar.

I shrugged. A cover-story doesn't have to be believed to be effective: it only has to distract the listener from the questions he should have asked.

"What can I say? My life's an adventure."

Yet another stranger arrived at our table and stood looking down at me. I glanced up at him, seeing the dark-blond hair shared by half the northern Ruillin and the sort of hard, habitual dishonesty one usually sees in back-rooms charms dealers. I restrained a groan: this place was just like a river ferry, except that the boat wouldn't dock anytime soon.

"Hello," I said, mostly because I wanted the man to go away.

"Hey… Ya wanna buy a flasher?" he said.

I glanced at the bag slung over his shoulder. I could guess at its contents: illicit flash-weapons, probably one-offs—or pieces spent, abandoned, and halfway-recharged at some old sun-circle. Not that any nobleman, or any man of honor for that matter, would be caught dead holding such a thing. A flasher is a coward's weapon, designed to use borrowed arcane power from a safe distance to do things better handled by an honest blade.

"You wanna wind up in the river?" I said darkly, and met his snake's eyes with a cold stare.

The man's mouth twisted; he strolled towards the other end of the table, and I caught his gaze again.

In how many pieces? I mouthed soundlessly, forming the words so they were easy to read on my lips.

He grimaced again and moved away.

"So," Loeg said, as if nothing had happened. "Tell me true: the stories are real?" He glanced again at the Tana.

"Depends which stories you mean," I answered. "No Tana ever enchanted me—but while I was on the other side of the mountains, I met people who remember Armoan's day."

"Damn," the mummer said softly.

I nodded.

"But the Tana?" the mummer pursued.

I gave him a rueful smile. "No easier to come by than human women. And they're in charge."

But myths like that don't die easily. It was easy to see in his eyes, the only part of him that still showed truth behind all the paint: the fault lay with me, though what defect I might carry wasn't easy to see. That was true enough, in its own way; but he thought it meant he would succeed where I had failed.

And who was to say about that, after all. I possessed no great understanding of the Tanaan: that became more evident every day.

Whatever his personal flaws might be, the mummer was too polite to share his thoughts aloud.

"In charge?" he echoed. "Of what?"

I thought about the answer, then surprised myself with a laugh. "Of everything."

He smiled. A man who doesn't fear a woman with a sword would only see it as spice, an added challenge to conquer. I was almost nostalgic for his uncomplicated view.

"Will you introduce me and my friends?"

I raised my eyebrows; Loeg held up both hands. "Only respect to your lady, of course."

I smiled a little. "Do yourself a favor and remember they're armed."

He laughed and rose, so I climbed to my feet, too. At the other end of the table, we had introductions all around: I met Suros, the mischievous redhead costumed as the Hero who waited to accost Amien with some joke or sketch he expected to torque the old man; Tindell, the Rogue or Lord, who had danced with Tru this afternoon on the ferry; and Sainrith, Donnall, and Corro, the Damsel, the Farmer, and the Druid, this afternoon's drum-and-pipe dance-band. Amien returned and had to be introduced all around as well, using the name *Rinnal Ruthin*.

"Hey," Suros said to Amien. "Mug of beer?"

Amien cast the redhead a speculative look. "Thank you?"

Suros grinned and scampered to the bar. The rest of the mummers slipped free of their conversations, as if some signal had passed among them, and withdrew behind the little curtain they had erected at the back of the platform. Suros returned, handed Amien his beer, and grinned again.

"Sit right down, now," the mummer said, radiating mischief from boots to hair. "We think you'll like this one!"

I restrained a groan. Amien watched the mummer hurry across the room to join his fellows behind the curtain; the Tanaan settled at the table again, expectant. After a short time, Suros, Sainrith, and Corro re-emerged: the Hero, the Damsel, and the Druid would play this scene.

Sainrith now sported a filmy blue scarf—and a shocking-red wig, which rested askew atop his long dark-blond hair, transforming the Damsel into a deliberately-failed rendition of a night butterfly. Corro had put on a cheap torc of tarnished brass and a grey wig that had clearly seen better days. I shut my eyes against the impulse to rise and interrupt their play; already I could see what they were about. They meant to perform the *Night Butterfly and the Druid*, and tonight the Druid was Amien.

I'd seen several versions of this skit before. Mummers' humor sometimes gets lower, but it's rarely more deliberately offensive. Whatever the conceit of the sketch's opening, in the end it boils down to a contest between the night butterfly and the Druid over the man with whom they share the stage. Sometimes their pawn is the Hero, sometimes the Farmer, occasionally the Fool. The Druid campaigns to keep the pawn engaged in a holiday ceremony so dull the poor man keeps falling asleep; the night butterfly endeavors to corrupt him. The punchline delivered by the night butterfly is always the same: *Give him an hour with me, and he won't just believe in the goddess, he'll worship Her too!*

Sainrith's bright red wig and blue scarf made my encounter with the night butterfly at Goibniu unfold in my head: the power of the river rushing into me when I began to relax in her presence; the half-second's tangling of the woman and the goddess in my mind. My first encounter with Laverna, out on the flats, had been no more than six hours old, and already I found it difficult to hold myself separate. Finally I understood why men up and down the Ruillin still worship Her; She is far more present here than Lady Tella. *Give him an hour with me...* My throat felt unaccountably tight.

Affront gathered predictably in Amien's face as the little skit progressed; I realized he'd never seen it before. How long had it been since anyone dared disrespect him? Centuries, I supposed. And there isn't much call for humor that dresses down the true religion at Aballo or any royal court: the *Night Butterfly and the Druid* is the stuff of the low rooms and lawless ferries of the Ruillin. And tonight I saw new layers in it, myself: not until this evening had I realized how little the true gods are loved by the common folk of the Ruillin. Tonight the Night Butterfly seemed not only the Ruillin's totem but her champion. Suros's arrow had flown true.

Watching Corro as they neared the climax of the skit, I realized how closely he mimicked Amien: not only the torc and wig marked him out; Corro had perfectly reproduced Amien's proud bearing and gravelly voice. How closely had the mummers been watching him? Corro was a talented player, to be sure; but to have absorbed that much in a minute or two would be nothing short of miraculous. *Seems a group of Tanaan defended the Lady's Well outside Goibniu from an attack by the Avengers of Esus.* Had the story that accompanied us out of Goibniu included the detail of a wizard participating in the battle?

It would be naïve to hope that it had not.

Had the mummers connected Amien with the tale of a wizard in the company of Tanaan? Had they, like this morning's windcaller, seen the torc and deduced what it meant? Was I, then, also to interpret the poorly-rendered night butterfly as a commentary on Letitia and our attempt at concealing her? I glanced away from the platform, to the place in which Loeg sat: seeing his eyes on me and Amien, a classic Fool's mask on his features but a predator's assessing patience in his gaze. Meanwhile Amien's ire condensed into a palpable cloud around us.

I manufactured a grin, leaned in close to the wizard's ear.

"This is funny," I whispered. "This is the funniest thing you've seen all month."

The wizard shot me a look. "They're doing *me!*" he whispered.

"And you are not a member of the initiate," I hissed back. "So this is funny."

The wizard moved restlessly, then suddenly stilled; understanding swept over his face, followed by a feral grin. "There's nothing in the Code that prohibits turning mummers into mules."

"Give him an hour with me..." Sainrith said, up on the platform; the half-empty room rang with laughter, and we joined the crowd.

Tonight's dinner consisted of pie made from some old, tough game-bird, potatoes, and bitter winter greens. It made me oddly nostalgic for Ilnemedon, where the first, tiny spring greens must be available by now. As we finished eating, three harpists arrived: none of whom I recognized, to my relief. None of them seemed to notice me at all, though they stared predictably at the Tana.

After a bit of tuning, a few half-complete melodic lines, and a sotto voce discussion that suggested a last-minute change of plans, they began to play on a cittern and a reed flute. For the moment the drum sat alone on the floor; after the first phrase from the flute, I understood why. They had decided to play *Coradon's Lament*, the story of Coradon, righ of the place that would later become Ilesia, and his seduction and eventual ruin by the Tanaan Lady Ara of Nimah. No doubt the harpists meant it as a tribute to the Tana. At least it wasn't the *Ballad of Carina*.

Coradon's Lament is a standard, and always well-received in taverns; I hadn't played it in years. Now I added it to the list of songs I must deconstruct and try to find the truth of: I finally understood that Nimah was a real place, not mythical, and the whole thing was shot through with all the misconceptions about Tana I had breathed for so many years. I was grateful most of the Tanaan couldn't understand it, too embarrassed to even look at Letitia.

Finally it ended, to applause from all the human men in the room; if the harpists understood it had failed to achieve some sort of rapport with the Tana, they gave no sign. But afterward the singer picked up the drum, and they returned to the more fertile ground of dance tunes. Immediately the mummers came bounding back to our table and invited the Tana, who seemed completely oblivious to the subtexts of the mummers' last sketch, to dance. Tindell claimed Tru again, Easca smiled and rose to dance with dark-eyed Corro, and Letitia crossed the room to the open dance-space with Loeg. Donnall, still dressed as the Farmer, and Sainrith, who had returned to his guise as the Damsel, made a comic business of joining in: so hilariously overdone in their play-courting that the whole room soon laughed.

Except the Tanann, I noted. Behind their studied neutrality I saw a flavor of jealousy few human men ever achieve, a drive that managed to transcend emotion. Their faces might be still and calm, but I had spent years reading the bodies of warriors, and theirs all looked like the final moments before swords are drawn.

It puzzled me: the Tans had been as oblivious to the import of the *Night Butterfly and the Druid* as the Tana; and with the exception of Iminor's commitment to Letitia, there were clearly no romantic bonds among any of them.

Every time we came within range of night butterflies, Tuiri and Mattiaci in particular lit up with charm I had never seen in them, indeed had rarely seen anywhere; and the others, if less adventuresome, were clearly as compelled by the night butterflies' provocative dress and what doubtless counted among Tanaan as their exotic appearance. I hadn't seen so much as a hint of sexual tension among the Tanaan, which was surprising in a mixed-gender crew of beautiful people. And yet tonight the Tans were ready to explode.

I was in no position to judge, of course. The sight of Letitia in the embrace of the black-and-white painted Fool made something uncomfortable try to unfold inside my chest, something that deepened when I saw her eyes on me across the room. It was only for a moment, but the intensity of it echoed through me until I had to look away. Instead I focused on the men with whom I sat, watching their narrow jaws go hard.

After the first two songs the dancers switched partners: Letitia with Tindell, who suddenly looked much more Rogue than Lord and whose boldness seemed only to amuse her; Easca with Donnall, who I overheard playing his Farmer role with very dirty overtones, making Easca first blush—when had she learned enough Ilesian to understand such talk?—and then smolder; Tru with Suros, who approached her with a reverent wonder that made me suddenly like him, after all. This time Loeg played the Fool in high form, dancing with Sainrith the Damsel.

Finally I'd had enough of watching the Tans seethe. I rose and moved to a place in which I could lean across the table, speak in an undertone and still have them hear me.

"You don't like it?" I said, looking around at them. "Cut in."

"Cut what?" Iminor said.

Oh, sweet Lady Tella. How are these things settled on that side of the mountains?

"Cut *in*," I repeated. "You go to the man who is dancing with the woman you'd like to dance with, tap his shoulder—*politely*—" I engaged all their gazes, one by one. "And say, 'Excuse me'. They will know what you want. Unless they're itching to fight—and believe me, none of these fellows are—they'll just bow and hand her over. And then it's your turn to dance."

I looked around at them again, watching the ideas turn in their minds. After a second I remembered there were still twice as many of them as there were Tana.

"It would be a courtesy if you all took turns," I said. "Then the mummers won't have to take it personally. Three of you go in first, dance with our friends; at the next dance, the other three come in. All very friendly. And remember to smile if one of the mummers cuts in afterward."

They all looked increasingly thoughtful. Finally Iminor nodded and rose, Mattiaci and Nuad on his heels.

"Does the phrase *international incident* mean nothing to you?" Amien said as I sat down again.

I shrugged. "I think I just averted one."

He nodded, thoughtful, watching the little drama unfold; I followed his gaze. Iminor executed his maneuver properly if a bit too intently; Mattiaci surprised me by making it seem charming. Nuad drew soldierly discipline around him and brought all his considerable courtesy to bear; and then Iminor danced with Letitia, Mattiaci with Tru, and Nuad with Easca, and I was stunned by what I saw in their faces and tender embraces. Now, finally, I understood: only a few nights remained until Bealtan. Whatever depth of meaning most humans bring to Bealtan observances, that festival is severalfold more critical to the Tanaan, who still practice the old rite, each and every one—and for whom it marks their sole period of fertility during the year. Of course the intensity must begin days before the festival.

Sudden wistfulness overcame me at having missed this twelvenight in the Four Realms. I must go back next year. I looked at Letitia again, and once again found her eyes on me, but I couldn't tell whether she wanted me to dance or—in the way women sometimes do—wanted me to see her dancing with another. Emotion roared through me; I bit it fiercely back. I would not play this game. It was entirely possible I was playing it alone. I rose and returned to the bar for another beer, then carried it out to the inn's front porch.

I could still hear the music through the open windows, but there were other things to look at here: long northern evening fading into starlight; Telliyn climbing over the round, ragged cones of the mountains on the Ruillin's other side; river mist creeping between the buildings. The cool serenity felt strange, divorced from reality; but I suspected the Ruillin was more or less the same as ever. I tried to remember what it had been to play in these inns in the evenings, alternately suffering and embracing the disconnection from everything I had once thought important: marking the days by sets played, women bedded, songs and histories taken apart and examined for traces of the sort of truth that had eluded me since the life I expected fell apart. What little I truly remembered of those years here and in Ballarona felt like tales from another man's life.

Inside, one of the harpists began a song on a set of pipes fitted with a bag and bellows in the northern style; the sweet melancholy of it closed around my throat. But it also made me realize the dancing must have stopped of its own accord, and wonder why: I pushed away from the wall and went back inside, encountering the Tanaan progressing back up the ill-lit stairs. Iminor looked fiercely neutral again, Letitia angry: no way would I ask the question begging for release behind my lips.

I fell in with Amien, following the Tanaan up the stairs with Amien on my heels. No one made any pretense of conversation. As the staircase reached an intermediate landing and folded back on itself, I glanced up at Letitia again: this time I was certain her eyes were on me, with a smolder whose like I hadn't seen on her since Irisa in her gaze; I forced my attention away lest I find myself trying to manufacture explanations. Out of some tiny storage compartment on the landing came the unmistakable ozone smell and arcing, sulfurous bolt of a flash-weapon.

Amien sent a bolt of his own into the lightless hollow on the stair; seemingly all the Tanaan dove on top of Letitia. The wizard beat me to the landing and wrested the flash-weapon from the attacker's hands before the afterimages had subsided from my vision. The man collapsed in a dark-clad, delicately smoking heap.

"Secure the mora," he said evenly to the Tanaan. Sudden satisfaction broke across his equine face, plain even in the poor light. "I've finally got something I can use."

"Ah," I breathed, pleased understanding settling over me. The operative part of any flash weapon is a charged crystal, which the weapon taps to produce a would-be arcane casting. The better ones use crystals charged by wizards. Though some inferior substitutes use mechanically generated quick-charges, those weapons are generally only good for a single use. The Bard of Arcadia had no need to resort to such measures, of course: the weapon in Amien's hands almost certainly contained a crystal that had been charged by the Bard's Wizard—which, in all likelihood, still bore his arcane signatures. Possibly even his name.

Learning our enemy's name would change everything. Stronger, much more targeted magics can be brought to bear when one knows the intended object's name; a man's name is the core of a useful binding. And the intelligence of the mundane variety we might gain would be nearly as important.

Amien's face was composed, but deep eagerness gleamed in his dark eyes. He watched the Tanaan pick themselves up and glanced at me; I smiled.

"I've got this," I said, with a nod towards the body. "I'll be up in a minute."

He grinned and raced upstairs after them.

I knelt at the edge of the little storage enclosure, checking the body to see what I could learn. His left sleeve concealed a redsnake tattoo, the mark of a kharr insider. Just to be thorough, I checked for the mark of Par at the nape of his neck, but of course it wasn't there. His hands bore the sort of calluses any craftsman's might, though some instinct made me suspect he was a smith. It didn't matter, in the end: the important detail was beyond dispute. I wrestled the body all the way inside the storage alcove and jammed the little door shut behind him; with any luck, by the time the body was discovered we would be gone.

"Kharr," I said to Amien as I entered the room, but he was already absorbed in his investigation: he'd pulled the crystal free of its housing and sat before the fire with the thing in his hands, thoroughly entranced. I stirred up the blaze, checked on the drying-progress of my things, and examined the harp for signs of warping. I wished I could play it to pass the time; no way could I leave the room until Amien returned from his investigations. A wizard in such a trance is even more vulnerable than a man asleep.

On the other side of the room, Tuiri and Fiacha had settled to the floor and begun yet another dice game. I wasn't that bored yet. Nevertheless they seemed to feel my gaze and looked up at me.

"Everything all right?" I said to them.

Tuiri blushed. "Well, Lord, the mora—"

I waved him off. "I don't need to know. Amien's been all right?"

They glanced past me to the wizard. Fiacha shrugged.

"I guess so," he said. "He's just been sitting there, quiet…"

I nodded. "That's fine." I wandered around the room again, trying to think of something to do. Amien was writing Sanglin a letter, I remembered; I tried to imagine who I should be sending what might be last thoughts and came up with no one with whom I wanted to share the contents of my mind. If I died tomorrow, the lords of the gorsedd would hold a day of mourning as soon as they got the news, then elect a new ard-harpist. No knowledge they needed would perish with me. Finally I stretched out on the bed and stared at the ceiling. I would not think about Letitia's eyes on me. Neither would I allow the illicit energies creeping around my awareness access to the parts of me that sang in response to their touch. I proved both of those resolutions hollow.

Gradually anxiety began to replace my boredom. Amien was taking a very long time. Some men are better than others at hiding their signatures among the folds and recesses of their arcane workings, and it was only to be expected that a man who could do the things I'd seen from the Bard's Wizard would have techniques few men ever conceived. But he also wouldn't be the first or last wizard to lay a mind-trap on something that might fall into an enemy's hands.

I sat up and looked at Amien. He hadn't moved. The fire needed stirring up again; how long had I been woolgathering, myself? The knights had given up their dice game and sat shoulder to shoulder, backs to the room's outer wall, holding a wistful conversation about the Bealtan they were missing at home.

"Amien," I said. The wizard didn't seem to hear, so I rose and walked towards him. I laid a hand on his shoulder and spoke his name again, got no response, grasped his shoulder and shook him. The crystal remained folded in his hands, his gaze fixed on nothing mundane eyes could see. I said his name again, loudly enough that it was probably audible from the hall and the adjoining rooms. I tried speaking into his mind, knowing it was useless.

I looked up; both knights met my gaze, wide-eyed.

"Is he all right?" Tuiri said.

I sighed. "Probably." I looked down at the wizard again, considering next options. I must go into his awareness myself and hope he hadn't become snared by something that would entangle me, too. I wondered where the closest practicing wizard was: probably Coran's House Healer Athramail, at Ilnemedon. Assuming he hadn't already left for Teamair, which was less likely than I wished. I should tell the knights who to go to for help if I became ensnared too; but that would require confessing things. A lot of things. Instead I knelt before the wizard, pulled the crystal from his surprisingly-resistant fingers and grasped his hands, leaned my forehead against his, and dove.

Amien's radiant energies engulfed me, as familiar as the sounds and shadows of a home long left behind. He was aware of me now, as if I stood at his shoulder while he pursued some absorbing task; he leaned against me, shoulder to shoulder as it were, staring down the trail of the knowledge he sought. Lattices of transparent crystal rose all around us, reflecting red and gold as if caught in some blazing sunset, climbing to impossible heights and depths and stretching in ragged ranks of nearly-regular faces, beyond the edges of awareness. Amien's mind focused on a trail of deeper red that darkened towards black, which seemed to lead endlessly further into the crystal and stretched an equally interminable distance behind the crystal-heart we occupied. I didn't have to encompass the whole structure in his mind to recognize that it was a circular path he pursued; I was glad I'd pulled the crystal from his hands before I stepped into this trap.

Hey, I thought, and tugged at his awareness.

Wait. Look there.

I looked ahead, down the trail of deepening, twisting darkness through the facets, suddenly remembering the labyrinthine paths inside the Great Barrow on Ilunmore—and the place I had slipped *through* into something I still wasn't sure how to categorize. It would be so easy to succumb to this beckoning trail and the promise of answers just around the edge of the next chamber.

No, this isn't working, I thought—and then something shifted. Through the lattice, behind the lattice, somehow both within its chambers and very far away, another awareness stared through the red-gold glow. I recognized it; now I understood who this trap was for. Amien had been merely the bait.

There was no time to do this delicately: I grasped Amien and wrenched us both into ordinary consciousness, half-surprised I could. The room in the inn screamed into being around us; Amien fell across his own knees, skull clutched in his fingers.

"Fouzh!" he groaned into his knees. "What the fouzhir hell!"

"I'm sorry," I began.

"Didn't you see how close—"

"My lord, you'd been at it for hours. We both know—"

He picked up his head, wincing as if every movement generated lightning-strikes in his brain, to stare at me in dismay.

"Hours," he said quietly. I nodded. He began to nod and decided against it.

"Well, he's got *my* name now," Amien said quietly. "Not that *that's* much of an accomplishment. Even the damned windcaller knew…"

"My lord," I began regretfully; he reached out and laid a hand on my shoulder.

"That was a fouzhir elementary trap," he said.

"Best damn execution I ever saw," I answered. He grunted, as if he suspected he was being managed. For a moment we stared at one another in silence. A half-formed flicker of the way things would have been, had I remained at Aballo, passed between us. Regret condensed inside me again.

"Well done," he said finally. "Thank you. Could you look in my herb-kit for some butterbur, and check downstairs to see if they've got any wine?"

I nodded, laid a hand on his shoulder, and rose. Halfway down the stairs, true cognizance of what had happened caught up with me; the headache haunting the edges of my brain roared in like the tide. I paused for a moment in the dim passage, grasping the rail, trying to catch my breath. Had I been wrong to stay with Letitia, after all? Even if I had been the first to reach the assassin, I wouldn't have been the one to try my hand at seeking our enemy's name in the crystal: not as long as Amien was here and capable. But our enemy's plan had encompassed that choice.

No doubt the assassin had been aiming for Letitia; but the Bard's Wizard had known he would fail. The attempt on her had been no more than a feint. The true operation had very nearly succeeded.

Butterbur and wine reduced my headache to the occasional stabbing moment and visual halo; eagerness to be gone from this place swept over me until I could no longer sit still. The Bard's Wizard knew where we were, to a level of exactitude that would make it a simple matter to send mundane forays against us; there was a body in a storage hollow on the stair, and I wanted to be far away when it was discovered. I fidgeted and paced while Amien called everyone together in our room, then discovered I still needed to stand while he delivered the news.

"You don't have good tidings," Letitia said, watching him pace before the fireplace.

The wizard shook his head. "It did not go well. I wasn't able to learn our enemy's name—clever bastard laid a very effective trap in that crystal, and I was lucky to get out of it with my mind. I've got a bitch of a headache as things stand," he confessed.

A collective sigh went up from the Tanaan.

"What's worse, there's no question our enemy now knows my name—not that that's a game-changer, since my name is well known to wizards everywhere, but he is now operating under no doubts that I am with you," Amien said to Letitia. "Worst of all, he knows we're in Dromineer. He can easily deduce we'll be on the ferry in the morning."

Letitia gasped. "We should leave now!"

"And go where?" I said. "The city gates are locked."

She looked at Amien again. "Then are you going to work wards?"

He shook his head, then winced. "It's tempting—but I think it would be the wrong move."

"But he knows where we are already!"

"He knows we're in this *city*," the wizard said. "The likelihood that the Bard sent only one assassin looking for you is small. Wards would allow him to pinpoint us precisely; unwarded, we're harder to find. And it will take time for him to find out which assassin discovered us, more time yet to find out where. Ellion?" He looked at me.

"I agree," I said. "It goes against every instinct I've got, but it's the best strategy. For tonight, Mora, I recommend we sit. There is really no place to go tonight; better to post watches and wait for the sun and the tide."

Letitia pursed her lips, staring at me. She wore a composed expression, but the vulnerability in her eyes made my hands itch for a weapon. Finally she nodded.

"What about tomorrow?" she said to Amien. "He'll know we're on the ferry, you said. What do we do instead?"

I met Amien's gaze; he gave me a quizzical look and a little, one-handed gesture of offering. I nodded.

"I think we get on the ferry," I said.

"What?"

I shrugged. "There's no good solution, Mora. He expects us to be on the ferry; he can be expected to attack the ferry. Which, actually, means it's the thing we're least likely to do. Especially when you consider the full history of this campaign, and the fact that we have always tried to avoid the traps we could anticipate."

Her regard shifted; sudden, impulsive faith warred in her eyes with a resolve not to trust me, and I felt as if her gaze quested all the way into my soul for some fact that would settle the matter. I fought off the feeling of nakedness her glance could raise, submitting to her examination. I shouldn't be trusted: we both knew it. And I so wanted to be worthy of trust, especially hers.

"There is really no usable road between here and Ballarona," I said. "The tide reshapes these coasts every year, and we'd need a local to guide us safely through. I haven't seen anything here that made me inclined to trust the locals." I glanced at Amien. "I only wonder whether it's just these two cities, or all of Mumhan that is already as good as in the Bard's hands."

Amien grimaced and gave a careful nod.

"Taking evasive action would require time we can't afford," I continued, looking at Letitia again. "Had we time, I'd take the Tellnemed ferry instead, and continue through Ilesia. But Amien will never make it to the Moot if we do. Riding upriver on the Saone only takes us farther from our goal. What we need—" I looked at Amien. "Is something to cover our movements in the morning, so the enemy must guess what we do."

"A fog," Amien said, smiling a little. He looked at Letitia. "We're not just talking about weather here, but an arcane fog."

I nodded. "One that obscures a healthy distance around the city, so he can't be sure what route we took until too late. Is there sufficient power here?"

Humiliation flared in Amien's eyes: not at the question, I knew, but at the fact that it was valid. His jaw hardened. "Even if I spend so much that you carry me onto the ferry, I'll make it happen."

I nodded and returned my attention to the Tanaan. "Under that cover, the moment they open the gates on the ferry ramp, we cross—and hide below until we sail."

"And you think that because he's not sure we're on the ferry, he won't attack it?" Letitia said.

So the brehons had not yet ruled on me. As well they should not.

I raised my eyebrows. "Even he has only so many resources. Each attack costs him. In his seat, I would wait until I knew where my quarry was, and spend my forces where they mattered. If he knows you travel with Amien, he knows you are bound for Aballo. He has only so many days left before he'd have to sacrifice everything else to reach you—but that day has not yet come. He will marshal his resources."

She looked at me for a long moment. "Are you sure?" she said finally.

I sighed. "No. But so far, every decision he's made was the one I would have made myself. I don't think he'll start making mistakes now."

Letitia stared at me further. After a moment I saw the decision in her eyes.

"As you advise, my lord," she said. "In the morning we take the ferry to Ballarona."

The Ruíllin-Aerona Basín

The Aerona Basin and Ruillin River

Chapter 22
Everything Has Its Price

Tuiri woke me and Amien an hour before dawn. We dressed without lighting a lamp and, under cover of the deep, moonlight-blocking dark granted by the mountains to the west of the city, crept on foot the little distance to the city wall. We found one of the small stairways leading to the wall's top, which are the sort of breach of sound military practices that cities accustomed to peace eventually indulge in—in this case, for the benefit of the ship captains—and walked the narrow parapet until we found a spot from which we could see all the way across the city.

Amien looked around, turning in a complete circle, planning his working. The beginnings of dawn glimmered behind the mountains on the opposite shore. He glanced at me.

"Time."

I nodded and extended my hand. "Lean on me as you will."

Astonishment flared in his eyes, though he managed to keep his face still. After a moment of silent staring, he nodded and grasped my hand.

Lending one's own native power to another is not the same as an arcane draw. This would not be my working, would be no violation of my vow, though I would experience everything he saw and did. I understood that is not how the sharing of power goes for men who aren't telepaths; understood Amien would feel me only as a wellspring of power, like a sacred site or the power in his own core, that he might draw on. The one-sided intimacy raised in me a strange melancholy—which I could ill afford. I pushed it aside, trained my attention on the way Amien conceived the fog with which he would blanket Dromineer.

He called up the power of the shrine to Par, which felt like the sort of charge that gathers in a wool blanket beside the illicit energies knocking against the edges of my awareness, then reached beyond the eastern wall and pulled on the mists beginning to rise from the river's surface. With those mists he seeded a mental conception of a fog that rose from the river, stretched past the wall on which we stood, blanketed the city, and sent feathering fingers to the south and west and north. I found myself smiling, a deep pleasure stirring in my chest as thought transmuted into form and a cold wet fog settled all around. He pulled on me, spinning my energy into a delicious electric cloud that caught me up in tingling delight as it interwove the physical fog, building a fluid framework that slipped and gathered as pleasantly as the silken cloud of a lover's hair: in the air, around the city, suffusing my consciousness. Through it the haze feathered down to the ground and up towards the sky, almost as high as the places where the thermals would soon begin to flow. It fluttered and glittered through me, not the grey and white of a typical morning river fog, but a shimmer that began with the hues of the rainbow and spiraled into colors mundane eyes will never see, blanketing everything in a deadening haze that even a clairvoyant could not penetrate. Droplets of mist clung to my hair and mail; sprinkles of invisible color caressed my skin. The sun rose and bounced from the fog, dazzling; rills of electric pleasure chased one another up my spine.

Amien made a final, irrelevant gesture with his free hand, released me and smiled. "Thank you. Are you all right?"

I grinned. I would have willingly lent him the power from my very bones, so long as I got to feel the working flow through me. "Fine. You?"

His smile deepened; he shook his head as if amused. "Fine. Let's go."

Down on the ground, Dromineer lay under an eerie arcane quiet that made my black heart sing. The trill and chatter of the birds fell silent; the cocks in the yards held their morning calls. Even the wheels of wagons moving through the fog sounded muffled. We slipped into the inn, where people already stood clustered at the windows, and climbed the stairs. The looks on the faces I saw at the windows made me want to laugh; I didn't even allow myself to smile. In short order the party stood ready, so we trooped back downstairs and out to the stable.

"You're not going out in that?" the ostler said.

I held back a grin, shrugging. "In the fog? Sian, if I lay abed every time we had fog in the morning—" Now I did smile. "Let's just say I'd need company in there, or I'd be bored half the month."

The ostler shook his head. "That's not fog."

"Really?" I said. "What do you call it?"

I left him trying to puzzle out an answer, mounted, and rode out.

From the top of the ramp that led down to the ferry docks, I saw similar consternation on the deck of the Ballarona ferry. The boarding gate stood open, but the crew clustered on the deck, staring skyward. Amien's fog stretched more than a mile out into the river; the demarcation between fog and morning sunlight shone as a fall of sunbeams out on the water. Beneath the fog, the air on the water lay as preternaturally still as within the city wall, and even the waves ran quiet.

"The windcaller's going to have quite the morning," Amien observed.

"The tide alone can get them under way," I answered. "All the captain will need is a bit of courage."

We sat in the saddles a moment longer, watching. The fog muffled whatever was said on the deck, but hearing the words was hardly necessary. Everyone on board was spooked.

"Everything has its price here, you said," Letitia said thoughtfully. "I wonder what his courage will cost."

I turned and looked at her; she pulled the thong from the end of her braid and shook her hair free. It fell in ripples and spirals of gold across the spider-silk of her mail shirt, gleaming in the muted light. I wanted to bury my face in it.

"Im," she said. "Give me the purse."

"*What?*" he blurted, then seemed to remember himself. "My lady, I don't—"

She cast him a steady stare, holding out her hand until he put the purse into it. She nodded and fastened it to her own belt.

"Ready?" she said to Amien.

A wondering smile spread across the wizard's face; he nodded and led us down the ramp.

The entire crew turned to stare at us as we approached. Somebody whistled, long and low; I saw more than one hand fold into a gesture invoking Laverna's protection.

"Now I've seen everything," one man said.

I glanced around, reading the deference in the rest of the crew—and realized he was the captain. His dark-blond warrior's tail and bristling mustache, well-groomed though they were, gave a strange impression of ferocity; but his face bespoke wonder.

If I could read men, Letitia could read both her people and mine. She put on a smile and met the captain's eyes.

"Good morning, Captain," she said. Amien reined, letting her ride ahead. I doubted anyone noticed: they were all busy goggling.

"Good morning," he managed; her smile deepened.

"This is a beautiful ship," Letitia continued as if he were the only other person present, riding across the gangway and dismounting within arm's reach of the man. I was not the only person on shore who stiffened. "What is its name?"

The impulse to correct her did no more than flicker in his eyes. The sailors of the Ruillin call their ships by the feminine pronouns, which seems to be a tribute to the goddess they all worship.

"*Rhian*, Lady," said the captain. "Her name is *Rhian*."

"Beautiful," Letitia said again, nodding. "We're bound for Ballarona this morning, sian. Are you sailing there?"

He raised his bushy eyebrows, quizzical. "I hope so—but this fog…"

She smiled and shrugged. "We see them like this at home all the time. Sail out to where the sun shines, and your windcaller will have no trouble at all."

Now he gave her a long look, eyes narrowed. "Do you know ships, Lady?"

"Not as well as I'd like, sian." This she delivered with a languorous look composed almost entirely of slow-sweeping eyelashes. She'd been watching the night butterflies too, I realized. The captain was entirely sunk.

"Sail out to the sunlight, you say?" he said, a sudden rough edge to his voice.

"I hope you'll tell the other captains," she said guilelessly. "I'd hate to see them miss a day of sailing just because of a little fog."

A smile I didn't like at all crept across his lips. "Just so. And in return for your kind advice, let me show you around while we sail. There's a lot to see."

Letitia smiled. "What is our fare, sian?"

"Oh, only the pleasure of your—"

"But my friends, sian, and our horses. Surely—"

He glanced across the gangway as if he had forgotten the rest of us were here. "Ah. All of you, for Ballarona?"

She nodded, reaching for the purse and opening it. His eyes lit at what he saw inside. Amien cued his horse and crossed the gangway, slipping out of the saddle even closer to the captain than Letitia stood.

"Oh, annu, let me get that," he said, folding her purse back into her hand, apparently oblivious to the captain's annoyance. "The usual, I assume?" he said to the captain.

"And another fifteen for the horses."

Amien nodded. "Just so." He paid the fare and beckoned the rest of us across the gangway. Letitia stepped back to let us all pass. I cast her an inquiring glance as I threaded my way between her and the captain, but she just smiled and turned the full force of her charm on him again.

"We're going to go—downstairs?" she said.

"Below," the captain supplied, warmth creeping into his voice again.

She smiled more broadly. "So much to learn. We're going to go below until we sail, sian. We haven't breakfasted yet. I'm sure you're very busy during this time of the morning, but I'd be pleased to see you once we're under way? If you like." Again she employed the eyelashes.

The captain bowed. "It will be my pleasure."

"Don't forget to tell your friends about sailing into the sunlight," she said, and caught up to the rest of us.

"You are surely the wickedest woman I have ever seen," I said in the Tanaan language, smiling at her.

Her answering smile was modest. "We're not under way yet, my lord."

By the time we had settled the horses, the captain had sent a man to share Letitia's advice on sailing into the clear with the other captains docked at the wharf—and another man back into the city, to cry the news that the ferries would sail at the inns and in the street. We climbed down the narrow stair to the lower deck and occupied most of the chairs in the rear salon.

On the other side of the room, a fortune-teller and a cards-dealer sat gossiping; they stared as if we were invading their territory, but we stuck to the Tanaan language and pretended we couldn't understand either their words or the intent of their stares. After a while I went out to wander among the stalls and salons of the lower deck until I found a food vendor who was already selling, then bought half of what she had on hand and brought it back to the group.

Once we'd eaten, there was nothing to do but wait. It took considerable discipline to resist the urge to pace. Tuiri and Fiacha managed to draw the rest of the knights into a time-killing dice game; but I had no stomach for dice this morning. I had a prickly sense that the only dice that mattered had been cast long ago and were still tumbling all around us.

Gradually people began to board: I heard footfalls and voices out in the corridors beyond the salon we occupied, heard the sounds of trunks and other heavy objects being loaded onto the deck above. Late in the morning the cards-dealer withdrew to her business in a neighboring salon, and the fortune-teller arranged her nest on the other side of the room. Again and again the dice skittered across the floor, until I was certain I'd be hearing the sound in my dreams.

Finally the sound of the tide on the outside of the hull stilled; we all looked up, exchanging breathless glances. A few minutes later, the ship began to move.

"Praise Endeáril," Iminor breathed.

"The question is whether the other ships will sail as well," Letitia said quietly.

Tuiri packed up the dice; the knights climbed back into chairs. We all sat and waited. After some interminable space of time, the ship scooted suddenly forward; the familiar tug of power against the base of my spine told me, even from below the waterline, what the windcaller was about.

"There he goes," Amien said. "The windcaller has the sails."

Smiles broke across Tanaan faces; I couldn't help breathing a sigh of relief myself. We rose and began gathering up our possessions; suddenly the captain stood in the doorway, predatory gaze on Letitia.

"My lady," he said, voice too smooth. "May I give you the tour?"

She smiled and slung the pack across her shoulder. "Thank you, sian," she said, and crossed the salon to join him. Iminor looked like a gathering storm.

"Remember your role," I said quietly in the Tanaan language. "Be as jealous and suspicious as you like, but do it as her brother."

He turned a murderous look on me. "Is this your moment to *cut in*?"

"I doubt it," I said, much more mildly than I felt. "Even the mummers remarked that the lady and I have little enough use for one another. Ours is a political marriage, after all. And the Ballarona ferry is usually full of fetching women…"

The Tan scowled so fiercely that Amien finally waved him off.

"Welcome to the Ruillin," the wizard said. "The one thing you cannot buy here is the truth. Does a lady not complain on a ferry, everyone's honor is assumed to be intact when they disembark. Let's go see if the Tellnemed ferry sailed."

Brilliant blue skies and white-tipped water greeted us as we stepped onto the deck above. Gulls wheeled and dove in the ship's wake, hunting; wind snapped and barked in the sails. I raised a hand to shade my eyes and scanned the waters around us, spotting the Tellnemed ferry and a brace of smaller traders' vessels. Up at the ship's prow, Letitia stood with the captain, looking fascinated as he pointed out things in which I had no interest. Her golden hair whipped behind her like a pennant, dazzling.

"Well done Letitia," Amien said quietly.

"Well done, indeed," I replied. I looked around to find the knights and relieve them of all duties but watchfulness; but they had already spotted the ships and moved on to more compelling things, so I glanced around for some way to pass the time.

"We shouldn't all watch her at once," I observed. The wizard nodded. "I can see there's no calling Iminor off, but I'm going to wander for a bit."

"I think I like the view from right here," Amien said with studied casualness.

I nodded. "Just so. I'll check in with you in a while."

I strolled about the deck. The *Rhian* was built in the same way as all the Ruillin ferries: there was little to explore. Down the east-facing side of the deck I went, mentally tallying the day's passengers, glancing periodically across the water to the shore. From here the high dome of the temple to Lady Tella at Tellnemed was just visible, stunning blue-and-gold in the brilliant sunlight. The crowd on deck looked essentially the same as they ever do, except for the fact that the uniformly-directed gazes of certain clusters made it easy to spot the places where the Tanaan passed the time.

Glancing inside the covered part of the deck, I spotted the mummers who had dogged our steps yesterday. Though, in fairness, I supposed we had dogged theirs. They had already been at the Ship and Anchor when we arrived. Today's performance seemed to be the same as yesterday's, except that Sainrith and Corro had switched roles: yesterday's Damsel was today's Druid, and vice versa. If they were going to perform the same routine for days on end, I supposed, they must switch roles periodically or go mad.

I circled behind the covered deck, glancing up at the sailing deck above. Atop the roof—doubtless there was some other, nautical word I didn't know—over the area in which the mummers performed sat a small, squat box of a room that I imagined must be the captain's. A ladder fixed to its side led up to the highest spot save the masts, where a windcaller sat in the high seat. To his right stood a crewman who periodically touched the ship's yoke to adjust the course. I surmised the captain performed that task when he didn't have Tana to seduce.

I glanced again at the little room beneath the windcaller's seat. The captain must not be allowed to take Letitia into that place, even if she didn't object. A glance down the deck at Iminor suggested the man would die in his tracks did he so much as try. I had never seen the Tan throw a knife, but every skill I had seen him employ was exemplary. I had little doubt he could manage a knife, too.

As I came back up the other side of the deck, I spotted Letitia and the captain on their way down the stairs again. She laid a hand on his arm as if for balance, which I knew was unnecessary; he leaned in closer than needed. Iminor began striding straight across the deck towards the stair; Amien intercepted him, drew him to the opposite rail. After a moment I followed Letitia and the captain below. From the base of the stairs I heard the typical hum of the cards-room; the clank of tankards in the floating tavern; Letitia in courtly mode, asking the captain so many questions that I didn't doubt she'd be ready to command or at least competently purchase such a vessel by day's end. I climbed back up into daylight.

Amien caught my gaze and crossed the deck to meet me, Iminor in tow.

"You *left* her down there?" Iminor said, outraged.

I glanced at Amien, then met the Tan's gaze. "It occurs to me, ouirr, that no one is going anyplace for a few hours, and the lady is armed."

Amien nodded thoughtfully.

"She sounds perfectly comfortable," I continued. "By end of day she'll have enough information to offer him a fair price for the ship."

Amien chuckled.

Iminor scowled. "I don't see—"

"I know," I said. "But it is every Beallan's dream to take a run at a Danaan woman. And she knows her own will. There is a fine line between our appearing concerned for our lady's well-being and the sort of obsessive guarding one would expect of the crew protecting—" Even in the Tanaan language, I had to choose the next words carefully. There is no such thing as privacy on the deck of a ferry, and names sound much the same in any language. "—certain ladies under death-vendettas. We need to be sure of remaining on the safe side of the line."

Iminor gave me a long look. "Your definition of *safe* leaves something to be desired."

I sighed. "As usual, ouirr, we are in a situation in which there are no clear-cut answers. I think we need to maintain a watch over her—loosely. The man doesn't want to kill her."

"No," Iminor growled—then flushed and spun away.

"Bealtan," Amien groused, watching him stalk across the deck. "You think it's bad with just nine of 'em."

"I still hope to see the real thing one day."

Amien's mouth curved into an unwilling smile; he glanced away into memory.

Letitia? Iminor's voice skipped across the aether. It took everything I had to avoid startling at the broadcast.

Im?

Are you all right?

Letitia's broadcast crackled with irritation. *I'm on the same boat you are! Don't distract me!*

I just— Iminor began, defensive.

Let me work! Letitia snapped, and the aether went quiet again. I crossed to the rail and busied myself with the view of Tellnemed, determined not to meet Iminor's gaze.

The afternoon dragged on; periodically we spotted Letitia, ever cheerful, meeting our glances with swift reassuring looks and returning always to the captain. I wondered why she thought it necessary to keep him on the hook all day, but knew with uneasy certainty that she must be right. She'd taken accurate measure of every human thus far. Including me.

Meanwhile the Tanaan entertained themselves and a significant portion of the passengers with the sort of flirtation one usually sees only in soldiers too long from home. Which, I realized, was exactly what they were. Their behavior fit perfectly into the licentious atmosphere of a ferry, but the loss of military decorum in women struck me so strange I couldn't help but watch. When Letitia and the captain returned to the spot in which Iminor and Amien stood at the rail, I seized on the distraction and followed. She unbuckled her sword belt, unslung her pack, and handed both to Iminor.

"We're going to climb up in the rigging!" she said, green eyes shining.

"*What?*" we all said.

"You can't wear a sword up there; it'll tangle. So I need you to take my things—"

"Annu, are you sure?" Amien said. The captain shot him a look, which he ignored.

"Imagine the view!" Letitia said. "We'll be back in a while; I'll wave to you."

"Keep both hands on the *ropes*," Iminor growled.

"It's fine," Letitia said, and followed the captain across the deck.

"It's *not* fine," Iminor muttered.

"She's surefooted, and well-balanced, and—" Amien said.

"It's *not fine!*" Iminor repeated. "None of this is *fine!*"

I sighed. "Do you trust her?"

The Tan cast me a look of astonishment. For a moment he was silent.

"What choice do I have?" he said finally, an ache in his voice that made something uncomfortable happen inside my chest.

"Then *trust* her," I sighed. "And keep an eye out."

We stood on the deck and watched as Letitia trailed the captain up the wide nets of the rigging, a cat following a bear up a tree. Westering sunlight made her hair glow in a dozen shades of gold and white, skipped shimmering from the spidersilk of her mail. She appeared not at all nervous, but something that felt like my heart was blocking my throat. Gradually I realized everyone on deck stared, as absorbed by the climb as I. I shaded my eyes with a hand, acutely aware of my utter helplessness.

Trust her. What fool had said that?

Finally, much too high, they stopped. She seemed to ride the shifting mass of rope as unconcernedly as he, and after a brief lively wave in our direction looked eagerly outward: pointing as they talked, twisting around so blithely that I was certain she'd fall.

But she didn't, and eventually they climbed back down.

"Sian," said someone at my elbow.

I turned and looked: Sainrith the mummer, yesterday's Damsel and today's Druid, looked up at me. His right hand grasped a wooden sword of the type mummers use for mock battles.

"Could you help me with a bit of fun?" he said.

I manufactured a smile. Anything that would get the crowd's attention off Letitia was a good thing. "It's what I live for."

Sainrith grinned. "Thanks. Come be my translator." He beckoned, and I followed him across the deck to the place in which Easca lounged with Nuad against the rail. They watched us come, amusement written in their angular faces.

"Sian," Sainrith said. "Please tell the lady I wish to issue a challenge."

I chuckled and relayed the message. Her mouth twisted in an unsuccessful attempt to hide a grin.

"We duel," Sainrith continued. "The prize is a kiss."

This time I didn't try to restrain the laugh. Once I'd translated, Easca grinned and unsheathed her weapon, then assumed a formal dueling posture. By the time Sainrith had copied her maneuver, they were completely surrounded by spectators.

"First blow goes to the challenger," I reminded him, and he waded in. She trounced him soundly, of course, grinning the while, then pulled him close and kissed him yet more vigorously, to cheers from the assembled crowd. I could see his knees wobble. Finally she pushed back and released him. The sudden, deep red of her lips sang against her luminous skin, emphasizing the translucence of her teeth.

"Tell him we duel again for the next one," she said to me, mischief and lust warring in her amber eyes. "Location of the kiss to be chosen by the victor."

I laughed and translated again, then wandered across the deck to see what was happening under the roof. I paused just inside the doorway for a moment, letting my eyes adjust to the dimmer space; at the front of the room, Loeg packed the mummers' last few props while a dark-haired harpist sat on a stool in the middle of the platform, retuning a cittern. They both glanced at me; Loeg smiled, grin dangerous behind black-and-white paint.

"Ellion!" he said.

Now the harpist was staring at me. "Lord?"

Oh, holy fouzhir hell. For all the time and energy we spent protecting Letitia's identity, it would be Amien's or mine that blew the game in the end. Loeg turned a look of profound interest on me.

"*Lord?*" he echoed, something darker than mischief in his tone. I waved dismissively; Loeg turned his penetrating gaze on the harpist, who flushed.

"Am I mistaken, Lo—sian?" the harpist temporized. "Lord Harpist Ellion?"

"And here I thought I was the one with a tale to tell," the mummer pursued.

I sighed. If only I had been ready for the danger of recognition, I might have sidestepped it. In hindsight, as usual, the error was glaringly obvious.

"Could you not repeat that, please?" I said to the harpist.

But the damage was done, of course: at the very least, word would get back to the Harpist Gorsedd Hall that I had been seen on a Ruillin ferry this twelvenight—in the company of a group of Tanaan. Oh, who did I imagine I deceived? Surely everyone was making the connection: *in the company of the Lady of Finias.* Cold gathered inside me.

"You have a tale, sian?" I said to Loeg, in vain hope of distracting him.

His dangerous smile deepened. "Oh, indeed I do!" he chortled. "Here is today's meal: the Lady of Finias came to Dromineer on a magical fog—and is on the Ballarona ferry."

I swallowed a long string of profanity while Loeg watched, satisfaction in his dark eyes.

"Really," I said finally, in the calmest voice I could muster. "Is that the plot of your next performance?"

"Perhaps you'll write a song about it," he rejoined.

"Oh, no doubt," I answered, in a tone that made it into a blatant lie. "Right after the ship takes flight and sails us all the way to Teamair for the Fair."

"Wait, I only booked passage to Ballarona," the harpist said, trying help-fully to build the jest. We both glanced at him. Silence stretched among us, an odd contrast to the merriment out on the deck.

"Of course you realize," Loeg said after a long moment, in full Fool style. "I must reconsider everything you ever told me."

"I suppose this means the marriage is off," I retorted.

"Ours?" he said, still in Fool mode. "Or the nuptials of the Lady of Finias? Assuming she lives that long."

No man with an ounce of sense will argue in public with the Fool, even if he knows the player's name; but I couldn't help staring at him, and I knew my gaze was too intense for a man who hopes others won't think past the desig-nation *harpist*. A moment of crystalline calculation flickered in Loeg's eyes; his gaze slipped past me, to something out on the deck.

"Let's just say it has been a day for shocking revelations," he said finally. "And it's not even dinnertime." He performed an ironic bow and brushed past me on his way outside. I sighed and sank onto a bench in the back row, leaning my forehead on the heels of my hands.

"Lord?" the harpist said after a moment.

"Yes?" I sighed.

"I don't want to—I recognize this may not be—Where have you been, Lord? Ilnemedon's talked of little else."

"Oh, really?" I groused. "Surely they've got more important things to think about. The war, for example, or the election of the ard-righ…"

He just stared at me, and finally I really looked at him. He was younger than I by almost a decade, with the black hair and pale eyes of Nagnata. Or Tellan. And like most young gorsedd members, he heard about things after they happened, and just tried to keep up with the news and the songs.

I sighed. "If I'm still alive after Bealtan, you can come and ask me then."

"Do… Do you expect to be, Lord?"

I shrugged. "Like all men, I hope to be." I didn't want to contemplate the tales of this conversation that would travel the chambers of the gorsedd hall; I changed the subject. "Listen, as you observe, I've been—otherwise occupied of late. I need news."

The young harpist nodded, visibly gathering his thoughts. "Well, Lord, you know about the ard-righ, and the Moot."

I nodded.

"You—" He hesitated. "—know the Bard of Arcadia has set a price on the neck of the Lady of Finias."

I just raised an eyebrow, regarding him steadily.

He cleared his throat. "Had Regia fallen to the kharr by the time you… left?"

"Yes."

He nodded. "And Esunertos?"

It took everything I had to avoid reacting physically: the ruined city of Esunertos, once the capital of fallen Esusdia, has stood deserted since Lady Tella's final battle with the last holdouts for the old god Esus—in Whose name the Bard of Arcadia now crusaded. The place could be of no significant stra-tegic value—except to a wizard who didn't fear tapping black energies. For the Bard's Wizard, it would be almost as important as Uisneach and Teamair. The assaults both arcane and mundane he could stage with that power at his disposal would have spurred the righthe to collective action even before the Moot, had anyone understood. I suspected we'd already experienced a foretaste of what he might do, in the operations he accomplished in the Four Realms.

"There wasn't even a battle, was there?" I said.

The young harpist cast me a creditably analytical look. "No, Lord; why?"

I shook my head. "Go on."

"Taillte in Granniu."

Taillte had looked to the one-time nation of Esusdia, before Lady Tella's war against Esus. So total had been the warfare that the entire nation crumbled: the people of Esusdia scattered, and where once the righthe of Esusdia ruled, now only wilderness and bog-land remain. The few remaining border cities and towns, Taillte among them, now look to the surrounding nations; and over the centuries people shortened the region's name to *Usdia*. Few even among harpists remember Esusdia anymore. Even their language is lost.

Esunertos had been Esusdia's capital, and from there the Esusdians had controlled the river Riga, the primary watercourse from Teamair to the sea. Taillte had been Esusdia's most important outpost on the river Aerona. Was the Bard trying to control the routes to the Moot at Uisneach and the Fair at Teamair—or to resurrect Esusdia from the cold ashes of its pyre?

"And," I said, because the harpist's inflection suggested the list was not complete.

"Canoviu."

"On the Aerona, on the Granniu-Mumhan border."

The harpist nodded. "And Sulis, in Nagnata."

An outlier, that. I didn't see its strategic significance. But I knew I didn't yet see the Bard's strategy and objectives—assuming he had such things at all.

"And what places are under threat?" I asked.

"Well… Nemetona," the young harpist said tentatively.

"The one on the Aerona."

"Yes."

I nodded: if the Bard really were trying to control the Aerona, it was a sensible target. And it spurred a horrifying insight.

"And Ballarona," I said, trying to maintain an even tone.

The young harpist nodded, looking worried. "They say the Bard will be there any day."

"And you're sailing *to* Ballarona?" I narrowly avoided allowing my voice to crack.

"Do you have any idea how long I've been trying to get this gig?" he answered, then evidently remembered after the fact who he addressed.

I laughed. "I see. If you live past Bealtan, I predict you'll thrive. Where else?"

"Slieve Mish."

The Nagnata capital. Sulis was no outlier: after Mumhan fell, Nagnata would be next, and then Fhergail Conwy of Deceang would face the hopeless task of defending his nation when he had no useful borders: a particular challenge with the sea-port of Priaochan, less than a mile into his coastal waters, already studiously neutral. Kharr control of the Deceang capital at Dias Diorwig, coupled with possession of Priaochan, would make a blockade of the Ruillin practical. It would be only a matter of time for Ilnemedon after that.

I nodded. "What is your name?"

"Marten, Lord. Marten Whitebeam."

I nodded again and stood. "Thank you, Marten."

The young man's color rose a little; he smiled as I turned to leave. "Lord—"

I turned back, meeting his pale eyes.

"*Is* the Lady of Finias on this ship?"

I managed a laugh. "Marten, no matter how I answered that question, you would be a fool to believe me. Best of luck to you."

I strode out to the deck, looking for Amien. It is the nature of a Ruillin ferry that practically every person on board had heard the rumor of the Lady of Finias on this ship by now, and that tale would accompany us into the city: moving, in the miraculous way of gossip, even faster than a man on horseback might. We couldn't just meander through the streets to the inn at which we were expected: a wholly new plan was needed—now.

But I could find no one I knew. Even Loeg and the mummers seemed to have disappeared into the dazzling orange-and-green light of sunset. And Ballarona's once-familiar satellite towns were slipping past on the western shore. I walked the stairs to the lower deck and paced through the corridors, peering into the salons. In the floating tavern I found Mattiaci, Tuiri, Ogma and Fiacha dancing with a collection of brilliant-tressed night butterflies while a couple of harpists bashed out a tune on a cittern and a drum. I spotted most of the mummers at a table at the back of the room: still in costume and makeup, drinking ale. Loeg wasn't with them. Neither was Sainrith.

The lower deck of any Ruillin ferry boasts a number of small storage areas and other cubbyholes into which passengers eager for a bit of privacy can disappear and enjoy one another's company. After ten years of living on the Ruillin, I knew where to find them all; and I suspected I might find Easca if not other people I knew among those little mystery-places if I tried. I wasn't worried enough to ruin anyone's ferry ride, however. Not yet.

After a circuit of the lower deck I went back upstairs. The high places of Ballarona peered over the horizon to the west: we'd dock in a matter of minutes. Now, finally, I found Amien, Iminor, Nuad and Tru: leaning against the rail, apparently watching the city approach. But every few seconds one of them glanced around as if seeking the rest of the party. I crossed the deck to stand among them.

"We have a problem," I said without preamble.

"You *think*?" Iminor snapped. I had thought they were simply unable to see Letitia at the moment; now I suspected they were wholly unable to find her.

"Where's Letitia?" I asked.

Amien gave vent to an explosive sigh. "Good damn question. We've been all over this deck and the lower—"

"I have, too—"

Amien nodded, dark eyes on mine. "And obviously she's not up on the sailing deck or in the rigging."

"Has anybody started knocking on the hidey-holes on the lower deck?" I asked.

"The what?" Amien said.

A smile commandeered my mouth. "There are a number of places on the lower deck that are quiet, dark, and just the right size for a man and his friend."

Iminor rolled his eyes. "Of course you'd know."

I ignored him. "Fortunately, they'll ring the docking bell in a few minutes, and that's generally the signal for everybody to come out. The time to check those places is probably a few minutes after."

"Just as we're docking," Iminor growled.

"Unless you take pleasure in interrupting trysts," I said. The Tan glared at me; I just raised an eyebrow and looked at the others again. "Most of the knights are down in the tavern—"

The docking bell rang; my heart thudded.

"Well, then," I said, more calmly than I felt. "One of you take the top of the stairs; one of you the horse corral; the others the gangway entrance. I'll go downstairs and send the knights around and start checking the hidey-holes. Once the gangway's down, let's have people on either side of it, just to be sure. And once we've got enough bodies up here, somebody find the damn *captain*." I cast a swift glance among them, seeing agreement, and hurried down the stairs again.

In the tavern, the dance had ended, but the knights were still busy flirting with the night butterflies.

"Excuse me," I said in the Tanaan language, loudly enough to command their attention. All four glanced guiltily at me; I beckoned, and they gathered in a little knot around me as people began making their ways upstairs.

"No one can find the mora at the moment—calm faces, please," I said quietly. "Ogma and Fiacha, I want you checking this deck, the others upstairs to help with covering the upper deck and the dock. Check in with Nuad," I added, glancing at Mattiaci and Tuiri. "All of you, whoever finds Easca, relay the order. And keep an eye out for the captain. Nobody steps off this ship without one of us seeing who it is."

They all nodded.

"Go," I said, and strode out to start checking hidey-holes. About half of them were still occupied; I checked the open ones for clues that Letitia might have occupied them and possibly left something behind. But I knew that if Letitia had decided to grant the captain the fulfillment of his dreams, he had a much better space at the top of the ship. Before long I would have to check there, despite the absolute prohibition against passengers invading the sailing deck of a ferry. Unless I managed to soothe the sensibilities of the crew, that would mark the last time I was welcomed onto such a ship. Particularly since Loeg knew my name.

The ship drifted to a halt and bumped delicately against the dock. Gradually the lower deck emptied, except for the entertainers and vendors and whatever staffs they maintained. After a few minutes the last disheveled couples stumbled blinking out of their warrens. I sent Ogma and Fiacha on a final circuit and climbed up to the main deck.

The bright skies under which we sailed had dissolved into lowering grey clouds shot through with orange and green and a prickle of approaching lightning; almost all the remaining light blasted horizontally from the gap between the mountains, half blinding me after the softer light of the lower deck. The tide crashed so powerfully southward it seemed as if the river might empty, but the air hung profoundly still. Passengers were still filing down the gangway, but more crew than passengers now occupied the deck. The crew seemed engaged with the same things sailing crews are always about at the end of a day's journey: pulling down the sails, clearing away the detritus of dozens of passengers, wiping down the decks and rails. Sailors are supposed to be weather-attuned, but none of them seemed to feel the sudden urgency in the air. None of them even looked at the darkening sky. I couldn't see the dock at the base of the gangway from here, typical for low tide; but the ship seemed to be riding even lower than usual for the Ballarona dock—which is river-bottom-scraping low on a normal day, by the time the ferries empty. This twelvenight was the spring tide, I remembered; I had a vague sense that spring tides spelled higher high tides and lower lows, but I didn't know whether that could account for the way the water seemed to drain away from the land.

I spotted Nuad looking fierce but not overtly threatening at the top of the gangway; the only other member of the party within eyesight was Easca, on watch at the top of the stair. She still had a bit of mummer's makeup smudged across her neck, but her braid hung reasonably straight. The only sensible thing to do was to treat her like any male knight: she'd been off duty, and by the time her presence was necessary she turned up. No doubt she'd get plenty of correction from Nuad, anyway.

"Any word?" I said.

Relief flickered in her face, but it was relief at not being called to task—again, I surmised.

"Haven't found the mora yet, Lord."

I nodded.

"Ra Nuad's on the gangway, Lord Iminor's with Tuiri and Matti down on the dock."

I nodded again. "And Amien?"

She frowned a little. "Has the corral, I think."

"Understood. Send Ogma—" Black energies swept up my spine, igniting desire I couldn't allow myself to satisfy. Far to the south, lightning flared out on the water. A contingent of Básghilae came pelting down the ramp to the dock and tangled in the crowd climbing up from the ferry, who met them with screams and panic and tried to flee back across the gangway again. I meant to brace myself against the black energies that would splatter across my awareness as the Básghilae fed, but instead I discovered myself suddenly, fully open. Sparks of several lives shot straight into me, setting me alight.

"Amien!" I shouted. The name echoed from the bluffs above the Ballarona dock, reverberated against the wall of the enclosure in which entertainers play. The wizard was already running across the deck, casting bolt after bolt of brilliant green against the ghouls. Thunder rolled across the water, as if in answer. The deck began to fill with panicked people; Iminor, Tuiri and Mattiaci formed up to hold the gangway against the Básghilae; sailors came running from the lower deck, carrying weapons that ranged from short swords to long knives.

Out of nowhere the captain was there; Nuad barred him from the gangway; the sailors and the rest of the Tanaan converged on that altercation while the Básghilae forced the knights on the dock back onto the gangway, step by backwards step. Suddenly all I cared about was Letitia.

Letitia! I broadcast. *Letitia!*

...Ellion? Her mental voice was incredulous.

Annu, where are you? I sent, for her mind alone.

After a barely-perceptible hesitation, her targeted thought came to me, carrying mingled relief and terror. *In Rob—In the captain's cabin. He's locked me in!*

I nodded, irrelevantly. *Did—* I couldn't form the question I wanted to ask, couldn't even allow myself to think it lest she hear. *Are you hurt?*

Just stupid.

I glanced around. Amien stood atop the rail, casting at Básghilae on the shore. Iminor had managed to turn his horse almost entirely sideways on the too-narrow gangway, and battled the ghoul at the front of the pack while Mattiaci bolstered him from the rear. Nuad, Ogma, Fiacha, Easca and Tru had formed a standing half-crown at the gangway entrance with Tuiri and his horse blocking the gangway at their backs, pinning almost a dozen wailing passengers between the fights and felling sailors by the handful.

It's all right, I sent. *I'll have you out in a few minutes.*

What's happening?

I sent her the mental equivalent of a shrug. *Fighting. Give us a bit.*

Take your time, she sent, in a composed tone completely belied by the wave of anxiety beneath.

Hold fast, I answered, and turned my focus on the battle. There was nothing I could do about the Básghilae until the battle on the deck had been won, and I needed the captain's keys: I slipped around the side of the entertainers' enclosure, swung myself up to the rail, drew my knife and ran along the rail the way one might tiptoe across the top of a wall, until I could jump down to the deck behind the captain. I grabbed him by the hair and laid the knife across his throat, letting it bite just a little.

"Your head is already in my belt," I growled into his ear. His sword clattered to the deck.

From the rail on the other side of the gangway, Amien gave vent to one of the ear-splitting whistles that had been the terror of Aballo apprentices for centuries. Everyone on deck paused. And saw.

"I have the captain," I said, as if everyone wasn't already aware. "Lay down your arms."

Predictably, some fool lunged at Easca. She cut him down; I let the knife bite more deeply.

"Do it!" the captain yelped.

Finally, they did. I pulled him backwards, across the deck, to the stairs leading up to the sailing deck, and stumble-pulled him up the flight without releasing my grip on his hair or the knife from his throat. Everyone on deck watched. It all felt stranger than a dream of playing in a tavern naked. But after a moment we stood outside the door to the little room.

"Open it," I said quietly, and let him move just enough to pull a key from his pocket. He fit the key to the lock and turned it; I drew the knife across his throat, let him slip to the deck, and stepped across his body to open the door. I heard the roar as the fighting on the deck started up again, but all my focus was on Letitia.

She raced towards me. Without thinking I pulled her close, buried my face in her hair, drew back to kiss her brow.

"Art thou all right?" I said softly, lips still tracing her hairline.

In the half-second required for her to digest the unfamiliar words, I realized what I had done. Holy fouzhir hell.

I stepped back. Evidently she had been taught the forms of the Ilesian language's intimate address, but she'd never used them: puzzlement shifted to understanding and then to something I couldn't name.

"Yes," she breathed. Her eyes shone. I couldn't decide whether to kiss her or run and hide. "Thank you."

"You are the person who deserves thanks," I said. A tremor swept up my spine. All at once the sounds of the battle below us crashed into my awareness again.

"Wait a minute?" I said, pleased that I sounded almost reasonable. "We're not done."

I stepped out to the sailing deck again—and encountered the windcaller. I'd seen him, earlier, while he sat in the high seat calling the winds for our voyage; I was certain he hadn't noticed me until now. He looked up from the captain's body and the blood pooling on the deck; our eyes met.

Like every man of the arcane orders, I knew, he was sworn to serve Aballo and the true gods. And I knew he recognized me for what I was. But he was also a member of the crew my companions were dismantling—and I saw, with sudden horrifying insight, that he had understood what the captain was about today. And he supported it. I didn't want to imagine why, didn't want to believe a wizard, even one of a lesser order, could conscience such a thing.

The windcaller reached for his sword; I drove the knife into his trachea and sliced, then stepped back to allow him room to fall. Below me, on the main deck, the last few sailors laid down their weapons and backed away from the knights, hands spread before them; on the other side of the gangway, the remaining Básghilae were retreating beyond the top of the ramp. The passengers on the deck and those trapped on the gangway surged towards the exit; Amien gave vent to another horrific whistle, and people looked at him, but the running feet trampled on.

"Don't touch them!" he shouted, loudly enough to be heard at the far end of the deck. "If you touch a—an Avenger, you will die. Step carefully!"

He jumped down from the rail; the knights cleared out of the gangway and drew aside to let the panicked surge of passengers pass. I moved back to the cabin doorway.

"Letitia!" I hissed. "We've got to run!"

She nodded and scurried out to the deck, gave voice to a strangled noise and raced down the stairs behind me. By the time we reached the corral, Amien and the rest of the knights were already there.

"I'm all right!" she said impatiently, in response to a dozen questions, and turned her attention on Amien. "My things?" Strangely, she looked as if that question were of vital importance.

"With Iminor?" the wizard said, fingers flying over the tasks of preparing his horse.

She nodded; we all mounted as quickly as possible and raced across the deserted deck and gangway.

"Im!" Letitia shouted as we crossed. "My things?"

"Got 'em!" he shouted in response; we pelted up the ramp. Halfway to the street I realized we had never discussed a change of plans. There was only one place in this city I could think to hide.

"Follow me!" I called and raced to the front of the pack, and we galloped through darkening streets towards the Orchid, a tea-house of the sort notably lacking from the northern Ruillin. If Marla didn't still own the place, we were sunk.

The sky lowered, charcoal and purple; wind whipped up from the river, smelling of energies far blacker than lightning and rain. An illicit thrill tingled up my back; I urged the horse faster, and he willingly complied. But after a moment I realized we were pulling away from the group and slowed him again.

Somewhere not too distant, barely audible above the noise of the horses' hooves, I heard the roaring sound of a festival-day crowd. I glanced down the streets we passed; as we crossed Spring Street, I looked down to the Spring Square—and saw: it was a festival-day crowd, but they celebrated no festival I wanted to see. The unmistakable energies of a crowd's devotions to a god hung upon the air—but the Presence they invoked was one I had never before encountered. My throat tightened; I fought down the temptation to cast a tendril of awareness towards the delight hovering in that square.

"The Bard is here!" I called, raising my voice just enough to be heard over the hoofbeats.

Amien and several of the knights swore; finally we reached the Bormo Way, and I turned down that street. I could see from here that the gate at the end of the street was already locked.

But the Orchid looked the same as ever, right down to the orchid-and-teapot plaque beside the front door and the warm light behind the tall second-floor windows that looked out, over the city wall, to the confluence of the Ruillin and the Aerona. I led us around to the back, to the little covered carriageway between the rear entrance and the stable behind it. A couple young boys raced out to meet us, eyes widening at the presence of the Tanaan.

I slid out of the saddle. "Tell Marla it's Ellion Tellan," I said to the taller, redheaded boy; he nodded and raced inside.

"Ellion, of all the places in Ballarona..." Amien groused.

"What is this place?" Letitia said.

The back door of the tea-house flew open; Marla stood in the lamplight of the doorway, looking at me. She looked fine, maybe even better than five years ago; the years that stood between us were visible only in a few tiny lines around her eyes, and her black hair seemed untouched by grey. In typical perspicacious fashion she took in the whole situation at a glance.

"Let's get them in *quickly*," she said to the boys, and covered the distance between us. Her subtle, exotic perfume brought a number of distracting memories to mind.

"Ellion Tellan," she said, eyes shining.

"You're looking well," I answered warmly.

She reached for my hand, glanced around again, and made the politic decision to only kiss me on the cheek. I returned it; her face was as silken-soft and warm under my lips as I remembered. She smiled and glanced around again, gaze settling on the Tana.

"Oh, my dears, you and I can get *very* rich," she began.

"Marla," I said gently.

Nothing got past Marla, ever; she performed a fluid curtsy, gaze on Letitia, and I realized she had already suspected who I traveled with.

"Welcome, Lady," she said. "You honor us."

Letitia shook her head, still visibly puzzled. "All the thanks are yours, Lady. We're in—a difficult spot."

"So I see," Marla said, her habitual composure very nearly covering her amazement at the Lady of Finias addressing her so. "Will you come in?"

"Thank you," Letitia said, and let Marla lead her inside; the rest of us followed. We climbed the paneled stairs to the second floor and walked out to the main salon; and the familiar feeling came over me that time simply does not pass inside the Orchid. My old friend the standing four-octave harp, which I suspected Marla had purchased for me, stood in the far corner; the rugs underfoot and the drapes covering the walls between the windows were as fresh and richly-toned as ever, the seats at the pristine tables as welcoming. The place was empty of patrons, but I recognized several of the girls—and evidently they remembered me. We smiled at one another, but I pushed aside the impulse to exchange pleasantries as if there were nothing more urgent afoot than a visit to a friend with whom sensual play was only the first of the things shared.

"My dear friend, we've put you in a tight spot," I said to Marla.

She waved dismissively. "I knew when I invited you in—"

I shook my head. "I may have brought the battle to your door. The Lady has many enemies, and today I've managed to gain her a few more; you want us out of sight."

Marla paled, but just a little. "The cellar or the attic?"

"Cellar," I said, relieved she hadn't offered us one of the girls' play rooms. It would have been too strange and distracting to see Letitia in such a place.

But Amien said, "The attic," with a firm shake of his head.

I looked at him. "There are windows up there."

"Exactly. The higher I am above what's going on in that square, the more effective—"

"The easier we are to find, and—"

"Have you seen that storm coming in?" Amien snapped. Involuntarily I glanced out the windows at the mass of purple and black clouds racing north on the Ruillin and the waves crashing up, out of the river's steep banks, to splash across the River Road. "I've got to gather up a counterattack, and I'm not sure who hasn't already left for the Moot!"

"He's not here!" I retorted. "Only the Bard! They hold Esunertos!"

"What?" Amien breathed. "How—"

"I found out this afternoon. Right around the time I understood everyone on the Ruillin knows exactly where we are today. Let's not make her that easy to find."

"Esunertos," Amien said, mostly to himself. "We have got to get the hell out of here." He looked at me again. "I *need* the attic."

I glanced away: I knew he was right. I was choosing between Letitia's safety and Marla's; a better man would have hesitated over the answer, but for me it was no choice at all. Whatever the name for the flavor of affection I carried for Marla, whatever pain and guilt it might cost me to do so, I would sacrifice her for Letitia. I had done it already.

"All right," I said. Cold fingers closed around my heart. "Let's go."

Marla nodded and led us upstairs; I could barely look at her. We passed up another softly-lit, paneled staircase hung with a series of erotic engravings, to the third floor; followed her down the long corridor of private rooms, where rugs muffled the sound of our boots on the wood; and paused to watch Marla unlock a door at the end that opened to reveal another stair. The walls here were unfinished: the stones and mortar stood exposed. Faint, purple-tinged light trickled down from the windows on the level above. I hung back as Amien and the Tanaan mounted the stair, reached out to lay a hand on Marla's cheek and meet her solemn grey eyes.

"I'm sorry," I said. "Thank you."

She smiled, just a little. "Even were you not here, I would have opened the door for her."

I swallowed, suddenly out of words, and kissed her softly. It was wrong, but my lips thought otherwise.

"It is good to see you, too, though," she said. She picked up my hand, laid the key she'd used to unlock the attic on the palm, and folded it shut. Then with a final, wistful smile, she stepped into the corridor again.

"Is it too—? Could you—?"

"What do you need?" she said gently.

"A messenger, to the Knight Inn." It was not a safe mission, not with the Bard of Arcadia in the city today. But we needed a force augmentation, and Rohini was supposed to be there waiting.

She nodded. "I'll send one of the boys up," she said, and shut the door.

Chapter 23
A Name Written on the Wind

The attic had only two windows: one looking east, over the Ruillin, and one looking south over the Aerona. Both showed roiling black clouds lit by streaks and sheets of lightning. Every few seconds, the blue-white glare illuminated crashing waters and windswept banks, cast the people in the attic in stark eerie light, and exposed the trunks, old furniture, and things less readily identified that Marla's staff had stored up here. Between flashes, the attic was nearly dark. Amien and the Tanaan had stacked their gear in a corner, but no one removed arms or mail; even Letitia had buckled on her sword again. Several of the knights moved cautiously through the narrow spaces of unoccupied floor as if looking for something. After a few seconds, Mattiaci crowed, "Aha!" and held up an object that the next flash of lightning revealed as a glass lamp with as much as an hour's worth of oil left in the reservoir.

Amien called fire with a little gesture; the lamp flared into light, casting a pool of illumination around Mattiaci that moved towards the broader space at the top of the stairs as he did. He set it on a table near the window; Amien picked it up and moved it to the surface of a low trunk near the stairs. Beside the trunk stood an upholstered bench.

"Ah," Letitia sighed, and sank onto it, wincing as she settled. Horror, grief and rage chased one another around inside me: I saw now that she had endured more than the realization she'd made a mistake in the captain's cabin. I wished I could kill him again, more slowly.

But her face reflected anger and disgust rather than the despair I would have expected of a human woman or man who had been raped. I couldn't decide whether my sense that the assault hadn't progressed that far was hope or wishful thinking, but her glance invited no discussion: I swallowed all the things I wanted to say and watched the knights settle in a loose circle on the floor. Finally I added my gear to the heap in the corner and sat. Amien still stood behind me, staring morosely out the window.

"They hold Esunertos," the wizard said.

"Yes," I said. "And by morning, Ballarona."

"And therefore all of Mumhan," Amien said thoughtfully.

I shrugged. "Were I Cuilean of Mumhan, I'd gather my tiarna at Presatyn after Bealtan and throw my vote at the Moot behind whichever man saw value in securing the upper Ruillin."

"That's not Deneth Cooley," the wizard observed.

"No, it's Fhergail Conwy, though he'd be a fool to throw his forces in that direction. We can only hope the rest of the righthe will see it. That's what the Moot is for, ultimately."

He turned and looked at me for a long moment, thoughtful. "If they elected you, what would you do?"

Something turned over in my chest; I found myself on my feet, pacing away. Outside, lightning struck so near that the house shook; the little flame in the lamp went out, and everything was dark.

"I don't have current intelligence," I said.

"Answer the damn question," Amien said evenly.

He was right: I knew what I would do. But I also knew it was beyond the combined resources of whatever armies might muster after the Moot.

"Take back Esunertos," I said. It was a battle only the wizards could win, and even for them the cost would be high. A fey desire to lead that fight ignited inside me; I pushed it aside.

"Yes," Amien said, as if the answer were both surprising and inevitable, and lit the lamp again.

I turned to look at him. "And then go after Macol, where it started. And by that time, I would have true intelligence on our enemy, and his ultimate sanctum would be my final target."

Amien smiled, just a little. "So Cuilean shouldn't vote for you, either," he said lightly.

I recognized the joke, but my throat clenched anyway. I produced what I knew to be an unconvincing smile. "Fear not."

For a moment the room was silent. Lightning flared again, not quite so near this time.

"Well, what else did we learn this afternoon?" Amien said.

"We learned that Ellion is a mindtalker," Iminor said, falsely cheerful. Heads all around the room whipped around for better views of his sardonic smile, then shifted to stare at me.

"Now all we have left to learn is how many *private* conversations he has listened to."

I glanced at Letitia; her beautiful face held a remote, brittle look, and her eyes were on something outside the window. I met Iminor's eyes.

"Where I come from, ouirr, if a conversation is private, we do not *broad-cast*," I said coolly. "If I have heard any of your conversations, it was because they were more or less shouted in my presence."

He scowled.

"Not that I found any of them—" I began.

"Gentlemen," Amien said tiredly. "If you are going to kiss, get it over with."

Someone, probably Mattiaci, failed to contain a snicker. Iminor flushed absolutely crimson, but I remembered too many times when someone had said the same thing at Aballo, where the suggestion is neither an insult nor necessarily a misdirected arrow; where members of Amien's workshop had said the same thing to Deaclan and me. I found it impossible to look at anyone; in my peripheral vision, I saw Amien glance out the window again.

"What intelligence do we have?" he said to the window.

I cleared my throat. "The tale spinning round the Ruillin today went like this: the Lady of Finias came to Dromineer on a magical fog and boarded the Ballarona ferry." I sighed. "By now, of course, the tale is further embellished with her and her wizard killing nearly everyone on board. We've ridden our last ferry."

"Fouzh," Amien said, sounding completely unsurprised. "I fouzhir hate the Ruillin."

I nodded. "Further, in addition to Esunertos—Taillte and Canoviu in Granniu, and Sulis in Nagnata, are now in kharr hands; and Nemetona and Slieve Mish are said to be under threat."

Amien grunted. "If I were Cuilean, I'd be wondering whether Presatyn were the place to hold my muster, after all."

"There is that," I said.

Someone knocked on the door at the base of the stairs; I rose and ran down to answer, drawing my sword at the bottom of the flight. The person on the other side of the door was the tall redheaded youngster who had announced me to Marla, and now his expression was pure terror.

"Sorry," I said, and sheathed the weapon. "Come in."

He swallowed, eyes huge in his white face, and carried a lamp inside. I shut the door behind him and gestured for him to precede me up the stairs.

In the attic, he stopped and looked around, glanced back at me, and belatedly made room for me to step up to the floor.

"Lords, Mistress Marla said you need a messenger?" he said, sounding surprisingly composed.

"Yes," Amien said, with the smile he used with new apprentices. "Thank you. We need you to take a message to the Knight."

"On High Street," the boy said, nodding.

"Yes," Amien replied. "The message is for a woman named Aedrini."

"Like the month," the boy said. I wondered what story lay behind Rohini's choice of that particular cover-name and whether she knew the tales of the old goddess for whom that month is named.

Amien nodded. "She'll be dressed like—like a knight, like the ladies you see here. She's very tall, hair as red as yours, done in a long braid down her back. Eyes that'll freeze your balls right off."

The boy swallowed.

"Not really," I said, shooting a look at the wizard. It is men, not boys, who come to Aballo, young though they may be, and all of them aware of their own power. Clearly he'd forgotten the difference. "You'll be all right. But she's a little—" I glanced at Amien, guessing. "Intense?"

The wizard nodded. "When you find her, tell her you have a message from Rinnal Ruthin. If she knows who that is, you've got the right person; ask her to come and meet us here."

The boy nodded thoughtfully. "The Knight. Aedrini. Rinnal Ruthin."

"Yes."

The boy handed me the lamp, sketched a bow, and fled back down the stairs. I set the lamp on the trunk beside Letitia and walked back down to lock the door behind him.

"So how do we get out of Ballarona?" the wizard said when I reached the upper floor again.

"Charter a ship, assuming we can," I said.

He nodded. "Were I a loyalist ship captain, I'd take any fare going south in the morning."

"Were I a loyalist ship captain, I would have gotten the hell out of here today," I rejoined.

Amien grunted. "And with this storm, no one is going anywhere."

"Not on the river," I agreed.

He looked at me as if I'd said something insightful. "Maybe we should ride out. It's—what?—fifty or fifty-five miles of crow-flight to Dias Diorwig—call it a long day, maybe a little more in weather. And then another two or three days to Aballo, depending on tides... That puts us on Aballo on—" He frowned. "The nineteenth."

"Two days before Bealtan Eve," I said.

"It's doable."

"Except," I said.

He cast me a look of despair; I raised my eyebrows.

"The thing is, you don't just ride across the Aerona here. The place where it should have been possible to ford, right before the drop to meet the Ruillin: they call Bormo's Well. The tides there are insane. There's a window of maybe twenty minutes every day when it's possible to even sail through there, and only the captains who work the Aerona every twelvenight will chance it."

Amien cast a glance heavenward, as if for support he already knew wasn't coming. "So where do you cross?"

"Presatyn."

"*Presatyn?* That's—what?"

"Another day on the road, all told," I said.

Amien sagged. "*If* everything goes right, which it hasn't yet, and if I fly from Aballo to the Moot." He shook his head. "I've got to handle this storm. And we've got to charter a ship, here."

I rose, nodding. "I know a few—"

"Yes, and how many know you?" Iminor interrupted.

We both glanced at him.

"What?" I said.

"You obviously know this place pretty well," he said. "You did more than pass through. How many people here know you? How many people will connect you with what happened this afternoon?"

I sighed. "Ouirr, at this point I would say Ballarona is divided into two camps, only one of which we'll get any traction with at all."

The Tan looked at Amien. "We should get your friend to charter the ship."

"I can promise you the kharr don't like her any better than they like me," I said. "If even half the stories of the Essuvians here in Mumhan are true—"

"Fouzh," Amien growled. He met my gaze, warning. Again I wondered about the nature of his relationship with Rohini: the Essuvians' situation in Mumhan was public knowledge, but he seemed to think I was about to compromise her reputation.

"I'm not saying it's her fault," I said evenly. "But the situation remains."

"What?" Iminor growled.

I glanced at him and sighed. "It's been more than a year since the Essuvians lost Uxellia to the kharr. They could only survive so long on their reserves out in the desert. The Chiefs—the Essuvian tiarna—still remembered one thing from their people's ranging days, and that was how to take their knights on the road and live off the land. On the other side of the mountains, it was cattle they lived on. For the past year it's been the spoils of the lands they rode through. Why none of the righthe offered Rohini and her Chiefs proper sanctuary— why Conary Mourne never offered them refuge at Teamair—"

I shook my head. "It's done. But it's a mess. Rohini and whatever knights she can muster will be the best blades possible against the Básghilae; they've been fighting that action longer than we have. But we'll get no welcome in any place we enter in their company, unless it's the house of a righ."

I glanced at Amien again, seeing frustration that no truth could ease, and returned my attention to the Tan. "All either of us can hope for is to find a loyalist captain, because the loyalists see how little choice the Essuvians had, while others just see what they did to survive. I absolutely agree that we should ask her to tap any captain she's got access to. But it would be a mistake to sit here and wait for her to succeed. I'm going out, too. Hopefully all the loyalists left in Ballarona tonight are not in this house."

"Agreed," Amien said, reluctant. "Also any intelligence you can gather about which of the Ruillin righthe may not yet have left for the Moot—"

"—so we can involve their House Healers against the storm—"

Amien nodded. "And meanwhile I will see what I can do about counteracting the damn thing from here. When you get back, maybe we'll go outside and see if we can find a way up onto the city wall…"

"Because that sounds safe," Iminor said.

The wizard glanced at him. "Any time you'd like to take over my job…"

"I'm trying to suggest that maybe it's important you remain alive," the Tan retorted. "Seems to me that's more important than reaching your Moot on time."

Amien frowned at him, but thoughtfully.

"Yes," he said finally. "Thank you."

I dug into my pack, pulled out my jacket, and slipped it over my mail shirt. Belatedly I realized Letitia hadn't weighed in. I looked at her: lamplight slid like liquid gold through her shadowed hair, making her braid into something as mysterious and complex as any spell-weaving. Her angular face and abyssal eyes were unreadable in this light; her gaze ranged beyond places any human might understand. Her body was here, I realized, but her awareness was distant; horrifying imaginings crowded around me again.

"Letitia?" I said gently.

She looked at me, still half-tangled in whatever memory or dark imagining had snared her.

"Art—" Not the intimate form *again!* "Are you—? Should we assume you agree with the plan?" A damning blush heated my face; I had to get out of here, now.

She frowned, thoughtful.

"To try to charter a ship and sail on?" Amien said.

She blinked at me. "Of course, my lords."

I nodded. "I'll be back as soon as I can," I said, and fled down the stairs.

Thee? When had I progressed to *thee* with Letitia? When had I allowed personal affections to dictate tactical decisions—sacrificed noncombatants to strategic objectives—become afflicted with *celibacy?* How was it possible I had fixed all my devotion to a woman I was simply never going to have?

I strode through the third-floor corridor; a lamp still burned there, but the second-floor salon was dark. Evidently Marla had given up hope that any patrons might turn up tonight. I found my way through the room by memory and the illumination of lightning, then scurried like a hare pursued down the back stair: I was clearly coming apart like a poorly-made shirt, and I needed to get out of here before I was called on to hold a sensible conversation.

I made it through the door and walked out to the street; wind tore the breath from my throat and then shifted to drive rain into my face. The power of the storm raised ripples of gooseflesh over my entire body, but my mind still spun. I couldn't make it latch onto anything useful: it shuttled senselessly between Letitia racing into my embrace this afternoon and the pain in her face as she settled on the bench. *Thee.*

My judgment was utterly compromised; my effectiveness as a commander was sadly blunted; I had given my word not to leave again. Worst of all, I didn't *want* to. Something perilously close to the surface of my mind wanted to wrest her from Iminor, to earn the right to celebrate Bealtan with her, to insert myself into her life. As if I could actually go back to Fíana after this whole thing was over and become the mor to her mora. As if, through her choice of me, my life might slip miraculously back into what my stars had promised: only better, more wondrously than I had ever imagined. All rights and pleasures within my grasp, and her chiefest of them all.

Thee. Gods, I was a fool.

Every so often, as I walked through the rain-drenched city, I heard skirmishing in the distance; but the moons hid behind the storm, and for the first time in my experience no one had lit the lamps on the streets. Powers Whose names I suspected but knew better than to confirm rang on the air, knocking against the edges of my awareness; the sounds of running and shouting and the periodic report of a cannon called up memories I'd thought long expunged. I thought about the people I'd known while I lived here: wondering whether they still lived in this city, whether they'd gotten out before the fighting started, whether they were all the loyalists I'd assumed they were. I didn't spare the time to seek any of them out; none of those relationships had been close. Marla had been the only person here with whom I could be even half of my true self. And I didn't walk down towards the end of the Balloo Road, where the Mumhan palace stands: Brion Cuilean's problems were on the long list of things I couldn't solve tonight, and I suspected he was already at Teamair. I wouldn't want to be the one to bring him word of what had happened in his absence.

All the loyalist taverns were as empty as the Orchid; a couple were actually locked. Yet another thing I'd never seen in Ballarona before tonight. I drew my sodden jacket about me, pointed the top of my head into the wind, and headed towards the docks: there was nothing for it but to go down there and try to read between the lines of the ships' names for clues to which might be loyalist-owned. I wondered whether Marla's boy had found Rohini, whether she might already have managed to engage a ship.

On the bluff above the Ruillin, at the top of the ramp leading down to the docks, I paused, looking out. The air was different here. Inside the city, it felt like a winter rainstorm: a phenomenon uncomfortable and possibly dangerous but with its energetic potential firmly based in the physical. Here the wind was still fierce, but only a few incidental drops of rain fell; the electricity on the air raised thrills that only began with the promise of lightning. A dozen ships pitched and rolled in the furious waves, the strings of lights on their rails dancing in the darkness, but I couldn't focus on them: within, throughout, all around the roiling black-purple-red of the clouds that stretched to the mountaintops and beyond, a fluid arcane mirror-box reflecting the seductive power of the Ruillin and redoubling it in endlessly-repeating black delight opened to my glance, revealing a fluid lattice of power that shifted and shifted again, inviting me into a dimension of delight that made the fog Amien had crafted this morning into a child's copy of a master's painting. A thousand shades that only appeared black until glimpsed through arcane vision swirled around me, tentacles of energy questing after an awareness that might understand them. Their motions slipped through extramundane colors into notes no harp or cittern or augmented pipe-set ever rendered, skipping in shuddering pleasure that tripped up my spine and lit a desire that should send me racing for cover. Instead I followed the shifting colors, the inexplicable pleasure of raw power that only seems to manifest in the body, the paths of the weaving that answered the Ruillin with something deeper and darker, dark air to its dark water, until the whole working unfolded in my incautious mind—and I saw its maker. His grey eyes met mine, a thousand miles away, close enough to feel his breath on my lips; and I read his name in a zephyr with too many dimensions to fit into the mundane world.

Nechton.

This was how it would feel if a hole opened in the sky and I fell through.

Astonishment and desperate urgency blasted me back into my own body, and I pulled a shield around my mind as quickly as I was able—then turned and sprinted back to the Orchid. The spell's terrible beauty echoed through me as I ran; my breath tangled in my throat at the memory of the colors and sounds I had tasted. I shook with the need for more, stumbled, and flailed my way back through the rain and into the Orchid's rear entrance. I clattered up the stairs, panted through the unlit public salon, blinked at the blistering light in the third-floor corridor, scrambled to unlock the attic door. At the top of the stairs, a woman stood among my companions: this must be Rohini. She was as tall as Amien had said; the shape of her profile and the long stretch of her legs and torso revealed Tanaan ancestry, and the sword at her side would have been too much for many men. Her stance and voice made it clear she was arguing.

"No, we've got to—" she said firmly in the Tanaan language, then paused and glanced down the stairs at me, hand moving to the hilt of her sword. "Is that him?"

Immediately Letitia hove into view above me, leaning out beyond the rail at the top of the landing. "*OhSweetLordthankyou,*" she breathed.

I pelted up the stairs; Rohini said, "Then let's go."

Letitia looked at me. "They want to sail *now*? Up the Aerona?"

I nodded. "We need to take whatever exit we can make." I glanced at Amien. "My lord, I have our enemy's name."

"The Bard?" Rohini said contemptuously. "That—"

"The wizard." I looked at Amien again.

He shook his head, relaxing; a smile began on his face. He glanced at Rohini, but she had turned her intense black eyes on me.

"How?" she said.

And thus ended the last of my defenses. I glanced at Letitia. "I read the spell. The storm."

Utter astonishment registered in Letitia's face.

"What?" Iminor blurted. "*Now* you're a—?"

I sighed. "I trained at Aballo. Yes. I don't practice." I looked at Amien again. "My lord, it's Nechton."

A strangled noise escaped Letitia. "Nechton? The mora Carina's… Nechton?"

I nodded. The wizard stretched out a hand, steadied himself against the back of a chair. Even in this light it was clear he'd gone ashen.

"Well, then," he said, gravelly voice even rougher than usual. "Let's get the hell out of here."

Chapter 24
The Shadow of the Sun

Rohini was not completely without allies in this place: she'd managed to bribe someone to unlock the Bormo Gate. The sound of it banging shut behind us echoed hollowly on the wild air.

Outside the gate, her personal contingent waited: a dozen rough-edged men in shaggy black cloaks and brass-finished helms whose spear-tips glinted under the lightning and whose torches had long since gone out. They divided themselves without consulting us, half to the front of the party and half to the back, and if Rohini found anything to question in it she said nothing.

We raced down to the Aerona Road and galloped beside the rising tide. The power of the storm wrapped itself around me again, begging me to open my mind and let it in. The world kept dissolving into lightning and extramundane colors; again and again I hauled myself closed, or tried to. It was hard to remember where I ended and the edges of the arcane storm began. When the party reined, I was late in noticing; my horse had to veer off the path to avoid a collision. I shook my head hard, but it didn't clear.

"Are you all right?" Amien said.

I glanced at him: he seemed as insubstantial as a lacewing against the intense presence of the storm.

"Oh, gods, this storm—" I began, and then clamped my jaws around the rest.

"Fine," I grated. "Thank you."

The boat Rohini had engaged rocked and shimmied beside several others at the Aerona dock. I was surprised to see other fools out here preparing to sail; but I supposed we were far from the only people desperate to get out of Ballarona tonight. I had to pull off my jacket and throw it over my horse's head before he would cross the pitching gangway.

We secured our horses, sent our gear down through a narrow hatch to the lower deck, distributed ourselves in the areas the captain, who had to shout to be heard over the wind and waves, designated—and held on as the crew cast off and the tide took the boat.

The boat raced and jumped; waves splashed over the rails and crashed across the deck; lightning revealed far too much about the state of the waters we sailed and the proximity of the other boats out here with us, and then its absence made my eyes ache with trying to see what we would strike first. The energies of the storm snared my mind again, bound me with my own refusal to admit them, catapulted me into a place in which nothing existed besides denial and desire until I remembered I had a purpose and a name and reclaimed my own body, inch by quaking inch. For an interminable time which I had been told would last no more than twenty minutes, the uncontrol in which we rode echoed redoubling against the arcane tempest that had ensnared me; and then, suddenly, the waters unrolled into calm, steady currents pushing us upriver. A few minutes later the storm was far enough behind that the moons emerged and lit up the world, and rational thought became possible again.

Soon I was able to find my boundaries, to look at the people around me and see them as whole and concrete rather than the constantly fracturing and reforming energy-shadows that most people become when the mind is open too far. Amien and Nuad sat near me; I realized the wizard had seen how the storm laid me open, had recruited Nuad to quietly guard me until I settled into the mundane world again. I leaned my shoulder against Amien's, oddly peaceful: it was almost like coming out of a trance and discovering a group of colleagues and the glow of a ward-circle around me. He offered a smile that nearly concealed his agitation and looked forward again, letting me find my feet.

The boat on which we sailed seemed to be out on this bizarrely picturesque, moonlit waterway alone. I wondered what had happened to the other vessels. Gradually I remembered we were sailing up the Aerona, which meant we were bound for Presatyn; but we had not thought beyond that, and all our assumptions must be taken out and re-examined.

"Is the lower deck ours?" I said to Amien. "We've got to recast our strategy."

"Damned certain we do," Amien said. "Are you all right?"

I nodded.

"Nuad, could you tell them we're ready?" the wizard said. The Tan nodded and walked around to the other side of the little charthouse; the wizard turned his penetrating gaze on me again.

"You're certain of what you saw," he said. It was a question, even though he had made it into a statement.

I called the memory to mind: the terrible delight of dark air reflecting and redoubling through a mirror-box of power so complex it couldn't manifest entirely in the physical world; the troubling sensation of intimate proximity with its author; the arcane signature, always impossible to eradicate on something that passes beyond the physical realm, but so cleverly and elegantly concealed that only a wizard with the fortitude or poor judgment to encompass the working's full black glory would ever find it. It whispered through my mind again: not just the name, but the flavor of its colors and the wild caress of its unearthly sounds.

"Ellion?"

I remembered the question. "Yes."

The wizard cast me a long, quizzical look.

"How long has it been?" he said finally.

"What?"

"Since you stopped."

I couldn't believe he'd asked the question. "You know. Since—" I swallowed, glancing away. "My parents."

The wizard shook his head. "No, since you've drawn power at all."

I frowned at him. "I made a vow, my lord. I won't—" I knew too well how very easy it was to forswear myself, and it usually started with the assertion that it would never happen. "I've upheld it."

Now he was staring at me, as if I'd said something truly unbelievable. Who knew better what a poor job I did of keeping sacred vows, after all: I glanced away.

"Great Lord Ilesan," he said finally. He shook his head. "Let's go."

Illuminated only by a couple small lamps, the lower deck of the boat was empty except for the Tanaan, our gear, a few oddments of sailing supplies, and Rohini—whose intense black gaze made me want to turn around and climb right back up to the deck. That desire deepened when I realized everyone else had also chosen this moment to stare at me.

"Are you—all right?" Letitia said finally.

I shook my head, embarrassed, then realized it would be misinterpreted. I waved the question away, trying to find something on which to focus.

"Fine," I said. "I'm fine, thank you."

"Every time someone has said that today, it's been a lie," Iminor observed quietly.

I shrugged. "I really am all right."

"As you say," the Tan answered. "So how long have you been a wizard?"

"What?" I blurted, reeling all over again. "I'm not—" But I was still too entangled in the arcane to manage the lie. I sighed. "I don't practice."

"That's not what I asked you," Iminor rejoined.

I glanced at Amien, looked away. "I studied at Aballo... a little more than ten years ago."

Iminor cast me a speculative look. "For how long?"

Where was this going? "About two years."

"Twenty months," Amien said quietly. I nodded.

"That's the standard term?" Iminor pursued.

One side of Amien's mouth twitched.

"No," I admitted.

"And did you—" Iminor gestured vaguely, groping after words he lacked. "Do wizards have certification? Like bards?"

"Something similar. Not the same," Amien said. "And yes. He is fully... qualified."

Iminor looked from me to Amien and back. "Who was your teacher?" His eyes said he had already deduced the answer.

"Who do you think?" I rejoined. It felt like tangling with a brehon, and I could smell the logical trap building. "Could we come to it, already?"

Iminor gave me a long, assessing look, something darker than simple distrust in his eyes. "So why aren't you a wizard anymore?"

"Now you're asking him to violate vows," Amien said crisply. "Certain things can't be discussed outside the initiate. Let's move on, please. Shall we sit?" All at once the weight of the things I'd learned tonight seemed to fall on his shoulders. "I really think I'd like to sit."

"Yes," Letitia said fervently.

We settled in a loose circle on the floor. The hull emitted the creaking noises I had long ago learned are normal but nevertheless didn't find comforting. On the upper deck, the captain called out some order muffled by wind and the narrow opening above us, which probably would have meant little to me if I stood beside him. It made me acutely conscious how little I understood of anything just now.

"Nechton," Amien said after a moment, gaze on his steepled hands. "I... can't quite believe he's alive. I—" He swallowed. "Carina defeated him, but she didn't kill him."

Pain manifested in Letitia's face, and for a second I thought she would speak; instead she curled her long white fingers around the chain of Carina's talisman, pursing her lips.

"Why?" the wizard continued. "I would have..." He sighed. Some dark thought crossed his face; he drew in breath, hesitated, finally spoke: "The Shadow of the Sun."

Sudden, awful understanding dawned over me. "I thought—You said it was destroyed, at the end of Nechton's War!"

Amien's mouth twisted. "I thought it was. We all thought he was dead. By the time anyone in the Order got to his workshop, everything inside had been burned—right down to the stone. We assumed the orb had been destroyed."

"But he's still got it," I said.

Amien nodded regretfully.

"He's still using it," I continued. "That's how—everything we saw in the Four Realms, every one of those workings, that's how..." I should have guessed. I had known before we reached Dianann that the only possible explanations for the assaults we endured in Fíana were a clairvoyant or a farsensing orb. I should have trusted what I saw rather than what I'd been told.

"What?" Iminor said.

The wizard glanced at him. "The Shadow of the Sun. It's a farsensing orb—an arcane tool that a wizard—or a seer—can use to gain access to things happening at a distance. People have been trying to create them for centuries;

Nechton is the only man who's succeeded since Hy-Breasaíl. I'm sure the Shadow of the Sun would be a very useful thing to a seer, but in the hands of a wizard, especially one who has abandoned the Aballo code... it's a nightmare. Nechton can use the thing to work remote magics that would otherwise be impossible—" Suddenly he was looking at me. "And particularly with access to the power well at Esunertos—"

Rohini drew in a hissing breath. "Wait—Esunertos—? It's of *magical* strategic value?"

"It may be as important as Uisneach," I said. "More so, from a practical standpoint."

"Fouzhir hell," she said.

Amien nodded. "Iminor, to try to answer your question before we get too far ahead of ourselves—the Shadow of the Sun is the most important weapon Nechton's got. No matter what else is in his arsenal. He created it before—before the earlier war, the one we've called Nechton's War for all these years—and it makes it possible for him to work magic at distance as reliably as if he were there himself. It's what he uses to control the Básghilae; it's how he was able to... out-outflank us... every time we tried to evade his attacks. I'm sure we don't even know half the tricks it allows him to pull."

And Amien hadn't enumerated half of what he knew. Nechton's operations in the Four Realms marched through my awareness, rearranging themselves in my understanding. Nechton had pinpointed Letitia's landing site on the night of the first attack because he could see her through the orb; the eerie, simultaneous withdrawal of the Básghilae that night and each time the balance of arms in an encounter shifted into our favor had been responses to his direct commands. The binding he'd laid in the Ériu House yard, the precision with which Básghilae had chosen victims whose shapes they could assume in order to get within range of Letitia: those things had also been accomplished directly, through the orb. He had seen us at will—still saw us at will, perhaps even now. He used the orb for farsight; he used the energies from the seemingly bottomless well of dark power at Esunertos to drive the things he handled directly; he used the Básghilae not only for military purposes but also to establish arcane connections for the workings that required a physical talisman on site. The depth and elegance of his strategy and techniques both chilled and fascinated me.

"So why—What does the name mean?" Iminor said. "When you say it in the Beallan language, it sounds like you're saying *the shadow of the—sun*?"

Amien nodded.

"What does that mean?"

Amien raised his eyebrows, glanced at his hands again. There was no way he'd give a useful answer to the question: the name comes from Aechering's infamous Shadow Working, arguably the ultimate work of black magic, which is widely assumed to be the operation Nechton performed in order to transform an inert sphere of crystal into the most potent arcane tool yet created. Aechering and his ideas are beyond the purview of polite conversation among wizards, let alone discussion with men outside the initiate. To touch on the topic of Aechering is to come perilously close to the subtle rot at the heart of the Aballo Order. Whatever Amien would admit even in this limited public,

Aechering's name would not come up.

"It's… a sort of a code name," Amien said slowly. "It's what we call it in the Order. No one is sure what name Nechton uses."

"More's the pity," I added.

Amien glanced at me as if I'd said something insightful. "Because, of course, if we had the thing's true name…" He sagged. "Not that we could do it at distance. Not that we even know where—"

The look on his face said he'd figured it out, at the same time I did.

"*Macol*," we said simultaneously. It had been the staging ground of Nechton's attempt to conquer the world four hundred years ago, the location of the workshop in which he had done his greatest, darkest, most successful work. There was no need to look further for his ultimate sanctum: we would find it there.

"No wonder!" I said. "No wonder the Bard began there; that was the ground his wizard needed! I hadn't seen the point of—"

I shot Rohini a rueful glance; she met my gaze with a sidelong look that bespoke wrath withheld.

"Without insult, Chief, it is a strange place for a base from which to conquer the world."

She didn't answer, but neither did her hand move in the direction of her sword; finally she shook her head. I shrugged.

Amien shook his head, too: slowly, bemusement in his face. "You were right, twice over," he said to me. He glanced at Rohini. "Wish you'd been there. He called it, earlier tonight: take back Esunertos, and then re-take Macol." Half a smile staged an assault on his mouth; Rohini just shook her head.

Abruptly he sobered. "Re-taking Macol isn't a military operation."

"Gods, which part of this *is* military?" I said.

The wizard nodded. "It will all come down to defeating Nechton."

Once again his most important thoughts went unsaid, but I knew what they were, at least some of them: Carina Ériu a Fíana had been the one person to stand toe-to-toe with Nechton and survive. Nechton had defeated the great Tol, then Prince of the Order, in senseless single combat little more than a month before Carina arrived at Macol. Tol's right hand Helmedach, who evidently had all of Tol's bravado but not nearly as much Talent, had found it necessary to fall on that same sword. By the time Carina met Nechton, Amien had succeeded Helmedach to the Prince's seat. He at least understood the limits of his power. No living member of the Order was likely to do what Tol failed.

But evidently Carina had.

"Letitia?" Amien glanced at her. "Carina… wouldn't talk about what transpired during her encounter with Nechton, not to me. Did she…?"

Letitia shook her head. "The first I heard of Nechton was from Ellion."

On the night we met, by the Crearu. In the last moments before everything unraveled. The irony was so thick I grew suddenly restless.

"The *Ballad of Carina*," I said.

"You said—" Letitia hesitated. "You said it was true."

"I thought it was."

"But we know *nothing*," Rohini said.

Amien pursed his lips, gaze on something inside his own head. "No. We know she defeated him, though we still don't know exactly how. We know she let him live, though we have no idea why. Also—"

His voice vanished. He cleared his throat, but now he sounded as if his throat were full of rocks. "We know she's dead."

Letitia put a hand over her mouth.

"It's not outside the realm of possibility that he would have joined forces with the Bard if she were still alive," the wizard said to Letitia, gaze apologetic and voice still choppy.

She met his gaze in silence, eyes bright with unshed tears.

"But if she were, annu, he wouldn't be seeking *you*."

Renewed horror broke across Letitia's face; she drew back, as if a few extra inches between Amien and herself might make his words go elsewhere.

"He fears you can do whatever she did," the wizard said, as much to himself as to her. "Because you have the same Talent."

Letitia frowned. "This little—?" She shook her head. "Amien, I don't have a Talent. Not like you do." She glanced at me, glanced away again. "All I have is this little... gift. It is of no practical use."

Amien shook his head. "Carina proved otherwise. You just haven't learned to use it."

"Use it?" Letitia echoed, incredulous. Her voice still skated the edge of a sob. "I don't know how it was for my mother, Amien, but with me—"

She shook her head. "Here it is, the start and finish of it. If I meditate on the light of the sun, the Holy Mora sends a little bit of it into me. It's—it's difficult to describe, except that it's wonderful and warm, and I feel Her closeness, and if I am tired Her Power will relieve it for a while. But it's not a weapon. I can't fling bolts of sunlight at Básghilae and have them drop dead; I can't make a wall of sunshine to hide from my enemies; I can't even wrap it around myself the way you do my personal wards. That's all there is to it. It's just a little... gift."

The wizard shook his head. "I wish I could have seen what she did, or learned from her afterward. All I know is that she had some understanding of this—gift—and the way the energy of light might be used against dark magic. That was the key, as I understood it: dispelling Dark with Light. I always imagined it as lighting a lamp to drive away darkness, but—" He shrugged. "What I can tell you is that her talisman, Iliria, which you still wear, was specifically crafted to allow her to store that power, so she might call on it when needed."

Letitia frowned, grasping the diamond in her narrow fist. "Because the sun isn't always shining," she said thoughtfully. She sighed. "And it worked?"

Amien raised his eyebrows, smiling a little. "She seemed quite satisfied with it." His smile faded; his eyes fixed on memory. "When she—After it was over, when I saw her after Nechton—After the battle... She didn't wear it after that, at least not until we parted company a month or so later. I had thought it might be lost."

"I found it... just recently." Letitia looked as if the admission were somehow humiliating.

"A stroke of luck," Amien said. Sudden insight broke across his face; he turned to me. "You know what we must do."

I nodded: it was obvious. Amien had been right, all along: the only place that held any possibility of safety for Letitia was Aballo. Once we disembarked at Presatyn, late at night though it might be, we must ride west with all possible haste. There was no reason to believe any windcaller we might engage would be a match for Nechton: the only sane thing to do was travel over land, and the Moot date be damned. But the intelligence we had now was critical: Amien bringing the news to the righthe and the wizards was the only hope of defeating the Bard.

The solution was clear: we must part company. I must ride with the Tanaan, Rohini, and Rohini's men to Bealingas in Usdia, whence we might cross on tides and natural winds to Aballo. Then the only problem would be opening the wards on the Aballo harbor without violating my vow.

The idea of stepping onto the soil of Aballo shouldn't raise this excitement in my chest. The thought of celebrating Bealtan with Letitia at Aballo shouldn't be knocking around in my head. My traveling to Aballo was nothing but a danger, to me and everyone involved, but I could not fulfill my duty otherwise.

Amien nodded, too. "We've got to go straight to the Moot. It's actually fortuitous that we had to go in this direction tonight—"

"*What?*" Letitia and I said simultaneously.

Amien spread a quizzical look between us. "Isn't it obvious? The righthe— and the members of the Order—need the news. If Ellion hadn't found Nechton's name, there's no telling how long we would have been knocking our heads against it militarily, when that isn't the issue at all. Our first operation must be to take back Esunertos, which will contain what the Bard can do east of the Riga; our second major objective must be Macol, and the focus of that will be to get Letitia safely into position."

"What?" we said again. Iminor joined the chorus this time.

The wizard sighed, looking at Letitia. "Annu, I understand that you don't feel sufficiently confident to take on Nechton one-on-one, but I think it would be a start if you—possibly working with a core group, we'll have to discuss it—could capture and destroy the Shadow of the Sun."

"You've lost your mind," I said flatly.

Amien frowned. "Which part of this doesn't make sense? All our objectives must be about containing Nechton's reach. The two greatest problems are Esunertos and the Shadow of the Sun. We handle those things, and the rest can be managed militarily."

I frowned, too. "You're right that Nechton is the issue, but—"

"Of course we will have to refine the details! But I—"

"*No!*" My vehemence surprised even me; several of the knights startled. "Would you send an untrained Talent up against a man of four centuries' experience? That's what you're talking about doing here!"

"No one can train Letitia! All we can do is support—"

"And how can you even contemplate destroying the orb? Think of the learning you'd be throwing away!"

"Think of the evil that went into its creation!" Amien retorted.

"Bollocks!" I snapped. "Have you even *read* Aechering? All of him? Or just that one working?"

Amien recoiled, and I knew he hated the fact that I'd uttered the name in front of outsiders even more than he objected to what I said.

But it was a valid question. No matter that Nechton is rumored to be the one man besides Aechering himself who successfully completed the Shadow Working; no matter that Aechering never seemed to question whether a working was black or white magic so long as it succeeded. Or maybe it is because of these things: Aechering's Shadow Working is the one operation in all the centuries of arcane history that every wizard will eventually work up the courage to read. Not only to read: to gawk at or slaver over, as if it were some sort of arcane pornography, or to endlessly debate the proper translations of the words whose original meanings have been lost.

Not that any of the men who read the working would contemplate attempting it or try to unravel what Aechering really meant: that would be to look too far outside their ordered worlds. Not that they would admit a more than prurient interest in the man's theories, which cannot be truly encompassed without the reader confronting the darkness in his own soul. For most men the Shadow Working is merely something to have seen, like the unfortunates whose sole support comes from traveling with the misborn shows and allowing strangers to gawk at their deformities.

"I'm not advocating working from Aechering, but his *ideas*—" I pursued.

Amien scowled, furious; I waved the line of reasoning away.

"Whether or not the theory about its creation is right," I said, trying to sound reasonable, "the fact remains that it's the only farsensing orb anyone has managed to create since Hy-Breasaíl. It should be studied, not destroyed. What if it could be turned against the kharr? Would it still be evil then?"

He stared at me for a long moment. Everything was quiet but the creaking of the hull.

"The source is tainted," he said heavily.

I sighed: that was a senseless attitude, but I had long since learned to recognize the times when reason wouldn't reach him.

"Even Aechering's grimoires remain in the library," I said. "If the orb is not to be used, at least let it be studied. And send trained men to capture it, not a woman of completely untried—"

"I'm not talking about sending her in there to do battle!" Amien interrupted. "That is why we need you!"

"The *hell* you say!" The words tore out of me before I was conscious of deciding to speak. I found myself on my feet, the boat pitching beneath me. Or maybe it was the world; no one else seemed to find any difficulty in keeping his or her seat, though Letitia's face had achieved a terrible pallor.

"Me working magic is the *last* thing—" I clamped my jaws around the rest. However I might desire it, I couldn't be trusted to do right if I drew power. I couldn't be relied on to recognize the difference between good and evil: how ravenously I hungered for all the flavors of illicit power, how perilously close Nechton's workings came to seducing me proved that.

"I know it's been a long time for you," Amien was on his feet now, too, sounding bizarrely reasonable. "I'm not asking you to go *duel* the man—"

But that was what he wanted, and it was what it would eventually come down to. Suddenly my hands itched for the draw of power; a thrill of black arcane lust swept up my spine. I thrust out my hands between us, as if my outspread fingers would stop his words.

But he pressed on. "I'm not a complete fool: we need a full-on arcane offensive, not some honor-duel. And we need—I need you to be my War-Lord."

"What?" I said, too stunned to even argue.

Amien cast me a look that said the point was perfectly obvious. "I felt it when you let me lean on you this morning. How deep your Talent has become, even while—" He shook his head; I reeled further. "I need you to order the battles. I need your strength."

"Don't you—How can you not understand?" I said. "You of all people? I made a vow. I can't—"

"Surely She will overlook it, if the power you draw is for the defense of others."

"It's not that simple!"

"Explain it to me!"

Words piled up in my throat; I choked them back down. *First explain to me the difference between me and Nechton,* I wanted to say. *Tell me who will point out when something I desire is wrong. Who will stop me when I am too mad to understand?*

"No," I said.

Amien frowned. "What do you mean, no?"

"I mean *no!*" Sudden, desperate fury swept over me. I needed to run, but I had promised Letitia I would not abandon her again. "I mean do not ask me to work magic! Do not send an untried, untrained woman to do the work of a whole team of wizards! Do what you promised, and keep her *safe!* Gods, Amien, if for once you could think about the person rather than about how they fit into your damned *plan*—"

"How many cities have to fall before it's enough?" Amien retorted. "You tell me: how long will it be before they hold both Uisneach and Ilnemedon, if things go on as they are?"

Two months. No more. I could neither entertain the possibility nor concede the point. I shook my head again. "So let the armies fight containment. Let the wizards go in against Esunertos, and then Macol!" Amien was already formulating his next objection; I talked louder and faster: "Let Letitia be *safe*—"

"As long as he holds the Shadow of the Sun, nothing else we do matters! As long as we cannot defeat him directly—"

"If you send her in there, without preparation—"

Amien waved the objection away. "Of course not now! It'll be more than a twelvenight after Bealtan before we can put even an advance force in Macol. Meanwhile we—"

"Carina was born before the Deluge," I said, struggling for calm. "Magic was not just in her blood, it was in her life every day. How long did she take to master Iliria?"

He shrugged. "It was quick. It seemed entirely intuitive for her."

"Because she knew what she was doing!" Letitia said. We both looked at her. "Ellion's right, I haven't the faintest idea how or even whether it's *possible*—"

"If the mora Carina did it, it's possible," Iminor said flatly. He glanced from her to me, gaze shifting into pure loathing, then looked at her again. "The fact that—All the things he has done to try to ward you off—means Nechton knows it, too."

Letitia shook her head. "I don't think we know—"

"You have a responsibility!" Iminor said. "You are royal because the goddess put you there! We are given responsibilities when She sets us apart!"

Terror and betrayal warred in Letitia's face. "How can you—"

"We are needed; we must serve!" Iminor said. "Of course you're afraid; I am too! But we don't get to choose how we will be needed, and we don't get to refuse because we're *scared!*"

Letitia leapt to her feet. "You don't—"

"Your knights have been steadfast in your defense!" Iminor snapped. "They are not the only ones—"

She spun away and bolted up the narrow stair; he stopped, gawking. After a few seconds he jumped up and raced after her. When the hull bumped gently against a dock, I scrambled up the stairs, too—just in time to see Letitia leap across the narrow gap between the deck and the dock, stumble and catch herself, and race away, towards the lights of a town I assumed was Presatyn. After another second of staring Iminor leapt across the gap, too, landing neatly on the dock. Letitia paused, spinning to face him, and extended a long arm to point at him.

"No!" she shouted. "You may not!" She spun away and ran again; Iminor stood where he was, hands sliding over his mouth.

"Well, that was productive," I said.

Amien shot me a look. "If you had not gainsaid every fouzhir thing…"

Fury swept over me again. My hands itched, and just drawing the sword wouldn't do: I wouldn't be satisfied until we had it out with raw power, right here; until I returned to something like sanity with yet another sin I would never balance on my soul. I leapt from the deck to the dock and started down the same path Letitia had followed.

"The mora said *no*," Iminor pointed out behind me.

"Good thing I'm not Fíanan," I grated, and broke into a run.

Chapter 25
All Her Secrets

Letitia was fast. I hadn't realized how fleet-footed she was. By the time I reached the end of the wharf, she seemed to have vanished on the night air. By the time I stumbled upon the site of Presatyn's sacred well, she had been and gone: wet footprints led out of the little cherry-blossom-strewn enclave and vanished into the dust of the street, and I knew she'd dunked herself in the waters to kill Amien's wards.

I would have done the same thing, if Amien had some arcane tie to me. I would have done whatever was necessary to gain a little privacy tonight. Finally, there was something to be grateful for: Nechton might see me if he chose, but at least Amien didn't. But it also meant that no one with the possible exception of Nechton knew where she was or whether she was safe; I hastened through the moonlit streets of the little town, looking for her.

Presatyn was oddly active tonight, in the way a town will get during the dead hours when both moons are close to full. Some of the best nights I could recall in Ilnemedon began during these too-bright dead hours, when the nap that should have been merely the evening's first sleep became all the slumber of an eventful night. But in an unfamiliar place, packed streets during the dead hours seem like harbingers of chaos.

The taverns were still busy despite the hour, light spilling from their windows and the lamps beside their doors. Savvy street vendors had taken advantage of the opportunity and were doing brisk business in skewered meat, fried meat pies, and some drink made from winter apples and uisquebae. People bound for the Fair at Teamair crowded the streets, and wherever they went it was as if the Fair had expanded all the way to Presatyn: I passed buskers of every possible talent, groups of staggering men and women whose drunken laughter echoed on the night air, night butterflies and a couple of men staging an improbable, entirely insufficiently-moonlit bout with naked swords. The buskers' competing musics and poems rang against the buildings and the trunks of the cherry trees, and pink-white blossoms rained down under the moonlight until the place looked like late-season snow.

On the long porch of a tavern, lit by torches and the light of the moons, I found Loeg and his troupe performing the same damned satire I'd been seeing for the past two days. The crowd thought it far funnier than I did. I couldn't figure out how the mummers had beaten us here. At least they weren't performing the tale of the Lady of Finias on the Ruillin: I wondered whether Loeg or the young harpist Marten would be the first to work something up.

At the edge of the porch, finally, I spotted Letitia: small and soaked, the sodden spidersilk of her mail clinging so seductively to her long delicate frame that I wondered she'd been able to reach this spot unmolested. That made me think of the captain of the Ballarona ferry again. The fury that simmered beneath my surface flared; I fought it back down. The man was dead; there was no one here who deserved the bite of my blade. I pulled off my jacket, stepped into an empty spot at Letitia's back, and settled it about her shoulders.

She startled—and came around swinging. I ducked beneath the blow, caught my jacket just as it touched the ground.

"It's you!" she breathed, green eyes shining as if I had somehow rescued her. The sweet, seductive energy that Amien's wards always obscured hung around her again, surprising an odd hitch in my throat.

I nodded. "Let's get out of here."

Danger gathered in her face. "I'm not going back to the boat."

"Nothing could be further from my mind," I said. "Give me a minute, and I'll get us a skin of something. We need a holiday."

"Damn certain," she said. It occurred to me that it was the first time I'd heard her swear. "Get uisquebae."

I nodded. "The very thing," I said, and gently grasped her elbow. Her unique, tantalizing energy tingled delightfully against my fingertips and palm. I guided her past the edge of the performance and inside. Loeg caught my eye as we passed, with a wink I couldn't decide how to interpret.

Either everyone was suddenly packaging their uisquebae in bottles or I'd been had again: once more I paid too much, caring just as little as last time. I waited just long enough for the barmaid to open it and escorted Letitia back out to the street. We passed the laughing crowd; I paused and offered Letitia the first swig. She gave an odd little salute with the bottle, then raised the thing to her lips and drank, grimaced and handed it back. I tipped the bottle and let the blessed fire pour down my throat. My anger cooled a little; a zephyr roused from nowhere and carried Letitia's exotic musk-rose-and-something-more scent into my core.

This time I offered her my arm; a surprising little thrill skittered through me as she snuggled close, and for a while we just walked, passing the bottle back and forth, the dampness of her mail shirt gradually soaking into mine. When the bottle began to seem in danger of growing empty, we took it to the vendor with the apple-and-uisquebae drinks and got more. Eventually we reached the little grove in which the sacred well resided; I realized I'd been heading there all along. I paused, giving Letitia an inquiring look.

"Yes," she said, a sudden smile blossoming. "That will do."

We walked through the gate, into the midst of the circle of flowering cherry trees. Moonlight filtered through the petals and branches, glowed in the rippling waters of the spring; the subtle power of the well wrapped gentle tendrils around me. The sounds of the crowd in the street outside receded almost to nothing. I looked around, at the devotional ribbons tied to the trees and the little bundles of flowers around the well's periphery: struck by the quiet, benevolent energy of this place, the present sense of a goddess Who would only do Her people good. I tipped my head back, looking at the branches and the stars above. The beauty of the place crashed through me; I stood transfixed.

"I want to sit," Letitia announced, with the abrupt certainty of the drunk, and settled on the grass beside the spring. Again she grimaced as she landed; my throat knotted.

"Annu!" I said. "You're hurt!"

She shrugged. Belated anger crossed her angular face. "He bit me."

"What?"

She shrugged again. "It's not bad; it was through my clothes. I don't think he broke—"

It wasn't my place to ask, but I couldn't contain it. "What *happened*?"

She reached for the bottle, had another swig of uisquebae. "Would you believe it was the wards that saved me? When he started—trying—and I fought him… and the dog was miles ahead of me; he'd already gotten me to take off the sword…"

I hissed, remembering, and settled beside her. I hadn't recognized the ploy, either, all my worry focused on her safety up on the rigging.

Her mouth twisted. "He put a knife to my throat—"

My hands clenched, beyond my control.

"—but as soon as the blade touched…"

"The wards flared," I said.

She nodded. "It scared him. He backed up and started cursing me, but of course when he tried again, there they still were. Finally he just backed off and locked me in."

I gathered her against me, kissed the top of her head. "Of all the things…"

"I know."

I offered her the bottle again; she drank.

"I'm glad you got out without anything worse."

"Thanks to you."

I kissed the top of her head again. "I was—glad to do it."

For a moment we were silent. I let the wondrous fog of uisquebae roll around in my brain, admired the moonlight in the cherry blossoms and the gentle fluttering of the ribbons tied to the branches.

"This damn thing is soggy," Letitia announced, and pushed herself to her knees. "I'm taking it off."

She unfastened the clasps of her mail shirt. I had a formless sense that it was dangerous, but I helped her pull it over her head anyway. The way her sodden clothes clung to her body made it nearly impossible for me to keep my hands politely to myself. She snuggled against me again; this time, for the first time, I felt the angular softness of her body under my arm and hand. Desire pounded through me; for a moment my head whirled.

"So," she said thoughtfully, still nestled against me. "Who are you, Ellion Tellan?"

I sighed and drank more uisquebae.

"You're a wizard."

I felt myself stiffen. "I don't practice."

She gave voice to a strange, short laugh. "Well, are wizards born... or made?"

Damn. "Born."

She nodded, hair tickling my neck. "You are a wizard."

The truth of that simple statement caught me. I had known since I vowed to stop—since before I made that vow—that nothing could change who I was at my core. I had long since discovered that no amount of ignoring all the things arcane senses told me did anything to blunt those senses: it just made me hunger at the slightest provocation. As if I had committed to total celibacy and then taken on a harping gig at a tea-house.

"I am a fool," I said.

She chuckled. "Let's have a contest. I've got you beat."

I found myself smiling. "I find that doubtful. I got started much earlier."

"Really," she said, sounding intrigued. "When?"

I had another drink, thinking. "When I decided to go to Aballo."

How great a fool had I been, after all? As heir to Tellan, already beginning to assume the tanist's role, I had let myself be drawn away on a promise of which I had not the faintest understanding. Any sane man would have thought my life already more than enough.

"Why did you go?" Letitia asked, and relieved me of the bottle. She no longer grimaced after each sip, and in fact she was no longer sipping. That might prove perilous; I reached for the bottle. Once it was in my hand, there was no choice but to drink again.

"Why?" she repeated.

I looked through the bottle, at the way everything on the other side grew foggy and bent. And for no reason I knew of, I told the truth. "Because the goddess Called me."

Letitia gave a quick, surprised little gasp and drew back to look at me. The dampness of her clothing had soaked right through my mail to touch my skin, and now I was cold.

I shrugged. After a second, a slow smile started on her face, and she snuggled against me again.

"You *did* understand," she said, sounding satisfied. "About the Touch of the goddess. I knew it."

I nodded and leaned my cheek against the top of her head. "I understood."

"But instead of binding you to your land, She sent you away?"

I shook my head, the silk of her hair sliding against my cheek and neck and tightening the screws on my desire again. "She Called me to Her. At Aballo I learned…"

I hesitated, the enormity of what I needed to convey beyond my limited command of Tanaan. There was probably no way to explain it, even in Ilesian, and to try to do so would most likely end with me violating the vow of silence concerning Aballo practices I had taken.

I sighed. "After I was done there, She sent me home."

Home. How simple a word, and how deceptive. I realized I still thought of Tellan as my home, even though I would never return. Melancholy welled in me; I reached for the bottle again.

"And yet…" Letitia hesitated. "Even though you did Her Will, you lost the throne."

Anger burst through me again; I withdrew, rose, began to pace. It wasn't fair, and I burned for revenge. But after a moment of seething, I remembered.

"That was my doing," I grated. "Not Hers."

"No," Letitia said with utter, drunken sincerity.

I nodded, throat tight, and waited for the questions. Of course she wanted to know what I had done; everyone wanted to know. The duel blasted through my memory again, the raw, angry glorious power of it, and instead of the guilt I should have felt, what hung on me was the mind-wrecking delight of powers no wizard sworn to the true gods should ever touch, the horribly seductive sense of the possibility of becoming just like Them. I couldn't remember why it would be wrong.

"It should take more than one mistake," Letitia said. "True effort should count for something."

I found myself looking at her, surprised. Where were the prying questions, the prurient interest in my transgressions? How was it possible that she had already forgiven me, without even knowing what I had done? Something inside me eased open, just a little.

"You didn't go back to Aballo?" she said.

How could I? I would have been just as forcefully rejected there. The wizards had closed ranks in public, and no one beyond Tellan's borders knew what had happened; but I was still the biggest disgrace they had endured in centuries. And at Aballo I would truly have been a celibate man in a tea-house. For a while. I would quickly have been forsworn, and irretrievably damned.

"I vowed to give up the practice," I said. "I went to live on the Ruillin, and got serious about the harp, and…"

"And shortly they declared you their leader, because that is just what people do," she laughed.

I found myself smiling. "They didn't bring it to me; I went and got it. There's a cloak, you know—it looks like something Loeg would wear—and I just…" Truth caught up to me.

Hid, I thought. *Tried to pretend I was someone else.*

"That seems like a pretty good idea," Letitia answered, and I realized she'd heard the thought.

Terror dropped out of the sky, nearly crushing me. I had spent the past month in the company of telepaths and neglected the simple precaution of mental shields. How much had they heard?

"How often does *that* happen?" I choked.

"What?"

"You heard the thought."

Letitia frowned. "Did I?"

I nodded, throat tight.

She looked thoughtful; for a moment she was silent.

"I don't remember having heard you think before tonight." She gazed up at me in further pensive silence. "I like it. You're beautiful on the outside, but I think your inside is much more interesting."

I should have laughed. Instead I found myself staring at her, sudden emotion welling painfully within. I swallowed, but my throat didn't ease.

"Thou'rt beautiful, too," I croaked. "If I were less drunk I would have something more artful to say."

"This is better," she replied, voice barely above a whisper and emerald eyes locked on mine.

"Then I shall stay drunk," I said, closed the distance between us, settled beside her and picked up the bottle again. She snuggled against me; my arm wrapped itself around her of its own accord, and I realized belatedly that I was caressing her, savoring the softness of her waist and the delightful angles of the girdle of bones beneath the flesh of her hip. I forced myself to stop, banished the readiness raging through me. She gave voice to a sigh of pleasure, snuggled closer, and laid a hand atop my thigh, which made it necessary to banish my aching need all over again. I was less successful this time, but managed to keep things below the level of embarrassment.

But then she shifted, wrapped her arm around me, turned and climbed into my lap: facing me, mouth just inches from mine and knees to either side of my hips—and I forgot how to ward off my body's inevitable response. All the blood raced away from my brain. She stared into my eyes, utterly serious. I let my hands settle on her waist, telling myself it would be rude not to, finding my fingers resting on the cold smooth skin of her back where her shirt had hitched northward and the waist of her pants dipped south. Even cold, the texture of her skin made my head whirl.

She was a virgin. Virgins never have any sense of the meanings of the things they do, not when it comes to loving. They are forever promising things they don't understand. I held myself still, hardly allowing myself to breathe, but all the apocryphal stories of Tana and the way they simply take the men they want stampeded through my head. I thought of Easca in some storage cubby with Sainrith, getting makeup all over her neck and gods only knew where else. I reminded myself of the difference between a woman of experience, who is ready for a quick simple tumble, and a virgin, who knows only what she feels. But my breathing quickened anyway, and my fingertips couldn't help but move, just enough to take in her miraculous textures.

She reached up, tangled a hand in my hair, raked her fingers through it until the thong that bound it back fell free and it tumbled forward around my face. Her gaze was still locked on mine, and I realized she meant this, at least; I couldn't guess how much more she meant, and I suspected whatever unfolded here would not be drunken forgetfulness of her commitment to Iminor but rather a rebellion against it, something born of anger as much as desire.

A better man would have stopped and questioned her motives. I pulled the thong from her braid, slid my fingers through the silken mass to trace the curve of her scalp as she closed her eyes, arched her neck, leaned into the caress with such abandon that I very nearly grabbed and pressed her to me.

But no. She had suffered an unwanted advance already today. And I wasn't sure what the choice would mean, because I might not like Iminor, but even in the midst of desire and uisquebae I recognized how much more bound me to him than to any of the men whose wives I ordinarily seduced. I had not yet done something truly wrong.

She opened her eyes, gaze lit with something that felt like the caress of fire in the hands—and touched my mouth with her fingertips, tracing my lower lip with her thumb. I turned my face into her palm, kissed her hand, aching with a flavor of need whose like I couldn't remember: both relieved and oddly terrified when she slid her hand away, down my jaw, and leaned in to kiss me.

But then her lips touched mine, and everything else vanished. I forgot myself, wrapped urgent arms around her, buried my hands in her hair while she crushed against me, her suddenly-heated skin and cold damp clothing sending wildly conflicting messages into me, the thing I most wanted pressing through the mail shirt and against my groin so I shuddered and growled. Fire raced all over my body; nothing existed beyond burning need and its miraculous answer, but just outside the bubble of unreason hovered the knowledge that I was doing something that couldn't be undone. I pulled back, gasping for breath.

"Letitia," I breathed. "Annu."

"Shut up," she whispered, breath feathering my lips. "Shut up."

But I didn't. Instead, when she stopped my mouth with her own, I opened my lips to her, and she to me, and I realized we were still within territory she knew. I grabbed lean handfuls of her this time, cupping the curves of her bottom; she leaned into me with such fervor that I gasped and pulled back lest I push her too far. Her eyes burned into me; her long fingers sought the clasps of my mailshirt; I recognized, with the remote wisdom of drunkenness, the stupidity of allowing it but couldn't find it in myself to care—and then it was off, and her breasts pressed into me and she came to rest against my groin, and I was very nearly lost.

"Wait," I breathed. "Wait."

She frowned. "What?"

It took me several seconds to figure out what was wrong.

"Wait," I said again, and returned to caressing her slowly, trying to give my brain time to catch up; savoring the soft delicious energy that hung on her, the veil of invisible light that caressed my fingers as it let them pass, stretched out to reach me in all the places where I leaned close, sent a glow of warmth into my consciousness. Gradually it dawned on me, as the silken skin of her neck slipped along beneath my fingertips, as blind need shifted into the sort of desire that allows things to build and last: whatever happened, however things changed when we stepped inevitably back onto that boat, I stood on the threshold of something miraculous. I might not be the first human ever to bed a Tana, but no doubt I was the first to enjoy a virgin. I would carry the secret to my pyre. It was only right to bring all the art of which I was capable to bear, to allow myself to remember and her to truly enjoy. But I looked into her face, seeing something that began with anger and drunken lust but hinted at the possibility of more—and nearly lost myself in her eyes again. I leaned in to brush my lips against hers.

"No regrets," I whispered against her mouth, feeling her tremble under the caress. "No regrets. Or stop me now."

"No regrets," she whispered, and the tremor infected me, but I shifted my grip and drew her to her feet, still unable to tear myself away from her mouth; lifted her, carried her from the center of the little circle to a spot in the moon-light-dappled shadows beneath a tree. She melted into my arms as we settled, let me stretch her out in the shadows and tangle myself around her—and then, somehow, her hands were unbuckling my sword, unbuttoning my shirt, sliding across the skin of my chest while she trailed kisses and delicate devastating teeth along my jaw, until I almost lost myself again, diving into her long white neck and very nearly giving into the urge to bite. Instead I employed every trick of the lips and tongue and gentle tooth I knew, and she gasped and writhed and gave voice to maddening noises—and I found myself lying on top of her, mouth full of her succulent lips, fingers working buttons by the sheer miracle of muscle memory. I drew back as the last button opened: head whirling, vaguely aware that I had lost any semblance of the style whose reputation I so carefully cultivated in Ilnemedon—and stopped without planning it, dumbstruck by the wonder.

I prayed I would remember: Letitia lay in the grass, moonlight gleaming in her ardent emerald eyes and the tumult of her golden hair, Amien's talisman glittering on its delicate chain, the long stretch of her neck unfolding into the clavicles I had glimpsed on occasion and the soft perfection of her breasts; all bathed in the seductive glow that no one but a wizard would ever see. For a moment I forgot how to breathe. I had completely lost track of reason, and if I didn't recover now, it would be over much too soon.

Playfulness. Style. Those were the things I needed, the things that usually came as effortlessly as the knack of flirtation I had lost somewhere in Fíana. I tried to remember what the rakehell of Ilnemedon would have done. I bent to kiss each breast in turn, the soft silk-and-velvet textures under my lips and tongue sending me spiraling towards uncontrol again, and moved on to the thing that would allow me to recover a more playful mood: I shot her a wicked grin, bent and grasped the talisman with my mouth, steadying it between my tongue and the roof of my mouth as I moved it aside so I could kiss her heart.

My head fired; the talisman lit me up with a power more brilliant and immediate than the delight that hung on Letitia when her wards were gone, and for a moment everything was as bright as day. My mind fell irretrievably open; Letitia's awareness hung within me like a bright fog, and all at once I knew exactly what she wanted, which caresses would answer the places that begged for my touch. I kissed the power back into her chest, surprising a low sound from her; sudden, unconquerable need pounded through me. It was too late for style; it didn't matter: I dove in to her breasts again, raining kisses downward as I undressed her, giving voice to a wholly unexpected moan as her hand found its way inside my pants and closed around me. Finally I recognized that I was as open to her mind as she was to mine, and she had read my desire as easily as I read hers. The vulnerability of it should have frightened me; instead it roused in me a strange wildness.

"This. Yes," she panted, as I twisted around to taste her mouth again. Her fingers moved, making me moan once more.

"Thou. Art," she whispered in Ilesian.

"Thine," I breathed. I didn't know when it had happened, didn't care. There was no longer any need to deny.

"Show me," she said, half a moan; once again I saw what she wanted. I let her pull off the rest of my clothes, until I was as naked in body as I was in my soul, and gave her everything a man can safely give a woman on whom he does not intend to father a child: not with style, but with a tenderness that welled from some place whose name I didn't know, serving her every need with my pleasure until she wilted, spent and trembling. Finally I lay back, gathered her against me, lay there staring at the branches above us: listening to her heart slow, to her breathing shift as she sank into sleep.

An odd peace descended over me; uisquebae unrolled a new layer of fog in my head, and through it I watched cherry blossoms flutter on a light breeze that somehow failed to reach the ground, admired the profusion of stars strewn across the moonlit velvet of the sky, breathed in the scent of the waters in the well, the soft earth on which we lay, the mystery that was Letitia. Her presence beside me and her warm softness under my hands felt unassailably right; for the moment everything outside this little enclave seemed very far away. It would have been easy to begin imagining ways in which this moment might become permanent; but for all the ways in which uisquebae dampens pain, it always unlocks the bare truth as well: this was a moment, no more. There had never been, never would be a battle between me and Iminor, and I had won nothing but the privilege of becoming her secret refuge. The best I could do was savor this moment and try to remember.

Suddenly, strangely, I found myself on familiar ground, but everything was different than ever before. I had never bothered trying to count the number of women I had seduced, nor the—thankfully smaller—number of husbands I wound up dueling when those women forgot about discretion. Over the years the patterns of it had become so familiar that I could predict each affair's unfolding, and I knew the emotional stages we would endure. After the thrill of the trespass came the woman's regret, followed by her decision to try to hold on to everything: the husband who gave her comfort and status, the lover who made her feel bold and wild. I became the dark little secret, the repository of all other inadmissible truths; it became my role to introduce her to the tastes for the illicit and transgressive she hid, possibly even from herself. Her discretion would be absolute—until, suddenly, it was not. Sometimes the breakdown in discretion came from a yearning for the thrilling danger of revelation; sometimes it was because the woman wanted, whether consciously or not, to extract the same kind of attention from the husband she betrayed; sometimes, but rarely, it was because she had developed a temporary infatuation and mistook it for genuine attachment. In any event, whatever caused the breakdown in discretion, the number of days remaining in the relationship might be counted on one's hands. That was the part I liked least, because the end of that countdown was nearly always marked by a duel, by another death for which everyone knew who to blame even though nothing was ever proven or recorded: none of it ever my idea, but usually, after all the damning and generally truthful words uttered in the run-up to the duel, a proceeding I regretted little until afterward. But the more times I ran that course, the deeper the regret grew. There were days when that part of it made me want to give up on women altogether.

This time, though, while I saw the road stretching before me, the terrain looked completely different. It was easy to see the possibility of investing everything I had, everything I was, in this doomed affair; the idiotic part of me that had fixed its devotion on her could go right on maintaining a gambler's face in public, dedicating my sword and wit to her defense, even while I marked the days by the stolen moments she gave me: until the war was won or I died in her defense, either outcome tracing a downward spiral towards something that would only seem like tragedy to the one experiencing it. To do otherwise would require changing the depth and nature of my devotion. In the glow of illusory closeness that always comes after the first tryst, the path of seemingly romantic self-destruction beckoned.

Surely it didn't have to be that way. Surely, with the application of some mental discipline, I could choose otherwise: to chart a path in which I accepted any subsequent trysts with Letitia as something that existed outside ordinary reality, as if they were arcane operations performed in an Aballo workshop; to allow myself to see tonight's tryst for what it was, a long-overdue lancing of some pocket of overactive emotion in me. I had learned, with Marla, to be both a lover and a friend. Couldn't I do that again here? Couldn't I regain the perspective, the clarity that allowed me to navigate these waters in Ilnemedon?

Yes, I decided: I could. I could accept whatever emotion Letitia might endure—surely it was all different for Tanaan, anyway—and count myself lucky that the Tanaan evidently had no tradition of dueling over lovers. I could allow my infatuation, deep as it was, to drain away. I could walk away when it was all over, carrying secrets and memories no one else would ever have.

I lay there, letting the idea of allowing myself to love Letitia, like the rest of them, as a friend and companion-in-arms, while enjoying the occasional tryst as time and circumstances permitted, to roll around with the uisquebae fog in my head. It was a good idea: all the things that made me want to devote myself so deeply to her were also reasons to hold her in the highest esteem as a friend; and if the madness of not having a woman I desired had been cured tonight, she was no less delicious than she had been three hours ago.

By the time the pale light of dawn began and Letitia stirred and woke, I was ready to smile at her, to meet her eyes and salute her awakening with a kiss. The delight of her flavors and textures raised me to readiness again, but the madness of it had receded a little.

"Ohhh," Letitia breathed, her gaze traveling down the length of me. "I had been about to say that *that* was a thing we shouldn't do again, but…"

My newfound perspective allowed me to find the rakehell of Ilnemedon, finally, to draw him on like a favorite shirt. I smiled and leaned in to kiss her, feathered my lips past her eagerly-offered jaw, whispered into her neck: "But now? What will it be?"

"Ahh…" she breathed. "Surely no one will miss us any more than they already do."

"Surely not," I answered, and kissed her again. It was all coming back to me now: in sudden, great waves of remembered surety. I gently stretched out her arms, spread myself along the full length of her: following all the cues women don't even know they give, building her desire and her pleasure towards the point at which even a moment's pause drives a lover beyond reason. The glow of her gentle power infiltrated me, but I didn't reach for her mind: that intimacy would throw me off balance all over again. Artful pleasure was enough this time. When I slipped inside, a moment of roaring emotion overtook me; but I was ready for it this time, and rechanneled it into the more controllable sort of passion. The wave of need pulled me under, and style was once again lost to me; but after a few moments of barely-conscious loving, I remembered my training, rode the waves of pleasure without succumbing to the release, ushered her shuddering and exclaiming across the line of climax and back again, and beyond the line once more. The echoing insanity spun me out into the places beyond the mundane realm, until I saw her shimmering energies even more clearly than I saw her face; felt them pulse all around me on the waves of her pleasure; shivered at the sudden sensation of her awareness within me once more, the intimacy of it inciting a wave of emotion that could only be managed by gathering her close, burying my face in her neck, hiding within the silken shield of her hair. When she shuddered towards exhaustion again I drew gratefully back, kissing her and trying to pretend there was not a knot in my throat, and began pulling on my clothes.

Letitia stretched languorously, watching me from eyes filled equally with the intoxications of pleasure and uisquebae, then finally rolled up to sit and began dressing as well. After a moment she paused, still only half dressed, looking at me again. Early morning light lay soft on her face, but her expression was suddenly serious.

"Do you know how far we are from—Teamair? Where the Moot will be?"

She had shifted back, from the intimate address, into the more formal "you". For a second the choice stung; but then relief set in. It might be significant of nothing more than unfamiliarity with the intimate forms of Ilesian; whatever her reason, hearing and saying *you* would help me remember. It didn't feel right, but I knew it was.

"Maybe five or six days," I said.

She nodded. "And how far to Aballo?"

"Eight or nine, if things go well."

"A person couldn't get to both places before the Moot, correct?"

I shook my head. "No. We're at the decision point."

"I have to decide, then," she said thoughtfully, and sighed. "I have to go."

I paused, foot halfway into a boot, looking at her. Fear for her welled in me. "Annu—Letitia, I meant what I said last night: to send anyone who has Talent but not training up against Nechton is insanity. I hope you don't hear it as an insult, but—you've seen what he can do. I've seen…" The memory of the arcane storm overtook me again; for a moment it was all I could see. "Even more. Maybe, if you can master whatever Carina knew, then we might talk about how to safely—"

She treated me to a bitter-edged smile. "Safe doesn't enter into it, Ellion. We both know that. Iminor's right: I've been given a duty. My clan's honor requires that I step up."

I sighed and pushed my foot all the way into the boot, then walked to the center of the enclave to retrieve my mail shirt. If she couldn't be dissuaded, I must insist on so much arcane and military support for her that what she could or couldn't do became irrelevant, must accompany her to ensure she didn't come to harm. And in the mean time I must renew my efforts to send the whole plan tumbling off the ledge. I shook out the mail, returning to the place in which she sat, watching with half an eye as she worried at some further decision and finally resolved it.

She fixed me with a direct stare. "I need to tell you something, Ellion. But it is a secret that must go no further."

Ah, yes, here it was: in this regard at least, a Tana was the same as a human woman. Now that I had become her secret, all the others she carried would come spilling out between us. It was not only a way of easing the pressure of the transgression: it was a test of my discretion. I had lost track of the number of times I'd performed this little drama: I knew my lines. I was surprised to discover that this morning it felt unfair.

"All your secrets are safe with me," I said anyway, with a manufactured smile, and pulled the mail shirt over my head. The extra layer between us helped, just a little.

"Amien is wrong," Letitia said.

"How so?" I said, reaching for my sword belt and buckling it on as I moved: towards the spot in which the thong for my hair and the bottle of uisquebae, which had begun to seem tempting again, lay. A little less pain, a little more clarity: those were what I needed.

"The mora Carina didn't defeat Nechton." The hitch in her voice completely undermined her calm delivery.

"What?" I said, all but skidding to a halt. The sector of my mind responsible for rational thought scrabbled hopelessly for purchase. My hand closed around the bottle, but it had lost its appeal.

"I don't know why that worries me, since with the Spear broken, I'm just going to wind up sacrificed to the goddess anyway..."

"What?" I said again.

Letitia closed the distance between us, reached for the bottle, took two healthy swallows and grimaced. I took it back.

"Oh, yes," she said, with the sort of calm only uisquebae can bestow. "The Great Spear of Fíana. It's broken. It's in my pack."

I refused to say the same thing again. I cast around for something slightly more lucid to say instead.

"Um," I said finally.

"Of course you realize I'll be the last Ériu to wear the Mora's Torc."

"Oh, Letitia," I said.

"I am not looking forward to trying to explain myself at the House of Donn." She sighed, glancing past me to the sacred well. "Assuming they let me in."

"Oh, Letitia," I said again. "Why didn't you say something?"

330

She met my gaze, despair in her eyes. "What, in front of all those people? Ellion, do you realize that even with only seven knights left to me, I still travel with representation of five of the eight great-clans? Let alone all the people from outside Fíana. How could I bring that disgrace on my clan?"

I swallowed. "But you're... Are you the one who broke it?"

Letitia shook her head.

"Then how can—"

"I will be the one who arrives for investiture without the Spear. It won't matter who broke it; the Spear was a gift of the goddess, and—" Her voice caught. "A sacrifice will be required to restore the balance. That sacrifice will be me."

It was poor judgment, but I gathered her against me, as if I could somehow ward off the doom that way. Pain welled in me. "Maybe you just shouldn't go."

She shook her head. "That would be a disgrace, too. With all the things the mora Carina did... It's up to me to make it right." A tremor ran through her; I clutched her more tightly. "Even if Clan Ériu loses the moraship, our honor..."

"Well, can't someone fix it?"

She gave voice to a bitter laugh. "It's wrought of findargat. The men who do the maintenance on the city windmills in Irisa have been trying to figure out how to work with findargat for years; they can't move it. No matter how hot they get the forges..."

"Findargat," I said. Memory hovered just out of reach.

"Remember those sculptures in Arian?" Letitia said. I remembered, finally: the immense, graceful harp and the huge improbable scales looking out over the destruction of what had once been a breathtaking city. The sad contrast between the beauty of the energies I'd tasted in the collapsing tavern and the boundless grief and anger outside.

"Everything else shattered..." I said.

Letitia nodded and tucked her head into my chest. A horrifying wave of tenderness raced through me. I needed the uisquebae, but I needed to be able to think even more. I must re-cast everything, must find a way to change Amien's plan without explaining why.

"What happened?" I said.

She shrugged. "It was Nechton, I think. He and the mora Carina seem to have been engaged in... magical warfare..." She swallowed and reached for the bottle again, and I let her take it, sensing the shame the admission had cost her. Their goddess had forbidden magic, and yet the mora of Fíana had been practicing in secret. And losing.

"You found her journ—her grimoire," I said. Pieces of a puzzle whose existence I hadn't even suspected were falling into place.

"And the room in which she..."

"Practiced," I supplied. What had it been for Carina to grow up with magic as a birthright and then be expected to abandon it through no fault of her own? Was Nechton the reason she kept practicing after the Deluge, in defiance of the word of her goddess? What humiliation it must have been to battle such a master when she could neither seek aid nor admit what she did; to let people think she had won a battle whose outcome was clearly much less well-defined, to accept the shame of upholding the lie in order to protect the honor of her clan.

"What did you find?" I asked.

Letitia glanced at me, humiliation in her gaze.

"Withdrawn," I said. "I don't need to know, do I?"

"I don't think I really understood all of what I saw," she said in a small voice. She pursed her lips. "Though you probably would."

Oh, gods. I kissed her forehead and withdrew, overcome by the need to pace. The outcome of Carina's encounter with Nechton had been ambiguous at best: no wonder she wouldn't talk about it after it was over; no wonder she laid the talisman aside, withdrew to Fíana, refused to even tell her compatriots where she had been. I wondered what injuries she and Nechton had inflicted on one another, how much of the truth Rishan suspected or understood.

She hadn't been completely ineffectual: after their encounter, Nechton had no longer been able to provide his armies with arcane support, and he had fled Macol for some deeper lair in which to lick his wounds. And, apparently, continued to battle Carina in secret. It must have been almost entirely aetheric.

I had glimpsed his capabilities in the extramundane. If Carina had held him at bay for centuries, she must have had more Talent and understanding than anyone recognized. Maybe Amien was right, and there was some hope of Letitia becoming the one thing Nechton couldn't handle. Certainly Nechton seemed to entertain the possibility. Maybe the problem was only one of giving Letitia time and opportunity to develop.

But how long would it take, and how bad would things get while we waited?

How was it possible I was even contemplating this? Expecting Letitia to develop a level of practice analogous to Carina's was naïve—assuming my conjecture about Carina was right at all. Carina had come of age during the era of which I had learned from countless songs: with magic as every Tanaan's birthright, to be used in whatever ways suited his or her talent and conscience. She had absorbed with the very air she breathed a level of understanding it would take Letitia years of intensive training to develop, if it came to her at all. And Carina had been no more than marginally effective.

No matter what anyone feared or wanted to believe, Letitia was not the answer to Nechton. I must protect Letitia's honor, but I must also ensure that any serious effort was spearheaded by the wizards.

I stopped pacing, looking at her. "This only makes me more certain. You should be heading for Aballo, not Teamair. Macol is the last place you should go. We should consider taking Amien, and Amien only, into confidence—"

She shook her head vigorously. "Don't you understand? I'm dead anyway. Don't make me take the Ériu clan's honor with me."

I shook my head, too. "There has got to be a way."

She smiled, just a little. "If anyone could find it, it would be you."

Chapter 26
Hidden in Broad Daylight

Out beyond the sheltering branches of the trees at the sacred well, Presatyn glared with too much sunlight. The streets of the little town stretched quiet, blindingly bright and littered with the trash of the previous night's revel. The squeaking of wheels on early-morning milk-men's wagons made my skull threaten to split open. I hadn't even reached the stage of true hangover yet: I was still more than a little drunk. I wasn't looking forward to a day on the water.

Letitia and I walked without speaking, oddly comfortable in our silence: as if everything that needed to be said between us had been, and now only the battles remained. The first battle loomed at the edge of the dock, rocking disconcertingly on the too-brilliant water and looking far more threatening than so small a boat had any right to. The people on the deck were already staring at us.

"Screw it," I muttered. "Let's go back to the well." The remaining uisque-bae, which I had whimsically poured out as a libation for the gentle goddess Who hosted us in safety last night—refusing to think about what such an action meant, from a man sworn to the true gods—suddenly seemed a terrible waste. Letitia laughed, as humorless as I felt.

By the time we reached the gangway, our entire party stood on deck. Even the crew seemed to be staring. It all felt too familiar, though this moment usually occurred when I walked back into a party or a ballroom from which I'd slipped away in the company of someone else's wife. Too often it was the beginning of the endgame I hated; sometimes, though less frequently as the years wore on and my reputation developed a life of its own, it could be defused by simply behaving as if my conduct had been above reproach, by looking my would-be rival dead in the eye. It occurred to me that this was not Ilnemedon, and the people on that boat most likely knew little or nothing of my reputation. It was definitely worth a try.

I handed Letitia onto the gangway and followed her across. Iminor stood within arm's length of the other end, blue eyes fairly blazing. All the pain I glimpsed behind his neutral mask was my fault, and I didn't even have the excuse of tactical necessity this time. Fleetingly I wished he would challenge me, so I could let him slice me open.

"Mora," he said, entire armies of conflicting emotions running beneath his even tone.

She answered his stare with a cool, remote regard. "My lord."

I met his gaze as I stepped onto the deck; he didn't bother trying to contain how much he hated me this morning. Either I had misunderstood the rules under which the Tanaan operate or he had forgotten them.

"Good morning," I said: not pleasant, precisely, but more than civil.

The Tan recoiled, still staring at me. "How drunk *are* you?" he demanded, a month's mounting resentment turning his voice into the bite of a snake. My self-loathing eased, just enough for me to adopt the time-tested shield of irony.

I shrugged, stepping past him with a manufactured smile. "I've been drunker. Still far from easy prey. You'll note the mora's still alive."

For a few seconds he stared as if formulating a truly withering response; finally his mouth twisted and he stalked off.

"Where is the captain?" Letitia said, to no one in particular.

A man stepped out from the staring knot of crew, pulled off a weather-beaten blue hat and sketched a bow. "My lady."

Letitia nodded, then looked as if she regretted the motion. "How far can we sail on this river?"

The captain glanced at Rohini, who still seemed to be staring at me and not much appreciating what she saw. He squinted at the chief as if weighing profit against the cost of stretching the truth, and returned his attention to Letitia.

"Ya c'n sail all th' way to Lake Nanno, if ya've a mind, Lady. But it's slow goin' after Nemetona."

Letitia looked as if she would nod again, then decided against it. "How far to Nemetona?"

"Th' day, Lady."

She glanced at me. I sighed and ruefully nodded.

"When can we sail?"

Again he glanced at Rohini and Letitia, and then at me, clearly wishing for the familiar rhythms of business among men. "If ya're ready, now."

"Yes," Letitia said. "Let's go." The captain bowed again and began issuing orders to the crew. Letitia turned and walked to the back of the boat, settling with her spine against the charthouse wall and her gaze on something beyond the rear rail. I crossed the deck to the prow and looked out: I had long since learned that my only hope of comfort or even dignity after too much strong drink was to look forward as the boat sailed, with the wind in my face. I offered up a brief prayer for smooth sailing, then realized the only sensible recipient was a goddess with Whom I should not engage in contact.

Longing for the time, not so many months ago, when Lady Tella was all I saw welled in me. I wanted to ask Her to turn Her gaze on me again, to help me find all I needed in Her as I once had; but after everything that had happened, the request was too presumptuous. Her intervention for me at Tyra seemed impossibly long ago.

The boat launched in short order, into a mercifully-smooth current. I kept my gaze firmly directed on the river ahead. Before long my mind was running over the puzzle of Nechton, Carina, and her seemingly less-effectual heir. Was it possible the subtle, delicious energy that hung on Letitia, which lit me up when we made love, might somehow become a weapon? That it could defeat the master capable of the working in which I had nearly lost myself last night? Free of last night's insanity, I couldn't believe it. Beautiful as that energy was, deep as my sudden, unexpected ache to taste it again might be, I couldn't imagine it packing sufficient force to do more than make a wizard hunger for more.

No, Letitia must not be sent anywhere close to Nechton. I must get either her or Amien to give up this senseless plan. I must fit together a strategy for wresting the Shadow of the Sun from Nechton without her; then one or both of them might begin to see reason. Amien had been right in one regard: the mission would be best accomplished under cover of a full-scale military assault. I would need intelligence about the terrain and current situation in Macol.

After some uncounted span of time I noticed Amien standing beside me at the rail, evidently waiting for me to emerge from thought. The need for blood grabbed me by the throat again; my head was already spinning past reason, toward readiness for a duel. I grasped the rail and fought it down. What was needed now was persuasion.

"What?" he said, in a passably calm voice.

I decided to take the question at face value. "Need to know more about the situation at Macol."

The wizard grunted, nodding. "Haven't been there in years, myself. Rohini can brief us."

"That's a start," I allowed. "But we'll still need current intelligence."

Amien nodded again. "The Moot."

"Gods, not that long, I hope."

The wizard sighed. "Are you familiar with Esunertos?"

I shrugged. "I've seen it from across the river. You?"

"The same."

"We'll need intelligence there, too," I said, and glanced at him. Now I saw he misinterpreted my thinking about the campaign as willingness to assume the role he wanted. Ire flared in me again.

One battle at a time. First I must secure Letitia.

"I talked to Letitia," Amien said, looking out over the river again. "She's willing."

This time I failed to contain my anger. "No, she feels bound by the honor of her clan!"

Amien's mouth thinned; I remembered we stood on the open deck, and the wind might not cover all my words.

"She expects to die in the attempt. I think she's right," I continued, voice quieter but words growing increasingly clipped, beyond my control. "And if you could look past your feelings for Carina, you'd see it too!"

So much for persuasion. The words bubbling up behind that outburst were even less diplomatic, and he looked ready to unload a few choice phrases himself; I turned away and strode down the deck, to the rear of the boat. Letitia still sat with her back to the charthouse. The talisman dangled between her hands, winking in the sunlight; her eyes fixed on the sun, but the delicious glow I knew she could generate was absent. The boat rocked under my feet; suddenly I wanted to vomit. I swallowed hard and walked forward again.

The hours and the river unrolled with agonizing slowness; my nausea ebbed and flowed as fiercely as the Ruillin, but I clung to my scant remaining dignity and swallowed against the too-bright sun, the surprising heat, and the persistent rocking of the boat. The sun climbed overhead and dropped down to stare into my aching eyes. By the time the boat reached the confluence with the Aban and the town of Nemetona, I had realized Rohini was traveling without her House Healer. I had never met the man, but I still counted it a blow: we could have used one more competent swordsman, one more Talent for Letitia's defense. I would have to find out what the situation was, once I was sure I could hold a civil conversation.

At Nemetona, Amien and I accompanied the Tanaan towards the city gate, while Rohini and her men forded the river to camp on the Deceang side. Their political situation must be at least as bad as I had suspected, the situation of the Nemetona loyalists as precarious as the young harpist Marten had said. I wondered whether upriver traffic for the Moot and Fair was shifting Nemetona's balance in favor of the loyalists, at least temporarily, or I had once again failed to understand.

Amien stood looking after Rohini and her men, deep worry in his face: I realized he hadn't truly believed me about the plight of the Essuvians until now. I found no pleasure in being right where he had been wrong: just signaled Nuad to wait while Amien stared across the ford and offered the wizard half a smile when he finally returned his attention to our party and mounted. The final hour of daylight softened the spare terrain we rode, shadowing the blank spaces and hard edges among the rocks and scrub grass, casting the sparse cottonwoods in red-golden light that made them look more substantial than they were.

I'd heard and read about the region between the northern bank of the Aerona and the upthrust to the piedmont that loomed in the distance: in this cold, arid zone thrives the hardy silkspider, cousin to the desert silkspider that produces the fantastically fine and expensive fabrics so desired by the upper classes across the southlands. Here on the Aerona they harvest and spin the heavier spidersilk that goes into the making of mail like Letitia, Amien, and I wore, and from which rope makers craft the nearly-indestructible spidersilk ropes and cables that are indispensable to siege engines and overland campaigns. The spidersilk growers who live in these lowlands trace their ancestry to the upper tiers of Uxellian society displaced after Nechton's first would-be conquest: predecessors in a sense to Rohini's people, pushed aside when the victorious ard-righ granted the Essuvians dominion over Uxellia after Nechton's defeat. The silk growers of the Aerona lowlands share ties I had never taken the time to examine with the fine-spidersilk weavers in Ballarona and Ilnemedon, and presumably with the growers of spidersilk in Uxellia: comprising a strange, nearly separate society whose spare enclaves and dour manners repel everyone who lives outside their walls. I had never done more than skirt the edges of the Weavers' Enclave in Ilnemedon: there is no entertainment to be had within, and the place always felt strangely hostile. But the Aerona lowlands stretched quiet and still to the northeast, as if no one lived here at all.

Nemetona itself reminded me of Dromineer: the first tier of the city, situated outside the wall on the riverbank, is filled with smithies and smelters and other low temples of the smith-god, Whose power rumbled beneath the rough streets and wafted on the smoke of the forges. The energies slipped into the crevices of my still-aching head with a disturbing familiarity, troubling me further when their soft rumble eased away the pain in my skull. I couldn't find it in myself to want the headache back, nauseating as it had been, but I couldn't shake the feeling that the lack of pain was wrong.

Once I stopped my unconscious clenching of all the muscles in my head and neck, the gentle power of Goibniu's Consort, understood in Nemetona to be the goddess of the local river, bubbled through me as well. Suddenly I recognized how deeply I thirsted: a real thirst of the body, the quenching of which would revive me. We passed a little well, just outside the city gate, and I felt its restorative power even without drawing near. But I was ready neither for the humiliation of stopping the party and admitting that I needed to drink nor for the more private admission of the benevolence that had touched me, here and last night. I rode with the group through the gate.

Inside, the little neighborhood shrines we passed as we climbed towards the more refined districts at the top of the bluff bore dedications to the true gods—though I sensed that the local river goddess was simply wearing Ara's face and going right on with Her relationships with the locals, accommodating the Presence of the true gods but not sparing Them much concern. Was the Aerona the frontier for the true gods? Was Their worship only lip service, north of the line? I had lived in Ballarona for five years without noticing anything amiss: had something changed, or had I been simply too enmeshed in Lady Tella, even after Her rejection, to see? There was no way to answer the question.

The inns along the street leading up to the city center buzzed with activity: traffic for the Moot and Fair, I assumed; probably more Fair than Moot down in this area. Presumably the tiarna, the righthe, and the people who followed them in hopes of making sales or securing patronage headed for the top of the bluff. Street vendors and buskers narrowed the way; meandering people clogged the traffic further. Even on horseback, we encountered spots in which we had to slow to accommodate the mayhem. I didn't see Loeg or any of his crew, and wondered whether we had finally outpaced them. Any sane person would have rested at Presatyn after last night.

In the city center at the top of the bluff, the atmosphere shifted again. This circle felt comfortable and right: suffused with accustomed energies and the aromas of foods I understood. The streets here seemed calm after the commotion in the roads below, but we still had to try three inns before we found one with sufficient space for all of us: the Brown Bull, a sprawling solidly-constructed edifice of three stories with an honest-to-the-gods portico rather than the sort of haphazard porch typical of garden-variety inns. That exterior and the richly appointed receiving room told me all I needed to know: we would pay far too much for everything tonight. I couldn't have cared less. The walls were solid wood; the fireplaces in the rooms would be decently-sized, ready for the merest beckoning of a wizard or strike of a tinderbox for fire to set them alight; two beds stood prepared to accommodate four men. I would have a glass of brandy tonight: not because I needed it, just because I could. I gratefully gave over the care of my horse to the busy but more-than-competent stable staff and carried my possessions up to the room.

Somehow I had managed to beat Tuiri and Fiacha here: the utter peace of the room enveloped me. For a moment I just stood, drinking in the quiet; then the door opened behind me and Amien entered.

"Civilization," I sighed.

"Too little of that lately," he agreed, depositing his burdens. He turned and shut the door, and stood staring at me as if gathering his thoughts. I'd seen that look enough times that dread of what he would finally say erupted, surprising me. I maintained a calm face.

"You would do well," he said at last, in the controlled tones that any Aballo apprentice knew to presage serious consequences, "to leave my personal history out of our strategic discussions. Whatever relationship you imagine I had with Carina a Ériu—"

The door opened; Tuiri and Fiacha walked in, engaged in some lighthearted conversation that immediately stopped.

"—rest assured it does not enter into what I do this month," Amien finished, face still and eyes intent.

I stood amazed, staring at the wizard. Behind him, our Tanaan roommates had frozen into utter stillness. Amien's mouth twitched; he turned on his heel and stalked out to the corridor: closing the door behind him, leaving me staring at the place where he had been. I shook off the paralysis, sighed, and dumped my things in a different corner, standing and staring at them in the vain hope that coherent mental function would resume.

"Are you... all right, Lord?" Tuiri said. "You're looking a little green again."

I sighed. "I'm fine," I said, walking to the window and looking out to the street. "Thank you."

"As you say, Lord," Fiacha said, in tones that said I was completely transparent but they were prepared to accept the lie as not particularly relevant to them. I sighed again, nodded, and took myself to the bathing room.

The place was more civilized than I had dared hope: it might have been Ilnemedon. An attendant greeted me as I entered. He ushered me to one of a dozen small private bathing chambers, mixed the water for me, and compensated for my forgetting my own razor with one from a long rank of gleaming implements on a shelf; he even worked some incomprehensible magic on my clothes while I bathed. I settled gratefully into the hot water and steam, soaking up civilization.

Last night unfolded itself in my mind, moments and memories as disordered as if thrown into the air. Letitia awash in moonlight, her soft power casting a glow that caressed my skin and lit up my mind. Clinging to the pitching deck of the boat out of Ballarona, lightning and waves crashing across the deck and Nechton's magnificent black spell enveloping me. Letitia's gaze holding me fast as she pulled the thong from my hair. The world-disordering incandescent moment of slipping into her mystery. Amien watching me as if he'd already named me his War-Lord, as if the only details he couldn't predict were the time and place of the duel with Nechton that he planned for me. Amien's lips drawing back to bare his teeth when I uttered Aechering's name.

The Shadow Working. The Shadow of the Sun. How had the former created the latter? Memory bounced me into an ill-lit corner of Aballo's library: the aromas of leather bindings and ancient parchment filling the air, Aechering's ideas my mind. I could still see the page, Aechering's spidery crabbed writing and his absentminded habits with the pen. And the words.

Hakaid the shadow of the Sun
And open the Abyss
Let the heir of Tílimya
Woo the Virgin Star
Join the Sun and the Moon in Darkness
Thus results the Union of Silver and Gold
Blend the Essences in the vessel of life
The Elixir cythe
Earth, Fire, Water and Air to command or release at will
In the Crucible where pain is ecstasy and Death is Life
Hidden is plain
The reach of the shadow of the Sun is infinite

The imagery of it took me, as ever. How could a man trained to unravel the meanings of esoteric texts not adore Aechering? His puzzles are all but impenetrable, but the secrets he presents the persistent reader never fail to open the mind to previously-unsuspected wonders. The Sun has a shadow, and it may be the key to everything. Absent this working, how would anyone ever suspect?

If only someone living knew what *hakaid* meant. I wondered how Nechton might have cracked open this working without the proper translation—or where he'd found the meaning.

But it was only an intellectual exercise. It is one thing to read Aechering's work, another to practice from it; even at my most immoderate I hadn't done the latter. It was beyond contemplation now. I pushed the verses from my mind, shaved and washed, and pulled on blessedly fresh clothes. And at last I felt like myself, or the version of me who dwelled in Ilnemedon in peacetime: clean, presentable, hair hanging free, my hand comfortable without a blade; ready to face both my companions and whatever subset of polite society occupied the inn's main room.

A harpist was already playing as I entered: some original composition for the instrument alone that provided suitable background to dining. I didn't recognize him, and he didn't seem to notice me: I settled gratefully at the long table occupied by my companions, taking in the pristine cloths and fine crystal glasses on the table and the road-weary smiles of the people around me. Iminor shot me a glare as I sat, on general principle it seemed; but Letitia met my gaze with a calm mask and eyes that lit with recent memory, then answered my cordial smile with one of her own.

Yes, I thought. We could do this. Discretion would be key.

"They're serving beef tonight," Nuad said to me. "We thought you'd approve...?"

"Dear gods, yes," I sighed. "Thank you."

"Where's Amien?" Letitia asked.

I shrugged. "You haven't seen him? He stalked off in a bit of a snit a while ago..." I shrugged again. "I'm sure he'll turn up when he's ready to look at me."

Letitia nodded pensively, glancing around the room again: I realized she must be waiting for him to rebuild the wards she'd wrecked last night. My imagination stood ready with a vision of what it would be to do the job myself; I fought it off, but found myself tingling anyway.

Shortly dinner arrived, the beef accompanied by early spring greens that must have been brought in on ice from much farther south; mixed winter squash; fresh, hot, proper bread; and an entirely respectable Deceangi red. The flavors of properly cooked foods proved even more intoxicating than the wine; I was struck, as always after too long on the road, by wonder at the fact that I had taken such things for granted not too long ago. The Tanaan were somewhat more cautious in their enjoyment, but before long they ate with gusto as well.

After dinner the harpist gave way to a group playing dance music; no sooner had they struck the first chord than Iminor stood at Letitia's elbow, inviting her to dance. She allowed him to hand her up with a courtly smile that didn't quite reach her eyes. Tru and Easca rose to dance with Mattiaci and Nuad. I ordered a glass of brandy and sat savoring it while I watched the dancers, Tanaan and human alike, step and twirl to the music. Eventually Amien arrived, settled in the empty spot remaining beside me, greeted me and our Tanaan roommates with a civil nod but no actual conversation, and ordered a brandy of his own. Tuiri and Fiacha rose and crossed the room to cut in for a turn at the dance.

"I spoke to our friends," Amien said, still not looking at me, and I knew he meant Rohini and the Essuvians. "They need to travel the south bank tomorrow; Mumhan is mostly closed to them, especially west of the Aban."

I nodded. "I imagine Granniu's not much better."

"They didn't get on with the Weavers *before* things got this bad."

It was only to be expected: the Essuvians had supplanted the Weavers in their own land. It would be too great a mental gymnastic to assign the blame properly, to a group of frightened righthe four centuries removed. I thought about the silk-growing community in Uxellia, the nexus of the Weavers' closed society, still living in the midst of lands that had once been theirs; and two seemingly-unrelated strands of events wove together in my mind.

"What was the extent of their involvement in the fall of Macol? The Uxellian Weavers, I mean."

The wizard shrugged. "Ask Rohini."

"I wonder if she knows."

The wizard shot me a forbidding look and returned his attention to the dance.

Tru and Tuiri crossed from the dance floor to the table, smiling. She kissed him on the cheek as he settled, then turned her bright gaze on me.

"Lord, would you like to dance?"

Unexpected emotion welled in me at her sweetness. I mustered a smile.

"Thank you," I said, rose and let her lead me across the room, her lean strong hand folded around my own as if she thought I might think better of it and bolt. I hadn't danced since the death of the ard-righ: Ilnemedon had mourned his death for a full month; and during the days before I left I'd had no stomach for the tentatively-resuming social scene, where I knew speculation about the Moot and the election of the next ard-righ would be the twelve-night's obsession.

Tru was as lightfooted on the dance floor as on the battlefield, as lean and sinewy and surprisingly delightful in my arms as she looked; she met my gaze in an astonishing intimacy wholly unfraught with dangerous overtones as we danced, so honest in her regard that a knot formed in my throat. She didn't let me lead so much as dance with me, which I surmised was a Tanaan peculiarity. I had never before considered how much of the way we dance arises from our roles off the dance floor, how the expectation that the man will set the tempo and choose the next steps would have a completely different meaning to a people of whom the women are in charge. I wondered if she expected me to let her lead.

"If you were at home for Bealtan, how would you spend the Eve?" she asked, sometime during our second dance.

Home. I shoved aside thoughts of how it would have been in Tellan this year, realized I would have been at the Moot anyway, finally concluded she had meant a much simpler question.

"In Ilnemedon?" I said, and laid my cheek against her soft hair. "A party, probably. You know most Bealla don't celebrate the rite, not the way the Danaan do." There would be any number of illicit observances, but they generally come down to simple sex rather than the sort of sacred practice that humans used to make of the holiday, and which Tanaan still do.

"What?" she blurted, drawing back to look into my face. "Then how do you—?" She shook her head. "That's very sad."

"Yes, it is." A blasphemous opinion, that; but tonight it seemed true. I had never before considered how reserving the rite to the wizards and the righthe cuts people off from the gods, diminishes the experience of what is properly a truly holy day. "But I will look forward to raising a glass with you."

"It will be very strange, so far from home," Tru said thoughtfully.

I nodded, thinking how much stranger it would be for Letitia, who had expected to marry and ascend her throne the following morning. How pleasant the idea of that festival had seemed less than a month ago, and how the thought of her marrying Iminor made ice form in my chest now.

Fool, I thought, and changed the topic. "What do you think of the Beallan realms thus far?"

"Have we visited your home yet?" Tru said carefully.

I smiled, shaking my head. "I lived in Ballarona for a time, and I worked a job or two in Dromineer; but these days I live in Ilnemedon, farther south."

"But that is not your home, either," Tru said, perspicacious grey eyes on mine.

I shrugged, and offered her the cue that should have resulted in a neat twirl, but which just confused her. After a few steps we regained our rhythm.

Tru nodded. "Irisa isn't my home, but I like it well enough."

Suddenly Easca stood beside us, grinning.

"*Excuse me*," she said in carefully-enunciated Ilesian. I withheld a laugh; Tru's sudden grin deepened the temptation. They bowed elaborately to one another, laughing until half the eyes in the room were fixed on us; Tru planted a light kiss on my cheek and stepped away. I smiled and drew Easca into my arms.

"Thank you," I said.

Easca grinned. "Some of the knights had a wager going about whether you could dance at all."

I laughed. "Who lost?"

She cast me a coy smirk. "I don't think it would be appropriate for me to say."

"I'm just disappointed I couldn't get into the pool!"

Easca danced in the same way as Tru: nimble, graceful, with no intention of ceding me control. Her bright amber eyes met mine frankly, the respect with which she had always addressed me melting into true fondness.

"I'm actually a very good dancer," I said, "in the Beallan style. I could offer you any number of supporting witnesses from Ballarona and Ilnemedon..."

She laughed, then looked thoughtful. "The Beallan style?"

"On this side of the mountains, the man is expected to lead the dance."

Astonishment flickered in Easca's eyes, but then she laughed again. "Of course!"

"It's up to the man to set the pace, to choose the steps—it's all done with cues, pressures of the hand or hip—"

"And the woman is expected to both figure out what he means and go along with it," Easca finished, as if the scheme were perfectly insane.

"Well, how is it done in the Four Realms?" I asked.

Easca looked thoughtful; after a moment she smiled. "The dances are much more... codified. There's no need for someone to decide what steps will be followed: it's all decided in advance. Partners can exchange cues about small decisions—" A grin broke across her face. "To tell you the truth, and if you ever repeat this I'll deny it, the way a man gives and receives cues is one of the main ways a woman decides about him. Especially during the Bealtan season."

I laughed. "So how am I doing?"

For a second her face was a mask of shock; then she laughed so hard she made us both stumble. "Oh, you're impossible. You clearly want to be in charge of everything."

"Well, of course," I said, laughing too. "But I know exactly what I'm doing."

Easca laughed again, shaking her head. "Well, that's one thing when it's just a tumble, isn't it? But on a twelvenight when you may be picking the father of your child...? No, a woman needs someone who can be relied on to cooperate."

"To listen, you mean," I said, smiling.

She shrugged. "That's a matter of taste. Would you choose a partner who always listened?"

I thought about this. "Always *listened*? Yes. Whether she always followed my cues..."

"Oh, I suspect you want that, too," Easca said lightly. "No matter how amusing it might be to play with a woman you couldn't rule, when it came down to the serious stuff..."

"Ah, well," I sighed, mock-regretful. "Then I will simply have to content myself with toasting your nuptials, whenever that occurs."

Easca smiled. "Don't hold your breath."

Halfway back to the table, I heard someone call my name. I paused, seeking the voice, and recognized Suibne Taidgh, third son of the Granniu righ, with whom I had shared innumerable nights in gambling halls and ballrooms across Ilnemedon.

"Ellion Tellan!" he said again, grinning; I wove among the tables to meet him. I had never done more than shake his hand in Ilnemedon, but here it was perfectly obvious that we must embrace; even as we stepped back he let a hand linger on my arm, as if we had grown much closer in our absence. It felt absolutely, inexplicably genuine.

"Where the hell have you been?" Suibne said, moss-green eyes intent in the midst of his cordial grin.

I shrugged. "Out and about."

Suibne gave me a sidelong look. "On a pleasure outing with a party of Tanaan and the Prince of the Aballo Order."

I manufactured a laugh. I'd sat at enough gaming tables with Suibne to know how well he read people, and of course there was no concealing the Tanaan; but I hadn't realized he was acquainted with Amien. Or had he deduced it?

"Oh, yes, it's been nonstop delight," I said. "Why are you traveling so late?"

Suibne shrugged. "Coran Mourne finally left Ilnemedon two days ago. Of course no one would leave until Himself did, but everyone was already in Fair mode. It's been nothing but parties!" His affable expression didn't flicker, but he grasped my elbow and steered me out of the center of the room, dropping his voice. "You're escorting Herself to the Moot?"

I glanced at him, maintaining the smile. "Where did you hear that?"

Suibne waved dismissively. "I have *eyes*."

I allowed myself a chuckle. "That you do, my friend."

"So?"

I sighed. "It would be inappropriate..."

"Then I have heard nothing. I never saw her at all. But you should stable your horses here and fly with me; the last thing you want is to ride upriver in the midst of gods-only-know-who, and I've got an airship big enough for all your friends."

"Oh, I wish we could," I said. And I did: an airship wouldn't reach Teamair any faster than we would, but Suibne would be well-rested and safe throughout the journey. As long as we didn't climb into the basket with him. "But we expect to need our horses after the Moot, so it really doesn't make sense..."

Suibne shot me an assessing look, covering it with a smile. "Ah, well, then, stop at Sucello on your way. I'm sure everyone would appreciate a night behind good walls."

I wanted to stop and stare at him, but there were too many eyes in the room: I forced myself to continue moving, letting him steer me towards the table at which my companions sat, while the enormity of what he had offered reverberated in my head. Sucello was the final place on the road to Teamair in which a loyalist might hope for any sort of security. The city occupies the narrow neck of land in which the headwaters of the Elen, the western shore of the Nanno, and the road to Teamair converge; and the Granniu righthe have a long tradition of holding that passage neutral and safe for Moot traffic, no matter what tensions may stand among travelers on the pilgrimage. The fortress itself enjoys commanding placement as well as excellent construction; only a fool would attempt its conquest. Any guest of the Taidgh family can expect to enjoy a night of complete safety.

But we weren't just any guests, and Suibne was sharp enough to be perfectly aware what he was inviting: not only Letitia and her escort but the enemies pursuing her.

"My friend, your hospitality is legend," I said finally.

"My pleasure entirely," he said, and then we arrived at the table, just as Letitia and Iminor returned from the dance. The rest of the Tanaan were already there, and they all looked curiously at Suibne.

"My lady," Suibne said to Letitia, offering her an elaborate bow and a roguish grin.

Letitia glanced at me. I chuckled: flirtation was as automatic to Suibne as breathing; what could be more compelling than a chance to take a run at a Tana, a royal no less?

"Letitia, allow me to present my friend Suibne," I said. "We have many of the same friends in Ilnemedon."

Speculation flickered in her eyes for a second, but she seemed to understand, or maybe she had been taught: when royals are introduced by first names only, everything is understood to be outside the purview of everyday rules. If I did not claim royal rights for her, neither could royal obligations be put on her in this meeting. I wondered whether she had absorbed the significance of my equally-nonspecific introduction of Suibne.

"My friend," I said to Suibne, "these are Letitia and Iminor—and these are our friends Nuad, Mattiaci, Tru, Easca—" Suibne offered Tru and Easca equally dandy bows, making me smile again. "—Ogma, Tuiri, Fiacha—and I believe you know Amien."

"A pleasure to meet you, sian," Suibne said to Amien.

"Likewise," the wizard said, and glanced at me.

"Suibne just invited us to stay with him at Sucello on our way to the Fair," I said to the wizard. "Naturally I said *yes*."

This time Amien smiled. "Your hospitality is legend. It's been some time since I've seen your…?"

Suibne laughed. "My father will be delighted to have you as our guests." He glanced at Letitia again. "As will I."

She gave him a courtly smile. "I'll look forward to it. Amien—" She glanced at the wizard; he nodded.

"It's been a pleasure to meet you, Suibne," she said, and extended a hand. He took it up in a well-practiced gesture, converting the offered handshake to a kiss on the wrist. Letitia just smiled again, glanced at Amien, and walked out with the wizard on her heels.

"Will you sit with us?" I said to Suibne. "The brandy's decent."

Suibne smiled and settled in Amien's seat, signaling the man who served our table for a brandy. "Thank you. When did you leave?"

I thought about the question. "Beginning of last month, more or less."

This earned me a look of surprise. "Seems longer."

I shrugged. "Mourning started at Ardan, remember."

"Yes," Suibne said, as if I'd solved a mystery. "That's right. And afterward all anybody talked about was the Moot. *Who will muster against the Bard? Who will be ard-righ?* Of course the only proper answer to *that* question was *Coran Mourne.*"

I shifted in my seat, restless.

"At least the betting pools were more interesting," Suibne continued. "I think I spent more time in gambling halls than anywhere else during the last twelvenight, just to get away from all those people telling one another what they wanted to hear."

"Well, who do you expect?" I said, mostly because I didn't want him to ask my opinion.

Suibne shrugged. "Expect? Coran. Like for it…?" He shrugged again. "None of them inspire me. I can't decide whether Cooley's a fool or in league with demons; I *know* Conwy's a fool, and I worry that he'd haul the entire muster east to protect the Ruillin; Coran's smart enough, but…" He sighed; I controlled the impulse to rise and walk away, wondering why I had thought opening this vein was a good idea.

"It just feels as if we're waiting for a candidate who won't come to the Moot at all," Suibne continued. It occurred to me how very different this was from our usual conversations, which tended towards the topics of happenings at the gaming tables and who was dueling over what offense. "As if we're waiting for Lugh Lámfhada, and all we've got is…" He shook his head, then cast me a quizzical look. "What?"

I smiled a little, shaking my head. "Strange to sit with you in this place and talk about these things. Everything is out of sorts this month."

Suibne glanced up the length of the table, as if he had just remembered our companions.

"Yes," he said to me, then distributed his gaze around the table again, mischief playing over his face. "I'm sorry, I've been remiss," he said to the Tanaan. "Human politics bore even us. Let's talk about something more interesting. What is the rakehell of Ilnemedon like when he's not at home?"

I groaned, feeling myself blush; then relief swept over me. "They don't speak Ilesian, Suibne."

But Easca cast me a glance comprised of equal parts mischief and speculation, and said carefully, "*Rakehell?*"

Iminor translated, smug; I glanced away, blush deepening and competing with an inexplicable desire to laugh; Easca repeated the question in Tanaan for the benefit of the other knights. Immediately they were all staring at me. After a second Mattiaci laughed; a second later it had spread to all of them. Suibne watched them: grinning, but a wonder in his eyes that he forgot to conceal when he turned his gaze on me.

"Am I to infer that you are… *well-behaved* on the other side of the mountains?" he said.

I shrugged. "We've been busy. You know."

Suibne laughed. "This is going to completely destroy your reputation! No women fighting over you?"

"That doesn't happen—"

"No *duels*?"

"Suibne," I said.

"No *drinking*?"

"I wouldn't go that far."

"Well, thank the gods for that." Suibne laughed again, looking up the table at the Tanaan. "Thank you. You have made this trip worthwhile! Ellion, I'll be holding this over your head for years to come."

I found myself smiling. "Oh dear gods."

Suibne rose, raised his glass to the group, had another sip of brandy and set it aside. "Safe travels, friends. I'll see you at Sucello."

I rose too, meeting his dark-eyed gaze; he grinned and embraced me again. "A pleasure."

"Likewise, you rogue."

He laughed and stepped away from the table; upstairs, in the inn's eastern wing, Amien drew up the power of the earth on which Nemetona stood to encircle Letitia in safety. Not only the familiar earth-energies but the wild power of the smith-god blasted through me; my vision was suddenly full of Amien's hands hovering over Letitia's narrow feet and the emerald glow of the ward's first tendrils unfolding into physical being, as if I were seeing the operation through Amien's eyes. A dozen mingled flavors of need ripped through me; I wrenched myself free of all of it, caught myself against the back of the chair Suibne had occupied.

"Fouzh," I heard myself say; I straightened up, grasping after ordinary consciousness. I blinked; my companions' faces swam into view, most of them watching me with varying degrees of dismay.

"Well, then," I said to no one in particular. "I'm going for a walk."

Outside, cold wind raked the top of the bluff, sending clouds scudding in front of Arliyn where she hung less than an hour above the horizon. I paced the road we had traveled on our way in, south towards the river and the lower circles of the city. It would have required the merest shift of attention to know exactly what Amien was doing: to see his strong, heavily-veined hands tracing paths of protection around Letitia's silken body, to know the tingle of summoned power against my skin even at this distance. Instead I pushed the awareness away, casting about for something mundane to which I might fix my eyes and mind.

But the roads at the top of the bluff were quiet; the only traffic was men walking from one inn to another in search of some new entertainment and the comings and goings of entertainers and rich men's staff. I flung myself down the steep climb to Nemetona's commercial district, where the Fair-month revel spilled out of the inns to the street. Here the buskers and street-vendors held sway, and the throng of people cushioned the blows of the wind; but it was all too ordinary to focus on. The jostling traffic clogged where some busker had set up in the middle of an intersection; the only way open led down a side street, towards quieter residences and craftsmen's closed shops. I wove through the narrow opening, escaped into the quiet of the minor lane, strode down the darkened way as if I had some destination in mind, watching Arlyn hide and peep behind the roofs. The tug of Amien's working had gone quiet, but I found myself listening for more.

I couldn't remember what it was to hold myself closed, to live behind an invisible wall that shunted aside all but the most persistent arcane energies. I hadn't felt this naked to power since my initiate. And unless I could persuade someone whose opinion mattered that Letitia should turn aside, I was bound for the Moot, where every wizard in the human realms would gather to lace the air with so many disparate arcane energies that I would twitch as if bound by a lover and tweaked to within a fraction of release. It would be only a matter of time before Amien's scheme for me to step up as his War-Lord seemed like sense. Already it felt like the come-hither stare of a voluptuous but utterly indiscreet woman: I knew following the impulse would end in disaster, but the lure was just so damned strong…

No. I had made a vow. I had the capacity to choose. No matter what other mistakes I made, I would not draw power. My value to Letitia lay in my ability to sort through all the intelligence, whether military or arcane, and find a way to keep her safe without compromising her honor. I could do that without violating my vow; I must rededicate myself to that path.

At the road's left hand, up against the wall of the bluff, stood a little shrine: I smelled the water of a sacred well, felt the gentle power that arises in a place where people regularly pray. I turned and stepped down the narrow walkway, as if I might find Lady Tella here, as if drawing Her about me might ward off my awareness of all the things I couldn't afford to touch. But She wasn't here: niches around the well were populated with votary images on which the name *Aerona* lingered, and only one of them bore any resemblance to Ara, even though it was Her name chiseled into the rock. The seductive, benevolent Presence I had touched at the well outside Nemetona's wall and in Presatyn last night gathered around me: not the familiar majesty of Lady Tella, merely something sweet and welcoming and safe. The energy of the well beckoned, inviting me into that peace, offering me a flavor of strength unlike anything an Aballo wizard had ever called on; instead I hurried out to the street again.

Farther from Nemetona's central road, across another street whose name I didn't know, the neighborhood I walked shifted again: ornate half-timbering gave way to squared-off buildings with flat roofs and shuttered windows. There was no wall here, but I recognized the architecture: I had stumbled into Weavers' streets. Everything lay quiet under soft moonlight; oddly familiar energies teased at my memory, driving me forward in search of explanation or source. The smart thing to do would be to turn around, to make my way back to the inn; a rebellious, resentful sense that curiosity was my only yearning that could be gratified made it impossible to lay aside that meager satisfaction, and I followed an aroma that was not physical through the quiet, twisting streets.

Was this the energy that had always repelled me in Ilnemedon? Tonight it felt exotic, like a spice I had enjoyed on some long-ago spree and only half remembered. Eventually I found it hanging all around me, running beneath the surface of my awareness, in much the same way the energies of the smith-god did. But this wasn't the smith-god: this energy walked the earth and reached up towards the heavens, tapping roots into subterranean powers outside the smith-god's purview and spreading searching fingers among the stars, weaving structures both subtle and mundane. There was danger here, but also hidden knowledge that made my breath catch with curiosity, made it hard to remember why I shouldn't just open myself and learn.

At the end of a road, against the city wall, I came upon another shrine. An immense, ancient oak stood at the center, gnarled of branch, split and scarred with innumerable lightnings, but with new leaves unfurling on every branch and shimmering in the cold wind like dark reflections of the stars. I tasted old sacrifices here, lives spilled out to feed the god, energies that had opened twisting paths beyond the mundane realm, unfolding—in a sudden rush of recognition it all unfolded—in much the same way Nechton's working on the Ruillin had last night. This space, these energies: they belonged to Nechton, even though the name hanging on all the devotions here was *Esus*.

For a fraction of time too small to measure, it all came together in stunning, blindingly blasphemous logic: wittingly or not, the Weavers looked to Nechton. The title *Avengers of Esus* was no mere conceit; the devotionals to Esus that followed in the wake of the Bard were no coincidence. Nechton Glyndwr, the Bard's Wizard, had somehow managed to become Esus, somehow tapped the power of a god.

I shook myself, actually shaking my head as if that might clear it. That couldn't be right. No human, not even a wizard, could become a god: gods are born, not made.

And yet I could almost taste the possibility of it. If a wizard can tap the energies at a sacred site, many of which arise from the devotions of the people who worship the gods, then why should it not be possible to tap directly into the power, to assume the god's Mantle? It wouldn't make a man a god; but it would make for good theatre, irrevocably change the political landscape, possibly even raise enough power to be useful.

The only thing that would prevent such a scheme from working would be the existence of the god. And therein lay the puzzle. The true religion teaches that the old gods are figments, constructs of imagination worshipped in ignorance and error; that Their appearances in the histories are misapprehensions or conflations or outright lies. That Esus, widely worshipped though He had been, was as mythical as the rest. Two months ago, I had been as certain of this as any adherent of the true religion; but since then I had tasted the power of a number of gods, on both sides of the mountains, even while Lady Tella held

Herself aloof. It was not as easy to dismiss the possibility of Esus as a living, breathing entity as it had once been. Nechton could not successfully feign becoming Him if He truly existed: not and survive for long.

Was it possible, then, that Nechton drew on the power of this old god the way a wizard of the true religion can call on the power sites, or in certain cases the gods Themselves, of the religion to which true believers look? That there was a network of sites dedicated to Esus, created and in some cases maintained by His worshipers even after His defeat by Lady Tella at Esunertos?

Without conscious decision I found myself stepping into the heart of the shrine, to stand in the lattice of shadows beneath the oak's limbs. From this angle the oak stretched impossibly huge, laying claim to spaces far higher and broader than any single tree might occupy. Arliyn hung among the branches; new leaves and stars mingled shimmering in the cold air. I stretched out a hand, laid my palm against the trunk, fingers spreading across a broad, old scar left by a lightning strike. The naked wood lay smooth and surprisingly warm beneath my hand. The energy of the place encompassed me, or I encompassed it, and as we saw one another I realized the warmth beneath my hand was a reflection of my presence: the reality of the Presence in which I stood was much colder and deeper, not Nechton but some Source he understood and which I had thus far only tasted. A vision came to me of hanging bound to this tree for the infinite and momentary space of nine nights, sacrificing self to Self: becoming this energy, learning the truths I sensed hidden within its scarred heart. If this Presence was Esus, that was the sacrifice He required; if I might become Him, He might also become Me. The perfect symmetry of it made the moment spread out to infinite, eternal stillness. The power tasted like rapture, but it was the understanding I truly craved.

Behind me, someone stepped into the shrine: I sensed the extra presence in the energy shimmering throughout my being more than through senses mundane, as the touch of his feet interrupted the circuit between me and this Being the common folk call Esus. I turned, looking at him and he at me, taking in the situation through that timelessness in which I stood. The old man, the broad flat planes of Weavers' blood in his face and dark-blond hair faded to a mix of grey and brown, served this shrine in the way a druid of the true religion might serve a shrine of Lord Ilesan or Lady Tella. Not a Talent of the sort who might draw power and do something with it, he was nevertheless sensitive enough to understand the import of my presence here and sworn to some commitment that required him to eliminate the threat I represented. The long knife in his hand glinted with cold starlight; I realized, far too late, that the veneer of civilization at the top of the bluff had lulled me into laying aside my sword. It had been only appropriate up there; here, I was no better equipped for this encounter than my opponent.

In this moment of expanded consciousness, it hardly troubled me. I saw, with the god's cold gaze, the symmetry of what would unfold: the way whatever blood was spilled would feed Him; His disinterest in the details of which blood He drank. I reached unhurriedly into my boot, eyes still on the guardian, and drew my knife. There was no need to speak.

He was fast, as deceptively wiry-strong as a whip of hardy spidersilk; I had probably killed no more men than he. His grey eyes saw past the façade of ethics I held up to the world and myself, straight into the black depths of my soul, and neither condemned nor endorsed it. My native power was not cause for fear, rather potential food for the god—and the reason he ultimately left enough of an opening for my knife in his heart. As if it had been not blades but Wills that settled the contest. He voiced only a small noise of surprised pain, dispassionate eyes meeting mine in the split-second before he sagged in my grasp. I pulled the knife free, and—prompted by some geas or compulsion I couldn't name—slit his throat, spilling his blood over the roots of the tree. The god would have His due; I had no idea how to reconcile what I knew to be necessary in this moment with what I ordinarily believed to be true.

I wiped the blade on his sleeve and sheathed it; I stepped back, head threatening to unhinge from my neck with the power that suddenly reverberated in this space. And I understood: all unwitting I had gained the right to possess this place, encompass this energy, sacrifice myself and master all the knowledge the Presence here had to offer. My companions would leave me for lost; they would never find me so far in the depths of the city; I wouldn't care. A new portion of my life would begin, like the next song in a cycle, culminating in the inevitable battle when Nechton arrived to re-take this source.

But I couldn't do that. I was sworn to the true gods, tonight's—and this morning's—sacrifices not withstanding, and Letitia wasn't safe here: not in this city, nor in any city in which either the Bard held sway or the Weavers held outposts. We needed to get Letitia out of here with all possible haste, to join Rohini and the Essuvians on the opposite bank of the river and put as much distance between Letitia and these people to whom Nechton was attuned as possible. But I didn't need to walk down to the bottom of the bluff to know the city gate was closed. The tiarn who held this place doubtless still thought he could lock the danger out.

With a last glance up at the impossible spread of the tree, I left the shrine and retraced my steps towards the top of the bluff: walking at top speed but resisting the temptation to break into an attention-attracting run, wishing I had figured this out before my companions retired for the night. I could only hope Nuad had not been as lulled as I by the familiar trappings of civilization and had required the knights to set watches.

The side streets lay as quiet and still as they had on the way out; the mayhem on the main road continued unabated. But now I saw it differently: the innocent-seeming revel was a potential cover for a kharr assassin or Weaver spy; every mummer's troupe or itinerant puppet-show might harbor the Bard's traveling shrine to Esus in the back of a cart. Now, finally, I read the threat under which Nemetona lay in the buskers' satires and the amulets to illicit gods affixed to rough leather neck-thongs. And at last I wondered: were the rumors of the threat to Nemetona based solely on some Weavers' plan to fell the place from within—or should I have been watching for the arrival of the Bard? He could have arrived here by airship, as early as tonight; it would be easy for some kharr insider to bribe the right person to unlock the gate and let him in. If someone in the throng through which I wove and pressed had marked me as a member of Letitia's party on the way up this road earlier, they could follow me to discover which inn she occupied now.

How careless had I been, assuming that once we left the Ruillin we would outpace the rumors. Suibne had known exactly who Letitia was, without being told. At least his loyalties could be counted on: he was royal. Commoners might be seduced by the lies the Bard peddled, but loyalists knew what the man was really selling: anarchy and mob rule, the replacement of the true religion with the worship of Esus.

Suddenly, there in the midst of the crowd, I finally grasped the depth of the Bard of Arcadia's—and Nechton's—intent: they planned to turn the true religion back on itself, to elevate Esus into the true gods' place—with Nechton as the Prince of Esus's shadow of the Aballo Order, or maybe His avatar—and the Bard of Arcadia His ard-righ. It wasn't just about deposing the righthe: they intended to overthrow the true gods.

On the heels of that realization came another: would I but take the initiation Esus offered, I might supplant Nechton, might become Esus's Prince or avatar myself. And I would have no need of a Bard to play ard-righ: I could assume those duties as well, both roles united in one man in a way that would result in far profounder strength for that once-and-future god. The elegance of it commandeered my mind, sending ripples of desire into my core: for the understanding that dark god offered, for the heady energies that would become mine, for the unexpected fulfillment of the promise of my stars.

What if this was the thing they had portended all along?

Abruptly the desire rippling through me became a tempest; I could barely see through the need, could no longer force my legs to move towards the top of the bluff, where I must lay the offered power aside. Had I not been promised these things? If Lady Tella would not give them to me, was it wrong to turn to One Who would?

I knew the answer. I had made a vow that bound me to the true gods, even when Their well-deserved rejection stung. I had vowed to lay aside the practice of magic, knowing that such cold hunger for power as I was exhibiting tonight would send me inevitably into evil. And oh, how right had I been! The man who stood in the shrine to Esus and met that god's cold uncaring Eye with an equally uncaring soul: he was the true essence of me. Not only would I violate the vows I had made at Aballo and Tellan, I would utterly negate the trust Letitia had placed on me. And if I didn't protect her, who would? Take this step now, and I would find her blood on my hands as surely as that of the shrine's guardian. And of my parents. I could have this power—or some semblance of honor. I could not have both.

The revel swirled around me, traffic in the street flowing past me as if I were a rock in a river. Potential subjects they were, potential tools for gaining the throne I had been denied, potential weights on my soul. I would not be that man; I must remember how to be the man who could rescue Letitia, could encompass all the things her enemies would throw against her. I must leave this promise down here in the lower districts and accept the diminishment that would come as I climbed that steep ascent. And if I took new understanding with me, I could not share it: not without confessing what I had done to gain it, not without confessing the black depths of my desires. How would that understanding change anyone's actions, after all? It must be enough that I would make it possible for the loyalists to thwart their enemies: there was no need for me to endure the humiliation of the truth.

I would have offered Lady Tella a pact: my protection of Her interests in exchange for Her protection of mine. But that is not how gods operate: I understood that only too well. Instead I forced my legs to move again, climbed the steep rise to the illusory safety of the bluff: to ensure Nuad had set up watches and sit down to conduct my own, to monitor the aether for arcane signatures only I would recognize, until someone unlocked the gate at the foot of the city and I could herd all those clueless potential victims to whom I had bound my heart across the ford.

Chapter 27
Seeing in the Dark

From histories that predate the Transition from Hy-Breasaíl, from tales of men who walked the lands ruled by the Hy-Breasaílian gods, we know something of the Eternal Realms. While the Danaan aspire to eternal reward in the House of Donn, on this side of the mountains we hope to reach Tír inna n-Óc. And while a person who is neither heroic nor particularly evil will spend some time in the Grey Lands, the Fields of Asphodel, before returning to the lands of the living for another life and trying again to achieve the reward—sages also tell us of a third destination after judgment, for those who are truly evil.

That place is Tílimya's Abyss, and it is named for its lord, the ancient god Who imprisons and metes out the punishments of those so consigned. When Cron and the gods of Hy-Breasaíl were defeated by Their Children and consigned to the Abyss, it was Tílimya Who held Them there. Tradition holds that when our gods arrived here and defeated the Ones Who had gone before, those defeated gods were consigned to the Abyss as well. Presumably Esus is among them. So too are murderers and oathbreakers, those who do violence to women and noncombatants, and others the gods judge too evil to be allowed back into the world.

There is no escape from the Realm of Tílimya, which is surrounded by the flaming river of blood called Dóiteán, encircled by triple walls of adamantine, and guarded by a hydra with fifty black, gaping jaws. Within those walls are only the Abyss and the Fortress that houses the Well of Tílimya, whose waters are capable of restoring a man who drinks them to life. The only way for someone who crosses the river Dóiteán, whether living or dead, to return to the realms of the living is to persuade the Well's Guardian that he should be allowed to drink. Fail in that endeavor, and even a hero will be consigned for eternity to the torments of the Abyss. Even, we are told, a god.

Sitting across the room from the place in which Amien lay sleeping, my mind spread like a net across the aether, I found ample time to consider my encounter with Esus. If Esus really were imprisoned in the Abyss, how did He manage to reach into the world of the living? If He was not imprisoned, then why make Nechton or even me His lieutenant rather than re-engage the true gods with His own, presumably far greater, Power? Was it possible Nechton had assumed His mantle and even now played the part of the god with the Bard's followers, getting away with the deception because Esus was trapped in the Abyss? Had I agreed to take Esus's initiation, would He have sent me against the true gods—or against Nechton? As so often happened when I considered mysteries that touched on the gods, I came up with no satisfactory answers.

After a night with mind trained on the aether, I felt no more grounded in the mundane. Amien woke as soon as the first rays of sunlight crossed the sill; I met his eyes from my chair by the door, watching his gaze shift into a flavor of assessment that took in my extramundane entanglement as no uninitiated eyes might. He grunted and rolled up to sit, eyes still on mine.

"What?" he said.

"Nothing yet," I said. "But we need to get the hell out of here."

"Care to explain?"

I'd rather have a nail pried off. "When we're secure."

The escort assembled in short order. This morning the energies and unexpressed emotions running beneath their surfaces came through more clearly than their words or physical aspects. Tru and Easca glowed with the approach of Bealtan estrus and the mounting pressure of needs that surpassed the sexual; the male knights radiated surging will to be the first and last to drink at those wells; Iminor spun those energies up to a blinding intensity overlaid with a flavor of animosity that I hadn't seen in a decade and couldn't have found less compelling. Amien's long-familiar energies jarred against the background of wild, diverse, oddly harmonious powers surrounding this place; his wards hung on Letitia again, smudging her delightful energy until it was practically undetectable.

I bit back my annoyance at the way it dimmed her glow, put a little extra effort into the problem and found, for a moment, the alien priestess staring back at me in the clear morning light. Now, finally, her physical beauty came into focus, her succulent mouth and long white neck and the spare curves against which the spidersilk mail shimmered and slid. Knowing the flavors of her mouth and the feel of her lean body beneath me did nothing to diminish the fascination she always roused.

I could eat you, I thought. I felt rather than saw the tremor that passed through her.

Feeling's mutual, she sent, on a targeted transmission for my mind alone. The smolder of her regard ignited something inside me; I wrapped my hands around the reins to keep them from developing other agendas. I knew our mutual gaze had gone on too long, long enough that it was becoming noticeable, but it took me a while longer yet to tear myself away.

"Let's go," I said and cued my horse. Amien shot me a look but fell in beside me, and we rode down, through the lower levels of the city, out to the ford and across the river. Already the road on the south bank was busy with Fair traffic on carts, donkeys, and the occasional plodding horse, the river surprisingly full of rich men's boats dawdling west against the tide.

Rohini and her contingent were ready and waiting when we arrived. We remained mounted as they climbed into the saddles, and then we all headed up to the river road. Rohini distributed her men to the fore and rear again. It was the proper strategy, but riding in the center of such a large group felt strange, as if I had somehow become a noncombatant; I nudged my horse forward until I could settle in beside Rohini.

"Good morning, sian," I said. I could not recall ever having addressed a woman as *sian*, but I had the sense that Rohini would interpret *Lady* as the throwing down of a gauntlet. I would find enough ways to offend her without succumbing to the obvious.

She shot me a quizzical, suspicious look, but replied with a civil nod. "Good morning."

Amien slipped into position on my other side, squeezing whatever lieutenant had been riding at Rohini's right hand to the edge of the narrow road. He dropped back behind us; Rohini spared him a glance but returned her attention to me.

"What's your plan today, sian?" I continued.

She raised her dark-auburn brows. "Hard to say. Were my men and I alone on this urgent a journey, I'd be aiming for Laetrif tonight: the days are running long. Will your crew last that far?"

"Hard to say," I answered. Most travelers to the Fair would make the journey between Nemetona and Laetrif a three-day trip; I was confident Letitia would last two-thirds of the distance, but the final third was a gamble. "It's not the knights who concern me..."

Rohini nodded, absorbing the things I hadn't said. "Let's just see how the day unfolds."

I nodded, too. "Just so. I haven't really met your men yet, sian..."

"Feel free," she said: permission to circulate among them and introduce myself, given from one commander to another; a pleasant surprise after all the dark and assessing looks I'd received from her.

"Thank you," I replied. "But I can't help noticing one particular absence."

She cast me a look of surprise, which faded into one of understanding. Amien gave a half-amused grunt.

"His name is Brinner?" I said: her House Healer, a man I had never met but who I was certain Amien must have hand-picked for her.

Rohini nodded, glancing briefly at Amien before returning her attention to me.

"He and my—" The word *tanist* hovered on the air, but at the last second she amended it. Difficult to have a tanist without a throne to which he might succeed. "—kinsman are moving the clan to the Precinct. He'll meet us at the Fair."

Rumor placed most of the exiled Essuvian clans in the northern reaches of increasingly hostile Mumhan; the neutral ard-righ's precincts would afford them safety for the duration of the Fair. A better ard-righ than Conary Mourne might finally offer them sanctuary after the Moot.

"That must be taking the better part of a twelvenight," I said, in a tone I hoped suggested sympathy for their plight: the overland trip to the ard-righ's precinct would be slow going for a group so full of noncombatants, and they would need whatever protection, military and arcane, they could get. But all I really cared about was the fact that Letitia would have to do without that blade and extra measure of arcane support.

"I appreciate your help more than I can say," Amien added, obviously a repeat of words uttered earlier.

Rohini smiled slightly, nodding to Amien. "And I yours."

The dusty road curved and climbed a short rise; a little distance ahead, a group of Fair travelers with donkeys eased their animals to the edge, making room for us to pass. In the midst of the fields beyond, an old spreading oak stood atop a mound with the unmistakable look of a long-forgotten tomb, rising from the early morning mist as if from a dream. Through the shimmering air I glimpsed myself hanging on that tree, felt the coiled power in and beneath the barrow into which the ancient roots tapped. The pull of that place rang in my head until I could hear nothing else, grabbed at my throat until I could barely breathe. Already I felt the morning sun fade into eternal starlight.

I wrenched myself free. Amien and Rohini continued to speak earnestly about things of no consequence; something that wasn't dust clogged my throat.

"Well, then," I said, apropos of nothing. "With your indulgence." I reined, ignoring the annoyance in the glances they shot me as they rode forward, and tried to occupy my mind with meeting Rohini's men.

The man we had pushed back a rank was Busadi Ausc, Rohini's second-in-command: a typically black-haired, broad-featured Essuvian with grey eyes and a sort of laconic grace. Mind still too broad, I read straight down to his core without meaning to, seeing through the hard layer of indifferent ethics imposed by the necessity of survival in hostile territory to the honor and multilayered devotion beneath. Given a cause he believed in, he could be trusted utterly—unless and until what was necessary interfered with Rohini's well-being. I spoke with him for a few moments about irrelevant things, remembering none of the details of what he said: mind too full of truth for anything else to lodge there.

Around him rode Magav, Luxin, Thurro, Olin, and Uxenti, each of whom hailed from a different Essuvian clan. Together with the men at the back of our strangely-large train, they had been Rohini's personal guard before Macol fell. Their allegiance to the woman they served had survived the loss of her title; their native Essuvian reserve prevented them from admitting the truth I read: hand-picked by Rohini herself, they had been chosen not on the basis of rank or clan affiliations but for character and talent with arms. I managed to stretch a part of myself sufficiently close to the mundane world to offer them the observation that Letitia's knights had been chosen in much the same way, representing the best Fíana had, and to relate a bit about the long mobile siege they had endured in her defense: remotely pleased at the shift I saw in their attitudes towards the Tanaan, remotely surprised at myself for caring.

Finally I dropped back to ride with the Tanaan: answering Iminor's civil nod and venomous stare with a disinterested nod of my own, settling in beside Nuad to contemplate all the reasons why Iminor was right to hold me in so little regard. I saw, with utter, emotionless clarity, the dangerous unanswered hungers in me, the way I had spent the past decade starving myself of things I needed as much as food and water and sleep; the ways in which my attempts to compensate for that missing nourishment with the empty thrills of sex and gambling and duels had drained me further still, had opened a gulf between me and all the people who would never understand even the most basic aspects of the truth at my core. How all of it had conspired to cut me off from the sustaining power of human affection until I walked as little more than a shadow among them. How little humanity was left to me, after all.

I could be cured, if I chose it: I saw this, too. But I wasn't sure who I would become if I were, or what path the cure would take. We climbed a steep rise and passed a sun-circle, complete and shot through with veins of gleaming schist, at the top of the ridge; the energy of the place infiltrated me until my bones hummed in sympathy. Compulsion to turn aside and enter that space competed with my awareness that I was already, perhaps irretrievably, more than a little bound to that energy and could reach it just as easily in mind as in body. I had to get Letitia to safety, and I might finally have enough men around me to do it. I slipped the bonds gathering about me and rode on.

Hakaid the shadow of the Sun.

Mile after mile the road stretched; group after group of travelers bound for the Fair ceded us the road, prompted by the compulsion to get out of the path of a horse of which humans are all but unaware and to which they are all utterly bound. Periodically we stopped to rest and water the horses, to eat and see to their care, and to stretch the muscles of legs and backs. I stared down at the river flowing at the base of the bluff and the boats plying patiently against the tide; I gazed across fields of wheat and flax at cairns and barrows and standing stones, wondering that no loyalist seemed to understand how much the old ways still held, even in Deceang; I participated absently in conversations I forgot as soon as they ended, seeing only the beautiful essences of my friends and the smudge of irritating energies that hung about Letitia.

The reach of the shadow of the Sun is infinite.

The knots of travelers through which we rode were even less present to me; their chatter and laughter and road-weary arguments drifted past me like smoke from a distant fire.But when Básghilae approached from some little site dedicated to Esus a mile or so distant, I felt them before I saw them, smelled the sudden surge of now-familiar energies cresting around us, saw the way the horses' ears pinned back long before any of the riders noticed something amiss. I reined, and whistled: loudly enough to be heard over all the conversations threading through our train.

"Básghilae," I called, pitching my voice to carry all the way to the back. Rohini shouted out some command I half-understood, in the Essuvian language;

Busadi took it up, embellishing her instruction with specifics that made even less sense. I sent the Tanaan into a half-crown around Letitia, with the sharp drop to the river at their backs. As the Básghilae crested the ridge of the road less than half a mile distant, the Essuvians at the front of the train raced out to meet them: alternately weaving among the traffic and trampling along the verge in a magnificent flying wedge, lances at the ready. Once they moved I realized how many noncombatants had frozen, trapped, between the approaching Básghilae and the place in which we stood.

"Run!" Letitia shouted at them. "*Run! Go back!*" Her voice escalated towards a shriek; they swiveled panicked stares from her to the approaching Básghilae and back again, and stood as if rooted to the road. She gave voice to an inarticulate cry comprised of frustration and despair and cued her horse forward, nudging him between Tuiri and Ogma. All the knights began to shout at her; suddenly the world returned from the distance it had occupied all day, blasting me with brilliant westering sunlight and long shadows and the trampled-earth smell of a well-traveled road.

"Letitia, no!" I shouted, banishing her back to the circle with an outflung arm. She met my gaze, and once again I saw the hopeless desperation that lay in her eyes at the Presatyn well. And I understood: if I wanted her to remain under protection, I had to give her cover in a way that also shielded as many noncombatants as possible.

"Fine!" I snapped. "Forward!"

I spurred my horse into motion; the Tanaan surged forward, circling around the frozen mass of humanity to stand between them and the approaching Básghilae, hurriedly re-forming against the ridge. I turned and walked my horse back in the direction we had all come, motioning the other travelers ahead of me.

"Run!" I said to them, still moving. They moved reluctantly out of my way, but mostly towards the sides of the road.

"That way!" I said, trying hopelessly to sound less frightening than the riders thundering towards us, casting shooing motions at them with both hands. "Run, you fools!"

"*RUN!*" Amien bellowed, and finally they seemed to get the point and began scurrying—just as the second half of Rohini's contingent surged towards the battle and the Básghilae closed in behind me. I turned again, drawing my sword, spurring my horse forward to meet the onslaught as the Essuvians tangled in the retreating noncombatants and pushed through to help.

The energy in which I'd been enmeshed all day bloomed across the road, wrapped itself around me again; I collided with the first ghoul, meeting his dead gaze as our blades crashed. The energy driving him was the same as the heady dark sparkle hanging all around, more potent than I had ever seen in the Básghilae: overlaid with the memories of human lives and the signatures I recognized as Nechton's—and shot through with something deeper and subtler, which I didn't recognize but discovered I could choose not to address. Now, finally, it was almost like doing battle with a living man; I still crafted all my tactics to create an opening that would allow me to take his head, still avoided touching him—though I was no longer certain that was necessary, at least for me. But the wild energies he carried didn't distract me. I was full of them already.

It should have horrified me. All I felt was relief. The patterns of the battle and the dispositions of the forces snapped into place in my mind, the way they always had; without effort I tallied successes and failures, ghouls defeated and noncombatants who fell to Básghilae, even in the midst of my own engagement. Traces of human lives splashed against me, lighting me up a little more each time but not spinning me beyond control; I felled the first dead man, moved on to the next, experienced no surprise when the power Amien cast at Básghilae began to fly astray again. I knew the energy he needed, could have drawn it more easily than a knife. It would have changed everything. Instead I poured more vigor into the mundane battle.

"It's too thick here," I called across the road to the wizard, remotely aware that I should have made an effort to sound alarmed or at least surprised. "He owns this place!"

Amien spared me a startled glance and returned to plying his sword. The engagement surged up and down the road as the Básghilae pressed towards Letitia and the massed Essuvians felled and drove them back, only to be pressed backwards again. Only the Tanaan stood firm in the midst of the chaos, breaking the Básghilae who came at them like a wall of jagged rock. Behind them, Letitia sat at the ready, sword in hand—but all her attention was on the noncombatants on whom the Básghilae fed, face a mask of despair.

Finally, late as usual, the horror in which we were engaged snapped into focus in my mind. I saw, with terrible clarity, how monstrous I had become: how little troubled I was when people not under my protection became victims; how willingly I drank the blood of enemies myself; how my hunger had eaten up all my compassion. I was like some weapon forged of human blood and bone, like Nechton's Shadow of the Sun: effective enough for its purpose, but crafted and fed on evil. *The source is tainted*, Amien had said of the orb. And I hadn't understood what he meant. I had long since absorbed the poison myself.

Did vowing not to draw power and upholding that vow really make any difference? How could it, if I was damned already? A short distance away, one of Rohini's men gave a despairing cry which was rapidly taken up by his countrymen; I finally maneuvered the dead man I fought into leaving enough space for my blade to pass through his neck. He fell, and I glanced towards the uproar, seeing nothing unusual—then wondered at myself for thinking this whole situation somehow normal, unsure whether I should laugh or fling myself off the bluff to crash on the rocks below. I could do neither now: another dead man was on me, a massive fellow with a sword most men would have wielded two-handed. He met my gaze across our clashing blades, and behind his eyes I saw Nechton. It was like looking into a mirror and remembering I was hideously deformed.

Smashing the mirror wouldn't change anything, but I needed to do it anyway. I waded in as if I might kill the evil in myself by besting one more ghoul, as if keeping Letitia alive might somehow restore my humanity or even my honor. I used craft and misdirection against the weight of the heavier blade, turning my opponent's own momentum against him—and then, just as the opening I'd been developing in his defenses materialized, I felt Nechton pull all the remaining Básghilae back. The pull resonated against my spine, echoed in my mind; and with one final glance at me Nechton turned my opponent aside, sent them all racing across the fields and out of sight. For several seconds I just sat, sword still in mid-air, the shock of what I had experienced resonating through me. I had never felt a colleague's arcane maneuvers so clearly outside a group working or shared circle. My throat ran suddenly dry; I swallowed, but it didn't ease.

Finally I sheathed my sword and looked around, taking in the situation. The circle of knights around Letitia loosened; she slipped from the saddle and headed straight for the area in which the noncombatants fell. A group of Essuvians converged on a Básghil corpse at the edge of the road, dismounting and staring down. I glanced at Rohini, who sat white-faced in the saddle a little distance away.

"What?" I said.

She shook her head and glanced at me, the black eyes that always seemed so judgmental looking haunted now. "His name was Navar. He—" She swallowed. "We lost him right around the time Macol fell."

I looked at the Essuvians clustered at the edge of the road again, finally understanding. "You... *knew* him?"

In my peripheral vision I saw her nod.

"I'm sorry," I said, and actually meant it. My throat felt tight; I looked at her again. "There are no words."

Her narrow jaw stiffened. "Whatever's necessary." She met my gaze. "Whatever's necessary to end this, we must do it. No matter the cost."

I wanted to agree, but I feared part of the cost would be Letitia. And I would give up a thousand Essuvians to keep her alive. It would accomplish nothing to say this: I nodded instead, glancing around again to assess the damage.

Two dozen noncombatants dead; half again as many Básghilae destroyed; one Essuvian injured by a Básghilae blade. His bleeding was minimal: it had been a glancing touch with the tip of a blade in the little gap between greaves and mail. But I saw the death-energy swirling into him, trickling in like water through a crack in a dam. This was the energy I'd failed to identify in the dead man earlier, the piece of the puzzle of Nechton's working I hadn't yet unraveled: the death-spell the Básghilae wore and carried on their blades. My earlier curiosity about the power vanished; only the pain of another brave man's death and disgust at so low a tactic remained.

"Your man Luxin," I said quietly to Rohini. "He's been hit."

"Ah, *fouzh*," she moaned, and cued her horse towards him. She drew up beside him, looking into his face, and astonished me by leaning across the intervening space to wordlessly embrace him. Pain gathered in my throat; Manannan's handsome face flitted across my mind. After a moment's silent embracing Rohini sat straight in the saddle again—then in a single motion drew her sword and took Luxin's head.

"*Fouzhir hell!*" I blurted. I'd almost forgotten how hideous it is to decapitate a living man. Rohini turned her blood-spattered face towards me, hell in her eyes.

"What did you—He had days yet!" I barked, knowing the line separating my prerogative from hers lay far behind me.

"Days?" she retorted, voice raw. "Days of his body charring itself from the inside? Days of fighting the need to kill and eat his companions, knowing he'll lose in the end?"

"What?" I breathed. "That's not how the Tanaan—"

"Pheh," Rohini said, and turned back to the man she'd beheaded. Busadi drew up on his other side; together they extracted his body from the saddle. It took me a long time to figure out what to say.

"I'm sorry," I said. All the resonance had gone from my voice.

Rohini glanced at me, meeting my eyes for a moment. "Different for the Danaan?" she said in a more composed voice.

"Much." My voice still didn't sound like it should.

"Next time we'll send them to the front," she said, as if the matter had been decided.

I couldn't work out whether that should be interpreted as a compliment. After a moment of silent staring I crossed the battle-space to the spot in which Letitia knelt among human corpses. She looked up at me as my shadow fell across the bodies, devastation and crushing guilt in her face. I slid from the saddle, stood gazing at her. Amien and the rest of the Tanaan gathered nearby.

"Why can't we stop this?" Letitia said to me, in a raw voice that warned of tears.

"Letitia," I said gently.

She shook her head vigorously, warding off words I hadn't yet formed with an outflung arm.

"No!" she said, half a sob. "There's no answer I can accept! This is *my fault!*"

"Letitia," Iminor said.

She glanced at him, sudden decision in her face, and turned her gaze on Amien. "Get me off this road. I won't ride it anymore."

Hope sprang in me that she meant something broader than that simple statement: she would turn aside, make for Aballo. Something inside me unclenched: we could have her safe in days. Strike out overland now, and we would leave the Fair traffic behind, reaching the river Sabrin in less than a day. From there we could sail on natural currents all the way to Aballo. With favorable winds we might reach the isle by Bealtan.

But she pressed on: "The north bank is quiet. And the distance must be the same. I won't—"

Suddenly Rohini was there. "Mora, the north bank is in enemy hands."

"This one isn't?" Letitia retorted.

Rohini shook her head, lips thinning.

"Fine!" Letitia said. "You keep to this road; put me and my knights on a boat. I don't care if I reach the Moot by Bealtan! We'll catch up to you when we can. At least no more noncombatants—"

"Do you see any boats here?" Rohini rejoined. "There's no choice but to ride!"

"So let's *cross!*"

Rohini shook her head again. "I can't guarantee your safety up there. This road is bad, but that one's worse."

Letitia glanced at me, a desperation in her eyes that left me powerless against the need to act.

"One's as bad as the other," I said quietly, knowing the mistake even as I made it. Rohini's head snapped around to stare at me.

Too late to back out now. "If Nechton has ties to the Weavers, he's also tapped in to every old power site dedicated to Esus."

Amien turned an incredulous gaze on me. Immediately everyone else was staring at me, too.

"I—" Amien began. He shook his head, visibly swallowed words, and said, in tones that bespoke careful control, "Nechton has ties to the Weavers. Not the Bard. Nechton."

"Well, the Bard does, too," I said just as carefully.

"You're short on straight talk lately," Amien said in a neutral voice.

I sighed. "Yes. It's all of a piece: Nechton and the Weavers, the Bard and the Weavers—Have you managed not to notice that they're all worshiping Esus? Or how live those sites are?"

The wizard was still staring at me, increasing dismay in his long face.

"The change in the Básghilae?" I pursued. "How about the fact that the power's running against you again?"

Amien shook his head slowly. "This was the problem at the inn last night."

I shrugged. "Not that I could have slept through it anyway."

The wizard gave me a long look, and I knew he hadn't been aware of anything except the backwards flow of arcane energy in the last half hour. I had the sinking sense that he guessed I'd been consorting with Powers no man sworn to the true gods should even know.

"If there is no difference," Letitia said reasonably, "there is no reason not to ride away from the crowd, and take the danger with us."

Rohini flung her hands into the air, shaking her head.

"You don't ride with banners, Chief," Letitia pursued.

"We don't need them," Rohini said. "Our enemies know—"

"Your enemies don't kill noncombatants! Mine do! Do what you will; I go no farther on this road!"

Rohini cast a wild glance at Amien, but the wizard just sighed. The glance she turned on me was as ill-disposed as all the looks I'd received from her yesterday.

"If you would, *sian*," she said to me, voice cold. "Take your knights and find us a crossing." Iminor gave voice to a strangled noise. "See whether you can find a place isolated enough to camp undisturbed for the night."

I nodded and glanced at Iminor: a horror I didn't understand lay in his eyes.

"Give us a sense of the lie of the road going west, and whether it is sufficiently—" Rohini swallowed, what words I didn't know. "—quiet for us to pass without dragging the mora into our battles."

"I seem to be dragging you into mine," Letitia said, sounding like a mora again. Rohini just cast her a cold-eyed stare.

"I may be a few hours, sian," I said to Rohini.

She nodded, but Iminor shook his head. "*All* the knights? Surely that's not—"

Rohini turned an affronted stare on him. "Ouirr? I've given my word to protect the mora! We've already lost a man! What do you want—"

Iminor flushed, shaking his head, and held up his hands in a conciliatory gesture. "Ouirr, I mean no disrespect—"

"That's funny!" Rohini snapped.

Amien laid a hand on her arm. "My friend, he is—" The wizard shook his head, casting Iminor an apologetic glance. The Tan flushed more deeply.

The wizard shrugged. "None of us measure up to his standards where the mora is concerned. I pray you, don't take it personally."

Rohini turned her dark eyes on him. After a moment the intensity in her face softened.

"I apologize, Chief," Iminor said quietly. "Lord Amien is right; I... I fear I am sometimes too vigilant."

Rohini addressed him with a silent, dark stare that stretched so long I grew uneasy. Finally she gave a tight nod and turned her attention on me again.

"In the meantime, we will prepare pyres," Letitia said.

"What?" Rohini snapped.

Letitia cast her a glance that said it was perfectly obvious. "I just got two dozen people killed! I've got to—"

Rohini shook her head. "Lady, you have—with respect, Letitia, you have no idea what you're asking! Just to prepare enough wood will take more time—"

"We have a wizard," Letitia said reasonably, looking at Amien.

"No!" I said. "Do you think his magic is free? All the energy he's got must be reserved for your defense! Assuming he can be effective in this zone at all! Did—"

"But you can," she said silkily, eyes on mine and a smolder in her gaze that sent my immediate, defensive rage tumbling into confusion.

I stared at her, heart thudding in my ears. I could neither admit she was right nor discuss why it was impossible; to say anything was to open a vein I'd never staunch. Instead I turned and mounted again, cast my glance across the gathered knights and said, "Let's go."

A strangled noise escaped Iminor. He swallowed and said, "Nuad, you're with us, please."

Rohini shook her head and stalked away; the rest of the Tanaan climbed into their saddles and followed me back down the road, in search of some track leading to the riverbank below.

Our shadows stretched out before us; the road grew quiet. Periodically the smoldering glance Letitia cast me while suggesting I might work with Esus's Power flitted through my mind. Before long we were the only people within sight.

"Where is everybody?" Mattiaci muttered.

"Setting up camp for the night," I said in a calm voice. "Bealla don't see as well as Danaan at night; for us the travel day is shorter."

"But you see in the dark," Tru said reasonably.

I heard myself laugh; the terrible truth of it tore more laughter from me. This time I heard the edge of madness in it and forced myself to stop.

"Not as well as you," I said, trying to sound composed.

After a couple miles we found a steep, narrow track leading down the face of the bluff to the river bank below. Over the course of the day I'd seen the space between the bluff and the water widen and narrow, ranging from a few feet to half a mile or more. This was a wider area, and from the top of the bluff I saw the glint of water among the grasses and cottonwoods that bespoke marshland. But there was no time to be choosy: we slipped out of the saddles and led our horses down the precarious trail in the fading light.

At the base of the bluff, we mounted again. I pushed aside my sense that I should put one of the Tans and his superior night-vision at the front of the line and took that spot myself: were someone to step into quicksand or an ambush, it should be me. We picked our ways, single file, through deepening shadows and twisting, uncertain paths as the sunset faded and will-o-the-wisps blossomed all around.

"*Ehh,*" Tuiri rasped.

"Sweet Lord, why does it have to be marsh demons?" Ogma groaned, evidently by way of agreement.

But I would take any light I could get in this place, even light that made the hair on my neck stand up. There would be no choice but to let one of the Tanaan take the lead on the way back. Probably with a torch.

We pressed on, through deepening streamlets and burgeoning marshlight, until we reached a little bar of dry land topped by a hillock, on which a lone willow stood illumined by so many will-o-the-wisps that they seemed to merge into a single entity. The Tanaan shifted nervously in the saddles; a strange sense of foreboding closed a cold hand on the back of my neck, too. It was nothing more than the aftermath of too many tales of demons in the marsh, of echoes of the stories that make marsh-lights into the souls of the recently dead. Another commander might have tried to mock the group out of their fear; but if I didn't believe the folk-tales, I still felt the wandering energies that give rise to will-o-the-wisps against my skin: better to let the Tanaan master the things their senses told them in their own ways. From the hillock I spotted the broader expanse of the river a short distance ahead: we were nearly there, and a precarious-looking cairn on the narrow flat beside the shore suggested I'd guessed correctly: the trail down the bluff had led to a ford.

"Almost there," I said, and climbed back down to mount again.

"Praise Endeáril," Mattiaci said.

I cued my horse and started forward; some odd, half-familiar shift occurred, and for a fraction of time a blue haze competed with the green glow of marshlight at the edges of my vision. Something fell to the ground behind me. The mud beneath my horse's feet opened into nothingness; the sound and concussion of an explosion rocked through me and were gone; the world vanished, replaced by limitless, empty darkness in which the only sound was Lady Tella's voice speaking words I didn't understand.

The world crashed into being around me: I was in the saddle, the horse bolting through darkness and afterimages of incomprehensible brilliance, cold water splashing up to dampen my pants and gloves and hair. I yanked on the reins, but the horse was having none of it, and I couldn't see anything: there was nothing to do but to hang on, to crouch behind his neck and hope he didn't do anything too stupid.

Suddenly, in a place my ears suggested was the middle of the river, he stopped: standing in the water trembling, sides heaving. I leaned forward to murmur lies in his ears and try to calm myself enough to persuade him things were all right.

They weren't. I knew they weren't. But I would have to convince the beast to turn around, to go back and face whatever had just happened.

Gradually sight resumed. As the haze in my eyes rolled back, I saw: we stood in the middle of the river, water rushing past us. The water flowed from left to right, which meant we were facing north. My boots were full of water. The opposite bank lay dark and quiet; both moons hung nearly overhead, casting everything in pale terrible light. I twisted around in the saddle to look back, seeing a fire on the marsh I'd left behind. None of the Tanaan were in evidence.

A moan forced its way up from my chest. I knew what I would find, but I persuaded the horse to turn, coaxed him back across the river to the shore. Once we were out of the water I reined, as if I could somehow prepare myself, then nudged him forward. I forced my throat sufficiently open to call the knights' names, dragged us towards the things I didn't want to see. Again and again I shouted, but no one answered.

After a time I found a blasted hillock with the remains of an old willow lying in pieces on the smoldering ground, trailing branches into the water below. Here, finally, I discovered the answers I hadn't wanted, in terrible pieces of people whose lives had been my responsibility, whose deaths were my fault in a way not even Manannan's had been. Tru's sword, with a scrap of belt yet attached to the scabbard; Easca's strong delicate hand, still clutching a length of the reins; a head with face turned into the water, as if Ogma were bobbing for apples at a midwinter fest: these things burned themselves into the backs of my eyes, inciting a howl that lay inexplicably trapped in my chest.

Marsh gases can knock a man out, and they can ignite in the presence of a torch. But they don't just explode for no reason: there must be a cause. Tonight's cause was the same as that of the ledge collapse at the top of the Muir Pass: someone who knew how to craft the sort of precise explosions one generally sees only in mining and sieges. The reason why this place had exploded was me, and the only reason I sat here shaking was that Lady Tella had intervened to spare my life, somehow plucking me out of the midst of the disaster. Why She would remove me and allow all those far worthier people to die I had no idea. I wished She had let me join them, wished She would grant me understanding or at least give me some indication of why my continued existence had any merit at all.

How could I have allowed this to happen? I had known there was a price on my neck since Tyra, had known my enemy didn't care who else he harmed since the pass. I had allowed my emotional entanglement with Letitia to persuade me to ignore the things I knew to be true. If my failures as a commander had killed Manannan, it was my failure as a human that had killed all these people. I should have let them escape me at Goibniu.

Something shifted and dropped; the fire surged, in a great bloom that suddenly occupied the clearing the way the will-o-the-wisps had. The horse whinnied and turned to run, and I let him. I should have leapt to the ground and gone with my friends, at least as far as the place where the worthy and unworthy part ways for the last time; instead I hung on as he ran, turning him back towards the path we had climbed from the top of the bluff, telling myself that if I didn't return, Letitia would sit exposed far longer than necessary. But I knew the truth, and I could find no real reason why I should return: only some binding I had cast over myself without noticing, which I was powerless to resist or dissolve.

When I reached the spot in which we'd fought our most recent engagement, I saw: Amien had thrown up wards, right there in the middle of the road. The shimmering emerald wall circled around to meet itself, stretched up towards the stars and out of sight. What had happened in my absence? I slid from the saddle, opened a little portal in the ward-wall, and slipped through, drawing the horse in behind me.

Several of the men inside cried out. Amien just turned his head to look at me, his aura of anxious waiting shifting into horrified understanding.

"What the hell?" Iminor croaked, giving the utterance a rhetorical inflection that I took to be an expression of surprise rather than a real question. I answered it in the only way possible, with a rueful shrug.

"I assume it wasn't a secure crossing," Amien said, voice scraping with pain.

Appalled comprehension blossomed in Letitia's and Iminor's faces; Nuad was suddenly on his feet, striding out as if he might pass beyond the wards. Letitia put her hands over her mouth and burst into a storm of tears that very nearly wrecked my tenuous composure. The trapped howl redoubled inside me, crushing my heart so I could barely breathe; I had to look away, to stare at the energies of the wall slipping from leaf-green to moss to emerald and across every hue of green yet imagined, studying the formless patterns as if I might reduce them to something I could explain in mundane terms.

"No," I croaked, too consumed by the truth I couldn't admit for the shame of my lack of vocal control to touch me at all. "It was not. We need to keep this road. I'd like to move—" My voice gave out. "Now. What's—" I forced myself to look at Amien. "My lord, you raised wards?"

The wizard shrugged. "Finally noticed the pattern." His mouth twisted. "For all the fouzhir good it did. Have you noticed that the mora's consort always senses when things are about to go to hell on us?"

In my peripheral vision I saw Iminor's head snap around to stare at Amien. Letitia was staring at Iminor.

"What?" Iminor breathed, face fading into a pallor so deep he looked wan even in the green light.

The wizard shrugged again, looking at him. "Lady Tiaran is your grandmother? It's not unusual for Talent like that to pass…"

Iminor shook his head. "But men don't…"

Amien put on a pale smile. "Oh, young ouirr, they used to tell Rishan the same thing." He looked at me again, smile fading, then glanced across the circle of people to Rohini.

"Well, then, we ride to Laetrif?" the wizard said to her.

She nodded.

"Perhaps in the morning I'll be able to charter a boat," Amien continued, eyes still on hers. "And we will see if I can summon a wind on a river without our enemy knocking us halfway back to the Ruillin. You'll join us?"

Rohini gave him a rueful look and a shrug. "It's not as if the Moot will accomplish anything before you arrive."

Chapter 28
The Silence of the Circle

We followed the river road all night. First Telliyn and then Arliyn crossed the sky to hang before us; in my mind, I hung bound to a tree whose branches spread among the stars. Dark energies infiltrated me: winding their ways into my bones, finding those bones had always resonated to the notes they sang. One by one, the people I loved floated away, casting me glances oddly free of reproach and spreading themselves across the sky to become stars. When the last of them had gone, I saw the truth of my solitude, heard the leaves rattle in the branches to which I was bound like the last breath in a dying man's chest. I would hang here until I achieved understanding, until I had been purged of the senseless human emotions that incited all the costly errors I made. But those emotions clung to me, and even while I saw them for what they were, I could not pull their teeth from my flesh.

Laetrif's city gate stood open by the time we arrived. We rode through; no one challenged or seemed to much notice the Essuvians with whom we rode. The energies that had entombed me all night stretched through the gate with me, trailing like an invisible umbilicus to a tree somewhere beyond sight. Even Rohini had never been here and had no useful intelligence regarding the loyalties of any of the inns on the road that ran along the city wall: we just worked our ways from one to the next until we found one that had half a dozen rooms free, saw to our exhausted horses, and stumbled inside.

Rohini's men were only one less than an even dozen: there was no reason for Amien and me to take any of them as roommates. Nuad and Iminor had lost the companions with whom they had been sharing rooms, too, of course; Amien cast a long look between me and Iminor, sighed, and let a separate room for the Tans. Letitia glanced at him, met Rohini's eyes, and said, "With respect, Chief, I'd prefer to be alone tonight. Today."

Rohini nodded, looking none too disappointed. "I understand, Mora. I'll send a couple of my men to watch your door."

Letitia shook her head, grief and exhaustion writ large in her face but mouth set in a way I had long since learned meant danger to the unwary. "*Alone*. Thank you."

"Letitia—" Rohini began, glancing at Amien for support. But the wizard disappointed her again.

"You'll let me ward your door," he said to Letitia, making the statement into a question.

That prospect pleased her hardly more, it was easy to see. But she gathered her composure sufficiently to say, "Thank you, my lord." Rohini shook her head, scooped up the lock in Amien's hand, and stalked off.

Amien and I followed Letitia upstairs. He saw her settled in her room, cast a subtle binding over her door that would be invisible to any but a wizard but which would both secure her door and tell him if anyone tried to pass. I stood at the door of the room we would share: watching, feeling the too-regular lattice of the binding jar against the flowing energies that surrounded the place. When he was done I opened the door to our room and let him precede me inside. The binding down the hall still pricked like a burr at the edge of a cuff.

Inside, the wizard paused only long enough to kick off his boots and fell headlong into the bed. Within seconds his breathing had shifted into sleep. I recognized that I was exhausted, too; but I couldn't settle sufficiently to lie down. I spent a few minutes staring out the narrow window, looking down at the street and beyond the city wall to the docks at the foot of the bluff. Most of the boats I saw had the look of vessels preparing for a day on the water. I wondered what choices Amien would find for us when he went down there this afternoon.

I unbound my hair, pulled off my sword and mail shirt and sodden boots, and set them all beside my harp case. I realized I hadn't done more than load and unload the harp since Dromineer. Fierce, deep longing for the release of playing raced through me, but I was afraid to open the case and look inside. For a moment I just stood there staring at it. Finally I opened the clasps—and a weight settled in my chest.

I'd ruined it. Three days ago it seemed I might rescue the harp with careful attention; now the beautifully-carved frame lay covered in mildew, and the front of the sound chest had warped. The inside of the speckled-hide case bore a fuzz of black mold.

I sank to the floor, leaning my forehead on my knees. There was no point in carrying the harp further; the only decent thing would be to give it a pyre. Assuming it would even burn. How terrible that the ard-harpist would do such a thing; what a lie my election to that position was.

What a lie I proved every commitment this month. What sort of commander let the knights entrusted to him take a blade meant for his own heart? Enough swordsmen might defend Letitia against all the Básghilae Nechton ever crafted, but nothing could protect her from the danger I brought inside her boundaries. I was no true champion: if I could not sever the binding between us, I must make her understand well enough that she would dismiss me of her own will.

Down the hall, a new flavor of power blossomed. Yet another shortcoming cut into me like a dull knife: I focused instantly on all the energies I must not touch, yet I could not hold my responsibilities sufficiently in mind to give them even the minimum of their due. But this untouchable bloom told me Letitia remained as wakeful as I: it was her gentle power teasing my edges, raising a storm of need in my chest. I must confess to her, while I had the strength to do it; I must be gone before the rest of them woke. I closed the case again, the way a man will shut the eyes of a murdered friend; I hauled myself to my feet and slipped down the hall. I eased my hand through the lattice of Amien's wards: feeling his attention on me for a moment as he registered the contact and then recognized me; feeling him relax under the mistaken impression that Letitia would be safer with me in the room. And I knocked on the door.

"My lord?" Letitia said from the other side, sounding surprised.

"It's me," I said, then fought down the temptation to laugh at my own presumption. *Me.* As if there were no question she would recognize my voice. But Letitia opened the door immediately, stood staring at me through the arcane lattice: hair unbound and armor off; Amien's wards smudging her delicious energy and his talisman dangling across the front of her shirt; a lifetime's worth of guilt and terrified frustration lurking behind her composed mask.

"We need to talk," I said.

She stepped back, gesturing invitation. "Come in."

I nodded and slipped through Amien's binding, closing the door behind me. She stood just a step away, eyes intent, waiting for me to speak; I had no idea where to begin. I should have worked it out before walking in, and already I was growing distracted by all the flavors of need she roused in me, by the sorrow that would drown me the second I stepped back out the door. I willed myself to focus, at least long enough to do a proper job of opening the vein.

"Letitia, I—" I swallowed. "Mora. The loss you suffered last night was entirely my fault—" Her mask fell away, revealing all the pain beneath. My heart threatened to explode. "—and I need to explain—"

"No!" she said. "Those knights were my responsibility—I was the one who insisted we must cross—"

I shook my head. "Annu, thou'rt—" Oh, dear gods. "I'm sorry—" I had meant that as an apology for the error of intimacy, for claiming a relationship we would never have—but then I truly heard the words, and a vein opened; but it was not the right one.

"Oh, gods," I croaked, voice gone absolutely to ruin again. "I'm sorry, Letitia, I'm so sorry, I shouldn't even be here, I should have given all of you safe distance at Goibniu, and instead I got everyone—"

She touched her fingers to my lips, stopping the torrent of words. The tenderness of the gesture tore away the last measure of self-containment left to me: I shut my eyes against the pain trying to force its way up from my throat and turned my face into her palm. A tremor wracked me—and her hand slipped around to the back of my neck, compelled my mouth to meet hers. Amien's wards buzzed against me; down the hall, his eyes flew open, and he looked straight into the truth of my transgression. I drew back, but Letitia pulled me to her again.

"No," I breathed, but raw pain and need exploded through me, and I found myself devouring her, found my hands dragging through the nets of his wards and dispersing them. I gasped in yet more guilt and clasped her so fiercely that I lifted her feet from the floor. My breath came in ragged sobs; a little whimper escaped her throat, and I drew back in fear of whatever injury I'd inadvertently caused. But her desperate eyes met mine in a way that made it clear the injury had happened hours ago; she commandeered my mouth again, and heartbreak and passion tore through me until I fell apart.

"You must dismiss me," I croaked, and buried my face in her neck, hiding inside her hair. But already my mouth was on the silk of her neck, and my teeth grazed her skin as if I might open up her veins, too, might drink her life right here.

"I *need* you," she breathed, hand closing around the back of my skull.

"I'm going to get you killed." And oh, gods, how I wanted to bite her, to feel her flesh yield and hear her cries of confused pleasure and pain. But I must not mark her. She was not mine.

"You're keeping me alive," she rejoined, with a near-logic I was insufficiently coherent to counter, and began undressing me.

The faces of our companions swam through my muddled mind; again I saw them spread out into stars. It should have cooled my ardor; my breath sobbed in me again. But I found myself trembling with redoubled need, discovered my fists full of her shirt and the garment flying past her hair without even tangling. And all conscious thought ceased.

I clasped her fiercely, not caring how I interfered with her efforts with my buttons; I lifted and fell across the bed with her, pulled off her clothes, let her peel me bare. Nothing remained of the world of the living but Letitia, and I wanted only to crawl inside her and find oblivion. There was no elegance between us this time, no gentle melding of minds: only sobbing breath and pounding desire and the unanswerable need to somehow put back the lives I had destroyed. I held off on the release, but just barely; the incompletion of it wrecked me yet again. When it was over I fell back, drew her across me, clasped her as if her slender body might shield me from the horror I carried.

Gradually we quieted, though the occasional shudder still passed between us, and my heart still felt as if it would burst. I stroked her hair, as much to soothe myself as to comfort her. Outside, the sounds of morning in a city rose around the building; the bells of boats on the river rang against the walls. After some uncounted interval Letitia wrapped a grip of astonishing intensity around me, head still on my chest, and said, "I do not release you, Ellion Tellan. Say what you will. You offered me your service, and I have need—" Her voice dried up.

Terrible relief washed through me; I hated myself for giving in. "At least let me take you to Aballo."

She raised her head, cast me a quizzical look. "How am I to capture the Shadow of the Sun from there?"

"Seems to me you should be less concerned about his weapon than your own," I said. There was no point, less than no point, in sending her against Nechton; if she would recover her family's honor, addressing the issue of the broken Spear would accomplish much more.

But Letitia's mouth twisted; she glanced at the talisman trailing across my chest and sighed. And rolled away to lie on her stomach.

"Of course you'd know," she said, eyes on something miles away and a bitter edge to her voice. "I don't know what I'm doing wrong."

"What do you mean?" I said carefully, bewildered.

"Well, I'm supposed to store—the Light energy, the power of the Holy Mora, in there—right? But I can't."

Now I understood: she thought I'd meant Amien's talisman. I frowned without planning it: watching Letitia's despairing face, thinking about the energy that raced through me when I held the diamond in my mouth at the shrine in Presatyn. I hadn't been seeking power, only trying to render a moment of intensity into something more playful; it had charged me without my even being aware of the possibility.

"But you *are*," I said.

She turned her head to look at me, sudden hope fading into fear of hoping at all. "What?"

"You *are* charging it." The talisman lay on the blanket, in the shadow Letitia cast; the chain traced a sinuous path around her neck. I picked up the diamond, held it between fingertips and thumb, let it roll across my palm. It sparkled as if lit from within, just a little brighter than the light in the room could explain; the memory of the gentle power it carried flashed through me, rendering the world mere shadows across my mind. I glanced at her again. "Oh, yes. You are."

Tremulous hope turned her wide-eyed.

"I'm not sure how," I said. "But the energy's getting in." The precision of the diamond's facets, the grace of its form, even the sweet manner of its mounting made my eyes want to trace its line again and again. Its energy was an invitation written on my palm.

"Maybe you're making this harder than it really is." I met her eyes. "That's a common novice mistake."

She stared at me, lips parted; her regard shifted. Now it held that same smolder with which she'd addressed me while suggesting I work with Esus's Power last night. I saw, finally: it ran both ways, this strange perilous current between us. Her awareness of my power and that closed-off part of my life lit her with a desire almost as complicated as what she incited in me.

It was the last thing I would have expected: what sane woman would find any appeal in a wizard too disgraced to practice? The taint of potential evil should disqualify me in the eyes of anyone who knew even part of the truth. A dangerous tingle spread through me; but answering her look would mean things I was too muddled with lack of sleep to work out. I dragged my focus back to the matter of the talisman.

I put on a reassuring smile. "Maybe you just need to relax and trust yourself."

The smolder still lay in her eyes, intensifying; my heart quickened, beyond my control. A hint of a smile graced her lips; her gaze turned inward, in a manner I'd seen times beyond counting at Aballo. But after a moment she sagged again.

"Maybe I'm not the one who's... charging... it at all. Maybe it's all leftovers or something. I just can't see how."

I shook my head. "It doesn't feel like leftovers. It's hot. Look, I never even touched it with my mind; all I did was put it in my mouth and—*bam!*"

"Bam," she repeated.

"The power was there. It lit me up."

This time the smile that came over me was genuine, but she just gazed solemnly at me. And I saw: she'd been chewing her own liver over this. She was so knotted up she'd never relax enough to be effective.

I saw what was necessary. For any other wizard it would have been simple: he would have taught her the process of charging, by demonstration and practice. But I could not draw the power necessary for that lesson; I sensed without asking that she would never admit her difficulty to Amien and allow him to help. It had somehow fallen into the category of things that would bring disgrace: things she would sooner die than confess.

There was no choice: I must do what I could, without drawing power. Maybe if I showed her the power already in the talisman, let her feel how light transformed through her into something infinitely more intoxicating than the original source, she would recognize whatever she was already doing. That was ninety percent of the battle, after all: acquaintance with the power sought. It is where every wizard's initiation starts.

"Look," I said, catching and holding her gaze. I popped the talisman into my mouth again: the smooth facets and precise angles like candy on my tongue, the chain trailing from my mouth like the reins on some faery horse. I touched it to the roof of my mouth.

This time it wasn't just my head that fired, but every power center along the length of my spine: cascading in a series of flares that fed one another like a sequence of explosive charges, building in intensity as the power descended, raising me instantly to desperate aching readiness for a joining that would only begin with the physical. Incandescence blasted me beyond reason, stretching me until I lost track of where I ended and she began. I could think of nothing beyond the necessity of sharing the energy with her, of rousing in her the madness she wrought in me: I flung myself across the bed, eyes still echoing with brilliance so intense that light and dark seemed to trade places, rolled her over and delivered the kiss of power in the place where it would have more effect than her heart.

The power redoubled in the transfer, knocking me out of every mundane orbit, spinning through me in raw pleasure that echoed yet again. She gave voice to the sort of scream that usually precedes a lover losing consciousness. But she didn't faint: instead she twisted around to take me again, surrounding me with the sort of ecstasy that presages total loss of control. Simultaneously another echo hit me through our accidental mindlink, grown somehow stronger yet. I heard myself cry out, found myself moving in desperate shivering thrusts while her brilliance permeated my entire diffusing being.

I was binding myself, felt it happening; couldn't imagine what it meant. When she found her completion, need came over me like a tempest: to surrender the magical essence with which I might conceive a child, to consign myself to utter oblivion, to seal the binding. I could only avoid the release by pouring my own energy into her instead. After the mayhem ended I was atypically sweaty and half-drained; and all I wanted to do was kiss her, as if by perpetuating the physical circuit I might find some of that surrendered energy flowing back into myself.

"Did you feel that?" I panted.

She fell back and laughed, giving voice to the sort of wondrous madness that a truly mind-wrecking working will leave behind.

I found myself laughing too, but quietly. "That's the energy you're creating. That's what's in the talisman. Once you've found the connection, the rest will go more easily."

"Oh, I think I will need far more than one lesson," she purred, gaze wandering the ceiling.

I smiled. "Lady, I might die."

She laughed again, low in her throat. I stretched out beside her, listening to the slowing of my heart and the incomprehensible normality in the street outside. It seemed impossible that life could be continuing as it ever had, somewhere outside these walls: that people might spend today on exactly the same pursuits as ever, with the Fair and the Moot as happenings of seemingly no more than passing importance, with the things bent on our destruction beyond their direst nightmares. I couldn't imagine whether it would be a source of relief or a disappointment to find events of such wildness and importance passing one entirely by. I couldn't imagine what it was to be a person who might answer such a question.

It seemed as if we lay inside a bubble, in some space in which reality had been suspended or somehow banished. In a few hours we would step out of it, climb onto a boat if we were lucky, tread the shores of reality again; but for now, we existed outside. I lay still for a moment, letting that idea roll around in my mind: there was something important about it that my mind was failing to grasp.

Finally, slowly, the significance of this extraordinary moment stumbled into the light. Separation from ordinary reality is the first imperative of truly powerful magic: the farther from the mundane realm one stands, the more influence one accrues. In this separate space, so far removed from the commonplace that we stood even beyond the bizarre crucible of blood-prices and pursuit we'd occupied all month, we might make choices in the sort of stillness one usually finds only inside a ceremonial circle, might find our decisions rippling far beyond the place in which we lay. So how should I use this moment? In what direction should I seek to move us?

Once I asked myself the question, the answer was obvious: Aballo. With Letitia safe there, I might give my whole attention to the strategic issues of defeating her enemy. There she had the greatest chance of finding someone who knew enough about the ancient Tanaan metallurgies to repair Fíana's Great Spear. And through investigating that weapon we might discover much about Carina's centuries-long war with Nechton: if I had guessed correctly, and she was the one who wrecked the Spear, that damage must have occurred in one of their engagements. How many of the energies of that battle still lay on the fragments Letitia carried? What treasures of intelligence about Nechton would we discover in Carina's grimoire? In centuries of battle she must have learned much about his strengths and weaknesses, his methods and preferred practices, even the sort of mundane details that would offer a strategic mind avenues of attack he would never think to defend.

Frustration mounted in me, propelling me to sit: for almost a month I'd had access to some of the best sources of strategic and tactical information available, and it hadn't even occurred to me to wonder about them.

"What?" Letitia said, turning her head to bestow a sleepy-eyed glance.

"Carina's grimoire," I said. "Her journal."

Letitia's gaze turned wary. "What about it?"

"Where is it?" I asked. Letitia rolled out of bed and plucked her shirt from the floor.

"Believe it or not," I continued, "her engagements with Nechton were probably the most success anyone ever had against him."

Letitia glanced at me and pulled the shirt over her head.

"I need to learn—"

"No," she said, glancing at me and then away. "I'm sorry—my lord, honor precludes—"

"Again?" I blurted, recognizing in that one unplanned utterance how far past exhaustion I had run. I had lost all semblance of discretion: I should beg her pardon, stumble away and sleep until it was time to leave. But the part of me that is unable to release an unsolved puzzle had its teeth in this one now.

"Letitia," I said, striving for a tone of gentle reason, "if I have not yet demonstrated my circumspection to you, I beg you tell me what it will take. That grimoire holds the intelligence I need—"

Letitia shook her head, golden hair scattering across the smudged white silk of her shirt. "I'm sorry. The dead must be allowed their secrets. Bad enough that I have read—"

"I can't believe she would rather you—"

I couldn't allow myself to say it, couldn't even think it. I swallowed and gathered myself to try again.

But Letitia's mouth was set. "It's not for me to say what she would choose. It's for me to guard her secrets."

"Well, can't we work around the places you can't allow—"

Again Letitia shook her head. The Tanaan concept of honor seemed to be growing stupider by the second.

Unless the secrets Letitia protected were just this damning. Wild, fierce curiosity roused in me; my mind spun imaginings that defied belief, and I was too tired to hold them at bay. Carina as a devotee of Aechering; Nechton fighting her cloaked in Esus. Duels that razed entire cities. The ruin of Arian flashed through my mind.

The truth, I knew, was much less dramatic. But for someone unacquainted with arcane practice, it must seem shocking just the same.

"Annu," I said gently. "Many of the things wizards take for granted as matters of practice would shock you. Some of the things we do would bring any-one else before an executioner. I promise you, none of what I might read of Carina's writings is likely to strike me as at all outlandish, and the vows I have taken to protect the silence of the circle—"

Letitia shook her head again. "I wish I could."

I closed my eyes against frustration and rising fear; and I began to see things differently. For all the well-deserved humiliation it brought on me, it was a lucky thing I had not confessed fully, fortunate I didn't leave. Even now, even in this privacy, there remained secrets she would die rather than reveal. I must protect her despite herself, must find some way to get at the truth she hid.

My presence was less a risk than what would certainly happen if she came within range of Nechton. As long as she didn't fall victim to the danger pursu-ing me, I would endure the dishonor of whatever other damage I caused. If I didn't stay with her, who else would recognize how unprepared she was for the burden Amien expected her to carry? Who else would guard her back?

I swallowed and pulled a semblance of calm about me, opened my eyes and met her gaze. "Then let me see the Spear."

She stared at me, intent and distractingly charming in her shirt and nothing else, for several seconds. She nodded, crossed the room, hefted her pack and carried it to the bed. I pulled on my clothes, but I had done no more than lace my pants and reach for the first button on my shirt before the pack opened and pieces of the Great Spear of Lugh Lámfhada, Fíana's Gaé Assail, tumbled clanking across the blanket. The jumbled wreck of the greatest weapon ever forged glinted in the morning light.

I fought down the impulse to reach for the pieces and begin rearranging them as if they were a child's puzzle: I would get only one first touch, and that would be the moment when I might usefully encompass the Spear and explore whatever memories and residual energies previous hands had left behind. But I could very nearly see the form the weapon had taken when it was intact; though there was so much more to it than any spear or lance I had ever seen, calling this weapon *Spear* had been inevitable.

There had been a long, narrow shaft of intricately pierced and carved stone—and Iminor was right: it seemed to be the same stone from which was formed the Tuaoh, the great Hy-Breasaílian righ-stone that Amien tapped with disastrous results atop the Temple Mount on Ilunmore. A once-beautiful orichalus-plated findargat housing enclosed the fragments of the shaft, wrap-ping the stone in sweeps and spirals and complex lattices of gleaming red-gold. Where the shaft had broken, the housing lay twisted and fractured, in irregular patterns that suggested whatever destroyed it had been more com-plex than a simple smashing against a stone.

A sort of grip and pommel at one end reminded me of the hilt of a sword; but this area was longer and considerably thicker than the parts of a sword it called to mind, even in proportion to the shaft, and the weapon had clearly been far too long to wield in such a fashion. Whatever its purpose, the hilt area was densely inlaid with squares of some crystalline material that winked in the subdued light and marred by a long, jagged crack wide enough to accom-modate a fingernail. The weapon's tip, which protruded beyond the housing, bore no cutting point: only a graceful, flared pyramid that called to mind the top of the obelisk that stands in the great plaza at Teamair. It was the most profoundly male weapon I'd ever seen; strange to think of women wielding it. Tangled around the whole disaster was a long, gleaming strap wrought of a sort of mesh or mail as thick as the leather of a boot but sinuous as silk. I didn't recognize the material.

I realized Letitia was staring at me, not at the weapon. I glanced at her, reading fear, embarrassment, and hesitant hope in her lovely face.

I nodded. "Incredible. Who besides you has touched it?"

Surprise manifested in her eyes. "I—No one besides the previous morae. That I know of. It was in a locked trunk inside the mora Carina's private..." She faltered, obviously uncertain of the word she needed.

"Workshop?" I said. "The room in which she practiced?"

Letitia nodded. "As far as I know, that room had stood locked since—since she left. I suspect she locked it behind her; she hadn't cleaned up from her last..."

"Working," I supplied. "What did you see there?"

Letitia glanced away. "She had... drawn... on the floor. And the walls."

"Blood or chalk?"

Letitia's eyes fixed on me again, astonishment written in her face.

"Both," she said, voice barely above a whisper.

I nodded. "A circle on the floor." A common technique for practitioners who lack the power to cast true wards.

"And—writing. I couldn't read it."

I nodded again. "What was on the wall?"

Letitia folded her hands in front of her mouth, almost as if she were praying; but a desperate tension was developing around her eyes. I'd reached the limit of what she could allow herself to admit.

"The goddesses," she whispered, not looking at me. "I—think it was the goddesses."

That was interesting. No wizard who believed he was practicing in defiance of the Will of his goddess would call Her into his workshop.

"Tell me," I said softly. Letitia's face shifted into despair. "Are there still people in the Four Realms who practice magic?"

"No!" Letitia said quickly, as if the idea were too terrible to contemplate. She glanced at the Spear again, turned her gaze on me. Some peculiarly Tanaan expression I couldn't fathom came over her.

"No," she said again, quietly. "As far as I know, the practice of magic is long gone."

More's the pity, I thought, but didn't give it voice. Letitia's chances would be so much better if the tradition had remained alive. But I was in no position to criticize people who turned away from the Work.

"Well, then," I said evenly. Excitement and dread sparked in me: I fought both down. I would no more be drawing power for this investigation than I had when I showed Letitia the power inside her own talisman: energies would run through me, and I would feel their charge, but it would work no change on anything but me, would be no violation of my vow. As recently as Dromineer I had assisted in a very similar operation. It was only long habit that forestalled me now.

"I need to touch the Spear," I said in a calm voice. "Is there a reason why I should not?"

"Is it... dangerous?"

I shrugged. "I have no reason to expect so. I just want your permission."

She gave me a long, unreadable look. I met her mesmerizing eyes; the contact nearly pulled me out of myself. Finally she nodded.

"Proceed, my lord."

I nodded and reached for the weapon's cracked hilt. The nubbly texture of the inlays rolled satisfyingly beneath my fingers and palms; the hilt's cylindrical form invited my hands to encompass it. The sinuous strap clung to a fastening on the finely-etched pommel; the other end tugged against the jumble of fragments on the bed. But I couldn't address that now; layers of old, rich energies permeated the metal and stone I held, teasing my unguarded mind so immediately open that they rushed into me too fast to regulate. I recognized the traces of Letitia's energy as they passed; glanced over layer upon layer of women whose minds and energies hovered just beyond my capacity to comprehend; felt the paths traced by millennia of bright broad energy manifesting from sources to which the stone held no intrinsic connection, saw them circulating among spiraling veins and crystalline structures and moving according to the personalities and mental idioms of the women who held it. Deeper, much longer ago, I sensed men's energies, too.

That mystery and the temptation to investigate it further sent my focus back into my own awareness. I realized I had been merely absorbing, allowing countless centuries to flit through and move beyond me, into spaces of memory only gods might touch. This was my opportunity; I wished I'd been able to take it when I had sufficient time and strength to make a long study of it, but there was no choice but to extract from it what I could. I gathered up my meager focus and reapplied myself, drawing my awareness almost into the here-and-now, pulling back to the surface to regain my bearings.

Here were Letitia's familiar, delicious energies again. Immediately beneath those delightful ripples lay a mindshadow of stunning quickness and intensity, a presence shaped by long temperance from blinding arrogance to an intriguing blend of determination, self-awareness, and passion wrapped around an unbreakable core. This was a woman who had spent centuries confronting the immediate possibility of her own death and somehow come to love it. Was she the Carina with whom Amien had fallen so desperately in love? More likely this was the woman she became, after countless years of facing Nechton.

But there was little time to examine her energies; the contact tripped me into the memories she'd left on the Spear, sent me tumbling from physical connection with the here-and-now and into a place that incited a shock of recognition in me: the summit of the Temple Mount at Ilunmore. The sun circle of gold-flecked stones stood half-wrecked again, and the subterranean hum of the Tuaoh ran half-apprehended beneath Carina's awareness. I was vaguely aware of my suddenly-distant body pitching face-first into a jumble of fragments on a bed.

Carina settled over me like a fog. Through her I felt cool breezes stir her hair and move in her jacket, felt the weight of the Spear through the strap slung from her shoulder and the familiar way it couched against her arm and hip. The structures of her thoughts eluded me; they felt as upside-down as the power of any Tanaan sacred site, and though I heard her thoughts, I didn't understand them. But the rest of her tumbled through me in raw intensity, and I felt her *waiting*: for the arrival of someone she knew and anticipated and dreaded to face.

Through her eyes I looked up to the sky, watching the approach of a dragon. Even on the passive perch I occupied, the wonder of it blasted through me. Much as I might have wanted to believe otherwise, I had never apprehended such creatures as real. But here it was, and it was even more magnificent than I had imagined: powerful black wings, a dozen times broader than an eagle's, gleaming in brilliant late-afternoon sunlight; black scales reflecting green-purple-blue-gold; sinuous neck turning as its long deadly head fixed a cold gaze on her.

She raised the Spear, taking aim; warring emotions pounded through her and resonated in me, sending the casting of power the Spear issued wide of the mark. She knew she must kill the dragon or all should be lost: this came through to me with blinding clarity as she cursed herself for missing, ran again through the complex preparatory procedure I couldn't understand and prepared to fire once more. But her reluctance and regret mounted yet more strongly, dragging her hands as if through deep water, sending the casting that should have obliterated the dragon into a standing stone instead. The stone exploded, scattering fragments across the circle and into the air beyond the summit.

The dragon settled, wings blasting the astonishingly misplaced aroma of amnivaren across the circle, giving me only a glimpse of the luminous scales of its chest before it blurred and took on the shape of a man. He stood beside the Tuaoh, incandescently naked and rampant, so beautiful it was impossible for the eye to avoid assessing his proud erect flesh. He pinned Carina with the gaze I'd seen behind the eyes of countless Básghilae, his familiar fearless power and unmistakable dark energies amplified by passion. This was Nechton: grey eyes so intense most men would mistake the regard for coldness; a long cloud of black hair and the broad facial structures of an Essuvian or a Weaver; a well-proportioned body whose musculature bespoke long training.

Gods, he was gorgeous, in the way a sword or a killing storm can be. In the way only a wizard can be in the full mad glory of his power. Even when my lover is a man, I prefer to bestow, but for him I would have made an exception, trading places as often as necessary. The pounding desire that erupted in Carina seemed the only appropriate response; the preparatory sequence evaporated from her attention, and she stood staring, resignation and terror spiraling through her inevitable arousal until there was no way to separate the strands. When Nechton drew on the power of the Tuaoh, I felt it through Carina's awareness, though she didn't recognize exactly what he'd done; his eyes never left hers, and only a negligent gesture of his right hand indicated the forces at work when he used the power of the Tuaoh to break the Spear in her hand, sending fragments scattering and Carina herself into oblivion.

Like to like, I thought, finding my face full of fragments of a Spear and the part I had thought of as a hilt wearing a hole in my chest. I rolled away from the jumbled pile. Stone and orichalus shifted and clanked around me; the strap tangled around my wrist.

"Sweet Lord of Light!" Letitia blurted, somewhere behind me. I heard the door slam shut; she raced to the bed and crawled towards me. "Are you all right?"

"Fine," I said automatically, gazing at her. She was fully dressed again, though her hair still hung unbound.

"What happened?" she said.

"Where were you going?" I said simultaneously.

We both smiled. Her face held a surprising, hesitant relief mixed with embarrassment, and I realized she hadn't truly grasped what I was doing.

"Going to get Amien," she admitted. "You—you just *collapsed*, and you wouldn't answer me, and—" She glanced away. "I heard the knights talking about what Amien did with the assassin's weapon at Dromineer, about how he got stuck and—"

I nodded, understanding now. "I'm fine," I said again.

Belatedly the true import of her actions caught up to me. She would have revealed the evidently damning truth about the Spear, as well as my state of semi-dress and its obvious implications, to Amien—for me. My throat tightened.

"Thank you," I said, meeting her solemn gaze. The worry around her eyes tugged painfully at my heart. "Amien would have told you not to worry, that this is common—"

Now I realized my mistakes; frustration with my own foolishness welled in me.

"*I* should have told you. I shouldn't have been standing. I'm sorry, all this sleeplessness is catching up with me. You were right; it was Nechton."

"What?" Letitia said softly.

"It was Nechton who broke the Spear..." The memory washed through me again: the terrible beauty of the dragon, the equally troubling splendor of the wizard, the ease with which he drew on the Tuaoh. Desire I feared to quantify settled over me; I pushed it away.

"Right in her hand," I said, hearing the dreaminess in my own voice. "Gods, what a—" I banished that line of reasoning, fixed my attention on Letitia again.

"Your mother was an amazing woman," I said. "I wish I'd known her."

Letitia's composure crumpled; she turned away, rose from the bed. I hauled myself up to sit; the world twirled around me. I hardened myself against what I must say.

"But she was wholly unable to best Nechton." My voice sounded cold, even to me; I felt my heart shrivel. "You must let me take you to Aballo. This battle is not for—"

"No," she choked, still with her back to me. "I must do what I can."

I flinched at my next words—and said them anyway. "And die trying."

A terrible sound escaped her; she put her head into her hands. "If I must."

"No!" I said, launched myself from the bed, wobbled and pulled her to me; she pushed against me and broke away. "What if we can find a way to repair the Spear at Aballo? Won't that be enough?"

"What if Amien's right?" Letitia said, a sob in her voice. "What if I'm the one who can—?" She faltered.

A flash of absolute self-loathing shot through me, rapidly overtaken by anger. "This is a mission for a wizard. For a whole team of wizards. There needs to be an organized assault, under cover of a military operation, and—"

Letitia shook her head. "I have no doubt of that. But if there is a part I must play, then I will play it. We are all in the goddess's Hands."

I'd seen the work of those Hands. But the terrible resignation in Letitia penetrated straight to my core. It is incumbent on a general to recognize a battle he cannot win, no matter how passionately he wishes he might.

I sighed. "Then we must find a way to protect you."

"We must find a way to defeat him," she answered.

"That will be an integral part of it," I agreed. I found my mind running over the problem again. The objective she'd been given was a sound one, at least in principle: we must remove the Shadow of the Sun from Nechton's hands.

Though it was becoming increasingly evident that was far from a complete solution. It is generally understood to be impossible to shapeshift into something larger or smaller than oneself: all of one's matter must go somewhere after the transition, and one cannot become larger simply through Will. And yet Nechton had managed to manifest a dragon of enormous size and physical presence.

Or had it been physical presence? What if it had been a Nechton-sized dragon wrapped in a truly persuasive illusion? I had seen through Carina's eyes, after all: I had no way to be sure she had sufficient Talent to see through a glamour.

"Was that—all?" Letitia said hesitantly, snapping me back into the present. "What else did you see?"

It took me a moment to realize what she was asking. After another second of staring at her while waiting for my laggard mind to catch up, I realized she feared I had seen something dishonorable or humiliating. Again my curiosity about the contents of Carina's grimoire surged.

"There wasn't much," I said. "She was using the Spear to defend the Temple Mount at Ilunmore from Nechton."

Letitia gasped, suddenly pale.

"It—didn't go very well," I said. "He flew in, in dragon shape—" A small strangled noise escaped Letitia. "—and tapped the power of the Tuaoh to break the Spear. She... lost consciousness."

Letitia nodded solemnly. "But she didn't die."

I nodded, too. "We can assume that she was the one who picked up the pieces and brought them back to Fíana. It's an interesting question what Nechton might have accomplished afterward. His presence at Ilunmore suggests he probably had the opportunity to integrate the power sources there—which actually goes a long way towards explaining the success he had with remote operations in Fíana—"

Another strangled noise escaped Letitia; I glanced at her, seeing grief and horror tipping towards despair. Belatedly I realized how disconnected from the realm of humanity I was growing: all my focus fell on the arcane and strategic, and Letitia's feelings about Nechton in her homeland, natural though I recognized they must be, eluded me even now.

How long had it been since I'd eaten? How long since I'd slept? A wizard's natural power gives him the ability to stretch beyond human limitations for a time, but not to take his humanity with him. In short order I would be nothing but cold Will and an unquenchable lust for power.

"I'm sorry," I said. And I was, though only for the pain I'd caused: I knew everything I'd said was true. "I need to sleep and eat; you must, too." I realized I was ravenous, carrying a wailing cavern in the place where my stomach should be. "Do you want to go downstairs and see what they're cooking?"

She gave me a long, solemn look I couldn't interpret; finally she nodded.

"Excellent," I said, buttoned my shirt, and strode to the door. I opened it, gesturing for Letitia to precede me—and caught sight of Amien's ward on the door. Abruptly I remembered the wards I'd wrecked this morning, the way I'd torn them from Letitia's body with my hands. I felt myself blush and closed the door again.

"What?" Letitia said, turning a look of astonishment on me.

"Your wards. I—wrecked them, earlier."

"*What?*"

I felt my face grow redder yet. I glanced down, at my bare feet. How many other little things was I forgetting?

"When we were—Right after I came in, and we were kissing, I—When I touched the wards, Amien... was aware of me."

"Oh Sweet Lord," Letitia groaned.

"And I just—I didn't think, I just... ripped them away."

She stared at me, the smolder in her gaze returning. "I didn't think... That's not supposed to..."

I shrugged, torn between the need to squirm and the fire her eyes ignited in me.

"So he knows," Letitia said.

"If we're lucky, he thinks he dreamed it. He knew I was here, so he wouldn't—"

"What?"

I chuckled. "I came in through his ward on the door. Of course he knows I was in here; he trusted me to watch over you."

Letitia nodded slowly. "So now what? Do I go back to him and ask him to do it again? How do I explain—?"

"No. Then he'll know it wasn't a dream. I've got to..." Oh, dear gods.

Building personal wards is a simple operation: one need only draw up the energies of the earth on which the subject stands and wrap them around his or her body. Even an initiate can do it. Naturally better wards have considerably more subtlety, and a good operator will customize his wards to the subject's situation.

But I had vowed not to draw power. How was I going to accomplish it?

All at once I saw: use Letitia's power, and I wouldn't have to draw any of my own. The concept blossomed whole in my head, in the way a plan for a working so often will; my hands itched for the touch of power. A dangerous excitement began in my chest.

"Get undressed." A rough edge had developed in my voice.

Immediately she was staring at me, the renewed smolder in her gaze making my heart beat faster yet.

"This time we'll use your power. All I will do is show you how."

She opened her mouth as if to speak, changed her mind, kicked off her boots and held my gaze while her fingers unfastened one button after another, until the shirt hung open. I controlled the impulse to reach out and snake my hands beneath it; my throat tightened as she pulled it off and let it fall to the floor.

I didn't understand why it should torque me so to watch her undress, when she'd been naked in my arms just a while ago; still need spun through me with increasing intensity as she peeled away the rest of her clothes. By the time she was fully undressed I could hardly breathe; I knelt at her feet, looked up the lean silken length of her, and said, "Ready?"

She nodded; I encompassed her with my awareness, in much the same way I'd done with the Spear. She gasped. Immediately she was everywhere, a cloud of delight hanging around me and a compelling new set of layers and thoughts in my mind. A tremor rocked through her, echoing in my own body. I saw my own ardent face staring up at her with absolutely naked need; shifted my focus to the part of her awareness where thought and memory resided; then reached deeper, finding the dark spaces below the conscious mind, where it can be dangerous for a mindworker who would do no harm to touch. Below that, I found the path I sought: the conduit to the diamond.

There, I thought.

Joy and astonishment erupted in her and blazed through our shared mindspace. *What! How did you find—?*

I smiled. *Right there the whole time. Just draw that energy in…*

She tried to pull on it, but a fog of anxiety rose and the conduit grew suddenly elusive. Her frustration ripped through us.

Zhev! she thought, fear rising in frustration's wake. *What's the matter with me?*

I pushed the thought aside.

Hush, I thought, putting as much reassurance into it as I could. *Stop. Don't try to make it do anything.*

But you said—

Never mind that now. Just relax. Watch the light. It's beautiful, isn't it?

I drew a deep breath and released it slowly, pushing aside my tingling eagerness for the energy she would manifest. Self-doubt is the direst possible killer of arcane success; letting her see how urgently I wanted her to continue would only serve to raise her anxiety. A better teacher would have sent feelings of calm and timelessness into her. No teacher, particularly not an initiator, should have any sort of emotional entanglement with either the student or the outcome of the process. I was a terrible failure in both regards. The best I could do was to let her breathe through the anxiety, hope she would take my closeness as calming support, wait while she found her center. Finally her nervous fluttering calmed; she slipped into the sort of entrancement of self that is the nearest most will ever come to arcane consciousness; and she began to float in the light of her own power. I met her gaze.

That light is yours, annu. It is you. Let it be in you.

Joy surged through her, spilling into me, carrying such tender admiration that my heart stumbled back into the realm of humanity. She met my eyes with the sort of regard that usually signaled the necessity of a swift retreat; this time I found myself sinking into it, emotion swelling inside me until my heart threatened to block my throat. Light rushed into her, spilling through me; my whole being begged for more. Absent the amplification of us bouncing it back and forth, her power was minor, gentle: a faint echo of what I might have carried, only a sip of the river-sized drink I craved.

Yes! I thought. *There.*

It would be far easier to channel the energy for the working than talk her through managing this small sparkle; the power I needed surged below me, waiting for my grasp and the opportunity to become something new. It was hard to remember why I shouldn't open myself and let it in.

Now all you need to is push it to the outside, draw it around…

…?

Letitia thought about pushing. But instead of moving the energy where it was needed, she only made it race faster inside, until the glow in her became visible. Her incandescence snared me, occupying the whole universe; her gaze captured me, irresistible as gravity. Joining with her was my only destiny, amplifying her power and spinning it back to her the only objective that mattered. I could barely breathe through the need. It took me far longer than it should have to remember why I'd started this and what I'd planned, longer yet to decide on a different approach.

Well, then, I thought. *I am going to put my hands where the wards should be; you just think about touching my hands with the light, and follow them wherever they go.* I stretched out my hands to hover above her feet, feeling stray brilliance feather against my palms. Letitia reached towards my hair, and I felt her desire for the feel of warm silk sliding against her fingers and palms, then saw her remember her task and restrain the impulse.

Touch me here, I thought. The thought resonated with my unruly, multilayered desire; I couldn't care about the ways I was failing as a teacher. *On the palms of my hands.*

Letitia shivered. The tremor raced across my skin like the memory of fire in the hands—and then the tingle was there, against my palms. All the air in my lungs left me in a rush; my head swam.

"Yes," I said, a rough edge in my voice again. *Follow me.*

I traced the air around her body, describing her narrow feet and slender ankles, gliding up the lengths of her legs. The tingle of Letitia's gentle power danced against my hands as I moved, trailing a prismatic, barely-visible sparkle through the air and echoing in pleasure along the length of my every nerve. Around the luscious curves of the moons great and small, I found myself augmenting her power with my own passion, allowed myself the transgression of trailing a finger beside the beautiful mound that occupied the center of the universe; the petal skin under my fingertip and Letitia's mounting ardor spun my head past reason once more.

I nearly split with competing desires, needing to cast the working aside and bury myself in her again, ravenous for the continued play of power against my skin. Necessity decided me, and as I continued I realized how right the choice had been: I traced my hands up the length of her spine, letting gentle ripples of power cavort against my fingers and palms, breathless at the glow they cast in my wake. She leaned in close enough to trace her lips with my own as I wrapped my hands around her head; the feathering of power between our mouths tingled in all the cells of my body. I circled and closed off above her crown, delighting in the delicious ripple of light that followed. The colorless glow danced all around her, spectral as sunlight through a waterfall. I settled my mouth against hers, butterfly-light, for a taste.

Letitia's answering kiss was ferocious. After a moment of devouring me, she began to speak against my lips, fingers busy with buttons: "Oh Sweet Lord that was amazing! I could feel you all around me—and the light—and—Endeáril, if that's what magic is like then how do wizards find time for anything but loving?"

I laughed, wrapped arms around her to feel the twin delights of her skin and her gentle power against me, pulled her frenzy into a pace that would allow us to enjoy in consciousness.

"It's not always like that," I murmured against her mouth, and applied myself to enjoying her flavors and textures. I could make love with Letitia all day, and enjoy the process, but now I remembered: it was the other thing, the flow of power and the delight of directing it, that I truly craved. Soon I would be mad with the need for more, but for the moment I felt like one does after the first course of an elaborate meal: ready to slow down and enjoy, but far more aware of the depth of my hunger. I had no idea how to fill that need without breaking my vow.

It was a good thing I had a lover to keep me occupied until I figured it out.

Chapter 29
Beneath the Surface

They were serving lunch when Letitia and I finally arrived in the inn's main room. I took it as a mark of how far beyond hunger I'd gone that I ate two bowls of what was doubtless a thoroughly unremarkable stew, relishing it nearly as much as I had the meal in the top-flight inn at Nemetona. The company was simpler, too: we ate surrounded by tradesmen and travelers less readily identified, none of whom I recognized. Evidently the rest of our companions still slept.

I was thinking about climbing the stairs and lying down for a few hours myself when Rohini's man Thurro walked in. He hurried to our table to deliver the news that Amien had found a boat and the company was assembling outside the stable. So much for sleep: we sped upstairs to gather our possessions. I pulled on still-damp boots, donned mail and sword belt, picked up my bags and the terrible wreck of my harp, and accompanied Thurro and Letitia to the stable.

Someone had already tacked out my horse: I had only to load up my gear and lead him outside. In the yard I discovered most of the party already present, waiting beside their horses.

I met the second group of Rohini's men, to whom I'd forgotten to introduce myself yesterday: Corrib, Pirres and Seihar; the brothers Calbo and Tibas, between whom it was difficult to distinguish; and Retogen, who evidently hailed from the same clan as Olin. There were no young men among Rohini's crew, I realized: only Seihar looked as if he might match me in age, and the rest of them were probably a decade older. I suspected a year of sleeping outdoors hadn't improved anyone's looks; all of them were weatherbeaten and shaggy. But they shared a patient, spare fierceness and the sort of bone-deep bonds that require few words to be exchanged.

When Rohini's second-in-command Busadi arrived, they greeted him with the blend of respect and affection that represents the best a commander can hope to achieve. He assessed them all with a practiced eye, and I recognized the way he cataloged them: Corrib was sufficiently deficient in sleep that he would err in a way Busadi could predict and now planned to compensate for; Tibas carried his arm in a way that suggested a shoulder wound of long history was troubling him. Busadi himself was suffering the sort of stiffness that comes from an abrupt change in sleeping arrangements. Strange how unaccustomed comfort can make the muscles lock up.

Iminor and Nuad entered the yard. I greeted them with a polite nod, watching as Iminor continued to play the perfect consort: inquiring after the quality of Letitia's sleep, which she admitted had been poor; assuming most of her burdens without any commentary. Today it all had the quality of things done because they were appropriate rather than because they would be appreciated or even necessarily matter.

His careworn aspect was my doing. If I would never come closer to possessing Letitia than the occasional tryst, then why didn't I back away and give him the space he deserved? He was too noble to be so betrayed. I was diminishing all of us. Hadn't I decided to love Letitia like I did the rest of them, after all?

Finally I remembered: reality crashed over me, robbing me of breath. His grief was my fault, two dozen times over: the rest of our companions weren't going to wake up and join us. No crowd of familiar Tanaan faces would gather in this yard. We would go forward without our friends today.

How was it possible I hadn't thought of them since this morning? I hadn't even thought to cut my hair.

That wasn't my prerogative. I was the cause of their deaths, not the one bereaved.

I realized Iminor was watching me. Reluctantly I met his eyes, trying hopelessly to steel myself against all the flavors of condemnation he had every right to heap on me. There was nothing I could say.

But what I saw in him was shared grief and a surprised respect. As if he had just developed the suspicion that I might be human, after all.

Might have been, perhaps: after a second I glanced away.

Amien strode into the yard and unhitched his horse, abstracted worry written in his face. He glanced around, automatically tallying riders—then stuttered to a stop, gaze fixed on Letitia.

"Letitia!" he said, as if her very presence startled him. I knew he saw the wards I had created for her, as clearly and disconcertingly as I always saw his.

Horror swept over me: with one unplanned utterance he would bring untold humiliation on both Letitia and Iminor. Her honor would be completely wrecked on this side of the mountains, no matter what the Tanaan rules said; Iminor would be forced to confront the certainty that he'd been cuckolded at the precise moment when the matter was revealed in public, with no time to master his emotions in private or work out how to proceed. It would all be my fault.

I leapt into the saddle, tweaked the horse so he startled and reared, and let the inevitable fall take me, tumbling spurs over ears and landing hard enough to blast the air from my lungs. Immediately every eye in the yard was on me. Rohini failed to contain a smirk; several of her men guffawed. Amien cast me a long, considering glance as I lay there in the dust. Understanding passed between us.

He knew everything; of course he knew. He saw exactly what had gone into the creation of Letitia's new wards; he had been aware when I destroyed his, had doubtless absorbed far more than the bare facts during those few seconds of arcane contact. If he doubted whether he'd dreamed it, he doubted no more. And he recognized at least part of why I'd staged the fall: with a single, silent nod of acknowledgment, he turned his attention on Letitia again.

"Your wards appear to be in fine shape," he said in a calm voice. "Excellent. We shouldn't need to revisit them before Sucello, if at all."

Letitia nodded, eyes on the wizard and a flush spreading across her otherwise-composed face. "Thank you, my lord."

Amien glanced at me again, some decision I couldn't identify in his eyes; he closed the distance between us and offered me a hand up. I let him pull me to my feet.

"Do you have any further antics planned this afternoon?" he inquired drily.

I shook my head.

"Let's go, then," he said. He clapped a hand on my shoulder, as if I were still a member of his workshop and I'd made a respectable go of a difficult working, and returned to his horse.

The boat Amien had engaged stood waiting by the dock when we arrived. It looked, to my untutored eye, more or less the same as the one we'd left behind at Nemetona: large enough for the party and our horses, but not designed for the comfort of passengers or crew. At least I wasn't drunk this time.

After the crew cast off, I crossed the deck to stand beside Amien in the prow, grasping the rail as he raised a gentle westerly wind that filled the sail and moved the boat steadily against the current. For the first few minutes I hardly dared to breathe, anticipating an answering blow from Nechton that would send us all into the water. But it didn't come. For mile after mile we sailed smoothly upriver, gradually gathering a flotilla of rich men's boats ahead of us as we drew up behind them and propelled them more rapidly against the tide. Overhead, the sky stretched blue and nearly cloudless, unnerving in its bright serenity; birds dove after fish in our wake. The ease of it made the skin on the back of my neck crawl.

"What, he doesn't care?" Amien muttered at last.

I shook my head. "We are playing right into his hands."

The wizard glanced at me, a frown on his face that suggested he'd had the same thought.

"Damned if I know how," I said, answering the unspoken question. "Just one more reason to take her to Aballo instead."

He gave vent to an explosive sigh. After several moments of watching the boats ahead of us, he said, "Do you have intelligence I should know about?"

I had promised Letitia silence. She chose honor over life. It was one of the few things about her I truly understood, despite my own failure in that regard.

"No," I said, after what had probably been too long a silence. "But I am familiar with her power, and his."

Amien sighed. "Great Lord Ilesan, I wish I knew what Carina did."

I nodded. "My lord, I know we need to begin casting strategy—but I won't be of much use until I've slept."

The wizard cast me a thoughtful glance. "It's been—what? Since Dromineer?"

I nodded again.

A reluctant smile creased his long face, and I knew he was thinking about my self-inflicted sleeplessness at Presatyn and this morning. I felt myself flush.

"Go, already," he said, smiling as if my blush amused him further. "Sleep. We'll talk tomorrow."

"Thank you," I said. "Call on me as you will."

He laid a hand on my shoulder again, for just a moment; I mustered a smile and crossed the deck to the opening through which a man could access the hold.

The place was dark and windowless, the air too still. But it was cool, and the darkness tugged me immediately towards sleep: I lay down on the floor and let the gentle rocking of the boat take me. Water rushed past the hull, lending the interior a soft, soothing hum; the sweet power of the river goddess gathered around me again. I should have fought Her, should have sought to hold myself separate; instead I welcomed Her gratefully in. And in the safety of Her cool dark embrace I slept.

Ruddy sunset light shone through the opening at the top of the ladder when next I opened my eyes. For a moment I lay still, the gentle Presence of the river goddess fading from my awareness, piecing together where I was and why. Gradually I realized the boat was no longer moving: I hauled myself to my feet and climbed the ladder to the deck above.

The boat lay at anchor in the middle of the river, rocking softly in the tide. At least a dozen other boats had anchored nearby. All those other vessels had been riding Amien's summoned wind, I remembered: when we stopped for the night, they had wisely done the same. We would spend this night surrounded by strangers: far enough apart that our watches would detect any approach before it arrived, but the way sound carries across open water destroying any illusion of privacy. Even now I heard men speaking on several other boats.

I crossed to the rear of the boat and saw to my horse: seeing him fed and watered; brushing him and checking his hooves, for the comforting routine and contact it gave both of us rather than because the short ride we took this afternoon had made it in any way necessary. I spoke to him in tones pitched for his ears alone, offering senseless apologies for the loss of his friends and for making him ride yet another boat, which I knew he enjoyed even less than I. I looked up and discovered Amien leaning against the rail, watching me.

I shrugged. "He gets nervous. He needs a lot of contact or he gets a little crazy."

Amien nodded solemnly. "Me, too."

A halfhearted smile overtook me. "He misses his friends. He'd just gotten used to them…" I found it necessary to swallow against a sudden tightening of my throat, to look out across the water. "Last night was… bad."

Amien stepped away from the rail, leaned companionably across his own horse's withers. "What happened?"

I drew a deep breath, trying to harden myself against the memory. Of course we needed to discuss this: it was a tactical issue. We should have talked about it last night.

Belatedly I realized Amien was handling me as gently as I was my horse. The idea of being *managed* made me want to buck and throw off the bridle, but I couldn't figure out where it was. I tried to draw a general's necessary distance around me instead.

"We walked into a trap," I said, keeping my voice at a pitch that would carry the words no farther than Amien. I shook my head, glancing away. "The path to the river crossing was mined. How they knew where to lay the trap when we hadn't even conceived of crossing and it made no damn tactical *sense—who* knew to lay the mines…"

The *shift* occurred in my mind again; the horse and I hung in the midst of nothingness as the ground fell away and something dropped behind us; the explosion ripped apart the spot in which that something fell.

"How did you…" Amien's voice came from some indeterminate place beyond the nothingness. "How did you escape?"

A fist closed around my heart. There was no way I could explain, not even to Amien. Especially not to Amien. He would read all the wrong things into the fact that Lady Tella had intervened for me again. I wrenched myself into the present moment, taking in Amien's grave face and my own fingers tangled frantically in the horse's mane. I bent and picked up the brush, began smoothing away the snarls.

"I was at the front of the line. When the first mine exploded—he just bolted. By the time I could see again we were out in the middle of the river."

"Great Lord Ilesan," Amien murmured.

"I don't understand," I said. My voice sounded choked again. "How the hell did they know to pick that spot?"

Amien shook his head. "How does what we're doing now feed their strategy? I can't answer that question, either."

"I'd give a lot for twenty minutes with that orb," I muttered. Amien turned a long, troubled gaze on me. "Or one of the Bard's generals and a vial of ephedra salts. That would work, too."

Amien gave me another thoughtful look. I glanced down the length of the deck, watching Rohini's men settle in for the evening's rest. Letitia, Iminor and Nuad sat with backs against the charthouse, gazing across the water at the southern shore. Up in the prow, Busadi stood looking around with the sort of posture and attention that suggested he'd claimed the night's first watch; Olin strolled around from the far side of the charthouse and planted himself in the rear. I suspected he'd been maintaining a respectful distance over there for a few minutes, giving us time to finish our conversation. Amien glanced at him, nodded politely—and yawned.

"I'll split the arcane watches with you?" I said. "Why don't you get some sleep."

"Call if you need me," he said, yawning again, and stepped towards the front of the boat. After a few steps he stopped, turning to look at me again, face falling into the lines that suggested some discomfiting topic was in the offing.

"You were wrong the other day," Amien said finally in Tanaan, "when you said I make decisions because of the way I bollocksed things up with Carina."

I nodded. "I know," I said in the same language.

"Letting her go to Macol without me was the stupidest thing I ever did," the wizard continued, eyes on something in Letitia's vicinity. He sighed.

"I think—" He shook his head. "Gods, this sounds stupid. I think I thought that if I ascended to the Prince's throne—I would deserve the way she... Fouzh."

It took far too long for me to come up with something to say. For all that, it wasn't very good.

"Men are idiots," I offered.

Amien glanced at me, looked away again.

"I know I am," I said.

Amien laughed, finally meeting my eyes. "Your instincts are truer than mine ever were. You should consider trusting yourself."

My throat clamped shut at all the layers of meaning I heard in his words. I couldn't help it: I glanced away.

"Sleep well, my lord," I croaked, still looking across the water.

"Gods grant you strength," he said gently, and left me to ponder which gods he meant.

I closed the distance between the Tanaan and myself, slipped down to settle beside Nuad: my back against the charthouse, my gaze on the the southern shore. I should have held myself separate, should have given all my attention to monitoring the arcane. But some tension in my chest abated, just a little, as the Tanaan glanced at me, silently accepting my presence, and returned to whatever woolgathering they were about. Within minutes Letitia had fallen asleep on Iminor's shoulder. I pushed aside a futile wish to trade places with Iminor, reminded myself I had resolved to give him the distance he deserved, and turned my eyes across the water.

Nagnata looked serene from here, with moonlight tracing marsh grasses on the shore and fields of flax on the land above. The bluffs were not as tall here as they had been yesterday. The moonlit fields, the distant standing stones, the immense old oak spreading its fingers among the stars: they seemed little higher than the deck of the boat on which I sat. I sank into a quiet that was not quite a trance, spreading tendrils of awareness into the aether: the Presence of the river goddess running beneath my consciousness again, the Power that was Esus stretching out and encompassing all the parts of me that should know better and yet could not help but respond to His Call.

My bones hummed to the song of the darkness; a tree grew up through my spine, pinning my flesh in a place that was neither mundane nor arcane; stars sparked in my fingertips and tangled in my hair. Gradually the torment of human emotion receded to a manageable distance, and I gazed dispassionately at the contents of my own mind: fitting facts together like the puzzle pieces they were, seeking a solution to the intertwined and mutually antagonistic problems of Nechton and the Bard on one hand and Letitia's safety on the other. Every solution I found hinged on breaking my vow. It seemed likely that my vow was self-indulgent foolishness: that I was damned already, had been damned before I was born; that the only way I could truly protect Letitia was to accept that fact and do what was necessary. That honor in this case arose not from doing the bidding of the gods but rather Their Will, and accepting the role my stars had long since assigned. The cold, clear-eyed awareness that had overtaken me turned its attention on the part that clung to human emotions and futile illusions of honor, and tried once again to pry it free. But then another presence brushed against a distant tendril of awareness—and that recalcitrant, emotion-ridden part of me woke up and swept everything else aside.

The world tumbled into place. I wrenched myself free of a tree to which I might or might not be bound. Nuad slept the sleep of long exhaustion beside me. On his other side, Letitia stirred as if in a dream, pain in her face. The glow of the wards we'd crafted still hung around her; through the spidersilk of her mail shirt I sensed the spark of her talisman, grown oddly bright in the darkness. Nechton hovered nearby. I felt him reaching towards her: not physically, but aetherically—as if he might slip in through a dream.

I was moving before the things I had decided fully manifested in the conscious part of my mind: encompassing Letitia with my awareness, simultaneously scrambling to my feet and scooping her up into my arms as Iminor woke and stared at me, peripherally cognizant of his affront fading into fear. She was present inside me at least as much as in my grasp, her nighttime logic transforming our entanglement into my presence in her dream. That was true enough: I might not allow myself to draw power, but it was no impediment to the psychic defenses I needed to create, and I spun them around us like a wall of flames in a shared nightmare, casting blinds and mines in that circle's wake as I pushed it outward and locked it down tight. Nechton crashed into that border, spent some interminable time staring across it: penetrating grey eyes and sardonic smile meeting my own as if we stood separated by a mirror rather than an aetheric minefield.

I itched to push him away, to send his awareness blasting backwards through the aether; but so far, I knew, he had only glimpses of me, not arcane signatures. I should hold onto what meager tactical advantages I had. Instead I set Letitia down behind me in that dream-space, let my hand settle on the hilt of my sword. Nechton smiled as if that, too, fell into some tactical plan I wouldn't understand until too late—and then he was gone.

Letitia woke, crying out; drew back far enough to look into my eyes; and buried her face in my mail shirt. Wave after wave of trembling wracked her delicate frame. I grasped her more tightly, whispering nonsense into the top of her head, reluctantly meeting Iminor's gaze. Fear competed with a bare-ly-checked jealousy in his depthless eyes; I realized part of the reason I still grasped Letitia was for my own comfort, settled her feet to the deck and un-wound myself from her. No sooner had I stepped back than Iminor grasped her, soothing her terror with a gentle embrace.

"That was Nechton," he said to me.

I nodded; he nodded, too.

"I thought I was dreaming," he said after a moment.

"Yes," I said gently. "When it's aetheric, that's often how it is."

"Next time I dream him, I'll wake up," he said. Letitia laughed weakly against his mail shirt. "We should ask Amien to work wards."

I shook my head. "Not on the water. He needs contact with the earth."

Iminor sighed. "All we get to do is name our poison."

"Tomorrow night we sleep at Sucello," I said, trying to sound certain. "She will be safe."

For a night. There was no need to say it; the grim awareness passed among us without words. My mind rolled forward to the days separating Sucello from Teamair and the twelvenight separating Teamair from Macol; and I won-dered how long it would be before no possibilities remained but breaking my vow.

Chapter 30
View of the Abyss

I woke when the boat began to move again. Morning spread clear blue and cloudless across the sky; Amien's summoned wind blew forward across the deck, sending the tail of my hair fluttering ahead of me as I rose. I saw to my horse, dug some jerky out of the supplies, and gnawed on it as I crossed the deck to the prow, where Rohini and the Tanaan already stood gathered around Amien.

Yesterday's flotilla preceded us again, the gay silks of rich men's pleasure boats easy to spot amid the utilitarian sails of the more practical vessels. I couldn't imagine why a man would want to sail for pleasure, particularly not so much so that he would buy a boat for the purpose, but today I envied those men the food I smelled cooking on their yachts. I was pleased to discover that I couldn't hear any of them talking this morning, however, and silently blessed the wind that filled all those sails. At least I wouldn't have to hear them enjoying it.

I stepped into the little cluster of people at the prow, exchanging greetings. Letitia looked calm again, exhibiting no ill effects of last night's encounter except a hollowness around her eyes. Iminor met my gaze evenly, no hostility in his manner, though he edged closer to Letitia without seeming aware of it.

"A quiet watch, my lord?" I said to Amien.

He nodded, glancing at me. His eyes held the half-abstracted look that bespoke a sector of his mind still engaged in the wind he was crafting, and fatigue weighted his brow; but he addressed me with focused attention. "We were just discussing tactics that encompass psychic defense."

I nodded, including the rest of them with my gaze. "What I did last night was fairly basic. Letitia should be able to learn much of it."

Letitia stiffened. "Ellion—"

I shook my head, manufacturing a smile. "There's no arcane power involved in crafting psychic defenses; it's all…" I groped uselessly after words that didn't exist. "Mental?" I shrugged. "That's not the word. Anyway. What I did last night was no violation of my vow, and there should be no reason why you can't learn it. It's not—" I hesitated again. "Magic. Not really."

Letitia frowned thoughtfully at me, silent for quite some time. "I see."

"Meanwhile, Amien was saying that the fewer nights Letitia spends in places he can't ward, the better," Iminor said.

"Agreed," I said, and glanced at Amien again. "Though I'd include the places in which Esus has strong followings on that list."

The wizard sighed. "Can you chart a path to Macol that avoids all of them?"

"I'm not convinced I know where all of them are. Do you? The terrain continues to surprise me in that regard."

Amien nodded ruefully.

"I suspect that, should Letitia go to Macol, we might actually be well advised to sail her there," I continued.

"What?" Iminor said. "After last night—"

"Yes," I said. "She'll require constant arcane watches, but even with nothing but natural winds the trip will take considerably less time. Armies travel at half the speed we've been making on our slowest days; a twelvenight from Teamair to Macol is optimistic by half, and that doesn't even take the time required for musters and rendezvous into account. And I'm still not convinced her presence there is a tactical necessity at all."

Amien's patience thinned visibly. Rohini groaned and looked away.

"I thought we were agreed about the Shadow of the Sun," he said in a calm voice.

"Really?" I said. "I'd agree it should be captured. I won't agree it should be destroyed. And given the number of wizards and swordsmen who would be required to ensure Letitia's safety during the operation, I have yet to be convinced Letitia can do anything that team couldn't do in her absence."

Anger flashed in Amien's face, but Iminor held up a hand.

"Wait," the Tan said. "What sort of an operation do you have in mind?"

"One made under cover of a much larger military assault on the city. We'll need much more concrete intelligence before we can solidify things." I glanced at Rohini.

She treated me to a dark, skeptical look, then glanced at Amien. "What sort of intelligence are you looking for?"

"Well," Amien said. "We agree about the objective." His inflection made the statement into a question.

Rohini nodded. "Recapture the city, and take the Shadow of the Sun."

"So what we really need to know," I said, "is how to infiltrate the palace."

Rohini froze, staring at me.

"I've no doubt you know all the ways that place is vulnerable, sian," I continued. "It won't be my objective to do damage or reveal those breaches to anyone not a part of the operation; I'm talking about a small party of wizards, whose discretion can be trusted. And, for the sake of argument, Letitia. We'll be able to use arcane concealments on approach and in the outer reaches of the palace, but as we come within range of the man's workshop those will be less than useless."

Rohini nodded slowly, something in her gaze I wasn't certain how to quantify. "What is your plan?"

I shrugged. "You know how these things go, sian; reality is always the death of our plans. We'll plan this thing down to the last detail, and then we'll get in there and things won't go as expected."

Rohini gave a philosophical shrug.

"I would take maybe six wizards." I glanced at Amien, and he nodded, but it was a gesture indicating attention rather than consent. "Who those wizards would be depends on who survives Esunertos, who turns out to be required elsewhere, et cetera."

"But you have a preferred team in mind," Rohini prompted.

I glanced at Amien again. "Well. Amien will have considerable input, naturally. At first glance I'd say Sanglin and Dandem—Brinner if he's available; he's dealt with Nechton before. I'm thinking you'd take the lead of the arcana-military aspects of the mundane assault," I said to Amien, who nodded.

"Oregen's in the service of the Deceang righ?"

Amien nodded again.

"Conwy's not likely to give him up without a lot of fuss," I mused.

"Especially not if he's elected ard-righ."

"Would you spare me Dáire?" The man had been armsmaster at Aballo during my tenure there. Evidently he'd held the post for more than two centuries, and there had yet to come a man to Aballo who could best him with a sword. I wondered idly how I'd fare against him now.

Amien gave me a long look. "If we agree he comes in for that mission and goes straight back to Aballo afterward. It makes me feel naked to think of him away from the isle even that long."

I nodded—and realized I'd gotten tripped into a side issue. "We can discuss how to fill out the team later. Let's come back to the palace at Macol. Did you mean to slip in quietly, Chief, how would you do it?"

Rohini grimaced and glanced across the water. She sighed. "Your objective is the wizard's… workshop."

I nodded.

She sighed again. "You know there are two."

"What?" I said, but Amien nodded.

"I'd forgotten that," he said. "No man dedicated to the true gods could work in the space Nechton used for all those years. Berngal, who served Armoan's son Conis—Armoan never did sleep in the palace, just pitched tents on the family lands—persuaded Conis to build an annex he could use. I suppose Nechton's workshop stood sealed for all that time."

Rohini nodded. "It was the stuff of ghost stories when I was young."

"Too bad no one thought to burn the place," Amien mused.

A faint smile flickered across Rohini's mouth. "It was not for lack of trying. Anyway, Nechton's workshop stands at the western edge of the compound, in a separate tower. I've never gone beyond the ground floor."

The image blossomed in my mind: a round tower with a peaked roof, like the sun-towers of Hy-Breasaíl; like the sun-tower in which we'd camped at Uriah. The magic still hanging in the tower at Uriah after so many centuries raced across my mind again. Sudden, desperate curiosity about what I would find in Nechton's workshop overtook me; I had to struggle to bring my mind back to the military issues.

"A round structure?" I said. "Like a sun-tower?"

"A sun-tower?" Rohini echoed.

"You may have seen them in Banbagor? Tall, narrow, peaked roof? Since the Deluge they haven't seen much use…"

She gave me another long look. "You've been there?"

"Banbagor?" I shrugged. "I rode through it on my way to Fíana. You know the place."

"Not as well as I would like," Rohini admitted. "My mother and I visited periodically when I was a child." She shrugged, one of those peculiar Tanaan one-shouldered gestures, and a wholly irrelevant line of reasoning crystallized in my mind: I stood looking at the issue of a marriage between human and Tanaan. If a man fathered a child on a Tana, this was essentially what would result: a person who stood with one foot in either place, whose eyes looked human but whose bone structure bespoke the Four Realms. Was Bealtan her one moment of fertility during the year? I fought down the temptation to look at Letitia, to consider the issue in terms more personal yet.

"If I know the towers you mean, sian," she said, wrenching my attention back to the matter at hand, "I'd say yes: that's essentially what Nechton's workshop looks like."

I nodded. A man might defend the upper floors of such a structure almost single-handed: a direct assault wouldn't do. Letitia would need stealth—and eyes that could see through Nechton's most persuasive glamours. Even did I hold to my vow, I could manage the latter. But stealth in such a place requires current intelligence.

"Well, then, we'll need insiders in the party. Men who know the secret inner ways and the security flaws."

"I'll loan you one of my men," Rohini said.

I met her eyes. "Thank you. That will be invaluable. Who?"

Rohini glanced from me to Letitia. "At this moment I'm thinking of Seihar. He's fast enough to maybe keep up with a group of wizards, and he doesn't spook at magic the way some do."

"Excellent," I said. "I expect we'll need to wait until we're in the area to gather enough intelligence about Nechton's operational routines to know how to time things. Assuming your man Seihar can get us inside—that's where the real challenge begins. If we can get enough information to know when we can slip in and steal the orb without fighting, that's only a trouble-free entrance: the real problems will start when it's in our hands."

"What?" Iminor said.

I gave him a rueful grimace. "Nechton has strong arcane connections with the orb. He'll be aware when it's disturbed, even if he isn't present; he's likely to be able to direct power through it, even at distance, which will put whoever carries it in considerable danger."

"And *that* is why Letitia is critical to the operation," Amien said, sounding satisfied.

"What?" I said.

The wizard met my gaze, a grim smile spreading across his face. "Unless you're contemplating taking him on in direct combat."

This time the suggestion didn't shock me. I met Amien's eyes, seeing the look a man gets when he thinks he's achieved checkmate—and a glint that dared me to agree. And for just a moment I found myself contemplating it: imagining what it would be to stand inside a sun-tower that vibrated with centuries of dark energies, much of it power I could draw just as easily as Nechton might, and cast aside my bonds; to accept the fact that I had been damned before this all began, allow the fierce intoxication of power to overtake me, and see what would happen. It wouldn't matter if I died, as long as I took him with me. We'd spend the rest of eternity together in Tílimya's Abyss. Doubtless we'd suffer many of the same punishments. The fierce cold thing that kept overtaking me welled up again, and the itch of need began on my palms.

I fought it down. Amien was still staring at me, but now the flavor of it was different. I suspected the thing that was different was hope; my throat knotted. I swallowed against the pain.

"No," I said in a calm voice. "That's not what I intend."

"Then what you need is someone who can weather Nechton's power. Who can manage Dark magic with Light."

"Oh, dear gods," I groaned. "*That's* your plan? Send Letitia in there equipped with a fairy tale? *Just call on the faeries, Dear*—"

"Fouzh!" Amien snapped. "I'm suggesting that Letitia can learn to channel whatever Nechton may send through the orb to ground! That whatever immunity she has to the Dark magic, together with a discipline she's already halfway to knowing—"

"Oh, fouzh," I said, suddenly understanding. He was probably right, loathe though I was to admit it: she already knew how to channel the power of the sun, a source far too broad for most wizards to manage. Whether she could accomplish anything with that channeled power wasn't the issue: the fact that she could handle it without mishap was. The power she and I bounced back and forth when I touched her talisman sprang unbidden to my mind, mixing confusingly with the idea of her channeling a wizard's power rather than the sun—and ignited a flare of multilayered desire that made it impossible for me to focus on the conversation, to see anything but her. She met my eyes frankly, gaze shifting into a smoldering regard that spun my brain into another orbit altogether. But abruptly I connected with the fact that it was Nechton's power Amien meant for her to channel, and everything inside me ran cold.

I looked out at the water, trying to wrestle my emotions into submission. Assuming she could learn to channel power to ground rather than simply absorbing it as she did the light of the sun, Amien was right: she was the logical choice for that operational role. Even a wizard would be in more danger in that role than she. There could be no tactical reason to hold her back, only my instinct that she must be kept as far away from Nechton as possible. And that was born of emotion.

I steeled myself, returned my attention to Amien. Rohini watched me as if she'd decided I was a liability, after all.

"Yes," I admitted. "You're right. Assuming Letitia can master grounding."

The wizard nodded.

"And who will command the operation?" Rohini said.

We both looked at her.

"I will," I said.

Rohini cast me a quizzical look. "The party is to be composed of wizards, who will protect Letitia; Letitia, who may be able to manage the orb without coming to harm; one of my men, for inside intelligence; and you—why? You won't be working magic, you said."

I shook my head.

She raised an eyebrow: I suspected that was what she always did when moving her final piece into checkmate.

"Without insult, sian," she began. When a man says that, it is always the preface to something so offensive that swords must otherwise be drawn. "I fail to see why your presence is an operational necessity."

I'd been right: she recognized what a liability my emotional entanglement had become. And I couldn't fault her: it is sound strategy to remove a commander who can't manage the necessary distance from a critical operation. Still my hand itched for my sword.

That, of course, was further evidence against me.

"Nevertheless," I said evenly, glancing at Letitia. "I have given my word."

Rohini cocked that eyebrow again, but Amien nodded.

"Yes. Working magic or no, you're the man I want in that spot."

Early in the afternoon, Amien's summoned wind bore us through the mouth of the Aerona and into her source: the deep, still lake of Nanno. Perhaps two hours later we reached the lake's western shore and gratefully disembarked. My horse seemed as pleased to reach firm ground again as I felt: he took the bit willingly, whickered as I tacked him out, and stepped unhesitatingly across the gangway.

The city of Sucello spread across the western shore, stretching north and west along the foot of the bluffs that mark the upthrust to the northern highlands. The familiar energies of the true gods hung on the air here, casting unaccustomed serenity across my mind. With no illicit gods clamoring for my attention, I simply settled in among the escort as we rode westward from the docks and along the broad crowded streets that line the city. Afternoon sunlight lay thick on walls and kitchen gardens, lulled the street vendors into a torpor that took the edges off their haggling and come-on cries. By the time we reached the palace gate, the beginnings of a plan involving a bath, a good dinner, and a soft bed were coalescing in my mind.

We were expected, which meant Suibne was already here: the men at the gate welcomed us immediately inside, and the righ's seneschal met us in the portico. Inside, the Taidgh family palace reminded me of Mourne Palace in Il-nemedon: grey stone that felt cool and welcoming in this afternoon's plentiful sunlight but which would foster a suicidal gloom on a winter morn; a multitude of high windows for illumination and ventilation but narrow security-conscious slits at floor level; rich unselfconscious furnishings that invited the visitor to relax. Already I felt myself unwinding.

The seneschal showed us to a long string of guest rooms securely situated on a second-floor corridor, put more servants than sixteen people could possibly need at our disposal, invited us to use the baths in the grottoes below the palace, and left us to make what use of the hours before dinner we would. Most of the party headed straight down to the baths, but Letitia forestalled me and Amien before we had so much as set foot in our rooms.

"My lords," she said, one hand on each of our arms, glancing from Amien to me and back. "When can we get started?"

"What?" Amien said, puzzled; but the mixture of trepidation and guilty anticipation in her eyes told me what she was about.

"I must learn to—ground," she said. "I gather it's not a foregone conclusion."

"It should be no difficulty for you at all," the wizard said, shooting me a look. "Ellion is overcautious."

I nodded. "Just so." Nevertheless the worry in her gaze didn't dissipate.

"What we'll need," the wizard said thoughtfully, "is a quiet place to work. Outdoors."

"I'll go ask," I said. Letitia nodded and opened the door to her room; Amien walked the little distance to his own. I turned back down the corridor. At the far end, Suibne climbed the last few stairs and walked towards me.

"There you are!" he called, sounding immensely pleased. "I hope you're comfortable?"

"Comfort is a small word for it," I said, meeting him halfway and accepting the offered embrace. "Thank you."

"Not at all." I could hear the grin in his voice; but then he drew back to look into my face, and sobered. "Damn, but you look like hell!"

"Thank you," I said lightly.

"What the hell—?"

"It's been an absolute pleasure ride. Let me just say we're all more grateful than we can express for an evening of quiet."

Suibne gave me a long look, serious; but he took the hint and let the matter drop.

"If I might impose further on your hospitality…"

"Whatever you need."

I offered him a bow. "Thank you. The mora—that is to say, Letitia…"

"*Mora?*" Suibne echoed.

I shrugged. "That is her title in the Tanaan language. I'm sorry, I've spent more days speaking Tanaan than Ilesian in the past couple months. The word means *riga*, essentially. Except that among the Tanaan, it's the riga, not the righ, who rules."

"So the Lady of Finias… is the riga? The *mora?*"

"Of Fíana," I said, nodding.

"Fíana," Suibne repeated.

I nodded again.

"So what do they call her husband?"

"She's not married."

"Oh?" Suibne said, looking intensely interested now.

"But he would be her consort—" I repeated the word in the Tanaan language, and Suibne nodded understanding. "And even though she isn't actually married, she does already have one of those."

"That serious fellow."

I smiled despite myself. "That's him."

"Ah," Suibne said, nodding judiciously. "Too bad. So what does the... mora... need?"

"Thank you. The mora needs a space outdoors in which she might meditate."

Suibne nodded again. "Naturally you're looking for something secure."

"Yes."

"Would our shrine to Ara do? It's a private shrine, on the family grounds..."

"That sounds perfect. Thank you. How do we find it?"

Suibne smiled. "I'd be pleased to show you."

"My friend, your hospitality is legend."

Suibne waited patiently while I gathered up Letitia and Amien. He greeted them warmly and led us out of the palace and northward across the grounds to the woodland beyond. After a few moments we came to a small grove of blossoming cherry trees with a little spring in its midst, which stood overlooking the lake. It looked so much like the sacred grove at Presatyn that I found myself unable to look at any of them. Already I felt a blush climbing up the back of my neck.

"Yes," Amien said, sounding amused. "This is perfect. Thank you."

"Not at all," Suibne said. "Then I'll... leave you to it?" His inflection suggested he hoped for an invitation to stay. But in my peripheral vision I saw Amien nod.

"Thank you," Amien said again. I began a wholly irrelevant walk around the perimeter of the shrine, as if there might be some security issue I would uncover; I stretched out tendrils of awareness, even though I already knew the shrine's dedication. The name *Ara* hung on the air here, just as advertised, and the energy was reasonably robust for a private shrine; but beneath the devotions to Ara I sensed older dedications—and glimpsed the goddess those dedications invoked, finding Her attention suddenly on me. My fading blush renewed itself.

"Enough!" Amien barked. "Letitia, Ellion, look at me!"

I glanced at him: the amusement I'd heard in his voice had faded to frustration.

"Are we going to work through this, or do I need to leave you two alone?"

I cast about uselessly for something to say, stealing a glance at Letitia. A pretty flush spread across her translucent skin.

"Letitia, I am neither entitled nor inclined to question your choices in these matters—and Ellion, I expected more from you!"

He was right: I knew better. Aballo puts no value judgments whatsoever on the sexual lives of its members, and wizards are expected to either leave those matters out of the workshop or make practical arcane use of them. But his words rearranged themselves into a completely different sense in my mind, and untoward hilarity overtook me: I failed to restrain the laugh. Now both Amien and Letitia were staring at me, perplexed. For no reason I knew of, that made me laugh harder.

"I'm—Oh, gods, you expected *more*? Are you telling me it's possible to aim higher than the mora of Fíana?" My laughter took on a life of its own, beyond control. Amien cracked a reluctant smile; Letitia was blushing furiously now, but unable to restrain a grin. "Who would that be? A goddess?"

"Well, then." Amien waved me to silence. "Yes, it's about time for pointless hysterical laughter, isn't it? All right."

He stood there staring at me while I dragged some semblance of composure around myself. It took me longer yet to stop grinning.

"I apologize," I said finally, mouth still twitching. "Please proceed."

Amien stared at me a moment longer. He cleared his throat. "Well, then. Letitia, let's start with what you already know: drawing on the energy of the sun."

She nodded gravely at him.

"Would you mind...?"

She gave him a quizzical look, then nodded and turned her head unerringly to the place in which the sun hovered, west of the wooded hollow we occupied. As I watched, the tension drained from her body; profound stillness overcame her. And then I felt the aether shift around her, saw the familiar glow gather, watched the light cascade through her wards as if through a prism. My throat knotted at her beauty; my fingers stretched as if they might encompass her, might taste that delicious energy again.

"Yes," Amien said, layers of memory and emotion in his gravelly voice. "That's what I remember."

Letitia startled, turned and looked at him, glow fading.

Amien nodded. "What you're doing there is channeling but not grounding—allowing the energies in, but holding on to them rather than allowing them to pass through. What you need to learn is to open yourself sufficiently to allow the energies to pass through you: you may feel them, but they won't remain. It won't feel comfortable at first."

Letitia nodded solemnly.

"Why don't you take off your boots," Amien said. "You won't always need to be barefoot to ground; you won't always need to be in contact with the ground at all. Once you find the knack of grounding, you'll be able to do it from an upper floor, in much the same way we can work wards upstairs. But this is the place to start."

Letitia nodded again, kicked off her boots and stockings and looked at the wizard once more.

"Yes," Amien said. "Close your eyes. Feel the ground beneath you. What's there? Is it cool and solid—or warm and soft?"

Letitia stood silent for at least a minute. "I feel it," she said at last.

"Good. Can you draw on the sun again?"

Letitia opened her eyes. "I'm full."

A strange thing to say, that. I couldn't imagine what it would be to find myself sated with power, particularly after just one small sip of something so delicious. But Amien just raised his eyebrows pensively, nodding as if he didn't find it strange at all.

"What if you—gave that light you're holding to Ellion?"

My heart slammed in my throat, as if he'd suggested watching while we made love; a visible tremor swept through her, and she cast a guilty glance at me.

Amien sighed. "Just do it, yes?"

I nodded and crossed the grove to stand before her, holding out my hand. She met my gaze and put her hand into mine, but the only thing that passed between us was a thoroughly embarrassed glance.

"That bad, is it?" Amien said, impatient. "Dear gods, maybe Rohini's right."

Unexpected ire flared in me, but I kept my gaze on Letitia. "Maybe you should remember that one of the people here was never a member of your workshop, and grant her some patience."

Amien *harrumphed*.

"Give us two minutes," I said, still not looking at him.

"One," he retorted, and strode back down the path on which we'd entered.

"Well, then," I said softly to Letitia, offering her a bit of a smile. "You know I could pull on the talisman, but that's not the point here, is it? This is more like when we created your wards—when you thought about where to put the light."

She nodded. I realized I was leaning closer and closer, as if I might taste her, and she was meeting me in the effort. Strange that a woman I'd already enjoyed could make my heart race like this.

"So where are you going to put the light this time?" I whispered, mouth within inches of hers.

The smolder in her gaze ignited into something yet more immediate; I chuckled. "We don't have that long."

Her mouth quirked. "Then just take off your mail shirt."

Gods, I was hopeless: my fingers flew over the clasps as if possessed of independent intelligence, and I yanked the thing over my head and let it drop. But then her gaze shifted, desire and mischief fading into something deeper, and she laid a hand over my heart. Her sweet, delicious energy pulsed into me, echoing back an inexplicable ache.

"Oh dear gods," I heard myself say. My breath lost its way in my chest.

"That's essentially what grounding is," Amien said behind me. Letitia glanced past my shoulder at him, horrified again. "Except that the objective is to just let the energy pass straight through, without pause."

She still stared silently at him; he sighed and walked into the shrine. "Letitia, what do you want from me? All I want is to teach you a skill, to protect you, to defeat Nechton and the Bard. Who beds whom along the way is not my concern unless I'm one of the parties involved. Can we move on?"

"Yes," she said faintly.

"Learn from your nasclethéan," he continued; hearing that label applied to myself in this context rocked me so thoroughly that I barely heard the rest of his words. The ties between a man and his nasclethéan only begin with partnership in the Work; nasclethéana share arcane workshops and grimoires, military training and battles, and frequently beds as well. More often than not it is a lifetime commitment between men who measure lifespan in centuries; the sort of bond in which they finish one another's sentences on those occasions when speech is necessary at all and dream one another's dreams.

"Make use of it or leave it out," Amien continued, evidently oblivious to the incomprehensible hugeness of what he'd said. "Whatever is more effective is the right answer."

"Understood," Letitia said, just as faintly as before.

The wizard glanced at me; realization dawned in his face. "I shouldn't have used that word."

"No matter," I said, waving the error away, but my voice sounded thin.

Amien sighed again. "No matter. Well, then, let's try it again, Letitia—but this time, rather than letting the energy stop inside you, send it straight on through to the ground."

She nodded and turned to the west again. After a moment I felt the shift as she opened herself to the energy and it began to flow, saw rainbows arc along the wards we'd created—and then disappear.

"Oh!" she said, surprise in her voice. Then, "*Oh.*" She looked at Amien. "You're right. That was… strange."

The wizard smiled faintly. "No doubt. If we had time to do this properly, I'd have you spend hours on that technique alone—but I'm going to rush forward to the thing that matters: grounding when you're not in control of the energy. I'm going to have you hold…" He trailed off, thoughtful, then smiled and drew his knife. "Here. This." He grasped the blade and handed it to her, hilt first.

"Well, then. Here is our game. You will hold my knife. It's not exactly an arcane object, but I've been using it for many years; it'll do for this purpose. Hold it however you like, but don't let it touch the ground. And every so often—I'm going to send an arcane charge through it. Your task is to channel that energy to ground."

Letitia nodded.

"Ready? I'll give you this one for free. Here it comes."

I felt the little rill of power he sent into the weapon, a zephyr brushing parts of me that weren't physical. It was a gentle transmission, far less intense than the energies I'd poured into her when we made love yesterday morning.

Nevertheless she startled and dropped the knife as if it burned her. "Oh!"

"No matter," Amien said patiently. "Let's try again."

Letitia picked up the knife. Amien said, "Ready?" and sent another little charge into it. This time Letitia just absorbed it.

"You didn't ground," I said.

Letitia grimaced, nodding. But their next attempt was successful, and Amien began drilling her: sending power into the knife without warning her when it was coming, gradually increasing the strength of the charges until the very air began to tremble with rippling energy and the hair that always escaped her braid flew wild. Again and again she grounded; her face took on a breathless glow. My breath hitched against the back of my throat. I told myself it was the way she looked with power racing through her, the energies dancing on the air. But I needed to feel power flowing through me, itched to give it to Letitia, ached to have her bounce it back redoubled. This lesson should have been mine.

"Yes," Amien said finally, closing the distance between them. "Well done."

She smiled and offered him the knife; he sheathed it. She cast a smoldering glance at me. "My lord, will you play?"

The need in me flared higher. Hadn't I been doing essentially the same thing Amien just did, when I gave her my own power yesterday? It could be of no possible importance that the energy had flowed between us on a telepathic link rather than through the aether.

Using a different conduit wouldn't make it a violation of my vow. It should be my energy making her skin flush and the hair fly around her face. I couldn't stand by and watch Amien do these things that should be my prerogative, not when her eyes said she'd rather have me.

To hell with caution. I could remember how far I could safely go.

"Take off your mail." My voice sounded like I felt; Letitia drew in an audible breath and glanced at Amien. But he was a wizard: he had seen far worse than anything we might do here committed in the name of magic, had done far worse himself. I refused to follow her gaze. "Come on."

She looked at me again, the flush on her cheeks competing with the slow burn in her gaze, and reached for the clasps. I stood and watched, hands held firmly at my sides but already itching for what would come next. Amien was profoundly still; I pushed my awareness of him aside.

She pulled off the mail shirt; my heart thundered inside my chest as I closed the distance between us, stood close enough to feel her breath on my skin.

"Well, then," I said, forcing the words past the sudden tightness in my throat. "You know I won't draw power. But I will give you what I've got. And you will ground."

Letitia nodded; the mixed hunger and trepidation in her gaze made my breath hitch again. I stretched out my hand, still holding her gaze, and touched the fingertips of my right hand to her palm, sending a little rush of energy into her. Breath shuddered out of her, feathering my lips and firing me with deeper need; through the contact between us I felt the energy pour straight through to the ground. I realized that wasn't what I wanted at all.

"Yes," I said, and smiled for her anyway. "The next one may or may not carry a charge."

"Ready," she said, still breathless.

I withdrew my right hand, grasped her elbow in my left. The gentle power beneath my fingers and against my palm was a feather caress; I sent a broader charge into her, everything inside me protesting when she channeled it to ground rather than bouncing it back to me. Her gaze felt like fire in the hands; my heart tried to beat its way out of my chest. But a hollow disappointment was developing beneath it.

"No matter," I said softly, willing myself to believe it, and shifted to caress the back of her neck. No charge this time, just to keep things interesting. She shivered and drew in an audible breath at the touch, but her eyes reflected a thirst for more. I settled my palm against her chest and answered that desire with a cascade of energy that made her stagger for balance, made her wards arc briefly with rainbow hues. She grounded it, just as she should, eyes shifting into the wide half-emptiness of the power-drunk; but the transfer left an ache of incompletion inside me, even while I tingled for more. Without thinking I leaned in until I felt her ragged breath on my lips, and sent the next charge into her with the barest brush of my mouth against hers.

She staggered backwards. "Stop. Stop."

I found myself staring at her, bewildered.

I will disgrace us both, she sent.

Desire blasted through me. I could barely remember, much less care about, Amien's presence here: she filled all my awareness, and the need to shift this senseless grounding into play that would satisfy both of us made the blood roar in my ears. But if my honor was merely a distant memory, hers was still worth protecting: I stepped back.

Amien stirred, suddenly registering in my peripheral vision. I glanced at him, seeing a hunger I couldn't quantify overlaid with things that troubled me more: burgeoning triumph, plans for using both of us, the beginnings of conversations in which he would use the word *fate*. It would be only a matter of time before he renewed his demand for me to step up as his War-Lord. Before he persuaded me to abandon my vow.

Before I admitted I had only been waiting for an excuse.

"We need to get back, my lords." Letitia still sounded breathless. "We haven't much time."

There was no time to bathe before dinner. I washed as well as I quickly could and dressed in clothing a servant had somehow restored to freshness in my absence. I didn't feel clean, though I was presentable: I promised myself a bath before bed and went down to the drawing room in which the Taidgh family and their guests were to assemble.

Rohini's men were already there, barely recognizable with faces shaven and hair hanging free. Rohini herself looked lovely dressed for dinner, with dark-red hair streaming more than halfway to her ankles, but she seemed as odd as a mummer playing a woman in her dress. Another wave of loss at the absence of my Tanaan friends washed over me; I shoved it aside and greeted Suibne.

"Well, you look better," he said warmly. "A decent dinner and a good night's sleep and you'll be yourself again."

I bowed. "Thank you for your help this afternoon. The mora found that space invaluable."

He smiled, but his eyes saw far too much. "I wonder whether she recognizes the magnitude of her good fortune."

He wasn't talking about his hospitality, I realized: after a moment of puzzlement I understood who he meant, and a wholly different flavor of confusion came over me.

"When do you leave for the Moot?" I said, buying space in which to recover.

Suibne's knowing smile deepened. "In the morning. Flying with my parents, my brothers, and their wives." He rolled his eyes. "That's seven hours of *Why don't you settle down, already* with no way to leave the room."

I chuckled. "You have my sympathy. Feel free to compare yourself favorably to me."

Suibne laughed. "Oh, I plan to. Let me introduce you."

"Ah, your hospitality is legend."

A force on the tournament field in his youth, Muiredach Taidgh now sported steel-grey hair and the thick layer of hard fat around the middle to which so many warriors run in later years. I had long since learned better than to underestimate the battleworthiness of a man so adorned.

"We met at Teamair, sian," he said, shaking my hand. "At the last Moot, when Conary Mourne was elected."

"I remember." I should have expected this. I wished I could invent some excuse why I couldn't dine with them, after all.

"I was saddened to hear about your father's loss," Muiredach pursued. A fist closed painfully around my heart. "What a good man."

"Oh, and Orlais was just lovely," his wife Emer interposed. "She was always kind to everyone."

If we were going to have to discuss my mother as well, I might find it necessary to flee without any excuse at all. I bowed to buy myself time.

"What happened?" Óengarb was older than Suibne, I knew, but apparently he had never developed discretion. I hoped their eldest brother had more sense.

"Óengarb!" Emer said.

"An accident," I said in the calmest voice I could muster.

"I am sorry," Emer said, with apparent sincerity.

I bowed again, casting about for some new topic.

"Suibne says you were on the upper Ruillin this twelvenight," Muiredach said; I relaxed, just a little. "What's the mood?"

"Ugh, politics," Emer groaned. "Must we?"

"Indulge me for five minutes," Muiredach said.

"I will be brief, Lady," I said. "We were only there a few days. Sian, we saw—" I hesitated, trying to find words that would make sense to a royal. "It's not easy to distill in just a few words. Ballarona fell the night we passed through. Because we were trying to protect the mora's identity, we traveled among commoners and stayed in inns that aren't... loyalist haunts. I was—surprised to see how many among the common folk still worship the old gods. I don't have full intelligence on this, but there may well be a sense that... the Bard of Arcadia is in harmony with those old gods, and Their followers see the Bard as their ally."

Muiredach frowned, as thoroughly puzzled as if I had begun speaking the Tanaan language. "But what about—Brion Cuilean, for instance, or the Mumhan tiarna?"

I shook my head. "Sian, we saw none of them. I suspect Cuilean had already left for the Moot by the time Ballarona fell."

"Hm," Muiredach said, thoughtful. "Chalk one for Conwy, then, I suppose."

As if the only issue the Moot must address was choosing the next ard-righ. I restrained a sigh and left them to fawn over Letitia, crossing the room to examine the harp that stood in the far corner. It was a beautiful instrument: a standing four-octave triple harp, richly carved and solid of construction.

"You have an interest in the harp, Lord?" someone behind me said.

I glanced up, seeing a man so gangly and light of bone it seemed as if he might be capable of flight. This must be the Taidgh House Harpist: he was certainly no warrior. I wondered that we had never met.

"An excellent piece," I said. "A Tigernan, is it?"

Astonishment manifested in his dark eyes. "Yes! Do you play, Lord?"

I smiled. "Sian, I'm Ellion Tellan."

Shock flitted across the man's face; then he grinned and offered me a bow. "Énna Ualgairg. I missed the conclave at which you were elected."

I bowed in return: in one sense we were royal and lesser; but Énna was an ollamh, one of the lords of the gorsedd, and in another sense that made us equals.

"If I don't go back to Ilnemedon soon, there may well be another conclave," I said, manufacturing a smile. I wasn't sure I would suffer any loss but pride if they ousted me; the realization confused me yet again.

"*You* are part of the Lady of Finias's escort?"

I nodded. "I was out there on gorsedd business when everything fell apart. I've just been doing what I must."

"Gorsedd business?" Enna sounded skeptical.

"You know the Lady Carina Finias once retained a House Harpist?" I said. "This spring seemed like a good time to renew that bond, but it developed she was not in residence."

Enna gave me a long look. "Indeed."

Dinner reminded me how far west we had come. The company was seated strictly by rank, with no apparent thought for fostering lively dinner conversation. I settled into my spot between Emer and Suibne, facing Rohini: amusing myself with black imaginings of the torment that must have arisen from trying to balance the Lady of Finias and her consort with the unaccompanied Prince of the Aballo Order; considering the mathematical exercises that must have gone into the placements of Rohini and myself, with both of us once members of the College of Righthe but now deposed, both hailing from countries situated not only west of the Ruillin but west of the Riga. Did the circumstances of my deposement outweigh the fact that I was, once again, technically the tanist of Tellan? How did the handicap of Rohini's gender weigh against the fact that she had true hope of being restored? Both of us were exiled now, though mine was voluntary. A mad temptation to engage the people around me in an ironic attempt to reduce the equations to something manageable welled within; I fought it down, but failed to contain a smirk at the contents of my own mind.

"What?" Suibne said to me, sotto voce.

I shook my head. "Ask me later."

"I plan to be drunk later."

"That's the smartest thing anyone has said yet today." I offered him a little salute with my glass, and he returned it, a grin breaking across his face.

After a meal that might have been measured in years, we returned to the drawing room. A footman served brandy, which I accepted with relief; Énna the harpist walked into the room, paused in front of me, and offered me a smile and a courtly bow.

"My lord," he said. "Never would I ask a guest of this house to play, particularly not after so long a journey. But if it would please you to use my harp this evening, you have only to say the word."

I glanced past him, at the harp across the room; a sudden, deep hunger to play rose inside me. I probably didn't deserve the privilege after what I'd done to Bernatel's harp.

Énna smiled as if he understood, or at least recognized I needed to be persuaded. "It would be our privilege, Lord."

There was no graceful avenue of escape now: an unwilling smile came over me, and I rose.

"The pleasure is mine, sian," I said, and returned his bow. "Your hospitality is legend."

I settled on the chair that stood behind the harp, drew the instrument against my shoulder. A strange mixture of sadness and relief settled over me as it came to rest. I raised my hands to the strings and stroked a few chords to get a sense of its temper; it sang back to me with a rich, satisfying voice.

The harp had probably been tuned for *Fare and Fir*, a sensible choice for this company; but some of the strings had shifted, as strings will, settling the instrument into something very close to the key of the undeservedly obscure *Tílimya's Well*. I had neither heard nor played that song in a long time—but it seemed oddly right tonight. I reached into my pocket automatically: seeking my harp key, laughing at myself for looking for something I had certainly not thought to stow there—and discovered the thing under my fingers. I had been carrying it for all these twelvenights without even being aware of its presence. I adjusted the strings and glanced around the room.

The last time I had performed was Dianann; my audience had been composed almost entirely of the knights who would become so dear. Who would die because of the price on my neck and my lack of the decency to warn them off or withdraw. I forced the memory aside: I had claimed the privilege of playing tonight, and now it was my responsibility to perform. I began playing the themes of this piece the harp and I had chosen: setting the mood, acquainting myself with the strings.

"Lords and Ladies, indulge me while I lay the field for our companions from across the mountains," I said, and shifted to the Tanaan language.

"This is *Tílimya's Well*, the story of the hero Gwydion and his quest to retrieve the healing waters of the Well of Tílimya, which lies within the Fortress at Tílimya's Abyss. I wonder whether you've heard some variation on it before: the great Hy-Breasaílian righ Bran has been wounded in the groin by a spear, in the course of battle with the righ of Boreas; and as he wastes without healing the land withers and dies. A seer tells Bran that only the waters of the Well of Tílimya can save him—which I suppose could just as easily have been interpreted as a slap in Bran's face..."

"I think I've heard this, maybe," Letitia said thoughtfully. "Though our bards tell it somewhat differently."

I nodded. "Just so. Well, then, here is tonight's version of the tale: the righ lies a-wasting, and with him the land, and only the healing waters of the Well of Tílimya can restore him. He decrees that whoever can retrieve this elixir will become his tanist and inherit all of Hy-Breasaíl. Gwydion is a young man from some remote place, one of Hy-Breasaíl's champions but without prospects beyond that; when he asks the seer, the Danaan sorceress Niamh, how to proceed in accomplishing the mission, she favors him and grants him not only the knowledge he needs but certain talismans he will require.

"Gwydion takes the talismans the seer gives him and follows her instructions to reach the realms of the dead. He crosses the Fields of Asphodel and the River Dóiteán, gaining the Fortress at Tílimya by using the seer's talismans and demonstrating the virtues of a warrior. Inside, he meets the Guardian of the Well and persuades Her to let him bring back the water necessary to heal the righ. He passes Her test, but the outcome is not as simple as everyone expects. She offers him a choice: rather than return with the water of the Well and heal the righ, he may remain as Her Consort. Rather than tanist of Hy-Breasaíl, she will make him ard-righ of all the world—and immortal. But if he returns to Hy-Breasaíl with the elixir, saving the righ and the land, as soon as the injured righ drinks Gwydion will die.

"The choice seems obvious, but Gwydion is a champion, and sworn. He embraces the Guardian, kisses Her, and tells Her he has given his word: he must bring back the water from the Well She guards. This was the true test, after all: immediately Tílimya is revealed as the paradise of Tír inna n-Óc, and the Guardian tells him he may return to Hy-Breasaíl, heal the righ, and claim his earthly prize—or return once the world has been restored to claim Her Love. By now he understands She is the goddess, and he has earned his place at Her side. After restoring the righ to health, he passes beyond the realm of mortals, dwelling in pleasure with the goddess for eternity."

I allowed my hands to wander over the Guardian's theme, giving them time to digest. After a moment a shift occurred in Iminor's face that might have been a smile, except that it held no real humor.

"Perhaps in my next life," he said thoughtfully, eyes on mine, "I will be Beallan. Beallan men seem to have all the fun."

I was reading too much into the statement. Surely he didn't mean the accusations I heard. Nevertheless as I began the song I carried with me renewed regret for my betrayal of the bonds between companions-in-arms—and a strange terror that the depths of my faithlessness would be revealed.

I turned my mind firmly to the song and the performance I must give; but as I unwound the tale, I found Gwydion had become Iminor in my mind. It was not the righ Bran and Hy-Breasaíl who needed healing, but Letitia and Fíana; not a spear that had done her in, but me. On a sorceress's horse he rode, to a cliff beside the sea, whence he must pass through a cleft in the rock and into the lands of the dead. Tonight that passage looked like the way from Arian to the Devadore in my mind; but beyond the black basalt cavern with its wizard-dream fungus and dark-running streams, he found not the blue-green waters of the Devadore: rather the grey expanse of the Fields of Asphodel.

It was too easy to imagine him passing untouched by the petty failings that snare a man in the Grey Lands and reaching Dóiteán, the flaming river of blood. In that stream boil murderers and perpetrators of other bloody crimes;

I remembered all the murders I had committed, all the blood on my hands: blood shed in rage and cold fury, blood my sword drank in the names of military objectives, blood spilled beneath an oak to feed an illicit god. Murder lay on my soul, yes; how much less hope would remain for me when I finally broke my oath, too? Or would it change anything at all?

When the boatman arrived to bear the traveler across the river, I recognized him from a hundred other tales: Ankou, clad in his bones and a huge black cloak, the broad brim of his immense black hat pulled low over the glowing abysses of his eyes. When he travels the lands of the living, Ankou usually comes on a cart, preceded by a blast of cold dank wind; but who would notice such a wind on the banks of a boiling river of blood?

Just to gain the deck of Ankou's boat the hero must demonstrate both forbearance and timing, but when he meets the boatman, the traveler's real trial begins: the price of his passage is the truth of his greatest sin. It is only honesty that can redeem him. But how hard could that test be for Iminor? His greatest sin would be something I committed before lunch. I, on the other hand, would require a journey far longer than the crossing of a river to determine which of my multitude of sins was the greatest—and had every reason to fear that admitting the truth would see me cast into that flaming river before there was time to confront the greater perils beyond. I should probably start working on my answer to the question now.

Naturally Gwydion, or Iminor, faced the trial with insight and grace, and disembarked unharmed on the opposite shore. But as he turned his attention on the obstacles to entering Tílimya, I glanced at the Iminor who sat in the drawing room—and found my mind pulled irresistibly back to the present.

There is an unmistakable look that comes over a wizard in trance. For all the different flavors and purposes of arcane trances, they all look the same from outside; and Iminor had that look now. I unwound the rest of the song with less than half my attention, all the times I'd played it carrying me through. A quick glance around the room showed an audience in a sort of almost-trance, the mundane flavor of involvement that will capture listeners when a harpist is doing his job: no one else seemed aware of what had snared Iminor. But I remembered returning after the last attempt on my life, finding Amien had cast wards around the section of road they occupied—because he had deduced that Tiaran's Talent ran true, and her natural heir had been entirely misapplied as Letitia's consort. I had never before been in the presence of a seer in the throes of his gift, but I had no doubt whatsoever of what I saw.

One does not disturb a seer in a trance: I played straight through the long trial in the Fortress of the Well and Gwydion's encounter with the Guardian. Midway through, I finally managed to catch Amien's attention, and gestured with my eyes at Iminor several times before the wizard caught my meaning. He nodded and rose in silence, garnering curious looks from our companions which he waved away, and withdrew just far enough to encompass the room with the sort of circle one casts to protect a wizard in the throes. The song unwound to its conclusion; I drew out the final chords into the best transition to routine consciousness I could manage; still as the final notes hummed into silence Iminor gave a violent start and returned staring to something that was not quite ordinary awareness, horrified gaze on me.

"No!" he said, gesturing as if he would ward me off. He surged halfway out of his chair—then seemed to recognize where we were and sat down again.

"Zhev," he muttered, and rested his forehead against the palm of his hand, propping it against the chair as if it were too heavy for his neck to support. Letitia laid a hand on his knee, face a mask of worry.

"Iminor?" Amien said gently, crossing the room to settle on his heels before the Tan. He rested a hand on Iminor's free arm, looking up into the Tan's face. "Iminor. Where are you?"

The Tan shook his head, frowning. "Ah, zhev," he said again, and glanced at Muiredach. "My lord, I apologize. I can't seem to stop falling asleep."

"What?" Amien said.

Iminor shook his head. "I don't know what's the matter with me today. I fell asleep in the bath this afternoon, too. I just keep having the damnedest—" He shut his mouth abruptly, face still but horrified realization in his depthless eyes.

"No blood lost, sian," Muiredach said. "Our grottoes can do that to a man. My grandmother—well, she had a touch of the Sight, you know—and she would never bathe down there. Always said it brought on troubling dreams. My entire life, she always bathed in a tub upstairs…"

A visible tremor passed through Iminor; my throat knotted. I remembered too well what it is to have Talent begin intruding on what should have been a reasonably normal life. But he rose, shaking his head, and bowed.

"I'm just too many days on the road, sian. With your indulgence, I think I'd better retire. Amien—what's this…?" He trailed off, eyes beseeching the wizard to offer any explanation for his circle but the truth.

"It's no longer necessary," the wizard said, and banished it. "Will you be all right?"

"Oh, indeed," Iminor said, with an attempt at certainty that fell short of the mark. "I just need sleep."

"Pleasant dreams," Emer said, smiling a sincere and oblivious smile that made Iminor stare as if she'd taken leave of her senses. Finally he bowed and left the room. Nuad glanced from me to Amien and back.

"Excuse me," he said in carefully-enunciated Ilesian, rising; he bowed and followed Iminor out the door.

The servants poured more brandy, but I had lost interest in the whole proceeding. As soon as I politely could, I excused myself and sought out the grottoes that had given Iminor so much trouble. I still needed a bath: now even more than before. I needed to wash away the crawling feeling that while I had been imagining him as the hero pure enough to bring back the Water of Life from Tílimya's Well, Iminor had Seen true evil—and the shape it had worn was me.

Chapter 31
Dark Water

The waters of Lake Nanno and the well at the Taidgh family shrine to Ara are cool and sweet; a different source feeds the baths below the castle. Steam and the taste of sulfur greeted me long before I reached the base of the slick, winding stair one must descend to reach the grottoes; lamplight ran yellow up the grey stone of the walls.

At the base of the stairs, the narrow passage opened to a large, nearly rectangular pool the spring had carved from the stone. The dark rippling water lay hemmed by broad walkways, around which lamps on the sweating walls illuminated the rising steam. Several smaller chambers opened from the walkways around the pool; the resounding quiet of the place suggested I was down here alone.

Except for the goddess. She infiltrated me on the steam, hung as an invisible Presence in the shadows that gathered in the corners and small alcoves, hummed in stray echoes against the stone. This was not the gentle goddess Who welcomed me at Presatyn and sheltered me on the Aerona: this Being and I had glimpsed one another at the Taidgh family shrine this afternoon, and Her regard had left me uncertain of my welcome even as the fruitless habits of a man sworn to the true gods made me recoil from Her Presence. Down here, Her regard was further weighted by sulfurous vapors and untold tons of granite pressing down on me from above; it made me uneasy. I stepped carefully across the slick stone of the walkway and into one of the smaller alcoves, hoping the smaller space would reduce the stress of Her Presence, and shut the door.

Her Energy felt less oppressive in here, but the steam still swirled grey-white in the heavy air, making my mind melt towards dream. I would not stay long, just wash away the things I'd done and the disasters I'd caused since Nemetona: I pulled off my clothes, gathered up soap and a razor, paused long enough to unsheath my knife and settle it within arm's reach, and slipped into the water.

Why did I want the knife? It seemed utterly unwarranted. But that reminded me too well of how irrelevant my sword had seemed in the inn at Nemetona, and how naked that had left me in the streets below. If I were a fool—and there seemed little question of that—I would be a live one. And, for a while at least, clean.

The heat of the pool turned my muscles to jelly; the sulfurous vapors uncurling above its surface made my mind run blank. I sank into the water up to my chin, resting my arms on ledges beneath the surface that seemed designed for the purpose and finding my feet floating up from the base of the pool. After a few moments I remembered my errand, washed and shaved, then shut my eyes and submerged in the darkly-sparkling water. When I surfaced, the steam on the air and the water in my lashes made haloes around the lamps, and fatigue made the effect unreasonably interesting: I leaned my arms against the ledge again, rested my head against the lip of the pool, and floated.

Pale tendrils of vapor swirled and settled and rose again; after some measureless moments a dream wafted up from the water and infiltrated me. I knew it for what it was, and yet it held me below the surface of consciousness, making me breathe it in.

I hung on the tree again, feet trailing roots deep into the earth while my head lay in the midst of the milky-bright Way of the Gods that stretches across the sky. My hair and fingertips buzzed with stars. I looked across the vastness into Tilimya's Abyss, meeting Esus's gaze. His face bore a startling resemblance to the visage I saw in mirrors, but His eyes were the black of the deepest parts of the universe. And without words, understanding passed between us: I was to be His champion, to take back the Power Nechton usurped; to defeat the interloping gods and restore Him to His natural place at the center. I would become His Prince and ard-righ, and return the world to what it should be, and no one would miss the gods Who had temporarily occupied His place. Aechering's words rang in my head. I suspected it was Esus's voice I heard.

Hakaid the shadow of the Sun
And open the Abyss

Tonight the verses made sense, though I couldn't have explained them. I saw the reason and the symmetry in all of it. I unbound myself from the tree as easily as a man might rise from a chair—but once I stood on the earth, in the midst of the sun-circle surrounding the tree from which I had hung, a new decision swept through me; and I kicked down the standing stones and drew the god's Mantle about Myself, then used that newfound power to reach across the universe and shove Esus more deeply into the Abyss.

Abruptly I found myself sitting on a little boat, looking across a campfire at Tílimya's boatman Ankou. Instead of a flaming river, all the stars of the universe hung around us: stretching from the edges of the boat to places impossibly distant, shimmering in a breathtaking range of hues from pale blue-white to vibrant red to colors for which men have no names.

The reach of the shadow of the Sun is infinite, they whispered.

Ankou's immense black hat blocked out huge stretches of the universe; his cloak, pushed back from his shoulders, revealed the gleam of starlight on all his bones. He rattled on in affronted tones about Sissyphus and what the god Zev had done to the man. My head whirled with the aftermath of some magic I couldn't remember committing, and all I could do was nod.

Now I stood in the keep at the Fortress of the Well, smelling the power and pure life-giving freshness of the water within. The Well rippled and shimmered in starlight; reflections of cherry trees danced in the moving water, and pale blossoms rained down in the darkness, illuminated by some light I couldn't find. The goddess Who guards the Well looked at me from depthless Tanaan eyes as emerald-bright as Letitia's; but Her hair was dark as the spaces between the stars.

Let the heir of Tílimya
Woo the Virgin Star

I had the nagging feeling that I should recognize Her, that I had met or seen Her before. Somewhere a harp played the ballad *Tílimya's Well,* and I remembered my lines.

Who are You? I said to Her; I didn't speak, but the question echoed on the nonexistent air. In the ballad, when Gwydion asks that fateful question, the Guardian shifts from the form She first presents him, revealing Herself in all Her aspects from the wrenchingly hideous to the incomprehensibly magnificent, changing from form to form and on to another form again, until finally She settles on the aspect of a queen. But instead this half-remembered goddess with black hair and emerald eyes fixed me with an inescapable stare and said, again without speaking, *Well, who are* ***you****?* And I felt myself begin to shift.

The water rocked around me; I opened my eyes. Letitia bobbed up to the surface, shaking out her unbound hair across the water, and came to rest beside me, leaning one arm against the ledge that supported me and trailing the wet fingers of her other hand across my chest. The dim steamy room and the water in Letitia's hair conspired to darken her tresses from their usual gleaming gold, and her eyes were the same as those of the goddess in the dream; but she was still herself. I wanted to ask how Iminor was weathering his bout: early intrusions of Talent tend to be uncomfortable at best. But her eyes told me she hadn't come here to talk. I should take advantage of the opportunity to push it all away for a while.

Join the Sun and the Moon in Darkness
Thus results the Union of Silver and Gold

"Hand me the soap?" she said silkily.

"Oh, I don't think so," I said, and smiled for her: I wasn't feeling the smile yet, but I soon would be. Even now the ache of readiness gathered, and it intensified as I lathered up my hands and began to wash her, beginning with the hand that rested on my chest. I started with a smiling pretense of innocence, washing her hands and arms, cradling her against me so she could feel my desire as I washed her hair; but soon enough she had shifted to wrap herself around me until I nearly drowned in her kiss.

"Ah, but you are not clean yet," I murmured, and pulled back to wash her neck and back and linger over the task of soaping her breasts, while she gasped and tried again to wrap herself around me. I was on the verge of slipping inside when Iminor's jolt into wakefulness after his vision knifed through my head. Cold crashed through me at the memory of what I'd seen in his eyes, the way his gaze reflected my own evil back at me—and I pulled back and lifted Letitia to the walkway at the pool's perimeter, filling my mind with the textures of her feet and legs as I washed them, with her flavors and soft cries as I laid her back and kissed the space between. When she began to wail with the pleasure of it I could no longer remember anything but her, so I drew her into the water and applied myself to dragging us both into oblivion. Immediately all the pent-up need she'd raised in me this afternoon roared to life again; I quivered with the need for release, steam and unreason swirling through my mind until I couldn't remember why, could only remember I must not, nearly succumbing when she found release herself. And in that moment of near-unconsciousness, I felt a *shift* on the heavy air, heard glass crash and shatter on the stone floor.

The sound impelled my mouth away from hers; I glanced across the chamber just as a second glass vessel hit the floor. A man stood there, half occluded by rising vapors: a warrior in black with his face covered by an assassin's hood. Dark red smoke rose from the shattered mess on the floor: poison gas, a favorite of the assassins of the Order of Par. The vessels would have held saltpeter, a decoction of horse's urine, and things only the Order know in hermetic chambers; the explosive combination of ingredients produced a thick, noxious vapor that would mutate into harmless indetectability within minutes.

Poison gas, I sent. *Don't breathe! We've got to get out.*

I drew back and scrambled out of the pool, head swimming with steam and breathlessness and the madness of near-release; and I grabbed the knife and launched myself across the slippery floor towards the assassin, nearly falling on the slick stone. The assassin beat me to the door, but rather than racing out into the larger cavern, the man stood his ground as if planning to die in here with us. Smoke stung in my tearing eyes; I rushed the assassin, knife poised to slash his throat. But instead of the hood I expected, he wore a peculiar bug-faced mask. Its protruding snout and staring glass eyes sent cold racing up my spine; its thick material extended down his throat.

I shifted the knife to stab him in the gut, lungs screaming for air. The assassin bounced against the door; I staggered, feet slipping on the slick stone, and nearly fell. The assassin crumpled. I shoved him out of the way, gestured frantically to Letitia, hauled the door open and dragged us outside, slamming it shut behind me.

I sucked in a huge lungful of sulfurous air; rage, terror, and a bout of coughing crashed in on me. The coughing doubled me over so I had to lean against the wall: eyes streaming, body spiraling so far beyond control that darkness gathered around the edges of my vision and the ground seemed to shift beneath my feet. But raw anger catapulted my mind past that momentary problem. I had friends to avenge, and the man who had killed them lay inside that poisoned chamber.

"Did you breathe?" I panted as soon as I could form the words, glancing at Letitia.

She shook her head, still wracked with coughing.

"What the—?" she managed, and began coughing again.

"Fouzhir assassin!" I said, then stopped myself from saying more. Was I really going to admit that he'd come for me, that Letitia's presence had been merely incidental? That my enemy had mastered techniques that made Nechton look like a green apprentice, and he roused Lady Tella to personally intervene? If I did, and Letitia finally agreed to dismiss me, we would part with her having knowledge I could entrust to no one. It shamed me to realize I was not prepared to put that sort of faith in her.

I needed to question the assassin. I must do anything necessary to extract whatever he knew. How long had it been since the poison-gas vials hit the floor? My father's security master had drilled into me the necessity of waiting a full thousand-count before allowing anyone back into the room; but once, when it wasn't a drill, the man had gone back inside after only a hundred. I wondered whether the assassin's ungodly mask was capable of keeping the gas out of his lungs and I would find him hampered by nothing more than a knife in his gut. It would mean I'd have time to question him—but that he was the only one who was armed. Or dressed.

"Stay here," I said to Letitia. *Call me if anything at all is wrong.*

She nodded understanding. I drew a series of deep breaths, trying to over-saturate my body the way one does before a dive, and filled my lungs one last time. With a final glance at Letitia I opened the door just far enough to slip inside, and closed it behind me.

I stood there alone. The assassin had vanished as if on the steam, and he'd taken my knife with him. Only a small pool of blood and a mass of broken glass showed anything had happened here at all. Rage blasted through me; I needed to put my fist through something, but there was nothing in this room not carved from stone. A roar forced its way up through my throat; I choked it back down and looked for possible avenues of escape.

There was none: I knew this. It had been the same wizard who disappeared after our encounters at Irisa and Dianann, who somehow survived not only bleeding to death but immolation on a pyre. Nevertheless I hauled open the door and glanced out to the main chamber, hoping he might have found some underwater passage between the pools. Letitia glanced at me, surprised; the room behind her was empty except for steam and yellow lamplight. I shook my head and shut the door again, casting an idiotic glance around the room as if my enemy might have reappeared while my back was turned.

He hadn't, of course. Steam still hung on the air, but otherwise the air seemed clear; my eyes didn't sting. I drew a cautious sip of breath, as if that would keep me alive. My throat and lungs felt fine, so I began to breathe. It seemed I should check the depths of this pool for some underwater passage that might have taken the assassin in a different direction; but I doubted a man who had just been knifed in the gut could manage such an escape, and he'd needed no such exit at Dianann: only ten seconds of my inattention.

Fury mounted in me, and only some of it was for my enemy: I should have known he would escape as soon as I looked away. I should have withdrawn from Letitia's presence long ago, should have known better than to relax at all, ever, anywhere. I prayed he would return, so I could keep my undivided attention on him, take him apart by pieces, teach him the names of all my friends before he died in slow agony. I would extract the name of the man who had bought my death, but the pain I inflicted on my assassin would last far longer than necessary for that goal. And that would be nothing compared to what I visited on the man who hired him.

If I was to have this revenge, I must devote much more focus to the problem. Starting now. Unlikely as it was that he'd escaped by swimming through some underwater passage, it would nag at me if I didn't check. Long training for poison gas made me hesitate over filling my lungs in here, but the alternative was to step outside and get drawn into a discussion of the matter with Letitia. And I couldn't afford to tell her anything. I drew a deep breath, coughed again, then gathered up my self-discipline and forced sulfurous air into my lungs. My head swam a bit, but I didn't seem to be dying, so I dove into the pool.

The water stung my eyes. Lamplight faltered before reaching the bottom of the pool: I had to drag my hands all the way around the perimeter down in those last few feet of darkness. As my body's clamor for breath mounted, the pool became Tílimya's Abyss, my fruitless search not for pursuit but for escape. Behind me I heard men who had been here longer laughing.

Ellion?

Letitia's voice reminded me who and where I was.

All clear. Come in. I'm down in the pool. 'Ware the glass and the blood on the floor.

At least I had those things. Hastily I finished sweeping the base of the pool, finding only the fissure through which the waters entered, and pushed myself back up to the surface. Letitia stood just inside the door, staring at me.

"Where is he?"

I should have worked out a story before inviting her in. I shook my head and climbed out, buying time to formulate an answer; coming up with nothing. My head still swam.

"Good damn question," I said. "All I can tell you is he didn't swim out, and he didn't walk out the door. You might as well get dressed; I'm going to see what I can learn from the things he left behind."

"Don't pass out."

"I'll try not to."

"Should I stay?"

I should send her away for her own safety. "Please."

"How do I know when to get Amien?"

I glanced at her, considering. His discretion with her honor could be trusted, but he would ask all the wrong questions—while Letitia seemed to have made the error of trusting me. Faint nausea gathered in my throat.

"Give me an hour," I said finally. I picked up my shirt and dried the water from my hands, then knelt on the stone before the little pool of blood. Dipping my fingertips into it yielded no impressions beyond what ordinary senses might convey: it had cooled to the temperature of the stone and was beginning to congeal. I touched my fingertips to my mouth—and new awareness roared through me, blasting me so far beyond ordinary consciousness that I lost contact with the chamber in which I assumed I still knelt.

There was no trace of arcane power in the blood: the man was no wizard, of no discernible Talent at all. But through that blood I tasted the presence of things in his body that the blood brushed up against but had no congress with: things that didn't live, even though their energies ebbed and flowed as if they did; things more mundane that served to hold him together in the aftermaths of a seemingly endless series of dire injuries. Through that taste I knew, as if in my own misplaced body, the searings of arcane castings and flash-weapon discharges that should have killed him dozens of times; stab wounds and deep slices and near-dismemberments from knives and swords; bloody bruisings and broken bones inflicted with blunt objects and bare hands; the ravages of fire and explosion and even the deep-lung burns of poison gas. The blood remembered all this, and yet the body lived. I reeled under the weight of so much injury, finding myself lying with my forehead in the midst of a pool of cold sticky blood: the chill of the stone beneath me seeping into my bones, a dozen lifetimes' worth of injuries echoing in my body. I groaned and rolled away, finding Letitia sitting within arm's reach.

He wasn't a wizard. And yet he had the capacity to come and go like a wraith in a fireside tale, and he seemed to be absolutely indestructible. Unkillable. I reached out and touched Letitia, to reassure myself I still occupied my own body and we both still lived.

"What?" she said softly. Even from this upside-down angle the distress in her face was plain to read. "Are you all right?"

"I don't understand," I said, head still swimming.

"Are—you—all—right?" she repeated, in Ilesian this time.

I waved the question away. "Yes. Thank you. Gods, what the hell…"

Abruptly I realized I was still naked, and I was being far too honest. She needed to think I had control of the situation; I needed her to not think too deeply about what had happened here. I dragged my collection of phantom injuries to the pool, washed the blood from my face, and began pulling on my clothes. When I was dressed I cupped my hands in the pool and brought water to the place where my assassin had fallen, washing away the blood.

A room-darkening reel of exhaustion came over me as I knelt before the shards of glass near the door. Had there been someone I could trust, I would have called on him to examine the fragments. If I'd had any silk besides what I wore, I would have gathered them up for later examination, trusting the silk to hold the energies intact. But even more than rest I needed security: I drew a deep breath and released it, watching yellow lamplight wink in the shards.

"Maybe you should wait," Letitia said softly. "You must need rest."

I shook my head, still looking at the glass. "The longer I delay, the greater the chance of discovery. I can't afford even for allies to know…" Speak the truth or hold on to that slim shield of security; reveal the price on my neck or let her think it hung on hers: I'd backed into yet another corner with her. Silently I damned myself for a fool—and then for a traitor.

And then discovered I couldn't speak the lie.

I swallowed against sudden searing pain in my throat and reached for the largest of the shards. This time I was vaguely aware of Letitia trying to catch me as I collapsed.

I stood so close to where I had knelt half a second before that my mind twisted sideways, the disorientation fading into a lingering sense of falling-darkness/wrenching-drop: eyes full of inverse night sky swirling and resolving into an image of myself and Letitia in the pool, her wet incandescent beauty and the raw ecstasy in both our faces sending me reeling into a mix of sudden aching desire and the despair of *another damned noncombatant* who would die at my hand. My head flashed with raining fire on a field full of children and animals—a public square occupied by innocent people—*What the hell am I doing?*—and then I found myself spilling across Letitia, legs sprawled sideways, head ringing with someone else's need for an honorable death.

"Ohdeargods," I breathed, and pushed myself to sit. Nausea welled in me, so powerfully that I nearly gave in to it. I swallowed, coughed, swallowed again. "Oh dear gods."

"Ellion?" Letitia said, smoothing back hair from my brow. I froze at the contact, fought against the need to pull back from tenderness I didn't deserve and lost. Hurt manifested in her face.

"I'm sorry," I said, and reached for her hand. And just like last time I'd said those words, the magnitude of what I needed to apologize for crashed over me. This time I bit it back, but my voice took on a rough edge anyway. "Ah, I'm sorry, Letitia. You deserve better. There's a reason wizards never marry."

She cast me a look of shock. "Is that the rule?"

An unwilling smile came over me; I shook my head. "No, there's no rule. Except what our natures impose. There's some sort of poison in us, every one…"

And none more deeply poisoned than I. I shook my head again, rose and manufactured a smile, handed her up. I bent and gathered the shards of glass in my hands.

"Could you get the door?"

She opened it; I nodded thanks and followed her through.

"It would probably be best," I said, as we stepped along the slick walkway towards the stairs, "if we didn't mention this. To anyone."

"Yes," she said softly, and mounted the first step. "I appreciate your discretion."

Something inside me putrified. I felt the goddess's eyes on me again. I couldn't speak the lie, but I also couldn't speak the truth: I carried the damning shards upstairs and dumped them into the first fireplace I passed.

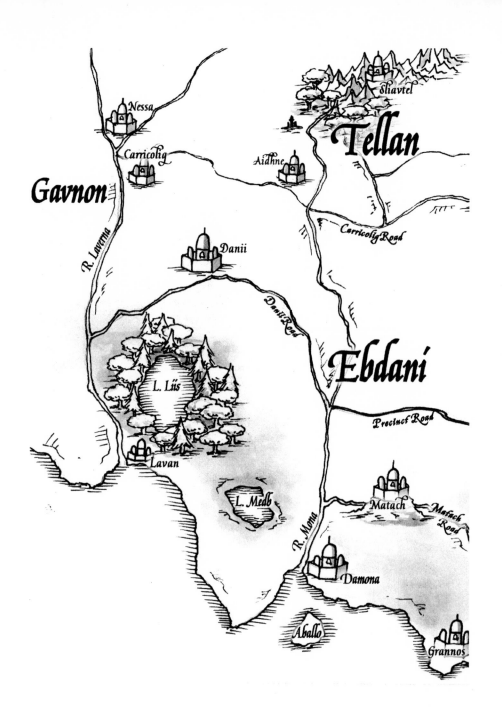

Nessa

Carricolig

Gavnon

Shavtel

Tellan

Aidhne

Carricolig Road

Danii

Danii Road

Ebdani

L. Lüs

Precinct Road

Lavan

L. Medb

Matach

Matach Road

R. Laverna

R. Mona

Damona

Aballo

Grannos

424

Ilnemedon: Royal Map Collection no. 887

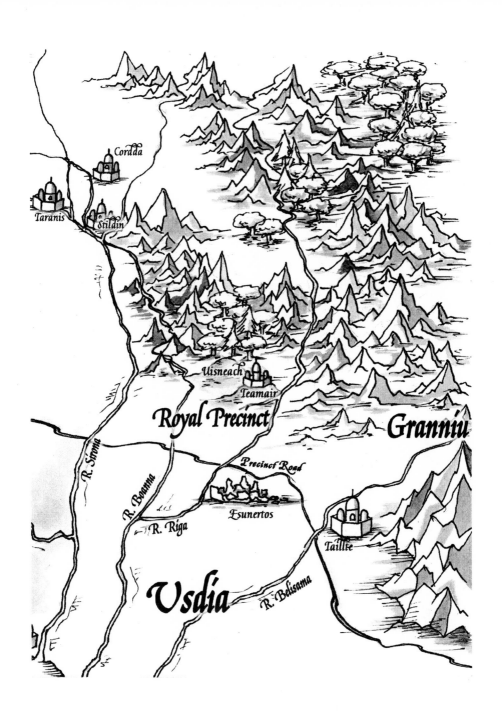

The Royal Precinct and Central Realms

Chapter 32
Abu al-righ

If my assassin had left me a hundred new questions last night, it was the thing he carried off that nagged at me. I could only suppose my knife had still been lodged in his gut when he performed whatever magic-without-Talent allowed him to disappear. No matter what prompted the choice to take the weapon rather than leave it behind, he left me with no recourse: this morning, I dug deep in my pack and found the knife I'd recovered from him a hundred years ago at Tyra, on the night I was foolish enough to think him dead, and I tucked it into the sheath in my right boot.

In the west, when men trade knives, it has deep significance. Not infrequently they will mark one another's flesh with the blades and share blood as well, but that fillip isn't necessary: exchanging knives amounts to a blood oath of brotherhood. It was a thing Tellan had instilled in me; I was surprised to discover it still lurking in the depths of my mind. There seemed a troubling symmetry to this exchange, despite the fact that the blood on both blades had been his.

Wizards know such rituals do not hold the force of magic. Western men know these things bind them to one another beyond life. All I knew was the knife fit perfectly into the sheath, but its clean smooth hilt worried against my calf as if it had been improperly finished. The things I'd read in his blood and on the shard of the vial hung on my mind like the awareness of a binding or a god; like some hideous portent in a song.

Hordes of Fair travelers crowded the road out of Sucello. These were the stragglers: by tradition the Fair begins a twelvenight before the Moot, which meant it had been under way before we entered the human realms. The people around us seemed nearly insubstantial, remote and mundane with their carts full of children and wares and their silly banners proclaiming support for one Moot candidate or another: no more than tools for gods and would-be ard-righthe. Nevertheless they appeared to be enjoying the trip far more than the party with which I rode.

Pleasantly-ordered urban environs gave way to small villages and increasingly isolated farm-holdings. The road unfurled, from places a man might call Granniu and be sure of the designation, to ill-defined Taillte and its pale excuses for satellite towns: where once men looked to the Esusdian righ at Esunertos; where later the tiarna tithed to the Granniu righ and locked the gates against dark spirits and rumors of old gods; where now the kharr held sway, turning the city's face towards Esus again. And Nechton and his ally the Bard.

Outside Taillte, we ignored the conventional wisdom of holding to the Precinct Road at all costs, turned and rode south into the forest rather than risk skirmishing with the kharr who held the place. Despite the proximity of the city, there were no trails here, nor even signs on the land that showed where hunters might range: as if everything south of the road had been somehow poisoned, and not even locals would venture there. We rode quietly towards the spot west of Taillte where distance and terrain conspire to conceal the road from the city, trying to make the best time we might; trees older than Amien gathered and hushed around us, whispering of long-abandoned communities and local deities Who had starved for lack of the people who once lived in this place. It reminded me of something, but I couldn't lay hands on what; when we finally rode out of the forest and back to the road, I was grateful to return to a less troubling route. Meanwhile the people who had prudently kept the road received us as if we had become Básghilae on our detour: drawing beyond the margins to allow us passage; halting and staring until we passed beyond whatever they imagined to be safe distance.

Silent as ghouls we trooped down the shank of the day and the increasingly deserted road. Forests faltered into vacant grasslands. Those abandoned places gave way to barren stretches of broken basalt, where westering sunlight fractured into ruddy reflection and black shadows. Across those blasted spaces came the energies I recognized as Esus, winding their ways into my faithless heart and magic-enslaved bones: lighting me up with pleasures whose transgression only increased their delight, until I caught myself and tried fruitlessly to realign my mind; laying themselves around my neck in the form of a torc no mundane eye would ever see and welding that ornament invisibly to my flesh. A whisper blew across the broken stone, stirring the tail of my hair and raising mixed terror and rapture up the length of my spine: *Abu al-righ.*

Hail forever. I hadn't heard that salute since my deposement: it is one only a righ may receive.

How much of last night's dreaming in the grotto had been the goddess of that place toying with me? How much had come directly from Esus? I felt the invisible torc around my neck as the seal on last night's mandate: take up Esus's cause; root out Nechton; return to the promise of my stars, serving Him as Prince and ard-righ; finally, when I had gathered enough strength to accomplish it, free Him from the Abyss. *Hakaid the shadow of the Sun.* As above, so below: then would both of Us be free. And the first task on that road would be the re-taking of Esunertos.

It was a thing that had to be done anyway. Who would care whether I did it in Tella's Name or that of Esus? What did it matter which god set me on the throne?

I wrenched myself into ordinary awareness, heart hammering. How was it possible I even allowed these ideas to roll around in my mind? I was sworn to the true gods; I had vowed to give up magic. I could not be a part of the arcane assault to re-take Esunertos, and it would be a terrible violation to render it into Esus's Hands after all those men dedicated to the true gods laid their lives on the line for its recovery.

I was supposed to be Lady Tella's man. I didn't need Her to accost me in grottoes to understand what She required. I could do no more for Esunertos than contribute to the development of Aballo's strategy: I resolved for the thousandth time to lay further ambitions aside.

But when the unsleeping eye the Riga traces around Esunertos hove into view, and red sunset light skipped from the water's surface and straight into my brain, the pull of the power still welling in that wrecked city raised a tempest inside me. I reined without thinking, peripherally aware that everyone around me had done the same.

"Sweet Lord Endeáril," Iminor croaked. I glanced at him: his eyes looked haunted. I couldn't recall him saying anything all day. I suspected I hadn't said much more. "Is that—Esunertos?"

"Yes," Amien said, in a voice that suggested he'd aimed for neutrality and missed. Wind sang across the river, carrying the scents of campfires and centuries-old arcane warfare into my suddenly tightening chest.

"I didn't realize you had a Deluge, too," Iminor said, gaze on the broken walls beyond the sunset-lit flow.

The truth of it crashed down on me: I wondered that I hadn't seen it before. I didn't know what had motivated their great goddess Dana, but history was clear on the destruction here: Lady Tella had reduced a city that once outshone Ilnemedon to a slag-heap because its people would not turn from Esus to Her. This had been the site of Her final battle with Him; even after all these centuries, the air still tasted of a goddess's rage.

"Deluge?" Amien sounded astonished. My mind was too full of black, ancient arcane energies to let me focus on him. "No, this was different."

The very rock still remembered arcane storms and plagues on the land and fire that rained from the sky. The noncombatants who had perished here turned my stomach, even while the energies that killed them raised terrible thrills along my flesh. It all seemed like the sort of arcane dueling that had cost me the throne, magnified a thousandfold. But it had been the goddess. I tasted bile.

"My lord, we should take the opportunity for reconnaissance," I said. I needed to understand; needed to see the difference between what She had done here and what the Danaan goddess wrought at Arian. We needed to know what powers would be in play when the wizards came back here after the Moot. I must rid myself of the hideous sense that Esus was not the One to blame for what happened to this land. The answers to all those problems lay on the opposite side of the sunset-flaming river.

"Agreed," Amien said, and turned to Rohini. "Shall we camp on this side tonight?"

"*Here?*" Iminor blurted. His voice cracked.

Power surged across the river, drowning out the argument that sprang up among them. I knew that power's flavor, knew the notes that resonated in my bones, but suddenly it rang as powerfully on the air as it had in the grove at Nemetona, on the night I first met Esus. Intoxication spiraled up from the ground, enveloping me; sunset's glow faded to eternal, moonless starlight. My companions' voices were barely audible, their words ranging over terrain impossibly remote.

"Well, are you going to ward the place?" Iminor demanded, his unaccustomed ferocity rocking Amien visibly backwards. "Or was Ellion right about that, too, and you can't even—"

In the midst of the river, in the place where Esunertos rose up from the flow, something shifted. I saw the city as it had been, as it would be, the red-shot basalt of its walls and towers rising like a more solid and angular echo of the glory that Arian once was. At the center, in the castle keep, stood an immense oak. From outside it seemed dead, scarred and leafless. But I saw the life coiled deep in its heart, waiting for something to revive it. I knew the touch it required.

Abu al-righ, the wind sang. The phrase tingled through me on the next breath I drew, and the invisible torc settled into a pleasant and altogether fitting weight around my neck.

"My lord?" Letitia's voice called me back to the barren place my companions occupied. I glanced at her, seeing the things that commandeered me reflected in a sudden hunger in her gaze.

"What would you see us do?"

I glanced across the river again. I needed to know; her future depended on the answers I would find.

"Trust our Essuvian friends," I said, eyes still trying to bridge the gap between today's destruction and the city's possibility. "And be prepared for the eventuality that what we learn may require us to decamp." Iminor opened his mouth and closed it again with an audible clicking of teeth; Nuad shifted in the saddle. "We won't be gone long."

"We'll be waiting when you return, sian," Rohini said, sounding satisfied.

I nodded and cued my horse; Amien fell in beside me. I'd read the histories of the battles that destroyed Esusdia; Beannchar in particular gives a wealth of detail on the terrain and the way Owain Mourne exploited it, making his volume one aspiring commanders still study. Today I could see little beyond Beannchar's complete failure to account for the arcane aspects of the war. But he'd left me one usable detail: east of Esunertos, it is possible to ford the Riga at the wide, open crossing commanded by the Precinct Road—or at a more secluded spot an hour's brisk ride to the south. I turned us southwest to ride across the broken plain towards the quieter crossing, which allows access to the isle of Esunertos itself. Or would, if that crossing were not too strongly secured. Amien wove a glamour around us as we rode, a sight-foiling haze that would conceal us from any lookouts but arcane ones—but which made it difficult to see beyond half a mile.

Daylight faded though the glow of evening to moonless dark. The aftermath of ancient arcane warfare hung on the air, alternately choking and intoxicating; I tried and failed to find some semblance of equilibrium, hauled my awareness back and back again to the military issues. But I already knew I was retaining no details beyond the arcane.

As the high ground traversed by the Precinct Road faded into the darkness behind us, I felt Nechton give the command. Just like last time, his Will tugged against my spine; his intention settled like fog across my mind. Horror erupted in me; I reined. Amien's horse clattered to a stop a moment later; he twisted round in the saddle to look at me, bewilderment barely visible in the fading light.

"Básghilae," I said.

"What?" Amien squawked.

I turned my horse's head around, spurred him to immediate speed. After a second I heard Amien follow; then all my attention fell on closing the gap between the Básghilae's arrival and my own. I felt them surge across the river and catapult across the open plain, unhindered by the moonless dark. I needed to go faster, to capitalize on my lighthorse's greater speed; I needed the eyes of a Tan. Or Esus.

Had there ever been any choice? I breathed in the velvet night in which Esus always enveloped me; the world shifted into visibility that revealed far more than obstacles over which my horse might stumble. Powers beneath the earth's surface and zephyrs of darkness on the air crowded around my peripheral vision, waiting for me to turn my attention on them; to turn them to the uses which only a wizard might make. Even without my touching them, those energies ignited me, crystallizing my need to protect Letitia into a Will of much greater breadth and clarity. Letitia was vitally important, though not for the reasons my blind human emotions would have me believe.

But turning my attention on that issue made the darkly-visible plain across which my horse flew fade from sight. I hadn't sufficiently opened myself to this power: that knowledge blew through me on a subtle blue-black breeze. There remained an initiation I must take.

There wasn't time to consider that, either; even after I released the issue of Letitia's significance for later, I still needed better visibility. I shredded Amien's glamour and spurred my horse faster yet, reaching across the aether for Letitia.

Annu.

I felt her startle across the miles. *Ellion! Are you all—?*

Básghilae on the way. I was remotely aware that I sounded far colder than a human should; no time for that issue, either. *I'm on my way, but they're going to beat me—Get ready—*

And then there was nothing to do but race through the darkness. Stars and cold invisible fire shimmered within my grasp, promising pleasures I'd foregone for a decade and sufficient energy to singlehandedly change the battle I must fight. Dread for my companions knotted in my throat. Everything about this night loaded the scales in Nechton's favor: the proximity of the power well across the river; the wide, barren terrain; even the moonless sky. I felt the shift in the Básghilae as they closed with my companions, the way the surge of my companions' terror became yet another source of energy. I urged my horse faster, even though I knew the horse capable of *faster* didn't exist. At last we crested the rise that traces the Precinct Road—and I spotted my companions' campfire. Even from here it dazzled my eyes.

"Yah," I said to the horse; his ears pinned back, but he surged bravely down the rise. Halfway there I discovered my sword in my hand, whistling against the rushing air.

Now I could see the disposition of the battle. Iminor, Nuad, and the Essuvians stood clustered around Letitia: all of them mounted, surrounded by more Básghilae than I had ever seen. Three of Rohini's men had fallen, but I couldn't identify them from here. More than a dozen Básghilae lay headless and defeated; their abandoned destriers milled restlessly a short distance away. Horses picked their ways among the bodies, trod on the remains of a dozen broken spears; firelight flashed in the blades of clashing swords. It hardly mattered where one additional man was deployed: I charged the closest Básghil, sweeping his head from behind—and gasped in surprise when the dark energies that powered him shivered up through my blade and into me. Immediately my head shifted, and the power blowing across these vacant lands blasted through me again; three more Básghilae converged on me before that first body hit the ground. A moment later Amien crashed in to engage the one at my left hand; gradually we shifted until our horses faced in opposite directions, stirrups periodically clashing as we jostled within a deepening ring of ghouls.

"Where the fouzh are they all coming from?" Amien muttered. But I didn't have to answer; we both knew. The only questions were how deep Nechton's reserve across the river might be and how much of it he was willing to expend. I swept a glance among the undead men surrounding us: in my peripheral vision each mounted Básghil seemed to double, and dozens more crowded restless and hungry just a short distance away. Even the abandoned destriers manifested shades of undead men.

There was nothing for it: we dug in and whittled away at them. Esus's Power whirled like uisquebae inside me; Nechton stared from behind Básghilae eyes. My companions' growing fatigue hung upon the air. Rohini's man Calbo took a thrusting wound through a joint in his armor and crumpled; his life energies lit up the battlefield like a rain of stars, knotting my throat with warring pleasure and revulsion. When Corrib went down beside him a moment later, I felt the energy of the battle shift.

We needed to withdraw, to find some better place in which to stand; but Letitia still stood utterly surrounded, and with this power racing through me I could see for miles: there was no better place within sprinting range. We could do nothing but chip away until the balance of forces shifted. Then Nechton would withdraw his troops. I glanced around, tallying swords: they outnumbered us by seven now. I applied myself to closing the gap.

But then Rohini's horse stumbled on the pieces of a spear, and her opponent whipped his blade through that half-second's opening. It slashed across her midsection with an audible impact, tangling in the wiry spidersilk; her personal wards flared in brilliant green and shades of black imperceptible to mundane eyes. She gave a short, surprised cry and tumbled from the saddle; Amien crumpled in mid-swing, falling across his horse's neck.

Suddenly he was all that mattered. The world shrank to the circle of Básghilae surrounding us, and I abandoned a developing opening in Básghil defenses to spin my horse on the spot, reach across the intervening space and grab Amien's reins. He didn't seem to be dead, just unconscious: I tweaked my horse so he reared, hooves flailing, and took advantage of that second of Básghilae confusion to drive the horse through a narrow opening to my right, pulling Amien's horse behind me. As we raced towards the rest of our companions, I saw: Letitia had slipped from the saddle to pull Rohini's inert body into the center with her; Básghilae all around the circle were pulling away from other engagements as if they might run her down. Iminor and Nuad began shouting at her.

"Letitia, *back!*" I heard myself shout; I had no recollection of forming the words. She glanced at me but dragged Rohini along with her, and then the shrinking circle of knights closed around her again. In the midst of the confusion Busadi backed his horse into the circle with Letitia, leapt from the saddle and hauled Rohini across his horse's withers, then scrambled up behind her. Letitia shinnied back into her saddle. I had to change the tempo.

I shouted, spurring my horse and yanking Amien's along; Busadi broke through the confusion to follow, the Tanaan and the remaining Essuvians trailing in his wake. Away from the road we raced, northwest across the broken plain: I would make for the river. If we could find a spot where the banks stood higher than the water, we could make a better stand.

The Básghilae had been fresh at the beginning of this engagement; we'd been riding all day. We never managed to pull away, just kept moving as they harried the back of our disorganized pack. After a few minutes of sprinting, Uxenti and then Olin took the bite of Básghilae blades and fell from the saddles; their horses never broke stride, just clung to the faint reassurance of the retreating herd. The terrible delight of stolen energy raced up my spine and was gone.

Finally the river loomed before us, its broad expanse barely distinguishable from the endless stretch of barren basalt in the dark. There was hardly any drop to the water: nothing here to guard our backs. But the horses were as tired as the men. Nothing for it: at least, while we fought, the horses might catch their breath.

"Busadi!" I shouted, and tossed him Amien's reins. "With Letitia!"

"Lord—" The argument tripped past his lips before he visibly thought better of it and gave a crisp nod. The rest of us circled around them at the shore: at least all of us would have better footing than some of the Básghilae. It was a pathetic excuse for tactical advantage.

Within a minute both Iminor and I had separated Básghilae heads from their bodies, and renewed hope rippled around the circle. I felt him as a solid presence at my left hand, relied on his defense of my flank almost as I would have done with Amien. And when next I looked back both Amien and Ro-hini had regained some semblance of consciousness; Rohini slid down from Busadi's horse and sent him back into the line, while Amien cast confusedly about for a sword I could only assume had been lost a mile or more back as we ran. Letitia shrugged and passed him hers, and he spurred his horse out to take up a position on Iminor's left hand. Still we were only ten now, with two of us injured and two disarmed: for all practical purposes, the Básghilae outnumbered us two to one.

I recognized the one battling Iminor: so immense he fought one-handed with a sword that should have required two, he was the one I'd been fight-ing when Nechton gave the command to retreat last time. Tonight he plied the weight of his sword and all the mass of his body against Iminor, who worked speed and subtle bladecraft to turn the heavier sword's momentum into a disadvantage—until the Básghil reared up in the stirrups and brought all his mass against Iminor: sword clashing against Iminor's and sending the Tan tumbling from the saddle; the sickening, unmistakable sound of a shat-tered blade splitting the air.

I must close the gap Iminor's fall opened in the line before Letitia; but pow-er flared, close by, and my head snapped around involuntarily to locate the source. An arcane casting flew from the blade of a Básghil a short distance away, streaking in brilliant red towards me.

A wizard not bound by a vow would have raised a shield, deflected the casting. I tried to dive from its path instead. But a shield erupted in the air around me anyway, sparkling in an array of greens that cast the darkness in brief emerald illumination—and flared into nonexistence as the bolt from the Básghil sword grounded in its flow. I hit the ground, rolling awkwardly around my sword; Amien slumped across his horse's neck again; the gap be-fore Letitia had become a highway through which the Básghilae might drive an entire wedge. I launched myself back into the saddle, glancing along the line just in time to see Iminor scramble to his feet and grasp a blade a defeated Básghil had dropped. I heard myself shout, heard Letitia wail despair—and the sudden, horrific flow of Nechton's death-spell from the sword into Iminor made my head spiral beyond control.

Iminor leapt into his saddle and engaged the massive Básghil before the man could reach Letitia; another arcane blast issued from the sword of the Básghil at my right flank; I bashed my blade against his, sending the casting wide, but the deflected power knocked my weapon from my hand. Nechton glared at me from behind the Básghil's eyes; power surged through the un-dead man again, and I was out of defenses: I launched myself across the space between our horses, dragging us both from the saddle.

I hit the ground with a thud I heard but didn't feel: fists full of a dead man's jacket and a cataract of arcane power blasting through me, lighting me up in black and red and colors the mundane world can't accommodate. A moonless night on a barren shore disappeared, and I hung in the midst of timeless dark-ness, staring through a corpse at Nechton's intense grey eyes while Básghil energy spun me so far past reason that I forgot to care about anything but the elation of it, vision questing into incandescent darkness to encompass my enemy. Rapture cascaded up from the base of my spine; without planning it I began wrapping my awareness around Nechton, seeking out the dark spaces beneath his conscious mind. He pushed me away, his focused will shifting into sudden dread; a flavor of desire ethical men fear to name erupted in me. We might be brothers, or lovers; I might consume him whole and begin considering dessert; he sank a dragon's talons into my arms.

Who the fouzh ARE you?

I laughed, because I knew and he didn't; abruptly he was gone. I lay on the ground in the darkness, clutching a corpse so long dead it should have decayed months ago, the sort of laughter that gets men locked away bubbling out of me. I was peripherally aware of Básghilae thundering away into the night, of my companions staring in horror; I forced myself to stop laughing, to roll away from the dead man and climb to my feet, to pause and assess the situation. That is a commander's first job, but I could hardly see the people and assets I meant to tally through the raucous delight of arcane consciousness.

We were ten now: Rohini staring dismayed at me, swaying on her feet with the broad sweep of a Básghilae blade blazing an inferno of pain across her midsection; Amien fading in and out of consciousness, his familiar energies shadowed by a troubling darkness; Iminor fully, horrifyingly aware of the death-spell swirling through him and regarding the blade in his hand with evidently detached interest; Letitia unhurt but half-blinded by guilt and grief, tears glittering unshed in her eyes. Nuad and Busadi, Thurro and Seihar and Tibas seemed uninjured except in soul. My sword had fallen a short distance away, beside the head of a Básghil I'd defeated: I went and retrieved it, slid it into the sheath, gathered my horse's reins in one hand and spent a few seconds reassuring him.

"Well, then," I said to my companions. "Can you ride?"

Rohini cast me a long, dark look. "Can you tell me who you are?"

A short bark of laughter escaped me. "I am the monster who's on *your* side. Let's find a place to camp."

Chapter 33
Darkness Incandescent

I sent Nuad forward to lead us through the darkness and find a usable spot, not realizing until afterward that I had simply assumed command and no one had argued. I couldn't focus on the issue: more stars than I had ever seen stretched above the barren waste we rode, and their energies played over my skin like the fingers of courtesans, begging me to open up and draw them in. Esus echoed around me, His Power thrumming on the silent air. The memory of those brief incandescent moments of connection with Nechton made thrills race periodically up my back, made my hands itch to turn the horse and ride west until I found him, made desires that would have shocked an ethical man gather in the power centers that trace a wizard's spine.

But I had vowed to answer none of those needs: I remembered this fact, though tonight I wasn't certain there was any sense in that decision. And I was responsible for the people with whom I rode. I glanced around at them, reminding myself who they were—and the intoxication of arcane power began to drain away.

Rohini rode in a haze of pain, the arcane wards that had shielded her altogether gone. It was a thing to add to the list of events that could knock out personal wards: contact with a Básghilae blade. The delicious shimmering net of spectral light that hung around Letitia might stop an ordinary weapon; might even stop the first blow of a Básghil. But after that she would be lost. I

437

couldn't allow things to progress that far.

Amien, meanwhile, slumped half-prostrate in the saddle: leaning heavily on the saddle bow, wavering between an expression that suggested a shattering headache and moments when I wasn't sure he was conscious at all. The shimmer of arcane power I was accustomed to seeing on him lay shadowed by swirling darkness. No member of the Order could best him: the annual Pardan games at Aballo ensure that all know who the greatest Talents are. If Nechton could inflict this debilitation on him through indirect contact, what would happen when the wizards returned to Esunertos after the Moot? The dire answer and the obvious solution to the problem hung around me like a cloud of flies.

Finally Nuad found a withered-looking copse of trees beside the halfhearted flow of some stream that fed the Riga and reined. At least it wasn't barren rock.

"Lord?" he said, looking at me. "It's indefensible."

"It's *all* indefensible," I rejoined. "I don't think it matters."

He nodded thoughtfully, the habit of trust and newfound dread of me warring in his gaze. "I don't expect we'll see them again."

"Not tonight," I agreed, and he gave voice to a humorless chuckle that said I was being dense. Finally I saw what I should have recognized immediately, what Nuad already knew: Básghilae would be useless against anyone who could drain their delicious energy. I wondered what weapon or tactic Nechton would roll out instead. I wondered how a man might follow up on the creation of the Shadow of the Sun.

I cleared my throat, glanced around as if anyone present might think my mind lay within a twelvenight's travel of the mundane realm.

"Yes," I said to Nuad. "It'll do."

Everyone slid or climbed or more than half-fell from the saddles. Thurro and Seihar set about building a fire. I relieved my horse of saddle and tack, but didn't even pay lip service to brushing him: just left him in Nuad's hands for food and water and turned to assess my companions' needs. Amien had Rohini on his horse's blanket already, peeling the mail shirt away from her injury while she denied any need for medical attention at all. I left them to it, hearing the patterns of long-standing arguments in their bickering, and turned to Iminor.

The Tan sat on the bare rock with the Básghilae sword in his scabbard, the depthless blue of his eyes reflecting the black abyss of night and cold pallor in his face. Letitia tended his horse nearby, with an air that suggested it amounted to penance for a crushing weight of sin. She glanced at me, guilt giving way to an instant of intimacy before the shame redoubled and she glanced away; when I glanced back at Iminor, his regard was as distant as the remotest of stars. I settled on my heels before him, meeting his dark stare.

"I'm not convinced you should be carrying that blade," I said.

"I fail to see how it makes any zhevir difference," Iminor rejoined evenly. "How long would you say I've got?"

Behind him, Letitia gave voice to a strangled noise.

I gazed at him, considering. Appropriate healer conduct dictates that one doesn't leave a question like that hanging, but I seemed to have lost track of my humanity again.

"Are you cold?"

The Tan shrugged. "Just my arm."

I nodded. Dark energies swirled through him like ink in water. But they weren't dissipating; in fact they still seemed to be gathering. Was it true that this spell ran differently in the Tanaan, slower and gentler in its working than the horrors Rohini described—or had we simply been seeing its effect at distance? The Básghilae were much stronger in these Esus-soaked places we'd been traveling lately; the spell might well be, too. Would Iminor's body begin consuming itself from the inside, as Rohini had predicted for her man Luxin? Would the things that made him such a righteous, shaming presence burn away to an inhumanity even I found necessary to eradicate? If it came to that, how would I be sure my blade was raised in mercy, and not because it would leave Letitia's affections free for me to enjoy?

That question burned my delicious intoxication away, taking the distance I'd enjoyed with it. This was a true champion sitting before me, a worthy consort: like Gwydion in *Tílimya's Well*, he laid down his own life for the one he swore to serve. If I used the excuse of the things Nechton's spell would do to justify the ending of his life, I'd never look Letitia in the face again—let alone meet my own regard in mirrors.

I forced myself to confront the blue-black abyss of his gaze. "Take off the sword. Let me see what's happening."

The Tan just raised an eyebrow, regarding me with frank skepticism.

"Indulge me," I said, shifted to kneel before him, and marshaled the will necessary to keep staring until he sighed and shook his head and unbuckled the sword.

"Thank you," I said, and held out my right hand. After another skeptical glance he put his left hand into it. His skin was warm, his fingers strong: I settled the fingertips of my other hand against his forehead, feeling an essentially normal flow of energies between hand and brain. I released his hand and drew back: the Tan sighed as if relieved.

"Now the other one," I said, and held out my left.

Again he sighed, but put his hand into mine.

Oh, yes, there it was: the skin was cold against my own. I touched his forehead with my free hand, and immediately lost track of everything else: Nechton's death spell shimmered all around my awareness. I saw it pour in from the hollow of Iminor's hand, wind its way up the muscles and sinews of his arm, trace lazy ink-swirling patterns into the rest of him. Tendrils of horrifying, delicious black energy wound around his heart, spiraled about his spine like streamers on a Bealtan-fest pole, shot up the narrow spaces inside that column to blast into his head. The black rage that followed in the energy's wake made me catch my breath at its depth and familiarity, at the way it echoed the tempests that so often stormed in me.

"Damn," I said softly. That wasn't healer conduct, either: I hadn't come nearly as close to the realm of humanity as I'd thought. Alarm flared inside Iminor, echoing into me; resentment came on its heels. I never would do anything useful, just ride around looking dangerous and picking fights with everyone. He should have known better than to hope.

"Well, let's see what we can do, then," I said quietly. "With your permission."

Surprise shocked through him; he met my eyes with that damnable look of unexpected respect he'd given me at Laetrif and nodded. It just reminded me how faithless I was, how little I deserved his esteem. Nevertheless I encompassed him; as soon as he condensed inside me, a developing vortex manifested in my mind. It spun slowly around him, drawing me into its circle and gaining speed even as I assessed its flow. Iminor wasn't the focal point, but rather the place where the maelstrom's mouth opened to swallow. The black rage in him was only a foretaste of the impenetrable dark at the origin of the abyss.

I turned my attention on the energies swirling within him. Cold gathered in my mouth like a mockery of water; the elusive poppy smell of death crowded around. I touched one of the streamers of black energy—and it shifted to wrap itself around me, a silken caress whose black hue burned away, revealing itself in luminous ripples of color and raising thrills of delight where it brushed against my flesh. I followed it beyond Iminor, beyond the mundane world, beyond any place of which the Aballo Order ever dreamed—into the deep velvet darkness, to grasp the heart of the spell.

The universe stopped. Everything created and as-yet-uncreated hung in breathless suspension while I encompassed the working's terrible magnificence. The spell was cunning, surprising, using the rules limiting such operations against themselves; it banked against the cold fire in the darkness between the stars, opening a conduit between the victim and a source of power so huge and frigid it was guaranteed to kill. The more the victim fought, the faster the spell would work, because the energy spent would just draw the cold in faster. Only by embracing that cold, dark fire could anyone who came into contact with this spell survive it. I reached out to grasp the deadly power, forgetting to fear.

I recognized it now: this was the magic that woke me on the morning of the ard-righ's death, wrapping me in crystal music and lightning flavor, its spectral spidersilk caress carrying a shattering breadth of arcane charge. But this time, with it occupying the dark spaces of my awareness, I saw it for what it was. The cold was a deception; its truth wasn't darkness: rather an intensity beyond mortal comprehension, a pleasure that exceeded any description a harpist or even a wizard might give: the inverse of the sort of white light that rains down upon a wizard at the moment of Union with a god. It stampeded through me in pleasure that tore a half-formed exclamation from my throat, burning away all my illusions of ethics and humanity, showing me how precious and inconsequential those ideas were and revealing Myself to me. This was what it was to be a god. This was what it was to encompass not only the good and generous but also the consuming and hideous. Of course its truth would destroy any mortal soul.

Except Nechton. Except me. Mortal though we were, neither of us should be described as human. To us the virtues of humanity did not apply.

Iminor, of course, was another matter entirely. He was something more virtuous than human, and he was looking at me, seeing straight into my depths: eyes full of awareness no mortal should ever have. But he lacked the Talent to control the power's flow: now that his connection with it had been established, there was no way for him to disengage. And no one else could do it for him.

You lying whore, he thought.

I should have expected this. While I'd been looking at him and the power he'd absorbed, he'd been seeing everything inside me. Our shared mindspace was filled with images and sensations and flavors that made me blush before him, all of them so suffused with Letitia that need erupted in me at the memories.

Behind his controlled tone boiled blinding rage. *You murdering, whoring sack of dung!*

It occurred to me that a Tan using the word *whore* constituted an entirely new flavor of irony. He extracted his hand from my grasp, reared up on his knees, and delivered a surprisingly heavy right cross that I saw coming and allowed to connect with my jaw anyway. My brain exploded with pain that made him wince and sever our connection; my head snapped around on its axis, making the vortex around us spin faster. The campsite flashed into my awareness as if it had just resumed existence: seven astonished stares fixed on us; Letitia's cheeks blazed as red as her cloak. She buried her face in her hands. I shook my head to clear it. My skull still rang.

"Yes," I said with a calm I didn't feel, forcing myself to meet his gaze. "I deserve that and more. You should probably kill me, or try. But first you should decide what to do."

The Tan gave voice to an inhuman laugh. "About what?"

"The spell."

He settled down to sit on his heels, staring at me.

I nodded. "It's as we thought: there's a spell on these swords, and now the power it invokes is in you. If I leave it this way, you will die."

Iminor's narrow jaw went hard; his pale lips grew almost white. "But you can fix it."

I raised my eyebrows. "It's not that simple. Once a wizard forges a connection like this, the connection exists. All anyone can do now is change *you.*"

Abruptly Iminor was on his feet, walking away. "Into someone who can enjoy the presence of evil?" He paused, pinning me with a stare that made something inside me shrivel. "Into something like *you.*"

I couldn't help it: I glanced away. "No, fortunately for all concerned, no one can generate something like *me.* The truth is more complex. There is a place in you that is open now, and power is flowing into you. It's not power that's meant to exist in people; very quickly it will overwhelm your natural energy. If you want to live, I need to create another opening, one that will allow the power to flow *through* you."

Iminor stopped pacing, fixing me with an abyssal stare. "But that's not all."

"No," I admitted. "This power—even passing through you, it will make changes you're not prepared for. There's a risk it will destroy who you are, destroy your soul."

"And then I *will* be just like you."

A humorless smile came over me, but I resisted the bait. "It will be painful. I can't say whether death is the easier option. Only you can choose."

Iminor stopped pacing, folded his arms across his chest. He glanced at Letitia, a flavor of rage so deep and encompassing in him that his face looked perfectly emotionless, then turned his black gaze on me again.

"If I begin to turn into—*you*... Will you still be able to kill me?"

Again I found it necessary to glance away. "That is not a power you should put into my hands."

"And yet there it is," the Tan rejoined.

I swallowed against the tightness in my throat. I couldn't look at any of them. "You will still be vulnerable to steel. But I suspect—can't prove, but I suspect... that the Básghilae death spells won't be able to touch you."

"Because the evil is already in me."

"Because the connection those spells depend on has already been otherwise grounded."

Iminor gave a snort of humorless laughter. "And still I make the mistake of thinking you capable of truth. Dance around this, then: will I still be alive?"

What a strange question. Was I still alive? I glanced again at the black incandescent power, feeling the connection that remained between me and it, tasting the flow that would pour into me if I but gave it leave—and that terrible laughter the touch of the Básghil incited in me threatened to erupt in my throat again. Alive? I hadn't been this alive in a decade.

I met the Tan's cold gaze. "Yes, indeed you will. You'll just be different."

Iminor's mouth twisted; he stared at me, contempt in his gaze and fear radiating so powerfully from him that I found it necessary to push the energy away. Breathless silence hung all around.

"Do it, then," he said finally, voice crackling with controlled rage. "And goddess forgive what I do after."

He settled before me, fixing me with a cold expectant stare. I nodded and held out my hands; his mouth twisted, but he put his hands into mine, and I encompassed him again. All his rage and fear blasted through me; breath shuddered out of me, and I twitched against the impulse to withdraw.

"No," he said aloud, the word echoing through our shared mindspace. "Finish it."

I nodded, but terror still swirled in me, kicking up memories I hadn't examined in years. A clearing in Tellan exploded with channeled power as my father met my eyes; I stood over the first man I ever dueled with swords, Ballarona resuming existence in my awareness and rage boiling away to horror of what I had become; I sat in an ill-lit corner of Aballo's library with the dust-and-parchment aroma of Aechering's ancient grimoire rising in my throat, recognizing myself in his words.

I would never practice from that volume. I probably shouldn't even be redirecting the flow of this spell, even though I wouldn't draw power to do it. I could still read the words from Aechering's pages in my memory. Every day now I tested the limits of this vow I'd so hastily taken, and every day found them a little more elastic than I'd thought. I still itched to explore Aechering's great mystery. Would I recognize the true boundary when I encountered it? What if I had passed it already?

Iminor's humorless laugh echoed through me. *You know this is completely esoteric, right? It's not what you DO that makes you evil, fool.*

So be it, then. But the duelist in me couldn't resist the riposte. *Let me know what you think a month from now, braugh. Take a good look at the dark side of the world and let me know.*

This time it was Iminor who shuddered.

I turned my attention on the flow of power through his body. The opening was exactly where I remembered, in the palm of his hand. An unfortunate circumstance: if the opening had been in one of the median power centers, it would have been easy to establish a swift, balanced flow. As things stood, there was no choice but to let the power wind its distracted way through him. Again I traced the flow from his darkening hand, up through his cold-cramped arm and on a lazy trip around his heart and spine. The power circulated around the base of Iminor's spine and up the bony shaft, then spun around inside his skull. Only a few wandering rivulets flickered in his left arm and legs. The sensible thing to do was to create an opening in his head.

Which power center should I use? The one at the crown is both strongest and easiest to open; it should be possible to establish a reasonable flow there. Had the Tan not been a Talent, permanently opening his crown would be the obvious choice. But for a person already half-open to the whims of the gods, blocking that place open could be dangerous.

Or, with power constantly flowing out through that opening, might he actually find himself shielded from eruptions of Sight? What little I knew of seers suggested relieving him of those episodes would be a blessing to him; but it might be a disservice to the gods.

The waste in which we sat spoke more eloquently than any harpist: there was far too high a price on serving the gods.

Terror of my own thoughts erupted in me again; I pushed that line of reasoning away. I was sworn to the true gods. It was the one facsimile of virtue I had left. I must do the best for Them I could. If it was Their Will that this Tan survive, all that remained to me was to do what I could for him and leave the rest in Their hands. It wasn't as if anyone really knew how Sight worked, anyway. Maybe the power center at his crown had nothing to do with it at all.

Oh, truly, either do it or slit my throat, Iminor thought. *I'm sure the gods washed Their hands of you long ago.*

I couldn't allow myself to think about how wrong he was, not with all my awareness open to him: instead I filled my mind with the energy flowing through him, letting it blast me up and around inside his skull. It lit me up until I barely remembered why I'd touched it. From inside his head I rode the flow, up to the place where it swirled around the edges of the power center at his crown; turned my attention on that place and teased its petals open; rode the sudden blast of energy out into the night. I hung on the air, looking down on the campsite, rising higher and higher towards the stars. I saw him groan and pull away from my suddenly vacant and crumpling body to bury his face in his knees; saw Letitia race across the campsite and then visibly hesitate over which of us to attend first; saw the white-hot stare he turned on her.

"Iminor!" she breathed, reaching out towards him.

He rose, ignoring the offered hand and staring down at her as all the color fled her face. Silence stretched again.

"I didn't do it for you," he said at last, voice as cold as the spaces between the stars. "I did it for all those people who will never be safe until you do whatever the hell it is Nechton fears. Don't be a coward." He turned and stalked away from her, across the campsite, beyond the circle of firelight and into the echoing void, while she stood with hands over her mouth and a terrible devastation in every line of her body.

Now I saw: whatever her feelings for me, she loved him in a way that would bind them all their lives and possibly longer. Whoever she took into her bed, his presence would always occupy the corners of the room. The awareness sent me crashing back into my own body, suddenly too heavy for the air to hold. I breathed in cold-dust air and pushed myself back up from the stone, finding her eyes on me.

And oh, alas for Iminor: mind still entangled in the darkness, I glimpsed the terrible ties binding her to me as well. No wizard but me could ever undo them, and I had no idea how. Loeg could make this into a tragedy, but it would fail to win any sort of popular following. What sane person would grasp its sickness, after all?

"Well, that's done, then," I said, and rose.

"Thank you," she said softly.

A humorless laugh escaped me. I couldn't think of anything to say, so I nodded and walked past her to check on Amien. But before I reached the place in which the wizard sat, Nuad planted himself in my path.

I stopped short, staring at the Tan: too wrecked to defend against the intensity of his sudden hatred.

"You let Manannan die?"

My throat clamped shut; there was no defense I could offer. A better commander would have kept a tighter rein on Manannan; would have maintained sufficient vigilance that the Tan never took the hit of a Básghilae blade at all.

"You let Manannan die!" Nuad rasped. "You had the power to undo the spell—and you—" Nuad choked on rage; terrible, belated understanding arose in me. "You drank his memory with us, and the whole time you could have—"

I shook my head, trying to figure out how to explain. The man I had been a twelvenight ago still understood what it meant to keep a vow. I hadn't unraveled the spells involved until the last few days. But I knew the truth: I hadn't tried. It hadn't even occurred to me to try.

The shame of it crashed down on me; I glanced away, discovering Rohini's gaze on me. I felt as if she looked straight into the rot at my core. And remembered her man Luxin.

And Vandabala, who took a minor hit with an enchanted blade on the night of our first Básghilae encounter. What would have happened if I'd attended to him myself, rather than insisting Amien assume the duty? Even without knowing the spells beforehand, might I have unraveled them and spared his life? If rechanneling the spell for Iminor had not been a violation of my vow, then why had I held back from aiding those others?

Nuad had every right to demand satisfaction at swordpoint. In his position I would do the same. And I should let him slice me open. But I had given my word not to abandon Letitia.

I swallowed against nausea, forced myself to look into his face. Better not to dance around it, lest he say something in which I found an excuse to win the duel.

"I have no excuse to offer, ouirr," I said quietly. "Reasons, shortcomings, failures; no excuses." I waited, hands ostentatiously distant from the hilt of my sword, for the demand. But Nuad just stared at me. Gradually I realized the Tanaan tradition of dueling must have died with their magic and their warfare. He didn't have the words.

I restrained a sigh. "Ouirr, it is not my desire, but... do you seek satisfaction?"

Nuad's mouth twisted. "An honor-duel? Don't you lack a basic requirement for such an event?"

That, of course, was a dueling offense. Except that it was true. Nuad shook his head and walked away. For a moment I stood as if rooted to the spot; finally I remembered that I had not completed the task I'd so belatedly taken on, and closed the distance between Amien and myself. He stared up at me, face still and black eyes bottomless in this light. The haze of dark energy still hung on him, seeming to war with his natural power.

"My lord?" I said quietly. "May I examine you?"

The wizard's jaw grew tight. "Leave it, Ellion. We've had enough for one night. Just let me rest."

I pursed my lips, tried to gather up a different approach; something in his face softened, just a bit.

"Truly," he said. "Let me rest. Let's see what tomorrow brings."

I had no right to demand he submit. I certainly hadn't earned his trust or anyone else's. I inclined my head, turned away, finally went and tended my horse.

It's not what you DO that makes you evil, fool.

I assumed the first arcane watch again, with no intention of waking Amien for the second. The look he cast me as he retired suggested he knew and couldn't find it in himself to fight about it. Cold skittered up my back at what I saw in his face.

Soon everyone but Busadi—and Iminor, who I sensed at the confluence of the stream and the river—lay bundled in cloaks or sleeping rolls nearby. Busadi haunted the darkness just outside the circle of firelight; I cast my awareness wide, diffusing into a state that wasn't quite trance. And as everyone around me lapsed into exhausted sleep, the power in the darkness between the stars closed in and shimmered around my edges, filling me with a music never heard by earthly ears. It tingled over my skin like the spray of a waterfall, playing in a thousand shifting, spectral hues across the intense infinite dark of the sky and stretching time into strange irregular ripples. I should have pushed it away; instead I breathed in just a whiff of it. Aechering's Shadow Working unfolded itself in my mind for the thousandth time.

Hakaid the shadow of the Sun

And open the Abyss

Was it true that my stars marked me not for greatness but for great evil? If the Abyss was my destiny, there was no point in worrying about vows or the line between dark magic and light. I should just bring everything I had to protecting the people I loved. I should race to close the gap between Nechton and myself, so I might be ready for whatever he threw against Letitia next. So I might make it unnecessary for Amien to do more than marshal my resources. What would it mean to *hakaid* the shadow of the Sun?

Aechering lived and worked before the arrival of the true gods: before the war that destroyed Esusdia, scattered her peoples and killed her language. His work is full of words for which no one living is certain of the proper translation, words that are sources of endless debate at Aballo. Even men who will never read more than this one working debate the meaning of *hakaid* the way harpists argue about *Fare and Fir*; men who read all of Aechering have many more words to puzzle over. Some say *hakaid* means *to summon*, others *to know*.

I wondered whether anyone had ever pursued this working using the theory that *hakaid* means *to invoke*.

Did a man invoke the shadow of the Sun, what would happen? If the Sun is Ilesan, the Lord of Gods—and though the Sun can mean no more than *the male force* in certain contexts, *the Lord of Gods* is the primary interpretation for any such formula—then the operator who invoked the Sun's shadow would be consciously tapping the Dark. Tonight I knew the form it would take: that sparkle between the stars, invisible to mundane eyes, which killed good men and raised evil ones to raging readiness to become gods. I knew the rapture that would pound through me.

The energy should repel me. But all the depthless sky sang with my need.
The reach of the shadow of the Sun is infinite.

Tonight it was easy to imagine being the heir of Tílimya: mortal successor to that ancient god Who men see as the very Incarnation of evil. If He long ago mastered every form of evil men will ever conceive, it was in order to defend all of creation from the men and gods who must be imprisoned in the Abyss. It was easy to imagine stretching myself across the sky and gathering up all the energy waiting there, letting it blast me beyond reason and into a place in which no matter what Nechton unveiled, it would seem no challenge at all. But I knew: invoke the shadow of the Sun, tap into the Dark, and I would be planting my standard in opposition to the true gods.

Cold raced through me at the thought of making that declaration; my throat clamped shut. I looked across the campfire into the golden eyes of Ankou, Tílimya's boatman.

A sane man would have been terrified; I just felt the inevitability of it. I realized I had no idea which of my many offenses was my greatest sin. Why had he come for me now? I'd incurred no injuries today, and I still had much to do. Letitia and Amien still needed my protection. Could I persuade the Guardian of the Well to parole me long enough to see them safe?

Let the heir of Tílimya
Woo the Virgin Star

I found myself taking Ankou in, even now enmeshed in a scholar's habits of assessing facts. Strange that the descriptions in the stories failed on the single most important detail: clad in gleaming white bones and voluminous black cloak though he was, his grinning skull capped by an immense black hat, he definitely had *eyes*: nearly human, fleshly orbs with brilliant golden irises. They reminded me of something I couldn't lay hands on. What had happened to the empty glowing sockets I'd been led to expect?

"Ellion, braugh." He stood looking at me, ghoulish and cordial, the spread of his immense hat blocking out half the stars. "Been a while, hasn't it? Haven't seen you since Tellan."

"*What?*" I blurted. There are protocols that wizards are taught to follow, should a god or a demon manifest in the course of a working. Senseless utterances do not figure in any of them.

"Hel-*lo, you* called *me?*" There was no rancor in his singsong mockery. No sense that anything occurring here mattered at all.

"What?" I said again. I drew a deep breath, swallowed, tried again. "I don't think so."

"No, really!" He gave voice to a clear, unfettered laugh. "Oh, wallow in denial if you like. But we've got a lot to do. We were only just getting started, that day in Tellan, when that pain in the ass Fintan turned up and blew everything."

Fintan had been Tellan's House Healer in my youth. Ankou—if that was who this being was—meant my duel with Deaclan. The memory settled over me: sitting on horseback in a not-so-vacant glade in Tellan, trying to focus on the invisible shimmer that teased my peripheral vision and listening to Deaclan's horse approach. The prickle of remembered *presence* swept over me again.

"That was you?" I said.

Without planning it I cast out tendrils of awareness: a half-familiar *otherness* hovered all around. Racing power, laughter, and sheer wildness infected me; vast, unbridled consciousness tugged at me like an invitation to play. Hunger raged in me again.

"Yes," the ghoul said softly, voice rich with promise. "You remember? You were the one wearing the tanist's torc; I was in my bones…"

My fingers sought the place where no torc lay about my throat, coming up empty as usual. "I didn't see you. Just heard you."

"Never heard from you after that."

Gods, had I called him? How was it possible I had summoned this being without conscious choice—without being conscious of it at all? And not once, apparently, but twice. If a man could summon such a being without conscious intention, what other magics might he work without being aware?

"I haven't been practicing," I said finally.

"Oh, *no.*" The ghoul shook his head, dismayed. "If you don't practice, you get rusty. And you have no fun at all."

I didn't answer. The ghoul sat down, arranging the voluminous black cloak around his bony legs.

"Boyo," he said, "why do you have this Talent?"

A strange question, coming from a being who knows everything about the life of every mortal. I could only infer it was rhetorical, so I drew on the rhetorics I'd been taught.

"Because the gods created me so."

"Fouzh, *really?*" Even without flesh on his face, he managed to produce a look of utter disgust. "Just recite the parrot's answer? Come on, dig in!"

I glanced around. The fire crackled and danced between us, one of the myriad sources of potential pleasure I couldn't allow myself to touch. Stars crowded to within a hand's breadth of the circle of light it cast: stretching from the pole above us, down to the ground and seemingly past that boundary. Sleeping people lay all around us; I could neither hear nor see Busadi. But when I looked more closely at Letitia and Amien, I realized I couldn't see them breathing, though the color in Letitia's face told me she yet lived. The constant wind across the barren plain had paused. I was no longer certain that plain still surrounded us at all.

Gods can control even time—and the fabric of the universe. Finally it occurred to me to wonder why no one calls Ankou a god, but only a boatman.

"You don't get the credit you deserve, do you?" I said. "How many people are even aware that you're a god?"

"*What?*" he said, bones rattling as he leaned towards me. His voice suggested I'd struck a nerve—which struck me funny, since clearly he had none. I was nearly successful in controlling the smile—and reeled in surprise at his answering grin.

"Don't change the subject, braugh. Why do you have this Talent?"

I wrapped my arms around my knees, allowing myself to sink into the problem. If I set aside the obvious answer—and being obvious, and yet a matter of the gods, was it not likely to be fallacious anyway?—then I was left with a much more concrete question: How—or *from where*—had I acquired this Talent? Natural philosophy recognizes different flavors of Talent: inherited Talents that are passed in the blood from father to son, including Sight and the druidic Talents that run in some families; the Talents granted by the gods, which allow wizards and windcallers to draw on natural forces and in some cases the Power of the true gods Themselves to accomplish the gods' Will. It does not account for power that stands separate from or even opposed to the true gods: wizards are taught that tapping into Dark, declaring oneself outside the gods' Embrace, is the short route to losing all access to power.

For all I knew that was true for most men. But that theory didn't account for Nechton, who was vastly more successful than Amien without any aid whatsoever from the true gods—and it didn't account for the things I'd seen on this journey, for all the old gods Who offered, nay all but impregnated me with, Their Power. Nor for the physical sources of energy that could be mine would I but consent: the stars, the dark fire that lay between them, the cold river of energy that circled the skies above like some inverse of Dóiteán.

My access to power was not dependent on the Will of the gods. It did not come from Them. The ghoul was right: the easy answer did not apply. But this conclusion led me back to the more difficult question after all.

Why did I have this Talent?

"I don't know," I said finally.

"Yes!" the ghoul snapped his bony fingers. "Now we're getting someplace! If we cannot say why you have a Talent, it is equally impossible to say with certainty what it is for. There is only the question of how you will use it."

"What if I use it for evil?"

"Ahhh..." He favored me with a disturbingly toothy grin, fleshy eyes gleaming. "What is your definition of evil?"

"What?" I said. "I thought we were supposed to discuss my greatest transgression."

The ghoul gave voice to a dismissive noise that should have been impossible to produce without lips. "That's apprentice-grade stuff. Let's dig in. Come on, what makes something evil?"

Déjà vu reeled in me. Why did I remember sitting around a campfire arguing philosophy? Where had I seen those eyes? For one wild moment those questions seemed more important than the definition of evil, even though my eternal fate might well hang in the balance. Oh, to be doomed to the Abyss because of an inability to lay the unanswered question aside.

I didn't think that constituted my greatest fault.

"Who *are* you?" I blurted.

"Hah! Who are *you*?"

Neither of us shifted form. For what might have been a moment or an hour I just sat there staring at him; he returned my stare. I discovered I couldn't answer that question, either. I looked at my hands.

"Well, there's your problem, then," the ghoul said, in a sympathetic tone. "If you've been taught to define yourself in terms of who you are to others, and then those definitions get ripped away, what do you have left? Only questions and doubts."

I glanced away, swallowing against pain.

"But none of those things is an excuse to refuse to do the things for which you are designed, to withhold the things the people around you need. If we can't say why you have a Talent, we can say without doubt that it is being wasted. And that may well be evil. At least when considered in context."

"I have a taste for things that harm others. *That* is evil."

The ghoul waved the statement away. "You have a taste for *power*. To a starving man even rotten food has a certain appeal."

"Oh dear gods."

"No, *listen*. There's an old story about a party that was trying to cross the mountains in winter when a terrible storm came in. They got lost—as it happened, less than a mile from the pass, but in that weather who could tell?— and they had no choice but to camp and wait it out. They managed to build themselves shelter, but after a time they ran out of food."

Old story? I'd never heard or read it.

"And when some of them died, the others did what was necessary to survive."

I swallowed against nausea. "They ate their friends."

"Does that make them evil? Or survivors? What if their religion taught them it was an expression of respect to consume their friends' flesh—reverently, and with remembrance? Would it be evil then? What if your gods didn't tell you that they must be your only source of sustenance, but rather that any power used in honor and mercy was as good? When you sleep with the river goddess in the hold of a boat, how is that different from lying with the goddess at Bealtan?"

I found myself on my feet. Now, finally, the dread I should have felt at his arrival had me by the throat. Was this even Who I thought?

"Are you some kind of demon?" I demanded. I couldn't imagine a being who judges mortals speaking such blasphemy.

He actually laughed. "No more than you are. Tell me this: When you perform the sacred marriage, who does it serve? Are you even sure with whom
you lie?"

Oh, that was unfair. The goddess—the priestess—is masked at Bealtan. To
penetrate that mystery would be to render the ceremony into nothing more
than sex. Or into something Dark.

Join the Sun and the Moon in Darkness
Thus results the Union of Silver and Gold
Blend the Essences in the vessel of life

In these contexts, the Moon is the goddess—or, sometimes, simply the female. If the operator who performed the working took *Essences* to mean the
magical sexual essences with which a man and woman might conceive a child,
was the vessel of life the goddess Herself? Or might it be the operator's assistant, the woman who might or might not wear the Bealtan mask?

What was the purpose of it, anyway? Why did I have this Talent?

"Yes," the ghoul said, as if he'd heard everything I hadn't said, every line
of Aechering's I couldn't eradicate from my mind. "You have honor, Ellion.
No matter what meanings you assign to things. If you know a definition of
evil that includes honor, you get to call yourself by that name. Otherwise your
greatest transgression lies in refusing to give the rest of us the benefit of who
you are."

I looked at him again. I couldn't think of anything to say. He rose, golden
eyes inescapable, and drew the voluminous black cloak about his bony frame.
He turned until I could see only the black expanses of his hat and cloak; they
flared impossibly wide, blurring into nonexistence—and then I stood there
alone, surrounded by sleeping people. The wind lifted the tail of my hair, sent
it forward to flutter in my peripheral vision. I felt far colder than its temperature warranted.

The reach of the shadow of the Sun is infinite.

Chapter 34
Season of Change

Are you some kind of demon?
No more than you are.

If that had been Ankou, he was not at all what I expected of a being who sat in judgment over mortals—whether or not he really was a god. The more I thought about it, the less certain I became of who or what I had seen.

It is easy enough, for a wizard or a god or a demon, to throw on an illusion; my failure to penetrate it meant only that my visitor, whoever he might be, was better at the game of glamours than I. He might well be a demon.

That would mean I was one, too, and no one had ever bothered to call my attention to it: for all the horrifying things he'd said, not once had I heard the telltale notes of untruth in his voice. And those are impossible to mask.

Are you some kind of demon?
No more than you are.

Wise men don't take advice from demons. Even when demons tell the truth, they shape it to their own ends. And evil men who would do good must be twice as wary: especially when the things demons say resonate with their own instincts. Nevertheless the ghoul's words echoed against the inside of my skull for the rest of the night, plying counterpoint to the seduction of all the powers gathering around the edges of my awareness.

Why did I have this Talent? I turned the question over and over in my mind, but failed to come up with any satisfactory answer. The stars wheeled past; the waning moons rose and faded into morning light; my companions shook off sleep and began preparing for the day. Amien still looked grey; his natural energies lay under dark clouds, and I couldn't be certain without touching him that those clouds were not still gathering, couldn't even scan him psychically without him being aware. And he had not granted permission. One of the hits he'd taken last night had been in Rohini's defense, but one had been for me, and the weight of it turned painfully in my chest. I crossed the campsite to stand before him.

"My lord—" Once again I'd failed to work out what I should say in advance. He frowned a little, puzzled; I cleared my throat.

"No more shielding for me, eh?" I said, pitching my voice so it wouldn't carry beyond his ears.

He laughed: a tired sound that made pain condense in my throat.

"I am grateful to you, my lord, but—"

"Are you going to start working your own, then?" Amien's gaze was a dare. Or a prayer, maybe.

I sighed. "My lord—"

The wizard shook his head. "I'm not losing you. Not after everything I went through to get you here. Gods know I had to go all the way to Fíana to find you."

An unwilling laugh escaped me. "I promise I'll attend the Moot, my lord."

Amien smiled. "In what capacity?"

"Fouzh," I growled, and went to check on Rohini. She was pale, her eyes too bright, the contrast between the deep red of her hair and the translucence of her skin contradicting her efforts to behave as if she were well. As I approached, she bent to gather her cloak from the horse blanket on which Amien had installed her last night, containing the impulse to voice the pain that suddenly flared around her. I understood: any righ or commander must mask his illnesses and injuries from the people he leads, so they may rely on his strength.

"How are you this morning, sian?" I asked, picking up the blanket and folding it so she wouldn't need to bend again.

She shrugged one shoulder. "Almost ready."

"Did Amien stitch you up?" I pitched my voice for her ears only, but she glanced around nevertheless.

"Wasn't necessary," she said, busy with folding and stowing her cloak.

"Chief," I said.

"*Leave* it," she hissed.

I nodded but wrapped stealthy tendrils around her: she was still unwarded, which meant Amien hadn't recovered sufficient strength for the working; pain that would have sent most men into whimpering huddles coursed through her midsection, radiating from a long rift that had opened when a heavy blade drove the wiry spidersilk of her mail into her flesh. It hadn't been stitched, and it should be. But no taint of magic lay on her anywhere: Amien's wards might not have done more than slow the blow, but they had turned aside the spell. Could we keep infection at bay, her pain would be temporary, and she would live.

"We'll be able to find privacy at Teamair," I said quietly. "You and I have an engagement."

She cast me a look of surprise that faded into understanding. But her gaze held no concession. "We'll see."

Finally Iminor turned up, outwardly calm but eyes full of things no mortal should ever know. He cast me a dispassionate glance; fear, hatred, and an uneasy sense of obligation warred beneath its surface. I slipped a tendril of awareness around him, observing the heady, constant flow of seductive power through his body and out through his crown—and the arcane bonds that lay between us now. The whole construct was stable; there was no reason to expect that the flow might cease while he lived. And in that moment of awareness-of-my-awareness, he saw it all as clearly as I did: whatever changes Nechton's spell and my reworking of it had wrought, his Sight was undiminished. In fact the change he'd undergone had strengthened it.

He looked at me through that augmented vision: a terrible understanding passed between us. All unthinking I had bound myself to both him and Letitia, with energies no one else could break and ties I had no idea how to undo. Even should we all survive this war, even did they return to Fíana and take up the lives they'd planned, this twisted thing would lie among us, undiminished by miles and time.

"Zhev," he growled, and turned away.

We broke camp; we climbed into the saddles and rode to the place where the Precinct Road crosses the Riga. Halfway across the ford I spotted a train of horses and wagons riding north on the opposite shore, following the weedy trail that had once been the Ard-righ's Road. At the front of the mass I saw the righ's banner of Ilesia.

Dread crashed in on me, just as fiercely as when that nameless ghoul cornered me with logic last night. The last time Coran and I spoke, I'd refused his offer to make me his ard-tiarn and War-Lord. I didn't know whether we were still friends. I controlled the impulse to turn the horse around, right there in the middle of the river, and head back the way I'd come: we would reach Teamair before midday, even did we fall in with Coran's train, and I'd given my word to see Letitia safely there. I'd promised to attend the Moot tomorrow— though this morning I'd somehow forgotten what that really meant: a commitment to watch Coran's election to the throne that should have been mine.

I realized I'd reined and was sitting stupidly in the middle of the ford. I cued the horse forward and rode up to the trail on the opposite side. Then there was nothing to do but wait while the slow train made up the distance. Sooner or later I would have to greet Coran and all the Ilesians who had made the trip in his company; I might as well salvage what grace I could.

Within a minute a herald in Ilesia blue-and-gold raced forward to meet us. I knew how we looked, how few and tired and unbannered; I knew all the calls and answers protocol demanded we endure now. Suddenly I had no patience for any of it.

"Good morning," I said as he reined. "The Aballo Prince, the Lady of Finias and her consort, the Chief of the Essuvians, and the ard-harpist. Tell your lord we wait on his pleasure." I might not be ard-righ tomorrow, but damned if I'd cede the road like some commoner.

The herald opened his mouth, closed it again, finally swallowed and said, "My lord." And with an appropriate dip of his banner towards us, he turned his horse and raced back. After a moment, Coran rode out from under his banner, spurred his horse to speed, and closed the distance between us. Never one for the dandyism of a dyed-coat mount, he had nevertheless allowed someone to tint his horse's mane: the white destrier now sported a froth of blue between his eyes and down his broad neck. Coran himself looked the part of ard-righ-apparent, dressed with his usual rich unconcern—but also a too-perfect plumed hat. Evidently he'd found time to have the righ's torc refitted. He made me acutely aware of my dishevelment.

He reined and slipped from the saddle before the horse had stopped moving: appropriate respect for the Aballo Prince. I slid to the ground as well, because to do otherwise would be unseemly: hearing Nuad and Rohini's men follow my lead, already thoroughly tired of protocol. When had I laid aside the habit of propriety? No doubt I had lost it somewhere in Fíana, along with the rest of the person who left Ilnemedon two months ago.

"My lord," Coran said to Amien, with an utterly proper bow. He glanced at me; the shift in his gaze said I looked even worse than I'd realized, and the change alarmed him. At least he didn't seem to hate me.

"Lord Coran," Amien said warmly and hauled himself from the saddle. I resisted the temptation to rush across the space between us, to catch him if he fell; but he dismounted without mishap, and the rest of them climbed from their saddles.

Suddenly Coran abandoned protocol, closed the distance between us, and embraced me. Through the contact I saw the way his clear, practical energies had been rechanneled into the necessity of managing far too many people and concerns, how heavily he drew on his natural constitutional strength in the face of too little sleep and too many cares. But the surprising depth of his affection came through just as clearly, sending regret and relief sweeping through me. My throat closed; I clasped him tightly in return.

"Dear gods, are you *all right*?" he said, pitched for my ears alone.

I nodded, stepping back to meet his eyes. "Thank you. Yes."

"We've talking to do," he said, still in an undertone, and returned his gaze to the rest of the party.

I made introductions: Coran greeted Letitia with a flavor of quiet wonder of which I had not realized him capable, met Rohini and Iminor with entirely sufficient respect, didn't blink once at my introducing the few others remaining in our party. He nodded to each of them, one warrior to another, and somehow the plumed hat and blue mane didn't undercut his warrior presence. He had truly expanded into the role of righ; I found myself pleased for him, as long as I didn't think about the election.

I realized the long train that followed him had caught up to us and now stood waiting; at least a hundred people watched us from carriages and horseback. At the front were Coran's brother Niall, his armsmaster Den and the men of his personal contingent; behind them I recognized a significant subset of the tiarna who regularly haunted Ilnemedon and their wives. Appearing so disheveled before Ilnemedon society should have embarrassed me; I was surprised to discover how little I cared. Why hadn't I realized they were not my people?

I had known. I just hadn't wanted to think about it.

"Lords, Ladies, will you ride with us?" Coran said.

I glanced at Amien: it would be inappropriate for the Aballo Prince to accompany any single righ through Teamair's gate before an election. In a very real sense the ard-righ is the Aballo Prince's War-Lord for mundane affairs, particularly in wartime: the Prince would be well within his rights to simply seat the man of his choice on the throne. The wizard met my eyes briefly, then turned his gaze on Coran.

"It will be our pleasure to ride with you a while," he said. "But we are bound for Uisneach."

Senseless shock raced through me: I barely felt ready to confront Teamair, let alone Uisneach. But it should have been obvious to me, and I didn't know what other obvious conclusions I was failing to entertain: while the righthe reside in Fair houses at Teamair, the wizards occupy the sacred center during the Bealtan season. It was the only sensible destination, not only for the Aballo Prince but also for the neutral parties under his protection. I couldn't consider whether I fell into that category.

Coran bowed. "Of course, my lord. You honor us with your company."

Amien smiled and nodded; we all climbed into the saddles again, and we moved to the front of the train. Coran nodded to the standard bearer, who gave the signal; everyone moved out.

I hadn't ridden with a train approaching this size since Tellan; today it felt unwieldy, confining. Irrelevant thoughts and misdirected energies swirled all around, bashing themselves against my awareness. I wanted to spur my horse away from the crowd, wanted to shout at them to contain their petty idiocies. How was it possible I used to willingly join their fractious company? My horse pinned back his ears, nervous; I laid a hand on his neck but had little comfort to offer him. Coran spoke courteously with Letitia and Iminor, but he kept glancing at me, worry behind his smooth expression.

Someone rode forward from the mass behind us, worked his way into the line beside me. I glanced at him, then failed to control the startle: at my right hand rode Caern Tirkeer, ollamh of the Harpist Gorsedd, the man I had defeated in the last election for ard-harpist. We had always been civil but never cordial. His reputation as a composer of the sort of works that men take to be significant was unexceeded, and as a teacher he had raised more men from the silver branch to the gold than any other two ollamh. He was the leader of the vocal contingent among the lords of the gorsedd who counted my election a political choice rather than one that would advance the state of music. Today I thought he might be right.

"Sian," I said, offering him what I hoped was a courteous nod.

"Nice to see you're alive," he replied with his usual gruffness. "I'm here on behalf of the gorsedd."

Of course: it is incumbent upon the ard-harpist to participate at the Moot, though none but the righthe may vote in the election of the ard-righ. The lords of the gorsedd would have felt the need to send someone. I decided not to ask whether they had voted me out in my absence. I wasn't sure how I would feel if they had: hurt and offended, of course, but once I got past the insult? I set the question aside.

"Just so," I said, nodding. "Did they send you with any sort of consensus?"

He shrugged. "No one favors electing the Bard to the throne, if that's what you're asking."

A laugh escaped me. It sounded no more than half-human in my own ears. "Indeed."

If I intended to invoke the position of ard-harpist as my token of admission to the Moot, I should clarify my status among the gorsedd. But the question was too difficult to ask in the midst of this crowd, the decisions into which it would force me beyond contemplation this morning. Instead I turned my eyes to the road ahead.

"You've been riding with the Lady of Finias?" Caern said after a moment.

I glanced at him and nodded. Any harpist worth the branch he carried would have had a song already more than half composed; would have stirring tales of battle and honor to pass along. I didn't want to talk about it.

"How long have you been riding?"

I thought back. "A month, maybe?"

Caern cast me a thoughtful glance. That last question had probably been a prompt to tell my story or at least relate some heroic anecdote.

"A difficult journey?" he said after a moment.

I glanced at him. He recoiled at whatever he saw in my gaze.

"Her enemies are serious about their objective," I said. "If you'll excuse me." I dropped back, worked my way across the ranks until I could fall in beside Coran's armsmaster Den.

"Lord!" He turned a genuine smile on me; something in me relaxed. The energies of the knights he led felt much more natural against my awareness, a welcome buffer against the continuing maelstrom of irrelevancy just outside their ranks.

"How are you?" I said, and settled in to let him talk. He'd always been a font of the sort of information generals crave; today he was as cordial as ever, but aware as any courtier of the crowd around us. He had grown into his new position, too; it raised in me a senseless nostalgia for the armsmaster who hadn't thought beyond the well-being of the man he served. Today I heard only news fit for public consumption: the convoy of ships that had carried Coran and his court from Ilnemedon to Grannos in Ebdani; the terrible storm they had endured at the mouth of the Ruillin. But the way his dark eyes met my gaze said he was giving me intelligence between the lines, and he wondered whether I'd absorbed it.

I had: for a righ on his way to the Moot to bypass the theoretically neutral port of Bealingas, the traditional landing for righthe on their ways to the Moot, for Deneth Cooley's harbor at Grannos spoke volumes about the strength of the kharr in coastal Usdia. How badly did it chafe Coran to accept Deneth's protection for his ships, when they would both stand as serious candidates at the Moot? But if Bealingas was not secure, to do otherwise with half a hundred noncombatants in tow would be insanity.

I should cast the decision as evidence in Coran's favor: the grace of a leader who would see to his people's safety before his own pride; evidence of the ability to coordinate his efforts with his peers, so critical in a man whose position comes from election rather than conquest. Assuming I was able to speak with any sort of grace about the prospect of Coran ascending the throne. That was by no means a foregone conclusion. I was proud for my friend, but the idea of him on the throne made me ache for an excuse to draw my blade.

I tried to focus on the storm they had endured en route instead: counting the days of their journey and ours, confirming the connection I suspected.

"We saw that same storm at Ballarona," I said quietly. "That was the night the city fell."

Den met my eyes. "Ballarona? Ah, no." He grimaced, shifting in his saddle in a way that bespoke a desire to return and secure Ilnemedon. "Lucky the Lady had the Prince with her, then."

"Indeed."

Den nodded. For a moment we rode in silence, dozens of other conversations threading around us. Most of them were too trivial to focus on. Even the ones regarding the Bard and his wizard were so far afield of truth or relevance that I found myself kneading the reins. When had I picked up that destructive habit? I forced myself to stop.

"Lord," Den said. "Did you ride all the way from Finias?"

I nodded.

"Did your contingent include anyone I might know?"

"No." A small, untoward relief engulfed me. "Fortunately, sian—no."

I nodded to him and rode forward again, settling in beside Amien. Too late I realized someone among this incessantly political mob would certainly over-interpret my claiming that spot; but to try to correct the tactical error would only add fuel to whatever fire I'd just started. I sighed; Amien glanced at me.

"What?"

"Civilization," I groaned.

He nodded. "Uisneach will be better."

A humorless laugh escaped me: Uisneach would be even worse. I tried to think of someplace that actually would be better, and failed. I longed for some quiet place in which to hide.

A little distance before the Teamair gate, we parted company. Coran invited me and my companions to attend tonight's Bealtan fest at Ilesia House in Teamair; the thought of it made the desire to bolt rouse so fiercely in me that it required all my will to simply remain still, to maintain a courteous façade while Amien smiled and thanked him for the invitation. Of course we must attend; nothing else would satisfy protocol but to answer the invitation of the ard-righ-apparent with grace.

Worse, I knew both Amien and Coran would withdraw from that party early, leaving me to contend with Ilnemedon society alone. Coran would slip out to perform the traditional pre-coronation Triple Sacrifice, and Amien would most likely be the wizard to administer it: Coran was ard-righ-apparent, after all. Amien couldn't officially sanction it, but neither would he let it pass him by.

"Ellion." Coran reached across the space between our horses, grasping my arm. I snapped unwilling out of the abstraction that had snared me, meeting his troubled eyes. "Will you have a glass with me before dinner?"

If only I believed it would be a quiet interlude between old friends, I would have leapt at the chance. In any event there was no turning the invitation aside, not with hundreds of eyes on us.

I offered him a horseback bow. "It will be my pleasure."

Uisneach surprised me. I couldn't have said what I expected of the place; but whatever my expectations had been, Uisneach ground them underfoot with a chuckle I could almost hear. The hill commands a view even more extensive than Teamair. But where the plateau atop Teamair is crowded with regular, meticulously-maintained squares and roads, and houses that are palaces in all but name, the long spiraling path up the hill of Uisneach ends in a broad expanse of green. Atop that summit, the only visible features are the Mooting Rock the gods Themselves fashioned in the form of a throne, the immense ageless oak that spreads broad limbs above it, and the lone wooden building the wizards occupy when in residence there. The quiet of the place enfolded me, even while the Presences of the god and goddess Who held this place infiltrated my consciousness. They surprised me, too, though by now I should have expected it: the Presences Who regarded me from some place no mortal eye can grasp were not Lord Ilesan and Lady Tella.

When you perform the sacred marriage, who does it serve? Are you even sure with whom you lie?

Pain gathered in my chest. Amien reined at the edge of the summit's clear expanse, drawing a deep, satisfied breath.

"Welcome," he said, looking around at us. "Without all of you we would never have come this far; thank you. We have room for all of you in the Mooting House, if you'll stay with us."

"Thank you," Letitia said softly; I echoed her words. This might be a reasonably quiet haven, if I could manage to avoid whatever wizards I knew who had made the trip.

"It would be a pleasure, my friend," Rohini said. "But I must find out what the situation is with the clans before I can say for certain."

Amien nodded as if he'd expected the answer. "And, Mora—" He turned his penetrating black eyes on Letitia. "It would be our privilege to host your Bealtan observances in our sacred grove."

Dread burst inside me. It was Bealtan Eve, wasn't it? The night for any ruler to renew his or her bonds with the land, to rededicate his rule to the gods. After all the dreams the idea of this night had sparked in me, the reality brought only pain. Of course Letitia must observe Bealtan with her consort, in public ceremony. There could be no stolen pleasure for anyone else. Terrible, unanswerable need crashed through me: I couldn't look at any of them. In my peripheral vision I saw Iminor glance away.

Letitia sighed. "Thank you, my lord, but no. We are a very long way from Fíana; I do not ascend the throne tomorrow. There will be no official observance for us tonight."

Amien nodded. "Well, you will find no lack of parties this eve. If you don't find amusement at Ilesia House, Ebdani House and Deceang House will certainly be hosting fests as well. I'm afraid things here will be quiet; the members of the Order have observances we must uphold."

"That is not necessarily a bad thing, my lord," Letitia said quietly, finally looking at him again. And at last it occurred to me that she must also mourn the throne she would not ascend tomorrow; that she no longer expected the life she'd been promised, even did we manage to win this war. It was unfair for me to compare my situation to hers; she had done nothing to deserve her disinheritance. Still I felt a strange closeness.

Four men crossed the gentle slope from the wooden building Amien called the Mooting House to the place in which we had paused. Wizards, all of them: I smelled the power long before they drew close enough for me to identify. Amien swung down from the saddle as if reaching his destination had restored his vitality; I climbed to the ground, too, hearing the rest of my companions do the same. By the time I'd gained the ground the wizards were close enough for me to see their faces, and it took everything I had to refrain from climbing right back into the saddle and cueing the horse for speed.

Why did it have to be Sanglin? If there had been any number of moments when I found it possible to imagine Deaclan as a nasclethéan, by the time I was nearing the end of my initiate it had begun to seem that Sanglin should dissolve his partnership with Amien and devote himself to practicing with me. Even Amien had seemed to see the inevitability of it. I didn't recognize any of the men trailing his wake: two must have passed through Aballo well before my tenure there, while the third was likely just past his initiate. But Sanglin bore me sufficient animosity for all four of them: the sudden agitation in his stride sent his bright red hair blowing back to reveal the hard, angry line into which his jaw had settled; the glance he cast me would have melted steel.

"My lord!" he said to Amien, sparing the old man a genuine smile and embracing him without preamble.

"I see the place still stands," Amien said, not releasing him. I heard the grin in his voice.

"Barely," Sanglin said lightly, stepping back. "You're here just in time."

"You can say that again." Amien was still grinning. "Mora Letitia Ériu a Fíana, Lord Iminor a Dianann, Chief Rohini Lanas, and Lord Ellion Tellan—" Now the wizards I didn't recognize were staring at me. With the Lady of Finias in their presence, what they found most fascinating was *me*. I feared to imagine what people at Aballo had been saying. "—allow me to present my second Sanglin Uaridnach; Domnall Techtmar, House Healer to Vellabor; Echach Duin, master of advanced studies at Matach; and Túathal Ua Machí, a member of my workshop."

They all bowed courteously enough, even Sanglin; though now that we were in proximity he refused to look at me. Within a minute everything had been arranged: Túathal was to conduct us to the stable behind the Mooting House, where we might see to our horses, while Domnall and Echach would ensure enough rooms were prepared. Rohini shifted restlessly.

"I need to see to my people," she said.

"Chief, you and I have an engagement," I reminded her.

Her mouth twisted. "It's not nec—"

How many times had Amien seen that protest before? He apprehended instantly what I was about and laid a hand on Rohini's arm.

"My friend, will you indulge him? I'll sleep better tonight."

"You won't sleep at *all* tonight," she rejoined.

"All the more reason."

She cast him a dark stare.

"What if I helped?" the wizard said, as patient as if she were a fractious child.

She blew out an exasperated breath. "I give you ten minutes."

"Oh, your generosity is boundless," Amien said, and led us to the Mooting House while Túathal showed the Tanaan to the stable. I hitched my horse to a simple post in front of the long, low structure, resolving to return as soon as I might: it is the way of Aballo that every man does what is necessary for himself. I knew we'd find no servants here, and no one would tend my horse in my absence. Inconvenient though I'd found the practice when I first arrived at Aballo, I had soon seen the peace and freedom in it; now I realized it was another of the things that had informed my life after I left.

Aballo had become a part of me, even while I thought it an aspect of a closed past; evidently I had become a part of Aballo, even while I stood disavowed. I had no idea what any of it meant: I followed Amien and Rohini through dim, quiet corridors, a strange foreboding prickling up my back. The spaces were too small; the shadows of these corridors would have concealed a dozen assassins. It would be far too easy to simply torch the place while half the wizards of the Aballo Order slept, and the gods they relied upon were not in residence here. The need to protect this place and these people from some phantom of my derangement itched on my palms, and though I saw it for the exhausted affliction of too long a siege, I couldn't push it aside. I chewed on my lower lip. Finally we reached a door that looked just like all the others. I followed them into the room behind it.

It might have been a dormitory cell at Aballo, except in wood: a single window illuminated a spare, narrow chamber that housed a bed, a small table with a single chair, and little else. From his pack Amien drew a healing kit; he motioned Rohini to the bed. She cast him a dark, silent stare, stripped off her armor, and sat.

I knelt beside her. "May I see?"

The taut lines of her shoulders softened; she drew up the front of her shirt to expose her midsection, revealing an angry slice, broad rather than deep, that disappeared beneath the waist of her pants.

"You need stitching," I said, looking up into her face.

"I know," she sighed.

"May I?"

"Thank you," she said, the words another sigh.

"Lie back, Ro," Amien said gently.

Once she surrendered, Rohini was a simple patient: she barely flinched at the numbing salve I spread along the edges of the gash, didn't complain at the long series of stitches the wound required. I found myself diffusing into a strange quiet occupied only by the work to be done and my hands doing it, emerging from that half-trance into a melancholy longing for the single-minded existence whose possibility I had always sensed but never laid hands on at Aballo: wishing I might somehow trade the trappings of wealth and position I'd accumulated in Ilnemedon for an opportunity to pursue the Work in peace, knowing even as I formed the wish that the longing I hung on this place was for a thing that would never exist outside my own mind. Aballo is as fraught with drama and politics as Ilnemedon, in its own inbred way. The only real difference would be the constant occupation with the processes of a faith whose tenets had seen far too many assaults by contrary truth of late.

Even could I find some sort of release from my vow, however much I might desire it there could be no place for me here. I tied off the stitches, rearranged Rohini's clothes into a semblance of dignity, climbed to my feet. Now, suddenly, she smiled.

"Thank you. That was excellent." She glanced at Amien. "Do you need to re-do my wards?"

Amien's shoulders sagged. Of course he did; but he had little more strength than required to keep his feet. Why hadn't he let me attend him?

"If you would lean on me, my lord," I said softly.

He glanced at me, something deeper than humiliation in his face. He raised his eyebrows and turned his gaze on Rohini.

"Well, then, this is the room where facts remain under lock and key," he said wryly. "You were wise enough to trust Ellion with your injury; now I need to trust both of you with mine. He's right: the… I took a couple hits of the arcane variety myself, last night, and I haven't regained my strength."

Alarm flickered in Rohini's eyes, but she covered it with a smile. "We are a pair, as usual."

He produced a wan smile of his own. "With the loan of Ellion's strength— and his presence here—I can do it. Or I can call on my second, Sanglin—"

Rohini shook her head. "Let's keep the number of people who know any of this as small as possible."

She began wrestling with her boots, and hissed at renewed pain; I knelt before her again. This time she accepted the help without a fight.

"I should sit with my back to yours," I said to Amien. He nodded understanding and knelt to wait for her; I settled behind him, my spine against his sinewy back—and as I opened my awareness to him, I saw: the same energy I'd rechanneled for Iminor now swirled in him. I drew back and spun to face him, surprising an exclamation from Rohini, who was already more than half undressed.

"You damn fool!" I blurted, barely noticing her dishabille. Amien flushed. "How could you not tell me! It's not so difficult—"

"What," Rohini said ponderously. "Is. Going. On. Now."

"I should have known," I said. And I should have. Gods, what a fool I was. "Did anyone wonder what happened to the death spell on the sword that hit you, Chief? Your wards deflected it. Guess where it went!"

"Oh, gods," Rohini moaned, sitting down abruptly. "But you can undo it—right?"

"He can rechannel it," Amien said. "Leaving Aballo with a Prince who is a permanent sink for dark magic."

"Better than a dead one!" I blurted, immediately regretting it.

Amien's mouth twisted. "Really? The law says a man with a physical defect may not be a righ. How can a man with a permanent attachment to dark power be Prince?"

I shook my head. "All magic is an affliction."

Amien hissed.

"My lord, it's true! You've said it yourself, although differently: when They give a man a Talent, the gods set him apart. They take from him any hope of a normal life, reserving him to Their own ends. This magic isn't changing you; until a moment ago I didn't even know—"

"It's changing me," Amien said. "I'll spare you the details of the things I think I sense today, but I know they aren't things of the gods…"

Like a god and goddess Whose names no wizard knew holding sway over Uisneach? I couldn't ask the question in front of Rohini, not even in a room where secrets went to die.

"When Nuad of the Silver Hand lost his arm, he stepped down from the throne and let Eochaid Bres take his place," I said. "No one suggested he should die. Please, my lord, if you need to step down, I won't fight you—but let me rechannel this spell!"

Amien gave me a long look. He swallowed, the apple of his throat bobbing visibly beneath the skin.

"Let me think on this," he said finally. "We will talk more tonight. Meanwhile—Ro, I'm sorry. I didn't realize until we talked about this that my working wards for you would only do you harm, with this spell in me. Let me call Sanglin."

Rohini shook her head. "I'll wait. Let me know what you decide."

Amien shook his head, too. "Ro, one way or another this spell will always be with me."

"I'll wait," Rohini said. "This secret does not leave this room."

Rohini and I stepped into the little corridor again. I pulled the door shut—and discovered Sanglin staring at me. I felt a blush creep up from my neck, though I couldn't have named any one thing that caused it. There were far too many reasons for me to choose just one.

"He needs rest," Rohini said to Sanglin, as peremptory as if he were an initiate and not Amien's designated heir. "See that he gets it. Ellion—" She surprised me with an embrace; I returned it as gently as I could. "I'll see you tonight."

I nodded, empty of words, and watched as she strode down the corridor with a swift strength that almost made me doubt her injury. I looked back to discover Sanglin's brown eyes still on me.

"I can't believe you're here," he said, anger crackling in his voice.

"It wasn't my idea," I replied.

For a moment that seemed much longer he just stared at me. A hundred memories of workshop experiences and moments of the goddess's Presence that we had shared fought for access to my conscious mind; I wrestled them back down.

"Hurt him again… and I will personally see you experience things that would make a devotee of Par weep in fear," Sanglin said.

I should beg his forgiveness right here, whether or not he would grant it. But if I opened that vein I'd never staunch it, and I must endure not only tonight but tomorrow; not only the wizards but all the righthe, and Ilnemedon's and Tellan's societies. I drew the habit of irony around myself instead.

"Missed you, too," I said, and went back outside to see to my horse.

He at least was pleased to see me. We went to the stable and tended his needs, including a thorough brushing and the long-overdue pleasure of a bath. After a good meal I took him to the area behind the stable, turned him out in a respectably-sized, sunny paddock to relax with his friends. Finally I carried my bags and the corpse of my harp inside, found the room I'd been assigned, and located the bath.

The slickness of the floor told me Letitia and Iminor had already been here, whether together or separately; the idea ran together in my mind with my bath in the grotto at Sucello, and inevitably to an all-too-vivid image of them sharing the water here. Sudden, terrible need and anger raged through me. I struggled to push them aside. All the rules for everything had been suspended while we rode across the world; now we were back in civilization, and the rules were closing in around us again. If I could be excused as much as any man for loving her, it was still incumbent upon me to step aside for her chosen consort, now that we had returned to reality.

Besides, *love* wasn't the right word for it. I tried and failed to imagine what word I should use for this madness instead.

Chapter 35
The Promise of the Stars

During those months when it stands, the city of Teamair is constructed entirely of wood: in token of the impermanence of any ard-righ's reign, which is subject to revocation not only by the gods but by his peers. Even the city wall is wrought entirely of logs. The place is occupied only during the month of a Moot, but during those days it is the center of the world: perennial, and yet temporary, like some bizarre wooden flower that blooms and dies in the space of a day. For the span of the Moot season there are more royal residences in Teamair than in the entire Ruillin basin: every royal family constructs a house there, and more than one puts up a separate residence for the tanist as well. Theoretically temporary shelters, they nevertheless strive to outdo one another in grandeur and density of carving, and each of them showcases its ornate exterior with live torches—the permanence of oil lamps being a violation of the requirement of *temporary* shelter—throughout every night of the season. Today I was acutely aware that the entire place was an even greater firetrap than Uisneach.

If I were the Bard, fire would definitely be where I started with this place. It wouldn't even require an arcane storm to bring it down. A mob of kharr with homemade incendiaries would be more than sufficient.

I rode past the ard-righ's palace on my way to Ilesia House. If the rest of the city was little more than half-familiar to me, that place lay etched upon my memory. I didn't even need to close my eyes to see the Star Chamber in which the ard-righ would preside. Today it was vacant except for staff, I knew; tomorrow evening men would be packed like fish in a net in that place for the new ard-righ's ascension. I found it impossible to imagine being among them.

I couldn't remember visiting Ilesia House last time I was here. I assumed I had: my father and I had attended all the parties on the night before the Moot. As a serious candidate for the throne, Conary Mourne must have hosted one. Nevertheless nothing about the place roused any sort of memory in me, and the aura of impending siege about the servants made me want to retreat to someplace much quieter.

Coran waited for me in a private chamber, standing and staring at a collection of maps spread across a table. The door stood open; I glimpsed the familiar look of concentration he brought to a chessboard now being directed at the maps. But then the seneschal announced me, and his look of intensity slipped through some expression that flashed by too quickly for identification and into a welcoming smile.

"Ellion!" he said, crossing the room to embrace me. "You're looking better. Did you get some rest?"

"A bit," I allowed. "How are you?"

Behind me, the seneschal shut the door; I let Coran lead me across the room, past the maps with their tactical markers, to settle in a pair of sumptuous chairs before the fire. The structure of this house might be impermanent, but everything else spoke of plans for an indefinite stay; the comfort about the room invited me to relax. But some ineradicable tension held sway over my spine, and Coran turned his chair away from the fire, looking directly into my face.

"What happened?" he said.

This was the man I remembered, not the politician who played the part of ard-righ-apparent for the emotional comfort of a train full of fools. A strange, untoward peace settled over me. I made him wait while I sipped his wine.

"Would you care to be more specific?" I parried.

Frustration and unwilling amusement chased one another across his broad face. Finally he settled on a quelling stare that must freeze entire rooms full of advisors.

"No, I don't think I would," he replied coolly. "You've a hell of a lot of talking to do. One day my father's dead and I'm trying to secure the one man who might outwit the Bard as my War-Lord; when next I look up no one has seen you in a month, and there's an Aballo herald cooling his heels on the steps of the Harpist Gorsedd Hall. What. Happened?"

"I went to Fíana."

"I gathered that. Why?"

"Some centuries ago, the Mora of Fíana was a Harpist Gorsedd client. I thought it was time to renew that bond."

"Bollocks!" Coran snapped, a flush rising on his face. "How is it *possible* you don't grasp the gravity of this situation?"

"On the contrary, my lord, I'd say I'm just about the only person who does."

"Don't you *lord*—What?"

"Oh, yes," I said. "While the righthe and the tiarna spend all their attention on the issue of who will be elected tomorrow, a much graver problem gathers around us. You know why those maps don't make any damned sense? This isn't a war for territory."

Coran frowned.

"Oh, yes, of course, the kharr are seizing cities. They hold Mumhan in all but name, and Nagnata will fall within the month. Gavnon will be next, assuming it hasn't already succumbed. But you're standing in a midst of an arcane war, and our problem is not the Bard. Not really."

"*What?*"

An unwilling smile overtook me. "Never let it be said that I am not your friend. Amien won't make this announcement until tomorrow, and you're getting it first. As we took our extended pleasure ride across the world, losing dozens of the best knights it's ever been my privilege to know—" Silently I damned the roughness creeping into my voice; nothing to do but ignore it and press on. "We learned the name of the Bard's Wizard, and you'll recognize it too. It's Nechton Glyndwr."

Coran sat back, gripping the arms of his chair. His face didn't change. "He's alive?"

"That's been a common question of late."

"I suppose you're halfway to done with a sequel-song to the *Ballad of Carina*."

Trust Coran to swallow the matter whole: there would be no need to spell out the terrible fact of Letitia's significance, nor to discuss how little we understood it.

"I've been a bit preoccupied with trying to keep her alive."

"Fouzh," Coran said thoughtfully, rose and began to pace. After a moment he stopped, looking at me. "Can you lay out the arcane war for me?"

"Up to a point," I said. "Without insult, sian, this is fairly heady stuff."

"Do *you* understand it?" His tone was rhetorical. Suddenly I remembered: he didn't know.

Dread sank fierce talons into my throat. "Yes."

Coran's eyes narrowed. He stared at me along the full length of his aquiline nose. "Why do I get the sense that we have just stepped into unexplored territory."

I glanced away, had another mouthful of wine. "I may have neglected to mention… that I studied at Aballo for a couple years."

"You—" I could almost hear him sorting through possible words to complete the sentence. I suspected not every word he considered was a verb.

"Really," he said, voice cold. I glanced away again. "What the hell have you been doing—" Again I heard him struggle with possible paths of conversation. "—as ard-harpist? In Ilesia? Is that why they deposed you: because you are…?"

I sighed. "A wizard? More or less."

"But you're not a wizard… are you? Oh, fouzh, Ellion, give me something!"

Labels. Men need them. Why hadn't I understood? *If you've been taught to define yourself in terms of who you are to others, and then those definitions get ripped away, what do you have left?*

"I'm sorry," I said.

Coran nodded, eyes suddenly distant. "You were right, weren't you? You can't be Tiarn of Louth. You can't be Ilesia's War-Lord. Why aren't you at Aballo?"

There was no answer I could give: I just sighed and had another mouthful of wine.

"Because they can't tolerate you, either," Coran said, sounding as if he wished he were amused. He shook his head. "Have the harpists unseated you yet?"

"I don't know."

This time Coran laughed, but there wasn't real humor in it. "Convey my condolences to them, will you? Tell them they're not the only ones feeling betrayed." He flung his empty wine glass past me to smash in the fireplace, turned and stalked out.

I resisted the temptation to spend the evening glued to the companions with whom I'd traveled; but I wished, with an intensity that actually made me ache, that we were back on the road instead. That was insane: in this place Letitia stood surrounded by well-nigh all the worthy warriors and wizards in the world. She could not be safer anywhere. But I craved the company of people who knew me for what I was and accepted it, whether or not they approved the choices I made. I wanted to hold real conversations without dancing around the things that must not be said: in public, prematurely, or at all. Instead I watched my friends as they sailed around the building looking like heroes in a song—and held the same conversations with a hundred irrelevant people while a sector of my mind mapped avenues of escape.

Amien's presence filled whatever room he occupied; he smiled and spoke with an endless succession of righthe and tiarna and lesser men with a grace that would have made me disbelieve anyone who told me about the spell gathering in his body, had I not seen it myself. His eyes met mine across the room, full of a pride and pleasure at my presence that I failed to understand. Iminor seemed completely unaware of the way the women admired his exotic warrior presence and the aura of mystery that lay around him, hanging on his few well-considered words. He had been competent when we met, if inexperienced; now I would match him against any champion and wager a nation's riches on the result. He didn't strut, but he finally knew his own worth. I wondered when he had stopped deferring to Letitia.

And Letitia: for the first time in a twelvenight I truly saw how alien her beauty was, how magical her eyes, how everything about her outshone every woman in the building. She was no longer the naïve young would-be mora I'd met in the wilds of Fíana, but a woman who knew the look and scent of her own death and had resolved to wrest some honor from it. I had completely failed to appreciate the last time I was alone with Letitia. I had failed to realize it was the last time.

Ilnemedon society swirled and crowded around me. They exchanged whispers about whose contents I couldn't find it in myself to care, even when

I knew they were about me; they tried to winnow my brain about Tanaan women, and an alarmingly high percentage seemed to consider it an established fact that I'd had Letitia. Those insinuations I put down with cold stares that ended conversation after conversation. When my hand began to itch for my sword, which perforce I had surrendered at the Ilesia House door, I took myself outside.

The Precinct spread out beneath me. The Fair houses of righthe occupying the top of the hill gave way to those of tiarna at the edge of the plateau; the city spilled down towards rich commoners' Fair houses lower on the slope. Beyond the wooden wall with its regularly-spaced torches, the campfires of thousands of travelers twinkled across the plain like a reflection of the sky. The great Bealtan bonfires would be just outside the city gate to the south; I couldn't see them from here, but I knew the wood stood stacked and ready, waiting only for Amien to come and perform the ceremony. The sounds of the revel in the streets and on the plain below carried on the night air. For the moment it all seemed to occupy a manageable distance.

But even here there was no peace. In short order Findabhair stood beside me, looking as luscious and indiscreet as ever.

"There you are!" she said. "I've missed you!"

I ignored the opening and bowed instead. "You're looking well."

She smiled. "Did you ride all the way from Finias with the Lady?"

I would have given much for a different topic. Everyone asked the same questions.

"Yes," I said.

"I hardly recognized you this morning. You looked like a wild animal." This was delivered in classic Findabhair form, intended as an invitation to demonstrate a flavor of wildness that would be the talk of the Moot season: mostly because she would insure it. She would revel in being the topic of the season's most delectable item of gossip, and would fan the flames even while she denied the allegations. Suddenly everything I hated about Ilnemedon society coalesced in this conversation, pinned itself to her empty soul. I found myself poised between looking for a weapon and flight.

"Madam, I *am* a wild animal," I said. "You would do well to stay indoors."

She cast me a long, silent pout. "You've changed," she sulked, and flounced back inside.

I sighed and tilted my head back to take in the sky. Long northern sunset had faded into a moonless night; the stars swarming beyond the edges of the torchlight looked oddly familiar. I strode out into deeper darkness, still looking up: finally I recognized what I saw. The constellations and sky-positions of my youth shone down on me, raising a sudden, terrible ache. I had forgotten how close together Teamair and Tellan lie, and that realization roused such pain in me that for a moment I couldn't see. I stood no more than a day's ride from Stildin, the little town on the Tellan border where I made the sacred marriage the month I returned from Aballo. A day's ride beyond that, I would reach the place I still dreamed as home.

Above me stood the immense stretch of the Hunter, which the common folk still call Beal-o-the-Oaks. He climbed up from the horizon, seeming from this angle to occupy half the sky. Centuries ago, all men invoked him as the god of the Bealtan holiday, called to him with the wildness that is part of every man's nature, offered up that wildness to feed the magic that would renew the land for another year. Now it is only the wizards, the righthe, and men who hold to the old ways in little villages that escape the notice of the druids who make that offering. *That's very sad,* Tru had said. I shouldn't agree, but I did. It was just one of the growing number of ways I was straying from the true path.

Eventually I noticed Amien standing beside me, eyes on the sky. He smiled and met my gaze, then looked up again. Gratefully I turned my glance skyward as well.

"Ah, I love the Bealtans of the lunisolar adjustment years," Amien mused, gaze still on the sky. "He looks so big and bright with the moons still below the divide."

If anyone but Amien had said that, every other man sworn to the true gods would have had to weigh the statement for blasphemy: to celebrate Bealtan without Telliyn presiding over the night is inauspicious. It smacks of a failure of balance. But I felt the same way. Something perilously close to my surface loved the idea of giving myself over to the wildness the Hunter, or Beal-o-the-Oaks, symbolizes, and following my own wild nature without feeling that She watched the things I did.

That was almost certainly a blasphemous thought. But it clearly didn't trouble Amien to think it. And I remembered how little my own blasphemy had troubled me, back in the days when I knew I stood with my feet on the path of the gods. With Lady Tella ever at my shoulder, I had known I could do no wrong.

If only it were possible to return to that.

"It's been quite the year, hasn't it?" Amien said thoughtfully. "Quite the month. Strange how different everything looked just a month ago."

I nodded. It had been a month, more or less, since Amien turned up at Irisa, doubtless full of anxious hope for a long-overdue reconciliation with the woman he had secretly loved for so long. Instead he got her daughter, and Básghilae—and me. I couldn't imagine which had been the greatest blow.

Once again I choked down a need to beg forgiveness. I must hold myself together until after the Moot.

"We've made good progress," Amien continued. A strange laugh escaped him. "Not that any of it has gone according to plan. But we got Letitia here alive, and she's begun learning to master her power…"

Finally I understood. His apparent capitulation and crafting a plan for her to do no more than carry the Shadow of the Sun while the wizards around her handled the arcane work: that had been the sort of tale one tells a child who is frightened of a surgery that must be performed. He still intended to train her into a simulacrum of Carina, oblivious to the fact that like Carina she would fail in the objective. I couldn't explain why his plan was worse than useless: I had promised Letitia silence.

But it sharpened my resolve: whatever strategies and offensives the righthe and the wizards planned tomorrow, my focus must be her. No one else could be allowed to grasp how defenseless she really was. Nechton could not be allowed to do her harm.

"But that isn't half the blessing finding you has been," Amien continued.

Something terrible burst in my chest, tried to claw its way out through my throat. "For a long time I feared I'd never work with you again—and gods, how I missed you."

"Ah, my lord, I've missed you, too." I had to force the words through a throat far too small to admit them. "After all the things I've done, all the mistakes I've made—"

Amien waved my words away. "That's in the past. Tonight we begin again. Do you realize tonight marks eleven years since your initiation? An auspicious number, that."

Eleven years. It seemed a lifetime ago, and yet the memory raced in too powerfully to turn aside: standing in Amien's workshop in the Presence of the gods with Sanglin, Dandem, and Oregen completing the circle around me; Lady Tella's sudden inexplicable manifestation in that space, Her heady scent wrecking what little sanity remained to me and Her cool soft hand on my cheek. *How fitting that you have come this night to stand before Me.*

Doubt not that we will meet again.

"Come with me tonight," Amien said softly. "We will call the fires together. You can renew your vows."

For a moment I couldn't breathe; then, just as suddenly, the breath beat painfully in my chest. If we called the Bealtan fires together, here at the Moot, he would be publicly designating me his heir.

"Afterwards, we'll take a few minutes and rechannel this damned spell. We'll have to talk about the best time for me to step down..."

"Oh, *gods*," I croaked. "My lord—I can't—"

He wrapped an arm around me. "I'm not abandoning you. I know you'll need to consider who you'll take as nasclethéan, but—"

"My lord," I said again. My voice still sounded hideous. "I *can't*."

Terrible disappointment swept across his face; just as swiftly he shook it off.

"Great Lord Ilesan, all you do is prove my point. I have never seen a man hold to a more terrible vow."

"All I do is figure out all the ways in which it might be stretched!"

"You need to make your peace with Her," he said, in a tone of patient understanding. "Bealtan seems like a time for that, too."

Where would I begin? Could it even be possible? Her interventions for me said that, against all reason, She still had some interest in me; but the farther I stretched the limits of my vow, the more I opened myself, the more gods and powers and terrible thoughts I allowed inside: none of which a man of the gods should ever admit. If I had held back from full Union with Goibniu the smith-god and Laverna of the Ruillin, still I had allowed Them to infiltrate me. I had done far more with Aerona and Esus. At Bealtan, when I should see nothing but Lady Tella, I trembled at the thought of returning to Uisneach, of confronting the Beings I'd glimpsed there this afternoon. Already I suspected I might know Their names. How could I be Prince and yet have such ties to so many illicit gods? How would I choose between upholding the teaching that only the gods of Aballo's religion are true—and speaking the truth as I now understood it: there are far more gods in the world than most of us like to admit, and Lady Tella did things in the name of war that would send a human righ before an executioner.

It is one thing for a man who may already be doomed to the Abyss to consider these things. It would be quite another for the Aballo Prince to drag all the world along.

"My lord… listen." Fear of what I must say stormed through me; I struggled to push it aside. "There are… things I'm trying to work out. You said… This afternoon, you said that this spell has made you see things that are not of the gods. I see those things, too."

Amien's breath caught audibly, but he didn't speak.

"I am—My lord, I *will* try—to come to peace with the goddess. But I don't—" I swallowed. "I'm afraid if we did that tonight, it would be an offense to the gods. That Their affront would be justified."

"And yet I still sense Her hand on you," Amien said.

I nodded, throat tight. "I have no idea what value She sees in me."

Amien laughed: a soft, regretful sound. "Well, not yet, then. For this year, you will be ard-righ."

"*What?*" I blurted.

Amien smiled. "It's been a long time since the Prince has invoked the privilege; it would have been simpler if you still held a throne. But in the end none of them have anything to say. It is my choice. This year, maybe, after the Moot ends the buildings will remain. Certainly the palace, if nothing else."

A delicate, phantom weight settled around my neck. *Abu al-righ.* But it didn't feel at all the way I expected: it was ungrounded and temporary, like the one place over which my reign would be undisputed. For all its importance during the Moot season, Teamair is barely a real city. What would it mean to rule a place in which no one lived? How would I feel when all my subjects packed up a few days from now and went home?

The surprising answer came to me: it would be a relief. Until Nechton was defeated, the responsibility of ruling a nation would only be a distraction. I could only be effective if the war were my entire focus. Still it felt strange and incomplete.

"My lord—I'm not sure…"

Amien laughed. "You're not sure? Well, I was on the summit of the Temple Mount on Ilunmore, when a certain wizard stepped into the circle—and the Tuaoh damn near shook the place apart! How many gods must speak before you're sure?"

If any more gods spoke to me I might finally go stark mad. I couldn't be the sort of righ Coran was: catering to the small minds and fearful hearts of people who lacked understanding of the things that mattered; fixing my mind on politics and allowing someone to dye my horse's mane. Let expectations of the ard-righ's role define me, let myself to get caught up in the mundane aspects of the war, which would be only a rear-guard action, while Letitia went forward without me—and the value I could offer her and the gods would be wasted. Especially since I knew what Nechton would do to the people who must face him in my stead.

In my stead. Oh, dear gods, *there* was the problem. Something inside me knew what I must do, and it was none of the things anyone else would admit to wanting: accept the fact that I was doomed to the Abyss, cast aside my vows and my morals, and lead the charge against Nechton. There would be a certain symmetry in a Prince tied to dark power and a demon, damned before he was born, as the Prince's War-Lord.

Was that what the gods intended? Had They thrown me away before I was ever conceived? I pushed aside a sudden sense of betrayal.

I looked at Amien. I realized it had been a very long time since I'd spoken, that he'd been waiting with his usual infinite patience for an answer.

"My lord... I'm lost. I need to see if I can hear Her Voice."

Amien nodded gravely. "Go to Uisneach. The sacred grove is yours. You should take Letitia."

I found myself staring without planning it; he offered me a quizzical smile.

"It's Bealtan. Tomorrow you will be ard-righ. There's a sacred marriage to be made."

Desire roared through me; I tried to dismiss it as reflex and failed. From the ard-righ's throne I could meet Letitia on more than equal terms, shift everything that lay broken and twisted between us into the natural fate of the world. Finally I would transform myself from a creature barely worthy of being her lover into her proper and fated mate.

But that was wishful thinking: even would Letitia allow me to come to her for the sacred marriage, it would resolve nothing. No matter what torc I might put on, I had no rights to her. If there were bonds both personal and arcane between us now, older and deeper bonds lay on her as well. It would take more than Bealtan to sever those.

And to celebrate Bealtan with her would be to miss the point: at long last, I understood. There is a reason why the priestess is masked: because it is better if the priest does not know her at all, if he sees only her role.

Most humans have forgotten, but it is incumbent on the wizards and the righthe to remember: Bealtan is for the goddess. On this night the priest or righ must stand before Her, offer Her everything he is, and hope She judges him worthy. Please Her, and She will bless his rule, receive him as Her consort for a year and a day. The small, human part of me who was ruled by emotions and other irrelevancies wanted desperately to come to Letitia for the sacred marriage, but the part of me who knew better saw it would only be a distraction. It was the goddess Whose Blessing I needed; there would be no resolving the insane tangle between Letitia and me, no sense in asking Letitia for the privilege of her Bealtan love, until I understood the goddess's Will and my fate. Until I defeated Nechton. How I might ever do that without violating my vow, how I would overcome the black lust that swept through me at the thought of it, how I would fit the things I'd seen and the gods I'd met this month into what had once been a well-defined relationship with Her: these were problems beyond my reach. My head whirled with unanswered questions and unconquerable need.

"Fouzh," I whispered. "I've got to go."

"Gods grant you strength," Amien said. "She has only been waiting for you to come back to Her. As we all have. Go: make your peace and renew your marriage. I'll be waiting when you return."

Chapter 36
Bealtan

A wall of flames encircled the Uisneach summit. Of course: all the wizards were vitally occupied with Bealtan devotions; no one could be expected to set those aside for the mundane details of a watch, and on this night it would be inappropriate to raise wards and separate the summit from the skies. The fire would do nothing more than keep mundane assaults and interlopers at bay; a wizard could penetrate that boundary. But if Uisneach is off-limits to anyone outside the initiate except on certain well-controlled occasions, the gods are understood to welcome all of Their initiate who would devote themselves. Even, perhaps, men with one foot already in the Abyss. I climbed from the saddle, opened a portal in the wall, and led my horse across the smoking ground and inside.

"Well done," I said, patting his neck. What a long way he had come from the horse who must be coaxed onto a boat. "Very well done indeed."

He whickered and nudged me. I released the wall, and it closed in on itself again. I led him back to the stable and turned him out, and then I began to walk. No one had told me where the sacred grove lay, though I suspected I would find it in the woods behind the ridge of the summit. I didn't feel ready to confront Whoever I might find there, anyway; I just walked through fields of asphodel and weedy flax, head whirling until the stars themselves seemed to reel overhead.

I didn't know what was wrong with me, though it was clear that there was something gravely amiss. I had been offered things that would have made any sane man leap for joy, and much as my mind saw the reasons why I should want them, my instincts shouted for me to thrust those opportunities away. All I wanted were the things of the Abyss and a woman who would never be mine.

At the top of the ridge I stopped, eyes automatically sweeping the skies for the Lady's Moon and coming up as empty as the saner part of my mind had expected. All I saw was the immense spread of the Hunter. Wind raced up the slope, sending my still-unbound hair fluttering behind me, carrying the scent of the Bealtan fires into my throat. I saw the dark power between the stars above me take shape, saw it fill in the spaces that men usually must complete with their imaginations if they would see the gods and heroes the constellations trace. Through that glimmer mundane eyes never see, I glimpsed the Face and Form of the Hunter, and put a name to Him.

Beal.

He was the One Who held the domain in which I stood, somehow reaching all the way from the Abyss to claim His due on the holiday that still bears His name. He looked at me across the void, and all the dark power that made up His ethereal form swirled through me, lighting me up until He seemed made of light, not dark; until pleasure raged like fire across my skin.

I knew Him. I had always known Him. He was the author of all the wildness I struggled to contain, all the insanity I had tried hopelessly to crush into a form that Lady Tella would approve. Ancient He was, older than any of the stars or the half-seen matter between them, older than thought; and yet, on this night, once again young, a Lover striving endlessly to woo the goddess Who occupied the center of everything: wagering everything He was on that one moment when He might give Her all of Himself, knowing before He began that He would never win Her.

I understood that, too.

I understood how He might find all the universe He created echoing with the scent of Her, especially on this night; might find it all but impossible to focus on anything else—and yet spare some relentless sector of His mind for the problem He now fixed to mine. Esus might want to free Himself from the Abyss, might promise me whatever He thought would move me to accomplish it; Beal thought much bigger than that. As the Lord of those gods imprisoned in the Abyss, Beal wanted to release all of Them, to restore freedom everywhere.

It was not for a bunch of young, upstart gods to usurp the place that should be His, to say what He might or might not do. Wasn't He the One Who had invented the rules and the place They used to trap Him? Shouldn't They all be free to follow Their Own consciences, to create as They chose? There was only one thing He and the gods He led needed: someone with sufficient fortitude to turn the key.

Hakaid the shadow of the Sun
And open the Abyss

I didn't need to ask what my reward would be; I knew He would say whatever I didn't even realize I was waiting to hear. What does One promise a man who has already been offered the titles of both ard-righ and Prince?

I couldn't breathe for terror of the answer.

I launched myself down from the ridge, down the dark and hidden northern side of the hill, crashing through bracken and entangling gorse until I discovered myself on a narrow trail. I stopped; something that might be the mundane world reshaped itself around me. I heard nothing but the sounds of my own harsh breath, saw nothing but darkly-shadowed tree limbs above. The pounding of my heart slowed, but my head still whirled at the very edges of reason, and the memory of dark fire chased itself across my skin: I started walking again. I needed to find the sacred grove, needed to hear Her voice or admit to myself that I could not. Either would serve to show me the path I trod.

Hakaid the shadow of the Sun
And open the Abyss
What if *hakaid* meant *to free*?

I pushed the question away; I walked faster, though I still wasn't sure where I was going. The path wove a route it was too dark to apprehend: across the northern face of the hill, climbing over the protruding roots of trees, skirting outcrops of stone that buzzed with a name it took all my will not to learn. Still Her awareness hovered around me. I struggled to hold myself separate, to fix my mind on the path.

Hakaid the shadow of the Sun
At last the trail spilled into a surprisingly level, regular clearing surrounded by ancient oaks and illuminated by torches: the sacred grove. I rushed in as if claiming sanctuary, senseless relief bursting through me. If I found Lady Tella here, I had a decade's worth of explaining to do, and I was far from certain She would accept any of it. Still that prospect seemed easier to face than the Presences outside this little circle of firelight.

I knelt in the center, looking around. I couldn't see who might have kindled those torches, couldn't imagine who would prepare this place for sacred ceremony and then leave; finally I set the issue aside. Everything happening tonight defied mortal comprehension. My task here was clear; I dragged myself towards a state in which I might hear the goddess if She chose to speak, opened my heart and mind. Beal and the goddess Whose name I worked so hard not to hear crowded around my periphery. I tried to ignore Them, tried instead to reach into that place in which it had once been possible to hear Her words.

Lady, I have no right to ask anything of You. But if You will grant this sad excuse for a servant the insight to understand what You require, I will strive to do Your Will.

The mundane world slipped away from me again. Time spread out into endless, breathless space waiting for someone to quicken it; my mind diffused into darkness and longing, for what I couldn't name. She had nothing to say to me, or else the Presences beating like moths against my edges drowned out Her Words.

Was that it, then? Was I already doomed to the Abyss? Or, as is so often the case with men not yet claimed by the gods, would She require more effort of me before She spoke? I wished I still possessed the grace to beg Her, if not for words, then for a sign.

Something changed. I looked up, into Letitia's mesmerizing eyes; the last of my boundaries fell away. The dark glow between the stars tumbled into me; Beal fit Himself into the spaces that remained; I realized there was only one thing in all the universe that mattered. I stood, caressing the face and savoring the silken hair I had no right to touch, mouth trespassing upon lips long since promised to another. Maybe I had been doomed before I was born; maybe only the Abyss awaited me. But before it claimed me I would give everything I was or could muster to see her safe. Even if what I could muster were gods so terrible They must be locked away. Even if I were the most dreadful of Them all.

Hakaid the shadow of the Sun
And open the Abyss

Letitia tangled her hands in my hair and devoured me as if I were not a form of poison. She trailed her lips along my jaw and sank her teeth into my neck: marking me for her own, raising such terrible need in me that I lost track of everything else, that I must clasp and press her against me. The heat and softness of her drove me wilder yet; within seconds I was trying to touch all of her at once, trying to beat a way past all our clothing and possess her utterly. But then she drew back, and I fell into her eyes, and I remembered.

It was Bealtan. Everything I was must be hers. It didn't matter that I had no idea what *hakaid* meant: all that mattered was that I dedicate myself to her. She was everything I would never again have: legitimacy, clear right and rulership, magic whose only outcome was Light. This was the goddess I must worship. There was no room in the Bealtan mystery for anything less, nothing to do but surrender my darkness to her.

Let the heir of Tílimya
Woo the Virgin Star

I unlaced her dress, trailing worshiping fingers and rapturous mouth across each silken bit of exposed skin; I let her peel me bare, the cool air on my flesh and the touch of her delicate hands echoing the caress of the dark power flooding through me; I knelt at her feet and unwrapped her like the mystery she was, breathing in her textures and flavors and wondrous sounds, fastening them upon my memory. When she settled across my lap, an instant of déjà vu raced through me; but then she took me, and conscious thought drowned. The delicious glow that hung on her annihilated the darkness in which I'd been tangled, crashing over me until I lost track of where I ended and she began.

No goddess ever had lips this sweet, hair this soft, skin this silken warm. Never before had a goddess given Herself to Her Consort with such abandon. This was no re-enactment, no ritual repetition: this was the real Bealtan, the one timeless night from which all imitations and legends would spread like ripples on a lake. Nothing less than absolute perfection would do; and I must remember all of it, because after tonight it would never come again.

Join the Sun and the Moon in Darkness
Thus results the Union of Silver and Gold

Nothing existed but her pleasure and the ways I might raise it; nothing mattered but all the inadmissible things I saw in her eyes. She diffused through me, raising tremors of delight and waves of brilliance throughout my being; I was powerless against the tenderness that swept through me and the sudden redoubling of desire that crashed in its wake. And in the midst of that naked insanity, I saw all the way down to her core, and she saw all of me. Through her I saw myself: a limitless well of passion and power, a bastion against danger—but also a wildness that could turn devouring at any second, against which there would be no defense. Her terror flashed through me—and transmuted into deeper desire.

Now I saw the truth of her, and it had nothing to do with the rules and rituals of Bealtan. Her position of control was not what she wanted; she needed me to possess her, dismantle her, set all the rules and pathways and absolve her of conscious thought. Rule and ritual be damned; the idea tore a growl from me, lit me with a deeper wildness than any power I'd yet known; there was no room in me for the surprising tinge of shame the desire for domination roused in her. It was what I had been born to do.

I grasped her and rolled, spreading her across the cool grass and claiming control; she cried out, trembling, and surrendered into my arms. I opened myself wider and deeper, encompassing all of her, finding other things infiltrating me as well: the light in her talisman lancing my eyes like too much summer sun; the ring of fire surrounding the summit and the Bealtan bonfires outside Teamair's city gate, flames guttering almost to nothing as their energies raced through me; Amien meeting my eyes across that sudden connection and giving voice to a laugh of pure, triumphant joy; the drunken boisterous half-aware crowd dancing their ways between the bonfires, their disparate thoughts and words and desires chattering through me as if an entire Ruillin ferry had manifested somewhere inside. Their energy poured through me, stretching me wider yet, infusing me with a flavor of pleasure unlike anything I'd yet tasted. I sent a little of it into Letitia, directing it into the places where it would please her most, stopping her rapturous wail with a kiss. Whether I was lost, whether I might yet be the goddess's man again: tonight I was only hers. This time, I would hold nothing back.

Blend the Essences in the vessel of life
The Elixir cythe
Earth, Fire, Water and Air to command or release at will

Source after source of power raced into me; there in the midst of the sacred and timeless I welcomed them all. All of them would be for Letitia. The elemental energies no mortal may command laughed through me and bloomed all around, wind swirling and the ground beneath us trembling in their wake. Stars tangled in my hair, tingled in the ends of my fingers, sparked ripples of delight that sent a not-quite human laughter bubbling up from my Abyss-dark core. Fear and need twined in Letitia again, sending me beyond the edge of reason; more minds skittered through my ever-expanding awareness, most of them unaware but Iminor meeting my eyes as he crackled through me, his sudden rage and anguish pouring the death-spell into me in a delicious rush.

Passion condensed into a wave of impending climax; I sank my teeth into her neck, the taste of blood on my lips and her shriek of pleasured pain catapulting me past inevitability into a place from which the universe spread out in raucous glory and Letitia's tastes and textures infused all of it, blending with the delicious light of the stars and the glory of the darkness between them. All the universe waited for my command.

In the Crucible pain is ecstasy and Death is Life
Hidden is plain

It was Bealtan: a dark Bealtan with the goddess beyond apprehension and Beal blanketing the world in darkness, a night on which the priestess surrendered to the priest. But still I must give her everything. Let it be an *everything* that surpassed anyone's darkest wildest dreams. The moment was on me; I let it happen, shiver trembling up into tingle, pounding towards rapture, cascading past unreason until only my pleasure and Letitia and the magic pouring between us existed. She cried out her ecstasy again; my insanity spun faster yet, and I let everything in my awareness, all the stars and Elements and human energies, tumble through me into her. I gave her my own magical essence; it shuddered out of me, taking something deep inside me with it. The universe crashed around me, but a void had opened inside.

The reach of the shadow of the Sun is infinite.

I struggled for breath; I sought the flavors and textures of Letitia's mouth, completing the physical circuit between us: a terrible, tender grief welling in me, the loss of all the things I would never possess a weight upon my soul.

It was over. I had stolen this Bealtan, had known all along I had no right to it, knew all the ways I was betraying everyone involved. I would do it again, if I could. But now there was an abyss inside me that nothing would ever fill.

Letitia clasped me tenderly, legs still tangled around mine; she caressed my face, eyes full of truths that could never be spoken. I had well and truly bound myself; hadn't realized until now how deeply I'd bound her as well. Were I damned, would this binding survive my descent into the Abyss? A wholly new ache gathered to blockade my throat. I should apologize; but the depth of the things for which I owed apology would wreck me. I must still endure tomorrow.

"I will not ascend the throne," Letitia said softly, emerald eyes tender and inescapable. "I have so little to offer you."

She shook her head, solemn, while my mind scrabbled hopelessly for purchase.

"Maybe this is the mark of what a true commitment should be, that you will come to me for no more than a heart's command."

"Annu?" I ventured. Now I suspected we'd been proceeding from entirely different assumptions and contexts. Again. As usual. Had we ever held a conversation in which we understood one another? "I—annu, *you* came to *me*. I had no expectations of anything beyond this night."

"Oh, c'choiri," she began, tender hand on my face again. Then comprehension snapped to life in her eyes. Hurt manifested in her face, the unmistakable ire of a righ who has been insulted on its heels. She pulled away, already reaching for her dress. "After—that night at Ilunmore, you said you didn't *care* if you were ever mor!"

"No, I said I didn't *want* to be mor of Fíana. I can't be a consort—"

"It's not as if you have prospects of your own!" It shouldn't sting me, but it did.

"Actually, Amien offered me the ard-righ's throne."

Why the hell had I said that?

She stared at me, dress still unlaced. "I thought you had to be a righ to be ard-righ."

I shook my head, mostly at my own idiocy. "Technically, no. I'm not sure I'm going to take it, anyway."

Letitia stared at me a moment more. She shook her head. "Sweet Lord, you're a fool."

"Yes," I said.

She flushed, narrow jaw suddenly taut; she jammed her feet into her slippers and stalked out of the grove. For a moment I could do no more than reel; then anger blossomed inside me. How was it possible that dedicating everything I was to her might be insufficient? I threw on my clothes without bothering to button my shirt, shoved my feet into my boots and raced after her. My love, my power, my devotion, my protection: these were sufficient so long as I stood one step below her? Demand equal status, and suddenly the rules changed? She had already gained the fields beyond the summit ridge by the time I caught up to her.

"So it's all right for me to lead the lovemaking, but otherwise you must be righ of the rise?" I snapped.

She stopped and slapped me briskly. White-hot anger surged through me. A second's terror flashed in her face—followed immediately by a storm of renewed ire, reluctant worship, and shame. I felt my mouth twist into something that was not a smile.

"Really," I said, remotely surprised at how cold I sounded. "As long as we've established what I am."

I should have understood. If human men think all Tana are wanton temptresses, Tanaan women have little more respect for men. Particularly foreign men. My royal status and military command had partially shielded me with the women of Letitia's contingent. But to a Tanaan royal I must be little more than a courtesan who knew how to handle a blade. The wonder was not that she took me into her bed when she was already committed to marry: it was that she would have made me her consort, when a much more suitable candidate had already been promised her long ago. Bealtan must truly have gone to her head.

"Fear not," I said. "Tomorrow you will be sane again."

I turned and walked back the way we had come: up to the top of the ridge from which I had spotted Beal. This time I found Amien sitting there, watching me approach.

"Well, then," he said as I sat down beside him. "You're back."

He meant *back to practicing magic*; I shook my head.

"That was just Bealtan."

Amien frowned. "Not funny, Ellion."

"But true, my lord."

He sighed. For a moment we were both silent.

"What the hell did She say?"

Nothing, I wanted to say. But if I hadn't heard Her words tonight, I had received signs aplenty. She had sent me the greatest of all possible gifts on Bealtan, and I had failed to accept it. All I had needed to do was submit, as the Bealtan priest should. Instead I had chosen wildness thrice over, proven myself unready to yield to Her Call. Instead I let illicit powers and old gods move my feet from the path.

She hadn't needed to answer. All She needed to do was show me myself.

I sighed. "Neither yea nor nay."

But I wasn't sure that was true: Her silence might well have been the answer. It was tempting to think of myself as an unbroken horse, as a being who must be shown the ways of righteousness before I was worthy to serve. But the truth was I had been trained, and by a master: I'd gone feral, like a lighthorse abandoned too long.

And Whose fault was it that I'd been abandoned?

Horror swept through me at the thought. Question Her distance in the face of my many transgressions, and there was no telling what I would find it in myself to question next. The ruin of Esunertos swam before my eyes; in my peripheral vision I glimpsed Beal recondensing overhead. I'd been right to turn aside from the Prince's throne. Who could say how far I had to travel back towards Her before I would be worthy of that post—or whether I would ever cover that distance at all?

"Ard-righ, then," Amien sighed.

That wasn't right, either: a twelvenight from now I would be righ of nothing but a vacant hill. Or, worse yet, a city of empty wooden façades begging for the comeuppance of a torch. But it would give me the rank I needed to set strategy and tactics, and that might allow me to defeat Nechton. And protect Letitia.

I would never be her consort. She would never be mine. But I had given both my word and my heart, and nothing would stand in the way of her safety. Not while I lived.

"Yes," I said, eyes on the ring of fire below us. "But don't expect me to carry it like Coran; I don't have time. I'll send the Ilesians to support you and the wizards at Esunertos—" Amien stirred, restless; I ignored it. "—and Conwy of Deceang and the other eastern righthe to secure the Aerona and Nagnata. Then they should be able to re-take Ballarona. Meanwhile Rohini and Cooley of Ebdani will muster with whatever righthe still stand in the west, and they will re-take Liis and Regia and move on to Macol. Letitia and I will handle the Shadow of the Sun."

Now Amien turned to look at me. Even in my peripheral vision I could see him grin.

"Don't look at me like that. She has not released me from my vow. I'll still need wizards."

Still Amien smiled as if in possession of a wonderful secret; I knew he believed it was only a matter of time before I secured that concession, as well.

It was much more likely that what I secured would be a place in the Abyss. That Nechton and gods Whose names I didn't even yet know would push me into a place in which I cast aside the last of my vows and succumbed to the lure of all the things I wouldn't allow myself to touch. Already those things crowded around me, the crystalline song of the dark power between the stars, the tastes and colors of the stars themselves, the power in the earth beneath me, the Powers of all the gods waiting for me to unravel the Shadow working and turn the key. A ripple of intoxication fluttered through me; illicit delight lit my skin. I knew the truth: I didn't need Them to push me. I only needed an excuse. The only real question was what would happen in the space between that final greatest transgression and my inevitable fall into endless empty darkness.

Maybe that fall had already begun.

"All right, then, *my lord*," Amien said, amused. "Now let *me* tell *you* how it will be."

I had long since crossed the line separating my prerogative from his, I knew. Once again I couldn't find it in myself to care: I just turned my head to look at him. His amusement deepened.

"I've missed that look," he said, laughter running beneath his words—then laughed aloud at whatever he saw in my gaze. "Well, then. I'm not a fool: your military strategy will stand. I give you absolute authority there. Meanwhile you will work to resolve matters with the goddess—I trust you know better than to argue like this with Her—"

An unwilling grin overcame me.

"Because it is not meet for the Aballo Prince to carry such an affliction as I do, and when you rechannel this damned spell, you will only be buying yourself time. I don't need ceremony to declare you my heir, and I have already informed Sanglin and the rest of the members of the Order who are here tonight."

A little of the wind went out of my sails. I didn't want to imagine that conversation.

"Also, I know you and Sanglin have a great deal to sort through—and I know you'll want him as your second. *You* are the one on whose shoulders that yoke rests."

He was right: that situation was my fault, and up to me to correct. "Yes, my lord."

Amien nodded, satisfied. A better man would have let the conversation rest there.

"But this year," I said, "all I really care about is Letitia and you. And Nechton." For just a second, I felt his awareness—as if he watched us through his Shadow of the Sun. A moment of arcane contact rushed through me, cloaked in the darkness of limitless aetheric space, overlaid with that wild sense of looking into a mirror he always gave me: *brother-lover-enemy*. I tingled with things no man of the gods should ever admit.

From impossible distance, shoulder warm against mine, Amien offered me a faint smile. "In that regard, we are all in your hands."

Glossary

Aballo   Island off the coast of Ebdani; seat of the Aballo Order. Rendered generally inaccessible except to Aballo's initiate by a combination of tides and arcane defenses.

Aballo Order   *Ilesian.* Religious/magical organization headed by the Aballo Prince. Initiates are termed *wizards*, and are distinguished from other initiates into magical orders by their level of ability. From this order are drawn the so-called House Healers attached to royal houses worldwide. *See also: druid, House Healer, windcaller, wizard.*

abu al-righ   *Ilesian.* "Hail forever to the righ."

Aechering   *Ilesian.* Wizard who lived and practiced before the arrival of the true gods; author of the Shadow Working. *See also: Shadow Working.*

Aerona   *Ilesian.* 1. River flowing from Lake Nanno in Granniu to the Ruillin, demarcating the Granniu-Nagnata, Granniu-Deceang, and Deceang-Mumhan borders. 2. A goddess of the old religion; patroness of the river of the same name.

aisling   *Ilesian; arcane.* A flavor of trance typically used in dreamwork, including, but not exclusive to, dream-sendings among wizards.

amhainseacht   *Ilesian; arcane.* A flavor of trance typically used in dealings with beings of other realms.

Amma   *Danaan.* Grandmother.

amnivaren   *Ilesian; arcane.* An herb used to facilitate arcane consciousness. May be burned in a censer or brewed as tea.

Ankou	*Ilesian.* Boatman of the Abyss. *See also: Dóiteán, Realm of Tílimya.*
annu	*Ilesian.* A term of affection; only applied to females.
Ara	*Ilesian.* A goddess of the true religion; consort of Par, patroness of farming, childbirth, and the hearth.
Ardan	*Ilesian.* Festival of the goddess Ara, celebrated in early spring.
ard-harpist	*Ilesian.* Leader of the Harpist Gorsedd, elected by the organization's ranking members. *See also: Harpist Gorsedd.*
ard-righ	*Ilesian.* Presiding member of the College of Righthe, vested with little authority over the righ or tiarna of any nation besides the one he rules. Elected by the righthe of all the nations, his primary function is as War-Leader in international operations. *See also: College of Righthe, righ, tiarn.*
ard-tiarn	*Ilesian.* Literally, "Lord Most High"; a title conferred by a righ to raise a member of his peerage to a higher standing than the other tiarna. Frequently also a righ's War-Lord. *See also: tiarn.*
argentel	*Danaan.* A brilliant, colorless gem; softer but brighter in luster than the diamond.
Arliyn	*Ilesian.* The smaller moon, named in honor of the goddess Ara, with an orbital period of 47 days. Though not of sufficient size or proximity to generate significant tides in its own right, Arliyn's influence can be seen in the magnitudes of double spring and double neap tides. *See also: Telliyn.*
Armoan	*Ilesian.* Ballad of the Essuvian hero Armoan Lanas, ancestor of High Chief Rohini of the Essuvians, and the role he played in the defeat of the renegade Nechton. Together with the *Ballad of Carina,* encapsulates popular understanding of the history of Nechton's War. *See also: Nechton's War.*
Armoan Lanas	Historic High Chief of the Essuvians and eventual righ of Uxellia, leader of the Essuvian offensive against the Uxellian capital during Nechton's War. *See also: Essuvian, Nechton's War.*
Ballad of Carina	*Ilesian.* Ballad of the Tanaan Lady Carina Finias, Carina Ériu, a Fíana, and her defeat of the renegade wizard Nechton. *See also: Carina Ériu a Fíana, Nechton Glyndwyr, Nechton's War.*
Bard of Arcadia	Leader of a popular rebellion against the righthe threatening the southern (human) realms. *See also: kharr.*

Bard's Wizard	Renegade wizard recruited by the Bard of Arcadia to the rebellion against the righthe.
Básghil	*Ilesian. Pl.* **Básghilae.** Magically-crafted undead.
Beal	*Ilesian.* A god of the old religion, patron of land and righship.
Beallan	*Danaan. Pl.* **Bealla.** Human.
Bealtan	Spring festival of fertility and a ruler's bonds with the land.
Beannchar	*Ilesian.* Military historian. Notable writings include a volume on siegecraft and a history of the Ilesian War.
Breasaílian	*Danaan, Ilesian.* Of or pertaining to Hy-Breasaíl. *See also: Hy-Breasaíl.*
brehon	*Danaan, Ilesian.* Scholars and practitioners of the disciplines of the law.
briocht	*Ilesian; arcane.* A spell, largely or fully verbal.
c'choiri	*Danaan.* A term of affection; *darling.*
Carin and Alannin	*Danaan.* A composition for the harp by the bard Alannin a Fea celebrating his love affair with Carina Ériu a Fíana. *See also: Carina Ériu a Fíana.*
Carina Ériu a Fíana	Former mora of Fíana; heroine of the *Ballad of Carina. See also: Ballad of Carina, Carin and Alannin, mora, Nechton's War.*
City of the Winds	Epithet for the Fíanan capital, Irisa.
College of Righthe	*Ilesian.* An assembly comprising the righ of every southern (human) nation; those eligible to vote in the election of the ard-righ. *See also: righ, ard-righ.*
Conary Mourne	The most recent ard-righ and righ of Ilesia, recently assassinated.
Coradon's Lament	*Ilesian.* Ballad about Coradon, righ of the nation that would later become Ilesia, and his seduction and eventual ruin by the Tanaan Lady Ara of Nimah. *See also: Nimah.*
creadhon	*Ilesian.* A profanity.
Cúchulainn	An ancient hero, the topic of countless songs and tales, on whom warriors are taught to model themselves; central hero of *The Siege of the Brown Bull.* Human lore teaches that the old god Lugh Lámfhada fathered Cúchulainn on a mortal woman; the Danaan believe Cúchulainn became the god Lugh after his encounter with the Green God that is described in the ballad *Fare and Fir. See also: Fare and Fir, The Siege of the Brown Bull.*

Cullinn	Clan that ruled the nation of Fiatach, later Ilesia, before the arrival of the true gods. *See also: Ilesian War, Owain Mourne.*
Dana	*Danaan.* The great goddess of the Danaan religion.
Danaan	*Danaan.* The Danaan people or language. *See also: Tanaan.*
Dana's People	*Danaan.* Epithet by which the Danaan people refer to their race.
Deaclan	A former initiate of the Aballo Order.
Deluge	A Danaan catastrophe.
Dian Cecht	*Danaan.* A god; patron of healers.
Dóiteán	*Ilesian.* Part of the geography of the Realms of the Dead: a flaming river of blood around the Realm of Tílimya. *See also: Tílimya's Abyss.*
Donn	*Danaan.* A god; Lord of the Dead and of the Danaan hero's paradise. *See also: House of Donn.*
druid	*Ilesian.* A priest of the true religion. Any magic undertaken by druids is likely to be of the divinatory or subtle-influence type; Talents capable of true physical magic are more likely to be trained as windcallers or, more rarely, wizards.
eipiciúil	*Ilesian. Pl.* **eipiciúilae.** Historical ballad.
Endeáril	*Danaan.* A god; consort of the goddess Dana.
Essuvian	A formerly nomadic people originating east of Ilesia; until recently overlords of Uxellia. The Essuvians aided the righthe of the southern (human) nations in defeating the renegade wizard during Nechton's War and were granted dominion over the nation he ruled: originally under the auspices of the ard-righ but later as a matter of succession. Oral histories suggest the Essuvian clans may have been part of the Esusdian exodus after the Ilesian War. *See also: Nechton's War, Ilesian War, Esusdia, Weavers.*
Estra	Festival of the Spring equinox.
Esunertos	One-time capital of the nation of Esusdia, now abandoned. *See also: Ilesian War, Esusdia.*
Esus	*Ilesian.* A god of the old religion; patron of war.
Esusdia	One of the first nations founded after the Transition, later destroyed by war; now a zone of wilderness and waste bounded by Ebdani, Nagnata, Granniu, and the ard-righ's precinct. The few remaining border cities and towns of the former nation of Esusdia now look to the surrounding nations; over the centuries people shortened the region's name to Usdia. *See also: Esunertos; Ilesian War; Transition.*
Fáilias	*Ilesian.* Corruption of the name of the Danaan nation of Fáill.

Fair	*Ilesian.* Annual spring gathering during the month of the Bealtan holiday at Teamair in the ard-righ's precinct. During years in which a Grand Moot is held, the event attracts people from all over the southern (human) nations.
Fare and Fir	*Ilesian.* Ballad detailing an encounter between the hero Cúchulainn and the Green God. *See also: Cúchulainn.*
Fergus in Exile	*Ilesian.* Ballad from *The Siege of the Brown Bull,* an ancient song-cycle. While the cycle features the hero Cúchulainn, this song tells the story of Fergus, the betrayal of whose trust was one of the proximate causes of the War of the Brown Bull and the tragedies that resulted. *See also: War of the Brown Bull.*
Fiatach	*Ilesian.* Original name of the nation of Ilesia, later changed by the righ Owain Mourne. *See also: Ilesian War, Owain Mourne.*
Fields of Asphodel	*Ilesian.* Part of the geography of the Realms of the Dead. After death a person who is neither heroic nor particularly evil will spend time in the Grey Lands—the Fields of Asphodel—before returning to the lands of the living for another life and trying again to achieve the reward of paradise. *See also: Tílimya's Abyss, Tír inna n-Óc.*
findargat	*Danaan.* An indestructible metal of silver hue.
Finias	*Ilesian.* Corruption of the name of the Danaan nation of Fíana.
flash-weapon	*Ilesian.* A weapon intended to afford men of little or no arcane talent the ability to wield an equivalent of an arcane casting. The operative part of any flash weapon is a charged crystal, which the weapon taps to produce a would-be arcane casting. Higher quality flash-weapons use crystals charged by a wizard. Though some inferior substitutes use mechanically generated quick-charges, those weapons are generally only good for a single use. Trained warriors, particularly noblemen, find the the use of flash-weapons beneath contempt.
flashmen	*Ilesian.* Warriors responsible for wielding flash-weapons. Generally employed by tiarna or wealthy commoners, neither of whom can gain the opportunity to retain wizards. Warriors, particularly noblemen, generally view flashmen with contempt, considering the flash-weapon a coward's tool.
Four Realms	*Danaan.* Collective term for the Danaan nations Banbagor, Fáill, Fíana, and Muir.
fouzh	*Ilesian.* A profanity.

Gáe Assail   *Danaan.* The Great Spear of Fíana: the treasure of Fíana and the mark of office of its mora. Originally belonged to the god Lugh Lámfhada.

geas   *Ilesian, Danaan.* A vow or obligation placed on a person. May have the force of a curse.

Goibniu   *Ilesian.* 1. A god of the old religion; patron of smiths. 2. A city in northern Mumhan named for the smith-god.

golden branch   *Ilesian.* The mark of office of an ollamh, one of the lords of the Harpist Gorsedd. *See also: Harpist Gorsedd, ollamh, silver branch.*

Gorias   *Ilesian.* Corruption of the name of the Danaan nation of Banbagor.

Grand Moot   *Ilesian.* Gathering of all the righthe and certain other parties designated by the Aballo Prince to settle matters of international urgency and/or elect the ard-righ. *See also: ard-righ.*

Great Barrow   *Danaan.* A mountain at the northern end of the sacred isle of Ilunmore; the burial chamber of the Danaan's great leaders. Danaan tradition holds the barrow within the mountain is literally the path to the underworld, the doorway through which the ancient Danaan emerged from the Lady's Underground Ways during the Transition, their retreat from Hy-Breasaíl. *See also: House of Donn, Hy-Breasaíl, Lady's Underground Ways, Transition.*

Grey Lands   See **Fields of Asphodel.**

grimoire   *Ilesian; arcane.* An arcane practitioner's book of notes, records, and spells, recipes and methodologies. A grimoire is personal and typically private.

Gwydion   Hero of the ballad *Tílimya's Well.*

hardy silkspider   A cousin to the silkspider of Uxellia, adapted to the region of Granniu between the northern bank of the Aerona and the upthrust to the piedmont, that produces a silk of extreme strength. *See also: hardy spidersilk, silkspider, spidersilk, Weavers.*

hardy spidersilk   A silk of extreme strength produced by the hardy silkspider of Granniu. While the silk of the hardy silkspider lacks the lightness and luster of the product of its western cousin, its strength makes it ideal for industrial and military applications. From hardy spidersilk is crafted lightweight, comfortable, nearly indestructible mail, and ropes and cables for siege engines and ships. *See also: hardy silkspider, silkspider, spidersilk, Weavers.*

Harpist Gorsedd	*Ilesian.* Professional organization of musicians. Admission to the gorsedd is achieved primarily through apprenticeship; certification to full membership is dependent upon the mastery of certain bodies of work and other demonstrations of competency. Ollamh, the so-called lords of the gorsedd, must be certified by a group of sitting ollamh, based on mastery of further bodies of work and original contributions to the art. The gorsedd is led by the ard-harpist, an ollamh elected to the position for a term of five years, whose election may be nullified at the will of the majority of other ollamh. Members are entitled to carry the silver branch as a mark of office; ollamh are entitled to carry the golden branch. *See also: ard-harpist, golden branch, ollamh, silver branch.*
House Healer	*Ilesian.* The title given to an Aballo wizard in the service of a royal house. While wizards are trained in the techniques of healing, most of the health needs of any royal house are actually met by professional healers. A House Healer's duties are understood to be mostly or entirely arcane. *See also: Aballo Order, wizard.*
House of Donn	*Danaan.* Part of the geography of the Realms of the Dead: the paradisal destination after death of heroes. Seat of Donn, the Danaan Lord of the Dead. *See also: Donn, Tír inna n-Óc.*
Hy-Breasaíl	The legendary paradise from which both Danaan and human/Beallan people are held to have originated; the ancient realm of the gods.
Ildan	*Ilesian.* Festival of the god Ilesan, celebrated at the fall equinox.
Ilesan	*Ilesian.* A god of the true religion: the Lord of Gods, patron of storms and esoteric learning.
Ilesian War	The war of ascension of the true gods. Upon the arrival of the true gods in the southern (human) realms, the goddess Tella revealed herself to Owain Mourne, a would-be druid in the nation of Fiatach (later Ilesia). Tella made Mourne into a conduit for her Will and power, though his arcane talent was all but nonexistent. With the goddess's support he rapidly ascended to the leadership of his heretofore-minor clan and led them to gain the throne of Fiatach a few years later. Within ten years the newly-renamed nation of Ilesia had forcibly converted Deceang and Mumhan. During the Ilesian conquest of Nagnata, the goddess Tella appeared personally to the Prince of the Aballo Order, who accepted Tella's emissary and sealed the acceptance of the

Ilesian War (cont'd)	true gods. Nevertheless the conquest of Esusdia and Ebdani was bloody; the Esusdians were completely intractable, and the Ebdanii, who held the ard-righship during this era, had great military resources. In the course of the battle for Esusdia, Tella destroyed the capital city, Esunertos. Most of the remaining Esusdians fled to the western badlands, forming a nation named Uxellia; several clans withdrew to the highlands east of Ilesia, becoming the Essuvians. One of the clans of Nagnata, who accepted Tella without a fight, received the land of Tellan; the leading clan of the new nation took that name as well. Within twenty years of the goddess Tella's first contact with Owain Mourne, all the southern (human) realms with the exception of Uxellia had converted to the true religion, and that nation would follow within a generation. *See also: Esusdia, Essuvian, Esunertos, Owain Mourne.*
Iliria	A talisman. Originally belonged to Carina Ériu a Fíana.
kharr	*Ilesian.* Literally, "anarchist(s)": participants in the rebellion against the righthe led by the Bard of Arcadia. Intelligence suggests kharr insiders wear a tattoo of a redsnake on the wrist. *See also: Bard of Arcadia, redsnake.*
Lady's Underground Ways	*Danaan.* The underground paths by which the ancient Danaan followed the goddess Dana from Hy-Breasaíl during the Transition. Reputedly terminating within the Great Barrow on Ilunmore, beyond that point the route traverses areas beyond the mundane realm, tracing a path that includes the House of Donn. *See also: Great Barrow, House of Donn, Hy-Breasaíl, Transition.*
Laverna	*Ilesian.* A goddess of the old religion; goddess of the River Ruillin and patroness of whores; consort of the smith-god Goibniu.
Lugh Lámfhada	Among the Danaan, a god; not the patron of anything in particular but instead celebrated for his many talents. Among humans/Bealla, Lugh is considered a god of the old religion, now understood as an ancient, ancestral hero. Legend holds that Lugh gained admission to the court of the gods because he was the only one who could demonstrate competence in all the skills of the gods.
Lys	*Danaan.* One of three primary goddesses; patroness of the hunt and seers.
machnamh	*Ilesian; arcane.* A flavor of trance typically employed in meditation.

madding   *Danaan.* The semi-centurial period of growing new teeth. The process is excruciatingly uncomfortable; a person in a madding phase is not held responsible for much of what he or she does or says.

Magh Tuireadh   Ancient battleground of the Danaan on Hy-Breasaíl. The Danaan fought two historically significant battles there: the first against the Fomor, in which the Danaan won hedgemony over Hy-Breasaíl; the second against humans, which they lost. *See also: Hy-Breasaíl.*

Moot   *See **Grand Moot**.*

mor   *Danaan.* The consort of a mora.

mora   *Danaan. Pl.* **morae.** Ruler of a nation; understood to be female.

mummers   *Ilesian.* Entertainers who perform plays, skits, and satires, usually employing stock characters: the Fool, the Lord, the Rogue, the Hero, the Damsel, the Druid, and the Farmer.

Murias   *Ilesian.* Corruption of the name of the Danaan nation of Muir.

nasclethéan   *Ilesian; arcane. Pl.* **nasclethéana.** A wizard's work-partner. *See also: Aballo Order, wizard.*

Nechton Glyndwr   Renegade wizard who attempted the conquest of all the southern (human) realms. An initiate of the Aballo Order, he served as House Healer to Uxellia before usurping the Uxellian throne and embarking on a campaign to rule the southern (human) realms. *See also: Armoan, Ballad of Carina, Nechton's War.*

Nechton's War   War of conquest staged by Nechton Glyndwr, renegade wizard of the Aballo Order. While serving as House Healer to Uxellia, he gained control of the throne and began a campaign to conquer all the southern (human) realms. After years of gradually losing territory to the renegade, the ard-righ entered into a deal, brokered by Rishan Tailltiu a Muir, with High Chief Armoan Lanas of the Essuvians, in which the Essuvians agreed to aid the righthe in defeating Nechton in exchange for overlord status in Uxellia. Meanwhile Carina Ériu a Fíana and Amien Cughlin, who would become Prince of the Aballo Order before the end of the war, developed a plan for her to employ a little-understood talent for channeling the power of the sun to defeat the renegade. By the time she reached Nechton's stronghold, two successive Princes of the Aballo Order had died in arcane duels with Nechton. Nevertheless she was evidently able to defeat the renegade. *See also: Armoan, Ballad of Carina.*

Nimah	Danaan outpost in the southern (human) realms, situated on Lethin Isle in the Ruillin; abandoned after the Deluge. *See also: Deluge.*
ollamh	*Ilesian.* A ranking member of the Harpist Gorsedd, one of the so-called lords of the gorsedd. In order to achieve this rank, a gorsedd member must be certified by a group of sitting ollamh, based on mastery of certain bodies of work and original contributions to the art. Ollamh are entitled to carry the golden branch as a mark of office and are eligible to be elected to or participate in votes concerning the position of ard-harpist. *See also: ard-harpist, golden branch, Harpist Gorsedd.*
Order of the Hidden Sun	*Ilesian.* A religious order devoted to Par, the god of warriors. While the tenets of the Order are sufficiently different from the standard teachings of the true religion to give the faithful pause, the Order is nevertheless devoted to the true religion and the Aballo Prince and trains the best spies, security masters, and assassins in the world. The original names and identities of initiates into the Order are carefully expunged, through methods proprietary to the Order; those initiated into full membership wear a small tattoo at the base of the hairline: a stylized sun rendered in black.
orichalus	A red-gold metal greatly prized by the ancient Danaan.
ouirr	*Danaan.* Honorific: *sir. See also: sian.*
Owain Mourne	Founder of the true religion and the ruling dynasty of Ilesia. After the arrival of the true gods, the goddess Tella appeared personally to him, investing him with her power even though he was of essentially no arcane talent in his own right. She raised him to the leadership of his clan, the righship of the newly-renamed Ilesia, and eventually to the ard-righship. During his tenure all the southern (human) nations converted to the true religion. *See also: Ilesian War, Tella.*
Par	*Ilesian.* A god of the true religion; patron of warriors.
Pardan	*Ilesian.* Festival of the god Par, celebrated in late summer.
Pirtanien	Historian. Notable works include histories of Hy-Breasaíl and the Transition. *See also: Hy-Breasaíl, Transition.*
pra-nu	*Danaan, Ilesian.* Literally, "sing the name": among Danaan, an expression of agreement or approval; "so mote it be" in prayer or arcane practice.

Precinct	The ard-righ's precinct: home of the ceremonial centers of Teamair and Uisneach, an area bounded by Tellan, Ebdani, Usdia and Granniu, held under the dominion of the ard-righ. *See also: ard-righ.*
ra	*Danaan.* Commander.
Ransmith	Wizard and author of a grimoire on methods of psychic warfare. *See also: grimoire.*
Realm of Tílimya	*Ilesian.* Part of the geography of the Realms of the Dead: the domain of Tílimya, Lord of the Dead. Surrounded by the boiling river of blood Dóiteán and insurmountable walls of adamantine, defended by a fifty-headed hydra, Tilimya's Realm encompasses the Fortress of Tílimya, which holds the Well of Life, and Tílimya's Abyss, the eternal prison of evil men and gods. *See also: Dóiteán, Tílimya, Tílimya's Abyss, Tír inna n-Óc.*
redsnake	A small, poisonous snake with red scales. Though few besides small children die from the bite of a redsnake, the venom is reputed to alter a man's mind. Intelligence suggests kharr insiders wear a tattoo of a redsnake on the wrist. *See also: kharr.*
riga	*Ilesian.* The consort of a righ; understood to be female. *See also: righ.*
righ	*Ilesian. pl.* **righthe.** Ruler of a nation; understood to be male.
seach	*Ilesian.* Minor nobility.
Shadow Working	*Ilesian; arcane.* An arcane operation, reputed to be the ultimate act of black magic, developed by the wizard Aechering. *See also: Aechering.*
sian	*Ilesian.* Honorific: sir. *See also: ouirr.*
The Siege of the Brown Bull	Ancient song-cycle featuring the hero Cúchulainn, detailing a war between the Hy-Breasaílian rulers of the nations of Chonnacht and Ulaid for possession of the legendary bull Donn Cúailnge. *See also: Cúchulainn, Fergus in Exile, War of the Brown Bull.*
silkspider	A spider, native to the desert of Uxellia, that produces a silk of extreme lightness and luster. *See also: hardy silkspider, hardy spidersilk, spidersilk, Weavers.*
silver branch	*Ilesian.* The mark of office of a member of the Harpist Gorsedd. *See also: Harpist Gorsedd, golden branch.*
sláinte	*Ilesian.* Health. Frequently used as salute or toast.

spidersilk	A silk of extreme lightness and luster, greatly desired by wealthy people of all the southern nations, which is produced by the desert silkspider of Uxellia. *See also: hardy silkspider, hardy spidersilk, silkspider, Weavers.*
stela	*Ilesian. pl.* **stelae**. Standing-stone.
tiarn	*Ilesian. pl.* **tiarna**. The titular lord of a territory. While some tiarna hold titles through royal grants, most are hereditary.
Tan	*Ilesian.* A Danaan man.
Tana	*Ilesian.* A Danaan woman.
Tanaan	*Ilesian.* The Danaan people or language. *See also: Beallan, Danaan.*
tanist	*Ilesian.* The heir of a righ. *See also: righ.*
Tella	*Ilesian.* A goddess of the true religion: consort of Ilesan; patroness of rivers, seas, and righship.
Telliyn	*Ilesian.* The larger moon, named in honor of the goddess Tella, with an orbital period of 24 days. The calendar marks its months by Telliyn's period. *See also: Arliyn.*
Tiana	*Danaan.* One of three primary goddesses; patroness of love and fertility.
Tílimya	*Ilesian.* A god, Lord of the Dead and jailor of evil gods. Though he predates the true religion, he is nevertheless accepted as real. *See also: Realm of Tílimya, Tílimya's Abyss.*
Tílimya's Abyss	*Ilesian.* Part of the geography of the Realms of the Dead. The destination after death of those who are truly evil; the prison to which the ancient gods of Hy-Breasaíl are consigned. *See also: Hy-Breasaíl, Realm of Tílimya, Tír inna n-Óc.*
Tílimya's Well	*Ilesian.* Ballad of the Hy-Breasaílian hero Gwydion and his quest to retrieve the healing waters of the Well of Tílimya in order to heal the Hy-Breasaílian righ. *See also: Hy-Breasaíl, Realm of Tílimya, Well of Tílimya.*
Tír inna n-Óc	*Ilesian.* Part of the geography of the Realms of the Dead: the paradisal destination after death of heroes. *See also: House of Donn.*
Transition	*Danaan, Ilesian.* The period of withdrawal from the ancestral paradise of Hy-Breasaíl. Danaan scholars posit a trip through the Lady's Underground Ways led by the great goddess Dana; human sources discuss sailing from the isle. *See also: Hy-Breasaíl, Lady's Underground Ways, Pirtanien.*

Tuaoh Stone	The great righ-stone that once marked the center of Hy-Breasaíl. The Danaan maintain it now resides atop the Temple Mount on the sacred isle of Ilunmore; human scholars disagree as to which of a number of standing-stones might be the true Tuaoh.
Turenn Thunderer	*Ilesian.* A god of the old religion; patron of storms.
uisquebae	*Ilesian.* A distilled alcoholic beverage made from malted barley. The name derives from "Water of Life". May, in certain circles, be called "Water of Beal".
Usdia	*See **Esusdia.***
War of the Brown Bull	Hy-Breasaílian war waged by the rulers of Chonnacht and Ulaid for possession of the legendary bull Donn Cúailnge: inspiration for the song-cycle *The Siege of the Brown Bull*. *See also: Cúchulainn, Siege of the Brown Bull.*
Way of the Gods	*Ilesian.* The band of light formed by thickly-clustered stars stretching across the night sky, dividing the sky into nearly equal hemispheres. While other stars may appear as discrete points of light, the stars of the Way of the Gods are all but indistinguishable.
Weavers	*Ilesian.* Clans of Uxellian ancestry, descendants of the original ruling class of Uxellia which was displaced by the Essuvians after Nechton's War. Weavers live as an almost entirely distinct society, residing in separate, typically closed, enclaves wherever they may make their homes. They grow, harvest, spin, and weave spidersilk or the related crop of hardy spidersilk. The largest concentrations of Weavers may be found in Uxellia, where the silkspider thrives and spidersilk is grown, and Granniu, where the hardy silkspider is found; Ballarona, the production center of hardy spidersilk products; and Ilnemedon, the center of the fine spidersilk trade. *See also: hardy silkspider, hardy spidersilk, silkspider, spidersilk, Essuvian, Nechton's War.*
Well of Life	See *Well of Tílimya.*
Well of Tílimya	*Ilesian.* Part of the geography of the Realms of the Dead. A magical well, located within the Fortress in the Realm of Tílimya. The waters have the power to restore the dead to life. *See also: Realm of Tílimya, Tílimya's Well.*

windcaller   *Ilesian.* A man of psychic talent capable of summoning and controlling winds. Windcallers are sworn to the gods of the true religion and trained under the auspices of the Aballo Prince, but typically perform no priestly functions. The talents of windcallers make travel by airship or on the extreme tides of the Ruillin practical and efficient. Ships that sail by sea find a windcaller convenient but not necessary. Few other than righthe and tiarna can afford to retain the full-time services of a windcaller, though access to their services is not as strictly controlled as those of Aballo wizards. A significant number of windcallers work as independent contractors or partners in sailing or airship concerns. *See also: Aballo Order, druid, wizard.*

wizard   *Ilesian.* An initiate of the Aballo Order, sworn to the true gods and trained at the sacred center of Aballo. Distinguished from other initiates into magical orders by their level of ability; their practice encompasses both religious and arcane elements. After their initiates, many, but not all, take appointments as House Healers attached to royal houses. *See also: Aballo, Aballo Order, druid, House Healer.*

zhamin   *Danaan.* A derogatory term for *Beallan*. *See also: Beallan.*

zhev   *Danaan.* A profanity.

Barbara Friend Ish

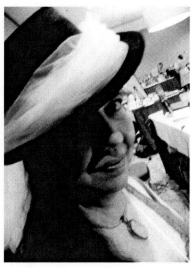

Writer, publisher, slave of cats: Barbara Friend Ish is Publisher, Editor-in-Chief, and Wild-Eyed Visionary for Mercury Retrograde Press, a small press dedicated to unconventional authors and works that might undeservedly slip through the cracks at bigger houses. After earning a Bachelor's in English from Rice University, Barbara divided her time between working with small groups of entrepreneurs who didn't know any better than to start their own companies and swimming against the current of the publishing industry, eventually co-founding Be Mused, an author services company devoted to helping authors and small publishers develop books. She founded Mercury Retrograde Press in 2007. She is insufferably proud of the authors with whom she works, including multi-award-nominated Edward Morris; Zachary Steele, whose debut novel was considered for the 2010 Sidewise Award; Danielle L. Parker, whose debut novel won the 2009 EPPIE; and talented fantasists Leona Wisoker and Larissa N. Niec.

Books edited by Barbara have been covered by *Library Journal, Publishers Weekly, Locus Magazine, The Midwest Book Review, SciFiDimensions, American Freethought, Baby Got Books, SFScope, SFSignal, Fantasy Book Critic, The Internet Review of Science Fiction, January Magazine* and *Green Man Review*. She has been featured in *The Atlanta Journal-Constitution* and on *Baby Got Books* and *SF Signal*, and has appeared at The Atlanta Book Show, RavenCon, Faerie Escape: Atlanta and Opus Fest.

For the past 23 years Barbara has been married to her one true love, one of the very first Cold-War-era Soviet émigrés. Together they have ridden the roller coasters of multiple start-up businesses (his and hers) and the raising of two children. Current projects include a garden entirely bereft of nutritional value and a search for the perfect bottle of champagne.

Born in Chicago, at various times in her life Barbara has called Philadelphia, Houston, New Jersey, and Atlanta home. She currently resides in Atlanta, GA, with her husband, her daughter, and two high-maintenance cats.

For more information on Barbara and her current projects, visit: **http://www.barbarafriendish.com**

Free eBook

Whether you're traveling across the world or just taking the train to work, sometimes you want the convenience of reading electronically. At the Mercury Retrograde Press website, readers who purchase the book in Trade Paper format can download the eBook version of *The Shadow of the Sun*—for free. Just enter the code UISNEACH on this form:

http://www.MercuryRetrogradePress.com/eBookform.asp

and we will email you a download link for *The Shadow of the Sun*, in whatever eBook format you choose.

Want More?

Visit the Way of the Gods page on the Mercury Retrograde Press website:

http://www.MercuryRetrogradePress.com/Worlds/TheWayoftheGods.asp

for even more on the world of *The Shadow of the Sun*—and a sneak preview of Barbara Friend Ish's next novel, *War-Lord of the Gods*.

Author updates

For information on appearances and new releases, visit:

http://www.MercuryRetrogradePress.com/Authors/BarbaraFriendIsh.asp

for announcements and news, or to register for updates by email.

Guardians of the Desert

by Leona Wisoker

GUARDIANS OF THE DESERT

BOOK TWO OF *CHILDREN OF THE DESERT*

LEONA WISOKER

Lord Alyea of Peysimun grows into her strength.

Deiq of Stass confronts his greatest weakness.

Lord Eredion of Sessin tries to live with his compromises.

Meanwhile, someone plots a brutal retaliation. . . .

Not long ago, Alyea Peysimun was a shallow young noblewoman maneuvering for personal power. Her first attempt at politics proved far more dangerous than she dreamed possible, and nearly ended her life. Now she is a desert lord, one of the powerful, little-understood southern elite. But power changes everything—including who to call *friend* and *enemy*.

Deiq of Stass has long hidden his dual heritage by passing himself off as a *mysterious quasi-noble*. He has a facility for lying and a strange sense of ethics; but he'll honor his promise to guide Alyea into her new life. To uphold that commitment, he must navigate more obstacles than even he could imagine—not least those within himself.

Eredion Sessin is the only desert lord who stayed in Bright Bay during King Ninnic's reign. He endured the worst of the insane king's excesses and helped to remove Ninnic from the throne; his guilt over the people he couldn't save is almost as deep as his self-loathing. He has come to hate all the ha'reye represent. And yet something deeper than loyalty binds him to Deiq, who he knows better than to trust.

As the truth of the ancient, mysterious ha'reye begins to emerge and those who oppose their ways marshal new strategies, the repercussions of Scratha's desperate gambit threaten to destroy a precarious balance that has held since the Split. And this time, there's no turning back.

LaVergne, TN USA
09 February 2011

215709LV00003B/2/P